The Western Story

A CHRONOLOGICAL TREASURY

1940 - 1994

The Western Story

A CHRONOLOGICAL TREASURY

Volume Two

1940 - 1994

Edited and Introduced by
JON TUSKA

Sagebrush
Large Print Westerns

Library of Congress Cataloging in Publication Data

The western story : a chronological treasury / edited and introduced
   by Jon Tuska
      p.   cm.
   Includes bibliographic references (p.   ).
   Contents: v.1, 1892-1939. v.2, 1940-1994.
   ISBN 1-57490-092-7 (alk. paper)
   1. Large type books. 2. Western stories. 3. West (U.S.)—Social
life and customs—Fiction. I. Tuska, Jon.
   [PS648.W4W46 1997]
   813'.087408—dc21   97-17588
                                                                  CIP

Cataloguing in Publication Data is available from
the British Library and the National Library of Australia.

The texts of the stories contained in this work, as well as all the
editorial matter, adhere as closely as possible to the original
manuscripts of all the authors included.

Sagebrush Large Print Westerns are published in the United States
and Canada by Thomas T. Beeler, Publisher, Box 659, Hampton
Falls, New Hampshire 03844-0659. ISBN 1-57490-093-5

Published in the United Kingdom, Eire, and the Republic of South
Africa by Isis Publishing Ltd, 7 Centremead, Osney Mead, Oxford
OX2 0ES England. ISBN 0-7531-5836-1

Published in Australia and New Zealand by Australian Large Print
Audio & Video Pty Ltd, 17 Mohr Street, Tullamarine, Victoria, 3043,
Australia. ISBN 1-86340-738-3

Manufactured in the United States of America by BookCrafters, Inc.

ACKNOWLEDGMENTS

DAWSON, PETER. "Retirement Day" first appeared in *Western Tales*. Copyright © 1942 by Popular Publications, Inc. Copyright © renewed 1970 by Dorothy S. Ewing. Reprinted by arrangement with the Golden West Literary Agency. All rights reserved.

FLYNN, T.T. "What Color Is Heaven?" first appeared under the title "Those Fighting Gringo Devils" in *Dime Western*. Copyright © 1942 by Popular Publications, Inc. Copyright © renewed 1970 by T.T. Flynn. Copyright © 1995 by Thomas B. Flynn, M.D. Reprinted by arrangement with the Golden West Literary Agency. All rights reserved.

CLARK, WALTER VAN TILBURG. "The Wind and Snow of Winter" first appeared in *Yale Review*. Copyright © 1944 by the Trustees of Yale University. Copyright © renewed 1972 by Robert M. Clark. Reprinted by arrangement with International Creative Management in association with the Golden West Literary Agency. All rights reserved.

JOHNSON, DOROTHY M. "A Man Called Horse" first appeared in *Collier's*. Copyright © 1949 by the Crowell Collier Corporation. Copyright © renewed 1977 by Dorothy M. Johnson. Reprinted by arrangement with McIntosh and Otis, Inc., in association with the Golden West Literary Agency. All rights reserved.

SAVAGE, LES, JR. "The Shadow in Renegade Basin"

PUBLISHER'S NOTE

The first two parts of this anthology, including an extensive introduction by Jon Tuska, are available in Large Print separately under the title *The Western Story: A Chronological Treasury, 1892-1939.*

CONTENTS

Part Three

STORYTELLERS OF THE GOLDEN AGE

Part Four

VISIONS OF DREAMS AND DANCING

Part Three

STORYTELLERS OF THE GOLDEN AGE

PETER DAWSON

JONATHAN HURFF GLIDDEN was born in 1907 in Kewanee, Illinois. Eighteen months later Jon's younger brother, Frederick Dilley Glidden, was born. The brothers—almost black Irish twins, as the expression went—grew up in Kewanee and were very close. Their father, who worked as the treasurer of the Kewanee Boiler Company, died of coronary thrombosis while on a fishing trip in 1921. He was little more than forty years of age. Their mother lived to a ripe age, dying in 1973, two years before her younger son and twenty-three years after her elder son.

Both of the Glidden brothers entered the University of Illinois at Urbana. Jon remained until he was graduated in 1929 with a Bachelor's degree in English literature. Fred transferred to the University of Missouri at Columbia where he was graduated with a Bachelor's degree in journalism. While Fred ventured to Canada where he trapped furs and took a number of odd jobs, Jon in the meantime married Dorothy Steele whom he had met while at the university and secured a good job with Cities Service Oil Company, selling gas conversion burners. He was based in Lexington, Kentucky. Fred, something of a fiddlefoot, had come somehow to work as an archeologist's assistant outside Santa Fe, New Mexico, and had married Florence Elder of Grand Junction, Colorado. Fred had tried various newspaper jobs, but none had panned out for him. He started writing Western fiction for the magazine market and was making a living at it when he wrote to Jon, urging

1

him to come for a visit. Jon and Moe, as Jon called his wife, visited Santa Fe and Fred launched a major campaign to convince Jon he should be an author of Western fiction. Jon's argument that Fred was the journalism major fell on deaf ears. Butch, as Fred called his wife, was writing, too. Her first story, titled "The Chute to Love," had been sold to *Rangeland Romances* for $50. Fred wrote as Luke Short, Butch as Vic Elder. Jon agreed to give writing a try.

Setting up a table and typewriter in the basement of the Lexington home, after eight hours of sales work Jon would write. He sent his stories to Fred who would return them with suggestions. Finally upon reading Jon's story, "Gunsmoke Pledge," Fred thought it good enough to send to his agent. The agent sold it to *Complete Stories* for $135. The name the agent, Marguerite E. Harper, chose for Jon was Peter Dawson and he would write under this name for the rest of his natural life, predominately Western fiction, but some detective and aviation stories as well, and a number of magazine serials later published as Western novels.

Moe figured it would require $200 a month for them to live if Jon was only to write and she was supportive of him in the effort. What he wrote was readily sold and soon he was earning more than the minimum Moe had set. By 1937, they had moved to New Mexico and bought an 18th-Century hacienda across the road from Fred and Butch in Pojoaque. In his Western fiction, Jon followed a very different course from the one Fred pursued. Fred preferred serials. Jon worked at the shorter forms, in part because the short story and short novel allowed him to depart from the obligatory structure in most serials of a hero, heroine, and villain, with the story ending in a romance. In "Owlhoot

Reckoning" in *Western Story Magazine* (8/20/38), the protagonist is forty-three years old and has spent his last fifteen years in Yuma State Prison. He has a limp in his right leg (other authors might have a character who limps but would not, as Jon, bother to tell the reader which leg was affected), a slight stoop to his shoulders, and an ugly, shiny scar on his right cheek dating back eight years to a prison riot. This character, Trent Stone, could never be a Luke Short hero, a man usually in his twenties.

Although he became a master of the short story form (the one film based on his work so far is an adaptation of a short story), Jon also wrote many excellent short novels. One of them—which he titled "One Man Hold-Out" and which was retitled "A Gun-Champion for Hell's Half-Acre" when it appeared in *Complete Western Book Magazine* (7/39)—concerns Ed January who refuses to sell his land as part of a sheep-ranching scheme. Bill Atwood, an old prospector killed on Ed's land while Ed is away, inspires Ed to reflect: "'The good ones always seem to go first. I hope it was clean and quick. That's the way he'd want to go.'" From this and numerous similar remarks throughout Jon's Western fiction, I surmise that the death of his father had a greater emotional impact on him than it did on Fred. This short novel, possessed of complex plotting, deft movement, fine characterizations, with a mystery that is illumined through delayed revelation, augmented by adept dialogue, is indicative this early of Jon's basic approach to his fiction. He worked at it, writing and rewriting, polishing, improving a scene with small but telling refinements. Jon also insisted on working at his own pace, which tended to infuriate Marguerite Harper, while Fred worked comparatively fast, completing a

3

60,000-word serial in as little as six weeks.

Jon was still writing for the magazine market, producing such fine short novels as "Ghost Brand of the Wishbones" which appeared as the "novel" in *Western Novel and Short Stories* (6/40) under the title "Half-Owner of Hell's Last Herd," when Street and Smith and Dodd, Mead announced a $2,000 prize for a first Western book-length novel. Fred had written serials for *Western Story Magazine* and *Argosy* but he had graduated by the late 1930s to writing for *Collier's*. With Fred urging Jon to try it, and Harper doing the same (largely because Street and Smith wanted someone who wrote "just like Luke Short"), Jon did. The result was **The Crimson Horseshoe** (Dodd, Mead, 1941) which won the prize and was run serially in *Western Story Magazine*. Even though Jon would follow this novel with a highly successful and distinguished group of Western novels, he also continued to write short stories and short novels.

It was a good way of life. Up and at work by 7:30 AM, working five hours, then breaking to polish well into the afternoon until Moe would come in softly and offer him a sandwich. The Second World War changed that. Fred was often in Hollywood and then in 1943 worked briefly in Washington, D.C., for the Office of Strategic Services. Jon entered the U.S. Army Air Force and attended Officer Candidate School in Miami in 1942. He was sent to London with the U.S. Strategic and Tactical Air Force. Jon was stationed in France, near Versailles, at the time of the occupation of Germany and was about to be deployed to the Pacific theater when Japan capitulated.

As Fred aged, he grew increasingly bored with writing Western fiction. His Golden Age was from 1938 to 1949. After that, he published less and less and virtually all of it is inferior to his earlier work. It was quite the opposite for Jon. He returned to Pojoaque and to writing, providing fiction for the magazine market as well as novels published by Dodd, Mead. ***Renegade Canyon*** (Dodd, Mead, 1949) was the first of four Peter Dawson novels serialized by *The Saturday Evening Post*.

In 1950 Jon was asked to return to service, this time as Assistant to Chief of Station in Germany. It was during this two-year tour of duty that he began experiencing severe angina pains. In fact, his stay in Germany was shortened by six months due to medical problems. He suffered his first heart attack while attending his twenty-five year reunion at the University of Illinois. He was living in New Mexico and writing, having just completed his serial, "Treachery at Rock Point," for the *Post*, when he went on a fishing trip to the Wagon Wheel Ranch near Creede, Colorado. It was while on this trip, much as had happened to his father, that Jon suffered his final heart attack.

Peter Dawson emerged in a period during which quite a number of outstanding authors wrote Western fiction and he still came to be recognized as a highly gifted and original talent. The more historical research he would do, the more he enjoyed what he wrote, and that sense of discovery and enjoyment continues to enhance the vast body of his work, a substantial achievement for any writer to have accomplished in a career that lasted only a little over two decades. Jon Glidden's Western stories remain remarkable for their precision, suspense, and the complexity of their narrative structures. Moreover, to the extent that a distinction can be made between plot and story, they are engaging for the interaction between various characters and the perceptive use of group psychology within frontier communities. Presently many of his finest novels, **Gunsmoke Graze** (Dodd, Mead, 1942), **High Country** (Dodd, Mead, 1947), and **Dead Man Pass** (Dodd, Mead, 1954), among them, are being reprinted in hard cover editions by Chivers Press in its Gunsmoke series.

"Retirement Day" was sent to Marguerite Harper on February 11, 1939. She was apparently not too fond of its off-trail plot, but it was sold for $45 on October 30, 1941 to the recently launched *Western Tales* from Popular Publications where it appeared in the February, 1942 issue. After the war, Jon would continue to do some of his best work for this magazine which, after this issue, changed its name to *Fifteen Western Tales* and, alone of Popular Publications' Western pulp magazines, emerged in late 1954 as a slick, bed-sheet size magazine. "Retirement Day" embodies several of the concerns and preoccupations Jon Glidden brought to the Western story, not the least of these being that a culture may be judged by the manner in which it treats its older members.

RETIREMENT DAY
1942

SLIM, THE APRON, POURED OUT A DOUBLE SHOT OF RYE whiskey and told old Joe Miles, "This is on the house, Joe. For old time's sake."

The half dozen men at the bar heard Slim and tried not to look at Joe, making small talk among themselves and not doing very well at it.

When old Joe said, "So long, boys. See you . . . well,

see you one of these days," they bid him good-bye with a forced cheerfulness and were relieved when the swing-doors up front hid his stooped slat of a figure.

"To hell with the railroad!" Slim grunted, rinsing Joe's glass and toweling it viciously. "To hell with all these new-fangled ideas! There's probably the last time we'll ever lay eyes on that old jasper. He's still a good man and they're kickin' him out."

"He's sixty-seven," someone ventured.

"He's as old as he thinks he is," Slim glowered at the speaker. "And until they gave him the sack, he was younger'n me or you. Listen here, brother . . . ," Slim leaned across the bar and wagged a forefinger in the man's face, not caring that his customer was a comparative newcomer and didn't know Joe Miles as well as he did the rest, "I've seen that old fool work three nights runnin' without sleep, freightin' food in here from the rail-head through a blizzard you'd be scared to stick your nose out into. I've seen him take a three-team stage over a washed-out hill trail you'd balk at walkin' a mule across. Don't tell me Joe's no good any more. When his old heart stops pumping, when they've throwed six feet of dirt on him, then he'll be ready to retire."

A stillness settled over the near-empty saloon. No one had a word to say. It was, in a way, the most fitting tribute paid Joe Miles that day.

Going along the street toward the stage station, old Joe hunched up his narrow shoulders and tilted his head down, so that the rain didn't hit his face but instead trickled down off the limp brim of his wide Stetson. He felt tired today, utterly weary for the first time in his keen memory. Maybe he was getting too old, like they said. He let himself get only so far along that line of thinking before he grumbled a ripe oath and hurried on.

He turned in off the walk at the office of the Blue Star Stage Lines, a weathered frame shack at the front of a huge hump-roofed barn. The man behind the wicket looked up from under his green eye-shade as Joe came in and said in an embarrassed attempt at joking, "It'd spoil things if you had good weather for your last run, eh?"

The oldster snorted, shook the rain from his coat. "What're they doin' with you, Len?"

"Makin' me bookkeeper down at Sands. I go down Tuesday, by train."

"Reckon I ought to ride the blamed thing myself just to see what it's like," old Joe said, smiling wryly, his lips a thin line below his cornsilk longhorn. "Maybe I ought to ask the railroad for a job, seein' as how they done me right plumb out of this one."

The door opened and a tall rangy man strode in, shaking the rain off his slicker. This was Ray Dineen, thirty and married. For ten years he had ridden shotgun alongside old Joe on the stage run out of this mining camp to Sands, the town on the plain, where the Blue Star had its division office, halfway along its main line.

Ray was making this last trip down with old Joe today, riding shotgun on the bank's regular week-end payroll shipment. Rumor had it that the money chest would contain an additional fourteen thousand in gold for the railroad crew working out of Sands. There wasn't going to be any fuss taking it through, since the rail officials weren't anxious to attract attention. Starting next week, the new spur would be finished and they would be sending trains through here and down to Sands and this short branch of the Blue Star Lines would be a thing of the past.

Ray Dineen said, "Hi yuh, Joe," and his face was serious. He had something to say and didn't know how to say it. Finally he blurted out, "I did every damn thing I could, Joe. Saw that young pup, Ted Baker, the new superintendent. What a boss! My age, and he's orderin' around men old enough to be his father." He shook his head soberly. "It's no use, Joe. Baker claims you're too old. He brought up that business about our gettin' drunk down in Vegas last December, too. Said I was lucky to be stayin' on after what happened."

Old Joe nodded. "Maybe we did raise too much sand that night. But we got here on time, didn't we, drunk or sober? And we didn't kill no horses or wreck no equipment." He shrugged, as though dismissing the thought. "What have they lined up for you, Ray?"

A little of his inward pride couldn't help but show in Ray Dineen's eyes. "They're giving me a try at the ribbons."

Old Joe's eyes lighted up. He smacked a fist into an open palm. "Drivin'? The main line! Ray, there's big pay, a future. I'll give you ten years before they make you division superintendent."

Ray shook his head. "But that's the job they should be givin' you. Hell, you deserve it. I don't."

"Don't go soft-hearted for me," Joe said. "I got plans for the future. Besides, I got a notion I ought to retire, live on my savin's."

"What savings? You borrowed twenty from me last pay-day." Ray Dineen's square face took on a bull-dog look. But then he saw the pointlessness of the argument, swore, and said, "Let's get her rolling. They're waitin' out there on the walk by the bank. They'll be sore if we don't hurry."

Five minutes later, slicker on, his Stetson pulled

9

down hard on his ears, old Joe wheeled the Concord down off the barn ramp and led his two half-wild teams of Morgans down-street under tight rein. No passengers were along this trip. Lately the load had been mostly freight, as today. Ray Dineen sat beside Joe, a double-barreled Greener cradled across his knees. As the Concord pulled in at the edge of the walk by the bank, where four guards waited with a brass-bound money-chest, the rain was coming down in a relentless spray whipped by the wind. The street was a sea of mud, fetlock deep to the horses; the town had a bedraggled, sodden look about it.

"Sling her up here where we can keep an eye on 'er," houted to the guards, pitching his voice to carry above the drone of rain on a nearby tin roof. He and Ray reached down, got a hold on one of the chest's leather handles, and heaved it to the boot beneath them.

While Ray lashed it in place with a length of half-inch rope, Joe called, "O' course we'll make it," in answer to a question Len Rivers, president of the bank, shouted from the doorway.

The teams slogged into the pull a moment later, and the Concord rolled out from the walk and down the street, past the stores and the awninged walks, past the few brick and frame houses and the many tar paper shacks along the cañon slopes, and finally out past the shaft houses of the Dolly Madison and Wee Willie mines.

Then the town lay behind and the stage was rolling along a winding trail through the high pines and scrubby cedars. Old Joe hadn't paid the town much attention purposely, for he hated good-byes and knew he might never again see the place he'd called home for thirty-four years. He'd live down in Sands from now on, get a cheap room and be handy for a job if any came along. The railroad was hiring men at pick and shovel work along the new right of way. Maybe they'd take him on.

"What did Rivers say?" Ray Dineen shouted above the downpour and the rattle of doubletree-chains and the creaking of harness.

"Asked me if I thought we could get across Graveyard Wash," old Joe growled. "As though I hadn't been drivin' this road long enough to know!"

Ray frowned. "I wondered about that myself. Sue and the kids are ahead somewhere in the wagon. They want to get to Sands before dark."

"They'll make it," old Joe said, expertly concealing the instant's tightening of worry inside him. Sue Dineen and Ray's kids, Ellen and young Tommy, heading down out of the mountains in a storm like this? Sue with a wagon-load of goods, furniture, bedding, all their worldly possessions. And she a frail woman at that, barely able to manage a team!

He was blaming Ray when he remembered that at one o'clock, two hours ago, the sun had been shining on a balmy summer afternoon. This had been one of those freak summer storms, with the clouds piling up behind the peaks for the last two days and spilling their rain when they rolled on over the mountains to hit the cold up-drafts on this side. It would be a good long rain if old Joe's weather eye was cocked right.

Joe decided not to worry. Sue had good enough sense not to head across Graveyard Wash if there was any water running. It was different with an old hand like him. He'd cheated the Graveyard more times than he could count on his gnarled fingers and crooked toes. He'd learned to gauge the water that foamed along the bed of that hundred-yard-wide wash that ran a torrent

11

each time it even sprinkled in the hills. He'd taken his stage across many a time with half a day's traffic of riders and wagons and rigs held up on the road on each side, all afraid to tackle the surging flood of water. Once he'd caught hell for it from the superintendent when the water boiled in over the floor below and soiled the dress of a woman passenger.

Four miles down-cañon old Joe hit the first wash-out in the trail, with a fifty-foot drop to the cañon floor on one side and a sheer climbing wall on the other. The Concord swayed dangerously, but was righted with perfect precision as Joe flicked one on-wheeler's rump with his whip and made the animal lunge into the pull. As the right rear wheel hit solid ground again and jarred the vehicle clear to the throughbraces, Ray Dineen suddenly groaned and doubled up with pain. He straightened a second later, but not before old Joe had shot him a glance to see his rugged face white and lined in agony.

Old Joe tightened the ribbons and drove home the brake. "Bouncin' too much, Ray?" he called.

Ray shook his head. "Gut ache. It must be something . . . ." A griping pain took him and he broke off his words and doubled over once more. His hand went to his side, below his belt. Then he caught himself and straightened up, taking his hand away. "Go on. I'll be all right in a minute or two."

"We'll stop at Ford's," Joe said. He knew the signs, had seen men taken with appendicitis before. He was wondering how long it would take John Ford to hitch his team to his buckboard and get Ray back to town. One thing they could all be thankful for was young Doc Slade, the sawbones who'd come in last year and started healing people instead of feeding them those sugar pills

12

old Doc Wheelwright had left in his office when he died.

They drove in at Ford's, a thirty-acre ranch in a clearing along the cañon, a quarter hour later. By that time the pain had hit Ray once again and then eased off.

Ray was stubborn and wanted to go on.

"What'll Sue and the kids do without me?" he kept insisting.

"I'll look after Sue," old Joe said. He met John Ford halfway between the yard fence and the house, explaining what he wanted.

"Sure, I'll take him in, right away," Ford agreed. Joe turned and started back toward the Concord, but Ford reached out and took a hold on his arm, saying in a lower voice, "But there's something you ought to know before you go on, Joe. Chet Richter and Barney Ryan went past here about an hour ago, headed out to the road."

"What have them two tramps got to do with this? I tell you Ray's sick, John. You hurry and get that team harnessed." He started out across the yard again.

"Listen, you bull-headed old fool!" Ford called. "Think a minute. I said Chet Richter and Barney Ryan. You're carryin' the railroad's gold, ain't you?"

"And I'll be carryin' you out to that wagon-shed unless you get a sudden move on!"

"Chet and Barney were fired last Tuesday for tryin' to lead the crew out on strike. They've been tryin' to work off their grudge against Paul Duval all week. Don't that mean nothin' to you?"

It did. Old Joe finally got it. What Ford could have said in as few words was that Chet Richter and Barney Ryan were a couple of hard cases, that they'd been fired for making trouble for Paul Duval, boss of the section gang working the railroad right of way below town, and that it wasn't out of the realm of possibility to suppose that they'd try and hold up the stage on the road and get even with Duval and the owners.

Old Joe faced John Ford with an angry light blazing in his watery blue eyes. He was worried, tired, and his patience was worn thin. "John, you ain't never got over shootin' that rustler twenty years ago. These ain't the old days. If Chet and Barney laid so much as a finger on that money-chest they'd have every railroad detective this side of Kansas City out after 'em. Now get that rig ready and get Ray to town to Doc Slade. And if Ray don't get there in time, you're answerin' to me . . . plenty!"

Old Joe felt lost and worried five minutes later, as John Ford, Ray beside him, drove his buckboard out of sight up-cañon, around a turning in the trail. He climbed up onto the seat and kicked off the brake. He cut the lead team across the ears with his whip, sorry the moment he'd done it. He had never abused his animals.

He settled to the long grind, and the rain turned into a downpour lashed by a cold wind, whipping up a spray off the rocks and trees that made it hard to see the road ahead. It was as miserable a drive as Joe could remember. He was cold to the bone and, in his sodden discomfort, without Ray's company, he was once more an old man, lonely, without hope, finished.

He had a few regrets, not many. Of course he should have saved his money through the years, put enough aside so that he could spend these last empty years in some degree of comfort, resting. Probably he should have married Martha Drew forty years ago, instead of being afraid to ask her and letting her wait so long she'd finally gone away with Spence Amsden.

But he admitted grudgingly that his good times and his throwing away his money had made up for most of the things he lacked now. When a man couldn't any longer work, he ought to crawl into a hole and pull it in after him.

He thought of John Ford, and of Chet Richter and Barney Ryan. He reached down and took the old Greener from the hangars under the seat and broke open the weapon, seeing that the buck-shot loads were fresh. Then he laughed.

"That's one thing you never was, Joe Miles . . . spooky!" he growled as he hung the shotgun under the seat again.

He hadn't thought much about the payroll but, now that he remembered it, he was thinking of the old days when the town up above was booming, when every gold stage carried gun-guards inside and out, and even then sometimes didn't get through with their precious freight. That was forty years ago, when the scum of humanity had flocked into these hills with the gold fever, when he'd worn a six-gun, the same as he'd worn his boots, and used it often.

But today wasn't forty years ago. The formality of sending a guard along with each payroll shipment was merely a habit of Len Rivers's, who was of the old school, Joe's school, that had lived the hard way. In case of real trouble, a driver was expected to hand over what was in the boot and let the insurance detectives take care of running down the thieves. Chet Richter and Barney Ryan! Two undersized, lazy tramps who couldn't give a real man a workout either with guns or fists. Men didn't know how to use guns any more, not the way they had forty years ago.

This country was settled, civilized; the stages were

giving way to the railroads. Joe Miles and his generation were giving way to men like Ray Dineen and Ted Baker, the new Blue Star superintendent, men who would bring in new and better equipment, run it faster and longer and make more money, advancing ahead of the railroads and maybe in the end going over to the railroads themselves. In this sober moment, old Joe saw that his going was symbolic of a dying age, and in his loneliness he was a little proud of his past, glad he wasn't beginning in this new era of change.

The cañon walls fell away and the trail cut in through the low foothills, and in the next two hours old Joe crossed three washes running water, one badly. The rain still held to a steady downpour. He heard the far-off roar of Graveyard Wash from a half mile's distance, and gauged its sound. It was running high; two more hours, he judged, would find it impassable.

His first sight of the wide wash brought a dry chuckle out of his flat chest. Muddy water boiled bank to bank across its hundred-yard width. Already there was better than a foot and a half of water, with three-foot waves churning up over the bars and the sand riffles. There was some driftwood, small seedling trees and bushes that had probably fallen in with caved cutbanks. Soon there would be larger trees. In fact, there was one down already, barely in sight upstream, a half-foot-thick cottonwood, branches sheered off along its straight trunk, its huge bole of spreading roots turning slowly in cartwheel fashion as it rolled lazily with the force of the current.

He drove as far as the down-grade cutting in the high bank, a pleasing excitement running along his nerves, making him forget how he'd felt back a ways. This was what his life had been, a series of small adventures

16

testing his ingenuity and toughness. Like this, getting two teams and a heavy stage across a roaring torrent. Few men could do it without letting an animal go down or bogging in quicksand. He could; he was still tough enough to do it right.

He pulled in the teams, letting his eye run over harness, the lashings on the boot; he tested the brake, spotted the line of the road opposite and lifted the reins to send his Morgans into the down-grade.

He heard the cry then, faint yet unmistakable.

"Ray! Ray!"

It was muted by the roar of the water, yet there was an emergency to the voice that brought him to his feet, looking downstream. Then it came again from downstream, "Ray!" and he was gripped in a paralysis of stark, sudden fear.

It was Sue Dineen's voice.

His bleak old eyes whipped over the angry waters. What he saw made him lift his whip. Twenty rods below, within a quarter of that distance of a sage-studded narrow strip of land still above water toward the far bank, he saw the wagon and the horse and Sue and the kids.

The wagon was bottom-side up, the wheels half out of water. Sue clung to the hub of the near front wheel, only her head and shoulders showing and the water foaming about her shoulders, pressing her in against the wheel. She was caught there; otherwise she'd be with the kids, who were standing above her on the overturned bed of wagon, only to their knees in water. One horse was down, drowned, his four stiff legs sticking out of the water. The weight of the carcass must have been dragging at the harness for, as Joe took that one fleeting look, he saw the remaining animal lunge and try to

17

break loose.

With the horse's lunge, Sue screamed. Joe heard it plainly and laid his whip to his teams. As the Concord lurched ahead, tilted into the down-grade, a distant explosion sounded out from behind. Joe looked back there. A hundred yards back along the trail he saw two riders coming in fast toward him. The one he recognized as Chet Richter aimed a six-gun and fired at him as he watched.

The Concord lurched badly, righted itself, and the Morgans shied down off the bank and into knee-deep water. Old Joe laid on his whip, forgetting that to trot a horse in fast water is unsafe. The off-wheeler stumbled, went to his knees and was up again. Joe held the horses to a walk, his eye on the wagon downstream. It might have been his imagination, but he thought that Sue was already lower in the water than when he'd first seen her.

All at once, fifty yards out, the right front wheel went down. Too late, old Joe remembered that there was quicksand out here. He whipped the teams and they were pulling clear of the sand when suddenly a bronc went down. An instant later the report of a shot cut into the steady roar of the rushing water. Joe looked back to see Chet Richter and Barney Ryan about to head their horses into the water after him. Barney had shot the horse.

The Concord's front wheel sank lower into the quicksand. Then, lazily almost, the stage went over on its side. Joe jumped, landed on the back of the animal alongside the downed bronc, and with his clasp-knife he cut the wounded, kicking horse from the tangle of harness. He slid off the back of the animal, stood on the long tongue of the coach. Then, the water boiling about his legs and threatening to drag him off his slender perch, he unhitched the lead team from all but their singletree.

The last thing he did before leaving the over-turned Concord was to edge back and cut the lashings from the front boot. He worked feverishly while he watched Barney Ryan and Chet Richter wade their ponies on through the water toward him, Richter brandishing his pistol and calling something unintelligible above the roar of the water. The chest slid out from the ropes, stuck on a metal brace. Old Joe kicked it viciously and it finally slid into the water with a sucking splash to sink out of sight.

He shook his fist at Ryan and Richter, twenty yards away now and coming fast. Then he freed the one remaining wheel bronc with a few deft slashes of his knife and threw himself on the back of one of the leaders. He drove them away from the stage, clear of the tongue, and cut obliquely out at a walk toward the over-turned wagon.

He was almost even with it; every muscle in him strained to use the ribbons as a whip; yet he knew it meant disaster and a quick death if the horse he rode lost his footing on the shifting sandy bottom. He looked back once to see Chet Richter sitting his pony alongside the stage, holding Ryan's. Ryan was aboard the Concord, kicking in a window, probably in search of the money-chest. Old Joe laughed harshly at the thought of how futile their search would be.

Working in toward the wagon now, he called encouragingly, "Steady, Sue! I'm comin'."

Then he happened to look upstream. There, less than forty yards away, rolling relentlessly down in line with the wagon, turned the huge bole of the uprooted cottonwood, enough weight in rock and soil in its roots to crush the wagon like matchwood.

"Ray!" Sue called. Then she saw who it was. "Joe! Hurry!" Her voice jerked him out of his momentary paralysis.

Tom, Ray's ten-year-old boy, was holding onto his sister, Ellen. His straight yellow hair, like his Dad's, was plastered down across his forehead. He was crying, calling out in a choking voice to his mother, trying to reach down to take her hand.

The water was up to Sue Dineen's neck, occasionally boiling up over her head so that her call to Joe as he drove the horses alongside was a gasp. "Joe, I'm caught. My legs are under the wagon. Take the children, Joe. Please! Get them away before it's too late."

Joe slid off the back of the horse, holding the reins tight. "Hold on a minute longer," he called. He darted a glance at the oncoming cottonwood. It was closer, but rolling out of line. There would be time enough now. The water sweeping up his thighs, he waded over and took Ellen under one arm, Tom under the other.

Tom fought, screaming, "Don't leave Mother!" until Joe said, "We'll get her out. Now you act like a man, Tom." He carried the children back to the horses, and lifted them onto the back of the nearest. "Hold on tight to the belly-band," he shouted, and clamped their hands to the leather. Then he left them for the wagon again.

He was working with an intent coolness now, not wasting a move. He caught up the one rein of the frantic bay horse still hitched to the wagon. Somehow he backed the animal and then headed him downstream. He gathered the one rein and all at once lashed out fiercely, yelling his lungs out in a high-pitched sharp yell. The horse, frightened into violent action, lunged against the harness. Joe whipped the animal unmercifully. The wagon slid, turned on its side, and then rolled on downstream as though its weight was no more than a packing box's.

Sue tried to stand, couldn't, and went under. Joe was swept off his knees as he lunged to stop her from being dragged on with the current. He went under, then, miraculously, caught a hold on her skirt and held it.

He struggled to his feet, picked the girl up and carried her to the horses. She was a dead weight in his arms, limp, but somehow Joe managed to throw her over the back of the horse alongside her children. He slapped her face hard. She stirred and her eyes opened.

He yelled, "Plenty of time now, Sue. Grab a hold and I'll climb on with the kids." She heard him, pulled herself onto the Morgan's back and took a hold on the heavy collar, a wave of thankfulness flooding her eyes as she saw that her children were there beside her.

Joe worked on around her horse and in alongside the other. On the way, he saw the cottonwood, its huge bole towering twice as high as his head, ten feet to one side. He was relieved that it had finally rolled out of line with them.

All at once the lower roots tilted crazily. They must have struck a boulder, for the weight of the bole fell outward and whipped the trailing stem of the tree out of the water. It rose from the current in a blinding sheet of spray. The Morgan shied. Old Joe, a weak hold on the harness-strap, was dragged off his feet.

The horse lunged, Joe's boots came down into the surging water, and his hold broke. He fell face down into the muddy roiling water, his last glance toward the Morgans showing them lunging into a run. Then he was under, rolling over and over along the gravelly bottom. His lungs fought for air, but he held his breath. Then he

21

managed to strike out with hands and knees and slow the force of his rolling weight. The next time he turned over, he was facing squarely downstream, with the current at his back. He struggled to his feet, his head above water and his lungs dragging in pure cold air. He got one full breath before the water swept his legs from beneath him and he was down again.

This time he was under longer, fighting, trying to remember what little he knew of swimming. Once more his head was above water; once more his lungs gasped for air. He struggled to his knees, to his feet. He spread his legs far apart, bracing himself against the mighty suck of the water. He looked downstream. The rolling bole of the cottonwood, trailing its slender trunk, was now nothing but a shadow in the blur of rain, fast disappearing. The horses were out of sight.

He screamed time and again, "Sue! Sue, answer me! Tommy! Ellen!" but his voice was only a feeble croak in the rush of water and the torrent of the storm.

The strength left his legs and he knew he was going down again, and this time he didn't care. He was too tired to care. He looked dully downstream once more. Coming toward him, dragging the broken front axle and one wheel of the wagon, was the remaining horse of Ray Dineen's team of bays. The horse was plunging wildly, crazed with fear, straight up the stream.

Joe struggled five steps and caught the one trailing rein as the horse lunged by. He held on, dragged hand over hand up the rein until he was alongside the animal. Then, in a last desperate effort, holding to the harness collar, he pulled the horse's head in toward the far bank, his legs dragging along the wash's rocky bottom. The bay stepped on him, tried to kick him, but he was lucky enough to keep his body out of line with the slashing

22

hoofs.

Five minutes later the bay was standing head down on the stream bank, and old Joe was lying on his back in the sand, arms aching.

When he could move, he started walking downstream, looking for some sign of Sue and the children. All he could remember was the plunging horses; the children couldn't have held on. He walked back and forth until dark, and all he found was the blue sweater Ellen had been wearing, caught on the branch of a dead willow two miles below the road. He gave up then, knowing the answer.

He walked back as far as the road and sat on the bank, looking out at the rushing waters through the darkness. There was four feet of water running now, nothing showing of the Concord but one rear wheel idly turning in the current. The rain had stopped. Later, the sky cleared and the stars came out. He walked a half mile looking for Ray Dineen's bay horse and finally caught him. He found signs along the road that told him Chet Richter and Barney Ryan had ridden back into the hills. He gave them little thought, thinking mostly of Sue and those two kids of Ray's.

At midnight, when he judged he could get the horse across the wash in the receding water, he began to think seriously of what to do. The first thing was to get to Ray, to break the news as gently as he could. He'd tell him how Sue had fought to save the youngsters and then how he'd fought to save them all. He had waited here because the nearest ranch in toward the hills was eight miles away and he was afraid the tired bay couldn't carry him that far. But if he could get the gelding across the wash, there was a homesteader, Caylor, who had a place within a mile.

He cut the one long rein and made two shorter ones of it, fastening them to the bay's bit. He finally climbed onto the bay and headed him into the water, deeper than any he'd ever put a horse into; but he made it.

Caylor's place a mile down the trail was deserted. The corral was empty; the wagon Joe had often seen in the barn-lot on his way past was gone. So was the homesteader's team. But there was a saddle in the barn, and Joe took the hull and threw it on the bay. He was worried about the tired horse being able to carry him the four miles in to Sands.

The bay horse walked most of the four miles, and during that long hour and a half the ghosts of Sue and Ellen and Tommy Dineen rode with Joe. When he saw the winking lights along the town's street, he felt his first reluctance to face what lay ahead. He'd have to make a report to the sheriff; there would be questions, maybe accusations. He'd have to get the superintendent, young Ted Baker, out of bed and report the loss of four horses and all his equipment.

Of course they'd find the money-chest; the damned money-grubbers would dredge the bed of the wash for ten miles for their payroll.

But that wouldn't bring back Sue and Ellen and Tommy Dineen.

He was a quarter way along the street when he noticed the scattered crowd along the walk far ahead in front of the lights of the Blue Star stage station. It was late for such a crowd; but then a fight or a noisy drunk or maybe a man hurt could attract these countless loafers who never seemed to sleep.

From far out of the distance came the wailing long note of a locomotive's whistler. Old Joe read a personal insult into the sound. But for the locomotives and the twin ribbons of steel cutting across the plain, he'd still have his job, have it until he died, and Sue and the kids wouldn't have been on their way down today.

He was even with the first stores along the street and riding down toward the group in front of the Blue Star when someone on the walk shouted suddenly, "Look! It's Joe Miles! Either him or his ghost!"

Men stepped down off the walk, looked his way. Then another man shouted, "It ain't no ghost!" and started running toward him. Half a dozen more followed. The swing-doors of a saloon across the street burst outward and a line of men filed out. More came from a saloon further along and joined the quickly gathering crowd in the street. Someone shouted, "Get him and bring him over here!"

Old Joe didn't know what was happening. He tried to turn the bay, but he wasn't fast enough. Hands reached up and pulled him out of the saddle. He was hoisted to two pairs of shoulders, even though he struck out feebly to shake loose the holds on his legs.

Men crowded those who were carrying him. A few hats went into the air and the shouts grew frenzied. They carried Joe across to the Blue Star stage station. All he knew was that these men were cheering, that they weren't mad. Abruptly he was lowered and pushed up onto the walk to face young Ted Baker, the new Blue Star superintendent, who stood in the office doorway.

Baker held up a hand to command silence. He was smiling as the shouts died away and a stillness settled back along the crowd. Old Joe shook loose a man who was holding him and waited, an ugly twist to his wrinkled face.

"Well, Joe, we hardly know what to say," Ted Baker began.

"You could start by tellin' me what the hell all this ruckus is about," said Joe. "I don't feel like jokin'. Something's happened. If you've planned this as a send-off, you young squirt, you can lay off and listen to some bad news.

"This afternoon I hit Graveyard to find a woman and two kids drownin', Ray Dineen's kids. Tryin' to get 'em out, I lost your outfit, horses and all. And I lost Sue and the kids, too. Now the whole pack of you clear out and let me . . . ."

"Joe," Baker cut in. "Joe, Sue and the children are across at the hotel, in bed. Alive! Safe! Larry Caylor brought them in, in his wagon. They thought you'd drowned. We all thought you'd drowned. The sheriff has a posse rounded up, ready to start looking for your body at sunup."

Old Joe Miles stood there a good five seconds, while the expectant hush held the crowd. Tears came to his eyes, streamed down his grizzled cheeks. Then, before any of them could reach out to catch him, his knees buckled and he fell full length on the walk in a dead faint.

Ted Baker was more worried than anyone else. For a half hour he paced the hallway before the hotel room where they had carried old Joe. The doctor was in there with Joe, trying to bring him around. The medico was an ornery old devil who insisted on having the room cleared before he went to work.

Finally the door opened.

"What about it ?" Ted Baker asked quickly. "Will he live?"

"Live!" the medico snorted. "There's nothin' wrong with that old cuss. A little tuckered out, maybe, and

26

bruised a bit. He'll be fit as a fiddle in the mornin'."

Baker took the chair alongside as Joe sat up. Baker pushed him down again, said, "Take it easy, Joe."

Neither of them said anything for a couple of minutes. Then Baker began, "Sue Dineen told me everything that happened. She thought you'd drowned under that tree. She told me about Chet Richter and Barney Ryan. They were shooting at you, weren't they? They tried to take that payroll, didn't they?"

Joe nodded. "I reckon. But your money's safe in the wash. I wasn't thinkin' much about Barney and Chet. It was the girl, and them kids. I can't see yet how they got away safe."

Baker shook his head, his glance touched with admiration. "Because of you, Joe,"—Baker had never before condescended to talk to his driver in this familiar off-hand way. Joe hardly knew what to make of it— "There'll be a reward out for saving that payroll, Joe. It'll amount to maybe five or seven hundred dollars. There's another thing I'd like to talk over."

"Shoot," old Joe said, hoping young Baker wasn't going to go sentimental over his thanks or make more excuses about letting him go.

"It's this, Joe. We've tried Ed Salzman for a year as superintendent on the southern division. He isn't working out well. I've done some thinking. We can run this efficiency and this new system into the ground. What we need is to keep the best of the old-timers, men who can pull us out of a tight spot when we get in one, like the one today. This superintendent's job is mostly inside work, nothing like you're used to. But I was wondering if we could make you decide to stay on a few more years and take it?"

Old Joe swallowed once, trying to clear his throat so

he could say yes. Baker understood. He got up out of his chair and went to the door. "I suppose you'll want Ray Dineen for one of your drivers, won't you?"

Joe thought of something, sat up suddenly. "I forgot to tell you about Ray," he said. "This afternoon he . . . ."

"I know," Baker cut in. "A man just rode in with a note from Doc Slade to Ray's wife. Ray had his appendix out this afternoon. He's in fine shape." He looked at his watch. "Get some sleep and I'll see you in the morning, Joe. We'll whip this line into shape and make it pay."

Old Joe couldn't get to sleep for better than an hour. It didn't worry him much. He had always insisted that a man who slept too much was old or soft, and he wasn't either of these.

T.T. FLYNN

THEODORE THOMAS FLYNN, JR. (1902-1979) was born in Indianapolis, Indiana. He was graduated from Indianapolis Technical High School, but decided against entering college. Instead, he enlisted in the merchant marine where he worked initially as a stoker in coal-burning ships and then as a ship's carpenter. Quitting the sea, Flynn and a friend on a lark paddled a canoe along the Ohio River and then down the Mississippi to New Orleans. What changed his life was meeting a woman named Mary, familiarly known as Molly, and marrying her, probably in 1924—Flynn was always ruthlessly secretive about his life. He went to work for the railroad, first as a brakeman, and then got a job in a roundhouse. It was at this time that he first began to write fiction. When Flynn was fired from his roundhouse job for writing on company time, he was convinced one could not write part-time. It had to be a full-time vocation, or none at all. In early 1925 Flynn became a client of literary agent Marguerite E. Harper. With the story "A Matter of Judgment" in *Adventure* (10/30/25) Harper began getting Flynn published in the higher paying pulp magazines.

Living in Hyattsville, Maryland, with Molly, Flynn continued to work capably and quickly at stories with a variety of settings. Because Molly suffered from tuberculosis, Flynn moved with her to New Mexico since the climate there was reputed to be salutary for lung ailments. Molly suffered terribly before she died. A perceptive reader could deduce that Flynn had witnessed her passing since his descriptions ever after of deaths in his fiction could only have been written by a man with first-hand knowledge. There are no grimaces or grins on his corpses, only the frozen vacancy, the terrible silence, the pallor as the blood vanishes from the surface of the skin.

Now that Flynn was settled in Santa Fe, he bought himself a large Chrysler Airstream trailer with which he traveled extensively. A New Mexican woman of Spanish, Apache, and German descent helped bring Flynn through his grief and depression after Molly's death. They married in 1930 and their daughter, Mary Cecilia but known as Cela, was born in 1932. The marriage, however, did not work out and Flynn always blamed himself when he spoke to Cela about it. Flynn was married for the last time to Helen Brown, a woman twelve years his junior whom he met on a trip to New Orleans. With Helen he had two sons, Thomas, later a physician, and Richard, later an Episcopal minister.

Following this marriage, Flynn gave up permanent living quarters and just traveled with Helen and the trailer—at any rate until young Tom was born. Part of the year the Flynns parked the trailer near Fred Glidden's home in Pojoaque and would visit with Fred and his brother, Jon, who lived across the road. Flynn had been such a staple at *Dime Detective* and *Detective Fiction Weekly*, editor Rogers Terrill, in launching *Dime Western*, had wanted a Western story from Flynn and Harper agreed to ask him to write one. The next year, when *Star Western* began publication in the wake of the earlier magazine's success, Flynn was again among the inaugural contributors. It is to Ted Flynn's early fiction in these magazines that we owe the paradigm of a Western story in which the protagonist is seen to endure the tribulations of Job, where the losses pile up and the odds become more and more heavily stacked against him. It fit the bleakness of the Depression years and it certainly influenced the fiction written later by the two Gliddens.

After dozens of Western stories in *Dime Western*, *Star Western*, and in other pulp magazines, Flynn began contributing regularly to Street & Smith's *Western Story Magazine* in 1938. In fact, in the period between 1932 and 1952 Flynn contributed over 100 Western novelettes and short stories to the magazine market, although he did not abandon other kinds of fiction, especially detective and crime stories. Subsequently, Flynn also wrote five Western novels published in paperback Dell First Editions, the best known being **The Man From Laramie** in 1954 which ran first serially in *The Saturday Evening Post* and was filmed under this title by Columbia Pictures in 1955. It is now available in a hard cover reprint edition from Chivers in the Gunsmoke series.

In the years following 1960, Flynn's obsession with the race track and his following the horses from track to track increasingly consumed all of his time. His final novel, and in some ways one of his very best, **Night of the Comanche Moon**, remained in manuscript until it was published as a Five Star Western in September, 1995.

In January, 1978, Flynn and Helen moved to Baton Rouge. His son, Tom, recalled that his father's "last years were spent . . . traveling back and forth to the racetracks . . . and trying to get me to 'invest' in his handicapping scheme. He was a very bitter man during the last twenty years of his life, and totally consumed with the racetrack to the point that I avoided visiting when he came home." Flynn had developed arrhythmia of the heart. Today this condition can be corrected by a lithium implant in the heart that maintains a constant heart beat even when the electrical impulse from the brain to do so is interrupted. One night, at dinner with Tom Flynn and his wife, Linda, a cardiac nurse, I suggested that had Ted been a little more fortunate he might still be living by virtue of such an implant. "But," Tom said pointedly, "I doubt he would have wanted one."

As T.T. Flynn continued to fashion his Western stories over a span of thirty years, they became increasingly a comedy of manners, in which the first step in any direction can often lead to ever deepening complications. He also became increasingly concerned with the emotional and psychological dimensions of his characters and, already by the late 1930s, his preoccupation with mortality had become transfused with an examination of dysfunctional families and relationships. Mike Tilden, Rogers Terrill's successor as editor of *Dime Western*, after reading "What Color Is Heaven?" insisted that Ted alter the ending. He himself changed the title to "Those Fighting Gringo Devils" when it appeared in the May, 1942, issue. Now, with its ending restored, the interrogative title Flynn gave this story, with its reference to storming the heavens with an eternal question verily out of the Gospel of Saint Matthew, shimmers again with all the passionate wondering and intimations of the deeper reality which he had intended to suggest by means of it. His daughter, Cela, perhaps put it best when she reflected on the last visit her father paid her shortly before his own death. Ted spoke to her about his beloved Molly. "She died in his arms," Cela recalled. "He never stopped loving her. . . . He talked a lot about her, and brought out her picture in the leather case, which I had seen numerous times in the past. Why I was named after her. Why I meant so much to him. He said then he would be with his love soon."

"WHAT COLOR IS HEAVEN?"
1943

I
"HOME-COMING"

WHEN THE STAGE GUARD OPENED FIRE AT THE PILED and tumbled rocks off-side the road, Rick Candleman had the quick feeling that once more the Iron Hat range held bad luck for him. Eight years had passed since that night he had tangled with Rufus Madden and then had lathered a horse away from the Iron Hat country.

And the news that Rufus Madden hadn't died after all caught up with Rick in the Argentine. He had stayed on down there under the Southern Cross. Now he was visiting home again—and, before the stage got him to Laguna, trouble was breaking in his face. The stage guard's roaring shotgun was the signal.

Rifles among the rocks answered the guard's gun. A bullet dropped one of the four stage horses. The tangled mêlée in the harness brought the stage to a swerving, reeling stop. The girl sitting opposite Rick exclaimed under her breath. Through the dust swirling around the stage they could hear the driver swearing as he fought the reins.

The other two passengers were men. The wizened, nattily dressed little man at the girl's side was a drummer for the hardware trade. Beside Rick was a blocky, broad-shouldered cowman with a black mustache and black, challenging brows. And as the stage stopped, the cowman reached under his coat.

"Better not, friend!" Rick warned. "They mean business! We got a lady here!"

The cowman blurted, "Don't sit there an' be yellow! Grab a gun!"

"Haven't got a gun. You'll have it all to swing . . . and get us shot up, too, if you play it like this!"

The wizened drummer sat with open mouth. The cowman glared at Rick. The girl eyed him with an intent, tense look.

She wasn't afraid, Rick decided. He might have expected it from the hot red glint of her hair, and from the provocation in her look when the cowman had climbed on the stage at Mission Wells and ogled her.

And now, while the stage still rocked and the driver fought the plunging horses, the guard's body rolled off the top, struck the road hard and stayed where it landed.

"One dead already!" Rick said curtly.

The cowman half rose to his feet, looked out at the body. The fight went out of him and he sat back heavily.

"Couple of rifles lined on us over there in the rocks," Rick said, looking out. "Only one man showing himself. You wouldn't have had a chance!"

"Plenty of chance if I'd half a man to help me!" the big fellow snapped under his breath.

One outlaw was running out from the rocks to the stage. He carried a six-shooter and wore a shapeless yellow slicker in the blistering midday heat. An old black hat was pulled low over a bandanna mask. He knew what he was about.

"Toss down that Laguna bank box!" he called to the

34

driver as he came down through the big rocks.

The driver's voice cut back through the settling dust. "Ain't no bank box for you this trip!"

"One started from the railroad! It better hit the ground fast or the boys'll open up! Half a minute's all you get!"

"That's half a minute too long, damn you! Ain't no box here for a pack of low-down thieves an' killers!"

Rick had noticed the driver as the stage loaded at Mission Wells. A lean, dried-out old fellow with a huge drooping mustache, the driver was the type to take a stubborn stand and hold to it.

The little dudish drummer shrank back in the seat. "They'll k-kill him, won't they? They'll kill all of us if they start shooting?"

"Likely," Rick agreed.

The gunman outside the stage spoke venomously behind the bandanna. "Time's almost up!" He had no interest in the passengers.

The drummer whimpered: "Ought to be something we c'n do!"

"Not much," Rick told him. "That dead horse has got us hog-tied."

The cowman snorted.

The red-headed girl said suddenly: "They'll kill that driver if he stays stubborn!"

"Maybe not," Rick answered without much conviction.

"Of course they will! And maybe us, too!" She was off the seat as she spoke. "I'll stop it! If he won't tell them about that box, I will!"

Rick caught her arm as she opened the door. But she jerked away and stepped quickly out into the open. Rick followed her out irritably. This was a hair-trigger business. She could make it worse with a word.

"They put an old carpetbag on top that was heavy enough to have gold inside!" she called rapidly to the gunman. She stepped away from the stage, pointing to the top. "It's that green bag, between the two leather cases!"

The six-shooter threatened Rick to a stop. But the gunman chuckled behind his bandanna to the girl. "If every stage carried something purty an' helpful like you, lady, it'd make this business a cinch!" Then the venomous threat snapped in his voice again as he addressed the driver. "Throw off that carpetbag!"

Dust spurted as the carpetbag landed heavily a foot from the dead man.

The gunman kicked the bag, nodded satisfaction. "You saved the stubborn old coot's skin," he told the girl. "Set over there on a rock while he cuts that dead horse loose an' rolls on."

She started to obey, then stopped at Rick's cold voice. "The lady's riding the stage with us."

"She *was*, you mean. Git back in there. The lady's stayin' here."

Rick hesitated, shrugged, climbed back into the stage and slammed the door. And without sitting down he snapped under his breath to the blocky cowman: "Gimme that gun!"

Startled, the man reached under his coat without asking a question. Rick caught the gun from his hand, turned quickly in the cramped space between the seats. His shoulder drove the stage door open, and he plunged out to what was probably the end of Rick Candleman.

Two rifles, maybe more, were lined on the stage. But Rick was counting on one slight advantage as he catapulted back into the open. None of the outlaws was expecting a play like this.

The gunman in the slicker had half-turned to look at the girl. Rick was on the ground, crouching, dodging, before a rifle up the long, boulder-strewn slope fired to bring him down.

The bullet missed, screamed off the rim of the back wheel; and the gunman, not half a dozen steps away, whirled for trouble.

By then Rick was where he wanted to be. The slicker-clad figure was shielding him somewhat from the rifles. And he had hit the ground with six-gun cocked and ready. He fired first, two shots almost as one. He hit the man's gun arm, shattering it.

Rick heard the girl cry out as he plunged forward. He knew her fear and it couldn't be helped. Better to frighten her a little now, better to put her in some danger than to let the stage roll on and leave her here.

The man in the slicker had dropped his gun. He was hurt and rattled. He turned to run, inviting a shot in the back. Rick held back the shot, caught him, grabbed the slicker collar and yanked him to a stop.

"Tell 'em to hold those rifles!" Rick panted, gouging the gun muzzle into the man's back and holding him close for a shield.

The rifles stayed silent and the man in the slicker bawled, "He's got a gun in my back! Hold it, boys!"

Rick backed his prisoner toward the stage and called to the driver. "Cut that dead horse out of the harness!"

The girl had not moved. Rick blurted at her. "Climb in the coach! You're all right now!"

But he wasn't so sure she was all right. A rifle bullet could drop the prisoner and Rick Candleman, too. The gunners hidden up there in the rocks might think the Laguna bank shipment was worth losing one man. But the guns were silent as Rick backed to the stagecoach.

37

The girl came to his side.

"Get in!" Rick snapped at her.

Standing at the stage step, she said a queer thing. "You look like a Candleman. You're Rick Candleman, aren't you?"

"Yes," Rick answered, wondering why she hadn't asked the question before. He was struck again by her coolness, her self-possession. And then the last thing he expected to happen caught him off-guard and stunned him.

The red-headed girl spoke in husky warning and put a gun muzzle in his back. "I'll stay here! Drop your gun and the stage can go on!"

She had gotten out of the stage with a woman's leather hand-purse which must have held a small gun. And because he had looked into her face and eyes and judged her, Rick did not doubt her warning.

An instant later he was blindly angry at the fool figure he'd cut. She had intended all along to stay here with the outlaws. She'd known there would be a hold-up. And because she was pretty as a red-headed jungle cat and probably twice as merciless, Rick did not try to argue.

"I'll drop nothing!" he said savagely. "Pull that damned trigger and I'll still have time to get this curly wolf in front of me!"

"He should be killed anyway for letting you cripple him," she answered with a lack of emotion that made Rick's nerves crawl. And she spoke past Rick's shoulder in the same unmoved tone. "Get up in the rocks, Slim."

Blood was dripping off Slim's wrist and hand. Sweat stood out on his neck. But more than pain and sweat from the hot slicker inspired his hoarse reply. "He'll shoot if I try it!"

"So?" the girl said, and suddenly she was speaking in Spanish like a native. "Does it matter who shoots you now? Quick, before I do myself!"

The man took a hesitating step away from Rick's gun. Nothing happened, and he took a longer step. Then, with blood dripping off his fingers, he began to run up the rocky slope as if death already were at his heels.

And Rick, with the strange prescience that greater dangers than his gun threatened the fellow, let him go.

"You see," the girl said behind his shoulder, "now there is nothing left. Must I shoot you?"

Rick shrugged and tossed the gun down beside the green carpetbag and the dead man.

The old stage driver had been using a pocket knife with furious haste on the harness of the dead horse. The knife was still in his hand as he turned back toward his stage seat, saw the outlaw running and Rick tossing down his gun.

"What'n hell?" the old man gasped.

"Take a look," Rick said with ironical bitterness. "And then get your stage out of here fast . . . if you can."

"But . . . but the lady! What's she . . . ?"

"She ain't a lady!" Rick rasped.

He heard the girl chuckle under her breath and he held that against her, too. He was angry as only a strong man can be angry and she was laughing at him.

"You heard *Señor* Candleman," she told the driver.

The old man gave Rick a startled look. "Candleman?" He spat. His big mustache was quivering as he looked at the rocks where the gunmen were hidden and then back at them. "I've done heard plenty," he said, and he spat again and added: "An' seen more!"

He climbed on the stage.

"*Adios*," the girl said to Rick; and she was laughing again as she finished in Spanish: "It's better you return to the Rio Tigre quickly."

"What the devil do you know about the Rio Tigre?" Rick snapped back in Spanish.

She had stepped away from his back. When he turned she was beyond reach, showing white teeth in a smile he would never like. The short-barreled gun she carried waved him to the stage step.

The driver had the reins and the whip. Rifles were waiting up there in the rocks. Rick glared at her and swung into the stage.

The long-lashed whip cracked like a pistol shot. The driver yanked the three remaining horses wide around the dead animal, swung the stage back into the road beyond, and they rolled toward Laguna.

Rick's hands were unsteady as he rolled and lighted a cigarette. Anger still ran hot and wild through his nerves. He paid no attention to the furtive, half-fearful looks the little drummer was giving him.

She had known his name—and that, perhaps, wasn't so puzzling, for he had the Candlemans' rangy build, high cheekbones, black hair and dark eyes that old Ross Candleman had given to his three sons.

But she couldn't have guessed about the Rio Tigre ranch, down there in the deep pampas of the Argentine. She had to know Candleman business to know that name. And once more Rick had the uneasy feeling that the Iron Hat range held bad luck for him.

II
"END OF THE MURDER TRAIL"

LAGUNA HAD NOT CHANGED IN EIGHT YEARS. THE

SAME dun-colored hills and distant mountains brooded under the hot blue sky. The stamp of the border country was in the low, thick-walled adobe houses, hugging the earth that had spawned them.

It was Saturday, and wagons and horses were thick at the hitchracks. The same saloons were doing the same brisk business that Rick remembered out of past Saturdays. The three-horse stage pulled up in front of the hotel and Rick looked for familiar faces in the crowd that quickly gathered.

The stage driver piled down, shouting: "Hold-up got the bank shipment! Might be a chance to git it back if a posse starts quick! Where's Dud Sloane?"

Rick saw the angular, familiar face of a young man about his own age and pushed through the crowd.

"Pat, you crop-eared maverick!"

It took an instant for a broad grin of recognition to flash on Pat Cody's face. His hand grabbed Rick's hand.

"I been lookin' for you, Rick! Your brother Dan told me he'd written you to come home."

For the third time Rick had that sharp uneasy sense of trouble waiting here for him. It wiped most of the smile off his face.

"I didn't get the letter, Pat. Must have left before it got there. Is Dan in town?"

"Haven't seen him."

"Why'd he want me to come home?"

"Figured he needed you, I guess."

"Trouble?"

"Always a little trouble one way or another, ain't there?" Pat Cody evaded. "Who jumped the stage?"

"Strangers . . . and a girl who rode from Mission Wells."

"*Girl?*" Pat said in amazement.

41

"A red-head. Pretty . . . and a hell-cat behind it. I've never seen one like her, and I've run across some wild ones since I left."

"A red-head?" Pat Cody repeated. He looked startled. His voice sharpened. "Didja see the men?"

"No."

Pat looked quickly around, as if scenting danger or trying to take in quickly what was happening.

The crowd had grown. The sheriff had arrived, star pinned on his scuffed leather vest, worry on his broad face as he talked with the old stage driver, the little drummer, and the blocky cowman. And so quiet had the crowd gone around the spot that Rick heard the cowman's rasping words.

"She asked if he wasn't Rick Candleman an' he allowed he was. So what does he do but throw down my gun an' let the feller lope away. An' then he jabbered Mex with her an' climbed back in the stage! I dunno what the name Candleman means around here, but I got my ideas after what I seen . . . ."

Pat Cody's hand closed on Rick's arm, his voice low and urgent.

"Rick, I was headin' out to the ranch. Got a little spread of my own now, a swell wife an' a couple of kids. Come along an' stay with us tonight."

"Right now," said Rick grimly, "I'll drop my loop around that lying loud-mouth talking to the sheriff!"

"Don't!" Pat pleaded. "There comes Rufus Madden on that horse!"

"Dan wrote me the old trouble I had with Rufe was crossed off by the law."

"What of it, Rick? Rufe's as ornery as he ever was. He's got a hand in the bank now, since his old man got heart trouble three-four years ago. Come on."

But Rick shook off Pat's restraining hand and pushed through the crowd.

Rufe Madden had dismounted behind the stage and shouldered to the sheriff. Rick reached them as Rufe was speaking angrily.

"There was twelve thousand dollars in the shipment! Maybe more! Sloane, why the devil don't you get after it?"

Rick stopped beside them, and it seemed to him the years rolled away. He felt the inner bristle that always had been there when he was around Rufe Madden since they were kids, meeting at the same little school house with Rufe's younger sister, Jean.

And yet it was like meeting a stranger, too. Rufe had grown heavier; and it all was bad meat, soft and puffy. Rufe's loose mouth had taken on a thick, vindictive set.

Dusty black pants were outside Rufe's boots; his dusty hat was pushed back on his curly black hair. His look slid off Rick and he jerked back with startled recognition. "What the devil are you doing here?" Rufe burst out.

Rick spoke to the sheriff. "I'm Rick Candleman. You've just heard one kind of talk about what happened out there on the road. Now I'll give you my say."

Sloane, the sheriff, had silver at his temples and his broad, slack, lazy face was beginning to look harassed.

"Tell it quick," he said without enthusiasm. "I got to get down the road after that money."

The sheriff's eyes were on Rufe Madden as he said it. He listened to Rick's terse story as if his mind were already on other things.

Rufe Madden conferred hurriedly in undertones with other men as Rick faced the sheriff and, as Rick finished, Rufe's harsh accusation cut in.

43

"I just heard how Rick Candleman tied in with that hold-up! He's a damn thief and a killer, Sloane, like all the rest of his name! Why the devil don't you lock him up and get going?"

Rick thought as he turned that he might have known something like this would happen. He should have stayed clear from the Iron Hat country. He should never have come back.

Then his hard fist smashed Rufe Madden's thick, vindictive mouth. And the fierce satisfaction that flooded him as Rufe went down was tempered by the knowledge that the years had closed up and again he had trouble on the Iron Hat range. Trouble once more with the Maddens. Wasted now were the memories of Jean Madden that had finally brought him back.

Rufe bounced up bellowing from a bloody mouth. Rick knocked him down again. This time Rufe stayed in the dust and the crowd surged back as Rufe snatched under his coat.

Rick wasn't armed, and Rufe could see it. But that didn't matter to Rufe Madden. It was as if that furious night eight years back were repeating itself, action by action. Rick could have told them all what Rufe would try to do and, because he knew, Rick moved fast and mercilessly.

A jump brought his sharp-heeled boot and full weight down with paralyzing force on Rufe's elbow. Rufe yelled with pain and Rick caught the arm, heaved and slammed the heavy figure over on the ground.

Fury out of the past and of the present kept Rick from stopping there. Rufe's hat had fallen off. Rick grabbed the black curly hair and drove Rufe's puffy face hard into the dust again and again. He would have stopped after a moment and taken Rufe's gun away and let him

44

up. But men caught him and hustled him back, holding his arms.

The red-faced sheriff jumped in front of Rick as Rufe Madden scrambled up. Rufe's face was smeared with blood and dirt and his eyes were half-blinded by dust as he pawed under his coat.

"Don't try it, Rufe!" the sheriff yelled. "I'll have to lock you up, too! A mess like this ain't gettin' the bank's money back! Grab Rufe, men! He don't know what he's doin'!"

Rick smiled crookedly. Rufe knew exactly what he was doing. Nothing the matter with Rufe's calculating mind, ever. But then, even Rufe Madden couldn't shoot a man who was shielded by the sheriff and held by other men.

Rufe pulled out a handkerchief instead of the gun and wiped eyes and face. A smile forced out on his bloody lips, already beginning to puff. He peered at Rick, then without a word he turned back to his horse, mounted, angled down the street and across to the bank, still wiping at his face.

"We'll settle all this after I git back!" the sheriff told Rick angrily. "Come along now . . . I'm gonna lock you up!"

Part of the crowd followed them to the jail. From a cell Rick heard the posse collecting out in front, heard the drum-beat of departing horses.

Rick rolled a cigarette, sucked in the smoke, and smiled crookedly at his bruised knuckles. All the trouble he could handle. The Maddens wouldn't let it rest at this. If there was any way of pinning that stage hold-up on him, they'd see that it was done.

Rick's smile left when he got to that point. His mind switched hard to the hold-up and the red-headed girl.

45

She'd known too much about him. The stage driver's manner had been peculiar when he heard the name Candleman. And Pat Cody's manner and words hadn't been any more reassuring. Rick looked up as a man stepped into the cells. It was Pat Cody, keys in hand, a grin on his angular face.

"Might as well move out while everybody's busy," Pat said as he unlocked the cell door.

"How come?" Rick demanded as he emerged.

"I deputied around for old man Sloane. He's a forgetful cuss," Pat said. "Likely to leave his keys anywhere. He hides an extra set in the bottom drawer of his desk, just in case. Thinks he's the only one that knows about it. He'll figure you found a mouse hole an' crawled through, an'll get drunk trying to puzzle it out. I got a horse for you out back with mine. We'll ride to my place, over on the north fork of the Sugarleaf, across the hills from your land."

No one noticed them as they kept off the main street, rode out of town, and put the horses into a lope.

"Let's have it," Rick said soberly. "What's wrong?"

"I figured you knew."

"Those two brothers of mine never were much on writing letters. If there was trouble, they'd be the last ones to bother me with it."

"Dan bothered you this time, Rick . . . only you didn't get it. I might as well tell you what everyone knows. Joe's gone bad. The Maddens claimed they caught him rustling. There was some shooting. Joe killed a man in the posse that tried to round him up and skipped across the Border."

Rick's low whistle was amazed. "Joe rustling? He's only a kid!"

"He growed up while you were gone," Pat said dryly.

46

"Dan says Joe told him he wasn't rustling. But it was too late then to matter. Joe threw in with a hard bunch of Border jumpers. Made no bones about it when he met the men across the line that he knew. They hole up over there under the wing of a half-breed named Sebastian Obrion, who cuts some ice as a politico in the Domingo section. And they raise plenty of hell on this side. Half the dirt that's done along this stretch of the Border can be laid to the bunch."

"And Dan couldn't straighten Joe out?"

"Dan's had his hands full with his own troubles," Pat said bluntly. "Word's been around for some time that Dan must have a tie-in with the Obrion riders. Don't matter that he's lost cattle like everyone else. Folks have got the idea those Border jumpers are always welcome at Dan's place and Dan cuts in on some of their pickings."

"Anybody who knew Dan would know it was a dirty lie!"

"A man gets to believing things he hears when he's being thieved out himself, Rick."

"It's because of Joe!"

"Sure . . . but there it is. A man got a black eye just working for Dan. Three of his hands quit before he wrote you. Left him with old Cady Sowers. Dan'll be glad to see you, Rick."

Rick said slowly, "Not after the extra dust I've kicked up in coming here. Last letter I had from Dan almost a year ago didn't mention a thing." Rick rolled a cigarette and kept his eyes on it as he said casually: "Dan's letter said Jean Madden busted up with a fellow she was going to marry. She made the jump since?"

"Nope. It was Curt Hanna. Likely looking fellow who bought out the Cross Bit spread after you left. Hanna's

47

done well. He's a friend of Rufe Madden's and has bought into the bank. It looked like a good match. Nobody ever heard that Jean and Hanna had trouble. Surprised everyone when Jean busted it off at the last minute and never said why. She and Curt Hanna still seem to be friends, too. Just one of those things, I guess."

"That red-headed girl in the stagecoach meant something to you," Rick said abruptly.

"And to everybody else who heard a red-head had a hand in the business and faded off with the men," Pat admitted. "This Sebastian Obrion is a red-head and so is his sister, Maisa. Their father was a red-headed Irishman named O'Brien. They Mexed up the name and dug in over there. Talk has it that Obrion's red-headed sister and Joe are next thing to married . . . if they ain't married. Anyway, Joe's crazy about her . . . and if the devil had red hair and skirts, he'd probably be her."

Rick nodded and rode in silence, thinking how bad it was. And when they crossed the deep, dry gash of the Arroyo Hondo, Rick nodded toward the brush covered hills rising west of them.

"I'll cut off this way to the home place. I want to see Dan."

Pat nodded in understanding. "Dan'll feel the same way. I haven't seen him in better'n a week, but I guess he's waitin' for you. If there's anything I can do, ride over and name it."

That next hour's ride was the hardest Rick had ever made. There wasn't much left to think about. Joe, the slim straight kid brother with blue eyes and friendly grin, had taken his way and would have to cut his own tally.

Dan, the older, was messed up and tangled up. He

48

might have a plan, but probably he didn't. Rick himself couldn't have arrived in worse circumstances. They both were tarred with the same black outlaw stick that Joe had brought home to the Candlemans.

Rick's throat tightened a little when he passed the home fences and swung over to a solitary cow and read the familiar CA brand on hip and shoulder. He rode faster toward the meeting with Dan. And when he reached the trickle of water in Gunshot Creek, Rick pulled up short, staring.

Gunshot Creek's sands were white and dry as usual. On the other side, upstream, the tall cottonwoods thrust into the late sunlight as Rick had remembered through the years.

The old thick-walled adobe house was there, too. But it was different. Windows and doors were gaping. Faint blue curls of smoke drifted lazily from where the roof should be. Buzzards were wheeling in the blue sky and the challenging nicker of a horse at the back corner of the house was the only life Rick could make out as he slashed his own horse into a gallop.

The creek bed hid him for a moment and, when he rode up under the cottonwoods, the strange horse and a rider were poised to leave. The man had jerked a rifle from the saddle scabbard and held it ready.

The place had been burned out. And the wheeling buzzards signaled death.

"What happened here?" Rick called roughly, and a second later saw the rider was a girl. Then he recognized the girl and a stifled gladness held him wordless as he rode to her.

"Rick!"

He nodded, seeing her for an instant in short dresses at school, and later slim and eager in the year they had drawn close before he went away. She was older now, lovelier in her mid twenties, and uneasily he noticed that her eyes were tearful.

"Dan said you were coming, Rick!"

"Where's Dan?"

"There!" Jean said huskily, pointing to the back of the house. "And Cady Sowers, too. Inside. I . . . I had to make sure before I left. Oh, Rick!"

III
"BREED OF THE DARK TRAILS"

THE AIR REEKED OF CHARRED WOOD AND DYING FIRE as Rick saw Dan Candleman lying in the back doorway. Sowers, inside the building, had not been so fortunate.

The heavy log *vigas* of the burning building had crashed in on Sowers. His body was half-buried in the roof wreckage. But Sowers had been dead from a head wound before the roof fell. Haystacks, the old bunkhouse, saddle shed and store house, all had been burned.

Jean was with the two horses, wiping her eyes, when Rick came back to her with a stony face.

"Any idea what happened, Jean?"

She shook her head. "I rode over to ask Dan again when you were coming. Rick . . . Dan didn't expect anything like this! He was worried, but not about *this*!"

Bitterly Rick told her: "Dan never could figure that men can be as dirty as they are." And with the same bitterness: "I tangled with Rufe again as soon as I got in Laguna."

"Was it necessary?"

"Maybe not. I could have agreed with Rufe." He told her what had happened. "Jean, you know Candlemans

50

and Maddens never got along. I didn't help my family any when I tangled with Rufe eight years ago and rode away from here."

"Rufe said the trouble was over me, Rick. I've always felt I was to blame."

Rick shrugged. "If it hadn't been you, it would have been something else. Joe hit the Candlemans harder when he went bad. This stage hold-up today makes it worse. Joe might have been back there in the rocks himself, sighting a gun on the stage. Chances were he was, if that red-head was his girl. Maybe that's why I didn't get shot when I jumped out and took a hand."

Jean stayed pale and silent, and Rick turned to the ruin behind them. "The Candlemans didn't do *this*. It was done before the stage hold-up. Dan and the old man in there couldn't have had much chance. Neither one has got a gun that I can see. They weren't looking for trouble. Dan opened the door and got shot down like a dog. And then Sowers got it and the place was fired over their bodies. It was murder, Jean . . . murder, to get the last Candleman out of the way around here! Who'd do that?"

Jean was pale. "I don't know, Rick."

He seemed to have forgotten her for the moment. "I didn't see much beef inside Dan's fences. Looks like the place is cleaned out. Joe wouldn't have done that to his brother. I wonder who knew I was coming home."

"I don't know," Jean said huskily. But her pallor was intense; something like fright was in her look.

Rick eyed her without comment. It was impossible to guess what was in his mind. "It's late. Better start home," he said.

"I . . . I can ride to Laguna and let them know."

"Laguna didn't help Dan while he was alive," Rick

answered her shortly. "I'll do what's needed here . . . alone."

Jean rode away without looking back.

Rick finished by firelight. The graves were under the cottonwoods beside the creek. No coffins, no shrouds. He'd been lucky to find an unburned shovel. Dan would stay here as he had lived, the last Candleman on the place. But not the last Candleman.

It was late when he reached Pat Cody's. Barking dogs brought Pat out.

"Trouble, Rick?" Pat guessed.

"A little." Rick got stiffly out of the saddle and tersely told his story. "Everybody around here knew I was coming back," he guessed.

"Dan told me he'd written you to come. Said he'd told Jean Madden, too. That's all I know of."

"That's good enough. Got a fresh horse, a rifle, and a gun?"

"Sleep on it, tonight," Pat urged. "If the men who killed Dan are around these parts, you'll be jumping right under their sights. The law's after you anyway. They'll have you where they want you."

"I'm riding south after Joe," Rick said.

"I'll get your outfit," Pat yielded. And when the fresh horse was saddled, sandwiches stuffed in the saddle pockets, rifle in the saddle boot, belt gun and cartridges strapped on Rick, they had a final smoke out under the stars.

"I hate to see you riding for trouble, Rick."

"I ran away once," Rick said slowly. "I thought I was staying down there in the Argentine because I was making money and liking it. But mostly I guess I was staying away from trouble. I knew if I came back there'd be Candlemans tangling with Maddens again.

It's been that way ever since Ross Candleman and Cory Madden settled in these parts and had their trouble over water rights in the year of the big drive."

"I know," Pat agreed. "But it don't have to keep up."

"I'll see you before I start back south," Rick said.

Two days later he was in the Domingo country south of the Border. From a cactus-studded rise he saw, far off, the blood-red sheen of the setting sun on water that would be the Laguna Domingo. The blot of low adobe houses and trees on the west shore of the lagoon was Domingo, crossroads for open and furtive trails a hundred miles in any direction.

He had been there once as a boy, with his father. He had thought Domingo pretty then, the three-sided little plaza opening on the placid lagoon; the sandy winding streets vanishing back among the low sprawling adobe houses and corrals. But big Ross Candleman had carefully barred the door of the low patio room behind a *cantina* where they had spent the night. And had slept with loaded gun under his pillow.

Years afterward Rick remembered the noisy music, loud talk, yells and singing of the night. Gunshots, too, and in the middle of the night a man's cry outside their door. In the morning he had seen drying blood on the patio flagstones, and understood with hot excitement that death had stopped outside their door in the night. Now once more in the town, Rick again had the feeling of death as he stepped inside the *cantina* where he had slept as a boy.

Massive ceiling beams were dark with age. Dull brass lamps threw heat into the smoky reek. Mexicans and *Americanos* were in the place. Girls from both sides of the Border. A drunken *peon* in rags snored in a dark

53

corner. Men were arguing at the end of the bar. A few couples were dancing. Later there would probably be more dancers and the night would be wilder.

Men looked him over as he drank at the bar. Strangers were under suspicion in a town like this until their business was known.

A Mexican barman with drooping black mustache and beady eyes shook his head when Rick asked where Joe would be. And a man who had stepped in at Rick's shoulder said: "You looking for Joe Candleman, too, stranger?"

The speaker was as tall as Rick, broader and a few years older. He was American, dressed in dusty gray broadcloth, a silver-mounted gun visible under his coat. Teeth flashed in his heavy handsome face and his eyes crinkled.

"I'm Pete Jones."

"I'm Pete Smith," Rick said briefly.

"Drink?"

"Another'll hold down the first one," Rick grinned.

They were smiling as they drank. Jones looked like a prosperous cattleman. "They say Joe Candleman ought to be back tonight sometime. He'll stop in here."

"Who says so?"

"Sebastian Obrion, his brother-in-law." Jones twisted his glass between strong white fingers and grinned, but his eyes were thoughtful. "You remind me some of Joe Candleman. Same build . . . something about your faces. Joe Candleman's a great boy."

"I haven't seen him lately," Rick said briefly. "Maybe you can tell me where his brother-in-law lives."

"Right now," said Jones, "he's back there at the corner table."

"Thanks," said Rick. "Thanks for the drink, too." He

wondered as he left the bar how crooked the American was. He looked like a prosperous cattleman who had crossed the Border to turn a shady deal in beef.

Then the man at the corner table took all Rick's attention. He was built in the shoulders like a bull. The hat pushed back on his head showed challenging red hair. Seeing the brother, you would know the girl who had ridden in the Laguna stage.

"I'm Joe Candleman's brother," Rick said bluntly. "Where's Joe?"

Obrion drained his beer glass. He could pass for either American or Mexican. But his smile was Latin.

"So? Dan Candleman?"

"I'm Rick Candleman."

"Ah . . . the one from South America?" Obrion stood up, chuckling as he dropped a heavy arm on Rick's shoulder.

"José is a brother to me. *Señor* Rick, you are of the family. Command me."

South of the equator you lived with such courtesy. Rick stayed blunt. "Where's Joe?"

"*¿Quien sabe?*" Obrion said expansively. "He will be here."

"A sign on the back bar says they've got rooms here. I'll put up my horse and catch some rest," Rick decided.

Sebastian Obrion rapped on the table with an empty beer bottle. The man who hurried to them was short, bloated, and swarthy.

"A room, hot water and a razor; anything my friend wants. And his horse will be put in my corral," Obrion ordered expansively.

It was done so hurriedly that a stranger could not doubt Obrion's power in these parts. In a patio room Rick washed, shaved in hot water brought in a bucket, and dropped on the bed and closed his eyes for half an hour.

He felt better when he got up. He dressed, blew out the lamp, and stepped out to see about Joe. Furtive movement in the darkness at the left of the door made him lunge suddenly that way.

He caught an arm—and, because he remembered this patio from past years, Rick was fast and rough in grabbing the stranger's throat and slamming him against the wall. The match he thumbed into flame showed a dapper little Mexican with fear-popping eyes and purpling face.

"Crawled out of a rat-hole to snoop on me, eh?" Rick snapped in Spanish.

"*Madre mi,* I was but find my room!"

"You found it! ¡*Vamos*!" Rick sent the man stumbling across the dark patio.

A low-vaulted passage led to a door in the end of the big barroom where music and noise were louder now. Rick was halfway through the doorway when he caught sight of the red-headed girl of the Laguna stage—Joe's wife.

He had expected to meet her here, had guessed Joe had been with her across the Border. And Joe's wife here in the *cantina* was not what stopped Rick in midstride. Sebastian Obrion's sister was the type who would go where she pleased in Domingo. No, it was the sight of Jean Madden at the same table, smiling at the man who called himself Jones, that wrung a stifled oath from Rick.

He could see Jean had ridden hard and long. She looked tired. She must have started south quickly after leaving Dan's body and the smoldering ranch house. Her friendliness with the lot of them at the table turned

56

Rick cold and bleak.

But Joe wasn't there. While Rick looked over the crowd for him, the dapper little Mexican Rick had shoved into the dark wall sidled to Sebastian Obrion's ear with a message.

Obrion had put a watch on Joe's brother and was getting his report. Rick turned back to his room, got his rifle, locked the door, and tossed the key out in the dark patio.

Years ago there had been another vaulted passage at the back of the patio and a barred door leading outside. The door was still there.

He had gone with his horse to Obrion's corral. He went back there now. The two *peones* in charge squatted beside a tiny fire at one corner of the shed.

The men showed no surprise. Strangers evidently came and went from Sebastian Obrion's corral at all hours of the day and night. And because Obrion's orders had covered everything he might want, Rick tried for a fresh horse.

"*Si, señor,*" he was told readily.

The fire flared as the other man dropped on a twist of hay. Rick peered at the uneasy horses. "That big bay ought to do."

"Another one, *Señor*. That is the horse of Don José Candleman."

"So, he's back, is he?"

"Don José is in the bed with a lame foot, *Señor*."

"Where's his house?"

"Where but the house of Don Sebastian?"

"I'll take that black horse," Rick said quickly and, when he rode from the corral, he had directions for finding Obrion's house.

A block beyond the plaza, facing the downslope to

the lagoon, Obrion's house looked big and massive, for all of being one story high. Iron bars covered the windows. The single narrow entrance through a roofed passage to the patio was closed by an iron grillwork gate.

The gate was locked. But a shadowy, blanket-wrapped figure rose up from the passage floor.

"I will see Don José," Rick said in Spanish, and it hardly seemed he could be talking about his kid brother.

"Don José is asleep, *Señor*"

"Wake him up."

"Don José will not see anyone," was the surly answer.

Rick grabbed through the gate bars, got the blanket, the shoulder under it, yanked the figure close against the gate. His gun jabbing through the bars stopped a warning cry.

"Open up!" Rick said viciously.

The place was bigger than he had suspected. There was a back wing and a back patio; and in a corner of that back wing the gateman knocked on the door of a lighted room. A lusty bellow of Spanish answered.

Rick pushed the gateman into the room and followed.

Joe Candleman was in a chair by a table with his bandaged left foot propped on another chair. Joe had been oiling a gold-mounted six-gun. He stared and lurched up with a delighted yell.

"Rick! My God, what're *you* doing here?"

It was hard to find the kid brother in this tall, muscular young fellow with a lean, reckless face. Joe was a man now. But he was more. Joe was hard. Even while he laughed delightedly and pumped Rick's hand, his eyes were gray and slatey and there were lines on Joe's face that should not be there at his age.

"Can this *pelado* speak English?" Rick asked.

"Only a few words," Joe said. "What's the idea of bringing him in here this way?"

"He tried to keep me out. Said you weren't seeing anybody. Your brother-in-law told me over at the *cantina* that you were out of town. He got me a room at the *cantina*, and then put a man watching me."

"So?" said Joe. He was smiling as he took a limping step, slapped the *peon*, and demanded why the house was barred against this visitor. He had to slap the man again before he got the whimpered answer that Don Sebastian's orders had been followed.

Joe cursed him, shoved him to a corner, and sat down. "I don't know what this means, Rick. I'll find out when Sebastian comes in. Horse pitched me off the other day and sprained my ankle."

"He should have broken your neck," Rick said in a level voice.

Joe went sulky as he looked up. "Never mind saying it. This is the way it turned out. It's my hard luck and my business."

It was like speaking to a stranger. Joe's gray eyes were slate-hard now. But Rick was hard, too. "It's my business when I find the name Candleman means something low-down and no-good. It was Dan's business, too."

"Dan gets along."

"He will now," Rick agreed. "He's dead . . . murdered. And the house burned down over him. I buried Dan myself before I started south."

Joe's mouth opened. He suddenly looked older, stricken. "Tell me about it," he said thickly.

Rick told him with cold, edged words

The handsome recklessness was gone from Joe's face as he stood up. He talked jerkily as he limped around

59

the room.

"Last time I saw Dan was a couple of months ago. He was worried about money to make a payment to the Laguna bank. But he wouldn't take my money. Said it was blood money."

"Wasn't it?"

"Hell, don't rub it in, Rick! I told Dan the Laguna bank wasn't any better. A man named Curt Hanna who bought into the bank after you left had been working with Sebastian Obrion since before I had my trouble and jumped the Border. Sebastian got drunk and let it out just before I saw Dan. That's how Sebastian always has luck when he sends men across the Border."

"That's all I need," Rick said. "It was worth riding here to get it. Dan was the kind to threaten this Curt Hanna and the bank that he was going to make trouble. I guess that's when he wrote me to come help."

"Funny, ain't it?" Joe said grinning crookedly. "Me an outlaw here across the Border . . . and the Madden bank back there in Laguna riding high and holy?"

"Funny," Rick agreed. "The Maddens got as low-down as you made the Candlemans . . . only they stayed smarter. Good-bye, Joe."

Joe had tied a rope-soled sandal on his bad foot, had put on gunbelt and coat. Now he caught a sombrero off a wall peg.

"Let's go, Rick."

Behind Rick in the doorway a woman said: "*Querido mi,* where do you go?"

Joe's red-headed wife had returned in riding clothes. A braided quirt still dangled from her wrist. She was, Rick thought, something half-wild and dangerously lovely as she smiled at Joe.

"Rick says he met you on the stage," Joe said. "We're

60

riding, Maisa."

She was not surprised at Rick's presence. Obrion had evidently told her he was here in Domingo. But she begged Joe quickly. "I'm just back . . . and you're leaving me?"

"I told you to let that stage alone, Maisa."

"But it was fun. Please, Josito . . . don't leave me tonight."

Joe answered her deliberately. "Maisa, you're like fire in the night near gunpowder . . . pretty as hell, but a man never knows what'll happen. I'm tired of wondering and not liking most of the things that happen. I hate to say it in front of my own brother . . . but, when they cut hang ropes for all of us, they'll need one for you, too. Now go to bed or figure out some dirt with your brother. I'm riding with Rick."

The wild, stormy side of her blazed at him then. "Joe, you fool! You can't go with him! Suppose your brother Dan is dead? You can't help him! You belong here with us! You've got to take what happens along with all of us!"

Joe took a step and caught her wrist. "What do you know about Dan? Did you and Slim and the boys kill Dan while you were over there taking that stage?"

"No, Joe! I didn't know about it until I got back! Sebastian told . . . ."

She stopped abruptly, frightened by the look on Joe's face.

IV
"LAST OF THE FIGHTING CANDLEMANS"

ONLY THAT LOOK ON JOE'S FACE KEPT RICK QUIET, coldly waiting for what Joe would do. And Joe, even a stranger could have seen, was meeting his own hell as he looked at his red-headed wife. The hell wrenched out in Joe's voice.

"So Sebastian had my brother killed?"

She was suddenly like a lovely trapped cat, too frightened now to flare and fight with her temper and willfulness. Joe was not hurting her arm, but a low moan of denial came from her.

"Not Sebastian, Joe! He didn't have anything to do with it. But he knows about it. Just today he knows, I think. And he's angry. He told me that your brother Dan was going to make trouble for Curt Hanna and his partner in Laguna. Dan warned Hanna there would be trouble. Curt Hanna's here in Domingo now."

"Why?" Joe asked through tight lips.

"For his share of the bank's money we brought back. Sebastian is with him at the *cantina*!"

Rick spoke to her quietly. "Curt Hanna is the big fellow who was talking to Jean Madden at your table?"

"Jean Madden?" Joe blurted.

And Maisa said: "We found her on the trail with a lame horse She was riding here to meet her brother."

"Why does she have to meet her brother here across the Border?"

Rick answered Joe's question with rough bitterness that had seethed since his sight of Jean at the *cantina* table.

"She followed Rufe here to warn him trouble's coming fast about Dan. She's a Madden. I used to think different . . . but there it is. Rufe must have started this way after I tangled with him in Laguna."

Joe glared at his wife. "Is Rufe Madden here too?"

She swallowed, nodded. "He came in the *cantina* just before I left."

Joe let go of her wrist. His voice was deadly. "Maisa, you got into my blood like a fever I couldn't shake off. I stood a lot. This is the end. Don't leave this room or let Gregorio out until I tell you to!"

"Joe, don't go! You'll get into trouble!"

"You heard me," Joe said, turning to the door.

Rick wouldn't have believed until this moment that tears would ever soften terror in her eyes as they did now.

"Josito!" she pleaded. "Sebastian needs those men from the Laguna bank! You know Sebastian. He thinks only of himself!"

"I know Sebastian," Joe said, and hobbled out behind Rick.

"Robbing that Laguna stage was kinda snapping at the hand that fed him, wasn't it?" Rick said.

"Not the way the Laguna bank is run," Joe grunted. "They'll claim they lost twice as much as Maisa and the boys got. It'll cover a lot that's already been taken out of the bank. Hanna'll get some gold from this end, too, as his cut. Everybody wins but the other stockholders in the bank. That's the way Hanna and Rufe Madden do business."

They fell into silence as they crossed the dark back patio. And the silence was a bond from the past . . . .

In the front patio Rick's hand dropped to his gun as they unexpectedly met Sebastian Obrion hurrying back toward Joe's room.

"José?" Obrion called, stopping.

"It's Joe tonight," was the short answer. "Joe Candleman and Rick Candleman. What the devil's the idea of having Rick kept out of the house?"

"So?" Obrion said. He chuckled. "Have you seen Maisa?"

"Yes."

"Then you know my friend Hanna is here from Laguna. And he's angry, Joe, because your brother Dan promised him trouble for the bank. *Dios* . . . what can I do? I told Hanna you were out of Domingo. It is better that you don't go to the *cantina* now, eh?"

"Sebastian, you're damned careful of me all of a sudden," Joe snapped.

Sebastian Obrion chuckled. "Okay, Joe. You're going to the *cantina*, no? But I told you."

"Yeah," Joe said. "I'll remember it. Is the Madden girl there with her brother and Hanna?"

"So now you ask me," Obrion said, shrugging his big shoulders. "At the *cantina*, Joe, if you got to know."

"Fine," Joe said. "Come along."

"Later. First I will see Maisa."

"I told you not to make a mistake about me tonight," Joe said in sudden warning. "Watch him, Rick, while I see why there's a light in that room over there where guests are always put."

"Por Dios, Joe!"

But Joe had already faded across the dark patio, limping toward a thin thread of light at a curtained window.

Obrion swore angrily under his breath. "I wash my hands of it. Good night."

"Hold it," Risk said, hand on his gun. "Joe knows what he's doing."

The door opened to Joe's knock, letting out yellow light. The murmur of voices came to them. Obrion again swore angrily.

Then the door closed. Joe started limping back to them. And Sebastian Obrion gave a shrill piercing whistle and jumped back.

Rick drew fast. He could have shot the man. But he was not here to kill Sebastian Obrion in his own house. The black shadows to the front of the patio swallowed Obrion's plunging form.

"Who whistled?" Joe called.

"Obrion. He's running out the front!"

Joe cursed. "I knew he was pulling a ranny on us! Come on!"

They bolted through the passage together, Joe moving as quickly as he could, his face taut in a grimace. But when they got outside, a running horse was fading off into the night, and Rick's horse was gone.

"We need horses first!" Joe panted. "This place is full of gunnies who cut wood when Obrion yells whittle. Let's get to the corral. Sebastian was lying, Rick. Jean Madden was in that room. He knew she was there all the time. Keep your gun handy!"

And as they moved side by side through the night, Rick held his pace in rein with Joe's. His brother muttered: "No use wondering who Sebastian's siding with! I could have told you. He's for anything that makes him money!"

Joe was gasping for breath from the strain as they ran down the alley that sided the Obrion pole corral. The tiny fire was burning at the corner of the saddle shed. The two *peon* hostlers were squatting beside it, smoking, as Rick emerged from the shadows, Joe directly behind him.

"Two horses saddled quick!" Joe called in Spanish. "My El Rey and another."

One of the hostlers threw an armful of hay on the fire as Joe started clumsily toward the saddle shed. And as the flaming hay blazed light over the corral, Rick yelled: "Down, Joe!"

Rick's gun fired at the corner of the saddle shed where a man had appeared with a rifle sighted at Joe. The licking flame above the dry hay made the target clear. The rifle bullet tore into Joe as Rick's gun fired.

The men dodged back into the shed. And Joe went spinning, staggering off to the right, hit badly, helpless, without even a chance to draw his own gun as he plunged to the ground.

Rick felt a cold shock in his left leg, heard the rifle shot back across the corral. His first hunch on the Laguna stage had been right. The Iron Hat range was poison for him. First, Dan dead in the burned ranch house. Then Jean Madden to mock the memories that had brought him on the long journey back. Then Joe, outlawed and gone bad. And when he had Joe back at his side, as a brother once more for a night, this ambush had dropped Joe with a treacherous shot. And here death was spitting across the corral at him.

But he could still move, still keep his feet—and Rick ran, now limping himself, to the fire. He heard a second rifle shot behind him. It missed him or hit Joe, crawling torturously on the ground. Rick ran through the fire, kicking hard, scattering blazing hay and wood embers in a shower of sparks, flame, and smoke. And in the flare of light it made, Rick dived to the ground at the end of the saddle shed.

The *peones* had vanished. Frightened horses were whinnying and raising dust as they bolted around the corral. And the scattered fire died to a duller glow.

The long gun's thin report came again across the corral. The bullet screamed away into the night. And from behind the gun a voice shouted: "He's there at the end of the shed, Curt! I hit him! Go out an' get him!"

But Curt Hanna was swearing, groaning inside the

adobe end wall of the shed, and he did not answer. Another rifle bullet drove dirt particles from the adobe wall into Rick's face.

"Curt, are you gonna get him?"

Rick answered with bitter fury out of the past years. "Try it yourself, Rufe! Or aren't you man enough?"

"I'm man enough!" Rufe's shout came back through the rising dust that was hampering his shooting. "I was man enough to get that damn brother Dan of yours! You'll be the last one, Rick Candleman! We got Dan first before you could get back. And soon as I found out you'd skipped jail, I started across the Border to catch you with Joe, if Hanna hadn't killed Joe first as he started out to do. I knew you'd head this way to hook up with him. We're sending the last of the Candlemans to hell tonight! And Sebastian Obrion's bringing his men to help. Come out and get it before some of Obrion's men drag you out!"

Dust was drifting thicker over the dying fire glow as Rick came out, his hands reaching for the top pole of the corral. He went over fast, falling on the dirt outside, and there was no shot from Rufe Madden's gun. The milling horses, the dust, the dying fire light might have kept Rufe from seeing him.

Half a dozen freight wagons stood outside the back of the corral. When Rick passed them and turned the next corner of the corral, he heard the obscene taunts of Rufe Madden ahead. He saw Rufe's dark bulk crouching, sighting a rifle through the corral poles.

"Come get the last Candleman, Rufe!"

Rufe Madden whirled, snatching the rifle back from the corral bars. It was too dark to see Rufe's thick, vindictive face, but he was caught by surprise. His hasty shot missed.

Rick ran at him, shooting. The first one missed. Rufe had time to lever in another cartridge and start to snap-shoot. He never pulled the trigger. Rick's lead smashed him on down to the ground.

Rick stopped for an instant to make sure it was done, and kept going to the corral gate which he jerked wide. Joe was flat on the ground in that dangerous mill of frightened horses.

A running figure reached the gate as Rick started in. He almost drove a bullet before he recognized Maisa Candleman.

"Where's Joe?" she cried at him. "I heard shooting!"

"Joe's down here under the horses!" Rick snarled at her. "Rufe Madden did it . . . but your damn brother's in on it! Going to wipe out all the Candlemans tonight. Get outa here before I forget you're a woman!"

But she darted into the corral. Rick followed her. And the nearest horses instantly found the open gate and led out a thundering, frightened stampede.

A gun blasted loudly in the middle of the corral and, when Rick plunged through the settling dust, he found Joe sprawled on his face, six-gun still in his hand. Beyond Joe, near a smoldering brand from the fire, lay big handsome Curt Hanna with his face to the stars and the ugly smashed hole of a .45 bullet in his right cheek. Joe had done that and collapsed again.

And when Rick turned back, he found Maisa Candleman down in the dirt and dust, holding Joe's head, crooning and crying to him.

"Joe, speak to me! My dear! My dearest *querido!* My big, brave *niño!* Joe, if you die, your Maisa dies too!"

"You're wastin' your breath!" Rick said harshly. "Here comes your brother and a bunch of his hard cases to finish it off! Get outa the way. Lemme drag Joe in the shed and make a fight of it!"

Maisa gave him no answer. He might not have been there as she caught the big .45 from Joe's hand and whirled up, facing the corral. Some light still came from the last embers of the fire. Enough to show the wild frantic passion on the red-headed girl's features as she stood over Joe and faced the gate with the gun cocked.

Rick had heard the shouts of running men, had guessed correctly. Sebastian Obrion had gone to the plaza for help. Now Rick knew what was coming; his crawling nerves cried to get under cover in the saddle shed. And yet he could not leave Joe out here in the open with his wife. Rick crouched, gun ready, waiting for the shot that would start the end of the Candlemans.

But the shadowy forms that ran to the outside of the corral stopped there uncertainly as they saw the girl facing them. Then Sebastian Obrion's angry shout came from among them.

"Come out, Maisa! Get back to the house!"

"Not until he's dead," she cried wildly back at her brother. "And when he dies, then I come to kill you, Sebastian! I swear it on our mother's grave! Tonight I promise you, Sebastian Obrion, I kill you for this thing you have done to my Joe! Shoot me now! If he dies, then I die, too, anyway! And now I shoot the first one who comes near my Joe!"

In the silence that followed, a rough amazed comment from one of the gunmen burst out: "Does she *mean* it? Sebastian, she's yore sister! It's up to you!"

Sebastian Obrion's reply through the corral bars was injured. "Maisa, this is not my work! Hanna and Madden came here to do this!"

She cried back: "What do I care about them now? They're dead! You are the one who can hurt Joe! Come

69

here, Sebastian, like a man, and face me over my Joe!"

"I don't think I can do that now," Sebastian Obrion refused out of the night. "But if Madden and Hanna are dead, Maisa, what have I to do with this? I didn't come across the Border to kill your Joe."

"You lie, Sebastian!"

"I swear it," said Sebastian reasonably. "If Hanna and Madden are dead, what do we gain by hurting my sister? Put up the gun so we can help Joe."

"I think he means it," Rick said.

"Where there is no money to make, he means it!" she choked, and lowered the gun and dropped to her knees beside Joe again.

Joe was stirring, speaking Rick's name painfully. Rick went to a knee quickly. Joe's dirt-crusted face worked in a painful grin.

"I heard most of it, Rick. Ain't she somethin' to love? I told her she was in my blood like fever, an' she was, an' always will be!"

"I don't blame you, kid," Rick said with a lump in his throat. "How bad you shot?"

"Can't tell. It's up under my shoulder. Kinda numbs me but there ain't any blood in my mouth yet. Rick, listening to Maisa made me think of something I almost forgot, the way things happened so quick. That Jean Madden was all tore up about you when I talked to her in the doorway. She came across the Border lookin' for you. Said Pat Cody told her you was headin' this way. Her brother Rufe had come home, questioned her sharp about you, and saddled for a trip. She figured Rufe was coming after you an' she out-rode him to get here ahead of him and warn you he was coming. Said she told Maisa and the others she was lookin' for Rufe, so they wouldn't stop her getting to you when you showed up.

Rick, she was near crying for worry about you."

"Joe," said Rick in a shaking voice, "you aren't lying to me?"

"Would I lie, Rick, when I'm this close to Heaven and with Maisa to think about for myself?" Joe denied weakly. "Seems like you ought to do something about Jean Madden, Rick."

"I came back from the Argentine to do it," Rick confessed. "Joe, they're going to take you to the house. I'll see you there."

Joe was grinning knowingly as Rick stood up and Obrion's men swarmed around the spot. They were used to bullet wounds. They'd take care of Joe as well as anyone.

But Rick turned back, pushed through the men and knelt again by Joe.

"Joe, I'm going back to the Argentine quick now. There's plenty of place for you and your wife down there . . . and nobody worries about what's happened in the past up in this part of the world. It'll be a home and a chance again."

Joe was still smiling faintly up at the dark sky, his face pale in the moonlight, when Rick suddenly realized that he and Maisa were alone, and turned blindly away. Maisa let out a scream and yanked Joe's body to her.

Rick rose then and passed silently among the Mexicans who had gathered around Joe in the corral, not seeing them. He vanished in the shadows of the night, but he had been walking in the direction of the room Obrion reserved for guests.

WALTER VAN TILBURG CLARK

WALTER VAN TILBURG CLARK (1909-1971) was born in East Orland, Maine, and in 1917 moved with his family to Nevada, the state which served as the setting for most of his subsequent fiction. He was graduated with a Bachelor's degree from the University of Nevada in 1931 and went on for a Master's degree in English, writing a thesis on the Tristram legend. He published a volume of poetry, *Ten Women in Gale's House and Shorter Poems* (Christopher Publishing House, 1932), and then accepted a teaching apprenticeship at the University of Vermont. While there he earned a second Master's degree, writing a thesis on Robinson Jeffers. Clark had personally met Jeffers at his Thor House on the California coast and was as impressed with the man himself and his way of life as with his poetry.

According to Max Westbrook in his biographical and critical study, *Walter Van Tilburg Clark* (Twayne Publishers, 1969), the two most significant influences on Clark's creative writing were Jeffers and C.G. Jung. Clark's first Western novel was *The Ox-Bow Incident* (Random House, 1940). It won him an immediate place in American letters. On the surface, this novel would seem to be concerned with the notion of frontier justice. It tells of three men encountered on the trail by a vigilante group and hanged as cattle rustlers only for them ultimately to be proven innocent. Westbrook's reading of this story, however, proceeds on a deeper level. "The subject of *The Ox-Bow Incident*," he wrote, " . . . is not a plea for legal procedure. The subject is man's mutilation of himself, man's sometimes trivial, sometimes large failures to get beyond the narrow images of his own ego. The tragedy of *The Ox-Bow Incident* is that most of us, including the man of sensitivity and the man of reason, are alienated from the saving grace of archetypal reality. Our lives, then, though not without possibility, are often stories of a cruel and irrevocable mistake."

The terrain, thus, is again familiar, encountered in one aspect or another in "The Last Thunder Song," "The Desert Crucible," and "Werewolf." Yet, none of the authors of these stories approached the Western story with quite Clark's profound erudition in addition to the stress he placed on human psychology, the psychology of the personal unconscious, the collective unconscious, and group psychology. In its way, *The Ox-Bow Incident* proved as shattering and powerful an influence on the way the Western story would be written as in their way Owen Wister's *The Virginian*, T.T. Flynn's early fiction for *Dime Western* and *Star Western*, or Ernest Haycox's serials for *Collier's* had also in their ways. T.V. Olsen openly admitted his debt to Clark's novel and the new dimension it opened for the way the Western story could be written. Les Savage, Jr., in his Western fiction also focused on the psychological dimension in ways that were far less apparent in the work of Western writers before Clark. Indeed, to a degree, it might be said that not a Western story written with a serious intent after 1940 is totally lacking in this heightened awareness of the psychological dimension of character. There are even intimations of it in the stories I have included by Peter Dawson and T.T. Flynn.

Because of the commercial success of his first novel and its sale to motion pictures, with William Wellman directing the screen version, Clark hoped that he could henceforth concentrate on writing fiction and leave his teaching career behind him. He published a number of short stories while he worked diligently on his very long and not very successful *The City of Trembling Leaves* (Random House, 1945). It is an initiation story in which setting and a sense of the land are negligible. This painful failure prompted Clark to seek his roots in the West. In 1946 he went to live in Taos, New Mexico, and returned to Nevada toward the end of the decade. *The Track of the Cat* (Random House, 1949), the distillation of this effort at spiritual renascence, is a story that demonstrates why two hunters are killed pursuing a panther, symbolizing the principle of evil in the world, because they do not understand it, and why two hunters who do understand it are able to slay the beast. Herman Melville's *Moby-Dick* was very obviously the paradigm Clark had in mind, but the primal inspiration evident in *The Ox-Bow Incident* is lacking in its immediacy and the later novel is ultimately only epigonal. It was, however, also sold for a motion picture adaptation and, upon release, became just a hunting adventure film.

Clark next published a collection of his short stories titled *The Watchful Gods and Other Stories* (Random House, 1950). Unfortunately, having been so gracious toward his first book, the critics became increasingly harsh in their appraisals of each book Clark published after it. In an essay titled "The Western Writer and the Eastern Establishment" in *Western American Literature* (Winter, 67) the late Vardis Fisher observed, "I read recently a surmise that Walter Clark, a fine artist, gave up writing because of the unfairness of some of his critics. If true, what a pity that he paid any attention to them!" This may well have been the reason Clark did quit writing. He returned to teaching, at the university level, and left behind only the fragments of an unfinished novel when he died. However, this notwithstanding, **The Ox-Bow Incident** assures him always of a pivotal rôle in having charted the course of the Western story in the new direction it would take in the 1940s and 1950s.

"The Wind and the Snow of Winter" is a short story from **The Watchful Gods and Other Stories**. It is one of the few stories Clark wrote that has much of the power and depth of his first novel. And the land *is* a character. Indeed, here as too seldom elsewhere, Clark was able to combine a vivid description of physical topography and characterization of a human personality with an eerie sense of metaphysical shadows and meanings less decipherable but somehow more potent as they are also in the best works by Zane Grey and Max Brand.

THE WIND AND SNOW OF WINTER
1944

IT WAS NEAR SUNSET WHEN MIKE BRANEEN CAME ONTO the last pitch of the old wagon road which had led into Gold Rock from the east since the Comstock days. The road was just two ruts in the hard earth, with sagebrush growing between them, and was full of steep pitches and sharp turns. From the summit it descended even more steeply into Gold Rock in a series of short switchbacks down the slope of the cañon. There was a paved highway on the other side of the pass now, but Mike never used that. Cars coming from behind made him uneasy, so that he couldn't follow his own thoughts long, but had to keep turning around every few minutes, to see that his burro, Annie, was staying out on the shoulder of the road, where she would be safe. Mike didn't like cars anyway, and on the old road he could forget about them, and feel more like himself. He could forget about Annie too, except when the light, quick tapping of her hoofs behind him stopped. Even then he didn't really break his thoughts. It was more as if the tapping were another sound from his own inner machinery and, when it stopped, he stopped too, and turned around to see what she was doing. When he began to walk ahead again at the same slow, unvarying pace, his arms scarcely swinging at all, his body bent a little forward from the waist, he would not be aware that there had been any interruption of the memory or the story that was going on in his head. Mike did not like to have his stories interrupted except by an idea of his own, something to do with prospecting, or the arrival of his story at an actual memory which warmed him to closer recollection or led into a new and more attractive story.

An intense, golden light, almost liquid, fanned out from the peaks above him and reached eastward under the gray sky, and the snow which occasionally swarmed across this light was fine and dry. Such little squalls had been going on all day, and still there was nothing like real snow down, but only a fine powder which the wind swept along until it caught under the brush, leaving the ground bare. Yet Mike Braneen was not deceived. This was not just a flurrying day; it was the beginning of winter. If not tonight, then tomorrow, or the next day, the snow would begin which shut off the mountains, so that a man might as well be on a great plain for all he

76

could see, perhaps even the snow which blinded a man at once and blanketed the desert in an hour. Fifty-two years in this country had made Mike Braneen sure about such things, although he didn't give much thought to them, but only to what he had to do because of them. Three nights before, he had been awakened by a change in the wind. It was no longer a wind born in the near mountains, cold with night and altitude, but a wind from far places, full of a damp chill which got through his blankets and into his bones. The stars had still been clear and close above the dark humps of the mountains, and overhead the constellations had moved slowly in full panoply, unbroken by any invisible lower darkness; yet he had lain there half awake for a few minutes, hearing the new wind beat the brush around him, hearing Annie stirring restlessly and thumping in her hobble. He had thought drowsily. Smells like winter this time, and then, it's held off a long time this year, pretty near the end of December. Then he had gone back to sleep, mildly happy because the change meant he would be going back to Gold Rock. Gold Rock was the other half of Mike Braneen's life. When the smell of winter came, he always started back for Gold Rock. From March or April until the smell of winter, he wandered slowly about among the mountains, anywhere between the White Pines and the Virginias, with only his burro for company. Then there would come the change, and they would head back for Gold Rock.

Mike had traveled with a good many burros during that time, eighteen or twenty, he thought, although he was not sure. He could not remember them all, but only those he had had first, when he was a young man and always thought most about seeing women when he got back to Gold Rock, or those with something queer about

77

them, like Baldy, who'd had a great, pale patch, like a bald spot, on one side of his belly, or those who'd had something queer happen to them, like Maria. He could remember just how it had been that night. He could remember it as if it were last night. It had been in Hamilton. He had felt unhappy, because he could remember Hamilton when the whole hollow was full of people and buildings, and everything was new and active. He had gone to sleep in the hollow shell of the Wells Fargo Building, hearing an old iron shutter banging against the wall in the wind. In the morning, Maria had been gone. He had followed the scuffing track she made on account of her loose hobble, and it had led far up the old snow-gullied road to Treasure Hill, and then ended at one of the black shafts that opened like mouths right at the edge of the road. A man remembered a thing like that. There weren't many burros that foolish. But burros with nothing particular about them were hard to remember especially those he'd had in the last twenty years or so, when he had gradually stopped feeling so personal about them, and had begun to call all the jennies Annie and all the burros Jack.

The clicking of the little hoofs behind him stopped, and Mike stopped too, and turned around. Annie was pulling at a line of yellow grass along the edge of the road.

"Come on, Annie," Mike said patiently. The burro at once stopped pulling at the dead grass and came on up towards him, her small black nose working, the ends of the grass standing out on each side of it like whiskers. Mike began to climb again, ahead of her.

It was a long time since he had been caught by a winter, too. He could not remember how long. All the beginnings ran together in his mind, as if they were all the beginning of one winter so far back that he had almost forgotten it. He could still remember clearly, though, the winter he had stayed out on purpose, clear into January. He had been a young man then, thirty-five or forty or forty-five, somewhere in there. He would have to stop and try to bring back a whole string of memories about what had happened just before, in order to remember just how old he had been, and it wasn't worth the trouble. Besides, sometimes even that system didn't work. It would lead him into an old camp where he had been a number of times, and the dates would get mixed up. It was impossible to remember any other way; because all his comings and goings had been so much alike. He had been young, anyhow, and not much afraid of anything except running out of water in the wrong place; not even afraid of the winter. He had stayed out because he'd thought he had a good thing, and he had wanted to prove it. He could remember how it felt to be out in the clear winter weather on the mountains; the piñon trees and the junipers weighted down with feathery snow, and making sharp, blue shadows on the white slopes. The hills had made blue shadows on one another too, and in the still air his pick had made the beginning of a sound like a bell's. He knew he had been young, because he could remember taking a day off now and then, just to go tramping around those hills, up and down the white and through the blue shadows, on a kind of holiday. He had pretended to his common sense that he was seriously prospecting, and had carried his hammer, and even his drill along, but he had really just been gallivanting, playing colt. Maybe he had been even younger than thirty-five, though he could still be stirred a little, for

79

that matter, by the memory of the kind of weather which had sent him gallivanting. High-blue weather, he called it. There were two kinds of high-blue weather, besides the winter kind, which didn't set him off very often, spring and fall. In the spring it would have a soft, puffy wind and soft, puffy white clouds which made separate shadows that traveled silently across hills that looked soft too. In the fall it would be still, and there would be no clouds at all in the blue, but there would be something in the golden air and the soft, steady sunlight on the mountains that made a man as uneasy as the spring blowing, though in a different way, more sad and not so excited. In the spring high-blue, a man had been likely to think about women he had slept with, or wanted to sleep with, or imaginary women made up with the help of newspaper pictures of actresses or young society matrons, or of the old oil paintings in the Lucky Boy Saloon, which showed pale, almost naked women against dark, sumptuous backgrounds—women with long hair or braided hair, calm, virtuous faces, small hands and feet, and ponderous limbs, breasts, and buttocks. In the fall high-blue, though it had been much longer since he had seen a woman, or heard a woman's voice, he was more likely to think about old friends, men, or places he had heard about, or places he hadn't seen for a long time. He himself thought most often about Goldfield the way he had last seen it in the summer in 1912. That was as far south as Mike had ever been in Nevada. Since then he had never been south of Tonopah. When the high-blue weather was past, though, and the season worked toward winter, he began to think about Gold Rock. There were only three or four winters out of the fifty-two when he hadn't gone home to Gold Rock, to his old room at Mrs. Wright's, up on Fourth

Street, and to his meals in the dining room at the International House, and to the Lucky Boy, where he could talk to Tom Connover and his other friends, and play cards, or have a drink to hold in his hand while he sat and remembered.

This journey had seemed a little different from most, though. It had started the same as usual, but as he had come across the two vast valleys, and through the pass in the low range between them, he hadn't felt quite the same. He'd felt younger and more awake, it seemed to him, and yet, in a way, older too, suddenly older. He had been sure that there was plenty of time, and yet he had been a little afraid of getting caught in the storm. He had kept looking ahead to see if the mountains on the horizon were still clearly outlined, or if they had been cut off by a lowering of the clouds. He had thought more than once, how bad it would be to get caught out there when the real snow began, and he had been disturbed by the first flakes. It had seemed hard to him to have to walk so far, too. He had kept thinking about distance. Also the snowy cold had searched out the regions of his body where old injuries had healed. He had taken off his left mitten a good many times, to blow on the fingers which had been frosted the year he was sixty-three, so that now it didn't take much cold to turn them white and stiffen them. The queer tingling, partly like an itch and partly like a pain, in the patch on his back that had been burned in that old powder blast, was sharper than he could remember its having been before. The rheumatism in his joints, which was so old a companion that it usually made him feel no more than tightknit and stiff, and the place where his leg had been broken and torn when that ladder broke in '97 ached, and had a pulse he could count. All this made him

81

believe that he was walking more slowly than usual, although nothing, probably not even a deliberate attempt, could actually have changed his pace. Sometimes he even thought, with a moment of fear, that he was getting tired.

On the other hand, he felt unusually clear and strong in his mind. He remembered things with a clarity which was like living them again—nearly all of them events from many years back, from the time when he had been really active and fearless and every burro had had its own name. Some of these events, like the night he had spent in Eureka with the little, brown-haired whore, a night in the fall in 1888 or '89, somewhere in there, he had not once thought of for years. Now he could remember even her name. Armandy she had called herself: a funny name. They all picked names for their business, of course, romantic names like Cecily or Rosamunde or Belle or Claire, or hard names like Diamond Gert or Horseshoe Sal, or names that were pinned on them, like Indian Kate or Roman Mary, but Armandy was different.

He could remember Armandy as if he were with her now, not the way she had behaved in bed; he couldn't remember anything particular about that. In fact, he couldn't be sure that he remembered anything particular about that at all. There were others he could remember more clearly for the way they had behaved in bed, women he had been with more often. He had been with Armandy only that one night. He remembered little things about being with her, things that made it seem good to think of being with her again. Armandy had a room upstairs in a hotel. They could hear a piano playing in a club across the street. He could hear the tune, and it was one he knew, although he didn't know its name. It was a gay tune that went on and on the same, but still it sounded sad when you heard it through the hotel window, with the lights from the bars and hotels shining on the street, and the people coming and going through the lights, and then, beyond the lights, the darkness where the mountains were. Armandy wore a white silk dress with a high waist and a locket on a gold chain. The dress made her look very brown and like a young girl. She used a white powder on her face, that smelled like violets, but this could not hide her brownness. The locket was heart-shaped, and it opened to show a cameo of a man's hand holding a woman's hand very gently, just their fingers laid out long together, and the thumbs holding the way they were sometimes on tombstones. There were two little gold initials on each hand, but Armandy would never tell what they stood for, or even if the locket was really her own. He stood in the window, looking down at the club from which the piano music was coming, and Armandy stood beside him, with her shoulders against his arm, and a glass of wine in her hand. He could see the toe of her white satin slipper showing from under the edge of her skirt. Her big hat, loaded with black and white plumes, lay on the dresser behind him. His own leather coat, with the sheepskin lining, lay across the foot of the bed. It was a big bed, with a knobby brass foot and head. There was one oil lamp burning in the chandelier in the middle room. Armandy was soft-spoken, gentle, and a little fearful, always looking at him to see what he was thinking. He stood with his arms folded. His arms felt big and strong upon his heavily muscled chest. He stood there, pretending to be in no hurry, but really thinking eagerly about what he would do with Armandy, who had something about her which tempted him to be cruel. He stood there, with his chin down into his heavy dark beard, and watched a man come riding down the middle of the street from the west. The horse was a fine black, which lifted its head and feet with pride. The man sat very straight, with a high rein, and something about his clothes and hat made him appear to be in uniform, although it wasn't a uniform he was wearing. The man also saluted friends upon the sidewalks like an officer, bending his head just slightly, and touching his hat instead of lifting it. Mike Braneen asked Armandy who the man was, and then felt angry because she could tell him, and because he was an important man who owned a mine that was in bonanza. He mocked the airs with which the man rode, and his princely greetings. He mocked the man cleverly, and Armandy laughed and repeated what he said, and made him drink a little of her wine as a reward. Mike had been drinking whisky, and he did not like wine anyway, but this was not the moment in which to refuse such an invitation.

Old Mike remembered all this, which had been completely forgotten for years. He could not remember what he and Armandy had said, but he remembered everything else, and he felt very lonesome for Armandy, and for the room with the red, figured carpet and the brass chandelier with oil lamps in it, and the open window with the long tune coming up through it, and the young summer night outside on the mountains. This loneliness was so much more intense than his familiar loneliness that it made him feel very young. Memories like this had come up again and again during these three days. It was like beginning life over again. It had tricked him into thinking, more than once, next summer I'll make the strike, and this time I'll put it into something safe for the rest of my life, and stop this fool wandering around while I've still got some time left—a way of thinking which he had really stopped a long time before.

It was getting darker rapidly in the pass. When a gust of wind brought the snow against Mike's face so hard that he noticed the flakes felt larger, he looked up. The light was still there, although the fire was dying out of it, and the snow swarmed across it more thickly. Mike remembered God. He did not think anything exact. He did not think about his own relationship to God. He merely felt the idea as a comforting presence. He'd always had a feeling about God whenever he looked at a sunset, especially a sunset which came through under a stormy sky. It had been the strongest feeling left in him until these memories like the one about Armandy had begun. Even in this last pass, his strange fear of the storm had come on him again a couple of times, but now that he had looked at the light and thought of God, it was gone. In a few minutes he would come to the summit and look down into his lighted city. He felt happily hurried by this anticipation.

He would take the burro down and stable her in John Hammersmith's shed, where he always kept her. He would spread fresh straw for her, and see that the shed was tight against the wind and snow, and get a measure of grain for her from John. Then he would go up to Mrs. Wright's house at the top of Fourth Street, and leave his things in the same room he always had, the one in front, which looked down over the roofs and chimneys of his city, and across at the east wall of the cañon, from which the sun rose late. He would trim his beard with Mrs. Wright's shears, and shave the upper part of his cheeks. He would bathe out of the blue bowl and pitcher, and wipe himself with the towel with yellow

85

flowers on it, and dress in the good dark suit and the good black shoes with the gleaming box toes, and the good black hat which he had left in the chest in his room. In this way he would perform the ceremony which ended the life of the desert and began the life of Gold Rock. Then he would go down to the International House, and greet Arthur Morris in the gleaming bar, and go into the dining room and eat the best supper they had, with fresh meat and vegetables, and new-made pie, and two cups of hot clear coffee. He would be served by the plump blonde waitress who always joked with him, and gave him many little extra things with his first supper, including the drink which Arthur Morris always sent in from the bar.

At this point Mike Braneen stumbled in his mind, and his anticipation wavered. He could not be sure that the plump blonde waitress would serve him. For a moment he saw her in a long skirt, and the dining room of the International House, behind her, had potted palms standing in the corners, and was full of the laughter and loud, manly talk of many customers who wore high vests and mustaches and beards. These men leaned back from tables covered with empty dishes. They patted their tight vests and lighted expensive cigars. He knew all their faces. If he were to walk down the aisle between the tables on his side, they would all speak to him. But he also seemed to remember the dining room with only a few tables, with oilcloth on them instead of linen, and with moody young men sitting at them in their work clothes—strangers who worked for the highway department, or were just passing through, or talked mining in terms which he did not understand or which made him angry.

No, it would not be the plump blonde waitress. He

did not know who it would be. It didn't matter. After supper he would go up Cañon Street under the arcade to the Lucky Boy Saloon, and there it would be the same as ever. There would be the laurel wreaths on the frosted glass panels of the doors, and the old sign upon the window, the sign that was older than Tom Connover, almost as old as Mike Braneen himself. He would open the door and see the bottles and the white women in the paintings, and the card table in the back corner and the big stove and the chairs along the wall. Tom would look around from his place behind the bar.

"Well, now," he would roar, "look who's here, boys. Now will you believe it's winter?" he would roar at them.

Some of them would be the younger men, of course, and there might even be a few strangers, but this would only add to the dignity of his reception, and there would also be his friends. There would be Henry Bray with the gray walrus mustache, and Mark Wilton and Pat Gallagher. They would all welcome him loudly.

"Mike, how are you anyway?" Tom would roar, leaning across the bar to shake hands with his big, heavy, soft hand with the diamond ring on it. "And what'll it be, Mike? The same?" he'd ask, as if Mike had been in there no longer ago than the night before.

Mike would play that game too. "The same," he would say.

Then he would really be back in Gold Rock: never mind the plump blonde waitress.

Mike came to the summit of the old road and stopped and looked down. For a moment he felt lost again, as he had when he'd thought about the plump blonde waitress. He had expected Cañon Street to look much brighter. He had expected a lot of orange windows close together on the other side of the cañon. Instead there were only a few scattered lights across the darkness, and they were white. They made no communal glow upon the steep slope, but gave out only single, white needles of light, which pierced the darkness secretly and lonesomely, as if nothing could ever pass from one house to another over there. Cañon Street was very dark, too. There it went, the street he loved, steeply down into the bottom of the cañon, and down its length there were only the few street lights, more than a block apart, swinging in the wind and darting about that cold, small light. The snow whirled and swooped under the nearest street light below.

"You are getting to be an old fool," Mike Braneen said out loud to himself, and felt better. This was the way Gold Rock was now, of course, and he loved it all the better. It was a place that grew old with a man, that was going to die sometime, too. There could be an understanding with it.

He worked his way slowly down into Cañon Street, with Annie slipping and checking behind him. Slowly, with the blown snow behind them, they came to the first built-in block, and passed the first dim light showing through a smudged window under the arcade. They passed the dark places after it, and the second light. Then Mike Braneen stopped in the middle of the street, and Annie stopped beside him, pulling her rump in and turning her head away from the snow. A highway truck, coming down from the head of the cañon, had to get way over into the wrong side of the street to pass them. The driver leaned out as he went by, and yelled, "Pull over, Pop. You're in town now."

Mike Braneen didn't hear him. He was staring at the Lucky Boy. The Lucky Boy was dark, and there were boards nailed across the big window that had shown the sign. At last Mike went over onto the board walk to look more closely. Annie followed him, but stopped at the edge of the walk and scratched her neck against a post of the arcade. There was the other sign, hanging crossways under the arcade, and even in that gloom Mike could see that it said Lucky Boy and had a Jack of Diamonds painted on it. There was no mistake. The Lucky Boy sign, and others like it under the arcade, creaked and rattled in the wind.

There were footsteps coming along the boards. The boards sounded hollow, and sometimes one of them rattled. Mike Braneen looked down slowly from the sign and peered at the approaching figure. It was a man wearing a sheepskin coat with the collar turned up round his head. He was walking quickly, like a man who knew where he was going, and why, and where he had been. Mike almost let him pass. Then he spoke.

"Say, fella . . . ?"

He even reached out a hand as if to catch hold of the man's sleeve, though he didn't touch it. The man stopped, and asked impatiently, "Yeah?" and Mike let the hand down again slowly.

"Well, what is it?" the man asked.

"I don't want anything." Mike said. "I got plenty."

"O.K., O.K.," the man said. "What's the matter?"

Mike moved his hand towards the Lucky Boy. "It's closed," he said.

"I see it is, Dad," the man said. He laughed a little. He didn't seem to be in quite so much of a hurry now.

"How long has it been closed?" Mike asked.

"Since about June, I guess," the man said. "Old Tom Connover, the guy that ran it, died last June."

Mike waited for a moment. "Tom died?" he asked.

89

"Yup. I guess he'd just kept it open out of love of the place anyway. There hasn't been any real business for years. Nobody cared to keep it open after him."

The man started to move on, but then he waited, peering, trying to see Mike better.

"This June?" Mike asked finally.

"Yup. This last June."

"Oh," Mike said. Then he just stood there. He wasn't thinking anything. There didn't seem to be anything to think.

"You knew him?" the man asked.

"Thirty years," Mike said. "No, more'n that," he said, and started to figure out how long he had known Tom Connover but lost it, and said, as if it would do just as well, "He was a lot younger than I am, though."

"Hey," said the man, coming closer, and peering again. "You're Mike Braneen, aren't you?"

"Yes," Mike said.

"Gee, I didn't recognize you at first. I'm sorry."

"That's all right," Mike said. He didn't know who the man was, or what he was sorry about.

He turned his head slowly, and looked out into the street. The snow was coming down heavily now. The street was all white. He saw Annie with her head and shoulders in under the arcade, but the snow settling on her rump.

"Well, I guess I'd better get Molly under cover," he said. He moved toward the burro a step, but then halted.

"Say, fella . . . ?"

The man had started on, but he turned back. He had to wait for Mike to speak.

"I guess this about Tom mixed me up."

"Sure," the man said. "It's tough, an old friend like that."

"Where do I turn to get to Mrs. Wright's place?"

"Mrs. Wright?"

"Mrs. William Wright," Mike said. "Her husband used to be a foreman in the Aztec. Got killed in the fire."

"Oh," the man said. He didn't say anything more, but just stood there, looking at the shadowy bulk of old Mike.

"She's not dead, too, is she?" Mike asked slowly.

"Yeah, I'm afraid she is, Mr. Braneen," the man said. "Look," he said more cheerfully. "It's Mrs. Branley's house you want right now, isn't it? Place where you stayed last winter?"

Finally Mike said, "Yeah, I guess it is."

"I'm going up that way. I'll walk up with you," the man said.

After they had started, Mike thought that he ought to take the burro down to John Hammersmith's first, but he was afraid to ask about it. They walked on down Cañon Street, with Annie walking along beside them in the gutter. At the first side street they turned right and began to climb the steep hill toward another of the little street lights dancing over a crossing. There was no sidewalk here, and Annie followed right at their heels. That one street light was the only light showing up ahead.

When they were halfway up to the light, Mike asked, "She die this summer, too?"

The man turned his body half around, so that he could hear inside his collar.

"What?"

"Did she die this summer, too?"

"Who?"

"Mrs. Wright," Mike said.

91

The man looked at him, trying to see his face as they came up towards the light. Then he turned back again, and his voice was muffled by the collar.

"No, she died quite a while ago, Mr. Braneen."

"Oh," Mike said finally.

They came up onto the crossing under the light, and the snow-laden wind whirled around them again. They passed under the light, and their three lengthening shadows before them were obscured by the innumerable tiny shadows of the flakes.

DOROTHY M. JOHNSON

DOROTHY MARIE JOHNSON (1905-1984) was born in McGregor, Iowa, and grew up in Whitefish, Montana. She was graduated with a Bachelor's degree from the University of Montana at Missoula. She worked variously as a stenographer before venturing to New York City in 1935 where she found employment, first with the Gregg Publishing Company until 1944, then with Farrell Publishing Corporation until 1950. It was while doing editorial work at these magazine and book publishing companies that she herself began writing in earnest (she had had only one short story published before leaving Whitefish). Her first book, ***Beulah Bunny Tells All*** (Morrow, 1942), is a collection of short stories about a fictitious schoolteacher previously published in *The Saturday Evening Post*.

It was also during this period that she began reading extensively about the Plains Indians and visited the museums in the area which specialized in their artifacts and cultures. It was as a result of this activity that she began to create her first Indian stories, selling them principally to *Argosy*, *Collier's*, *The Saturday Evening Post*, and *Cosmopolitan*. When queried as to the reason her work had gone so thoroughly in this direction, her truthful answer was that she was homesick for Montana. She returned to Whitefish on a vacation in 1950. When she was offered the position of news editor for the Whitefish *Pilot*, a weekly newspaper, she flew back to New York and stayed there only long enough to resign from her job at Farrell Publishing and to pack up her things. In 1953 she moved to Missoula to work as the secretary-manager of the Montana Press Association and the next year was also appointed an assistant professor of journalism at her former *alma mater*.

Bill Gulick, a frequent contributor of Western stories to many of the same magazines for which she wrote, once said of Johnson, "She was not a woman who needed to be liberated by legislation; she was born liberated, and never changed." She had nothing but contempt for political correctness in the Western story, or anywhere else. In a letter to the editor of *The Missoulian* protesting the newspaper's clumsy attempt to avoid "sexism" in its Help Wanted columns, she wrote: "The city of Missoula advertised for applications for the position of Ward 5 'alderperson.' This nicety makes me gag. There is nothing wrong with the last syllable of 'alderman' except to persons who just can't get their minds off sex. Sometimes I worry about the *huperson* race. (Signed) Dorothy M Johnson, a *woperson*."

Among the hundreds of Western writers with whom I have spoken and corresponded over the years, Dorothy M. Johnson was always the most crisply accurate in her assessments and the most poignantly amusing. Accuracy, in fact, even got into an obituary notice following her death from Parkinson's disease. Benjamin Capps, in his *memoria* for Johnson in *The Roundup* (1/85), cited Dorothy Powers's tribute to her friend in the Spokane *Spokesman-Review*. Johnson had insisted that the inscription on her headstone contain a single word: "Paid." Johnson had told Powers, "God and I know what that means, and nobody else needs to know." Powers's conclusion was "that Dorothy Johnson meant she had done her best to live a life that left nothing owing the world for her time and space in it.

Even in death she was—as always—accurate. But she was much too modest. That marker should really read: 'Accounts Receivable.' For this world is greatly in *her* debt—for laughter and literacy and love of life."

"A Man Called Horse" was first published in *Collier's* (1/7/50). It incorporates a theme common in Johnson's Western stories whereby men and women grow as human beings through humiliation rather than by conquest. The story was included in Johnson's first collection of her short Western fiction, **Indian Country** (Ballantine, 1953), dating from that early period during which Ian and Betty Ballantine published their Western story titles simultaneously in both hard cover and paperback editions. Jack Schaefer contributed a Foreword in which he observed that Johnson was "one of the few writers whose authenticity, integrity, sheer vigor and excitement were helping to build a body of true literature about the American West." Her second story collection, published as an original paperback by Ballantine in 1958, was titled **The Hanging Tree**. This appeared for the first time in hard covers in the reprint edition from Gregg Press in 1980.

Controversy never accorded the story began with the appearance of the motion picture version, *A Man Called Horse* (National General, 1970). "Rather than a tale of Indian life," Dan Georgakas wrote in "They Have Not Spoken: American Indians in Film" in *Film Quarterly* (Spring, 1972), *A Man Called Horse* "is thus really about a white nobleman proving his superiority in the wilds. Almost every detail of Indian life is incorrect. An angry Sioux writing to the *Village Voice* complained . . . that the Sioux never abandoned widows, orphans, and old people to starve and freeze as shown in the film." This posture concerning Sioux attitudes is also the one promulgated by Black Elk as recorded by John G. Neihardt:

I could see that the Wasichus [white people] did not care for each other the way our people did . . . . They would take everything from each other if they could, and so there were some who had more of everything than they could use, while crowds of people had nothing at all and maybe were starving. They had forgotten that the earth was their mother.

Whatever else he may have been, Black Elk was neither an historian nor an anthropologist. "Some old people, unwanted or without relatives, had no place to go," Royal B. Hassrick noted in *The Sioux* (University of Oklahoma Press, 1964). "These were forced to live alone at the edge of the encampment. Here they were given food and supplies by the generous young men who thereby gained prestige . . . but at best theirs was a tragic lot, too often filled with insecurity and despair." The same was true also for the Crow Indians, in history as in Dorothy M. Johnson's story. And, in the event, Johnson cannot be held accountable for any foolishness produced by Hollywood. Once, when I commented to her on how poor a film I thought *A Man Called Horse* to be, she responded with asperity, "If you think that one's bad, wait until you see *Triumphs of a Man Called Horse* [HBO, 1983]!" I did. It was the second sequel, and she was right.

There are two principal ways to end a captivity story: a captive may somehow secure freedom, or remain with the captors. "There was only one group lower in status than the women; that was the slave or captive group," Mildred P. Mayhall recorded in *The Kiowas* (University of Oklahoma Press, 1971). "This group held an impermanent status, for captives, showing fortitude and bravery, could be accepted into the tribe, usually by adoption into a family. For a girl, also, marriage with an important man might change captive status. Many captives did not desire to return to their own people." Perhaps the most telling difference between now and the 19th-Century American West is that there were *once* alternatives to the invaders' culture.

A MAN CALLED HORSE
1949

HE WAS A YOUNG MAN OF GOOD FAMILY, AS THE phrase went in the New England of a hundred-odd years ago, and the reasons for his bitter discontent were unclear, even to himself. He grew up in the gracious old Boston home under his grandmother's care, for his mother had died in giving him birth; and all his life he had known every comfort and privilege his father's wealth could provide.

But still there was the discontent, which puzzled him because he could not even define it. He wanted to live among his equals—people who were no better than he and no worse either. That was as close as he could come to describing the source of his unhappiness in Boston and his restless desire to go somewhere else.

In the year 1845, he left home and went out West, far beyond the country's creeping frontier, where he hoped to find his equals. He had the idea that in Indian country, where there was danger, all white men were kings, and he wanted to be one of them. But he found, in the West as in Boston, that the men he respected were still his superiors, even if they could not read, and those he did not respect weren't worth talking to.

He did have money, however, and he could hire the men he respected. He hired four of them, to cook and hunt and guide and be his companions, but he found them not friendly.

They were apart from him and he was still alone. He still brooded about his status in the world, longing for his equals.

On a day in June, he learned what it was to have no status at all. He became a captive of a small raiding party of Crow Indians.

He heard gunfire and the brief shouts of his companions around the bend of the creek just before they died, but he never saw their bodies. He had no chance to fight, because he was naked and unarmed, bathing in the creek, when a Crow warrior seized and held him.

His captor let him go at last, let him run. Then the lot of them rode him down for sport, striking him with their coup sticks. They carried the dripping scalps of his companions, and one had skinned off Baptiste's black beard as well, for a trophy.

They took him along in a matter-of-fact way, as they took the captured horses. He was unshod and naked as the horses were, and like them he had a rawhide thong around his neck. So long as he didn't fall down, the Crows ignored him.

On the second day they gave him his breeches. His feet were too swollen for his boots, but one of the Indians threw him a pair of moccasins that had belonged to the half-breed, Henri, who was dead back at the creek. The captive wore the moccasins gratefully. The third day they let him ride one of the spare horses so the party could move faster, and on that day they came in sight of their camp.

He thought of trying to escape, hoping he might be killed in flight rather than by slow torture in the camp, but he never had a chance to try. They were more familiar with escape than he was and, knowing what to expect, they forestalled it. The only other time he had tried to escape from anyone, he had succeeded. When he had left his home in Boston, his father had raged and his grandmother had cried, but they could not talk him out of his intention.

The men of the Crow raiding party didn't bother with talk.

Before riding into camp they stopped and dressed in their regalia, and in parts of their victims' clothing; they painted their faces black. Then, leading the white man by the rawhide around his neck as though he were a horse, they rode down toward the tepee circle, shouting and singing, brandishing their weapons. He was unconscious when they got there; he fell and was dragged.

He lay dazed and battered near a tepee while the noisy, busy life of the camp swarmed around him and Indians came to stare. Thirst consumed him and, when it rained, he lapped rain water from the ground like a dog. A scrawny, shrieking, eternally busy old woman with ragged graying hair threw a chunk of meat on the grass, and he fought the dogs for it.

When his head cleared, he was angry, although anger was an emotion he knew he could not afford.

It was better when I was a horse, he thought—when they led me by the rawhide around my neck. I won't be a dog, no matter what!

The hag gave him stinking, rancid grease and let him figure out what it was for. He applied it gingerly to his bruised and sun-seared body.

Now, he thought, I smell like the rest of them.

While he was healing, he considered coldly the advantages of being a horse. A man would be humiliated, and sooner or later he would strike back and that would be the end of him. But a horse had only to be docile. Very well, he would learn to do without pride.

He understood that he was the property of the screaming old woman, a fine gift from her son, one that she liked to show off. She did more yelling at him than at anyone else, probably to impress the neighbors so they would not forget what a great and generous man her son was. She was bossy and proud, a dreadful bag of skin and bones, and she was a devilish hard worker.

The white man, who now thought of himself as a horse, forgot sometimes to worry about his danger. He kept making mental notes of things to tell his own people in Boston about this hideous adventure. He would go back a hero, and he would say, "Grandmother, let me fetch your shawl. I've been accustomed to doing little errands for another lady about your age."

Two girls lived in the tepee with the old hag and her warrior son. One of them, the white man concluded, was his captor's wife and the other was his little sister. The daughter-in-law was smug and spoiled. Being beloved, she did not have to be useful. The younger girl had bright, wandering eyes. Often enough they wandered to the white man who was pretending to be a horse.

The two girls worked when the old woman put them at it, but they were always running off to do something they enjoyed more. There were games and noisy contests, and there was much laughter. But not for the white man. He was finding out what loneliness could be.

That was a rich summer on the plains, with plenty of

buffalo for meat and clothing and the making of tepees. The Crows were wealthy in horses, prosperous and contented. If their men had not been so avid for glory, the white man thought, there would have been a lot more of them. But they went out of their way to court death and, when one of them met it, the whole camp mourned extravagantly and cried to their God for vengeance.

The captive was a horse all summer, a docile bearer of burdens, careful and patient. He kept reminding himself that he had to be better-natured than other horses, because he could not lash out with hoofs or teeth. Helping the old woman load up the horses for travel, he yanked at a pack and said, "Whoa, brother. It goes easier when you don't fight."

The horse gave him a big-eyed stare as if it understood his language—a comforting thought, because nobody else did. But even among the horses he felt unequal. They were able to look out for themselves if they escaped. He would simply starve. He was envious still, even among the horses.

Humbly he fetched and carried. Sometimes he even offered to help, but he had not the skill for the endless work of the women, and he was not trusted to hunt with the men, the providers.

When the camp moved, he carried a pack trudging with the women. Even the dogs worked then, pulling small burdens on travois of sticks.

The Indian who had captured him lived like a lord, as he had a right to do. He hunted with his peers, attended long ceremonial meetings with much chanting and dancing, and lounged in the shade with his smug bride. He had only two responsibilities: to kill buffalo and to gain glory. The white man was so far beneath him in status that the Indian did not even think of envy.

One day several things happened that made the captive think he might sometime become a man again. That was the day when he began to understand their language. For four months he had heard it, day and night, the joy and the mourning, the ritual chanting and sung prayers, the squabbles and the deliberations. None of it meant anything to him at all.

But on that important day in early fall the two young women set out for the river, and one of them called over her shoulder to the old woman. The white man was startled. She had said she was going to bathe. His understanding was so sudden that he felt as if his ears had come unstopped. Listening to the racket of the camp, he heard fragments of meaning instead of gabble.

On that same important day the old woman brought a pair of new moccasins out of the tepee and tossed them on the ground before him. He could not believe she would do anything for him because of kindness, but giving him moccasins was one way of looking after her property.

In thanking her, he dared greatly. He picked a little handful of fading fall flowers and took them to her as she squatted in front of her tepee, scraping a buffalo hide with a tool made from a piece of iron tied to a bone. Her hands were hideous—most of the fingers had the first joint missing. He bowed solemnly and offered the flowers.

She glared at him from beneath the short, ragged tangle of her hair. She stared at the flowers, knocked them out of his hand and went running to the next tepee, squalling the story. He heard her and the other women screaming with laughter.

The white man squared his shoulders and walked

boldly over to watch three small boys shooting arrows at a target. He said in English, "Show me how to do that, will you?"

They frowned, but he held out his hand as if there could be no doubt. One of them gave him a bow and one arrow, and they snickered when he missed.

The people were easily amused, except when they were angry. They were amused, at him, playing with the little boys. A few days later he asked the hag, with gestures, for a bow that her son had just discarded, a man-size bow of horn. He scavenged for old arrows. The old woman cackled at his marksmanship and called her neighbors to enjoy the fun.

When he could understand words, he could identify his people by their names. The old woman was Greasy Hand, and her daughter was Pretty Calf. The other young woman's name was not clear to him, for the words were not in his vocabulary. The man who had captured him was Yellow Robe.

Once he could understand, he could begin to talk a little, and then he was less lonely. Nobody had been able to see any reason for talking to him, since he would not understand anyway. He asked the old woman, "What is my name?" Until he knew it, he was incomplete. She shrugged to let him know he had none.

He told her in the Crow language, "My name is Horse." He repeated it, and she nodded. After that they called him Horse when they called him anything. Nobody cared except the white man himself.

They trusted him enough to let him stray out of camp, so that he might have got away and, by unimaginable good luck, might have reached a trading post or a fort, but winter was too close. He did not dare leave without a horse; he needed clothing and a better hunting weapon than he had, and more certain skill in using it. He did not dare steal, for then they would surely have pursued him, and just as certainly they would have caught him. Remembering the warmth of the home that was waiting in Boston, he settled down for the winter.

On a cold night he crept into the tepee after the others had gone to bed. Even a horse might try to find shelter from the wind. The old woman grumbled, but without conviction. She did not put him out.

They tolerated him, back in the shadows, so long as he did not get in the way.

He began to understand how the family that owned him differed from the others. Fate had been cruel to them. In a short, sharp argument among the old women, one of them derided Greasy Hand by sneering, "You have no relatives!" and Greasy Hand raved for minutes of the deeds of her father and uncles and brothers. And she had had four sons, she reminded her detractor—who answered with scorn, "Where are they?"

Later the white man found her moaning and whimpering to herself, rocking back and forth on her haunches, staring at her mutilated hands. By that time he understood. A mourner often chopped off a finger joint. Old Greasy Hand had mourned often. For the first time he felt a twinge of pity, but he put it aside as another emotion, like anger, that he could not afford. He thought: What tales I will tell when I get home!

He wrinkled his nose in disdain. The camp stank of animals and meat and rancid grease. He looked down at his naked, shivering legs and was startled, remembering that he was still only a horse.

He could not trust the old woman. She fed him only because a starved slave would die and not be worth boasting about. Just how fitful her temper was he saw on the day when she got tired of stumbling over one of the hundred dogs that infested the camp. This was one of her own dogs, a large, strong one that pulled a baggage travois when the tribe moved camp.

Countless times he had seen her kick at the beast as it lay sleeping in front of the tepee, in her way. The dog always moved, with a yelp, but it always got in the way again. One day she gave the dog its usual kick and then stood scolding at it while the animal rolled its eyes sleepily. The old woman suddenly picked up her ax and cut the dog's head off with one blow. Looking well satisfied with herself, she beckoned her slave to remove the body.

It could have been me, he thought, if I were a dog. But I'm a horse.

His hope of life lay with the girl, Pretty Calf. He set about courting her, realizing how desperately poor he was both in property and honor. He owned no horse, no weapon but the old bow and the battered arrows. He had nothing to give away, and he needed gifts, because he did not dare seduce the girl.

One of the customs of courtship involved sending a gift of horses to a girl's older brother and bestowing much buffalo meat upon her mother. The white man could not wait for some far-off time when he might have either horses or meat to give away. And his courtship had to be secret. It was not for him to stroll past the groups of watchful girls, blowing a flute made of an eagle's wing bone, as the flirtatious young bucks did.

He could not ride past Pretty Calf's tepee, painted and bedizened; he had no horse, no finery.

Back home, he remembered, I could marry just about any girl I'd want to. But he wasted little time thinking about that. A future was something to be earned.

The most he dared do was wink at Pretty Calf now and then, or state his admiration while she giggled and hid her face. The least he dared do to win his bride was to elope with her, but he had to give her a horse to put the seal of tribal approval on that. And he had no horse until he killed a man to get one . . . .

His opportunity came in early spring. He was casually accepted by that time. He did not belong, but he was amusing to the Crows, like a strange pet, or they would not have fed him through the winter.

His chance came when he was hunting small game with three young boys who were his guards as well as his scornful companions. Rabbits and birds were of no account in a camp well fed on buffalo meat, but they made good targets.

His party walked far that day. All of them at once saw the two horses in a sheltered coulee. The boys and the man crawled forward on their bellies, and then they saw an Indian who lay on the ground, moaning, a lone traveler. From the way the boys inched forward, Horse knew the man was fair prey—a member of some enemy tribe.

This is the way the captive white man acquired wealth and honor to win a bride and save his life: He shot an arrow into the sick man, a split second ahead of one of his small companions, and dashed forward to strike the still-groaning man with his bow, to count first coup. Then he seized the hobbled horses.

By the time he had the horses secure, and with them his hope for freedom, the boys had followed, counting coup with gestures and shrieks they had practiced since boyhood, and one of them had the scalp. The white man was grimly amused to see the boy double up with sudden nausea when he had the thing in his hand . . . .

There was a hubbub in the camp when they rode in that evening, two of them on each horse. The captive was noticed. Indians who had ignored him as a slave stared at the brave man who had struck first coup and had stolen horses.

The hubbub lasted all night, as fathers boasted loudly of their young sons' exploits. The white man was called upon to settle an argument between two fierce boys as to which of them had struck second coup and which must be satisfied with third. After much talk that went over his head, he solemnly pointed at the nearest boy. He didn't know which boy it was and didn't care, but the boy did.

The white man had watched warriors in their triumph. He knew what to do. Modesty about achievements had no place among the Crow people. When a man did something big, he told about it.

The white man smeared his face with grease and charcoal. He walked inside the tepee circle, chanting and singing. He used his own language.

"You heathens, you savages," he shouted. "I'm going to get out of here someday! I am going to get away!" The Crow people listened respectfully. In the Crow tongue he shouted, "Horse! I am Horse!" and they nodded.

He had a right to boast, and he had two horses. Before dawn, the white man and his bride were sheltered beyond a far hill, and he was telling her, "I love you, little lady. I love you."

She looked at him with her great dark eyes, and he thought she understood his English words—or as much as she needed to understand.

"You are my treasure," he said, "more precious than jewels, better than fine gold. I am going to call you

107

Freedom."

When they returned to camp two days later, he was bold but worried. His ace, he suspected, might not be high enough in the game he was playing without being sure of the rules. But it served.

Old Greasy Hand raged—but not at him. She complained loudly that her daughter had let herself go too cheap. But the marriage was as good as any Crow marriage. He had paid a horse.

He learned the language faster after that, from Pretty Calf, whom he sometimes called Freedom. He learned that his attentive, adoring bride was fourteen years old.

One thing he had not guessed was the difference that being Pretty Calf's husband would make in his relationship to her mother and brother. He had hoped only to make his position a little safer, but he had not expected to be treated with dignity. Greasy Hand no longer spoke to him at all. When the white man spoke to her, his bride murmured in dismay, explaining at great length that he must never do that. There could be no conversation between a man and his mother-in-law. He could not even mention a word that was part of her name.

Having improved his status so magnificently, he felt no need for hurry in getting away. Now that he had a woman, he had as good a chance to be rich as any man. Pretty Calf waited on him; she seldom ran off to play games with other young girls, but took pride in learning from her mother the many women's skills of tanning hides and making clothing and preparing food.

He was no more a horse but a kind of man, a half-Indian, still poor and unskilled but laden with honors, clinging to the buckskin fringes of Crow society.

Escape could wait until he could manage it in

comfort, with fit clothing and a good horse, with hunting weapons. Escape could wait until the camp moved near some trading post. He did not plan how he would get home. He dreamed of being there all at once, and of telling stories nobody would believe. There was no hurry.

Pretty Calf delighted in educating him. He began to understand tribal arrangements, customs and why things were as they were. They were that way because they had always been so. His young wife giggled when she told him, in his ignorance, things she had always known. But she did not laugh when her brother's wife was taken by another warrior. She explained that solemnly with words and signs.

Yellow Robe belonged to a society called the Big Dogs. The wife stealer, Cut Neck, belonged to the Foxes. They were fellow tribesmen; they hunted together and fought side by side, but men of one society could take away wives from the other society if they wished, subject to certain limitations.

When Cut Neck rode up to the tepee, laughing and singing, and called to Yellow Robe's wife, "Come out! Come out!" she did as ordered, looking smug as usual, meek and entirely willing. Thereafter she rode beside him in ceremonial processions and carried his coup stick, while his other wife pretended not to care.

"But why?" the white man demanded of his wife, his Freedom. "Why did our brother let his woman go? He sits and smokes and does not speak."

Pretty Calf was shocked at the suggestion. Her brother could not possibly reclaim his woman, she explained. He could not even let her come back if she wanted to—and she probably would want to when Cut Neck tired of her. Yellow Robe could not even admit that his heart was sick. That was the way things were. Deviation meant dishonor.

The woman could have hidden from Cut Neck, she said. She could even have refused to go with him if she had been *ba-wurokee*—a really virtuous woman. But she had been his woman before, for a little while on a berrying expedition, and he had a right to claim her.

There was no sense in it, the white man insisted. He glared at his young wife. "If you go, I will bring you back!" he promised.

She laughed and buried her head against his shoulder. "I will not have to go," she said. "Horse is my first man. There is no hole in my moccasin."

He stroked her hair and said, "*Ba-wurokee*."

With great daring, she murmured, "*Hayha*," and when he did not answer, because he did not know what she meant, she drew away, hurt. "A woman calls her man that if she thinks he will not leave her. Am I wrong?"

The white man held her closer and lied, "Pretty Calf is not wrong. Horse will not leave her. Horse will not take another woman, either." No, he certainly would not. Parting from this one was going to be harder than getting her had been. "*Hayha*," he murmured. "Freedom."

His conscience irked him, but not very much. Pretty Calf could get another man easily enough when he was gone, and a better provider. His hunting skill was improving, but he was still awkward.

There was no hurry about leaving. He was used to most of the Crow ways and could stand the rest. He was becoming prosperous. He owned five horses. His place in the life of the tribe was secure, such as it was. Three or four young women, including the one who had belonged to Yellow Robe, made advances to him. Pretty

110

Calf took pride in the fact that her man was so attractive.

By the time he had what he needed for a secret journey, the grass grew yellow on the plains and the long cold was close. He was enslaved by the girl he called Freedom and, before the winter ended, by the knowledge that she was carrying his child . . . .

The Big Dog society held a long ceremony in the spring. The white man strolled with his woman along the creek bank, thinking: When I get home I will tell them about the chants and the drumming. Sometime. Sometime.

Pretty Calf would not go to bed when they went back to the tepee.

"Wait and find out about my brother," she urged. "Something may happen."

So far as Horse could figure out, the Big Dogs were having some kind of election. He pampered his wife by staying up with her by the fire. Even the old woman, who was a great one for getting sleep when she was not working, prowled around restlessly.

The white man was yawning by the time the noise of the ceremony died down. When Yellow Robe strode in, garish and heathen in his paint and feathers and furs, the women cried out. There was conversation, too fast for Horse to follow, and the old woman wailed once, but her son silenced her with a gruff command.

When the white man went to sleep, he thought his wife was weeping beside him.

The next morning she explained.

"He wears the bearskin belt. Now he can never retreat in battle. He will always be in danger. He will die."

Maybe he wouldn't, the white man tried to convince her. Pretty Calf recalled that some few men had been honored by the bearskin belt, vowed to the highest

111

daring, and had not died. If they lived through the summer, then they were free of it.

"My brother wants to die," she mourned. "His heart is bitter."

Yellow Robe lived through half a dozen clashes with small parties of raiders from hostile tribes. His honors were many. He captured horses in an enemy camp, led two successful raids, counted first coup and snatched a gun from the hand of an enemy tribesman. He wore wolf tails on his moccasins and ermine skins on his shirt, and he fringed his leggings with scalps in token of his glory.

When his mother ventured to suggest, as she did many times, "My son should take a new wife, I need another woman to help me," he ignored her. He spent much time in prayer, alone in the hills or in conference with a medicine man. He fasted and made vows and kept them. And before he could be free of the heavy honor of the bearskin belt, he went on his last raid.

The warriors were returning from the north just as the white man and two other hunters approached from the south, with buffalo and elk meat dripping from the bloody hides tied on their restive ponies. One of the hunters grunted, and they stopped to watch a rider on the hill north of the teepee circle.

The rider dismounted, held up a blanket and dropped it. He repeated the gesture.

The hunters murmured dismay. "Two! Two men dead!" They rode fast into the camp, where there was already wailing.

A messenger came down from the war party on the hill. The rest of the party delayed to paint their faces for mourning and for victory. One of the two dead men was Yellow Robe. They had put his body in a cave and walled it in with rocks. The other man died later, and his body was in a tree.

There was blood on the ground before the tepee to which Yellow Robe would return no more. His mother, with her hair chopped short, sat in the doorway, rocking back and forth on her haunches, wailing her heartbreak. She cradled one mutilated hand in the other. She had cut off another finger joint.

Pretty Calf had cut off chunks of her long hair and was crying as she gashed her arms with a knife. The white man tried to take the knife away, but she protested so piteously that he let her do as she wished. He was sickened with the lot of them.

Savages! he thought. Now I will go back! I'll go hunting alone, and I'll keep on going.

But he did not go just yet, because he was the only hunter in the lodge of the two grieving women, one of them old and the other pregnant with his child.

In their mourning, they made him a pauper again. Everything that meant comfort, wealth, and safety they sacrificed to the spirits because of the death of Yellow Robe. The tepee, made of seventeen fine buffalo hides, the furs that should have kept them warm, the white deerskin dress, trimmed with elk teeth, that Pretty Calf loved so well, even their tools and Yellow Robe's weapons—everything but his sacred medicine objects— they left there on the prairie, and the whole camp moved away. Two of his best horses were killed as a sacrifice, and the women gave away the rest.

They had no shelter. They would have no tepee of their own for two months at least of mourning, and then the women would have to tan hides to make it. Meanwhile they could live in temporary huts made of willows, covered with skins given them in pity by their friends. They could have lived with relatives, but Yellow Robe's women had no relatives.

The white man had not realized until then how terrible a thing it was for a Crow to have no kinfolk. No wonder old Greasy Hand had only stumps for fingers. She had mourned, from one year to the next, for everyone she had ever loved. She had no one left but her daughter, Pretty Calf.

Horse was furious at their foolishness. It had been bad enough for him, a captive, to be naked as a horse and poor as a slave, but that was because his captors had stripped him. These women had voluntarily given up everything they needed.

He was too angry at them to sleep in the willow hut. He lay under a sheltering tree. And on the third night of the mourning he made his plans. He had a knife and a bow. He would go after meat, taking two horses. And he would not come back. There were, he realized, many things he was not going to tell when he got back home.

In the willow hut, Pretty Calf cried out. He heard rustling there, and the old woman's querulous voice.

Some twenty hours later his son was born, two months early, in the tepee of a skilled medicine woman. The child was born without breath, and the mother died before the sun went down.

The white man was too shocked to think whether he should mourn, or how he should mourn. The old woman screamed until she was voiceless. Piteously she approached him, bent and trembling, blind with grief. She held out her knife and he took it.

She spread out her hands and shook her head. If she cut off any more finger joints, she could no more work. She could not afford any more lasting signs of grief.

The white man said, "All right! All right!" between

his teeth. He hacked his arms with the knife and stood watching the blood run down. It was little enough to do for Pretty Calf, for little Freedom.

Now there is nothing to keep me, he realized. When I get home, I must not let them see the scars.

He looked at Greasy Hand, hideous in her grief-burdened age, and thought: I really am free now! When a wife dies, her husband has no more duty toward her family. Pretty Calf had told him so, long ago, when he wondered why a certain man moved out of one tepee and into another.

The old woman, of course, would be a scavenger. There was one other with the tribe, an ancient crone who had no relatives, toward whom no one felt any responsibility. She lived on food thrown away by the more fortunate. She slept in shelters that she built with her own knotted hands. She plodded wearily at the end of the procession when the camp moved. When she stumbled, nobody cared. When she died, nobody would miss her.

Tomorrow morning, the white man decided, I will go.

His mother-in-law's sunken mouth quivered. She said one word, questioningly. She said, *"Eero-oshay?"* She said, "Son?"

Blinking, he remembered. When a wife died, her husband was free. But her mother, who had ignored him with dignity, might if she wished ask him to stay. She invited him by calling him Son, and he accepted by answering Mother.

Greasy Hand stood before him, bowed with years, withered with unceasing labor, loveless and childless, scarred with grief. But with all her burdens, she still loved life enough to beg it from him, the only person she had any right to ask. She was stripping herself of all she had left, her pride.

He looked eastward across the prairie. Two thousand miles away was home. The old woman would not live forever. He could afford to wait, for he was young. He could afford to be magnanimous, for he knew he was a man. He gave her the answer. "*Eegya*," he said. "Mother."

He went home three years later. He explained no more than to say, "I lived with Crows for a while. It was some time before I could leave. They called me Horse."

He did not find it necessary either to apologize or to boast, because he was the equal of any man on earth.

LES SAVAGE, JR.

LESLIE HUNTER SAVAGE, JR. (1922-1958) was born in Alhambra, California. When he was graduated from Hollywood High School in 1940, it had already long been his intention to pursue a career in art. This changed once he enrolled at Los Angeles City College and started writing fiction. His first professional effort was a story he titled "Bullets and Bullwhips." He sent it off to Street & Smith's *Western Story Magazine* and was delighted when it was accepted and he was praised by the magazine's current editor, John Burr.

There are perhaps two ways to view Savage's first Western story which was subsequently reprinted in *The Pulp Vault* #9 (10/91). In the light of the tremendously high quality of the stories he would be writing not even half a decade hence, it seems a minor effort. Yet that would be to take the story on terms other than its own. While it is true that in "A Colt for Captain Bullwhip" in *Frontier Stories* (Summer, 49) Savage would make gripping and astonishingly dramatic use of a bullwhip fight between two bullwhackers and even more so in his posthumously restored novel, ***Fire Dance at Spider Rock*** (Five Star, 1996), already in 1942 he had researched bullwhip techniques sufficiently to impress any reader. Moreover, even this early—at the very beginning, in fact—he created a protagonist who was "off-trail," so much so that when he is first encountered he has just come off a three-year drunk, a spiritually defeated man who is scarcely handsome and clean-cut in the way expected at the time of a Western hero.

Savage had written and had published two stories in

Star Western, one in *10 Story Western*, and one in *Frontier Stories* when he became a client of the August Lenniger Literary Agency. The first story Savage submitted to the Lenniger Agency was sold in April, 1943, to Fiction House and appeared as "Gunsmoke Ghost" in *Lariat Story Magazine* (11/43). His stories would appear elsewhere but much of the best of what he wrote in the 1940s was showcased in Fiction House magazines. Savage was the first author to receive star treatment there since Walt Coburn in the 1920s, even to having his photograph reproduced in issues of the magazines carrying his stories and his name was always emblazoned on the covers. It was in these stories that Savage developed his formidable backgrounds: the era of the fur trade, Santa Fe in the period the Mexican War and before, and overland freighting prior to the Civil War. Whereas, following the Wister tradition, most Western stories for decades had been set in the years after the Civil War, from virtually the beginning Savage harked back to earlier periods and he could invariably be relied on to tell a riveting story, highly atmospheric, assiduously accurate as to period, with characters vividly evoked. He came to have an intimate grasp of the terrain wherever he set a story, a vital familiarity with the characteristics of flora amid changing seasons as well as the ways of horses, mules, women and men on the frontier. He did this in an entirely natural and graceful manner, displaying only covertly specialized learning in a dozen disciplines from mining, geology, and period furniture to manner of dress, anthropology, and firearms. He might have been a poet because of the striking images he could conjure. Take this example from his last novel, **Table Rock** (Walker, 1993), in which he conveys zoological information by means of poetic imagery: "He knew those of the marten, the paws printed faithfully in pairs, each oblique to the other, like delicate embroidery in the snow."

Malcolm Reiss, general manager at Fiction House, was Savage's first mentor and he repeatedly encouraged him to experiment with his stories. This appealed to Savage's already keenly volatile imagination so that he would alter traditional patterns of the Western story, even iconoclastically, and upon occasion produce a story without any romantic interest whatsoever. Conversely, another ultimately frustrating tendency which Reiss permitted and New York book editors later would not was Savage's realism in presenting romances on the frontier between his protagonists and females who were mixed-bloods, full-blood Indians, Mexicans, or on one instance—in "The Lone Star Camel Corps" in *Frontier Stories* (Summer, 45) a Syrian woman—and in another, **North to Kansas** (a novel he was forced to abort in 1955 but which will eventually be published as he wrote it), a black slave woman.

Don Ward, who edited *Zane Grey's Western Magazine*, was Savage's next mentor. Most of Savage's early novels were condensed for single installment serial publication in this magazine because Ward was convinced of the integrity and power of Savage's fiction. This was fortunate for Savage because this magazine paid 4¢ a word which is more than any of the other pulp magazines did at the time.

In the late 1940s Savage's life underwent significant changes. He published his first novel, **Treasure of the Brasada** (Simon and Schuster, 1947), and the next year he married Marian Roberta Funck. Marian brought to this marriage her young son, John, whom Les called Butch and he later adopted him. He dedicated **Land of** *the Lawless* (Doubleday, 1951): "To Butch, My Son, and I could search the world and never find a better one."

To say more about how Savage was forced to conform to political correctness by book publishers in the 1950s would take us too far afield. Suffice it to say that this situation, forty years later, is now being corrected beginning with **Table Rock, The Tiger's Spawn** (Chivers, 1994), **The Trail** (Chivers, 1994), and even the story which follows.

While working on **Beyond Wind River** (Doubleday, 1958), Savage was more aware than ever that he was dying. He dedicated this book: "To Dr. Wendell Keate—Who Kept the Machine Running." He died on May 26, 1958, only a few days before his tenth wedding anniversary, from a heart attack brought on by a combination of his hereditary diabetes and elevated cholesterol.

Les loved the Western story. In his own time, as his agent and editors were only too cognizant, he was wont to wander off trail, but that was because the impulse was ever within him to propel the Western story unrelentingly in the direction of greater and greater realism and historical accuracy. Elmer Kelton, T.V. Olsen, Frank Roderus, Cynthia Haseloff, and Douglas C. Jones are only a few of those who took up this cause where Savage left off, so that today it is possible to publish Savage's stories and novels as he wrote them. Much as Stephen Crane before him (and whom he replaces in this second edition), while Savage continued to write, the shadow of his imminent demise grew longer and longer across his young life and he knew that, if he was going to do it at all, he would have to do it quickly. He did it well, better than most who have written Western and frontier fiction, ever. And so now, with his novels and stories being restored to what he had intended them to be, his achievement irradiated by his profoundly sensitive imagination will be with us always, as he had wanted it to be, as he had so rushed against time and mortality that it might be.

It was in 1948 that Savage began making his initial forays into the psychological Western in ways previously attempted by only a few, preëminently Max Brand and Walter Van Tilburg Clark. It was with these stories that Savage would have a great impact on other Western writers just starting out. "The Shadow in Renegade Basin," which harks back to the spiritual terrain of Greek drama, was submitted by August Lenniger to Fiction House under the title "Bushbuster"—which Savage's agent felt seemed more "Western" or, at least, more traditional than certainly was the story. Malcolm Reiss bought the novelette on May 4, 1948; but, once having it, he didn't know what to do with it. An author of Western fiction himself in the early 1930s, Reiss rewrote the ending to give it a ranch romance conclusion and finally published it in the Summer, 1950 issue of *Frontier Stories* under the title "Tombstones for Gringos." The themes of incest and fratricide were also modified. Yet, once they were, the Æeschylian notion of evil being visited upon generation after generation of a once great house was lost. It may also be worth noting, in regard to this tale, that one of the legends spun in Classical Antiquity about Teiresias, the blind seer who figures so prominently in Sophocles's Theban cycle of plays about Œdipus, is that his blindness was a punishment meted out to him by the goddess Artemis for his once having looked upon her naked body while she was bathing.

THE SHADOW IN RENEGADE BASIN
1950

I

IT WAS JUST ONE OF THE MANY MOUNTAINS FORMING
the Patagonias, a few miles north of the Mexican border,
but something made it stand out from the other peaks—
some singular, almost human quality of brooding,
dominating malignancy. Its dome rose toward the sky,
like a bare, scarred skull, and a line of stunted timber
grew in a strange, scowling line across its brow. Some
mineral in the land caused its shadow, settling across the
basin, to have the deep, mordant tint of wet blood.

Colin Shane had halted his Studebaker wagon at the
crest of Papago Divide to stare at the mountain, his
deep-socketed eyes luminous with the growing spell of
it. "Almost gives you the creeps, doesn't it?" he told his
brother.

Farris Shane stirred on the wagon seat beside him,
chuckling deep in his chest. "You got too much of Ma's
old Irish in you, Colin. All full of leprechauns and
fairies."

"I heard a miner talking about it in Tombstone," said
Colin. "El Renegado he called it. Some kind of legend
connected with the mountain. When he heard we were
planning to prove up on a homestead in Renegade
Basin, he got a funny look on his face, and started this
story. That was when you came in with word that Ma
was worse. I wish we'd stayed to hear the story, now,
somehow."

His face, turned somberly toward the south again, was

122

not made for much humor, some Celtic ancestry lending the gaunt, bony structure of cheek and brow a countenance as dour and brooding as the mountain. His body was neatly coupled for such a long man, negligible through belly and hips, the only broad thing being his shoulders.

His younger brother beside him was in complete opposition, a short, heavy-chested replica of their father, with all the Red Irish of the man in his flaming hair and blue eyes. His thighs were so burly with bulging muscle they had split his jeans out along the seams, and his red flannel shirt was rolled to the elbows over heavy forearms, covered with hair as gold and curly as cured mesquite grass.

"You don't stop mooning, we'll never make the river by nightfall," he grinned.

Colin tried to shrug off his sense of oppression, turning to peer through the pucker of the Osnaberg sheeting covering the wagon. "You all right, Ma?"

Laura Shane's pain-wracked body stirred feebly beneath the blankets, within the stifling wagon. "Drive on, son. I'm still kickin'."

As Colin turned back, shaking the reins, a dim shout came from somewhere down the road. The tired horses drew them toward the sounds till the wagon rounded a turn in the road, and the words were intelligible.

"Ay, you *rumbero*, you are killing my birds. Nacho, *por Dios*, I have not revealed a thing. I am only a poor *pajarero* . . . ."

The horses came down off the grade and around a big rock, and Colin could see the two struggling men, among the bizarre, ridged shapes of tall saguaro. There were half a dozen bright-colored birds fluttering and squawking around in the air, scattering their feathers over the two men fighting in the sand, and half a dozen *amole* cages lying on the ground, some with their spindled doors torn open, three or four still holding shrieking parrots.

One of the men was a swarthy, thick-waisted Mexican in a fancy *charro* jacket and gleaming *taja* leggings. His immense sombrero had been torn off, and his long, black hair swung in greasy length down over his vivid, savage face, as he held the other man pushed down to his knees in the sand, beating at him—a greasy, fat little man with a pock-marked face and a red bulb for a nose, squirming and struggling to dodge the brutal blows.

"Let the little guy go, you big tub o' lard," shouted Farris, jumping off the wagon before it had stopped.

The squawking birds and rain of sand kicked up by the struggling men had excited the horses, and Colin was still fighting to halt them when Farris reached the Mexicans. He caught the bigger one by an arm, swinging him around to sink a vicious right fist in that thick waist. Colin had never seen a man before that whom Farris could not down with such a blow, but the Mexican only grunted harshly, taking a step backward and bringing both arms up to cover himself. Farris looked surprised, then plunged on in.

Colin had the horses halted by now, and jumped off the seat. The Mexican had already blocked Farris's first blow with his left arm, and was putting his own fist in under it. Farris staggered back, and the Mexican followed, hitting him again. This stiffened Farris. His face was white and working and his whole body was lifted upward in a perfect, unprotected setup for the Mexican, as he brought his third blow in, low to the belly.

"Meddling little *gringo*," he snarled, as he struck. Farris jackknifed at the waist over that fist. The Mexican stepped back and allowed him to fall.

At the same time Colin had reached them, charging in with all the long, close-coupled whiplash of him. He had seen how little effect his brother's blows had on the man and knew, if Farris could not do it that way, he couldn't, so he threw himself bodily at the Mexican's knees.

Legs pinned together by Colin's long arms, the man went over backwards, striking the ground heavily. Colin fought up across him to grab that long, greasy black hair, beating his head against the ground. They were in among the squawking, squalling birds now, with the fat little Mexican jumping around them and clapping his hands together.

"Ay, ay, that's it, beat the black Indian to a pulp! ¡*Que barbaridad*! If anyone deserves this, it is Nacho. What a bull you are, *Señor* . . . ."

It was like trying to stun a rock. Nacho's face was twisted with the pain of the blows, but he still reached up with scarred, thick hands, pawing for Colin. Colin tried to avoid them, sparring from side to side and beating that head again and again into the ground. Then one set of fingers caught on his arm, closed on it. He shouted aloud with the crushing pain. The other fist groped inexorably for his free hand, caught it, pulled him in. He squirmed spasmodically in the grip, appalled by the strength of the man beneath him. Like a bear, Nacho hugged him in, till his whole consciousness was popping and spinning in crushed pain.

"Hang on a minute, Colin, boy," he heard from somewhere behind him.

Colin opened his mouth as wide as he could, sunk his teeth into the nose beneath him. There was a deafening

125

howl of pain, a spasm of wild thrashing. He hung on desperately. Neither would Nacho loosen his bear hug. He settled back, breathing through his mouth in a guttural, savage way, and began applying pressure once more.

Colin thought his lungs would burst. Ribs began to snap and crack. A terrible, maddening suffocation gripped him. Then he heard the sound. A dull, solid, whacking sound. Once. Twice. Three times. Suddenly the arms fell limply from around him. He lay a long time, sprawled across the body, gasping like a fish cast upon the land. Finally he lifted his head to see Farris standing weakly above them, leaning on the spare wagon tongue he had unleashed from beneath the Studebaker.

"Couldn't do much more," he panted. "My guts are all stove in. Never saw a man with that kind of punch."

Colin got to his feet, slowly. The little Mexican was scrambling around among the cages, righting them and slipping the raucous birds back into them, a comical, pathetic little figure in an archaic, hooded cloak and red Turkish trousers that ballooned out around the ankles.

"Come here, Pepita," he called to one of the birds perched on a saguaro. "Come little one, back to your cage. He is a macaw, *Señores*, from the land of the white Indians, in Darien. And Roblero there . . . come, Roblero, your castle awaits . . . Roblero is a white-necked raven. He even talks. Say something, Roblero."

"*Que un rumbero*," squawked the raven.

"We know all your birds now," said Colin. "How about you?"

"Ah," the little man cackled, turning toward them with a sly, upraised finger. "I am Pajarero. It means bird-catcher, *Señores*. You must have seen us in

126

Tintown. The place is made up of bird-catchers. Would you like to buy this tanager? Only three pesos. A rare bird, *Señores*."

"As rare as this one on the ground?" said Farris, turning his pale eyes to Nacho, who was beginning to regain consciousness now.

The sly humor left Pajarero as his eyes dropped to Nacho. He made the sign of a cross before himself as Nacho rolled over, lifting himself painfully to his hands and knees. Shaking his head, he looked up at Colin, and the intent was plain in his smoldering eyes.

"Do anything more and I'll clout you again!" growled Farris, moving in with the wagon tongue.

Nacho rose to his feet. His hand opened and closed above the butt of his holstered gun, but Farris could have struck him again before he got it free.

"There are many more days left in the year, *Señores*," he said at last and turned to walk out among the saguaros. Colin expected him to get out of range of that wagon tongue and then turn back, going for his gun. He took a breath that swelled his flat belly against the barrel of his own gun, stuck naked through his belt, just behind the buckle, and waited that way, to pull at it if Nacho turned. But the man disappeared among the tall, haunted cactus without wheeling back.

"You had better leave the basin before another of those days comes," said Pajarero, at last. "I have heard him say that to seven men. They are all dead now."

"We don't scare that easy," said Colin. "We aim to prove up on some government land here. We couldn't go on if we wanted. We're out of money and Ma's too sick. I don't even think the horses could pull another mile."

"Homesteading . . . here?" said Pajarero, in an awed

voice.

"What's wrong with here?" asked Farris.

"You have not heard about . . . El Renegado?"

"The mountain?" Colin asked him. "What about it?"

"Ooh . . . ," the man pouted his lips, pulling his fat head into his shoulders, "perhaps I had better not tell you."

Farris shifted his weight, with that wagon tongue. "Perhaps you had. I'm tired of all this mystery."

"Very well, *Señor*, very well," said the man, hastily. The pout faded from him as he turned toward the mountain. "Do you see how empty the valley is? Not a house, not a man. The richest basin in this area, more water, more grass, more everything than you could find within a hundred miles. Open to homesteading many months now. Yet not a house, not a man."

"Yes?" said Farris, cynically.

"It is said," murmured Parjarero, turning back to him, "that anyone who settles in the shadow of El Renegado is doomed."

II

THE TWO BROTHERS MADE CAMP THAT EVENING IN THE rich river bottom. Colin cut willow shoots for his mother's bed, laying them herring-bone to make a light, springy mattress. Farris found fresh meat in a mule deer back in the hills, and they had that and sourdough for supper. The Mexican bird-catcher had come with them, and ate sparingly as his feathered charges, for all his corpulence, regaling them with fabulous stories of his wanderings in search of birds. Farris's cynicism had kept him from elaborating upon what he had said about the mountain, and it was not until after supper that it

128

was again brought to Colin's attention. Laura Shane did it. She had eaten little and was feverish and, as Colin sat by her bed, she caught at his wrist with one veined, bony hand.

"I heard what that Mexican said this afternoon," she moaned. "He was right, Colin. Don't settle here. The land is cursed. I can feel it."

"Don't let your Irish blood get the best of you, Ma," soothed Farris. "The land's no more cursed than we are, just because we've been plagued with a little bad luck these last years."

"You're the practical one, Farris," muttered their mother. "Too much like your father. If you can't put your hands to a thing, it don't exist. It does for Colin. He knows what I mean. Don't stop here, Colin . . . ."

"We've got to, Ma," Colin told her. "It's our last chance. You know that . . . ."

He had meant to say more but it would not come. There was a figure in the firelight to stop him. He did not know exactly how she had gotten there. A woman. The dark, haunted face of a woman, tawny, dusky flesh and great black eyes that reflected the firelight opaquely. It was hard to separate her black hair from the night behind her. There was a jet rosary at the swell of her breast, immense black pearls and silver bracelets on her slender wrists.

Pajarero had risen from the fire, staring at her with wide, liquid eyes, gripped in some strange enchantment. Colin felt the same way, unable to speak. It had always been Farris who had been easy with the women anyway, grinning confidently, now, and wrapping his tongue around the blarney.

"Well, an angel stepped right out of heaven; how can the basin be cursed when they grow such beautiful flowers here, a little bit o' colleen wrapped up in Spanish lace and called *señorita*. We're the Shanes. I'm Farris, my brother Colin, and our mother, Laura."

"I am Christina Velasco," the woman murmured, her English accented just enough to give her husky voice a tenuous, piquant appeal. "My hacienda is on the other side of the basin. I heard your mother was ill. I wondered if I could help."

"With the gratitude of Erin to greet you," smiled Farris, holding out his hand. Colin could see the little lights kindling in his eyes, as they played over her body. She allowed the redhead to guide her over the rough, matted ground toward Laura Shane, but halted momentarily before Colin.

"You have not spoken," she said.

"When my boy has anything worth saying," Laura Shane said, from her sickbed, "he'll speak."

Christina Velasco inclined her head to one side in a thoughtful, studying way, smiling faintly at Colin. Then she moved on, passing Pajarero. He had been staring at her all the while with those shining eyes and faintly parted lips. She nodded at him in a gracious, dimly condescending way as she passed. A shudder seemed to travel through his whole body.

"*Señorita*," he whispered, dropping to his knees and reaching out one hand, as if to grasp the hem of her skirt and kiss it. But she pulled it up at that instant to avoid a hummock of dirty grass, and he drew his hand back sharply, a strange, apologetic line rounding his shoulders.

The woman knelt beside Laura Shane and spoke on a sharp, disgusted little exhalation. "You are letting her drink this water? How stupid. That's the first thing you should have stopped. Even boiling it does not help the

130

newcomer to the valley. There is some wine in my *carroza*. Please get it for me?"

The tilt of her head indicated the road, and Colin started off through the willows. He found the *carroza* to be an old Spanish coach, parked alongside the road. A man rose from where he had been squatting against the high back wheel, smoking a cigarette. He looked Indian, with a round, enigmatic face and sullen eyes, his smooth wrists tinkling with turquoise and silver jewelry.

"*Señorita* Velasco sent me to get some wine," Colin said.

The man nodded, opened the door, bent inside to get a clay jar. He handed it to Colin without speaking, and squatted back against the wheel, staring at Colin with unwinking eyes. Colin wended his way back through the matted undergrowth of these rich bottomlands to their camp. Christina was still kneeling beside his mother, washing her face now and murmuring Spanish in an unintelligible, soothing way.

"She's so feverish," she told Colin, reverting to English.

"You don't need to talk Yankee if you don't want," Colin told her in Spanish. "We were raised on the Texas border before we hit for Missouri."

She looked up in surprise, then asked him, "Have you anything for her?"

"The doc in Tombstone gave us some Dover's powder."

The woman made a disgusted sound, picking up her skirts as she rose, and headed for the undergrowth. Colin followed her in puzzlement. He found Pajarero at his heels, staring after the woman with that dog-like devotion. She called for a torch, and Farris thrust a length of sappy wood into the fire, bringing the light to

131

her. In a few moments she had collected what looked like a bunch of common weeds, carrying them back to the fire in her skirts.

In amazement, Colin watched her slender, aristocratic hands go about the work with such skill. She labored for hours with his mother, feeding her the romero tea, performing the mysterious, amazing healing arts of these Border people, learned slowly, painfully, through the long centuries when there was no doctor within a thousand miles. They were all dozing about the fire when Laura finally became quieter, drifting off into a troubled sleep. Christina rose from her side, waking Colin with the movement. He got up unsteadily, gazing at his mother.

"That's the first real sleep she's had in weeks," he said.

"It is well," said Christina. "She will feel more like traveling in the morning. You must bring her to my hacienda for a few days before you leave the valley."

"We aren't leaving the valley," Colin told her.

She whirled on him, a strange, wild look obliterating the almost Oriental calm of her face for a moment, then disappearing as violently as it had come, wiped away by some inward effort of her own. "You can't stay," she said intensely.

"You're not talking about the mountain?" he asked.

"How can you think of staying, if you know?"

"I don't know," he said. "Pajarero started to tell us, but he closed up tight when Farris scoffed at him. What is it?"

She stared up at his eyes in a fixed, fascinated way, held by the rapport the sincerity of his voice brought. She started to smile; then it faded before a puzzled frown drew her brows together. She began, haltingly at first, her voice gaining conviction at the quiet attention on his face.

"When Don Juan Oñate first made his conquest of this country," she said, "he established a *presidio* in this basin, with a priest for the mission, and a company of Spanish soldiers and their families. Commanding them was a young captain who fell in love with an Indian girl belonging to the tribe in the Patagonias. These Indians were so war-like that the priest had only converted a few of them, who were working in the mission as neophytes. The others planned to wipe out the *presidio*. Through his contact with the woman, the captain knew this, and could have saved his comrades. But he betrayed them, running off to the mountain with the woman. He was called El Renegado, and the mountain came to be named after him.

"The attack came near evening, when the shadow of the mountain touched the *presidio*. It was the changing of the guards, and with help from the neophytes inside, the Indians overwhelmed the garrison and wiped them out, women and children and all. The priest was mortally wounded but, before he died, he declared the ground touched by the shadow of the mountain to be cursed by the death of so many innocents. The basin is so shaped that all of it, during the course of the day, is touched by that shadow, and there is not one person to try and settle here who has not been blighted by that curse."

"Why are you here, then?" he asked.

She turned sharply away from him, as if to hide the subtle alterations hardening her face. "Because I am," she answered, finally, and then lifted her chin toward the east, dawn light making a cameo of her face. "The sun will be up in a few minutes. If you will wake your mother, I will go and prepare the coach for her. It will be more comfortable to her than that wagon."

He walked over to kneel by his mother, taking her shoulder gently. It felt cold. He shook her lightly. Her body reacted with the lifeless motion of a rag doll. He bent down to stare at her face. There was no sign of breathing. He gazed for a long, blank moment at her closed eyes, conscious of Farris's rising from the fire, to come over by him.

"I guess you won't have to get the coach ready," he told Christina, at last. "Mother's dead."

At that moment, the sun lifted its first brazen rays above the undulating silhouette of the mountains to the east. But its brightness did not seem to touch them, here. Colin realized why, at last. The bulk of the sun lay behind the ugly, brooding peak of El Renegado, throwing its shadow across the valley, to shroud their whole camp.

III

THERE WAS NOT MUCH WILL FOR LIVING LEFT IN EITHER of the brothers for several weeks after their mother's death. They buried her on a hill above the camp they had made in the bottoms, and remained there, hunting and fishing for the food they needed. It was Farris who seemed to recover first, finally coming up with the suggestion that they build a house. This hard work helped to take their minds off their mother's death.

After they had built a three-room adobe and some corrals, they made a trip north, over Papago Gap, trading some of their meager household goods from Missouri for onions and chile from the Mexican *pajareros* in Tintown. And farther north, among the

Papagos and Pimas, they found one butcher knife was worth a wagon load of melons and squash and Indian corn for seed crops. They got half a dozen peach and apricot trees to transplant about their house, and the fruit was beginning to ripen by June. And then it was that evening when Colin stood out among those trees, enjoying a cooling breeze after the heat of the late spring day, seeking satisfaction in what they had built here.

He did not find as much as he sought. He wondered if his mother's death was still too recent. Or was it something else? Farris came up behind him, smoking his pipe.

"You got Tina on your mind?" he asked.

"What makes you say that?" smiled Colin.

"You're looking off toward her place."

"Seems to me you're the one who should have her on your mind," Colin told him. "You've gone to see her every Saturday we've been here."

"You might as well have come along," chuckled Farris. "Seems all we talked about was you. Makes me jealous, she's so interested. Wanted to know why you didn't call. I told her you was shy with women."

"What did she say?"

"She said she didn't think that was true . . . you just moved a little slower than me, and didn't say anything until you could really mean it."

"I should think so," said Colin, with one of his rare, fleeting smiles. "With all your blarney." He sobered. "I guess I was thinking about her, in a way, Farris. We've got the house to a place where it needs a woman."

"The same thought's been in my mind," Farris murmured.

Colin turned to look at his brother in some surprise,

135

and Farris chuckled, poking the pipe at him. "We aren't going to be in competition, are we, Colin?"

For a moment, Colin wanted to answer it with a grin, but he could not. When it finally came, it was forced. "What chance would I stand, against a lady's man such as yourself . . . ?"

He stopped speaking to stare out at something beyond. The earth beneath him seemed to be trembling. Then there was the sound. A great, growing sound.

"Earthquake?" asked Farris, stiffening.

"Stampede!" cried Colin, with the first bawl of cattle reaching him. "Those blackhorns up the valley. Get your horse, Farris! If they come through our fields, we'll lose everything."

Their stock was fat, now, from the rich graze of the valley, moving restlessly in the pack pole pen behind their corral. Colin hooked a bridle from the top pole and swung the gate open, jamming it in the first mouth he found, swinging aboard without waiting for a saddle. It was one of the bays they had used in the wagon team, a good enough horse for this short run.

Colin raced out through their new orchard and across the alfalfa on this side of the river. On the opposite bank he could see them, now, a milling, bawling herd of blackhorns, trampling through the Indian corn just thrusting its tender green shoots from the soil.

"Keep them on that side or they'll ruin our alfalfa, too," shouted Farris, coming up from behind Colin on another animal, and both of them plunged into the ford toward the cattle. It did not look like a stampede to Colin. The cattle were headed in no definite direction as yet. They seemed to have milled in the cornfields, and now were being shoved unwillingly into the river by some unseen pressure.

Before the brothers were halfway across the broad, shallow ford, however, the leaders of the herd were plunging into the water. More and more cattle followed, and their direction was becoming more definite. Colin started shouting hoarsely in an effort to turn them back. The leaders spooked at his loud voice and oncoming horse, trying to turn aside, but there were too many behind them.

The true charge began with a burst, as the whole front rank seemed to break into a deliberate charge at Colin, bawling and screaming in the stupid, bovine frenzy that would carry them blindly forward when the primeval fright of the stampede finally reached them.

"Get out of the way, Colin!" yelled Farris, from behind. "You can't stop them now. They'll run you down . . . ."

Colin only half-heard him, urging his own spooked mount on ahead, in a deep, black anger that so many months' work could be wiped out in a few minutes. He was into the leaders, then, still screaming at them in an effort to start a mill. But their impetus carried his horse back on its haunches. The beast tried to turn and run with them. It stumbled on the rough bottom, and began lunging from side to side, squealing, losing its head entirely. Colin realized he would go down in another moment.

Halfway between the bank and the herd, Farris had started to turn his horse aside. When he saw what had happened to Colin, he wheeled the animal around and raced straight for the herd.

"Get back, you fool," Colin screamed at him. "You'll only get killed too!"

But Farris plunged right on toward him. Colin had managed to rein his horse around in the direction of the cattle, but he was pinched in between two of the leaders, now, and the animal had not yet found its footing. He felt it stumble again, heavily, and knew, with the knowledge born of a lifetime on horseback, that this time it was going down for good. Farris must have seen it too, for just as he reached the head of the herd, he wheeled his horse broadside, shouting at Colin to jump for it.

A dozen feet separated them. Colin lunged upward on his foundering, falling horse, got purchase enough with one heel on its off-flank to kick away, and jumped. He struck the side of a steer, caromed off, hit shallow water with both flailing feet. He ran three stumbling steps before the impetus of his jump robbed him of balance completely. The tail of Farris's horse was before his eyes as he went over. Blindly he clawed at it. He heard Farris shout, and felt the animal lunge forward under a kidney kick. It almost tore the tail from his hands, his arms from their sockets. He had a dim, vivid sense of little, bloodshot eyes and waving, tossing horns and churning legs, and realized Farris was running down the front ranks of the herd in a diagonal line, attempting to get out to the side before his own horse was caught up in them. The ford fell into deeper water, and then the tail was torn from Colin's hands as the horse stumbled and lost its feet, too.

He went under in a plummeting force, striking bottom, kicking off. He came to the surface, gasping for air, getting water instead, doubling over in a paroxysm of coughing that would have put him under again. He was too dizzy and disorganized to find control. But as he went down, panic paralyzing him, he felt a hand on his hair. He fought wildly, losing all sense in the terrible, primal fear of being drowned. There was a cracking blow against his jaw, and he seemed to sink into the delicious coolness of the deepest water . . . .

His next sensation was of gritty sand, and a muttering, a distant sound. He opened his eyes, tasting silt, coughing up a quart of water, before he saw Farris hunkered above him. He lay back, swearing at his brother affectionately.

"Damn fool. I ought to pin your ears back. You could have gotten killed."

"You *would* have," grinned Farris. "It makes us even for the time you pulled Nacho off me."

"Let's not start keeping score," said Colin, sitting up. "I couldn't count high enough for the tight spots you've pulled me out of."

He stopped talking to stare after that muttering, dying sound of stampeding cattle running across the valley. Before his eyes lay the trampled, ruined alfalfa fields, the little grove of transplanted trees uprooted and mangled, the ocotillo corrals wrecked beyond repair and all the animals in them stampeded off with the beef. Then, somehow, his attention was not on that. It was beyond, climbing the steep, scowling slope of that scar of timber forming a frowning brow, and above, to the somber, brooding dome of El Renegado, dominating the valley, and the night, with its malignancy.

IV

THERE WAS NOTHING THEY COULD DO THAT NIGHT BUT try and get some sleep. The house was still intact, though one wall had been knocked in. When Colin awoke the next morning, Farris was not there. The redhead's guns were not in evidence either, and Colin

139

decided he had gone hunting.

He spent the morning searching the river bottom for their horses. He found the bay he had ridden, up on the bank where it had dragged itself to die, with both front legs broken, and shot the hapless beast to put it out of its misery. Near noon he found the one Farris had forked, three miles downstream where it had been swept by the river. It was calmly cropping gramma, and sound enough to ride.

Colin returned to find Farris still gone. He put a saddle on the horse and started tracking his brother. He found fresh sign leading out across the river into the hills behind them. Within these foothills he came across other sign mixed with Farris's footprints, the mark of hooves, shod and unshod. He lost them in the general trampling the herd had made here, and was still trying to unravel it all when he sighted Farris hiking back down a rocky slope toward him. His face was so covered with alkali it looked like a death mask, and even this could not hide the strange expression of it. He did not seem to see Colin till he was close, and only then did he make an effort to change the look.

"What is it?" said Colin.

"Nothing. Been hunting. Nothing up there."

"Horses mixed in with those cattle tracks," said Colin. "A shod one in with the unshod. What is it, Farris? Why won't you tell me?"

"There's nothing to tell," the redhead's voice was lifted shrilly. "Now let's get back."

Colin reined the horse around to block his brother's move to leave, one leg coming against the thick, sweating chest of him. He bent forward to peer at Farris. "You went up to the woman's place last Saturday."

"What makes you say that?" said Farris angrily.

"You don't get that slicked up to irrigate our corn."

"All right," said Farris. "So I went up to the woman's place. What's that got to do with it?"

"That's what I'd like to know," said Colin. "What's that got to do with this?"

The redhead's alkali-whitened face lifted in a sharp, strained way, and that same expression flitted through his eyes. "Listen, Colin," he said, tightly. "Quit swinging this horse around and let me by, will you? I been on a long hike and I'm tired and my temper won't stand all this blather."

"Tell me what you found and I'll let you past."

"Nothing, damn you, I told you . . . ."

"It's got something to do with her. You're shielding her!"

"The hell I am. You know . . . ." Farris halted himself with an effort so great it twisted his face. He stood there for a space that had no measure, chest rising and falling against Colin's leg, dampening it with sweat. Finally, Farris reached up to fold his fingers around the stirrup leather, speaking in a grating restraint. "Listen, Colin, you and I have had our spats in the past, but this is different. I don't want to fight with you this way so soon after mother's death. Or any other time, for that matter. Leave the woman out of it, will you?"

Colin had quieted, for this moment, too, and the rapport they had known before was between them. He stared deeply into Farris's pale, blue eyes. "You really got a case on Tina, haven't you?"

"Colin," said Farris. "I think I'd kill the man who tampered with her . . . in any way."

Colin drew a deep breath. "Then I won't ask you what you found up there, Farris. Let go and I'll find out for myself."

"No." A tortured look passed through the redhead's face. "Please, Colin, there's nothing up there . . . ."

"Then why are you so bent on my not seeing it?" said Colin. "Let go, Farris."

"No."

"Farris . . . ," there was a deadly, final quality to the tone of Colin's voice, startling after their rising shouts, "I'll ask you once more. Let me go."

"Only if you turn around and come home with me."

Colin snapped his foot from the stirrup, shoved it against Farris's chest with the leg jackknifed, straightened that long, lashing leg with a vicious force. Farris went over backward with a shout, hand torn loose of the stirrup leather. Colin slipped his foot back into the oxbow and booted the animal forward. He heard Farris call his name, but did not turn around, and then he was over the crest and into the next shallow valley.

Each great, ruddy rock clung hatefully to its rough slope, scowling down upon Colin like some crouching, mordant demon. The scar of timber forming its brow was shadowed darkly, ominously, with no sign of life breaking the spell. Above timberline, the bald, lithic head thrust the seamed, scarred planes of its skull ominously toward the sky, like Lucifer defying Saint Michael and all the angels.

Irish inheritance of a deep mysticism gave Colin an acute sensitivity to such influences, and he pushed forward without trying to laugh away the real, tangible sense of awe, almost of fear, the mountain engendered in him. He did not try to cross its crest, but pushed inward on the mountains behind by rounding its slope beneath the timber. Following Farris's tracks, he at last realized he was on some kind of trail leading through endless tiers of varicolored rocks. They blocked off sight of the valley behind him, now. The air up here was stifling. His clothes were drenched with sweat. It seemed difficult to breathe, somehow. He kept glancing up at the mountain, as if seeking the cause in its malignancy. Then it spoke to him.

"*¿Que paso?*" it said, in a voice like the rustle of quaking aspens.

Colin halted his horse, shivering with the shock of it. He keened his head up toward the sound. It was not the mountain. It was a man, sitting on a rock above the narrow trail, grinning down on him.

Colin did not think he had ever seen such an age. The man's face was no more than a skull with parchment for skin, stretched so tightly the bones appeared ready to come through. The eyes stared, huge and feverish, from the gaunt coign of their sockets. The flesh of the hands was wrinkled and seamed, burned the color of ancient mahogany by the countless years of this land's sunshine, and the fingers shook with palsy on the butt plate of the ancient rifle that looked like a matchlock Colin's father had hung above the mantle in Missouri.

"You are one of Captain Velasco's men?" asked the ancient, in a strange, stilted Castilian. "Is he coming today?"

"I'm Colin Shane," Colin told him in Spanish. "Who are you?"

"Shane?" The man bent forward in senile belligerence, repeating the name in a shrill, suspicious way. "Shane? Shane? No one by that name with the captain. I've been waiting a long time. They say Don Oñate will be here soon. Did you see the inventory Captain Velasco made of his clothing? A true *conquistadore*. They say he has garters with points of gold lace in colors to match each costume. And doublets

143

of royal lion skin. Do you believe that? Six pairs of Rouen linen shirts. Why should a man have that many? He can only wear one shirt at a time. Shane." He seemed to snap back with a jolt. "Shane?" He bent forward again. "Are you one of the Indians?"

"I come from the valley," said Colin, staring at the old man, trying to find mockery in him. There was a weird, sardonic light to those old eyes, a secretive leer on his lips. Or had the sun done this? Then he made out what it was beside the old man. An ancient, rusted Spanish helmet, and a cuirass of tarnished metal, backed with rotting leather that was still damp with sweat.

There was something dream-like about it—the strange costume, the archaic dialect, talk of men so long dead—but the harsh reality of it was brought home to Colin by the lighted match in the man's hand. His own response came automatically, a sudden move to rein the horse away, halted by the flick of the old man's hand toward the touch hole. Colin stared down the immense bore of that ancient gun, unwilling to believe that it could still fire, yet held stony by the possibility of it. The old man bent toward him, cackling.

"I told him no more would come up from the valley. Fray Escobar's curse is useless. We're still alive, aren't we? And you die. One by one, you die. Even the Don himself will not escape alive. Velasco is master here. El Renegado is king."

"Don't bring that match any closer, you fool," said Colin, trying to keep his voice level. "I'm not with Oñate. I'm an Irishman. Shane. Does that sound Spanish? I'm not your enemy . . . ."

"That's what the last one told me and I let him by. He said he was an Indian bird-catcher from Tintown. Captain Velasco was in a great rage. He followed him out and killed him. He would have killed me if I wasn't such a faithful friend. Oh, no. Not this time. I'll kill you this time."

That ghastly cackle rang against the rocks. Colin stared at the lowering match, filled with an awesome helplessness. He gathered himself for a last, desperate effort, meaning to wheel his horse and drop off the side at the same time. The tension filled him till he thought he would burst, and the match reached the touch hole.

"Stop it, *Cabo*!"

It was a clear, cutting voice, from above in the rocks. The old man jerked the match away with a surprised moan. Powder in the touch hole hissed, went out. Colin stared at the gun, trembling all over and, for the first time, he felt the clammy sweat sticking his shirt to him. Finally he found himself staring upward. Christina Velasco sat a black horse with four white stockings on a huge rock fifty feet above them. She was moving it now, bringing it carefully, delicately down some narrow trail Colin could not see. Colin had not seen a woman in pants too often. They were *charro*, of red suede, tight fitting as another layer of skin, and he could not help staring. She had a *charro* jacket, too, with gold frogs embroidered across the lapels against which her breasts surged. There was a strange, dark look to her face, almost an anger, as she reached their level. Colin could not tell if it was directed at him or the old man.

"*Cabo*," she said. "Go back, now."

"But Captain Velasco told me to . . . ."

"I told you to go back," she said, sharply. "You're relieved."

"It's about time," muttered the old man, gathering up his armor. "Seems like I've been out here for years."

"You have, you old fool," muttered Tina, too low for

145

his ears. She waited till he had hobbled on up the trail and out of sight among the rocks, then turned to Colin. He was watching her with a strange mixture of suspicion, and something else he could not define.

"*Cabo*," he said. "Corporal?"

"The sun of this country can addle the brain, Colin," she said. "He is only a crazy old man who thinks he is back in the 16th Century with Don Juan Oñate."

"And Captain Velasco?" said Colin.

She shrugged. "All right."

"You didn't tell me you were descended from him."

"Just because my name is the same?"

"Are you?"

"All right," she said, in a sudden anger. "So I am descended. And so I didn't tell you. It isn't something one goes around bragging about. He was a traitor, a murderer, a renegade, and all his descendants . . . ."

She cut off sharply, and his black brows raised, as he asked her, "All his descendants what?"

"Nothing," she said, shaking her head sharply. "This is no place to talk. My hacienda is lonely. Will you join me in afternoon chocolate?"

They turned their horses down the slope, and she did not speak again till they were out of the rocks and into timber once more. Then he found her eyes on him, studying his face.

"What were you doing up there?" she asked.

"A herd of cattle stampeded across our land last night," he told her. "Ruined most of our crops for this year. We found some horse tracks mixed in with the cattle sign this morning. Farris found something up here but he wouldn't tell me what."

Perhaps it was the expression in his eyes looking at her, for she lifted her body in the saddle. "So you think

146

I've taken to stampeding cattle now?"

"I didn't say that."

"You might as well."

"All right," he said. "What *are* you doing up here?"

"I . . . I . . . ." she broke off, biting her lips, eyes dropping. She shrugged. "You wouldn't believe me anyway."

"Yes, I would, Tina," he said. "Tell me one straight thing and I'll believe you."

Those big eyes raised again, gratefully. "I can see the mountain from my hacienda. I saw you come up here and thought you might run into The Corporal. He's old and he's crazy, but he can be dangerous. I didn't want you hurt, Colin."

He inclined his head. "I'm sorry. I guess I should be thankful instead of suspicious. My apologies."

"That makes me feel much better," she smiled, and drew her horse over to lean towards him. "Now, if you will wipe that scowl off your face and come down to the house, perhaps you and I together can clear up just how you feel about me."

V

IT HAD ONCE BEEN A MAGNIFICENT, EXTENSIVE hacienda, with a high adobe wall surrounding an acre of buildings and corrals, but much of the wall was fallen in, now, and all but one of the patios was overgrown with yucca and gramma. They rode through a great gate into this one garden, where a stream gurgled through a little red-roofed well and peach trees dropped their delicate bloom across the sun-baked tile topping the wall. The Indian Colin had found by the coach that first night appeared through a spindled door, taking their

147

horses.

Smiling, the woman whipped dust from her *charro* pants with a quirt, and turned to walk toward a cane chair by a long table. Colin started to follow her, and it was then they saw the man.

He had been standing in the deep shade of the wall, smoking a cigarette, and Colin had the sense of eyes being on them all the time, in that sly malevolence.

"Nacho!" The woman's voice held whispered shock.

He smiled, pinching out the cigarette and dropping it to grind the butt into the earth with his heel. With a thumb, he pushed the brim of his sombrero upward till the hat was tilted back on his head at a rakish angle. Then he hooked his hands in the heavy gunbelt at his waist, and moved toward them in an unhurried, swaggering way, the chains on his great Mexican cartwheel spurs tinkling softly with each step.

"You consort with the *gringo* now," he told the woman.

"In my house, Americans are no more *gringos* than Mexicans are greasers," she said.

"Your house?" Nacho asked, brows raising in that mocking smile. Only then did he condescend to move his eyes to Colin. "Is this the day, *Señor*?"

Remembering what the man had said that first time, Colin lowered his head a little. "Any day you want."

"I'm glad you leave the choice to me," smiled the man. "You will not wait long, *Señor*." He turned to the woman. "I want to speak with you."

"You would ask me to leave my guest?"

"Not asking you, telling you."

"Whatever you want to say can be said right here," she told him.

Those spur chains tinkled again. His movement

148

forward was so fast Colin could not follow it till the man had grasped Tina by the wrist. She tried to pull away. Colin saw Nacho's knuckles go white. Tina's face contorted with the pain of the squeezing grip. She lifted the quirt to lash it across Nacho's face. He shouted with the stinging pain, and it allowed her to tear loose, stumbling backward across the garden. Tears squeezed from his squinting eyes as Nacho started after her. At the same moment, the Indian appeared once more through the spindled gate. He stopped, however, just within, making no move to stop Nacho. Colin spoke, then.

"Nacho."

Again, the utter, deadly quiet of his voice had a startling effect after all the violence and noise. It stopped both Nacho and the woman. Nacho turned back his way. Colin was standing perfectly straight, with no inclination of body or arm to advertise his intent, yet Nacho's eyes flickered momentarily across the stag butt of the big Paterson he had thrust through his belt just behind the buckle.

"¿Si, Señor?" Nacho said, in that mocking tone.

"Get out of this garden," said Colin.

"Now, Señor?" asked Nacho.

"I won't ask you again," said Colin.

"You won't have to," said Nacho. His draw was as blinding as the rest of his movements. He halted it so abruptly his whole body shuddered. His gun was only halfway out of his holster, and he held it there with a tense, bent arm, staring in unveiled surprise at the Paterson filling Colin's hand, pointed at the middle of his belly.

The Indian had started some overt move, too, over there by the spindled gate, and half stopped it as quickly

149

as Nacho, with sight of Colin's weapon. Tina let out a small, moaning sound. Nacho allowed his gun to slip back in its holster, raising his eyes to Colin.

"Get out and on your horse," said Colin. "I'll be watching you out of sight. And I'll have this in my hand all the way."

"There are still enough days left in the year, *Señor*," said Nacho, softly. He met Colin's gaze for a moment longer, his own eyes showing no particular defeat, smoldering with the banked coals of that subterranean hate. Then he turned, chains tinkling as he walked to the *zaguan*. He moved through the large gate and disappeared for a moment. They could hear the creak of saddle leather. Then he appeared again, spurring his horse cruelly into a headlong run. Colin inclined his head at the Indian.

"How about you?"

"That's all, Ichahi," said the woman. The Indian let those enigmatic eyes pass over Colin as he turned to go. Tina's glance followed Colin's movement as he thrust the Paterson back into his belt. Then she raised her eyes to his face, a new measure of him in their depths.

"I would not have taken you for a gunfighter," she said.

"I'm not," said Colin. "Dad always said a man had no right to use tools unless he could use them well."

A mingling of emotions brought a subtle, indefinable change to her face, and then left it with only a strange, withdrawn calculation. She walked over to sit on the long, comfortable bench beneath a peach tree. She toyed idly with a ring on her middle finger, pouting a little. Feeling awkward, standing in the middle of the garden, he finally joined her. His attention was caught by the ring's strange design.

150

"Looks like some kind of Mexican brand," he said.

She held it up for his inspection. "It is called a *rubrica*. In the old days, the Moors wore rings with designs on them . . . their initials, or something signifying their house . . . and, instead of signing their name, stamped this in hot wax on the paper, forming sort of a seal. The Moors carried it into Spain in their conquest. The design in this ring has been handed down through our family for generations."

"You're full of stories."

"You don't have to restrain yourself so nobly. You've been looking at me that way ever since *Cabo* mentioned Captain Velasco, up there on the mountain."

"I don't deny it. When you first told me the legend of El Renegado, you were very careful not to name the captain who betrayed his people. How are you descended from him?"

"There are many versions of the legend of El Renegado," she said. "One of them is a belief, as persistent as it is false, that the descendants of Captain Velasco are back in the Patagonias somewhere, a race, a people to themselves, really. Not true half-breeds, because the mating of Velasco and the Indian girl was so many centuries before, that the division of blood has almost been lost. They are supposed to be renegades, as he was, bandits, murderers, veritable ogres, capable of appalling atrocities, holding the simpletons of Tintown and the other settlements outside the basin in constant fear. You know how a thing like that can grow through the centuries. Every deed of violence within a thousand miles is attributed to this band."

"And there's no truth in it?"

"I am the only descendant of Velasco," she said. "He did have children, but they drifted down off the mountains into this basin years ago, adopting the customs and language of the Spaniards who had come into New Mexico by then. One of them did such service to the Spanish Crown that he was pardoned for his ancestor's crime, and granted the land this hacienda occupies."

He studied her face, finding logic in those curiously haunted eyes. He leaned toward her, a vagrant smile catching at his mouth for the first time.

"Will you forgive my suspicions?"

"I'm used to them. It is the usual reaction to the name, Velasco. I didn't realize how bad it really was till father died. It left me completely alone here."

She sat, staring moodily at the flagstones, and he had to say something, anything. "How did he die?"

For a moment, he thought a cloud had passed before the sun. The shadow crossing her face was that palpable. Then, instinctively, he glanced toward El Renegado.

"You aren't thinking of the . . . the . . . ."

"The curse?" she finished, head lifting in some sharp defiance. "You sound like your brother. I thought you were different. I thought you were sensitive to those things. Do you know how old I am? Twenty-five. Do you know how many days I've heard laughter in this house? Not one. In all my life, not one!"

She was standing now, staring at the wall, fists clenched at her sides, giving vent to some violent release that had been gathering force for a long time. "Do you know how much pain and tragedy and death I've seen? A grandfather paralyzed when he fell from his horse, sitting for ten years like a stone statue faced toward the mountain. A grandmother burned to death in the stables. A mother killed when she was thrown downstairs by her husband in a drunken rage. A son

152

killing him for it. A lifetime of loneliness because my name is Velasco. Not a man in the towns around here who has had the courage to look at me, for fear of the curse. How can I help but think of that curse, when I say anything, do anything, remember anything?"

He saw she was on the verge of crying and got to his feet sharply, catching her. She turned to him with a hunger which surprised him, molding her body into the circle of his arms, and then he was answering the hunger, pulling her against him with a savage passion he had not known himself capable of, cupping a hand under her chin to lift her face. His lips were still on hers when he heard someone call her name.

"Tina? Tina?"

The voice was unmistakable. It caused him something close to pain to pull his mouth away and turn toward the sound. All the romance of Erin had always given Farris Shane his way with women, and it was so typical of him to make a flourish of it that way, ignoring the half-open gate in the *zaguan* to come vaulting over the top of the adobe wall itself, from the back of his horse outside. Mouth still open from calling her name, he had already seen them before he landed.

His knees bent with the weight of his body striking the ground, then straightened, and he was staring at them with eyes already blackened by storm.

"Colin?" he said, in a small, unbelieving way. "Colin," he repeated, his voice now hoarse, angry.

"Farris," cried Colin, releasing the woman abruptly. "Don't be a fool."

"I *have been* a fool," said Farris, his tone so thick with anger he could hardly speak. "It was you. Behind my back. Knowing how I felt about her, and meeting her like this."

153

"Farris . . . ."

"I told you, Colin, how it would be."

The rest of it was lost as he rushed Colin in that blind, roaring rage. Colin tried to wheel aside, but Farris spun him against the wall. He caught Colin there, doubling him over with a vicious punch to the groin. Gripped in the nauseating pain of it, Colin would have fallen to the ground except for Farris there in front of him, pinning him against the wall.

Dimly, somewhere down in the pain-filled recesses of him, he realized that if Farris hit him once more he would be through. With Farris's body against him, holding him up, he felt the surge of muscle, shifting away from his own left side, that told him of his brother's right arm brought back for a second blow.

His long legs found purchase, and he shoved with all the strength of them, just as Farris struck. Tripping backward, Farris's blow lost all its force, falling weakly against Colin's shoulder. Colin kept shoving, his arms wound about the man's waist. Farris came up against something with a tumbling crash of wood and stone. He seemed to surge upward in Colin's arms, as if something had lifted his feet off the ground. Then all the tension left Farris's body. He fell backward. There was another sharp crack, something sickening this time.

It must have been Farris's head striking that oaken bench, for he lay sprawled on his back just beside it, darkening the flagstones with his blood. Colin swayed above him, staring at the growing red stain. Then, face twisting, he dropped to his knees beside his brother.

"Farris?" he said, in a weak, husky voice. There was no answer. "Farris?" Lifting the head up. "Farris?" Seeing the eyes roll open, white and sightless and dead.

"I'll . . . I'll get some water," whispered Tina,

standing above them.

Colin dropped his brother's head back. "He doesn't need any water," he told her, in a voice that did not belong to him. For a moment, he thought the blood had spread across all the patio floor, to darken it that way. Then he felt the chill of the garden, and turned his face upward. The woman was looking in that direction, too, an ominous fulfillment torturing her face. The sun was setting behind the Patagonias, and the shadow of El Renegado lay black as Farris's blood across the whole garden.

VI

CONSCIOUSNESS OF A GREAT HEAT CAME TO COLIN. HE tried to open his eyes. There was blinding brightness. He realized he was on his back, and rolled over. The grit of earth scraped his belly. He got to his hands and knees, opening his eyes again. He saw that there was barren land about him—great, ruddy rocks and steep, sandy barrancas. He had a dim, whirling memory. Farris was in it somehow. He sat down, holding his head in his hands, trying to think.

It returned then, like a blow, memory of the fight in the garden. Farris dead? He raised his head, unable to believe it. He was a murderer, then. Of his own brother.

In this torture, he stared around him, trying to make out where he was. There seemed to be mountains all about him, stark, barren, unworldly. He thought, for a moment, of a dream. But it was too real for that. More memory came, filtering in painfully, dim and tantalizing. He could almost see the man stumbling out through that *zaguan*, eyes blank and staring in the madness of realizing what he had done. Was it him? He

155

had wandered, then. He had run from the scene of his crime and wandered to this spot, too crazed with grief and guilt to have any lucid memory of it.

He looked at his shirt. It was in tatters. How long had he been wandering? He felt his beard. It was a rough stubble an inch long. It had been days. He tried to rise, fell back. On his second attempt he made it.

Now he knew a burning thirst, and began walking, aimlessly, hands outstretched, unable to see half the time that the sun was so bright. He stumbled and fell many times. The one thought in his mind was water. Then something else began replacing that. He felt his arms twitch, as if tensing to strike something. His lips moved in someone's name. He saw a face before him, and saw himself hitting at it. Farris. Farris, on the ground before him, with the blood darkening the flagstones. A scream of anguish escaped him and he dug his fists into his eyes to escape the vision, running from it, running with small, animal sobbing sounds, stumbling and falling again, losing sanity before the persistent, maddening memory that blended with reality until he could not tell them apart.

He ran on down the sandy, desolate slope, a tattered, babbling figure, sinking finally into the same apathetic state which had led him wandering so long with no memory of it.

When he became lucid again, the heat was gone, the burning thirst. He knew a great sense of coolness. Above him was a ceiling, laced with the herringbone pattern of the willow shoots they laid beneath the foot of earth forming the roofs of their adobe houses. Under these stretched the *viga* poles that were the rafters, forming dim, smoke-blackened lines from wall to wall. Then it was the face, the greasy, bland, grinning face,

156

and the man squatting back on his heels.

"Pajarero."

"*Si*," smiled the bird-catcher. "I found you wandering the Patagonias. *Loco* in the head. Ay. Does it torture one so, to kill his own brother?"

Colin's face twisted. "You know?"

"The whole basin knows," said Pajarero. "You and he fought in the woman's garden and he died in the shadow of El Renegado." He seemed to be looking beyond Colin. "Did you ever wonder why it was you who lived, and not he?"

Colin tried to sit up. "How do you mean?"

"He was the one who scoffed at Renegado. Sometimes the unbelievers are punished in strange ways for their heresy."

Colin's efforts to rise brought a chorus of squawks from the birds in the cages around the room. The bird-catcher rose from his hunkers and fluttered around from one to another, calming them.

"Quiet, Pepita. *Caramba*. Are you old women, that you screech at a mouse? Silence, Garcia. That does not befit a gentleman."

Finally he had them quieted down, and he shuffled over to a pot of stew simmering over one of the pot-fires on the adobe hearth, ladling out a bowl for Colin, muttering into his fat jowls. Colin sat amid the fetid sheepskin pallets, gulping the stew ravenously, following it with a dozen cold tortillas piled on a plate.

"We're in Tintown?" he asked Pajarero, at last.

"In the Patagonias," said the man.

"I thought you lived in Tintown."

"I live wherever my travels take me," said the man, grumpily.

Colin studied the man. "Why did you take me in,

157

Pajarero?"

Something withdrew in that round, greasy face. "You would have died out there. You had the fever. This is your first clear head in three days. I been nursing you like a baby."

Colin moved again, feeling the weakness in him. Even talk cost him an effort. But he had to know. "Why, though, Pajarero?" he insisted. "You know how I stand with Nacho. I think he's quite capable of killing you for taking me in this way. Don't you?"

The man squinted, as if in pain at the name, and Colin had it. "Maybe because I saved you from him that first time?" he asked.

"Well, well," muttered Pajarero, "so I am not so noble, so I had a reason for taking you in. Maybe you are the only one in the valley who has opposed Nacho and lived. I heard about that business with the guns. Poom!" He made a gesture of drawing a gun, index finger pointed. "So fast nobody saw it come out. So fast Nacho started first and still didn't have anything free in time."

"And you're hiding from him?" said Colin. The man made vague, shrugging movements with his shoulders and arms, pouting and muttering incoherently, moving over to pour coffee he had put on to boil "Why?" asked Colin. "Why was he trying to kill you that first day?"

"How would I know?" said Pajarero, turning away.

"Does he run a gang back here in the Patagonias?"

"I don't know *nada* about nothing."

"You mean you're afraid to tell. How is Tina mixed up in it? What is Nacho to her?"

"*Dios*," exploded the man, waving his hand so violently he spilled the coffee. "Haven't I saved your life? Is that not enough? What do you want? The history

158

of the New World? Drink your coffee and be thankful I have found it in my groveling little soul to do this much. Now, rest a while. I have to go and get water from the *tinaja*."

A *tinaja* was a natural rock sink in which rain water collected during the wet season. Colin expected the man back in a few moments, but time stretched out to an hour, two hours. He was stirring feebly within the stifling hovel, worried about the bird-catcher, when the man's grimy, weary face poked through the low door.

"*Agua*," he grinned. "Enough to last a couple of days if we do not wash."

"Don't mean to tell me it's that far away," muttered Colin.

"Over two mountains," chuckled Pajarero.

"You really are holed in," said Colin.

"*El Diablo* himself could not find us," smiled the man, secretively. "The Patagonias themselves are so inaccessible that no more than a dozen men have penetrated them in the last century, and this is the most inaccessible spot in all the Patagonias."

Colin knew it was useless to ask the man again why he was so afraid of Nacho. He settled down to recovering, dozing most of that first day, moving about some the second. He began to brood soon, about Farris, sinking into a black, ugly mood that lasted for hours.

"But it was not your fault," Pajarero pleaded with him, over and over. "You did not mean to kill him. You were only defending yourself. It was an accident, *amigo*, that bench."

When that failed, the man would try to amuse him by babbling about his experiences in Yucatan, or Darien, or some other forgotten section of Mexico, hunting birds. It helped, somehow. There was a naïve simplicity to

Pajarero, for all his travels, all his strange, exotic knowledge, that lifted Colin out of his depression. But there was always something behind the talk—in those quiet, expressive eyes of Pajarero's, in the way he watched Colin sometimes—a sense of pendant waiting. Colin had regained most of his strength by the third time Pajarero had to go for water. After the man had left, Colin went outside the door, hunkering down against the wall, squinting against the haze of heat the sun brought.

It was just a little one room adobe *jacal*, walls crumbling with age, a corral of cottonwood poles behind, holding Pajarero's jackass and a couple of mangy horses. On every side, the mountains lifted their jagged, barren steeps to the sky, utterly devoid of vegetation. A buzzard circled high above. The silence had a palpable pressure. Shadows lengthened slowly, crawling like black fingers across the rocks to touch Colin. They brought him a sudden chill. He stirred, realizing how long Pajarero had been gone.

He went inside, lying on the fetid sheepskins. He must have dozed, for when he awoke, it was night. A loafer wolf filled the darkness with its mourning. Colin moved restlessly about the building, looking off in the direction Pajarero always took.

When the moon began to rise, shedding a pale, unworldly light over the peaks, he went inside, pawing through the sheepskins till he found where Pajarero had put his Paterson. He shoved the gun in behind his belt buckle and went to get one of the horses. There was an ancient Mexican tree-saddle on the top pole of the corral. With this on the beast, he set off up the trail he had watched the bird-catcher take.

It was so rocky the hoofs left no mark, and he soon

lost his way. He was on the point of turning back when he realized the horse was tugging at the reins, trying to face the other way. A thirsty animal had some sense of water many miles away, and he gave the animal its head. The horse went at a deliberate walk, as true as if it had traveled the trail all its life, carrying him across one of the knife-like peaks and into another valley. The wolf was still howling off in the distance somewhere, when the other sound joined it. A faint mewing, like a sick cat.

He saw it, finally. Pajarero had been tied to a jumping cholla. Some of the longer spines had thrust clear through his body at the sides and other narrower portions. His shirt front was rusty with blood. There were the charred coals of a fire at one side, with several half-burnt stalks of Spanish dagger. Jumping off his horse and going to his knees beside the man, Colin saw what they had been used for. Pajarero's eyes had been burned out.

"*Agua*," whispered the fat, little Mexican, moving his head from side to side. "*Ruego de alma mia, Señor*, I can hear you . . . help me . . . ." He broke off, chest lifting with his sharp breath. "Nacho?"

"No, Pajarero," said Colin, gently. "It's Colin. Take it easy and I'll have you off this."

"No, no," bleated the man, like a weak child. "I die soon. Do not cause me more pain."

Colin settled back to his heels, holding the man. "Why did Nacho do this?"

"He wanted me to tell where you were." He made a ghastly attempt at a smile. "I'm proud of myself, *Señor*. When you go through Tintown, do me the favor of telling the other bird-catchers that Nacho is not so terrible. He could not even make Pajarero talk."

161

"This wasn't why he was trying to kill you that first time."

"I suppose not."

"Can't you tell me now, Pajarero? Who is Nacho?"

"There are some things even the wind dare not whisper, *Señor*."

"You're protecting Tina. It has something to do with her."

"Does it, *Señor*?"

"Why did you stay in the basin, knowing Nacho would kill you?"

"I have traveled two continents in the quest of rare birds," said the man, weakly. "There was one rarest, most beautiful of all . . . which I desired more than any other in the world. But I am only a fat, stupid little Pajarero, a comical clown of a bird-catcher and it was denied me. All I could do was flutter about inside its cage."

Colin's throat twitched as he realized who Pajarero meant. He remembered the dog-like devotion in the man's eyes that first time they had seen Tina, remembered how Pajarero had tried to kiss the hem of her skirt, on his knees. At the time, it had been almost amusing to him. The full pathos of it struck him now.

"Ay," said Pajarero, at his silence. "You see, now. And if I had it to do over again, it would be no different. For but one more look at her, I would take ten times this torture. They kept trying to get you to go, didn't they?"

"Tina?"

"She. Your mother. Even I told you how foolish you were to stay, once. And yet, you stayed. You had seen her, too. We are not very different underneath, *Señor*. Your plumage may be more brilliant, but inside it is the same. I would ask you as a dying favor, to leave now.

But I know how useless that would be. You will stay and be killed, because you have seen her. Renegado is fulfilled in strange ways."

He leaned back against the cactus, greasy face contorting in some last spasm of pain. Then he sank down, and the shallow breathing stopped. Staring down at the round, fat face, Colin felt a tear begin rolling down his cheek. He was crying. The pain of his anguish was the more intense because he could make no sound.

Later, he untied the man and gathered rocks for a cairn, piling them over his body. Then he gathered up the gum-pitched *morrales* Pajarero had been carrying the water in, slinging them over the withers of his horse, and set off on the trail. The rock and talus had given way to parched earth, here, which recorded the prints of four horses faithfully. By the moonlight, it was not too hard to follow.

VII

THE MOUNTAINS SEEMED TO RISE AND FALL ABOUT Colin, before him, behind him, like a gigantic sea, as he traversed peak after peak, valley after valley. He came to vegetation, ocotillo spreading from an arroyo like a fountain of gold, candlewood spouting a torch of flame from its spidery wands. And then, ahead, El Renegado, appearing suddenly behind a nearer range, like a great, somber skull, thrusting up out of its cerements.

The awe it brought struck Colin so forcibly he felt a vague nausea. It caused him great effort to push on, keeping his attention on those tracks. He knew he was nearing the basin now, and wondered if they were seeking him at his house. He plunged through creosote, yellow with flower, into a steep arroyo, still on the trail, finding it again as it came from the creosote into the sandy wash. Then the walls of the arroyo echoed and reverberated to crazy, cackling laughter, and that voice filled with the archaic accent of Castilian.

"Here is an *Indio, Capitan*. I have an *Indio, Capitan* . . ."

Recognizing the voice, Colin pulled up his jaded horse, staring about him. A gun crashed, and his horse leaped into the air with a scream. Colin threw himself off the thrashing animal before it went down, pulling his gun as he fell.

He struck heavily, rolling through deep sand to come against mesquite with a loud crackle. Stunned, he crawled into the bushes.

He could hear horses galloping back down the arroyo, now. Three riders burst around its winding curve into the broadening wash, with Nacho in the lead, spurring his horse, brutally. Colin raised to his knees in the bushes, holding his gun out till he had it point blank on the man's body, and fired. Nacho shouted in pain, pitching upward and backward off his animal, with arms spread eagled to the sky.

Colin saw the other two men wheel in the saddle toward him, trying to pull their horses up and fire all at once. It was too fast and too confused to be sure of hitting the men now, and Colin lowered his gun to shoot their horses out from under them, one after the other. The first animal went down by the front, tumbling its rider over the head, and the second veered off sideways suddenly, crashing into the rocky slope of the arroyo, and wiping his man out of the saddle. He flopped down to the bottom of that slope like a doll with all the sand gone, and lay moveless there. Further back, in the broader bottom of the arroyo, the other man lay on his

164

back, calling softly in pain.

"Nacho . . . Nacho . . . come get me, damn you. My leg's broke, my leg's broke . . . ."

This had all taken no more than a minute, but as Colin's attention was swept back to the spot where he had shot Nacho; he could not see the man. Blood stained the sand and made an unmistakable trail into the creosote on the other side of the arroyo. Colin searched those bushes for some sign of movement, unwilling to move, with The Corporal still somewhere up above him.

One of the horses he had shot lay kicking and writhing in the sand, and the other had fallen to its side, in death. Farther up the arroyo, where Colin had first entered it, was Nacho's horse. Nacho rode with split reins, and they had dropped to the earth. He must have been trained for ground-hitching, as most Mexican animals were, for he had spooked that far from the excitement, and then halted, fiddling around nervously.

Colin wanted that horse the worst way, with his own animal down. He decided at last that he had to find The Corporal before he could expose himself, and turned to worm his way through the cover of rocks and bushes up his side of the arroyo, seeking the spot from which the crazy old man had shot his horse.

"Nacho," called the man, from down at the bottom. "Come and get me, damn you, come and get me, my leg's broke, I say."

Almost at the lip of the arroyo, Colin heard a dim, muttering sound. He wormed through mesquite toward it. Through this brush, finally, he made out The Corporal crouched down over that ancient matchlock, fumbling with the pan. Colin must have made some rustle in the mesquite, for the old man's head jerked up. Colin felt his gun move abruptly to cover The Corporal.

The man leered blankly at him.

"Have you got a match, Comrade?" he said. "The Indians are down in the valley and I'm out of matches."

"You damn old fool," muttered Colin. He still kept his gun on the man, knowing a frustrating indecision. Before it left him, there was some movement down in the arroyo to attract his attention. It was in the creosote, up at the end where Nacho's horse had halted. The animal began fiddling again down there, ears pricked. Colin could not help raise up as he saw a man pull himself out of the creosote, clutching at a stirrup. The horse tried to dance away, but the man caught a leather, hauling himself erect.

It was Nacho. He must have crawled through the brush from where he had fallen to get his horse, knowing that Colin was looking for him. Colin started moving, trying to find a position that would clear the man for his gun. But Nacho was mounting on the opposite side of his horse. In desperation, Colin aimed at the animal.

"Watch out, *Capitan*," screamed The Corporal, from behind Colin. "The *bribón* is going to shoot you . . . ."

Colin half-turned in time to see the old man jumping at him, that gun clubbed. He ducked under it, throwing The Corporal over his shoulder. Nacho was racing down the arroyo now. Colin snapped a shot at him, but he was going too fast, and too far away.

Colin wheeled to where The Corporal's horse stood, a mangy crow-bait with trailing reins. The animal did not even shy when he ran up on it. He had to boot it unmercifully to get any movement. He passed The Corporal, trying to climb back up the slope from where Colin had thrown him, and then he slid the horse down the bank into the arroyo. Pushing the horse, he reached

166

the end of this to run out into a series of benches with Nacho in sight, crossing them.

Colin knew there was no use trying to catch Nacho, on this old nag, but he felt no desire to. It was a certainty in him, where the man was going, and he figured Nacho would be more sure to keep in that direction if he thought he was not followed. Colin allowed his horse to slow down, until Nacho ran out of sight into the timber at the footslopes of El Renegado.

With the mountain there, Colin knew where he was, now, and he took a southwesterly direction, not even bothering to follow Nacho's trail directly. El Renegado brooded over him the whole distance, some malignant portent in its air of patient, sinister waiting. He was tense in the saddle, with its spell, when he came out into the flats of the basin. The Velasco hacienda was ahead of him. He approached it through the cottonwoods growing in the river bottom. This cover brought him right up against the high adobe wall surrounding the place. Down this wall about fifty feet was a broad *zaguan*, the logical gate to use for anyone coming from the direction Colin had. And before it, on the ground, even at this distance, he saw the bloodstains.

Thought of Farris was in his mind, as he lifted himself to a standing position in the saddle, against the wall, grasping the tiles on top and hoisting his body over. A weeping willow dropped its foliage over the wall here, and in this momentary screen he reloaded his gun from the handful of shells he always carried in his pocket.

After this was done, he found himself unwilling to move. He was torn between a deep reluctance to find Nacho with Tina, and a bitter desire to finish this up, for Pajarero, for Farris, for his mother.

He forced himself from the screen of willow, dropping off the wall. There was a row of sheds ahead of him, filled with the muted stamp and snort of horses, and he realized he was in the back end of a stable yard. He moved through the reek of rotten hay and droppings, around the end of this row of adobe stalls. This brought him to the main yard, into which the *zaguan* opened. It was lit by flaring torches, and Nacho's horse stood hipshot and blowing next to a half-open door.

Colin stepped to the door, listened a moment. There were muffled voices from far within. Carefully, he pushed the portal open. He was staring down a long hall, lined with the niches in which they placed their carved wooden saints. Blood stains made a trail down the floor to another door at the end, partly ajar. Colin made his way to this. The voices seemed to lift away from him now. He saw beyond the second door a great room, lit by a dozen candles, filling the candelabra of beaten silver on a great oak table. The light drank in mauve *savanarillas* hanging on the walls, seemed to catch up the faded red of a Chimayo blanket draped across the adobe *banco* that ran all the way around the room to form a foot-high bench molded in against the wall.

At the far side of the room, a stairway rose, railed in wrought iron, tarnished and rusted with age. Finally he could wait no longer. He pushed the door open with a boot. Nothing happened. He stepped into the room, ducking over back of the table. Still nothing. He darted for the wall by the stairway. He was almost to the corner, where it would afford him cover from the steps higher up, when a shot rocked the room.

It caught him across the side of his thigh, filling him with the hot, inchoate sense of a burning, lashing blow, twisting him halfway around. His run carried him up against the wall at that corner, however, half-falling across the adobe *banco*. With this for support, he bent forward and sent a shot up the dark stairwell.

There was the scream of a ricochet, a sharp, withdrawing movement up there. He took that indication of retreat to jump on into the stairs, firing upward again, seeing the dim shape above. There was one answering shot, ripping adobe off in pale flakes from the wall at the side of his head. He fired a third time with the body full in his sights.

"¡*Por Dios*!," screamed Nacho, pain rending his voice. Then there was a heavy, thumping, sliding sound, as of someone dragging themselves down a wall. Colin's leg would bear his weight no longer, and he went down on the stairs before he reached the top. Lying there, with light from below still strong enough to see, he made out that the bullet had struck the great outer muscle of his thigh, going down in a long, deep flesh wound to come out at his knee on the same side.

"Nacho?" called a woman's voice, from up there. "Nacho, please . . . ."

It was Tina, her voice driving Colin to crawl on up the stairs. His head came over the top step, and he could see down another long hall. Light from its end was blocked off by the woman's body. He saw a low niche in the wall above him, and reached up to clutch at its edge, pulling down the wooden *santo* it contained as he struggled up. Tina reached him then, trying to keep him from going on.

"Colin, please, you can't do it, please!"

"Maybe you didn't see what he did to Pajarero," said Colin, twisting inexorably around her.

Tina's struggles to hold him became more violent.

"Pajarero? I can't help it, you mustn't, not Nacho . . . ."

"If I had more guts, it would be you, too," he said, tearing loose. He almost fell, then put himself into a headlong run that carried him in a stumbling, hurtling passage down the hall. He came to the head of the stairs giving off light from below, and saw Nacho on the landing, halfway down. The man turned, raising his gun. But Colin had his held level, waist high, and all he had to do was pull the trigger. It made a deafening crash. Nacho was punched heavily back against the wall. Then he pitched forward, rolling down the stairs to the bottom. Colin went down after him to make sure.

Nacho's dead right hand was thrust outward, a ring on the curling fourth finger. Colin stared at the design on it, the Velasco *rubrica*. The rustle of skirts brought his head around. Tina was staring at the ring with wide, tortured eyes.

"Are you satisfied now?" she asked.

He looked up at her with frowning eyes. "He's a Velasco?"

"My brother."

"And I thought," muttered Colin, staring blankly at Nacho. "I thought . . . ."

"You thought he was my lover?" she finished, when he would not go on.

Colin nodded dully. "You mentioned your father throwing your mother downstairs in a drunken rage, and a son killing him for it."

"That was Nacho," she said. "It changed him somehow. We tried not to blame him for killing father. It was such a terrible thing father had done. But it twisted Nacho. He had been such a good boy before. He turned into something wild, like an animal, running off into the Patagonias and gathering that bunch of filthy,

170

crazy *bribónes* around him, like The Corporal, taking advantage of the Renegado legend about the descendants of Velasco being back in there, just to maraud the countryside. And then he would come back for a little time, and be the boy he had been, giving me the company and companionship I craved so here, and I would know the hope that he was changing. That's why I wanted you to leave. He was still my brother. Can you understand the position I was in? I knew that one of you would kill the other if you stayed. From the first, it was obvious. He was my brother *and* my lover. Isn't that a happy choice? And now . . . now?" She sank to her knees beside Nacho, the tears running silently down her face. "Now one of you has killed the other."

"No wonder Pajarero wouldn't tell me your connection with Nacho," murmured Colin. "And it was you who stampeded those cattle and Farris found you up on Renegado that day?"

"Yes," she nodded, dully. "Ichahi and I did it. Do you blame me?" He was silent so long she raised her head, meeting his eyes, seeing what was in them. "I didn't know Farris was coming that day, though, Colin. I didn't plan *that*. You can't believe I did."

In a sudden, impulsive way, unable to put his answer into words, he reached out for her, lifting her to her feet, encircling her with his arms. For a long time they stood that close, finding comfort in the nearness, until he finally sensed the subtle tension flowing into her body. He felt as if something had touched him from behind, and realized they were no longer standing in the dawn sunlight. A shadow had dropped across them. They both turned as one, staring at the mountain, forming its somber, brooding silhouette against the morning sunrise. Tina made a small, tortured sound.

"You've got to get that out of your system," he said. "Nacho was causing everything as much as the mountain."

"Did he cause your mother's death?" she said. "Or Farris's?"

He felt something within him contract at the thought of Farris, and could not help its showing on his face, that dark, mystic sensitivity to the spell of the mountain.

"You'll take me away from here, Colin? You won't try to stay here any longer? You feel it as deeply as I do?"

"Where I am going, Tina, you cannot come."

"But where are you going?" she asked, arching away from him in sudden defiance.

"If you will show me where Farris's body is buried, I shall move him, so he can rest beside our mother's grave."

"And then?" she asked.

"Then," he said sadly, but with a dim light of hope in his eyes, "then I will begin all over again. I told you the night our mother died, Tina. *We* aren't leaving the valley." With the chill of that shadow in his very bones, tears now again in his eyes, he repeated the words slowly. "No, Tina. Where I am going, you cannot come."

Part Four

VISIONS OF DREAMS AND DANCING

LOUIS L'AMOUR

LOUIS DEARBORN LaMOORE (1908-1988) was born in Jamestown, North Dakota. He left home at fifteen and subsequently held a wide variety of jobs although he worked mostly as a merchant seaman. From his earliest youth, L'Amour had a love of verse. His first published work was a poem, "The Chap Worth While," appearing when he was eighteen years old in his former hometown's newspaper, the *Jamestown Sun*. It is the only poem from his early years that he left out of *Smoke From This Altar* which appeared in 1939 from Lusk Publishers in Oklahoma City, a book which L'Amour published himself; however, this poem is reproduced in *The Louis L'Amour Companion* (Andrews and McMeel, 1992) edited by Robert Weinberg. L'Amour wrote poems and articles for a number of small circulation arts magazines all through the early 1930s and, after hundreds of rejection slips, finally had his first story accepted, "Anything for a Pal" in *True Gang Life* (10/35). He returned in 1938 to live with his family where they had settled in Choctaw, Oklahoma, determined to make writing his career. He wrote a fight story bought by Standard Magazines that year and became acquainted with editor Leo Margulies who was to play an important rôle later in L'Amour's life. "The Town No Guns Could Tame" in *New Western* (3/40) was his first published Western story.

During the Second World War L'Amour was drafted and ultimately served with the U.S. Army Transportation Corps in Europe. However, in the two years before he was shipped out, he managed to write a great many adventure stories for Standard Magazines. The first story he published in 1946, the year of his discharge, was a Western, "Law of the Desert Born" in *Dime Western* (4/46). A call to Leo Margulies resulted in L'Amour's agreeing to write Western stories for the various Western pulp magazines published by Standard Magazines, a third of which appeared under the byline Jim Mayo, the name of a character in L'Amour's earlier adventure fiction. The proposal for L'Amour to write new Hopalong Cassidy novels came from Margulies who wanted to launch *Hopalong Cassidy's Western Magazine* to take advantage of the popularity William Boyd's old films and new television series were enjoying with a new generation. Doubleday & Company agreed to publish the pulp novelettes in hard cover books. L'Amour was paid $500 a story, no royalties, and he was assigned the house name Tex Burns. L'Amour read Clarence E. Mulford's books about the Bar-20 and based his Hopalong Cassidy on Mulford's original creation. Only two issues of the magazine appeared before it ceased publication. Doubleday felt that the Hopalong character had to appear exactly as William Boyd did in the films and on television and thus even the first two novels had to be revamped to meet with this requirement prior to publication in book form.

L'Amour's first Western novel under his own byline was **Westward the Tide** (World's Work, 1950). It was rejected by every American publisher to which it was submitted. World's Work paid a flat £75 without royalties for British Empire rights in perpetuity. L'Amour sold his first Western short story to a slick magazine a year later, "The Gift of Cochise" in *Collier's* (7/5/52). Robert Fellows and John Wayne purchased screen rights to this story from L'Amour for $4,000 and James Edward Grant, one of Wayne's favorite screenwriters, developed a script from it, changing L'Amour's Ches Lane to Hondo Lane. L'Amour retained the right to novelize Grant's screenplay, which differs substantially from his short story, and he was able to get an endorsement from Wayne to be used as a blurb, stating that *Hondo* was the finest Western Wayne had ever read. *Hondo* (Fawcett Gold Medal, 1953) by Louis L'Amour was released on the same day as the film, *Hondo* (Warner, 1953), with a first printing of 320,000 copies.

With *Showdown at Yellow Butte* (Ace, 1953) by Jim Mayo, L'Amour began a series of short Western novels for Don Wollheim that could be doubled with other short novels by other authors in Ace Publishing's paperback two-fers. Advances on these were $800 and usually the author never earned any royalties. *Heller With a Gun* (Fawcett Gold Medal, 1955) was the first of a series of original Westerns L'Amour had agreed to write under his own name following the success for Fawcett of *Hondo*. L'Amour wanted even this early to have his Western novels published in hard cover editions. He expanded "Guns of the Timberland" by Jim Mayo in *West* (9/50) for *Guns of the Timberlands* (Jason Press, 1955), a hard cover Western for which he was paid an advance of $250. Another novel for Jason Press followed and then *Silver Canyon* (Avalon Books, 1956) for Thomas Bouregy & Company. These were basically lending library publishers and the books seldom earned much money above the small advances paid.

The great turn in L'Amour's fortunes came about because of problems Saul David was having with his original paperback Westerns program at Bantam Books. Fred Glidden had been signed to a contract to produce two original paperback Luke Short Western novels a year for an advance of $15,000 each. It was a long-term contract but, in the first ten years of it, Fred only wrote six novels. Literary agent Marguerite Harper then persuaded Bantam that Fred's brother, Jon, could help fulfill the contract and Jon was signed for eight Peter Dawson Western novels. When Jon died suddenly before completing even one book for Bantam, Harper managed to engage a ghost writer at the Disney studios to write these eight "Peter Dawson" novels, beginning with *The Savages* (Bantam, 1959). They proved inferior to anything Jon had ever written and what sales they had seemed to be due only to the Peter Dawson name.

Saul David wanted to know from L'Amour if *he* could deliver two Western novels a year. L'Amour said he could, and he did. In fact, by 1962 this number was increased to three original paperback novels a year. The first L'Amour novel to appear under the Bantam contract was *Radigan* (Bantam, 1958). It seemed to me after I read all of the Western stories L'Amour ever wrote in preparation for my essay, "Louis L'Amour's Western Fiction" in *A Variable Harvest* (McFarland, 1990), that by the time L'Amour wrote "Riders of the Dawn" in *Giant Western* (6/51), the short novel he later expanded to form *Silver Canyon*, that he had almost burned out on the Western story, and this was years before his fame, wealth, and tremendous sales figures. He had developed seven basic plot situations in his pulp Western stories and he used them over and over again in writing his original paperback Westerns. *Flint* (Bantam, 1960), considered by many to be one of L'Amour's better efforts, is basically a reprise of the range war plot which, of the seven, is the one L'Amour used most often. L'Amour's hero, Flint, knows about a hideout in the badlands (where, depending on the story, something is hidden: cattle, horses, outlaws, etc.). Even certain episodes within his basic plots are repeated again and again. Flint scales a sharp V in a canyon wall to escape a tight spot as Jim Gatlin had before him in L'Amour's "The Black Rock Coffin Makers" in *.44 Western* (2/50) and many a L'Amour hero would again.

Basic to this range war plot is the villain's means for crowding out the other ranchers in a district. He brings in a giant herd that requires all the available grass and forces all the smaller ranchers out of business. It was this same strategy Bantam used in marketing L'Amour. *All* of his Western titles were continuously kept in print. Independent distributors were required to buy titles in lots of 10,000 copies if they wanted access to other Bantam titles at significantly discounted prices. In time L'Amour's paperbacks forced almost every one else off the racks in the Western sections. L'Amour himself comprised the other half of this successful strategy. He dressed up in cowboy outfits, traveled about the country in a motor home visiting with independent distributors, taking them to dinner and charming them, making them personal friends. He promoted himself at every available opportunity. L'Amour insisted that he was telling the stories of the people who had made America a great nation and he appealed to patriotism as much as to commercialism in his rhetoric.

His fiction suffered, of course, stories written hurriedly and submitted in their first draft and published as he wrote them. A character would have a rifle in his hand, a model not yet invented in the period in which the story was set, and when he crossed a street the rifle would vanish without explanation. A scene would begin in a saloon and suddenly the setting would be a hotel dining room. Characters would die once and, a few pages later, die again. An old man for most of a story would turn out to be in his twenties.

Once when we were talking and Louis had showed me his topographical maps and his library of thousands of volumes which he claimed he used for research, he asserted that, if he claimed there was a rock in a road at a certain point in a story, his readers knew that if they went to that spot they would find the rock just as he described it. I told him that might be so but I personally was troubled by the many inconsistencies in his stories. Take **Last Stand at Papago Wells** (Fawcett Gold Medal, 1957). Five characters are killed during an Indian raid. One of the surviving characters emerges from seclusion after the attack and counts *six* corpses.

"I'll have to go back and count them again," L'Amour said, and smiled. "But, you know, I don't think the people who read my books would really care."

All of this notwithstanding, there are many fine, and some spectacular, moments in Louis L'Amour's Western fiction. I think he was at his best in the shorter forms, especially his magazine stories, and the two best stories he ever wrote appeared in the 1950s, "The Gift of Cochise" early in the decade and "War Party" in *The Saturday Evening Post* (6/59). The latter was later expanded by L'Amour to serve as the opening chapters for **Bendigo Shafter** (Dutton, 1979). That book is so poorly structured that Harold Kuebler, senior editor at Doubleday & Company to whom it was first offered, said he would not publish it unless L'Amour undertook extensive revisions. This L'Amour refused to do and, eventually, Bantam started a hard cover publishing program to accommodate him when no other hard cover publisher proved willing to accept his books as he wrote them. Yet "War Party," reprinted here as it first appeared, possesses several of the characteristics in purest form which I suspect, no matter how diluted they ultimately would become, account in largest measure for the loyal following Louis L'Amour won from his readers: the young male narrator who is in the process of growing into manhood and who is evaluating other human beings and his own experiences; a resourceful frontier woman who has beauty as well as fortitude; a strong male character who is single and hence marriageable; and the powerful, romantic, strangely compelling vision of the American West which invests L'Amour's Western fiction and makes it such a delightful escape from the cares of a later time—in this author's words from this story, that "big country needing big men and women to live in it" and where there was no place for "the frightened or the mean."

WAR PARTY
1959

WE BURIED PA ON A SIDEHILL OUT WEST OF CAMP, buried him high up so his ghost could look down the trail he'd planned to travel.

We piled the grave high with rocks because of the coyotes, and we dug the grave deep, and some of it I dug myself, and Mr. Sampson helped, and some others.

Folks in the wagon train figured Ma would turn back, but they hadn't known Ma so long as I had. Once she set her mind to something she wasn't about to quit.

She was a young woman and pretty, but there was

strength in her. She was a lone woman with two children, but she was of no mind to turn back. She'd come through the Little Crow massacre in Minnesota and she knew what trouble was. Yet it was like her that she put it up to me.

"Bud," she said, when we were alone, "we can turn back, but we've nobody there who cares about us, and it's of you and Jeanie that I'm thinking. If we go west you will have to be the man of the house, and you'll have to work hard to make up for Pa."

"We'll go west," I said. A boy those days took it for granted that he had work to do, and the men couldn't do it all. No boy ever thought of himself as only twelve or thirteen or whatever he was, being anxious to prove himself and take a man's place and responsibilities.

Ryerson and his wife were going back. She was a complaining woman and he was a man who was always ailing when there was work to be done. Four or five wagons were turning back, folks with their tails betwixt their legs running for the shelter of towns where their own littleness wouldn't stand out so plain.

When a body crossed the Mississippi and left the settlements behind, something happened to him. The world seemed to bust wide open, and suddenly the horizons spread out and a man wasn't cramped any more. The pinched-up villages and the narrowness of towns, all that was gone. The horizons simply exploded and rolled back into the enormous distance, with nothing around but prairie and sky.

Some folks couldn't stand it. They'd cringe into themselves and start hunting excuses to go back where they came from. This was a big country needing big men and women to live in it, and there was no place out here for the frightened or the mean.

The prairie and sky had a way of trimming folks down to size, or changing them to giants to whom nothing seemed impossible. Men who had cut a wide swath back in the States found themselves nothing out here. They were folks who were used to doing a lot of talking who suddenly found that no one was listening any more, and things that seemed mighty important back home, like family and money, they amounted to nothing alongside character and courage.

There was John Sampson from our town. He was a man used to being told to do things, used to looking up to wealth and power, but when he crossed the Mississippi he began to lift his head and look around. He squared his shoulders, put more crack to his whip and began to make his own tracks in the land.

Pa was always strong, an independent man given to reading at night from one of the four or five books we had, to speaking up on matters of principle and to straight shooting with a rifle. Pa had fought the Comanche and lived with the Sioux, but he wasn't strong enough to last more than two days with a Kiowa arrow through his lung. But he died knowing Ma had stood by the rear wheel and shot the Kiowa whose arrow was in him.

Right then I knew that neither Indians nor country was going to get the better of Ma. Shooting that Kiowa was the first time Ma had shot anything but some chicken-killing varmint—which she'd done time to time when Pa was away from home.

Only Ma wouldn't let Jeanie and me call it home. "We came here from Illinois," she said, "but we're going home now."

"But Ma," I protested, "I thought home was where we came from?"

"Home is where we're going now," Ma said, "and we'll know it when we find it. Now that Pa is gone we'll have to build that home ourselves."

She had a way of saying "home" so it sounded like a rare and wonderful place and kept Jeanie and me looking always at the horizon, just knowing it was over there, waiting for us to see it. She had given us the dream, and even Jeanie, who was only six, she had it too.

She might tell us that home was where we were going, but I knew home was where Ma was, a warm and friendly place with biscuits on the table and fresh-made butter. We wouldn't have a real home until Ma was there and we had a fire going. Only I'd build the fire.

Mr. Buchanan, who was captain of the wagon train, came to us with Tryon Burt, who was guide. "We'll help you," Mr. Buchanan said. "I know you'll be wanting to go back, and . . . ."

"But we are not going back." Ma smiled at them. "And don't be afraid we'll be a burden. I know you have troubles of your own, and we will manage very well."

Mr. Buchanan looked uncomfortable, like he was trying to think of the right thing to say. "Now, see here," he protested, "we started this trip with a rule. There has to be a man with every wagon."

Ma put her hand on my shoulder. "I have my man. Bud is almost thirteen and accepts responsibility. I could ask for no better man."

Ryerson came up. He was thin, stooped in the shoulder, and whenever he looked at Ma there was a greasy look to his eyes that I didn't like. He was a man who looked dirty even when he'd just washed in the creek. "You come along with me, ma'am," he said. "I'll take good care of you."

"Mr. Ryerson"—Ma looked him right in the eye—"you have a wife who can use better care than she's getting, and I have my son."

"He's nothin' but a boy."

"You are turning back, are you not? My son is going on. I believe that should indicate who is more the man. It is neither size nor age that makes a man, Mr. Ryerson, but something he has inside. My son has it."

Ryerson might have said something unpleasant only Tryon Burt was standing there wishing he would, so he just looked ugly and hustled off.

"I'd like to say you could come," Mr. Buchanan said, "but the boy couldn't stand up to a man's work."

Ma smiled at him, chin up, the way she had. "I do not believe in gambling, Mr. Buchanan, but I'll wager a good Ballard rifle there isn't a man in camp who could follow a child all day, running when it runs, squatting when it squats, bending when it bends and wrestling when it wrestles and not be played out long before the child is."

"You may be right, ma'am, but a rule is a rule."

"We are in Indian country, Mr. Buchanan. If you are killed a week from now, I suppose your wife must return to the States?"

"That's different! Nobody could turn back from there!"

"Then," Ma said sweetly, "it seems a rule is only a rule within certain limits, and if I recall correctly no such limit was designated in the articles of travel. Whatever limits there were, Mr. Buchanan, must have been passed sometime before the Indian attack that killed my husband."

"I can drive the wagon, and so can Ma," I said. "For

the past two days I've been driving, and nobody said anything until Pa died."

Mr. Buchanan didn't know what to say, but a body could see he didn't like it. Nor did he like a woman who talked up to him the way Ma did.

Tryon Burt spoke up. "Let the boy drive. I've watched this youngster, and he'll do. He has better judgment than most men in the outfit, and he stands up to his work. If need be, I'll help."

Mr. Buchanan turned around and walked off with his back stiff the way it is when he's mad. Ma looked at Burt, and she said, "Thank you, Mr. Burt. That was nice of you."

Try Burt, he got all red around the gills and took off like somebody had put a bur under his saddle.

Come morning our wagon was the second one ready to take its place in line, with both horses saddled and tied behind the wagon, and me standing beside the off ox.

Any direction a man wanted to look there was nothing but grass and sky, only sometimes there'd be a buffalo wallow or a gopher hole. We made eleven miles the first day after Pa was buried, sixteen the next, then nineteen, thirteen, and twenty-one. At no time did the country change. On the sixth day after Pa died I killed a buffalo.

It was a young bull, but a big one, and I spotted him coming up out of a draw and was off my horse and bellied down in the grass before Try Burt realized there was game in sight. That bull came up from the draw and stopped there, staring at the wagon train, which was a half-mile off. Setting a sight behind his left shoulder I took a long breath, took in the trigger slack, then squeezed off my shot so gentle-like the gun jumped in my hands before I was ready for it.

The bull took a step back like something had surprised him, and I jacked another shell into the chamber and was sighting on him again when he went down on his knees and rolled over on his side.

"You got him, Bud!" Burt was more excited than me. "That was shootin'!"

Try got down and showed me how to skin the bull, and lent me a hand. Then we cut out a lot of fresh meat and toted it back to the wagons.

Ma was at the fire when we came up, a wisp of brown hair alongside her cheek and her face flushed from the heat of the fire, looking as pretty as a bay pony.

"Bud killed his first buffalo," Burt told her, looking at Ma like he could eat her with a spoon.

"Why, Bud! That's wonderful!" Her eyes started to dance with a kind of mischief in them, and she said, "Bud, why don't you take a piece of that meat along to Mr. Buchanan and the others?"

With Burt to help, we cut the meat into eighteen pieces and distributed it around the wagons. It wasn't much, but it was the first fresh meat in a couple of weeks.

John Sampson squeezed my shoulder and said, "Seems to me you and your Ma are folks to travel with. This outfit needs some hunters."

Each night I staked out that buffalo hide, and each day I worked at curing it before rolling it up to pack on the wagon. Believe you me, I was some proud of that buffalo hide. Biggest thing I'd shot until then was a cottontail rabbit back in Illinois, where we lived when I was born. Try Burt told folks about that shot. "Two hundred yards," he'd say, "right through the heart."

Only it wasn't more than a hundred and fifty yards

the way I figured, and Pa used to make me pace off distances, so I'd learn to judge right. But I was nobody to argue with Try Burt telling a story—besides, two hundred yards makes an awful lot better sound than one hundred and fifty.

After supper the menfolks would gather to talk plans. The season was late, and we weren't making the time we ought if we hoped to beat the snow through the passes of the Sierras. When they talked I was there because I was the man of my wagon, but nobody paid me no mind. Mr. Buchanan, he acted like he didn't see me, but John Sampson would and Try Burt always smiled at me.

Several spoke up for turning back, but Mr. Buchanan said he knew of an outfit that made it through later than this. One thing was sure. Our wagon wasn't turning back. Like Ma said, home was somewhere ahead of us, and back in the States we'd have no money and nobody to turn to, nor any relatives, anywhere. It was the three of us.

"We're going on," I said at one of these talks. "We don't figure to turn back for anything."

Webb gave me a glance full of contempt. "You'll go where the rest of us go. You an' your Ma would play hob gettin' by on your own."

Next day it rained, dawn to dark it fairly poured, and we were lucky to make six miles. Day after that, with the wagon wheels sinking into the prairie and the rain still falling, we camped just two miles from where we started in the morning.

Nobody talked much around the fires, and what was said was apt to be short and irritable. Most of these folks had put all they owned into the outfits they had, and if they turned back now they'd have nothing to live on and nothing left to make a fresh start. Except a few like Mr. Buchanan, who was well off.

"It doesn't have to be California," Ma said once. "What most of us want is land, not gold."

"This here is Indian country," John Sampson said, "and a sight too open for me. I'd like a valley in the hills, with running water close by."

"There will be valleys and meadows," Ma replied, stirring the stew she was making, "and tall trees near running streams, and tall grass growing in the meadows, and there will be game in the forest and on the grassy plains, and places for homes."

"And where will we find all that?" Webb's tone was slighting.

"West," Ma said, "over against the mountains."

"I suppose you've been there?" Webb scoffed.

"No, Mr. Webb, I haven't been there, but I've been told of it. The land is there, and we will have some of it, my children and I, and we will stay through the winter, and in the spring we will plant our crops."

"Easy to say."

"This is Sioux country to the north," Burt said. "We'll be lucky to get through without a fight. There was a war party of thirty or thirty-five passed this way a couple of days ago."

"Sioux?"

"Uh-huh . . . no women or children along, and I found some war paint rubbed off on the brush."

"Maybe," Mr. Buchanan suggested, "we'd better turn south a mite."

"It is late in the season," Ma replied, "and the straightest way is the best way now."

"No use to worry," White interrupted; "those Indians went on by. They won't likely know we're around."

"They were riding southeast," Ma said, "and their home is in the north, so when they return they'll be riding northwest. There is no way they can miss our trail."

"Then we'd best turn back," White said.

"Don't look like we'd make it this year, anyway," a woman said; "the season is late."

That started the argument, and some were for turning back and some wanted to push on, and finally White said we should push on, but travel fast.

"Fast?" Webb asked disparagingly. "An Indian can ride in one day the distance we'd travel in four."

That started the wrangling again and Ma continued with her cooking. Sitting there watching her I figured I never did see anybody so graceful or quick on her feet as Ma, and when we used to walk in the woods back home I never knew her to stumble or step on a fallen twig or branch.

The group broke up and returned to their own fires with nothing settled, only there at the end Mr. Buchanan looked to Burt. "Do you know the Sioux?"

"Only the Utes and Shoshonis, and I spent a winter on the Snake with the Nez Perces one time. But I've had no truck with the Sioux. Only they tell me they're bad medicine. Fightin' men from way back and they don't cotton to white folks in their country. If we run into Sioux, we're in trouble."

After Mr. Buchanan had gone Tryon Burt accepted a plate and cup from Ma and settled down to eating. After a while he looked up at her and said, "Beggin' your pardon, ma'am, but it struck me you knew a sight about trackin' for an Eastern woman. You'd spotted those Sioux your own self, an' you figured it right that they'd pick up our trail on the way back."

She smiled at him. "It was simply an observation, Mr. Burt. I would believe anyone would notice it. I simply put it into words."

Burt went on eating, but he was mighty thoughtful, and it didn't seem to me he was satisfied with Ma's answer. Ma said finally, "It seems to be raining west of here. Isn't it likely to be snowing in the mountains?"

Burt looked up uneasily. "Not necessarily so, ma'am. It could be raining here and not snowing there, but I'd say there was a chance of snow." He got up and came around the fire to the coffeepot. "What are you gettin' at, ma'am?"

"Some of them are ready to turn back or change their plans. What will you do then?"

He frowned, placing his cup on the grass and starting to fill his pipe. "No idea . . . might head south for Santa Fe. Why do you ask?"

"Because we're going on," Ma said. "We're going to the mountains, and I am hoping some of the others decide to come with us."

"You'd go alone?" He was amazed.

"If necessary."

We started on at daybreak, but folks were more scary than before, and they kept looking at the great distances stretching away on either side, and muttering. There was an autumn coolness in the air, and we were still short of South Pass by several days with the memory of the Donner party being talked up around us.

There was another kind of talk in the wagons, and some of it I heard. The nightly gatherings around Ma's fire had started talk, and some of it pointed to Tryon Burt, and some were saying other things.

We made seventeen miles that day, and at night Mr. Buchanan didn't come to our fire; and when White stopped by, his wife came and got him. Ma looked at her and smiled, and Mrs. White sniffed and went away beside her husband.

"Mr. Burt"—Ma wasn't one to beat around a bush—"is there talk about me?"

Try Burt got red around the ears and he opened his mouth, but couldn't find the words he wanted. "Maybe . . . well, maybe I shouldn't eat here all the time. Only . . . well, ma'am, you're the best cook in camp."

Ma smiled at him. "I hope that isn't the only reason you come to see us, Mr. Burt."

He got redder than ever then and gulped his coffee and took off in a hurry.

Time to time the men had stopped by to help a little, but next morning nobody came by. We got lined out about as soon as ever, and Ma said to me as we sat on the wagon seat, "Pay no attention, Bud. You've no call to take up anything if you don't notice it. There will always be folks who will talk, and the better you do in the world the more bad things they will say of you. Back there in the settlement you remember how the dogs used to run out and bark at our wagons?"

"Yes, Ma."

"Did the wagons stop?"

"No, Ma."

"Remember that, son. The dogs bark, but the wagons go on their way, and if you're going some place you haven't time to bother with barking dogs."

We made eighteen miles that day, and the grass was better, but there was a rumble of distant thunder, whimpering and muttering off in the cañons, promising rain.

Webb stopped by, dropped an armful of wood beside the fire, then started off.

"Thank you, Mr. Webb," Ma said, "but aren't you afraid you'll be talked about?"

He looked angry and started to reply something angry, and then he grinned and said, "I reckon I'd be flattered, Mrs. Miles."

Ma said, "No matter what is decided by the rest of them, Mr. Webb, we are going on, but there is no need to go to California for what we want."

Webb took out his pipe and tamped it. He had a dark, devil's face on him with eyebrows like you see on pictures of the devil. I was afraid of Mr. Webb.

"We want land," Ma said, "and there is land around us. In the mountains ahead there will be streams and forests, there will be fish and game, logs for houses and meadows for grazing."

Mr. Buchanan had joined us. "That's fool talk," he declared. "What could anyone do in these hills? You'd be cut off from the world. Left out of it."

"A man wouldn't be so crowded as in California," John Sampson remarked. "I've seen so many go that I've been wondering what they all do there."

"For a woman," Webb replied, ignoring the others, "you've a head on you, ma'am."

"What about the Sioux?" Mr. Buchanan asked dryly.

"We'd not be encroaching on their land. They live to the north," Ma said. She gestured toward the mountains. "There is land to be had just a few days further on, and that is where our wagon will stop."

A few days! Everybody looked at everybody else. Not months, but days only. Those who stopped then would have enough of their supplies left to help them through the winter, and with what game they could kill—and time for cutting wood and even building cabins before the cold set in.

Oh, there was an argument, such argument as you've never heard, and the upshot of it was that all agreed it was fool talk and the thing to do was keep going. And there was talk I overheard about Ma being no better than she should be, and why was that guide always hanging around her? And all those men? No decent woman—I hurried away.

At break of day our wagons rolled down a long valley with a small stream alongside the trail, and the Indians came over the ridge to the south of us and started our way—tall, fine-looking men with feathers in their hair.

There was barely time for a circle, but I was riding off in front with Tryon Burt, and he said, "A man can always try to talk first, and Injuns like a palaver. You get back to the wagons."

Only I rode along beside him, my rifle over my saddle and ready to hand. My mouth was dry and my heart was beating so's I thought Try could hear it, I was that scared. But behind us the wagons were making their circle, and every second was important.

Their chief was a big man with splendid muscles, and there was a scalp not many days old hanging from his lance. It looked like Ryerson's hair, but Ryerson's wagons should have been miles away to the east by now.

Burt tried them in Shoshoni, but it was the language of their enemies and they merely stared at him, understanding well enough, but of no mind to talk. One young buck kept staring at Burt with a taunt in his eye, daring Burt to make a move; then suddenly the chief spoke, and they all turned their eyes toward the wagons.

There was a rider coming, and it was a woman. It was Ma.

She rode right up beside us, and when she drew up

she started to talk, and she was speaking their language. She was talking Sioux. We both knew what it was because those Indians sat up and paid attention. Suddenly she directed a question at the chief.

"Red Horse," he said, in English.

Ma shifted to English. "My husband was blood brother to Gall, the greatest warrior of the Sioux nation. It was my husband who found Gall dying in the brush with a bayonet wound in his chest, who took Gall to his home and treated the wound until it was well."

"Your husband was a medicine-man?" Red Horse asked.

"My husband was a warrior," Ma replied proudly, "but he made war only against strong men, not women or children or the wounded."

She put her hand on my shoulder. "This is my son. As my husband was blood brother to Gall, his son is by blood brotherhood the son of Gall, also."

Red Horse stared at Ma for a long time, and I was getting even more scared. I could feel a drop of sweat start at my collar and crawl slowly down my spine. Red Horse looked at me. "Is this one a fit son for Gall?"

"He is a fit son. He has killed his first buffalo."

Red Horse turned his mount and spoke to the others. One of the young braves shouted angrily at him, and Red Horse replied sharply. Reluctantly, the warriors trailed off after their chief.

"Ma'am," Burt said, "you just about saved our bacon. They were just spoilin' for a fight."

"We should be moving," Ma said.

Mr. Buchanan was waiting for us. "What happened out there? I tried to keep her back, but she's a difficult woman."

"She's worth any three men in the outfit," Burt

replied.

That day we made eighteen miles, and by the time the wagons circled there was talk. The fact that Ma had saved them was less important now than other things. It didn't seem right that a decent woman could talk Sioux or mix in the affairs of men.

Nobody came to our fire, but while picketing the saddle horses I heard someone say, "Must be part Injun. Else why would they pay attention to a woman?"

"Maybe she's part Injun and leadin' us into a trap."

"Hadn't been for her," Burt said, "you'd all be dead now."

"How do you know what she said to 'em? Who savvies that lingo?"

"I never did trust that woman," Mrs. White said; "too high and mighty. Nor that husband of hers, either, comes to that. Kept to himself too much."

The air was cool after a brief shower when we started in the morning, and no Indians in sight. All day long we moved over grass made fresh by new rain, and all the ridges were pineclad now, and the growth along the streams heavier. Short of sundown I killed an antelope with a running shot, dropped him mighty neat—and looked up to see an Indian watching from a hill. At the distance I couldn't tell, but it could have been Red Horse.

Time to time I'd passed along the train, but nobody waved or said anything. Webb watched me go by, his face stolid as one of the Sioux, yet I could see there was a deal of talk going on.

"Why are they mad at us?" I asked Burt.

"Folks hate something they don't understand, or anything seems different. Your ma goes her own way, speaks her mind, and of an evening she doesn't set by

195

and gossip."

He topped out on a rise and drew up to study the country, and me beside him. "You got to figure most of these folks come from small towns where they never knew much aside from their families, their gossip and their church. It doesn't seem right to them that a decent woman would find time to learn Sioux."

Burt studied the country. "Time was, any stranger was an enemy, and if anybody came around who wasn't one of yours, you killed him. I've seen wolves jump on a wolf that was white or different somehow . . . seems like folks and animals fear anything that's unusual."

We circled, and I staked out my horses and took the oxen to the herd. By the time Ma had her grub-box lid down, I was fixing at a fire when here come Mr. Buchanan, Mr. and Mrs. White and some other folks, including that Webb.

"Ma'am"—Mr. Buchanan was mighty abrupt—"we figure we ought to know what you said to those Sioux. We want to know why they turned off just because you went out there."

"Does it matter?"

Mr. Buchanan's face stiffened up. "We think it does. There's some think you might be an Indian your own self."

"And if I am?" Ma was amused. "Just what is it you have in mind, Mr. Buchanan?"

"We don't want no Injuns in this outfit!" Mr. White shouted.

"How does it come you can talk that language?" Mrs. White demanded. "Even Tryon Burt can't talk it."

"I figure maybe you want us to keep goin' because there's a trap up ahead!" White declared.

I never realized folks could be so mean, but there they

196

were facing Ma like they hated her, like those witch-hunters Ma told me about back in Salem. It didn't seem right that Ma, who they didn't like, had saved them from an Indian attack, and the fact that she talked Sioux like any Indian bothered them.

"As it happens," Ma said, "I am not an Indian, although I should not be ashamed of it if I were. They have many admirable qualities. However, you need worry yourselves no longer, as we part company in the morning. I have no desire to travel further with you . . . *gentlemen.*"

Mr. Buchanan's face got all angry, and he started up to say something mean. Nobody was about to speak rough to Ma with me standing by, so I just picked up that ol' rifle and jacked a shell into the chamber. "Mr. Buchanan, this here's my Ma, and she's a lady, so you just be careful what words you use."

"Put down that rifle, you young fool!" he shouted at me.

"Mr. Buchanan, I may be little and may be a fool, but this here rifle doesn't care who pulls its trigger."

He looked like he was going to have a stroke, but he just turned sharp around and walked away, all stiff in the back.

"Ma'am," Webb said, "you've no cause to like me much, but you've shown more brains than that passel o' fools. If you'll be so kind, me and my boy would like to trail along with you."

"I like a man who speaks his mind, Mr. Webb. I would consider it an honor to have your company."

Tryon Burt looked quizzically at Ma. "Why, now, seems to me this is a time for a man to make up his mind, and I'd like to be included along with Webb."

"Mr. Burt," Ma said, "for your own information, I

grew up among Sioux children in Minnesota. They were my playmates."

Come daylight our wagon pulled off to one side, pointing northwest at the mountains, and Mr. Buchanan led off to the west. Webb followed Ma's wagon, and I sat watching Mr. Buchanan's eyes get angrier as John Sampson, Neely Stuart, the two Shafter wagons and Tom Croft all fell in behind us.

Tryon Burt had been talking to Mr. Buchanan, but he left off and trotted his horse over to where I sat my horse. Mr. Buchanan looked mighty sullen when he saw half his wagon train gone and with it a lot of his importance as captain.

Two days and nearly forty miles further and we topped out on a rise and paused to let the oxen take a blow. A long valley lay across our route, with tall grass wet with rain, and a flat bench on the mountainside seen through a gray veil of a light shower falling. There was that bench, with the white trunks of aspen on the mountainside beyond it looking like ranks of slim soldiers guarding the bench against the storms.

"Ma," I said.

"All right, Bud," she said quietly, "we've come home."

And I started up the oxen and drove down into the valley where I was to become a man.

WILL HENRY

HENRY WILSON ALLEN (1912-1991) was born in Kansas City, Missouri. After attending Kansas City Junior College for two years, he drifted west, working at odd jobs until he ended up in Los Angeles. He worked for a newspaper for a time and then found employment in 1935 with a company manufacturing animated films. Two years later Allen was hired by M-G-M as a junior writer in their short subjects department. It was first in midlife that Allen decided to try his hand at the Western story. *No Survivors* (Random House, 1950) was his first Western novel. It was published under the byline Will Henry because Allen did not want anyone in the film industry to know he was writing novels (something he later dismissed as a wrong-headed notion). While numerous authors of Western fiction before Allen had provided sympathetic and intelligent portrayals of Indian characters, Allen from the start set out to characterize Indians in such as way as to make their viewpoints and perspectives an integral part of the story he had to tell.

Allen's second novel was *Red Blizzard* (Simon and Schuster, 1951). Harry E. Maule, who had become Western fiction editor at Random House in 1940, rejected it. When another publisher accepted it, Allen's agent, August Lenniger, had Allen adopt a different pseudonym, reserving Will Henry for novels published by Random House. The second byline was Clay Fisher. It is probable that what Maule detected in *Red Blizzard* was Allen's tendency to impose an often superfluous historical framework upon what remained in essence a traditional Western plot. However, in view of Maule's rejection of this second novel, Allen's reaction—only natural under the circumstances—was to believe that he was able to write two totally different kinds of Western stories without himself being certain as to just how and why one was distinct from the other. Every time Maule rejected a novel, it became a Clay Fisher. In the event, there is really no difference between a Will Henry and a Clay Fisher novel except as an indication of the whimsies of Harry E. Maule's personal taste. Allen's next Will Henry novel was *To Follow a Flag* (Random House, 1953) and this story is as much a straight action narrative as the next Clay Fisher title, *Santa Fe Passage* (Houghton Mifflin, 1952).

Frequently, Allen could be intimidated by historical sources. He might add merely a dramatized floss to an historical account, such as his reworking of James D. Horan's version of Jesse James in *Desperate Men* (Bonanza Books, 1949) in the Will Henry novel, *Death of a Legend* (Random House, 1954). In *Reckoning at Yankee Flat* (Random House, 1958) by Will Henry, Allen provided a fictional account of the Henry Plummer gang. Since Professor Thomas J. Dimsdale wrote *The Vigilantes of Montana* (1866), this story has intrigued novelists. Allen may have been more meticulous than many of his precursors in depicting the actual historical events, but he could not succeed in bringing Plummer himself to life, relying instead on quotations from people who had known or seen the man. Yet, curiously, in the much later *Summer of the Gun* (Lippincott, 1978), with no historical context to intimidate him, Allen was able to create a truly vivid character in the gang leader, Fragg, whose fictional personality is much closer to that of the historical Henry

Plummer than the ambiguous shadow in **Reckoning at Yankee Flat**. Of all his attempts at straight fictional biography, perhaps only *I, Tom Horn* (Lippincott, 1975) can be judged a complete success. Indeed, it is more than that. It is a masterpiece, perhaps most fully realized not in the motion picture based upon it with Steve McQueen in the title role but in the full-length audio version from Recorded Books, Inc., as read by Frank Muller.

In general many of Allen's best novels deal with the failure of the frontier experience, the greed, the rape of the land, the apparent genocide, novels which end tragically because, in the history of the American West and given the premises built into these plots, such an outcome is inevitable. In this group belong two of the novels for which Allen won Golden Spur Awards: *From Where the Sun Now Stands* (Random House, 1960) and *Chiricahua* (Lippincott, 1972). Also worthy of inclusion are *The Last Warpath* (Random House, 1966), an inter-connected series of tales about the Cheyenne Indians (illustrating how Allen was basically a short story writer whose novels are often a patch-work of novelette-length sequences fused together but able easily to stand alone), and *Maheo's Children* (Chilton, 1968), a story of Preacher Nehemiah Bleek and his Indian orphans set against the background of the Sand Creek massacre. *The Gates of the Mountains* (Random House, 1963) is a highly romantic retelling of the Lewis and Clark expedition and is clearly not in quite the same class as these others, despite its having also won a Spur. The shortcomings in this last title, however, apply to an extent even to Allen's best novels where the use of historical sources tends usually to be somewhat improvisational. *Maheo's Children*, in fact, was first intended as a straight historical narrative to be published under the byline Henry W. Allen and Allen submitted it to Don Ward, at the time an editor at Hastings House, a publisher of Western history books. Ward sent a section of the manuscript to Mari Sandoz (who herself published several not altogether reliable historical accounts with this same publisher) and her reactions were contained in a letter dated July 26, 1964 to Don Ward, reprinted in *Letters of Mari Sandoz* (University of Nebraska Press, 1992) edited by Helen Winter Stauffer. "The foreword or introductory bit tells one right off that the author knows nothing of the Cheyenne religion," Sandoz commented. " . . . All Allen offers here is the usual uninformed white man idea of sun, rain, and earth gods. Living up on the Tongue [River] even a few days should have taught him better about the Cheyennes. If not, Allen can read, can't he?" The books Sandoz cited, however, are by George Bird Grinnell with their openly favorable view of the Cheyennes and biased portrait of the Pawnees. Obviously, Allen once more felt intimidated by historical sources and, therefore, turned this attempt at straight history into a fictional account intended now for a young adult audience. But he did get two books out of it, *Maheo's Children* and *The Day Fort Larking Fell* (Chilton, 1968).

The appeal of Allen's historical Western fiction to some critics has been his political and social perspectives. Betty Rosenberg in her Introduction to the Gregg Press' library reprint edition of *From Where the Sun Now Stands* in 1978 wrote: "The information . . . for realistic and honest novelization of the Indian wars was available. Lacking was a novel-reading audience willing to accept tragedy in place of romance. Such an acceptance would force the reader to recognize that Indian cultures and ways of life are sophisticated realities and their destruction wanton evil; that the invaders' Manifest Destiny was a blatant hypocrisy, an excuse to cover the theft of land and commercial exploitation; that missionary activities were a tool of subjugation; that the imposition of an Anglo culture upon the Indians was an unwelcome curse." The subject of this novel is the war against the Nez Perce Indians in 1877 and their subsequent defeat. These Indians did have a long tradition of peace and friendliness with the whites and in their terrible passage from Idaho through Montana to reach Canada, in which attempt they failed, they did not harm a single white woman or child because, in the words of the Nez Perce first-person narrator of the novel, "we had lived too long as brothers of the white man. Even in our last hours, we could not kill and mutilate his loved ones." As the 1960s progressed, such a sympathetic posture would become politically correct in viewing *all* of the Indian nations and tribes which, in its way, overlooked what made the Nez Perce stand out as victims and made this episode in their relations with Anglo-American culture such a poignant tragedy. For all of that, in Will Henry's *MacKenna's Gold* (Random House, 1963), Allen characterized the frontier buffalo soldiers as having "the hot blood of their savage African ancestors running wild in them"—an image right out of James Warner Bellah's *Sergeant Rutledge* (Bantam, 1960).

Possibly David Remley in his essay, "Sacajawea of Myth and History" in *Women and Western American Literature* (Whitson Publishing, 1982) edited by Helen Winter Stauffer and Susan J. Rosowski, in his critique of *The Gates of the Mountains* came closest to a balanced view of Allen's historical fiction. He found this book "full of the opposites of moral vision built into the Judeo-Christian heritage—the beautiful, the ugly, the saved, the damned; the free, the slave, the good, the bad. Will Henry's is a split vision which tells us much about ourselves but probably has little, if anything, to do with who the American Indian—and Sacajawea—really is, or was. Probably too the love La Charrette thinks Sacajawea feels for him and Clark 'or any white man'— not passion for one but brotherly love for all—is, in part, Will Henry's own need for reconciliation projected upon her. It is a need for forgiveness—for release from old guilt—sensitive whites seem driven to ask of the American Indian and of the whole vast brooding continent itself." Doubtless, such a critique can be seen to apply no less to subsequent, and even more neurotic and subjectively agogic, attempts at dealing with the American Indian by writers in the post-Will Henry tradition such as Richard S. Wheeler and Win Blevins.

After *Summer of the Gun*, Allen found it impossible to write another novel, although he was urged to do so by editors. After 1980 his memory began increasingly to fail so that by 1990 he would confess that he could no longer keep together the threads of any story. He stopped typing and his last letters were hand-written. In the years of our friendship, we must have exchanged 200,000 words with each other. I shall always miss his spiritual companionship. He was a good friend.

"I am but a solitary horseman of the plains, born a century too late and far away," Allen once wrote about himself. He felt out of joint with his time and what alone may ultimately unify his work is the vividness of his imagination, the tremendous emotion with which he invested his characters and fashioned his Western stories. At his best, he could weave an almost incomparable spell that can involve a reader deeply in his narratives, informed always by his profound empathy with so many of the casualties of the historical process. The story which follows first appeared in the Will Henry collection, **Sons of the Western Frontier** (Chilton, 1966).

THE TALLEST INDIAN IN TOLTEPEC
1966

WHERE THE WAGON ROAD FROM THE SMALL TOWN OF Toltepec, in the state of Chihuahua, came up to the Rio Grande, the fording place was known as the old Apache Crossing. This was because the Indians used it in their shadowy traffic in and out of Texas from Old Mexico. It was not a place of good name, and only those traveled it who, for reasons of their own, did not care to go over the river at the new Upper Crossing.

This fact of border life was well understood by Colonel Fulgencio Ortega. He had not forgotten the Indian back door to E1 Paso on the American side. That is why he had taken personal charge of the guard post of his troops at this point.

A very crafty man, Colonel Ortega.

And efficient.

It was not for nothing that the *descamisados*, the starving shirtless poor, called him the Executioner of Camargo. Chihuahua had no more distinguished son, nor another son half so well known in the ranks of the irregular *rurales*, which was to say the stinking buzzards of the border.

Now, with his men, a score of brutes so removed from decency and discipline that only their upright postures stamped them as human beings, he lounged about the ashes of the supper fire. Some of the bestial soldiers bickered over the cleaning of the mess kits. Others sat hunched about a serape spread on the ground, belching and complaining of the foulness of their luck with the cards and with the kernels of shelled corn which passed for money among them. The heat of the evening was stifling. Even with the sun now down at last beyond the Rio, it was still difficult to breathe with comfort. The horseflies from the nearby picket line still buzzed and bit like rabid foxes. It was a most unpromising situation. In all of the long daylight they had wasted at the ford, no fish had come to their net, no traveler from Toltepec had sought to pass the crude barricade flung across the wagon road.

"¡*Válgame*!" announced Ortega. "God's name, but this is slow work, eh, Chivo?"

The name meant "goat" in Spanish, and the bearded lieutenant who responded to it seemed well described.

"True, *jefe*." He nodded. "But one learns patience in your service. Also hunger. Hiding. Sand fleas. Body lice. How to use corn for money. How to live on water with no tequila in it. Many things, Excellence."

Ortega smiled and struck him across the face with the butt of his riding quirt. The blow opened the man's face and brought the bright blood spurting.

"Also manners," said the Colonel quietly.

Chivo spat into the dirt. "*Sí*," he said, "also manners."

Presently, the man on duty at the barricade called to his leader that someone was coming on the road.

"By what manner?" asked Ortega, not moving to rise.

"A burro cart."

"How many do you see?"

"Two. A man and a boy. Hauling firewood, I think."

"¡*Pah*! Let them go by."

"We do not search the cart, *jefe*?"

"For what? Firewood?"

"No, *jefe*, for *him*; these are Indians who come."

Instantly, Ortega was on his feet. He was at the barricade next moment, Chivo and the others crowding behind. All watched in silence the approach of the small burro cart. Had they begun to pant or growl it would have seemed natural, so like a half circle of wolves they appeared.

On the driver's seat of the cart, Díaz grew pale and spoke guardedly to his small son.

"Chamaco," he said, "these are evil men who await us. Something bad may happen. Slip away in the brush if there is any opportunity. These are the enemies of our leader."

"You know them, Papa, these enemies of our *Presidente*?"

"I know the one with the whip. It is Ortega."

"The Executioner?" The boy whispered the dread name, and Juliano Díaz, slowing the plodding team of burros, answered without moving his head or taking his eyes from the soldiers at the barricade.

"Yes, my son. It is him, the Killer of Camargo. As you value your life, do not speak the name of *El Indio* except to curse it. These men seek his life."

El Indio was the name of love which the shirtless ones had given the revolutionary President whom they had brought to power with their blood, but who now fought desperately for the life of his new government

207

and for the freedoms which he sought to bring to the *descamisados* of all Mexico, be they Indians, such as himself and Juliano and Chamaco Díaz, or of the Spanish blood, or of any blood whatever. To the small boy, Chamaco, *El Indio* was like Christ, only more real. He had never seen either one, but he knew he would die for his *Presidente* and was not so sure about the Savior.

He nodded, now, in response to his father's warning, brave as any ten-year-old boy might be in facing the Executioner of Camargo.

As for Ortega, perhaps the sinister appellation was only a product of ignorance and rebelliousness on the parts of the incredibly poor Indians of the Motherland. He understood this for himself, it was certain. But being a soldier was hard work, and the people never comprehended the necessity for the precautions of military control. This did not mean that one of the Spanish blood could not be gracious and kind within the limitations of his stern duty. The Colonel waved his whip pleasantly enough toward the burro cart.

"Good evening, citizen," he greeted Díaz. "You are surprised to see us here, no doubt. But the delay will be slight. Please to get down from the cart."

"*¿Qué pasa*, Excellence? What is the matter?" In his fear, Díaz did not obey the request to step down but sat numbly on the seat.

"Ah, you know me!" Ortega was pleased. "Well, it has been my work to get acquainted among the people of *El Indio*. Did you hear my order?"

"What?" said Díaz. "I forget. What did you say, Colonel?"

Ortega moved as a coiled snake might move. He struck out with his whip, its thong wrapping the thin neck of Juliano Díaz. With a violent heave, the guerrilla leader threw the small man from the cart onto the ground, the noose of the whip nearly cracking his vertebrae.

"I said to get down, *Indio*," he smiled. "You do not listen too well. What is the matter? Do you not trust your Mexican brothers?"

Díaz was small in body only. In heart he was a mountain.

"You are no brothers of mine!" he cried. "I am an Indian!"

"Precisely," answered Ortega, helping him up from the dirt of the roadway. "And so is he whom we seek."

Díaz stood proudly, stepping back and away from the kind hands of Colonel Fulgencio Ortega. He made no reply, now, but the boy on the seat of the burro cart leaped down and answered for him.

"What!" he exclaimed, unable to accept the fact anyone would truly seek to do ill to the beloved *Presidente*. "Is it true then that you would harm our dear . . . ?" Too late, he remembered his father's warning and cut off his words. Ortega liked boys, however, and made allowances for their innocence.

"Calm yourself, little rooster," he said kindly. "I said nothing of harming *El Indio*. Indeed, I said nothing of your great *Presidente* in any way. Now how is it you would have the idea that it is him we look for, eh?"

All of Mexico knew the answer to the question. For weeks the outlands had thrilled to the whisper that *El Indio* would make a journey to the United States to find gold and the hand of friendship from the other great *Presidente*, Abraham Lincoln. It was understood such a journey would be in secret to avoid the forces of the enemy en route. But from Oaxaca to the Texas border the *descamisados* were alerted to be on the watch for

209

"the Little Indian" and to stand at all times ready to help forward the fortunes of his journey.

Chamaco Díaz hesitated, not knowing what to say.

His father, brave Juliano, broke into the growing stillness to advise him in this direction.

"Say nothing, my son," he said quietly, and stood a little taller as he said it.

Chamaco nodded. He, too, straightened and stood tall beside his father.

They would talk no more, and Ortega understood this.

"My children," he said, "you have failed to comprehend. We do not seek to harm the *Presidente*, only to detain him."

If standing tall, Chamaco was still but a small boy. He had not learned the art of dishonesty.

"Why do you stop us, then, Colonel?" he demanded. "We are only poor wood gatherers from Toltepec, going to EL Paso."

"Just exactly my problem," explained Ortega, with a flourish of the whip. "You see, *pobrecito*, it is my order that every Indian going across the border must be measured against that line which you will see drawn on the dead oak tree." He pointed to the sunblasted spar with the whip. "Do you see the line on the tree?"

"Yes, Colonel."

"Well, it is drawn five feet from the ground, *chico*. That is just about the tallness of your great *Presidente*, not being too precise. Now the problem is that I, myself, am not familiar with this great man. I would not know him if I saw him. But we have his height reported to us, and I have devised this method of . . . shall we say? . . . ruling out the chance that *El Indio* shall get over the river into the United States and complete his journey."

"Colonel," broke in Juliano Díaz, going pale despite

his great courage, "what is it you are saying?"

Ortega shrugged good-naturedly.

"Only that if you are an Indian not known to me, or to my men, and if your height is the same as that of *El Indio*, and if I detain you, then I have prevented a possible escape of your great *Presidente*, eh?"

"You mean that you think I, Juliano Díaz of Toltepec, am . . . ?" He could not finish the thought, so absurd was it to his simple mind. Could this rebel colonel truly believe such a thing? That he, Díaz, was the leader, the great *El Indio*? Díaz gave his first hint of a relieved look. It may even have been the trace of a smile. There was, after all, and even with the sore neck from the whip, something ironic about the idea. "Please, Excellence," Díaz concluded, forcing the small smile to widen for the sake of Chamaco's courage, "take me to the tree and put me against the mark, that my son and I may go on to EL Paso. I have not been well, and we need the *pesos* from this wood to buy medicine in Texas."

"Chivo," snapped Ortega, no longer smiling, "measure this Indian!"

Chivo seized Díaz and dragged him to the tree. Pushing him against its scarred trunk, he peered at the line.

"He comes exactly to it, *jefe*. Just the right size."

"Very well. Detain him."

The matter was finished for Colonel Ortega. He turned back to the fire. He did not look around at the pistol shot which blew out the brains of Juliano Díaz. To a scrofulous sergeant, even with the startled, sobbing cry of Chamaco Díaz rising behind him, he merely nodded irritably. "Coffee, Portales. Santa Maria, but it is hot! Curse this river country."

What would have been the fate of Chamaco, the son, no man may say. Chivo was hauling him to the fire by the nape of his neck, pistol poised to finish him as well, with the Colonel's permission. Also, no man may say if Ortega would have granted the favor. For in the instant of death's hovering, a thunder of hoofs arose on the American side of the river and a rider, tall sombrero proclaiming his Mexican identity, dashed his lathered mount across the ford and to a sliding stop by the fire of the Executioner of Camargo.

"Colonel!" he cried. "I come from El Paso! Great news is there. *El Indio* is in the town. He has already been to see the American *Presidente* and is on his way back to Mexico!"

Ortega stepped back as though cut in the face with his own whip. The wolf pack of his men drew in upon him. Chivo, in his astonishment that *El Indio* had gotten out of Mexico and was ready to come back into it, dropped his rough hands from Chamaco Díaz. It was all the signal from above that the quick-witted Indian youth needed. In one scuttling dive he had reached the crowding growth of river brush and disappeared, faithful, belatedly, to his dead father's instruction.

Chivo, pistol still smoking, led the yelping rush of the guerrilla band after the boy. Ortega cursed on his men, raging about himself with the lashing whip.

"Kill him, you fools!" he screamed. "He must not get over the river. Shoot! Shoot! Stomp him out and shoot him. He must not warn the Americans that we know they have *El Indio*! After him, after him, you idiots!"

Deep in the brush, Chamaco wriggled and squirmed and raced for his life. The rifle bullets of the renegades cut the limbs about him. The cruel thorns of the mesquite and catclaw and black chaparral ripped his flesh. He could hear the soldiers panting and cursing within a stone's toss of his heels. He cried for his dead father as he ran, but he ran! If God would help him, he would reach the other side of the river and *El Indio*.

As the desperate vow formed in his mind, he saw ahead a clearing in the tangled growth. Beyond it, the waters of the Rio Grande flowed silver-red in the sunset dusk.

Riding through the twilight toward El Paso, the thoughts of Charlie Shonto were scarcely designed to change the sunburned leather mold of his features—not, at least, for the happier.

A job was a job, he supposed, but it seemed to him that all the while the work got harder and the pay less.

Who the hell was he, Charlie Shonto? And what the devil was the Texas Express Company? And why should the two names cause him pain, now, as he clucked to his weary buckskin and said softly, aloud, "Slope along, little horse, there's good grass and water awaiting."

Well, there was an affinity betwixt the likes of Charlie Shonto and the Texas Express Company, even if it hurt. The latter outfit was a jerkwater stage line that had gotten itself about as rump-sprung as a general freight and passenger operation might manage to do and still harness four sound horses, and Shonto was a "special agent" for the stage company. But Charlie Shonto did not let the fancy title fool him. There was a shorter term, and a deal more accurate, for the kind of work he did for Texas Express. If a man said it with the proper curl of lip, it came out something awfully close to "hired gun."

Shonto didn't care for the label. He didn't especially

relish, either, the risks involved in wearing it. But a "riding gun," be he on the driver's box with an L.C. Smith or Parker on his lap, or in the saddle with a Winchester booted under his knee, made good money for the better jobs. The better jobs, of course, were those in which the survival odds were backed down to something like, or less than, even money. So it was no surprise to Shonto to be sent for by Texas Express for a "special assignment." The surprise might lie in the assignment, itself, but the sun-tanned rider doubted it. It could be assumed that when Texas Express sent for Charlie Shonto, the "opportunity for advancement" was one already turned down by the Rangers and the U.S. Army, not to mention Wells Fargo, Overland Mail, or any of the big staging outfits.

Shonto clucked again to the *bayo coyote*, the line-backed buckskin dun, that he rode.

"Just around the bend, Butterball." He grinned dustily. "Billets for you and bullets for me."

Butterball, a gaunt panther of a horse which appeared wicked and rank enough to eat rocks without spitting out the seeds, rolled an evil eye back at his master and flagged the ragged pennant of his left ear. If he had intended further comment than this one look of tough disgust, the urge was short-circuited.

Scarcely had the comment about "bullets" left Shonto's lips than a respectable, if well-spent, hail of them began to fall around him in the thicket. Next instant, the sounds of the rifle shots were following the leaden advance guard in scattered volleys.

Instinctively, he ticked Butterball with the spurs, and the bony gelding sprinted like a quarter-mile racer for the near bend ahead. When he brought Shonto around that bend, the latter hauled him up sharply. Across the

Rio Grande a tattered company of Mexican irregulars were target-practicing at a dark, bobbing object in midstream. Shonto's immediate reaction was one of relief that the riflemen had not been firing at him. The next thought was a natural curiosity as to what they had been firing at. It was then the third message reached his tired mind, and his mouth went hard. That was a little kid swimming for the American side out there.

The night was well down. In the Texas Express office in El Paso, three men waited. The drawn shade, trimmed lamp, the tense glances at the wall clock ticking beyond the way-bill desk, all spoke louder than the silence.

"I wish Shonto would get here," complained the express agent, Deems. "It ain't like him to be late. Maybe Ortega crossed over the river under dark and blind-sided him."

The second man, heavy-set, dressed in eastern clothing, calm and a little cold, shook his head.

"Shonto isn't the type to be blind-sided, Deems. You forget he's worked for me before. I didn't exactly pull his name out of a hat."

Deems stiffened. "That don't mean Ortega didn't pull it out of a sombrero!"

Sheriff Nocero Casey, last of the trio, nodded.

"Deems is right, Mr. Halloran. I don't care for Charlie being late either. It ain't like him. If Ortega did hear we had sent for Charlie Shonto . . . ." He broke off, scowling.

Halloran took him up quickly. "It's not Shonto being late that is really bothering you, is it? I counted on you, Sheriff. I didn't dare import a bunch of U.S. marshals. I hope you're not getting cold feet."

"No, sir. It's common sense I'm suffering from. This

job is way out of my bailiwick. The government ought to send troops or something to see it through. It's too big."

Again Halloran shook his head. "The U.S. government can't set one toe across that river, Sheriff. You know that. It's the law. That's why we've brought in your 'special agent.' Mr. Shonto is a man who understands the law. He appreciates its niceties, its challenges."

"Yeah, I've often wondered about that," said the Sheriff. "But I won't argue it."

"Ah, good. You see, there is no law which says Texas Express cannot ship a consignment such as our invaluable Item Thirteen into Toltepec. It will be done every day now that the new Mexican Central line has reached that city."

Agent Deems interrupted this optimism with a groan.

"Good Lord, Mr. Halloran, what's the use of talking about what we can ship when that cussed Mexican Central Railroad starts running regular between Toltepec and Mexico City? They ain't even run one work engine over that new line that I know of. Them blamed ties that are laid into Toltepec are still oozing greenwood sap!"

Halloran's heavy jaw took a defiant set.

"Are your feet feeling the chill, also, Deems? I thought we had the plan agreed to. Where's the hitch?"

Agent Deems stared at his questioner as if the latter had taken leave of whatever few senses government secret service operatives were granted in the beginning.

"Where's the hitch, you say? Oh, hardly anywhere at all, Mr. Halloran. You're only asking us to deliver this precious Item Thirteen of yours to railhead in Toltepec, Mexico, fifty miles across the river, tonight, with no one

216

wise, whatever, right square through Colonel Fulgencio Ortega's northern half of the loyalist guerrilla army, guaranteeing to get our 'shipment' on the train at Toltepec safe and sound in wind and limb and then to come back a-grinning and a-shrugging and a-saying, 'Why, shucks, it wasn't nothing. It's done every day.' Mister, you ain't just plain crazy, you're extra fancy nuts."

"As bad as all that, eh?"

"Fair near," put in Sheriff Casey. "We don't know if that Mexican train will be in Toltepec. We don't even know if those wild-eyed coffee beans even got a train. All we know is that you government men tell us they got the train, and that it'll be in Toltepec if we get this Item Thirteen there. Now that's a heck of an 'if.'"

Halloran was careful. He knew that only these local people—Texans familiar with every coyote track and kit-fox trail leading into Chihuahua—could bring off the delivery of Item Thirteen. Nothing must go wrong now.

"If we took Item Thirteen five thousand miles, Sheriff, surely Texas Express ought to be able to forward shipment the remaining fifty miles to Toltepec."

"Huh!" said Deems Harter. "You got one whack of a lot more faith in Texas Express than we have. In fact, about forty-nine miles more. As agent, I'll guarantee to get your precious shipment exactly one mile. That's from here to the Rio Grande. Past that, I wouldn't give you a nickel for your chances of making that train in Toltepec. *If* there's a train in Toltepec."

Halloran shook his head, unmoved.

"I'm not exactly thinking of my faith in terms of Texas Express, Harter. It's Charlie Shonto we're all gambling on."

"Yeah," said Harter acridly. "And right now Charlie

217

Shonto looks like a mighty poor gamble."

"Well, anyways," broke in Sheriff Nocero Casey, who had drifted to the front window for another look up the street, "a mighty wet one. Yonder comes our special delivery man, and it looks to me as though he's already been across the river. He's still dripping."

Halloran and Harter joined him in peering from behind the drawn shade. It was the express agent who recovered first.

"Good Lord!" he gasped. "What's that he's toting behind him?"

Sheriff Nocero Casey squinted carefully.

"Well," he said, "the bright lights of El Paso ain't precisely the best to make bets by, but if I had to take a scattergun guess at this distance and in the dark, I'd say it was a sopping-wet and some-undersized Chihuahua Indian boy."

In the shaded office of the Texas Express Company, the silence had returned again. First greetings were over. Shonto and Halloran had briefly touched upon their past experiences during the war between the States, and the time had very quickly run down to that place where everyone pauses, knowing that the next words are the ones that the money is being paid for. Sheriff Casey, Agent Harter, Shonto, even little Chamaco Díaz, all were watching P. J. Halloran.

"Now, Charlie," said the latter, at last, "we haven't sent for you to review the squeaks you've been in before." He let the small grimace which may or may not have been a smile pass over his rough features. "But I did feel that some slight mention of our past associations might prepare you for the present proposal."

"What you're saying, Mr. Halloran, is that you figure your Irish blarney is going to soften up my good sense." Shonto's own grin was a bit difficult to classify. It was hard as flint and yet warmed too, somehow, by a good nature or at least a wry appreciation of life as it actually worked out in the living. "But you're wasting your talents," he concluded. "I've had a couple of birthdays since I was crossing the Confederate lines for you, and now I don't sign up just for a pat on the back from my fellow countrymen. I've learned since the war that a man can't buy a bag of Bull Durham with a government citation. Not that I regret my time in the 'silent service,' mind you. But a fellow just doesn't like to be a hog about the hero business. Especially when he did his great deeds for the North, then went back to earning his keep in the South. If you spend your time in Texas, Mr. Halloran, you don't strain yourself reminding the local folks that you took your war pay in Union greenbacks."

Halloran nodded quickly.

"Don't be a fool, Charlie," he said. "Harter, here, and Sheriff Casey were carefully sounded out before we ever mentioned your name. They are not still afire with the Lost Cause. We can forget your war work."

"I'm glad you told me, Mr. Halloran. Somehow, I still remember it every so often. Matter of fact, I still occasionally wake up in a cold sweat. Now I can put all that behind me. Isn't it wonderful?"

"Shonto"—Halloran's hard face had turned cold again—"come over here to the window. I want to show you something." He took a pair of binoculars from Harter's desk, and Shonto followed him to the drawn shade. There, Halloran gave the glasses to him and said quietly, "Look yonder on the balcony of the Franklin House. Tell me what you see. Describe it exactly."

From the other's tone, Shonto knew the talk had gotten to the money point. He took the glasses and focused them on the hotel's second-story *galería*, the railed porch so common to the southwestern architecture of the times. As the view came into sharp detail, he frowned uneasily.

"All right," he began, low voiced. "I see a man. He's short, maybe not much over five feet. He stands straight as a yardstick. Stocky build. Big in the chest. Dark as hell in the skin, near as I can say in the lamplight from the room windows behind him. He's dressed in a black Eastern suit that don't fit him, and same goes for a white iron collar and necktie. Black hat, no creases, wore square like a sombrero. Long black hair, bobbed off like it was done with horse shears." He paused, squinting more narrowly through the binoculars. "Why," he added softly, "that's a blasted Indian dressed up in white man's clothes!"

"That," said P. J. Halloran, just as softly, "is exactly what it is." They turned from the window. "Up there on that balcony," Halloran continued, "is the most important man, next to Lincoln, in North America. I can't reveal his identity, and you will have to know him as Item Thirteen, until you have him safely on that waiting train at Toltepec."

"What train at Toltepec?" Shonto frowned. "Since when have they built the Mexican Central on into that two-burro burg?"

"Since today, we hope," said Halloran. "The idea was that, precisely as you, no one knew the railroad had been laid on into Toltepec. Those last few thousand yards of track were to be spiked down today. The gamble is that not even Ortega and the *rurales* would hear about it in time. Or, hearing of it, not realize a train was waiting to be run over it."

"That's what I'd call house odds, Mr. Halloran. This Item Thirteen must be one heck of a table-stakes man."

"He's one heck of a man," answered the government operative. "Anyway, Charlie, the train is supposed to be waiting at midnight in Toltepec. If we can get Item Thirteen there, the train can get on down past Camargo by daybreak and out of Ortega's reach . . . if the train's waiting in Toltepec."

"Longest two-letter word in the world," said Shonto. "Go ahead, drop the other boot."

"Well, we know that powerful enemies lie between El Paso and Toltepec. There's no point explaining to you the type of enemy I mean. I believe you're familiar enough with Colonel Ortega and his loyal militia."

"Yes, just about familiar enough. In case you're still wondering how Chamaco and I got ourselves doused in the Rio, it was meeting Ortega's loyal army, or as big a part of it as I came prepared to handle. I'd say there was twenty of them. They were pot-shooting at the kid swimming the river. He got away from them while they were murdering his father. Butterball got excited at the rifle fire and ran away with me: bolted right into the river. Next thing I knew, I was in as bad shape as the kid and, long as I figured two could ride as cheap as one, I scooped him up and we made it back to the American side by way of hanging onto Butterball's tail and holding long breaths under water on the way. I have got to get me another horse. In my business, you can't be fooling around with jumpy crowbaits like that."

"When you decide what you want for Butterball," put in Sheriff Nocero Casey, "let me know. I've been looking for just such a *loco* horse."

"Charlie," broke in Halloran, "are you interested or

221

not? We've got to move soon."

Shonto nodded speculatively, a man not to be rushed. "Depends. You haven't dropped that other boot yet."

"All right." Halloran spoke quickly now. "The small man in the black suit carries a letter of credit . . . a U.S. letter of credit . . . for an enormous amount of money. Some say as high as fifty million dollars. That's fifty million U.S., not Mexican. It's to bail out his revolution down there." Halloran gestured toward the Rio Grande and Mexico. "I don't need to tell you, Charlie, what men like Ortega will do to prevent that letter from getting to Mexico City. The money means the rebels are through . . . loyalists, they call themselves . . . and that the revolution will succeed and will stay in power. As you have already learned when your horse ran away with you, Colonel Ortega has been assigned the job of sealing off the border in Chihuahua State. Now, it becomes your job to unseal that border."

Charlie Shonto's grin was dry as dust.

"Shucks, nothing to that . . . nothing that I couldn't do with ten or twelve companies of Rangers and a regiment of regular cavalry."

"Don't joke, Charlie." Halloran pulled out an official document and handed it to Shonto. "Here are my orders. You don't need to read them. But check that final postscript at the bottom of the page against the signature beneath the Great Seal of this country you and I fought for, when he asked us to."

Shonto glanced down the page, reading aloud slowly. "'Any man who may aid the bearer of these orders in the business to hand will know that the gratitude of his government and my own personal indebtedness shall be his and shall not be forgotten. [Signed] A. Lincoln.' Well now," he said, handing back the document as gingerly as though it were the original of the Declaration of Independence. "Why didn't you say so, Mr. Halloran?"

"Like you"—Halloran smiled, and this time there was no doubt it was a smile—"I always save my best shot for the last target. What do you say, Charlie?"

"I say, let's go. For *him* I'd wrestle a bear, blindfolded. Who all's in it?"

"Just you, Charlie. I've brought our man this far. Sheriff Casey and Agent Harter have handled him here in town. But from here to Toltepec, he's your cargo . . . *if* you'll accept him."

Shonto winced perceptibly.

"There's that word again. You got anything extra to go with it this time?"

Halloran picked up a rolled map from Harter's desk.

"Only this chart of the area between here and Toltepec supplied by the Mexican Government. You know this ground as well as any man on this side of the Rio Grande. Take a look at this layout of it and tell us if you spot any way at all of getting past Ortega's patrols, into Toltepec."

He spread the map on the desk. Harter turned up the wick, and the four men bent over the wrinkled parchment. Behind them, the little Indian, Chamaco Díaz, had been forgotten. He stood silently in the shadows, wondering at the talk of these Americans. Chamaco had been to school some small time in El Paso and knew enough English to follow the conversation in the rough. Lonely and sorrowful as he was, he knew who that other little Indian in the black suit was, and his heart swelled with love and pride for these American men, that they would talk of risking their lives that *El Indio* might live and might reach Mexico City with the

223

United States money which would save the *Presidente*'s brave government of the *descamisados* and *pobrecitos* such as his father, Juliano Díaz, who had given their lives to establish it. Now, Chamaco watched the four big Americans bent over the map of Toltepec—his part of the beloved Motherland—and he waited with held breath what the verdict of the one tall man with the dried leather face would be.

For his part, the latter was having considerable last doubts. The map wasn't showing him anything he didn't already know. Presently, he glanced up at Halloran.

"There's no help here," he said. "I was hoping to see an old Apache route I've heard stories of. But this map shows nothing that wouldn't get me and the little man in the black suit stood up against the same tree that Chamaco's daddy was stood up against. Ortega knows all these trails."

"There's nothing, then? No way at all?"

"Yes, there's that Apache brush track. It was never found by the Rangers, but they know it exists. They've run the Chihuahua Apaches right to the river, time and again, then seen them vanish like smoke into midnight air. If we knew where that trail went over the Rio, we might have a coyote's chance of sneaking past Ortega's assassins." Shonto shook his head. "But there isn't a white man alive who knows that Apache track . . . ."

His words trailed off helplessly, and the four men straightened with that weary stiffness which foretells defeat. But into their glum silence a small voice, and forgotten, penetrated thinly.

"*Señores*, I am not a white man."

Shonto and his companions wheeled about. Chamaco moved out of the shadows into the lamplight.

"I am an Indian," he said, "and I know where the old

224

trail runs."

The four men exchanged startled looks and, in their momentary inability to speak, Chamaco thought that he detected reproof for his temerity in coming forward in the company of such powerful friends of Mexico. He bowed with apologetic humility and stepped back into the shadows.

"But of course," he said, small-voiced, "you would not trust to follow an Indian. Excuse me, *Señores*."

Shonto moved to his side. He put his hand to the thin shoulder. Telling the boy to follow him, he led the way to the office window. He held back the drawn shade while Chamaco, obeying him, peered down the street at the Franklin House.

"Boy," he said, "do you know who that small man is standing up there on the hotel balcony?"

Chamaco's eyes glowed with the fire of his pride.

"Yes, *patrón*!" he cried excitedly. "It is *him*! Who else could stand and look so sad and grand across the river?"

Shonto nodded. "You think *he* would trust an Indian boy?"

Chamaco drew himself up to his full four feet and perhaps five inches. In his reply was all the dignity of the poor.

"*Patrón*," he said, "he once *was* an Indian boy!"

Charlie Shonto nodded again. He tightened the arm about the boy's shoulders and turned to face the others.

"Don't know about you," he said to them, "but I've just hired me an Indian guide to Toltepec."

The men at the desk said nothing, and again Chamaco misinterpreted their hesitation.

"*Patrón*," he said to Charlie Shonto, "do *you* know who it is up there standing on the *galería* looking so sad

225

toward Mexico?"

"I could take an uneducated guess," answered Shonto, "but I won't. You see, Chamaco, I'm not supposed to know. He's just a job to me. It doesn't matter who he is."

The Indian boy was astounded. It passed his limited comprehensions.

"And you would risk your life for a stranger to you?" he asked, unbelievingly. "For an Indian in a rumpled white man's suit? A small funny-looking man with a foreign hat and long hair and a dark skin the same as mine? You would do this, *patrón*, and for nothing?"

Shonto grinned and patted him on the head.

"Well, hardly for nothing, boy."

"For what, then, *patrón*?"

"Money, boy. *Pesos. Muchos pesos.*"

"And only for that, *patrón*?"

At the persistence, Shonto's cynical grin faded. He made a small, deprecatory gesture. It was for Chamaco alone; he had forgotten the others.

"Let's just say that I was watching your face when you looked up at that hotel balcony a minute ago. All right, *amigo*?"

The dark eyes of Chamaco Díaz lit up like altar candles.

"*Patrón*," he said, "you should have been an Indian; you have eyes in your heart!"

Shonto grinned ruefully. "Something tells me, boy, that before we get our cargo past Ortega tonight we'll be wishing I had those eyes in the back of my head."

Chamaco reached up and took the gunman's big hand. He patted it reassuringly. "*Patrón*"—he smiled back—"do not be afraid. If we die, we die in a good and just cause. We lose only our two small lives. Him, up

226

there on the *galería*, he has in his hands the lives of all of the poor people of Mexico. Is that not a very fair exchange, our lives for all of those others, and for his?"

Shonto glanced at the other men. "Well, Chamaco," he said, "that's one way of looking at it. Excuse us, gentlemen; we've got a train to catch in Toltepec."

He took the boy's hand in his and they went out into the street. Halloran moved to follow them. At the door he halted a moment, shaking his head as he looked back at the express agent and the sheriff.

"Do you know what we've just done?" he said. "We've just bet fifty million dollars and the future of Mexico on a Chihuahua Indian kid not one of us ever laid eyes on prior to twenty minutes ago. I need a drink!"

The coach bounced and swayed through the night. Its side lamps, almost never lit, were now sputtering and smoking. They seemed to declare that this particular old Concord wanted to be certain her passage toward the lower ford would be noted from the far side—and followed.

The idea was valid.

The lower crossing, the old Apache route, was the way in which a mind of no great deception might seek to elude examination by the *rurales* at the upper, or main, crossing. The driver of the old Texas Express vehicle, a canvas-topped Celerity model made for desert speed, held the unalterable belief that the Mexican mind was so devious as to be very nearly simple. It twisted around so many times in its tracks, trying to be clever, that in the end it usually wound up coming right back where it started.

The driver was banking on this trait. He was

depending on Colonel Fulgencio Ortega to think that, when the planted rumor from El Paso reached him by avenue of his kinsmen in that city, he would say, "Aha! This stupid *American* stage-line company thinks that if they announce they will try to cross with *El Indio* at the old lower ford, that I shall at once conclude they really mean to cross at the new upper ford, and that I shall then be waiting for them at the new upper ford and they can cross in safety at the lower place. What fools! I shall quite naturally watch both crossings, and this they realize full well. What they are trying to do is see that I, personally, am not at the lower ford. They think that if they can contest the crossing with my men . . . without me . . . it will be a far easier matter. Well, now! ¡*Ai, Chihuahua*! Let them come. Let them find out who will be waiting for their disreputable stagecoach and its mysterious passenger at the old lower ford! Hah! Why will they attempt to match wits with the Executioner of Camargo?"

Of course, if Colonel Ortega did not reason thus, the driver of the coach would have made a grievous error, for the entire plan depended on meeting the Executioner.

The driver, a weather-beaten, leathery fellow, wrapped the lines of the four-horse hitch a bit tighter. He spoke to his leaders and his wheelers, tickling the ears of the former and the haunches of the latter with the tip of his fifteen-foot coaching whip.

"Coo-ee, boys!" he called to the horses. "Just so, just so." Leaning over the box, he spoke to the muffled, dark-faced passenger—the only passenger—in the rocking stage. "*Señor*, it is all well with you in there?" He used the Spanish tongue, but no reply came in kind from the interior. Indeed, no reply came in any tongue.

A very brave fellow, thought the driver. His kind were not many in the land below the Rio—or any land.

"You are a very small boy," said the somber-looking little man. "How is it that you are so brave?"

"Please, *Presidente*. I beg of you not to say more, just now. We are very near to the place, and there is great danger." Chamaco spoke with awed diffidence.

"I am not afraid, boy." *El Indio* patted him on the shoulder. "Do I not have a good Indian guide?"

"*Presidente*, please, say no more. You don't know Colonel Ortega."

"I have dealt with his kind. I know him, all right. They are all alike. Cowards. Jackals. Don't be afraid, boy. What did you say your name was?"

Chamaco told him, and the small man nodded.

"A good Indian name. It means what it says. How much farther now, boy, before we cross the river?"

They were moving on foot through a tunneled avenue in the river's brushy scrub of willow and rushes. It was the sort of thoroughfare frequented by the creatures of the night. None but very small men—or boys—might have used it at all, and then only very small Indian men or boys. If the Rangers had wanted to know one reason, just one, why the Apaches raiding up from Chihuahua had been able to disappear before their eyes on the American side of the Rio, it would have been that they were seeking some "hole" in the brush which would accommodate an ordinary mortal, not a Chihuahua Indian. But Chamaco Díaz was not alone a small Indian boy; he was a patriot.

"*Presidente*," he now pleaded, "will you not be quiet? *Por favor*, Excellence! We are coming to it this moment."

The small man in the black suit smiled.

"You dare to address me in this abrupt manner!" he said. "You, an Indian boy? A shirtless waif of the Border? A brush rat of the river bottom? ¡*Ai!*"

"*Presidente*," said the boy, "I will ask it one more time. I know that you do not fear the Executioner. I know that I am only a *pobrecito*, a *reducido*, a nothing. But in my heart you live with the Lord Jesus. I will die for you, *Presidente*, as I would for Him, even sooner. But I have sworn to guide you across the river and to the rendezvous. I have sworn to get you to Toltepec by midnight this night. Therefore, why should we die, when you must live for the people of our suffering land? I am taking you to Toltepec, *Presidente*. And if you continue to speak along the way, I will die for nothing and Mexico will never get the money you bear and she will not be saved. But mostly, *Presidente*, you will be dead. I cannot bear that. You are the life of all of us."

They had stopped moving. *El Indio*, in a streak of moonlight penetrating the arched limbs above them, could see the tears coursing down the dark cheeks of Chamaco Díaz. He reached quickly with his fingers and brushed away the tears.

"An Indian does not weep," he told the boy sternly. "Go ahead, now. I shall be still."

Chamaco swallowed hard. He dashed his own hand quickly at the offending eyes. His voice was vibrant with pride.

"It was the brush, *Presidente*, the small limbs snapping back and stinging me across the face. You know how it is."

El Indio nodded once more.

"Of course, boy. I have been in the brush many times. Go ahead, show the way. I have been an old woman, talking too much. We are both Indians, eh? Lead on."

Straight as a rifle barrel, Chamaco Díaz stood before him a moment. Then, ducking down again, he scuttled on ahead. *El Indio* watched him go. Just before he bent to follow, he glanced up at the patch of moonlight. The beams struck his own dark face. They glistened on something which seemed to be moist and moving upon his own coffee-colored features. But then of course in moonlight the illusions are many, and the lunar eye is not to be trusted. Had he not just said, himself, that Indians did not weep?

The coach of the Texas Express Company splashed over the old Apache Crossing and came to a halt before the flaring bonfire and wooden barricade across the Toltepec road. "*¿Que pasa?*" the tall driver called down to the leering brigand who commanded the guard. "What is the matter? Why do you stop me?"

"*De nada*. It is nothing." Lieutenant Chivo smiled. "A small matter which will take but a moment. I hope you have a moment. *Yes? Very well. Colonel*," he called to the squat officer drinking coffee by the fireside, "the stage for Toltepec has arrived on time."

The Colonel put down his tin cup and picked up a long quirt Uncoiling the whip, he arose and came over to the barricade. He stood looking up at the coachman. After a moment, he nodded pleasantly enough and spoke in a friendly manner.

"Please to get down," he said.

"Sorry, I can't do it," replied the driver. "Company rules, Colonel. You understand."

"Of course," said the guerrilla chief easily. "Without rules nothing is accomplished. I'm a great believer in discipline. Did I introduce myself? Colonel Fulgencio

231

Ortega, of Camargo. Now do you care to get down?"

"*The* Colonel Ortega?" said the American driver, impressed. "*Jefe*, this a great honor. And these are your famed *rurales*?" He pointed with unqualified admiration to the surly pack stalking up, now, to stand behind the colonel and his lieutenant. "My, but they are a fine-looking troop. Real fighters, one can see that. But then, why not? On the side of justice all men fight well, eh, Colonel?"

Ortega ignored the compliments.

"Did you hear what I said?" he asked. "I wish you to get down. I do not believe I have met your passenger, and I think you should introduce me to him. My men will hold your horses."

His men were already holding the horses, as the driver was keenly aware. Also, he did not miss the fact the soldiers were holding something else for him: their rifles—pointed squarely at him. But he was the steady sort, or perhaps merely stupid.

"Passenger?" he said. "I carry no passenger, Colonel. Just some freight for Toltepec."

Ortega stepped back. He looked again into the coach.

"Freight, eh?" he mused. "Strange wrappings you have put around your cargo, *cochero*. A black suit. Black hat with round Indian crown worn squarely on the head. And see how your freight sits on the seat of the coach, just as if it were alive and had two arms and two legs and might speak if spoken to. That is, if fear has not sealed its cowardly Indian tongue!" His voice was suddenly wicked with hatred, all the smile and the pretense of easiness gone out of it—and out of him. "Chivo!" he snapped. "Please to open the door of this coach and help *El Presidente* to dismount!"

The stage driver straightened on the box.

"*El Presidente*?" he said to Ortega. "Whatever in the world are you talking about, *jefe*?"

"We shall see in a moment." Ortega nodded, in control of himself once more. "Hurry, Chivo. This *cochero* does not understand the importance of his passenger. Nor is it apparent to him that jokes about 'freight' which walks and talks like an Indian are not laughed at in Chihuahua just now. *¡Adelante!* Get that coach door opened, you fool!"

Chivo, grinning as only a dog wolf about to soil the signpost of his rival may grin, threw open the door of the Concord and seized the lone passenger by the arm. With a foul-mouthed oath, he pulled the small figure from the coach and hurled it viciously to the ground.

His surprise was understandable.

It is not the usual thing for a victim's arm to come off at the shoulder and remain in the offending hand of its assaulter while the remainder of the torso goes flying off through the night. Neither was it the usual thing for the poor devil's head to snap off and go rolling away like a melon when the body thudded to earth.

"*¡Santisima!*" cried one of the brute soldiers of the guard. "You have ruined him, you dumb animal!"

But Lieutenant Chivo did not hear the remark, and Colonel Ortega, if he heard it, did not agree with the sentiment, except perhaps as to Chivo's intelligence. For what the guerrilla lieutenant had pulled from the Texas Express Company's Toltepec stage was quite clearly a dressmaker's dummy, clothed to resemble a very short and large-chested Mexican Indian man who always sat straight on his seat and wore his black hat squarely on his head.

Moreover, Colonel Fulgencio Ortega was given no real time in which to comment upon his soldier's awed

233

remark or his lieutenant's amazed reaction to the arm in his hand and the head rolling free upon the firelit banks of the Rio Grande. For in the small moment of stricken dumbness which had invaded all of them when *El Presidente's* body had come apart in mid-air, the American driver of the Toltepec stage had wrapped the lines of his four-horse hitch, stepped to the ground in one giant stride from the precarious box of the old Concord, and all in the same motion slid out a long-barreled Colt revolver and buried its iron snout in the belly of the Executioner of Camargo.

"*Jefe*," he announced quietly. "if you make one false movement, your bowels will be blown out all over this river bank," and this statement Colonel Fulgencio Ortega had no difficulty whatever in comprehending.

"Chivo!" he cried out. "In the name of Maria, hold the men. Let no one touch trigger!"

"Yes, Chivo." The leather-faced American "*cochero*" nodded, spinning Ortega around so that the muzzle of the Colt was in his spine. "And so that you do not in greed seek to replace your beloved *jefe* in command of the *rurales* of Camargo . . . that is to say, that you do not in this moment of seeming opportunity make some move deliberately to get me to shoot him . . . permit me to introduce myself."

"Ah?" queried Chivo, who truly had not yet thought of this obvious course of treachery to his leader. "And to what point would this be, *cochero*? Do you think that I am in fear of stagecoach drivers?"

The tall driver shrugged.

"Well, I think you ought to have the same break I give any other man I'm paid to get past."

There was something in the way that he spoke the one word "paid" which penetrated Chivo's wily mind. He

234

hesitated, but two of the soldiers did not. Thinking that they stood well enough behind their companions to be safe, they moved a little aside from the pack to get a line of fire at the big American. The instant they were clear of their friends, however, flame burst from behind the back of Colonel Ortega—one lancing flash, then another—and the two soldiers were down and dying in the same blending roar of pistol shots.

"Shonto," said the stage driver to Chivo, the smoking muzzle of the Colt again in Ortega's spine. "Over there across the river, they call me Shonto."

"¡*Madre Maria*!" breathed Chivo, dropping his rifle, unbidden, into the dirt of the wagon road. "Carlos Shonto? *Por Dios, pistolero*, why didn't you say so?"

"I just did." Charlie Shonto nodded. "Now you better say something. Quick."

Chivo shrugged in that all-meaning way of his kind.

"What remains to die for?" he inquired. "You do not have *El Indio* in the stage. You have fooled us with the dummy on the ground over there. Somewhere, *El Presidente* is no doubt riding through the night. But it is not upon the stage for Toltepec. Another of our guards will get him. For us, the work of the day is over. Command me."

Shonto then ordered all the soldiers to drop their rifles and cartridge bandoleers. All knives, pistols, axes went into the common pile. This arsenal was then loaded into the stage along with Colonel Fulgencio Ortega, bound hand and foot by his faithful followers. The work went forward under Chivo's expert direction, the spirit of the *rurales* now totally flagged. With their chances of snaring *El Indio* had gone their interest in being heroes. Like soldiers everywhere, they were of no great menace in themselves. Deprived of leadership, they were just so many surly dogs quarreling among themselves. Shonto had gambled on this, and gambled exceedingly well.

Yet, as in every risk, there lurks the element of the unknown, the thing that cannot be depended upon except in the name of "luck." Shonto's luck ran out with the command he now issued to the scarfaced Chivo.

"All right, Lieutenant," he said. "Up you go. You'll be the *cochero* now. I'll ride shotgun. You savvy '*la escopeta?*'" With the question, he reached for the double-barreled Parker laid across the driver's box, and Chivo nodded hastily. He "savvied" shotguns very well. One did not argue with them at close range, not ever. But Shonto had made his basic mistake some time ago, when he had put the thought of succeeding to Ortega's place of power in Camargo in the mind of the brutal lieutenant. Such towering aspirations had never flooded his dark brain. True, he would have seen Ortega killed in a moment, should that suit his purpose. This much was exactly what Shonto had guessed. What the wary gunman had not foreseen, however, was that, until he, Shonto, had mentioned the matter, Chivo had never really thought about the possibility of promoting himself over his Colonel.

Now the prospect inflamed his jackal's mind.

"Whatever you say, *jefe*," he told Shonto, fanging a smirk which the latter hardly supposed was a grin of good nature. "You see, I climb to the seat gladly. I take the lines and am ready to drive for you. Come on. Let's go."

Shonto started to swing up after him. For one moment both hands were occupied. It was in that moment that the boot of Lieutenant Chivo drove into his face. Shonto fell backward, landing hard. The shotgun was still in his grasp but was useless from that angle. Above him,

236

Chivo was shouting the horses into motion. The coach lurched forward. Shonto made it to his feet in time to leap for the trunk straps in the rear. He caught one of them, held on, and dragged behind the moving stage for fifty feet. He still had the shotgun in his right hand.

The soldiers, sensing his helplessness, ran toward him. They seized clubs and picked up rocks on the run. Chivo, in response to their yells, slowed the stage, thinking to allow them to beat and stone the dragging American.

Shonto held onto the trunk strap. When the snarling soldiers were near, he raised the shotgun and fired it with one hand into their faces. The first barrel and the second blasted as one. The soldiers fell away, three to stagger and fall mortally wounded, two others clutching at their shredded faces, screaming in the agony of the immediate torture and the knowledge, even in their terrible pain, that they would never use their eyes again.

Chivo, on the driver's box, turned in time to see Shonto haul himself up over the rear of the Concord. He had no weapon, now, but neither did the *rurale* lieutenant.

Chivo knew the one way open to him and took it. Over the side he went, rolling to the ground and free of the speeding wheels, the excited teams running wild the moment he flung away the lines. Shonto, weaving precariously, made it to the driver's box and threw himself down between the straining horses to recover the lines.

His luck now returned. He was able to gather up the lines and return to the box, the coach under control and still upright on the wagon road to Toltepec.

But now he knew the wolf pack behind him had a leader again. He could guess how long it would take

Chivo to mount the survivors and take up the pursuit.

"Coo-ee, coo-ee," he called to the snorting team. "Steady down, you beauties. You've not begun your night's work yet. Save that pep and vim for the last lap!"

Where he had said he would be waiting beside the wagon road to Toltepec with *El Presidente*, there Chamaco Díaz waited when, half an hour's loping run from the Rio, Shonto pulled up his panting horses and hailed the underbrush. The Indian boy had guided his charge without fail and on foot through the night and between the prowling soldiers of Colonel Ortega's four miles south of the river. The ancient and secret Apache escape route from Texas, which the two had traveled to reach their rendezvous with Charlie Shonto and the stage for Toltepec, lay still unknown behind them. Shonto did not ask Chamaco where it ran, and the boy did not tell him. He was an Indian, even now, and Charlie Shonto was a white man.

Swiftly, then, the last part of the plan was put into operation. The four horses were unhooked from the coach. Four saddles and bridles were brought from the coach trunk, and the mounts were readied. Colonel Ortega was removed from the stage and hung over the saddle of one mount in the manner of a sack of grain. Shonto tied his hands to his feet under the horse's belly, halfway hoping the ropes would not hold. Where the rutted track of the road bent to go past the rendezvous, an eighty-foot bluff rose above the Chihuahua plain. Over this drop, Shonto and his two Indian friends now tossed the Concord's load of firearms. There was no time for more effective disposal. Mounting up, the party set out, away from the road, Chamaco leading, Shonto bringing up the rear with the pack horse of the Executioner of Camargo. The goat path along which the small Indian boy took them disappeared into the desert brush within a pistol shot from the wagon road. Shonto had no more idea where the trail led than did Ortega or *El Presidente.* No options remained in any event. Behind them, along the road from the river, they heard now the shouts of men of Mexican tongue and the hammer of horses' hoofs in considerable number. In a pause to listen, they all recognized the high yelping tones of Lieutenant Chivo, discovering the abandoned stage and guessing, amid a goat's beard of rotten curses, the manner of flight of his enemies. And more: from Chivo's murderous bleats, they made out that he had with him another patrol of Ortega's *rurales,* evidently encountered along the way. These new soldiers, whatever their number, would be armed and were clearly being commanded by the colonel's good lieutenant. All might still have been well—yes, surely would have been so—considering the depth of the brushland and the blindness of its cover. But in the press of time and because he had not thought ahead to the complication of Chivo's picking up more arms en route, Shonto had not taken the precaution he ordinarily would have of gagging the captive colonel.

He thought of it, now, as Ortega's galling shout echoed down the slope they were climbing.

"*¡Aqui, aqui, muchachos*! I am here! I am here!"

His head was hanging on that side of the horse nearest Shonto. The shout for help was cut off by the toe of the gunman's boot knocking out four front teeth and knocking out, too, the owner of the teeth. But the price of poker had just gone up, regardless.

"Chamaco," he said, "we have one chance: to split

up."

"Never, *patrón*."

"Listen, kid"—Shonto's voice went hard as quartz—"you do what I tell you. I'm running this show."

"No, my American friend, you are not." The denial did not come from the boy but from the small man in the black suit. "It is I who must say what will be. And I say we stay together. You are not with Spaniards, my friend. You are not with traitors who call themselves Mexicans. You are with Indians. Lead on, boy."

Shonto knew he was helpless. He knew, as well, that they were helpless, that it would be but a matter of minutes before the *rurales* would come up to them, blind brush or not. They were so close behind that they could follow by ear the sounds of the stagecoach horses breaking through the brush. The rifle firing would commence any moment, and a bullet, unaimed except by the noise of their ponies crashing ahead, would soon enough find all and each of them. There was no other end within reason.

Yet Chamaco Díaz was no victim of such knowledge. He had been supported by his *Presidente*, had heard him with his own ears say, "You are with Indians." What was not possible in the service of such a man?

"*Patrón!*" he now called to Shonto, voice high and sharp with excitement. "There is a way. Follow me, and don't worry about making noise. The Rangers from your Texas side of the river did not always obey the law!"

Their horses were plowing on up the slope now, and true to Shonto's fear the guerrillas were beginning to fire blindly at the sound of their progress. The bullets hissed and sung about them. But the boy's shout had intrigued Charlie Shonto.

"What's that?" he yelled back.

"The Rangers of Texas," answered the boy, laughing for the first time in Shonto's memory of him. "Many times they would run the Apaches right on across the river, *patrón*. Then the Apaches had to have a way on this side to 'lose' them. I know the way, *patrón*. Ride hard and jump your horse when I demand it."

Shonto wanted to know more about that "jump" business, but the guerrillas were too close now. All he could do was bend low in the saddle and hope the bullet with his name on it went astray. It did. They came to Chamaco's "jumping place" without a wound. The place itself was a declivity in the trail—dug by hand and centuries gone—where no rider, not knowing that it waited beyond the steeply descending hairpin turn which hid it from above, could ever lift his mount over it in time. The animal's momentum, coming down the roof-steep pitch of the decline, would have to carry it and its rider into the "Ranger trap." And this is the way that it worked with the eager *rurales* of Chivo. All of the horses of Chamaco's party, even the pack horse with Colonel Ortega's unconscious form, cleared the break in the trail, leaping it like deer because spurred to the effort by their desperate riders. But the mounts of the guerrillas, scrambling around the hairpin, snorting furiously under the urging of their savage masters—the scent of the kill hot in the nostrils now, so close were they—had no chance to see or to lift themselves and their riders over the yawning pit. Into the waiting blackness of the man-made chasm the first dozen horses and soldiers went screaming and kicking. Another dozen soldiers and their mounts piled up in the trail above and did not plunge into the abyss with the others. But neither did they seem to retain their previous eagerness for the blood of *El Presidente* and the

241

elevation of Lieutenant Chivo to the rank of Executioner of Camargo.

As for Chivo, himself, Shonto never knew if he was among the first group of riders, or the second. All that he did know was that, following the first spate of screamings from the fallen, he did not hear again the harsh yelping voice of the bearded lieutenant.

"¡*Madre*! Chamaco," he said to the Indian boy, in the first moment of stillness following the piteous cries from above, "what is in that Apache trench up there?"

"Tiger's teeth," said the youth, "their points burned to hardness of iron, their butts set in the cracks of the mother rock. I don't wonder at the screams, *patrón*. I've looked down in that hole."

"¡*Santísima*!" breathed Shonto. "A staked pit!"

"For a pack of animals, the death of a pack of animals." The Oaxacan accents of *El Presidente* seemed sad. "Let us go on and catch that train in Toltepec. There is so much work to do in Mexico. The people cry out to me, and there is little time, so little time, for me to answer them."

Shonto did not answer, feeling for the moment belonged to another. Chamaco understood the courtesy.

"Yes, *Presidente*," he said softly. "Please to follow your humble servant."

At once the small man in the black suit spurred his horse up beside that of the Chihuahua Indian boy.

"You are no one's humble servant," he said sternly. "Remember that always. You are a citizen of Mexico, a free man, humble to no one. If you believe in a god, you can thank him for that. If you believe in a man, you can thank a man."

"Yes, *Presidente*, I thank you *and* God."

"In that order, eh, boy?" A trace of warm amusement

crossed the dark Indian features. "But you are wrong about the man, *muchacho*. It is another *Presidente* whom I charge you to remember. See that you don't forget his name, citizen; you owe it your life. Burn it in your mind, if you are a true Mexican: Abraham Lincoln."

It was all downhill from there. Some minutes short of midnight, Shonto rode into Toltepec with his charges. By a quarter past the hour, "Item Thirteen" was aboard the waiting train. Steam being up and the dawn all too near, the parting was abrupt. Camargo must be run past in the dark. Also, for the benefit of good health, those who must remain behind when the train pulled out would do well to be drawing in American air come sunrise of that risky day. *El Presidente*, surrounded by his faithful guard aboard the train, was virtually "taken away" from Shonto and Chamaco. So, as well, was the one-time Executioner of Camargo. In a last-second view, *El Presidente* seemed to spy the tall American and the tiny Indian boy sitting their horses in the lamplight spilling from his car's window. Shonto and Chamaco thought they saw him wave to them, and they returned the wave, each with his own thoughts. If the Texas gunman saw the bright tears streaming down the dark cheeks of Chamaco Díaz, he said nothing of the matter, then or later. Each man was permitted his own manner of farewell. But when the train had pulled away from Toltepec—before, even, its smoke had trailed into the Chihuahua night behind it—Charlie Shonto knew all he ever cared to know of the ending of the story. His big hand reached through the dark to touch the knee of his companion.

"Come along, Chamaco," he said. "We had better make long tracks. It's forty-nine miles to the river."

The boy nodded obediently, saying nothing. They turned their horses and sent them into a weary lope.

As they rode, Shonto's rawhide features softened. He was watching the proud set of the thin figure riding by his side. He was aware, surely, that the small Indian man in the ill-fitting black suit had been Benito Juárez, the liberator of Mexico, his people's Abraham Lincoln. But that part of it did not impress the big gunman unduly. For Charlie Shonto, the biggest Indian that he saw that night was always a little Chihuahua boy who barely reached to his gunbelt. History would not record, Shonto suspected, the secret fact that Juárez had been spirited to the Capitol in Washington, D.C. History would never record, he knew certainly, the added fact of the strange manner in which the legendary *El Indio* had been returned safely to his native land. But Charlie Shonto and Texas Express would know the way that it was done, and so would the tallest Indian in all of Toltepec!

When he thought of that, somehow even Charlie Shonto felt better. As the shadows of the Toltepec hills closed behind them, he was sitting as straight in the saddle as Chamaco Díaz.

But of course not as tall.

ELMER KELTON

ELMER KELTON (1926–) was born on a ranch in Andrews County, Texas, and spent his youth and early manhood associating with cowboys and Western old-timers around the Midland-Odessa ranching country of West Texas. Kelton's great-grandfather, in his words, "came out into West Texas about 1875 with a wagon and a string of horses, started a big family and died young, leaving four boys to break broncs, punch cattle, and make a living as best they could, supporting their mother and two baby sisters."

Following graduation from high school, Kelton entered the University of Texas but his further education was interrupted by the Second World War in which he served with the U.S. Army Infantry in the European theater. Upon his discharge, he resumed his education at the University of Texas at Austin and was graduated in 1948 with a Bachelor's degree in journalism. From 1948 to 1963 he worked as a livestock journalist reporting for the *San Angelo Standard-Times* and, subsequently, spent twenty-two years as associate editor of *Livestock Weekly*. He had always wanted to write fiction, in particular the Western story, studying the Western fiction of Ernest Haycox, Luke Short, S. Omar Barker, Walt Coburn, and others. It was during his last semester at the university that he sold his first Western story, "There's Always Another Chance," to *Ranch Romances* (1st April 48). Some of Kelton's early fiction from this period has been collected in *There's Always Another Chance and Other Stories* (Fort Concho Museum Press,

1986). *Hot Iron* (Ballantine, 1955), a story set in Texas dealing with the cattle business (something in which even at this time Kelton was well versed), marked his debut as a novelist. *Buffalo Wagons* (Ballantine, 1956) followed, a story about hide hunters in the Comanche territory in the early 1870s, and it won him the first of six Golden Spur awards from the Western Writers of America. Perhaps ironically, Kelton's reworking of this novel as the much-expanded *Slaughter* (Doubleday, 1992) earned him his fifth Golden Spur.

As he matured as a novelist, Kelton came increasingly to be concerned with history and at the same time his fiction changed in tone and substance. "As a fiction writer," Kelton remarked once in an address to the Texas Folklore Society, "I have always tried to use fiction to illuminate history, to illuminate truth, at least as I see the history and truth. A fiction writer can often fire a reader's interest enough to make him want to dig into the true story and make him search out the real history to find out for himself what happened."

Kelton was not afraid to experiment and to expand the horizons of the Western story. *The Day the Cowboys Quit* (Doubleday, 1971) is centered on a little-known episode in the range history of Texas when the cowboys defied great landowners and cattle kings. However, as fine as this and other of Kelton's novels are, I believe his *The Time It Never Rained* (Doubleday, 1973) is one of the dozen or so best novels written by an American in the 20th Century. It is set in Texas in the 1950s during a seven-year drought. Charlie Flagg, the protagonist, is an aged man possessed of the qualities most admired by Kelton in human beings: determination, integrity, and endurance. Above all, the land itself is a character in this novel, the land around

Rio Seco and nearly all the attitudes and the behavior of the various characters are in some way responses to the land. Charlie Flagg can only persist, cling to the land, and hope to try again. He refuses to beg from the federal government; he asks only to live by his own lights and to be left alone. The old Comanche buried on top of Warrior Hill becomes a symbol for Charlie and for the strength of character invested in him. "'I'd be a lot more satisfied if Uncle Sam didn't hire so many left-handed nephews to run everybody's business,'" is how Charlie puts it. A significant enemy to human survival in *The Time It Never Rained*, and one more irrefragable than any stereotyped Western villain, is the federal government and its utter inability with its many wasteful and ineffectual programs to address real human needs outside of a narrowly political context that tends only to promote self-serving and unsympathetic bureaucratic posturing.

Kelton's sixth Golden Spur came for his essay, "Politically Correct or Historically Correct?" It appeared in *The Roundup* (9-10/93), the house organ of the Western Writers of America, and it is an apt critique of the writings of politically correct eco-extremists, most of whom "live in urban areas which they and their neighbors have forever blighted" and who "couldn't tell sideoats grama from burro grass." Not only is historical accuracy not on the side of their fanatical devotion to a revisionist presentism, but "they are judging past generations in the light of a current generation's attitudes. They are rewriting 19th-Century history to fit a 1990s political and social agenda. I can't help wondering how future generations are going to regard all this someday when they face the payday for our penchant for spending money we don't have and leaving

247

the note hanging over our grandchildren's heads." Looking back to the time of his own great-grandfather on the frontier, Kelton could only conclude: "I recognize that he was a product of *his* time, as we are a product of *our* time. If we were placed in his time I doubt that we would have done any better. We might very possibly not have done nearly so well."

Elmer Kelton's Western fiction is not character-driven, as is that of T.V. Olsen or Max Brand, to name only two authors in whose work this quality is preëminent, but it is concerned with character, in both the narrow sense and the general sense. His men and women are sensitively drawn people of integrity who suffer hardships in building their homes and working the land, who find the wages of changing times relentless, and whose struggles are of more than passing interest for their own lives and to future generations. Knowing full well—as that past-master, William MacLeod Raine, and numerous other authors of the Western story were aware before him—that these qualities in a story are not likely to attract accolades from the critical establishment, Kelton once observed how "for many critics a writer is important only when he savages his subject matter. If he writes with understanding and hope, with respect and love, he is considered trivial." Yet, because this is precisely what Elmer Kelton has attempted in his work, his appeal as his subject matter are likely to outlive the time in which his work was created, just as his contributions to the Western story have continually revitalized and enriched it.

When I was preparing the first edition of this anthology, I had read all of the short stories Kelton had written over the years, mostly for magazines, and found none that seemed to me the equal of his best novels. Therefore I suggested that I adapt an episode from *The Wolf and the Buffalo* (Doubleday, 1980) which had then only recently been published. The humility of the man was such that he honestly wanted to know what I thought of that book, was it really good? My answer is still yes, it is; and it remains in many ways the Western novel of his perpetuation as an artist, a celebration of the American spirit, chastened by the land, instilled by the Great Mystery with a profound reverence. It also records human suffering, and human defeat, and spiritual despair.

"Desert Command" was the title I chose for my selection from that novel. It was later anthologized in *The Horse Soldiers* (Fawcett Gold Medal, 1987) edited by Bill Pronzini and Martin H. Greenberg and yet again in *The Mammoth Book of the Western* (Carroll and Graf, 1991) edited by Joe E. Lewis. The episode deals with a troop of buffalo soldiers lost in the wastes of the Southwestern desert. It is a theme with which Kelton dealt earlier in "Apache Patrol" in *Ranch Romances* (2nd March 52) but not quite so well as here. The last line in this novel reads: "Old Rangers and old warriors would often smoke together and share memories of an open-plains era lost to them all." It has not been completely lost. Elmer Kelton is among those who have brought it to life again in his fine and memorable Western stories.

DESERT COMMAND
1980

THE CAPTAIN WENT THROUGH THE MOTIONS OF SETTING up a guard mount, but it was a futile effort. Most of these suffering men could do little to defend themselves should the Indians choose this time to attack. Gideon's vision was so blurred that he could not have drawn a bead. Sergeant Nettles could no longer control his limp. He kept his eyes on the captain and contrived not to move more than necessary when the captain looked in his direction.

Gideon asked, "Sergeant, why don't you take your rest?"

Nettles's eyes flashed in anger. "You tryin' to tell me what to do, Private Ledbetter?"

"No, sir. Just come to me that you had a hard day."

"We all had a hard day. Mine ain't been worse than nobody else's."

"You've rode back and forth, walked back and forth, seein' after the men. You gone twice as far as most of us. You rest, why don't you? Tell me what you want done and I'll do it."

"I want you to leave me alone. Ain't nothin' wrong with me that ain't wrong with everybody here."

"The rest of them got no arrow wound that ain't ever healed up."

The anger in Nettles's eyes turned to sharp concern. "It's all right, and I don't want you talkin' about it." He glanced quickly toward the captain and showed relief to find Hollander's attention focused elsewhere.

Gideon said accusingly, "You been hidin' it from him."

He could not remember that he had ever seen Nettles show fear of anything. But the sergeant was fearful now. He gripped Gideon's arm. "Don't you be tellin' him. Don't be tellin' nobody. Without the army, what could I be? Where could I go?"

"Lots of things. Lots of places."

"You know better than that. In the army I'm a sergeant, a *top* sergeant. I'm somebody, and I can *do* somethin'. Anywhere else, I'm just another nigger."

"Captain'll see for hisself sooner or later."

"Not as long as I can move. Now you git to your own business."

Sometime during the early part of the evening Gideon heard horses walking. He pushed up from the ground, listening, hoping it was Jimbo and the canteen carriers coming back. He was momentarily disoriented— dizzy—but he realized the sound was from the wrong direction to be Jimbo. It was coming from along the column's backtrail, to the west. He thought about Indians, but they wouldn't make that much noise. The clinking and clanking meant cavalry horses.

Captain Hollander figured it out ahead of Gideon. He walked to the edge of camp and did his best to shout. "Waters! Sergeant Waters! Up here!" His voice was weak and broke once.

The horses seemed to stop for a moment. The men— one of them, at least—had heard the captain. Hollander shouted again, his voice hoarser now. After a moment, the horses were moving again. The captain grunted in satisfaction. His good feeling was soon spoiled, for the horses kept walking, right on by the knoll.

"Waters!" Hollander tried again. Gideon took up the shout, and so did several others. The riders continued to move, passing the hill and going on eastward. The

251

captain clenched his fists in anger.

Gideon volunteered, "I'll go, sir. I'll fetch them back." Hollander only grunted, but Gideon took that for approval. He started down the hill, his legs heavy. He shouted every so often for Waters, but he heard no reply. When he stopped to listen he could tell that the horses were getting farther from him. He tried to run but could not bring his legs to move that rapidly. He stumbled over the crown of some dried-up bunchgrass and sprawled on his belly. He invested a strong effort into getting on his feet.

Behind him Hollander called, "Come back, Ledbetter. Let them go."

He wavered on the point of insubordination but found he could barely hear the horses any more. He had no chance to catch them. Wearily he turned and began the struggle back up the hill. It must have taken him an hour to reach the huddled company and fall to the ground.

Hollander stood over him, against the starlight. "You tried."

When he had the breath, Gideon said, "They just never did hear me."

"They heard you. Waters simply did not choose to stop. He's saving himself, or trying to."

A question burned in his mind, and he came near asking it aloud. *Are we going to save ourselves?* His throat was too dry to bring it out.

Nettles came over after a while to see if he was all right.

Gideon demanded, "What was the matter with Sergeant Waters? I know he heard me. I never figured him to panic out of his head."

"I seen him when the men commenced to groan. It was the groanin' done it. You ever wonder why he drank so much? It was to drive the groanin' sounds out of his mind."

"I don't understand."

"Old days, Waters was a slave catcher. It was him that kept the hounds, and him the white folks give the whip to when he caught a runaway. He didn't have no choice—they'd of took the whip to *him* if he hadn't done it. Now and again they made him keep whippen' a man till the life and the soul was beat out of him. I reckon them dead people been comin' after Waters ever since, in his mind."

The night breeze turned mercifully cool, but it held no hint of moisture. Gideon woodenly stood his guard duty, knowing he would be helpless if anything challenged him. He heard men groaning. The sound made his skin crawl. He could imagine how it had been with Waters. Across the camp someone babbled crazily, hallucinating. Gideon lapsed into sleep of sorts, or unconsciousness. When he awoke, color brightened the east. His head felt as if someone were pounding it with a hammer. His tongue was dry and swollen, his mouth like leather.

Sergeant Nettles lay on his blanket, his eyes open. Gideon crawled to him on hands and knees. He knew what he wanted to say, but his tongue betrayed him. He brought out only a jumble of sounds. He worked at it a long time before he summoned up a little saliva and forced his tongue to more or less his bidding. "You all right sir?" he asked.

Nettles nodded and pushed himself slowly from the ground. At the edge of camp, Captain Hollander was moving about, the first man on his feet.

Little effort was made toward fixing breakfast. The men could not eat. They could not swallow without water. The captain started trying to pack the mules. The regular packer had fallen behind yesterday with Waters. Gideon began to help. It was almost more than he could do to lift a pack to the level of a mule's back. Had the mules been fidgety, he could not have managed. But they were too miserable to move around.

He could see a little better this morning, for the rest, and his legs moved easier than last night, but the gain was of only minor degree. A stir among the buffalo hunters attracted his attention. He became conscious that many of their horses and pack mules were gone. They had strayed off during the night, or perhaps Indians had stolen into the edge of camp and quietly made away with them. The hunters staggered around uncertainly, accusing one another mostly by gesture, for they were as hard put as the troopers to convert gestures into understandable words. In a little while hunters and soldiers started a ragged march down the gentle slope and left the round hill behind them.

Grasping at hope wherever he could find it, Gideon told himself that perhaps Jimbo and the others had stopped at darkness for fear of losing the trail, and by now they were on the move again, coming to the rescue.

The morning sun was soon punishingly hot. Miles went by slowly and painfully, and Jimbo did not come. Far up into the morning, after a couple of troopers had slumped to the ground, Hollander called for a rest stop. They had moved into a sandy stretch of ground with low-growing stemmy mesquite trees and small oak growth shin-to-knee-high. Many of the men draped blankets over these plants and crawled under them as far as they could go for partial protection against the punishing sun.

Gideon turned to look for Sergeant Nettles. He found

him shakily trying to dismount from his black horse, Napoleon. Gideon reached to help him. He spread a blanket across a bush and pulled the corner of it over Nettles's head.

Young Nash tried to dismount but fell and lay as he had landed. Little Finley sat hunched, crying but not making tears. He tried to talk, but the words were without form.

Hollander was somehow still able to articulate, though he spoke his words slowly and carefully. He said it was his judgment that José had become lost and was not coming back—not today, not ever. The men who had gone on after him with the canteens must be sharing whatever fate had overtaken José.

Thompson argued sternly that somewhere ahead lay Silver Lake, and that it was no doubt José's goal. It couldn't be more than a few more miles—fifteen or twenty at most, he declared.

Hollander shook his head violently, his face flushed. If water were that near, and José had found it, Jimbo and the others would be back by now. The captain pointed southeastward. He still had his compass. Water anywhere else was a guess, and evidently a bad one. But he *knew* there was water in the Double Lakes. It was time to stop gambling and go for the cinch.

Thompson was aghast. "You know how far it is to the Double Lakes? Those darkies of yours—they're almost dead now. They'll never live for another sixty-seventy miles."

"They'll live. They've *got* to live."

Thompson insisted that water lay much closer, to the northeast.

Hollander countered, "You said that yesterday. How far have we come? How many more men can we afford to lose?"

"Go that way," Thompson insisted, pointing his chin across the sandy hills toward Double Lakes, "and you'll lose them all."

"There is water at Double Lakes. There is only death out here in these sands. Will you go with us?"

Thompson turned and studied his hunters. "No, we're trying for Silver Lake. It's there. I know it's there. I beg you, Captain, come on with us."

But Hollander had made up his mind. "I've already gambled and lost. I'll gamble no more on water that may not exist. Best of luck to you, Thompson."

The buffalo hunter saw the futility of further argument. "God go with you, Frank."

Hollander nodded. "May He walk with us all." Anger stood like a wall between the men, but each managed to thrust a hand forward. The two groups parted, the hunters toward the hope of Silver Lake and a short trail, the soldiers toward the certainty of Double Lakes, a long and terrible distance away.

The last time Gideon glimpsed the hunters, fading out of sight far to his left, four were walking, the rest hunched on their horses. Though he had not become personally acquainted and could not have named any except Thompson, he felt an ache of regret, a sense of loss as they disappeared into the shimmering heat.

He had no feeling for time. His legs were deadweights that he dragged along, one step and another and another. His vision blurred again. He trudged with his head down, following the tracks of the men in front of him. He no longer thought ahead, or even thought much at all. He fell into a merciful state of half consciousness, moving his body by reflex and instinct. His tongue had swollen so that it almost filled his mouth, and at times he felt he would choke on it.

He was conscious of hunger but unable to act upon it. He put hardtack into his mouth but could not work up saliva to soften it. It was like dry gravel against his inflexible tongue. He had to dig the pieces out with his finger.

Rarely did the horses or mules urinate but, when they did, someone rushed with a cup. The thought was no longer revolting to Gideon. Captain Hollander passed out brown sugar for the men to stir into the urine and increase its palatability. Some was given back to the horses, which at first refused but later accepted it.

By midafternoon, when the heat was at full fury, a horse staggered and went down. Hollander cut its throat to put it out of its misery. Finley came with his cup and caught the gushing blood and drank it, and others took what they could catch before death overtook the animal and the flow stopped. Some of the men became violently ill; the blood was thick and bitter from the horse's dehydration.

Hollander was compelled to call a halt. Men were strung out for half a mile. Orders meant next to nothing. This was no longer a column of soldiers; it was a loose and straggling collection of half-delirious men struggling for individual survival. Gideon saw Nash fall and wanted to go to help him but for a long time could not move his legs. Only when he saw Sergeant Nettles collapse upon the sun-baked sand did he muster the strength to stagger twenty steps and throw blankets over the men's heads to shield them from the sun. He slumped then, too exhausted to do the same for himself. He lapsed into a dreamlike state and seemed to float away like some bodiless spirit, back to the plantation. He heard the happy voice of Big Ella and the others there, and he splashed barefoot into the cool, flowing river.

The heat abated with sundown, and night brought a coolness which broke Gideon's fever. He roused to the point that he could look about him and see the other men lying in grotesque positions, many groaning, half of them suffering from delirium.

He rallied enough to crawl to Sergeant Nettles. At first he could not tell that the man was breathing. He held his hand just above Nettles's mouth and felt that faint but steady warmth of breath. Probably the sergeant was unconscious. Gideon saw no point in trying to bring him out of it. The Lord was being merciful.

Sometime in the night Captain Hollander started trying to get the men on their feet to use the cooler hours for easier miles. Gideon watched him impassively at first, until the man's strong determination began to reach him. Sergeant Nettles arose and began limping from one man to another. Gideon pushed to his feet and helped.

He heard Hollander say thickly, "Good man, Ledbetter. Get them going."

In the moonlight it was apparent that several horses had wandered away. Judas was gone. Gideon could not bring himself to any emotion over that. Half the men were afoot now, their horses strayed or dead. Many of the pack mules were missing. Nettles asked Gideon to count the men, to be sure they left none behind. He found it difficult to hold the figures in his head. His mind kept drifting to other things, other times, other places far better than this one.

Many blankets and packs were left on the ground as the company moved out. A couple of men dropped their carbines, and Gideon forcibly put them back in their hands. A little later he looked back and saw that one of the men was empty-handed again.

He dreaded sunrise, but it came. He sensed that they had walked or ridden many miles in the cool darkness. The heat was blunted the first couple of hours by a thin cover of dry clouds that held no promise of rain. These burned away, after a time, and the men and horses trudged under the full punishment of an unforgiving July sun.

A transient thought flitted through Gideon's mind. He wondered where the Indians were. It struck him as strange that he had gone so long without the Indians intruding on his consciousness. It occurred to him that it had been most of two days since he had heard them mentioned. Odd, that the mission which had brought the soldiers into this blazing hell had been so completely forgotten in the face of a more elemental challenge, simple survival.

A staggering horse brought the procession to a halt. Without waiting for the captain to give an order, one of the troopers cut the animal's throat, and several fought over the gushing blood. Gideon saw Nettles start toward the men to break up the fight, then go to his knees. Gideon took it upon himself to part the fighters, throwing a couple to the ground with more strength than he had realized he still owned. Little Finley's own horse went down on its rump. Finley stared dumbly, making no effort to join the struggle to capture its blood. He lay down on the short, brittle grass and wept silently, his shoulders shuddering.

Through all of it, Nettles sat helplessly. The spirit was still strong in his black eyes, but the flesh had gone as far as it could. Gideon managed to get the men under some semblance of control, making gruff noises deep in his throat because he could not force his tongue to form clear words. He felt the eyes of Hollander and Nettles upon him. Without being formally bidden to do so, he took command upon himself and motioned and coaxed and bullied most of the men into movement. Lieutenant Judson, weaving a little, got on his droop-headed horse and took the lead.

Soon only five men were left, Gideon and Hollander on their feet, the sunstruck Nash and shattered little Finley lying on the ground, Sergeant Nettles sitting up but unable to keep his legs under him.

By signs more than by words, Nettles conveyed his intention of staying with Nash and Finley until they were able to move. Then he would bring them on, following the company's trail to water. Captain Hollander nodded his assent, though Gideon saw sadness in the man's blue eyes. Hollander took the big black hand in both of his own and squeezed it for a moment, silently saying good-bye to an old friend. Hollander turned away quickly, not looking back. Nettles raised his hand again, and Gideon took it.

The sergeant mumbled, but Gideon made out the words he was trying to say. "Take care of them, soldier."

Gideon tried to assure him he would be back as soon as they found water, but the words would not come. He turned back only once, a hundred yards away, and took a final look at the sergeant, still sitting up, holding the reins of big, black Napoleon. For a moment, in spite of the heat, Gideon felt cold.

The column moved until upwards of midday, when the heat brought more horses to their knees, and more of the men. By this time the company was out of control. Now and then a man in delirium struck out on a tangent of his own, away from the main body. At first Gideon tried to bring them back but soon had to give up, for the effort was a drain on whatever strength he still held in reserve. He stopped thinking ahead but concentrated on bringing one foot in front of the other.

When Lieutenant Judson went down, slipping from the saddle and landing limply in the dry grass, the column stopped. The lieutenant's horse braced its legs and stood trembling. It no longer sweated, though a crust of dried mud clung to its hide. Hollander tried to rouse Judson but could not. Hollander gave a little cry and slumped to the ground, covering his face with his hands. By instinct more than reason, Gideon helped him to a small mesquite and threw a blanket over it to shade him, and to shield the captain's emotions from view of the men. The lieutenant's horse, untethered, began wandering off southward, dragging the reins, drawn by instinct in the direction of Concho. Gideon knew he should make some effort to bring it back, but he lacked the willpower to move. He sat with his legs stretched out before him on the ground and watched the horse stumble away to a slow death somewhere out there on the parched prairie.

After a time, Gideon became aware that the captain was trying to call him. Hollander motioned with his hand. Gideon crawled to the officer on hands and knees.

Hollander extended his silver watch, despair in his sunken eyes. Very slowly, very deliberately, he managed a few dear words. "Wife. Give to my wife and baby."

Gideon reached for the watch until the import of the captain's words penetrated his fevered brain. Hollander was giving up. Gideon looked slowly around him at the men sprawled on the ground, covering their heads with blankets if they still had them, hats if they did not.

If Hollander died, these men would die. Hollander might be no better man than they, but his was the leadership. His was the example they had been conditioned to follow, as they had been conditioned all their lives to follow one white man or another. It came to Gideon that if he accepted the watch, that would release the captain to die in peace.

He felt a flare of deep anger. The captain had no right to die! He had brought these men here; he had to live and take them out. Gideon drew back his hand. Shaking his head, he tried to form words first in his mind, then get them out on his dry, swollen tongue.

"No! You'll live. *You* give it to her."

The captain reached out with both hands, the silver chain dangling. His eyes begged, though his cracked lips formed no discernible words.

Gideon almost gave in to pity, but the anger was still hot in his face. Stubbornly he pulled back. The words came clearly in his mind, though he could not get his tongue to speak them.

You got a baby now, more than likely. You owe that woman, and you owe that baby, and you owe us! You goin' to live if I got to kill you!

Only the anger came out, not the words. But the captain seemed to understand that Gideon refused to release him from his responsibilities. Hollander turned his head away, in the shadow beneath the blanket. He clutched the silver watch against his chest, his shoulders heaving.

In a while he was somehow on his feet again. He motioned for Gideon to help him lift the delirious lieutenant onto the captain's own horse. Gideon tied the young officer in the saddle. Hollander struck out again southeastward, his steps slow and deliberate. He was setting a pace, an example. His shoulders had a determined set. Gideon sensed that the captain would not give up again. He might die, but he would not surrender.

Gideon had trouble distinguishing reality from hallucination. His head roared from fever, and it ached with a steady rhythm like a drumbeat. He imagined he could hear the post band playing a parade-ground march, and he tried in vain to bring his feet into step with it. His vision was distorted, the men stretched out of shape, the prairie rolling in waves. Cajoling, threatening, he got the men to their feet one by one and set them to following the captain. Some moved willingly, some fought him, but by and by he had them all on the move.

Stumbling, bringing up the rear so no one could drop out without his knowledge, Gideon moved in a trance. It occurred to him that a couple of the pack mules had strayed off on their own. Only two were left.

Each time a horse staggered and fell, its throat was cut, and the men caught the blood and gagged it down. The captain's horse gave up after a long time, going to its knees. Gideon struggled to untie the lieutenant but could not bring his unresponsive fingers to the task. He cut the rope and tried to ease the officer to the ground. He lacked the strength to hold him. He and the lieutenant fell together in a heap. Gideon looked up at the horse, afraid it might roll over on them. He dragged himself and the lieutenant away before someone cut the animal's throat.

That was the last of the horses.

He lay struggling for breath; the exertion had been severe. The men were like gaunt scarecrow figures out of a nightmare, their uniforms a dusty gray instead of blue, many hanging in strips and ribbons. The faces were stubbled, the beards matted grotesquely with dust and horses' blood as well as some of their own, for their lips were swollen out of shape and had cracked and bled. They no longer looked like soldiers, they looked like madmen—and Gideon feared he was the maddest of them all.

The packs were untied from the mules, and Lieutenant Judson was lifted aboard one of the last two surviving animals. Again Gideon tried to tie him on, but he could not coordinate his hands and gave up the task. Delirious or not, Judson would have to retain instinct enough to hold himself on the mule.

The ragged column plodded and staggered and crawled until far into the afternoon. Hollander motioned for a rest stop in an open plain that lacked even the low-growing dune mesquites over which a blanket could be stretched for shade. Hardly a blanket was left anyway. The men had dropped them one by one, along with everything else they had carried. Troopers sprawled on the ground, faces down to shield them from the sun. Gideon fell into a state more stupor than sleep. After a time, he felt someone shaking his shoulder. Hollander was motioning for him to get up, and to get the other men up. Gideon went about the task woodenly. He helped Hollander and one of the other troopers lift the lieutenant back onto the mule.

Gideon saw that Hollander was studying the other mule, which had remained riderless. The wish was plain in the officer's eyes, but Gideon saw there a reluctance, too. They were no longer officers and men; they were simply men, all in a desperate situation together. Hollander was uncertain about using the advantage that might save his life.

Gideon felt a sudden temptation to take the mule himself. He had the strength to do it. At this moment, he was probably the strongest man in the column. Nobody—not even Hollander—could stop him if he made up his mind.

The thought became action to the point that he laid his hands on the reins, and on the mule's roached mane. He leaned against the mule, trying to summon strength to pull himself up. But he could not, and he realized slowly that it was more than simply a matter of strength. It was also a matter of will. Sergeant Esau Nettles forcibly pushed himself into Gideon's mind. In Nettles's eyes, such a thing would be a dishonor upon Gideon and upon the company.

Gideon cried out for Nettles to leave him alone, but in his mind he could see the sergeant's angry eyes burning like fire, and their heat seemed to touch him and force him back from the mule.

Gideon motioned for Hollander to take the mule. Somehow his tongue managed the words. "Ride him. Sir."

He had not been willing to give Hollander release to die, but now he offered him release to live. Hollander stared at him with remorseful eyes. With Gideon's help, he got onto the mule's back. He reached down and took up the reins to lead the mule on which the lieutenant had been placed.

A momentary wildness widened Hollander's eyes. The thought behind it was too clear to miss: with these mules the white men could leave the black soldiers behind and save themselves.

Reading that temptation, Gideon stared helplessly, his mouth hanging open. He knew he could not fairly blame

Hollander, for he had almost yielded to the same temptation. One pleading word shaped itself into voice. "Captain . . . ."

The wildness passed. Hollander had put aside the thought. He pointed with his chin and motioned for Gideon and the others to follow. They moved off into the dusk, toward a horizon as barren as the one behind them. But the waning of the day's heat brought a rebirth of strength. Gideon kept bringing his legs forward, one short step at a time.

Darkness came. He knew men had dropped out, but he could do nothing any more to help them. He followed the cloudiest notion of time, but somewhere, probably past midnight, he heard a cry from Hollander. Fear clutched at him—fear that Hollander was stricken. Gideon forced his legs to move faster, bringing him up to the mules. He stumbled over an unexpected rut in the prairie, and he went heavily to his hands and knees.

Hollander was making a strange sound—half laugh, half cry. He pointed at the ground. "Trail," he managed. "Trail."

Gideon felt around with his hands in soft sand, trying to find solid ground to help him push back to his feet. Slowly he understood what Hollander was trying to say. He had stumbled into a trail—a rut cut by wagon wheels.

"Shafter," Hollander said plainly. "Shafter's trail."

Shafter. Of course. Colonel Shafter had been all over this country the year before, exploring it in a wetter, more amenable season. These ruts had been cut by his long train of supply wagons.

Lieutenant Judson seemed more dead than alive, responding not at all to Hollander's excitement, or to Gideon's.

Hollander pointed down the trail. "Double Lakes. Come on."

Gideon felt as if he were being stabbed by a thousand sharp needles. Strength pumped into his legs. He struggled to his feet and found voice. "Water, boys. Water, yonderway!"

The men quickened their steps, some laughing madly, some crying without tears. Gideon stood at the trail in the bold moonlight, pointing the troopers after the officers and the mules as they passed him, one by one. When the last had gone—the last one he could see—he turned and followed.

The mules moved out farther and farther ahead of the men afoot, and after a long time Gideon thought he heard them strike a trot. It was probably in his mind, for surely they no longer had that much strength. Unless they had smelled water . . . .

That was it, the mules knew water lay ahead. His legs moved faster, easier, because now they were moving toward life, not death.

It might have been one mile or it might have been five. He had walked in a half-world much of the time and had little conception of anything except his revived hope. But suddenly there it was straight in front of him, the broad dust-covered expanse of the dry playa lake, and the moon shining on water that had seeped into the holes the men had dug in another time that seemed as long ago as slavery. The soldiers who had reached there ahead of him lay on their bellies, their heads half buried in the water. Captain Hollander was walking unsteadily around them, using all his strength to pull some men back lest they faint and drown themselves.

"Not too much," he kept saying thickly. "Drink slowly. Drink slowly."

Gideon had no time for reason. He flung himself onto his stomach and dropped his face into the water. The shock was unexpected. He felt his head spinning. He was strangling. Hands grabbed him and dragged him back.

"Easy now. Easy."

He tried to scramble to the water again, even as he choked and gagged, but the hands held him. "Slow, damn it. Slow." The voice was Hollander's.

He lapsed into unconsciousness. It might have lasted a minute, or it could have been much longer. When he came out of it, he was hardly able to raise his head. The terrible thirst returned to him, but this time he realized he had to keep his reason. He pulled himself to the edge of the water and scooped it up in his hands. He realized that if he fell unconscious again it must be on the dry ground, lest he drown before anyone could respond.

The water still had an alkali bite, but that was no longer a detriment. Gideon had never known water so sweet. He rationed himself, drinking a few sips, waiting, then drinking again, always from his cupped hand. He became aware that some men had slid into the water and were splashing around in it with all the joy of unleashed children. That this compromised sanitation never entered his mind; he kept drinking a few swallows at a time. Almost at once, it seemed, his tongue began to shrink. He thought of words, and they began to pass his lips in creditable fashion. "Praise Jesus! Bless the name of Jesus!"

Finally, when he came to a full realization that he would not die, he lay down and wept silently, no tears in his eyes.

There was no guard duty, unless Hollander stood it himself. Occasionally the thirst came upon Gideon with all its furious insistence, and he drank. When finally he came fully awake, the sun was shining warmly in his face. Gradually he heard stirrings, men going to the water or from it. He pushed to his knees, blinking in surprise at a bright sun an hour or more high.

His eyes focused on Captain Hollander, sitting up and staring back. Hollander's face was haggard, his eyes still sunken. But he was an officer again. "Ledbetter, let's see if you can walk."

It took Gideon a minute to get his legs unwound and properly set beneath him. But finally he was standing, swaying. He took a few steps.

"Ledbetter," Hollander said, "I need a noncom. I want you to regard yourself as a corporal."

"And give orders?" Gideon was stunned. "I ain't never led nobody. I been a slave for most of my life."

"So was Sergeant Nettles."

"I sure ain't no Nettles."

"Most of us would still be out there in that hell if it hadn't been for you. Perhaps all of us. Like it or not, you're a corporal." He dismissed further argument. "We left some men behind us. I want you to pick a couple or three of the strongest, fill what canteens we have left and go back. Take a mule." He pointed his chin at Lieutenant Judson. "The lieutenant will ride the other to the base camp and bring up wagons and supplies. I'll send a wagon on after you."

Gideon sought out three men he thought had regained strength enough to walk. Almost everything had been discarded along the way, so they had nothing to eat except a little hardtack. The men drank all the water they could comfortably absorb so they would not have to drain the canteens later. Those would be needed for whatever men they found along the trail. Looping the canteens over the mule, he set out walking, his step improving as he went along. His mind was reasonably clear, and he began mentally upbraiding himself for not counting the men at the lake before he left. He didn't know, really, how many were still out. His memory of yesterday's ordeal was hazy at best. Men had dropped by the wayside—he could remember that—but he could not remember who or how many.

The rescue party came in time to a Mississippian named Kersey, lying in yesterday's blown-out tracks. It took a while to revive him, and then he clutched desperately at the canteen, fighting when anyone tried to pull it away for his own good. Gideon asked if he knew who else might be behind him, but the man could only shake his head. He could not speak.

Gideon left one of his three men with Kersey and set out walking again, northwestward. Before long his legs began to tremble, and he knew he was approaching his limit. He and the other two looked at each other and reached silent agreement. They dropped to rest, the sun hot upon their backs.

By night they had found just one more man. Gideon had managed to shoot a couple of rabbits, and the men shared those, half cooked over a small fire before sundown. They smothered the fire and walked on for a time to get away from the glow, in case it might attract Indians.

All day he had watched the unstable horizon, hoping to see Esau Nettles and Nash and Finley riding toward them. Now and again a distant shape would arise, only to prove itself false as the heat waves shifted and the mirages changed. His hopes ebbed with his strength.

Night gave him time to brood about Jimbo. He could visualize Jimbo and the men who had gone with him, following the trail of the lost guide until one by one they fell. Jimbo would have been the last, Gideon fancied, and he probably had not given up hope until he had made the last step that his legs would take.

More men had dropped out than Gideon had found. The others had probably wandered off in one direction or another. Some might find the lakes for themselves. The others . . . . He slept fitfully and dreamed a lot, reliving at times his own agony, seeing at others Jimbo or Esau Nettles, dying alone in that great waste of sand and burned short grass.

They moved again in the coolness of dawn, but the men had less of hope now to buoy them along. Though no one spoke his doubts, they were clear in every man's eyes.

The wagon came as Hollander had promised. The other men stayed behind to leave the load light. Gideon got aboard as guide. The driver and his helper had not been on the dry march. They could only follow the tracks, the trail of abandoned equipment, the swelling bodies of horses that had died one by one along the way. Riding silently on the spring seat as the wagon bounced roughly over dry bunchgrass and shinnery, Gideon drew into a shell, steeling himself for what he had become convinced he would find at the end of the trip.

It was as he had expected, almost. They found little Finley first. To Gideon's amazement, he was still alive. He fought like a wildcat for the canteen Gideon held to his ruined lips. Gideon was unable to keep him from drinking too much at first, and for a while he thought Finley might die from overfilling with the alkali-tainted water.

Like a candle flame flickering before it dies, Gideon's hopes revived briefly. Perhaps finding Finley alive was a good omen.

The hopes were soon crushed. They found black Napoleon, dead. As an act of mercy, Nettles had taken off the saddle and bridle and turned the horse loose on the chance it could save itself. The gesture came too late. Soon Gideon found Esau Nettles and the young trooper Nash lying beneath a blanket spread for shade over a patch of shin oak. Even before he lifted the blanket, Gideon knew with a shuddering certainty. They were dead. He dropped in the sand beside them, drew up his knees and covered his face in his arms.

In the wagon he could hear little Finley whimpering, out of his head. Anger struck at Gideon, sharp, painful and futile. For a moment the anger was against Finley, a liar, a sneak thief, a coward. Why should he live when a man like Esau Nettles had died? For a moment, Gideon's anger turned upon God. Then he realized with dismay that he was railing against the faith drilled into him since boyhood, a faith he had never questioned in his life. The anger exhausted itself. Only the sorrow remained, deep and wounding.

The trip back to the Double Lakes was slow and silent. Little Finley regained mind enough to be afraid of the two bodies and to move as far from them as possible without climbing out of the wagon. "They're dead," he mumbled once. "Why don't we leave them?"

Gideon chose not to dignify the question by answering it. His contempt for Finley sank deeper into his soul. He made up his mind that he would do whatever he could to force the little man out of this outfit, if not out of the army. He wanted to blame Finley for Nettles's death, though he knew this was not totally valid. Perhaps Nettles had realized he would never make it to the Double Lakes on that bad hip. Perhaps he had stayed behind with Nash and Finley so someone else later would not have to stay behind with him. The more Gideon pondered that possibility, the more he wanted to believe it; it gave reason to Nettles's death, even nobility.

As the wagon went along, it picked up the men who had stayed behind. Most had walked some distance in the direction of the lakes rather than wait to be hauled all the way. All looked in brooding silence at the blanket-covered bodies. Those exhausted climbed into the wagon beside them. Those who could walk continued to do so. Gideon got down and joined them, for he was feeling stronger. The exertion of walking helped the black mood lift itself from him.

Captain Hollander met the wagon as it pulled up to the edge of the lake. Gideon stared, surprised. The captain had shaved and washed out his uniform. It was wrinkled but passably clean, within the limitations of the gyppy water. Army routine had again prevailed over the challenge of the elements.

Hollander counted the men who walked and who climbed out of the wagon. He asked no unnecessary questions. He seemed to read the answers in Gideon's face. He lifted the blanket and looked at the bodies, his face tightening with a sadness he did not try to put into words. "We had better bury them here. This weather . . . ."

The digging was left to men who had come up from the supply camp, for they had the strength. Hollander had brought no Bible to read from, an oversight some might regard as indicative of the reasons for the company's travail. The captain improvised a long prayer asking God's blessings upon these men, these devoted servants of their country and their Lord, and upon any others like them who had met death alone on that hostile prairie, unseen except by God's own messengers come to lead them to a better land.

Three more men had wandered into camp during Gideon's absence, men who had lost the trail but somehow retained enough sense of direction to find the lakes. Toward dusk Gideon heard a stir and looked where some of the men were pointing, northward. He saw horsemen coming. His first thought was Indians. But soon he could tell these were soldiers. And the man in the lead was unmistakable.

Jimbo!

Jimbo spurred into a long trot, and Gideon strode forward to meet him. Jimbo jumped to the ground, and the two men hugged each other, laughing and crying at the same time.

In camp, when all the howdies were said and the reunions had lost their initial glow, Jimbo explained that the guide, José, had missed the Silver Lake he was trying to find and had come instead, somewhat later than he expected, to a set of springs just off Yellow House Cañon. Jimbo and the soldiers who followed had stayed at the springs long enough to recoup their own strength and that of their horses. Some had remained there with the buffalo hunters who straggled in, but Jimbo and three others had filled canteens and set out along their backtrail to carry water to the column they expected to find somewhere behind them. Hollander's decision to strike out for Double Lakes had thwarted them. They marched much farther than they intended and found no one. Fearing that the rest of the company had died, they had returned heavy-hearted to the springs, rested a while, then set out to find Double Lakes and the base camp below.

Captain Hollander's face twisted in remorse as he

listened. The hunters had been right; if he had followed them his troops would have reached water sooner than they did. Perhaps Esau Nettles and Private Nash would not be dead; perhaps others would not still be missing.

Lieutenant Judson tried to reassure him. "You used your best judgment based on the facts at hand, Frank. You knew this water was here. You couldn't know there was water where the hunters wanted to go. They were just guessing. What if they had been wrong? You had the responsibility for all these men. Those hunters could gamble. You could not."

Gideon knew Judson was right, as Hollander had been. But he could see the doubt settling into the captain's eyes. As long as Hollander lived, it would be there, the questions coming upon him suddenly in the darkness of a sleepless night, in the midst of his pondering upon other decisions he would be called upon to make in the future. To the end of his life, Hollander would be haunted by Esau Nettles and the others, and the unanswered question: did it have to be? Gideon looked at him. It was one of the few times in his life he had ever genuinely pitied a white man.

Gideon wrestled awhile with his doubts, then approached the captain hesitantly. "Sir . . . ." He took off his hat and abused it fearfully in his nervous hands. "Sir, you done right. Old Sergeant, he'd of said so hisself, if he could. He'd of said you *always* done right."

Hollander stared at the ground a long time before he looked up at Gideon. "Thank you, Ledbetter. There's not a man I'd rather hear that from than you . . . and *him.*"

Early on the fifth day, having sent out search parties and having given up hope that any stragglers still out would ever turn up alive, Hollander ordered the company to march southward to the supply camp. Water there was better, and timber along the creek would provide shade. The trip was slow and hot and dry, and Gideon found himself skirting along the edge of fear as terrible memories forced themselves upon him.

Late on the afternoon of the sixth day, a column of mounted men and two army ambulances broke through a veil of dust out of the south. A rider loped ahead of the column, pulling up in the edge of camp. He was the civilian scout, Pat Maloney, from the village of Ben Ficklin. He whooped in delight as he saw Captain Hollander and Lieutenant Judson standing beside a wagon.

"Frank Hollander! Dammit, man, we thought you were dead!"

He pumped Hollander's hand excitedly, but that was not enough. The ex-Confederate gripped the Union officer's arms and shook him in a violence of joy. "Tell you the God's truth, Frank, we come to hunt for your body. We thought every man jack of you had died."

His gaze swept the camp. Gideon felt the scout's eyes stop momentarily on him and Jimbo, lighting with pleasure at the sight of them.

Hollander replied gravely, "A few of us *are* dead. The best of us, perhaps."

Maloney looked around a second time, his face going grim as he missed Nettles. "The old sergeant?"

Hollander looked at the ground. "We buried him."

Maloney was silent a moment. "We thought from what we heard that we would have to bury you all!" He explained that Sergeant Waters had somehow made it back to Fort Concho, with two others. They had brought a report that Captain Hollander and all his men had been led astray by Indians on that great hostile plain, that they and all those buffalo hunters were dying from heat and thirst. They were certain, Waters reported, that no one except themselves had survived.

Maloney pointed to the approaching column. "You can imagine how that news tore up the post at Concho."

Apprehension struck Hollander. "My wife . . . Adeline. She heard that?"

"Everybody heard it."

"She must be half out of her mind. This, and the baby coming . . . . We'll have to send word back right away."

Maloney smiled. "You know I got me a new baby boy, Frank?"

Hollander seemed not quite to hear him. "That's good, Pat. Glad to hear it." But his mind was clearly elsewhere.

Maloney said, "Who knows? He may grow up to marry that little girl *your* wife had. Join the North and South together again, so to speak."

Hollander's eyes widened. He had heard *that*. "A girl, you say? You've seen it?"

"Went by there last thing before I left the post. She looks like her mother. Damn lucky thing, too, because her papa looks like hell."

The trip back to Fort Concho was made slowly and carefully, for more men were afoot than on horseback, and none had completely regained strength. At times even the civilian Maloney would step down from his horse and walk a while, letting some tired black trooper ride.

Messengers had carried the news of their approach ahead of them, so that most of the people of Saint Angelo were lined up to watch the arrival of men who had come back from the dead. An escort and fresh horses were sent out from the post. Hollander and

Judson and Maloney rode at the head of the column. Gideon was behind them, urging the men to sit straight and look like soldiers that Esau Nettles would have wanted to claim.

Ordinarily they would not have ridden down the street, but this was an occasion, and the escort wanted to show them off. Lined along Concho Avenue were civilians of all ages, sizes, and colors, white to brown to black. Most cheered the soldiers as they passed, though Gideon looked into some eyes and found there the same hostility he had always seen. Nothing, not even the ordeal the soldiers had been through, had changed that. Nothing ever would.

Two-thirds of the way down to Oakes Street, a seedy, bearded man leaned against a post that held up the narrow porch of a new but already-dingy little saloon. As Hollander came abreast of him the man shouted, "Say, Captain, why didn't you do us all a favor and leave the rest of them damned niggers out there?"

Hollander stiffened. He turned in the saddle, rage bursting into his face. He freed his right foot from the stirrup and started to dismount. Maloney caught his arm. "Frank, you ain't got your strength back."

Maloney swung slowly and casually to the ground, handed his reins to Gideon and walked up to the man with a dry and dangerous smile set like concrete. He crouched, and when his fist came up it was like a sledge. The man's head snapped back, then his whole body followed. He slid across the little porch, winding up half in and half out of the open front door.

Maloney looked first to one side, then the other, challenging one and all. Nobody took up his challenge. He reached down for the struggling man.

"Here, friend, let me help you up."

278

When the man was on his feet, Maloney hit him again, knocking him through the door and into the saloon. With a wink, he took his reins from Gideon's hand, swung back into the saddle and gave the silent Hollander a nod.

"You're welcome," he said.

T.V. OLSEN

THEODORE VICTOR OLSEN (1932-1993) was born in Rhinelander, Wisconsin, and continued to live in the area all his life as had Olsens in his family since his paternal grandfather emigrated there from Norway in 1890. Growing up, Olsen felt he labored under a considerable handicap in that he was creative, a loner, and an individualist with a dislike for taking orders. Those were once all excellent reasons to head out into the territories. In Olsen's case, they prompted him to turn his literary attention to the frontier. He discovered Luke Short the year between high school and college. He felt that while Ernest Haycox "was a matchless stylist" that his characters "with their distant, Homeric quality seemed less than human to me. Short's less intrusive prose, his warm treatment of characters as people, his attention to small details in their behavior, made for greater reader involvement . . . ." He discovered Les Savage, Jr., and Elmore Leonard in the pages of *Zane Grey's Western Magazine* and he read Walter Van Tilburg Clark's **The Ox-Bow Incident**.

Olsen was graduated from Central State College at Stevens Point, later part of the University of Wisconsin system, in 1955 with a Bachelor's degree. He had begun his own Western novel in 1953 and, once he had completed it, he sent it together with a reading fee of $35 to the August Lenniger Literary Agency. He titled it **Valley of the Hunted**. Six months later he heard from John Burr, the last editor of *Western Story* then working for Lenniger, that if he was willing to cut the novel by 15,000 words Doro Stiles, an editor at Ace Books, was interested in purchasing it. The advance was $1,000 and the next year it was published under the title **Haven of the Hunted** (Ace, 1956). This first novel, while indebted somewhat to Luke Short, is perhaps even more indebted to Savage and Clark for the complexity of its psychological motivations and the interactions of its characters.

It was apparently not easy for him to follow this novel with another and so, for the next two years beginning with "Backtrail" in *Ranch Romances* (1st April 56), Olsen turned to the Western short story. His success in the shorter form was at once evident since "Backtrail" was purchased for $3,000 by "Dick Powell's Zane Grey Theatre" and was televised in the spring of 1957 with Powell in the leading role.

By late 1957, Olsen turned again to the novel with a story he titled **The Kid From Nowhere**. Some revision was required by Doro Stiles but in the end it was accepted for publication as **The Man From Nowhere** (Ace, 1959). By the time this novel was published, August Lenniger took Olsen on as a personal client. Olsen wrote a new Western titled **Day of the Vulture** which Lenniger sold to Fawcett for an advance of $2,000 and it was published as **McGivern** (Fawcett Gold Medal, 1960). **High Lawless** (Fawcett Gold Medal, 1960) followed along with **Gunswift** (Fawcett Gold Medal, 1960) and **Ramrod Rider** (Fawcett Gold Medal, 1961). All had been written in 1960 and, from starting the year almost flat broke, Olsen finished it with a total of $8,000 in advances.

In an article titled "What Do Americans Want in Westerns?" in *The Roundup* (2/62), Olsen entered the controversy then at issue among members of the Western Writers of America between the traditional

Western and the off-trail Western. In describing what he felt the proper direction for the Western story, he also summed up the significance of his own tremendous contribution to what would become increasingly the direction of his own fiction: " . . . a commercial Western fictioneer of today would do well to regard each book as a new creative challenge in development of plot and situation and highly varied characterization, with mature and intelligent concepts of theme and treatment—but strive simultaneously to recapitulate more truly the traditional elements that have made the Western beloved of Americans: the historical feel of the place and the people and the times, the sense of freedom, of a wild and wide-open land, sex presented more honestly but still not sensationally, tough-minded men who did what they damned well had to and never mind about Mr. Jones, a swift, close-knit pace carried by lots of fast-moving action, and the decisive triumph of good over evil by a protagonist who can make mistakes and commit an occasional wrong because he is understandably human."

What in effect Olsen was accomplishing at the time in his own Western fiction was to remove the Western story from the idealized models which harked back to Greek drama and the epic poems of Homer and Vergil and to populate his stories with realistic human beings who, notwithstanding, are caught in the same web of moral questions as found in Classical precursors—is this right? is this wrong? how ought one live? what is most important in life? So-called main-stream fiction had long abandoned any pretense it had ever had at addressing such questions but Olsen, with other Western writers of his generation including Elmer Kelton, Brian Garfield, Noel M. Loomis, and Robert MacLeod, was asking them in a stronger voice than ever before, following the trail Les Savage, Jr., had blazed in which the focus increasingly is turned toward psychological motivations directly related to the historical events and circumstances and personalities of the period and place where the story is set.

It would be as Theodore V. Olsen that he would publish what to that point would prove his most successful novel, *The Stalking Moon* (Doubleday, 1965). It had occurred to Olsen in a flash of inspiration to combine the notion of a killer stalking a helpless family with a real-life Apache Indian who had had a penchant for killing Mexicans. At the WWA convention in Portland, Oregon, in 1964, Olsen was dismayed to hear from Harold Kuebler of Doubleday that he was thinking of rejecting the novel on the basis of the outline he had been provided. Author and editor thrashed out reservations on the spot and Olsen's proposals for a revision of the plot were accepted at once. Doubleday's marketing department was so impressed with the novel that, rather than issue it in the Double D library line, the decision was made to bring it out in a general trade edition. Several motion picture producing companies expressed an interest in the novel and it was finally sold to National General where it was produced starring Gregory Peck and Eve Marie Saint. In *The Stalking Moon*, as so often on the frontier, despite the savagery of the struggle to survive, there does emerge from the long battle a fundamental human decency that extends beyond any thought of racial or cultural or ethnic differences, beyond even any notion of civilization. It is this same theme which preoccupies another of Olsen's finest novels, *Blizzard Pass* (Fawcett, 1968). Yet in this story it is welded to a cognizance that human evil is a reality that must not be denied. Though limited in number, each of the cast of characters in this novel is etched so deeply and developed so poignantly that the narrative has an incredible depth. It has recently been reprinted in a hard cover edition in the Gunsmoke series by Chivers Press.

Beginning with *McGivern*, Olsen's novels have the same sort of visceral, wrenching involvement found in *The Stalking Moon* and *Blizzard Pass*. Once past the first chapter, it is nearly impossible to put them down. They are stories that work on two levels: the gnawing question of what will happen next combined with a profound emotional involvement with characters about whom a reader comes to care deeply. The events may be those of an action/adventure narrative but the characters provide such a rich texture to the stories that they carry forward the plot as readily as do the events. Above all, in common with Euripides, the universe of T.V. Olsen's West is one in which reason does not prevail and therefore all that happens is unpredictable, as it is also in life. All that remains to Olsen's battered and struggling protagonists, male and female alike, is their commitment to decency, to loyalty, to friendship, in a word to each other. The losses are great and irretrievable but the ordeals form a school for character that alone becomes decisive in an individual's life even if, as sometimes happens, he loses it.

There are no two characters alike in any Olsen story even if they have undergone similar experiences. Sara Carver in *The Stalking Moon* is one kind of American woman who survived Indian captivity. Miss Cresta Lee in *Arrow in the Sun* (Doubleday, 1969) is a wholly different case. She is made of such stern stuff that living with an alcoholic father who abandoned her at eight to an orphanage did not daunt her any more than the two years of captivity she spent with the Cheyenne Indians as the wife of war chief, Spotted Wolf. She may not be a good shot with a pistol or a rifle, but she is clever and determined and manages, finally, to elude her Cheyenne captors. It was Ralph Nelson, director of the film version under the title **Soldier Blue** (Avco-Embassy, 1970), who decided to append to this story a slaughter of helpless Indian women and children similar to the Sand Creek massacre. Olsen knew his history of the Indian wars too well, and had too much respect for the Indian nations that were once at war with the United States, to depict them repeatedly as helpless victims of a genocidal holocaust which, for the Vietnam War-era political activist, was found embodied in Dee Brown's **Bury My Heart at Wounded Knee** (Holt, Rinehart, 1971), a popular account albeit with an equivalent slant to the kind of history of Rome Spartacus might have written.

For five years Olsen researched and wrote his first major historical novel, **There Was a Season** (Doubleday, 1971), concerned with the young Jefferson Davis during the years 1828-1833 when he was a young Army lieutenant on the Wisconsin frontier and Davis's bittersweet love affair with Sarah Knox Taylor, daughter of Zachary Taylor, later hero of the Mexican War and President of the United States. Ted regarded it as his *magnum opus*. It was finally published in a paperback edition in 1994 by Leisure Books which has been systematically reprinting all of T.V. Olsen's novels.

As he continued to write Western stories, Olsen's horizons continued to broaden. Increasingly his male protagonists and female protagonists could only succeed when they pulled together, varying strengths in the one compensating for weaknesses in the other. He also opened the Western story to spiritual dimensions that have traditionally been shunned. The Navajo shaman, Adakhai—the character's name was borrowed from Savage's **Land of the Lawless** (Doubleday, 1951)—in **The Golden Chance** (Fawcett Gold Medal, 1992) is in touch with the spirits who rule the world. In **Deadly Pursuit** (Five Star, 1995) Adakhai is able to conjure visions both from the past and the future. As early as "The Strange Valley" in **Great Ghost Stories of the Old West** (Four Winds, 1968) edited by Betty Baker, Olsen began injecting elements of a meta-physical, meta-temporal, and supernatural nature into his fiction. They are surely to be found in "Jacob's Journal."

Ted Olsen and I were friends for twenty years. It was he who first introduced me to Les Savage, Jr.'s Western fiction. For his last years, I was his agent. In fact, while Les was my first estate client, Ted was my first living client. His sudden and unexpected death from myocardial infarction in 1993 was a devastating blow to me that has yet completely to heal. I found among his papers in the little cottage where he did his writing four unpublished novels in long-hand and four unpublished short stories. So even if death claimed him too early, new Olsen stories will remain forthcoming into the new century. Bill Pronzini had suggested to Ted that there should be another collection of his short fiction. The previous one was **Westward They Rode** (Ace, 1976). It is due to this suggestion that Ted took time between novels to write the story that follows. It was first published posthumously in *Louis L'Amour Western Magazine* (11/94) and will eventually be the title story in an Olsen short Western fiction collection (there are sufficient stories for two more such book-length collections).

"... Olsen is an efficient and compelling storyteller who more often than not uses his skill to touch on serious themes," Joe R. Lansdale concluded in **Twentieth Century Western Writers** (St. James Press, 1991). "... I can not but feel with the right press Olsen could command the position currently enjoyed by the late Louis L'Amour as America's most popular and foremost author of traditional Western novels." Yet, even having said that much, Lansdale may not have gone far enough since "traditional" is not a meaningful adjective when surveying Olsen's contributions to the Western story. He exceeded and went beyond traditional boundaries in almost all that he wrote. In common with such very, very select company as Les Savage, Jr., Bill Gulick, and Lewis B. Patten, Olsen never published a story that is less than very good and most are better than that. Were it not that the Western story has always been classed as category fiction, it would have been possible before this late date to recognize in T.V. Olsen one of the outstanding American literary novelists of the late 20th Century as well as one of the brightest lights in the firmament of the Western story, a man whose modesty and reclusive-ness worked at odds, always, with the wide readership his fiction deserved and will continue to deserve far into the future.

JACOB'S JOURNAL
1994

JUNE 8, 1886
Sarah is dead. I killed her with my own hands and buried her beneath tons of rock. I know she is dead. Yet

this forenoon I saw her . . . alive?

I do not know. But I saw her as clearly as I see the page on which I indite these words.

I was crossing from the commandant's office to the agency house—a longish walk of perhaps two hundred yards—when I became aware of being watched. Turning my head, I saw her. A woman standing on the prickly pear-and-chaparral-covered rise a little south of the agency house.

At first I took only passing note, supposing her to be the wife of one of Fort Bloodworth's officers or enlisted men. But something in the way she stood, absolutely motionless and watching me, as I believed, arrested my attention. Leaving the well-worn path, I started across the intervening hundred or so yards of nearly barren ground toward her.

I was quite close before I recognized her but, when I did, recognition came unmistakably. The sunlight lay full on her face and on the brightness of her red-gold hair.

It was Sarah.

I stopped, petrified with fear and incomprehension. Either I was experiencing an hallucination or I was a victim of some gigantic hoax. But the latter possibility, at least, seemed out of the question. None but I—I was positive—knew the truth behind my wife's sudden disappearance.

Screwing up my courage, I advanced slowly toward her. I was nearly to the rise when my nerve broke utterly and I shouted her name. Screamed it, more than likely.

Until that moment she had neither moved nor changed her expression by a hair's breadth. It was as severe and aloof as—damn her soul!—Sarah had so long been toward me.

Now I saw her smile. A lovely and alluring smile, one such as I had rarely seen on her face during our years together. And while she smiled, she slowly raised an arm and beckoned to me. Then she turned, not hurrying, and walked over the crest of the rise and out of sight.

When I had scrambled to its top, she was nowhere to be seen. She had vanished as if the rocky soil and scant vegetation had swallowed her up. Impossible! When I looked for any tracks which might help solve the riddle, I found nothing, not even the trace of a footprint. Still, the ground was so stony and impervious to ordinary sign that even a skilled tracker might have found nothing. Except . . . .

The fact comes to mind only now. As though, earlier, my mind had rejected the knowing. A hot wind was blowing off the desert, strongly enough to whip particles against my face. The woman on the knoll wore a voluminous dress with a wide skirt, identical to that in which I buried Sarah.

Yet in all the time I saw her, the woman's clothing, the drape of its fabric, was unstirring in the blast of wind. As though the wind could not touch her, could not have its way with her in any particular . . . .

With the last few sentences, the bold sprawl of Jacob Creed's rapid writing turned into a shaky, dashed-off waver. Then the entry suddenly ended.

Major Phineas Casement had been reading slowly aloud from the leather-bound journal he had slipped open at random, pausing often to squint at the words, swearing and muttering. Now he said a disgusted oath, slapped the journal shut, and tossed it on his desk.

"Good God, what a pack of nonsense! Sheer balderdash. The fellow must have been deranged."

"Possibly, sir," said Lieutenant Mayberly. "But every entry he made in that book, if you except this one persistent delusion, has proved out to a detail."

"I'm sure, Mr. Mayberly, I'm sure. That fine probing intellect of yours would do its damnedest to ferret out the whole truth, no matter where it led."

Major Casement reached for the humidor on his desk, extracted a cigar, and offered the humidor to Mayberly with an impatient thrust of his hand. Politely, as Casement had known he would, the lieutenant refused a cigar.

Major Casement pushed his swivel chair back from his desk and rose to his feet, grimacing as the movement peeled his blouse sweatily away from his back and paunch. Arizona Territory—Christ! you'd think that after a dozen years of being stationed at one or another of its raw frontier outposts, a man would be used to the furnace heat of its relentless summers.

He lifted a foot onto the chair, struck a match on the heel of his high cavalry boot, and lighted the cigar, glancing enviously at the younger officer, seated at ease in the room's only other chair.

Mayberly looked as cool as a January thaw. His double-breasted blue miner's blouse and blue trousers, with the yellow cavalry stripe down the outseams, were hardly stained by dust, not at all by sweat. His black, neatly blocked campaign hat rested on the knee of his crossed leg; his dark hair was neatly parted above a sober, cleft-chinned face. The subaltern was only a year out of West Point; Fort Bloodworth was his first assignment. Yet he'd blended into this inhospitable land with the adaptability of a chuckwalla lizard. A leather dispatch case was propped against his chair.

Major Casement swiped a hand over his sweatdewed, nearly bald head, clamped the cigar between his bulldog jaws, and slowly paced his narrow office, up and down. "The fellow was a heavy drinker, I'm told. How much of that *persistent delusion* of his came out of a bottle?"

"There may or may not be a way of telling, sir." Lieutenant Mayberly leaned forward to take Creed's journal from the desk. He flipped backward through the pages. "In any case, the journal entries which are of main concern to us begin at a much earlier date. May I quote from them?"

Major Casement rolled out an irritable plume of smoke.

It would be his duty to write up a full report on the whole unsavory mess to the Secretary of War and file a duplicate report with the U.S. Department of the Interior, since Jacob Creed had been the agent assigned to one of the hellholes they called their Indian reservations. Before doing so, the major would need as thorough a briefing as possible from his ultracompetent aide, Mayberly, whom he'd ordered to investigate the almost simultaneous deaths of Agent Jacob Creed and Colonel Richard Dandridge, Fort Bloodworth's late commandant. Major Casement had been hastily dispatched here to replace Dandridge, and Mayberly had already given the major a sketchy report on his findings.

"By all means, Mr. Mayberly," Casement said sourly. "The damned fellow's hand is so execrable I could scarcely make out the words. Read it aloud, if you please . . . ."

May 17, 1886

Today, after two months at this God-forgotten post, cautiously trying the tempers of the officers at Fort

291

Bloodworth as well as those of the headmen on the adjacent reservation, I made my approach to Colonel Dandridge. Not only is he in the ideal position to abet my scheme, he possesses the requisite qualities to implement it.

Beneath his façade of an efficient and highly regarded career officer (President Lincoln himself bestowed a Medal of Honor on him during the late conflict), Dandridge is a savagely bitter and disillusioned man. This in consequence of his being several times passed over for advancement to a brigadier generalship, due to favoritism toward officers of far lesser qualification who were, nevertheless, politically well situated . . . .

The echo of taps died away in the gray twilight. Lamps winked out as darkness closed over the parade ground of Fort Bloodworth. From the Chiricahua reservation to the south drifted the lone, keening bark of a camp dog.

Jacob Creed had locked up his sutler's post. Standing on the porch, teetering gently back and forth on his heels, feeling mellow as all hell, he took an embossed whiskey flask from his coat pocket, uncapped it and took a small swig.

Creed was a bearded, thick-set man whose coarsened features and bloodshot eyes showed little of his genteel background. His belly was badly burning from the effects of intermittent drinks he'd consumed during a day of haggling with the Apaches who came to trade at his post. By now the damned siwashes should be aware that no one left Jacob Creed on the short end of a trade. Yet they never ceased trying. Born hoss-traders (as well as hoss-stealers) they were. All the bastards were.

Creed chuckled quietly. He treated himself to another

pull at the flask. Things would be different from now on. A hell of a lot different.

As to bartering with him, the Apaches had little choice. Post trader Jacob Creed was also the Indian agent for the San Lazaro Reservation. In addition to his government salary, he received an allowance of federal funds to buy steers from local cattle ranches to furnish the monthly beef ration allotted the reservation Chiricahuas.

Behind the combination trading post and agency headquarters was a cattle corral. An issue chute was set up across the weighing scales adjoining the corral. And the steers were driven through the chute where the head of each family presented his ration ticket, had it stamped, and watched his cattle being weighed.

Colonel Richard Dandridge, as the fort C.O., was required to add his official presence to the weighing-out but, after their conference this morning, that would be a mere formality. Seething with his private bitterness, the aging career officer had been almost eagerly amenable to Creed's proposal.

For the hundredth time, Creed chuckled over the development.

It was simple. So damned simple. From now on he would buy up the poorest of the cull steers the ranches had for less than half the ordinary price, then pocket the balance of allotted moneys. A simple matter, also, to rig the scales so that the sorriest steer would be well within the minimum poundage allowed. One-third of Creed's swindled government funds would keep Colonel Dandridge's bitter-thin mouth silent. And the Apaches, unable to subsist on gaunt, stringy, possibly diseased beef, would be forced to trade at Creed's post for supplies.

Jacob Creed took another mild swig from his flask, capped it, and put it away. He took a step off the porch and damned near fell on his face.

Jesus! Was he that drunk?

Sure he was.

Why had he made the deal with Dandridge? Sold whatever dregs of gentle birthright he could still lay claim to for a mess of conspiratorial pottage?

Then, reflecting on Sarah and the miserable course his life with her had taken, he thought: *Why should I give a solitary shit?*

He straightened upright and lurched homeward along the sandy, thin-worn path to the agency house beyond the fort, considering (as he often did) ways in which he could repay her treatment of him.

Creed grinned crookedly. There was one sure-as-hell way . . . .

Even the most incorruptible man, when all his hopes and ideals have been repeatedly dashed by adverse fortune, may become approachable . . . .

"Damn the fellow's complacency!" Major Casement cut disgustedly into his subordinate's reading. "Did he fancy that *his* reason was any better or different from that of the man he bribed?"

Mayberly raised his brows. "Probably not, sir. I think it was Creed's wry, oblique way of telling himself as much. As I suggested earlier, his difficulty with his wife must have been a powerful goad behind all his actions."

"M'm." Casement rolled the cigar from one side of his mouth to the other. "Powerful enough to drive him to murder. Go on, Mr. Mayberly."

Again the lieutenant flipped back through the pages.

"I think, in the light of subsequent developments, that this entry is a revealing one, sir. It was made on the day Creed arrived with his wife on the stage from Silverton to take over duties at the San Lazaro Agency . . . ."

March 12, 1886

The conditions at our new post are not nearly as desolate as we had feared. The reservation itself is situated at a considerable height above the desert lowland to the south, to which much of the reservation land forms a striking contrast. Numerous stands of giant pine lend a cool and indeed attractive aspect to our new home, although they are interspersed with terraced open flats which, I am told, have defied the sorry efforts of my reservation wards to farm them. As if we could, in a brief decade or so, transform a race of nomadic warriors, barely subdued by us, into tillers of the soil!

The agency house itself is a gratifying surprise to us. I do not know what we expected to dwell in—perhaps an oversized hut of baked adobe. However, the agent who preceded me at this post was James Montoya, a man—I was told—of pure Spanish descent and a true aristocrata. *Clearly he chose to build after the fashion of his* hidalgo *forebears and, with all the splendid pine roundabout, found no need to build of stone or mud.*

The squared giant timbers that compose both the inner and outer walls were hand-shaped by adze and drawknife, fitted so beautifully together that one can hardly slide a knife blade between them, and the tiers of logs are fastened at all ends and corners with vertical iron rods. It must have cost him a pretty penny to import the highly skilled labor necessary to put up such an edifice. Most of the furnishings went with Montoya when he departed, but what remains indicates that they were opulent and costly. I was told, however, that his people have money. Of course the raw timber was free for the taking, and the rough labor (Indians and mestizos, no doubt) to cut the trees and trim the logs and transport them to the spot could be hired cheaply.

Salud, Don Jaime: *Your family must have been a large one. (As is more often the case than not, of course, with these Papists.) There are no less than a dozen spacious rooms, including six chambers on the second floor, three to a side with a hallway dividing them. Of particular interest are the two wide central balconies with their iron-wrought grillwork railings. Built off the center rooms on either second-story side of the house, one faces north, the other south. Thus, I should imagine, an occupant might enjoy sun or shade on almost any day, according to his preference.*

Even Sarah seems delighted with the house and its piney surroundings, and she is particularly taken with those charming balconies. Could this herald a change for the better in the steady dissolution of our married life? One can only hope . . . .

"Obviously it didn't." Major Casement plumped himself back into his chair, folding his hands over his paunch. "Eh?"

"No, sir." Mayberly turned a block of pages, going forward in the journal now. "Here's his entry for June 4th. It reads simply, 'Damn Sarah: Damn her soul to eternal hell: Last night . . . .' "

"That's all?"

Mayberly nodded. "His temper reached such a passion that his pen-nib slashed through the paper at that point, and a scattering of ink blots suggests that he flung the pen down in a rage. Whatever provoked the outburst apparently occurred on the previous day or evening. From the shakiness of the writing, I should say he was barely recovered from a monumental debauch."

Major Casement unlaced his fingers, tapping them on his paunch. "No entry for that date . . . June 3?"

"None, sir. The journal is full of gaps and omissions . . . for our purpose, at least. We can only speculate on the missing parts. My inquiries among our own garrison personnel turned up a few things that may help fill in the picture."

"Such as?"

"Well, it seems that Mrs. Creed *did* take a hankering to those second-floor balconies. She loved to sit of an afternoon on the one that faces north . . . on the side toward the fort."

"Is that where . . . ?"

"Yes, sir. Where Creed fell through the nailed-shut door."

Major Casement frowned. "I haven't paid a lot of notice to the agency house, but I'd assumed that it was a boarded-up window he went through. So there *was* a balcony there?"

"Until Creed had it torn off, sir. Lieutenant Verlain's wife told me that Mrs. Creed preferred the north balcony because it was cool and shaded in the afternoon. She was careful never to expose her creamy complexion, of which she was very proud, to the sun for any great time. In any event she would sit out and read or else let down her hair and brush it, a lengthy ritual." Lieutenant Mayberly cleared his throat. "Seems that some of our chaps at the fort . . . both officers and enlisted men . . . would get out field glasses and watch her from the barracks windows. It became a daily piece of business hereabouts."

"Did it now!"

"Sir, there's something mighty provocative in the sight of a beautiful woman brushing out her hair." Mayberly reached in his dispatch case and took out a photograph which he handed across the desk. "That is Mrs. Creed. A picture I found in her husband's effects. Mrs. Verlain verifies it is a recent one. You can't tell from this, of course, but her hair was very long and shining . . . like a waterfall of reddish gold, Mrs. Verlain put it."

Casement gazed long at the photograph. "A looker, Mr. Mayberly. A looker, all right. Creed had reason to be jealous . . . if that is why he had the balcony removed."

"That's why, sir. And he had the door that opened out on it nailed shut. For a while after that, Mrs. Verlain claims, Mrs. Creed had recourse to the south balcony, holding a parasol against the scorching sun. But it was awkward and uncomfortable and she soon abandoned the practice . . . ."

Creed sat in the deepening shadows of his sutler's store, drinking and brooding. He was coatless, his single badge of dignity removed, and his shirtsleeves were rolled up. Now and then he hooked his thumb into the ear of a whiskey jug, tilted it on a thick, hairy forearm, put it to his lips and drank deeply, afterward wiping his mouth on the back of his other forearm. He was not drinking idly. He was drinking to get deeply and sullenly drunk.

Damn the woman! He'd never used to drink like this.

Where had it started? When?

Ten years ago and in Washington City, he supposed muddily, if you wanted to go back that long and far. To

298

the beginning of a marriage. It had seemed an ideal match, everyone agreed. He was the young scion of an old New York family and, as the personal secretary of a U. S. senator, privy to secrets at the very pulse of power, destined for great things. She was the Senator's lovely socialite daughter, and they were thrown often and naturally into company.

The engagement had been as brief as propriety allowed, the wedding lavish and festive, and the aftermath stained with acid. Sarah's ideas of Perfect Marriage were gleaned from the purported precepts of HRM Victoria, discreet advice in *Godey's Lady's Book*, and murky tidbits from her mother ("A woman must learn *submission* to her husband, my dear, no matter how demanding he may seem.") All of this, along with too much festive champagne, had Sarah in a mildly hysterical state by the end of their wedding day. And Creed remembered his nuptial night vividly. The words she had screamed at him: "Oh my God, I never dreamed . . . *you hairy beast!*"

Words that still cut his memory like blades. Where could a marriage go from there except downhill?

Sarah had soon learned the submission that her mother had recommended. It was all that was required of her and all that she damned well intended to give. Not bad if a man could pleasure himself by embracing a waxen statue, but Creed had found and taken his pleasures elsewhere. Along with a concomitant erosion not only of his married life but of his career in government service.

The pit of his descending fortunes had been reached two years ago, with his appointment as agent to the tiny blister patch of a Jicarillo reservation south of here. Granted, his new assignment to the big San Lazaro reservation was a step back up. But then, once you'd reached the lowest rung on a ladder, where could you go?

You could fall off it on your face, Creed thought with the humor of stark misery, and took another pull at the jug, draining it.

A trapped fly had been bussing and batting monotonously against the fly-blown window beside his head. Suddenly furious, Creed took a backhand swipe at it with his right hand, shattering the glass.

"Goddammit all to hell!"

He stared at his badly bleeding hand for a half minute, letting out a string of ripe oaths. Then, awkwardly left-handed, he bound the cut up with his handkerchief. It did little to check the bleeding.

He got off the petulant jag-end of his temper by smashing the empty jug on the packed-clay floor. Then he closed up for the night, not bothering to lock the door, and maneuvered foggily across the parade ground. Mulrooney, Troop L's bugler, gave him a bad start by suddenly sounding tattoo just a few yards away. Creed was barely sensible enough to curb his impulse to call the bull-chested Mulrooney a God-dam' bog-trotting mick ———— .

He wove his way home along the narrow trail, barged into the agency house, tramped through the front and back parlors and into the kitchen, bawling, *"Sarah!"*

"You needn't shout. But as pixilated as you are, I suppose you wouldn't know the difference."

Creed hauled up in the doorway, glaring at her. Sarah was seated at the small kitchen table, picking at a plate of leftover chicken and biscuits. She gave him a radiant, meaningless smile and nibbled daintily at a biscuit.

"Where's my supper, Goddammit!?"

"You've already drunk it, haven't you?"

Creed started to lurch forward, but the whiskey had caught up to him with a vengeance. He had to grab at the doorjamb for support. "Goddammit . . . ."

"Don't tax your vocabulary, dear. If you have anything to tell me, you might be more at home, not to say lucid, with words of one syllable. Certainly not three."

Oh, Christ! Creed dropped his hot forehead against his bent forearm, braced against the doorjamb. *Ever since he'd had the damned balcony torn off*! Up till then, at least, they had always been tolerably polite, if cool, toward one another. He remembered her outraged cry as Miguel Ortez, the local handyman-of-all-trades whom he'd hired to demolish the balcony, had begun his work.

"Please don't, Jacob! I didn't know those men at the fort were . . . were spying on me. You can't blame me! Please . . . I love that balcony!"

Creed had felt a grim satisfaction in ignoring her plea. It was something to have finally broken through her cool and regal façade. All the years of his philandering and her silent knowledge of it had never touched a nerve. At least not so it showed. Now she was wringing her hands, pleading, driven literally to tears. And he'd grinned at her, unspeaking, while they'd listened to the shriek of pulled nails and the wrenching of boards as the destruction went on.

Afterward Sarah had locked herself in her room. Locked her door against him for the first time. Next morning, when he'd come down to breakfast, Sarah was composed and calm-eyed, even humming a little, as she set out a meal for herself alone. When he'd angrily asked where his breakfast was, she'd given him a gentle

301

smile and said nothing as she began to eat.

It was pretty much how things had gone ever since. They never took their meals together. If Sarah chanced to fix more than she felt like eating, she'd leave the remainder on a plate for him. By the time he got home, it would be cold and marbled with grease: a more pointed sign of her contempt than when she left nothing at all for him. Always a meticulous housekeeper, she now abandoned any pretense at housekeeping except for keeping her own bedchamber tidy and washing her own clothes and sheets. Creed abhorred the notion of lowering himself to housework. Although he knew he'd be giving the garrison gossips a field day, he hired Dolores Ortez, Miguel's wife, to clean the place once a week, wash the stacks of dirty dishes, and launder his clothes and bedding.

Creed raised his head and stared at Sarah. She patted her lips with a napkin and rose to her feet. Lamplight ran a silken caress over the red-gold corona of her hair. Smiling faintly, she said: "Do try to be less casual, dear. Your hand is dripping all over the floor."

Somehow it tripped off the last cinch on Creed's temper. In all their years together, however angry and frustrated he'd become, he had never laid a violent hand on her.

Suddenly now, red rage sizzled in his brain. It was uncontrollable. With a throaty growl he surged forward, gripped the edge of the table between them in both hands and flung it aside. It caromed against the wall with a crash of shattering dishes.

As easily as if she'd been expecting this, Sarah slipped around and past him, graceful as a wraith. She paused in the doorway and gave a soft, taunting laugh.

"Temper, Jakey. Is that any way for a petty household

tyrant to behave?"

Creed swung wildly around and after her. Sarah glided away, going through the back parlor and up the oak-balustraded staircase.

Creed's vision began to fuzz away as he stumblingly reached the staircase. Then everything tilted crazily in his sight. He wasn't aware of falling, but suddenly his chin crashed against the third rise from the bottom.

Befuddledly he lifted his head, waggling it back and forth, tasting blood. He felt no pain, but knew he had bitten through his tongue. Above him, Sarah stood at the head of the stairs. He had never seen a smile so radiant.

"Sweet dreams, Jacob. You'll have them exactly where you're lying now, I suspect. *Sic semper tyrannis.*"

She blew him a kiss and vanished into the upstairs hallway. Creed's head dropped; his chin hit the rise again. The three inside bolts on Sarah's door shot loudly, crisply into place as she secured them. Those were the last sounds Jacob Creed heard before he passed out . . . .

June 7, 1886

I have done the deed.

After several days of mulling over what further indignities I might inflict on that ivory-skinned bitch, I came to the conclusion that there were none. She was now armored in her mind against whatever I might do. There was no recourse left me but the final one. The most final of all.

The longer I mulled on how pleasant it would be to take that cool white throat between my hands, to crush it to jelly between my hands, the more forcefully the idea seized me. Sarah must die. And no way of encompassing her end could be more gratifying.

Yesterday I did not drink at all. I must be as keen and cold as steel to perpetrate the deed. I must make no mistake, leave no sign that might be traced to me. My only fear was that without the crutch of strong drink, my determination might waver at the last moment.

It did not.

I returned home at an early hour to be sure of arriving before she might retire behind the locked door of her chamber. I found her at supper. I throttled her in the midst of one of her tart and supercilious remarks.

God, but it felt wonderful. I could feel the strength coursing through my body into my hands, increasing momentarily, as I watched her face purple into death.

She scratched my hands rather badly, trying to tear them from her throat, but that is a trifle. The marks will soon heal. Let anyone, should I be suspect, prove how I came by them.

Making sure the body will never be found presented no great difficulty. I had already weighed the matter carefully. There was a place ideal for my purpose. Not five hundred yards east of the agency house is a deep arroyo lined with cutbanks of crumbling rock. At one spot was an overhang of massive rubble that, with a little assistance, would collapse in a slide of rocks so heavy that no flash flood would ever undermine them.

Accordingly, well after taps sounded, I left the agency house with the body across my shoulders, clinging to deep shadows against the light of a quarter moon. I laid her out (with hands folded on her bosom; peace be to her shade!) at the bottom of the arroyo beneath the cutbank. Ascending it, I struggled to pry loose a key rock that I was certain, if dislodged, would bring the whole mass of rubble crashing down.

It was quickly done and the evidence of my deed

buried forever. The pile of tumbled boulders looks as if it might have been thus for a thousand years . . . .

"The devil," muttered Major Casement. "And the story he gave out was that his wife simply . . . disappeared?"

"Yes, sir," said Mayberly. "No elaborate cover story. He was supremely confident. What was there that might prove otherwise?"

Casement shook his head slowly. "But to record the act with all incriminating detail in that journal. He *must* have been mad!"

"Well, sir, I've read that a madman may try to collect his scattered thoughts by writing them down. Of course he had the journal well concealed and had no reason to believe anyone would see it while he still lived . . . in which assumption he was correct. I spent most of a day searching the agency house for clues, for evidence of any sort, before I located this volume. It was in a hidden compartment at the base of an armoire in his room."

"And it enabled you to look for . . . and find . . . the remains of Mrs. Creed?"

"Yes, sir. Had only the vague description he gives here to go on. As Creed mentions, there was nothing but tumbled rock to indicate the site, and that could describe almost any spot the length of the arroyo. Which is a quarter mile long, more or less. So I enlisted the aid of our garrison's chief scout, Joe Tana. He is full-blood Pima."

"M'm. One of those fellows could pick up sign on the burned-out lid of hell. Which," the major added sourly, "a good piece of this country comes near to being. Go on."

"Lord knows how Joe Tana found the place, but he

305

did. Then I assigned a half dozen of our troopers to dig through the rubble. After a couple hours of wrestling giant boulders away, they uncovered the body."

"It was identifiable?"

"Just barely, sir. The fall of rock had crushed it beyond facial or physical recognition. And it had been there for well over a month. Only the clothing gave indication of sex." Mayberly paused, looking down at the journal. "The only sure identification was the hair that both her husband's journal and Mrs. Verlain describe so . . . vividly."

"'Like a waterfall of reddish gold'?"

"Yes, sir. You can't imagine . . . ."

Major Casement grimaced. "Unfortunately, I can. Go on, Mr. Mayberly."

"His entry for the following day records his first seeing the apparition of his wife." Mayberly flipped a few more pages. "Then a week later, this . . . ."

June 15, 1886

Came to an understanding with Colonel Dandridge today. Following Sarah's disappearance, which I duly reported, he ordered patrols out to search for her. When they turned up not a trace, he was inclined to feel that I knew more than I had divulged and bluntly told me so. Wherefore I told him just as bluntly that I have written a full account of our 'arrangement' anent the misappropriated government funds for the Apache beef ration and sent it under seal to my attorney in a city I did not name, with instructions that it be opened in the event of my death. I could as easily add a proviso that if I were to suffer imprisonment or detainment, or be held incommunicado *in any way, it should be opened. In that case I would have nothing to lose. Dandridge . . .*

everything . . . .

Major Casement lifted a quizzical brow. "Was there such a statement?"

Mayberly shrugged. "Apparently Colonel Dandridge believed so, as there's nothing to indicate that he took any action then or later. However, Creed has been dead for weeks, the news widely published, and no attorney, no claimant to his estate, has come forward. I've found no will and no mention of any living relative."

Casement signed. "Then?"

"All the entries for several weeks thereafter . . . when he troubled to make them . . . deal with mundane, everyday matters. As though he had casually laid aside the very memory of his wife. Then . . . ," Mayberly turned a section of pages to another marked place, "we come suddenly to the following . . . ."

July 20, 1886

The gradual cessation of heavy drinking has done wonders for the well-being of my mind and body. Indeed, my sexual vigor is far greater than it has been in years! Not only is this manifest in the state of my flesh, but my attention to comely females has intensified, at times almost to a frenzy I cannot control.

A liaison with one of the women of the fort, the wife or daughter of an officer or enlisted man, even if it could be managed, would be both difficult and dangerous to undertake. It is out of the question. Nor am I inclined, any longer, to cajole and flatter even a willing female. What god-damned bitches women are. I shall never again make the least obeisance to gain the favor of any of them.

Another solution to my need has formed itself in my

307

mind. I have examined it from every side and see no reason why it cannot be accomplished. In fact I shall implement it this very day . . . .

Creed squatted on his hunkers in front of the brush *wickiup* of Sal Juan, a leading headman of the San Lazaro Apaches. Facing him in a similar crouch, Sal Juan was a wolf-gaunt man whose barrel chest strained his calico shirt. His clean shoulder-length hair was streaked with gray, but the lines graven in his mahogany face told more of harsh living than of age.

Sal Juan's eyes were like obsidian chips and they smoldered with hatred. He had reason to hate, as Creed was unconcernedly aware, and he knew that a few short years ago Sal Juan—one of the fiercest of Apache war chiefs—would have killed him without hesitation for what he had just proposed. But Sal Juan's war-trailing days were past. He had surrendered to the *pinda-likoyes*, the white-eyes, so that the pitiful remnant of his half-starved band might be spared a final annihilation.

Presently he lowered his eyes, scooped up a handful of dirt and juggled it in his palm. "What will *Nantan* Creed give to take the daughter of Sal Juan as wife?"

"Horses. Goods." His years on the Jicarillo reservation had given Creed an easy command of the slush-mouthed Apache tongue. "What do you ask?"

Sal Juan raised his hate-filled eyes. "This thing you know as well as I."

"Cattle?"

"Fat cattle. For all the people of the *Be-don-ko-he*. From this time forward we will have fat cattle."

Creed dipped his head solemnly. "Fat cattle for all the people of the Chiricahua from this time forward. It will be as Sal Juan says."

Dandridge wouldn't go for his reneging on their bargain, he knew amusedly. But he wouldn't lift a damned finger to prevent it, either. He couldn't threaten Jacob Creed with anything Creed couldn't turn against him just as effectively. Not while he believed that a certain incriminating statement was in the possession of Creed's attorney.

What attorney? Creed laughed silently at the thought. Sal Juan again bent his head, his face a stone mask. Creed squatted patiently, letting him have all the time he wanted.

Creed shuttled his gaze past the headman to the girl. She was crouched on her heels grinding corn in a stone *metate* and her slim figure was lost in her shapeless camp dress.

But on other visits here he'd seen her moving about at one chore or another, walking graceful as a young willow, the lissome outlines of her body showing through the dress, letting you visualize all her tawny loveliness: gold-skinned, sweet-curving, secret-hollowed. Sweet sixteen and bursting with the just-ripened juices of her youth.

God. Just thinking of her was enough to make his mouth go dry, his hands grow moist. This close, even, seeing her ungracefully squatted at her squaw's work, set up a wild thunder in his blood.

"*Sons-ee-ah-ray* is a good daughter," Sal Juan said presently. "She is strong and works hard. She will breed strong sons."

Creed inclined his chin appreciatively. "This thing I believe."

"A young man called *Gian-nah-tah* has tied his pony before my lodge."

"Has the daughter of Sal Juan taken it to water?"

"Yes. It is her will."

"And Sal Juan's will? How many ponies can the young man give him?"

The headman held up all the fingers of one hand.

Creed spread the fingers of both hands. "I will give Sal Juan this number of ponies."

Supplementing Apache words with an English number, Sal Juan said flatly: "*Nantan* Creed will give seven times that number."

"Three times."

"Six times that number."

"Five times."

"Four."

"No. Five times that number."

Creed nodded. "Five times that number and fat cattle for all the *Be-don-ko-he* from this time forward. It is done?"

Sal Juan was silent. The gift of ponies weighed far less with him, Creed knew, than the welfare of his band. The burden of leadership outweighed even his hatred of Creed. Yet he hesitated.

Creed repeated, "It is done?"

"There is the chief of pony soldiers."

Creed let his beard part in a slow smile. "I tell you what, old man," he said in English. "You just leave *Nantan* Dandridge to me, all right?"

"You, him," Sal Juan said in the same language. "You dogshit. Both you dogshit. I spit on you."

Still smiling, Creed said mildly, "Uh-uh. No you won't. You think your folks have had it bad up till now? You've hardly seen the start of how bad I can make it."

Sal Juan made a fist around the handful of dirt.

Creed said patiently, "It is done?"

The headman did not reply. Something else was

troubling him, Creed realized. Giving up a hard-working daughter? Creed doubted it. Sal Juan had his share of women: two wives and a couple more unmarried daughters, neither of them a looker. But Apache standards of beauty were different from whites', and Sal Juan could easily spare one daughter.

"I have wealth," said Creed. "The daughter of Sal Juan will be treated well."

"It is another thing." Abruptly Sal Juan rose to his stocky height. "We will speak with *Skin-ya*."

Creed got up too, hiding his irritation. *Skin-ya*, that dried-up old buzzard bait! But Apache life was colored with superstitions of every hue. Signs and omens dictated the Apache's choices and actions. Nothing important was undertaken against the wishes of the prevailing spirits. These spoke most trenchantly through the *izze-nantan*, the man of medicine. So *Skin-ya*, the local crucible of mumbo-jumbo, must be consulted.

As he and Sal Juan passed through the village, drowsing in the midday sun, Creed held the girl hungrily in his mind's eye. *Sons-ee-ah-ray*. Morning Star. That's what the name meant and that's what he'd call her. He thought of the consternation he'd cause among the white contingent at the fort by taking a bride so soon after Sarah's disappearance. *A redskin bride*! The thought pleased him so much that he nearly laughed aloud.

As to the promise of a fair cattle issue he'd given Sal Juan, he would keep it for a while. As long as it suited him or as long as it proved convenient. You could never tell. The girl was a good worker; she'd fix his meals and keep that rat's nest of an agency house cleaned up. But she might go all to suet in a few years, the way a lot of these squaws did. In that case . . . .

They found *Skin-ya* seated cross-legged before his *wickiup*, head bent in meditation. Naked save for a breechclout, his wrinkled hide dyed to the neutral color of the arid land which had sustained him for eighty summers or more, he did not look up as the two men hunkered down facing him. He seemed in a trance. At last, slowly, he raised his eyes. They sparkled blackly in his shriveled mummy's face.

"Sal Juan," he husked, "would know the will of the *chedens* in the matter of his daughter's marriage."

Creed stared. "How did you . . . ?"

Sal Juan cut him off with a chopping motion of his hand. "Will *Skin-ya* make the medicine?"

Skin-ya fumbled inside a buckskin bag and took out the accouterments of his craft, spreading them on the ground. A fragment of lightning-riven wood, a root, a stone, a bit of turquoise, a glass bead, and a small square of buckskin painted with cabalistic symbols. He sprinkled them with *hoddentin*, the sacred powder ground from maguey. He sprinkled *hoddentin* on himself, on Creed, on Sal Juan; he scattered *hoddentin* to the four winds.

The ancient shaman sat in silence for a long time, eyes closed. He opened them suddenly, eyeing Creed. "There is a smell of *tats-an* about the *pinda-likove*. Also he walks with a ghost."

Sal Juan said, "What of *Sons-ee-ah-ray*?"

"Would Sal Juan wed his daughter to one who is *tats-an*?"

"I am alive," Creed said harshly.

"Soon you will be *tats-an*. You will not be present."

Jesus. These siwashes had such a damned polite way of saying you'd be dead before long. "*How?*" he spat.

Skin-ya struck his own neck sharply with the edge of

312

his palm and let his head hang grotesquely to one side.

"You lie," Creed said coldly.

"The white-eyes walks with a ghost," *Skin-ya* repeated imperturbably. "The *cheden* of a woman."

He raised a scrawny arm and pointed.

Sarah stood on a barren rise not thirty feet away. Heat danced on the flinty slope and he could see its shimmering waves *through* her body; they made it shimmer and waver too.

She smiled and beckoned to him.

With a hoarse cry he lunged to his feet and stumbled toward the rise and up it. The loose soil cascaded away under his driving feet and sent him plunging on his belly. He lay unmoving and stared. Before his eyes the smiling form grew dim and slowly faded and was gone . . . .

. . . Sarah. Then I did not imagine the other time. But that was on the day after the night I killed her, well over a month ago. Why has she come back? What does she . . . .

"Balderdash!"

Major Casement's cigar had gone out some time ago. He took the wet stub from his mouth and eyed it distastefully. "You've questioned these Apaches, of course?"

Lieutenant Mayberly nodded soberly. "Sal Juan says he saw nothing. But he believes *Skin-ya* and Creed did."

Casement snorted. "And I suppose the old charlatan *insists* he did?"

"Well . . . ," Mayberly nodded at the photograph of Sarah Creed on the commandant's desk. "I showed that to *Skin-ya* and asked if he had ever seen the woman. He said that was *her* . . . the ghost that walked with Creed."

"Preposterous! Do *you* . . . ?"

"Sir, I've merely reported what I was able to find out."

"All right . . . all right!"

"There's a little more. For the next day. His last entry."

"Very well." The major gestured resignedly with his cigar stub. "Get it over with, Mister . . . ."

July 21, 1886

After yesterday's experience in the village, I had no taste for returning home. I dreaded the prospect. What might I now encounter in the very house where I killed her?

I cannot doubt that I actually saw the abomination, for Skin-ya saw it first and directed my attention to it. Badly shaken, I returned to my store and steeped myself to the eyebrows in booze. It gave me the courage to return to the house where, in drunken hallucination, I might easily have seen the apparition again.

But I did not.

I have only the vaguest memory of getting out my journal and recording my second entry of the day, a lengthy and rambling one to be sure. Now, looking back over what I wrote at the time, I have tried to determine how much of it is fact, how much of it fancy.

I can no longer tell. My thoughts are too confounded.

Tonight I must not drink. I must go home cold and clear of head and confront whatever is there, surely and finally. I know something is there. But I must have the truth—

Creed scribbled the last words with an impatient flourish. He was standing at a long counter of his sutler's store, the journal spread open before him. For a

314

moment, pen poised in hand, he glanced over what he had just written. By now it was dark enough so that he had to squint to make it out.

What more was there to say?

Impatiently he thrust the pen back in the inkstand, closed the journal, and thrust it into his coat pocket. Then he skirted the counter and headed for the door, preparatory to looking up.

Creed paused. A sly tongue of thirst licked at his belly.

Liquid courage. Why not? He could use some. He turned quickly back to the counter, reached under it and pulled out a bottle of Old Crow. The best. Saved for a notable occasion. Perhaps now.

No, Goddammit!

Resolutely he stowed the bottle back out of sight. It was a time of reckoning. He had to be certain. No false courage. And no drink-inspired delusions.

Creed locked the door behind him and tramped hurriedly across Fort Bloodworth's parade ground. It was long after tattoo; all lights were out. The path to the agency house was paved by moonglow. Creed kept his head bent, not looking at the dark masses of brush to either side, as though he feared what he might see.

Is it all a damned trick? Couldn't it be a God-damned trick of some kind?

Those God-damned Cheery-cow Apaches hated his guts. They'd like to see him dead, Sal Juan most of all. Suppose that Sal Juan and that shrunken bag of bones, *Skin-ya*, had rigged all this between them. Mesmerized him into thinking he was seeing something that wasn't? Planted a fear in his mind that might trip him to his doom.

That was it, sure. A lot of God-damned hocus-pocus.

315

The only trouble was, he didn't believe a dust mote of his own rationale . . . .

The house loomed ahead, a flat black oblong against a cobalt sky. Creed's steps slowed. But he had to go in. Had to face whatever was there.

He opened the front door and left it open to the stream of moonlight as he crossed the room to a lowboy where a lamp reposed. He lifted the lamp's chimney, struck a match, shook it free of a sulfurous flare of sparks, and touched it to the wick.

Suddenly the door slammed shut.

Creed started and wheeled around. The tiny spoon of lamp-flame faintly picked out familiar objects of the room. Nothing else.

No wind at all. No draft. Why should the door . . . ?

Now the lamp-flame was guttering in the sudden stir of air from the slamming door. Heart pounding wildly, Creed cupped his hands around it, cherishing the flame. God, if it went out! If he were isolated in total darkness . . . .

The flame held and became steady again. Carefully he replaced the chimney and turned the lamp up high. Carrying it with him, treading with a slow care, he walked from the front parlor to the back one, where the staircase was.

Creed halted at the bottom step. The lower rises were picked out in a waver of shadow and saffron light, but the top of the stairs was lost in darkness. He sleeved away the cold sweat from his forehead. He started up the stairs, making his feet move independently of the congealed fear in his brain and belly.

It is up there. God! It's waiting. I can run from it, but it will still be with me. It will always be with me. I must face it out now, or . . . . Go on, Goddammit! Don't think about it. Just go on . . . .

316

He reached the top of the stairs and advanced into the hallway. It smelled musty and unused, like an exhalation from the tomb. He came to the door of his room, a central one whose one window faced south, along with a door that opened on the still-intact south balcony.

Creed opened the door, peered cautiously about, and went in. He set his lamp on the commode and crossed the room to the armoire. Squatting down, he slid back a small panel at its base, exposing the hidden compartment. He took the journal from his pocket, placed it in the compartment and pushed the panel back into place.

"*Ja-cob . . . .*"

The murmurous whisper froze him where he was, crouched on his heels. Creed did not want to look around. The blood thudded sickly in his temples. And then he looked.

She stood in the open doorway, appearing as real as if she were still flesh. Creamy flesh. Tinted as if the rich blood of life still pulsed beneath it.

The smile formed; the arm raised and beckoned.

Creed let out a mad roar. He surged at her, his hands lifting to grasp and crush. He plunged through her as if she were smoke. Momentum carried him on through the doorway. He crashed against the closed door opposite him.

The door of Sarah's room.

He swung around, wildly. His own doorway was empty now, framed by lamplight and nothing else.

"*Ja-cob . . . .*"

Where? He froze, straining his ears. No other sound. But he was sure. The cajoling whisper had come from behind Sarah's door.

He wrenched it open and flung it wide, the door banging against the inside wall.

She was in front of him. Smiling still, the arm beckoning. Moonlight from her room's one window, as well as lamplight from his back, picked her out, but more faintly now.

She was transparent. *Again.*

With a howl he dived at her, reaching and closing his hands, seizing hold of nothing at all. And when he wheeled around again, she was gone.

"Jacob. To me. Come."

Sarah's voice. Unmistakably hers. Not ghostly at all. Just words spoken in a calm, quiet tone. Yet firm and commanding.

She was standing close to the window and both her arms were outstretched now. She was not smiling any more. Only positive.

"God damn you to all hell!"

Creed shrieked the words as he dived at her. His hurtling weight smashed against a solid wall. Almost solid.

It yawned open abruptly with a snarl of ripped-out nails, a sound of splintering wood. Jacob Creed plunged on and out into a cool rush of night air, his arms flung wide to embrace nothing.

Falling, he had one last impression: the trailing sound of a woman's laughter . . . .

Lieutenant Mayberly closed the journal and laid it on the commandant's desk beside the photograph of Sarah Creed.

"What happened after he made that last entry, we can only surmise. When he didn't show up at his store the next day, Corporal Higgins of L Troop . . . who'd gone to the sutler's to purchase some tobacco . . . was curious enough to stroll over to the agency house and investigate. What had happened was plain. The door that opened on the north balcony . . . the door that had been nailed shut after Creed had ordered the balcony torn off . . . .was split nearly in half, dangling from a single hinge. Creed's body was on the ground beneath. Obviously he had smashed through the door . . . ."

"And died of course," Major Casement said irritably, "as that old shaman had divined he would? Eh?"

Mayberly gave a noncommittal nod. "Incidentally, sir, he did. Yes. Of a broken neck."

"Balderdash," the major said wearily. He nudged the journal with his thumb. "For God's sake, Mr. Mayberly, I don't doubt that you've investigated this matter with your usual thoroughness and efficiency. But how in hell can I assemble a report to the department that will make any sense of it all?"

"Sir, I'd simply relate what we've been able to tell for certain. Higgins immediately reported Creed's demise to Colonel Dandridge. I've checked Higgins's story. He says the colonel seemed apathetic, almost indifferent, to the news, and then dismissed Higgins with a disconcerting abruptness. Five minutes later, Sergeant-Major Carmody, at his desk in the outer office, heard a shot. He hurried to the inner office and found the colonel slumped across his desk, his service revolver clenched in his fist. He had shot himself through the head. No doubt because revelation of his complicity with Creed in cheating on the Apache beef issue would have wiped out the last remnant of his career."

"All that is clear enough, Mr. Mayberly," snapped Casement. "What concerns me is this blather about spectral apparitions. I don't see any way to avoid

319

alluding to it if I'm to submit a complete and truthful report on the business." He scowled, tugging at his underlip. "Suppose I can hazard a speculation that Creed was suffering from a massive delusion brought on by feelings of personal guilt or whatever . . . ?"

Mayberly cleared his throat. *As he always did when he found something difficult to communicate*, Casement thought irritably. "Out with it, Mister!" he barked.

"Perhaps you'd better see for yourself, sir." The subaltern cleared his throat again. He nodded at the journal. "It's in there. The last entry."

Casement's patience was worn to an edge. "You said you'd read off the last entry in that damned thing. What . . . ?"

"*Creed's* last entry, sir. But there's another one after it. See for yourself."

Major Casement picked up the journal and flipped impatiently through its pages to the end of Creed's almost indecipherable writing.

He stared at the place.

The short hairs at the back of his neck prickled; his throat felt stuffed with phlegm. He managed to clear it with a couple of mild "harrumphs," trying not to let Mayberly know that he was doing so.

"'Hem. Isn't it possible, Mister, that somebody . . . for whatever odd reason . . . added this final entry later on?"

"I doubt it, sir. I found the journal in the base of Creed's armoire, his own place of concealment. The handwriting, as you can see, is crisp and clear, in a backhand script. Quite different from Creed's broad, forward slanting scrawl. Too, as nearly as I can tell, it's a woman's hand."

"Preposterous," the major said in a fading voice.

"One more item, sir . . . ." Mayberly reached in his

320

dispatch case, pulled out a piece of paper and slid it across the desk. "I found this in Mrs. Creed's room. It is a letter she had begun to write to a sister in Boston, but never got to finish."

Mayberly paused, wrinkling his brow. "Don't ask me to explain *this* one, sir. I'm no handwriting expert. But I needn't be one, nor do you, to perceive that the hand which indited this letter and the one which made that final entry in Creed's journal are absolutely identical."

Major Casement stared at the letter. Then his gaze moved with a slow, dreading reluctance, back to the journal spread open on his desk. To its brief and final entry:

Poor Jacob. His fancies overcame him. He fancied that he saw a ghost. Sic semper tyrannis.

CYNTHIA HASELOFF

CYNTHIA HASELOFF (1945–) was born in Vernon (once known as Eagle Flat), Texas. The family story has it that Cynthia's father, stationed in Kansas during part of the Second World War, went AWOL in order to return his pregnant wife to Texas prior to Cynthia's birth rather than allow a Haseloff to be born outside the Lone Star State. Notwithstanding this bit of derring-do, the family did soon move to Cave Springs, Arkansas, where they became Texans in exile. Cynthia was named after Cynthia Ann Parker, perhaps the best-known of the white female Indian captives on the frontier.

As a child, Cynthia suffered from asthma and was often confined to her bed. In the Afterword to her first published novel, ***Ride South!*** (Bantam, 1980), she recalled that she "really soaked up" the stories and legends about the family and life in Texas that her mother told her. "I even told myself stories at night to put myself to sleep. And I remember vividly the night we all sat up as my father read the whole of a newly arrived biography of Sam Houston." The imaginary West in the form of Western films was a staple of family outings and so became part of the young Haseloff's nurture.

Haseloff was graduated from the University of Arkansas at Fayetteville with a Bachelor's degree in Art and Art History in 1965 and went on there to earn a Master's degree in Rhetoric-Public Address. It was Haseloff's early ambition to be a filmmaker and so she went on to earn a Doctorate degree in Film and Television in 1971 at the University of Missouri at

Columbia. Her first novel actually began as a screenplay. Haseloff had made a study of Dorothy M. Johnson's style and went so far as to copy Johnson's captivity story, "Lost Sister" (1956), in long-hand to study her narrative technique. Haseloff decided to turn her screenplay into a novel which she completed in 1974. It was rejected by a number of publishers over the next six years until Haseloff met a vice-president from Bantam Books at a seminar and the executive promised to have someone at Bantam read the manuscript. Bantam accepted the book. However, the publisher felt her gender would have to be disguised and so in that long tradition beginning with B.M. Bower through J.R. Williams, P.A. Bechko, L.J. Washburn, despite having no middle name or initial, she became C.H. Haseloff, according to the back cover blurb "one of today's most striking new Western writers."

A Killer Comes to Shiloh (Bantam, 1981), *Marauder* (Bantam, 1982), *Badman* (Bantam, 1983), and *Dead Woman's Trail* (Bantam, 1984) followed in rather short order. *Marauder* has more recently appeared in a new hard cover edition in the Gunsmoke series from Chivers Press. "If *Ride South!* is a traditional Western novel, Haseloff's approach introduced a female perspective rarely encountered previously in Western fiction by making her protagonist a mother searching for her children out of a sense of love and responsibility rather than out of a desire for revenge or fame," Vicki Piekarski observed in her entry for Haseloff in the second edition of the *Encyclopedia of Frontier and Western Fiction* (1997). "Leah's simple courage and determination to find them, when most others believe them dead, is adeptly juxtaposed against the revenge-seekers, opportunists, and legend-makers who are only interested in self-aggrandizement or self-promotion. In this and subsequent novels, many of Haseloff's characters embody old-fashioned values—honor, duty, courage, and family—that prevailed on the frontier and were instilled in the young Haseloff by her own 'heroes,' her mother and grandmother. Her stories, in a sense, dramatize how these values stand up when challenged by the adversities and cruelties of frontier existence."

The one thing that emerges quite clearly when reading any Haseloff novel is her admiration for the people who lived through the frontier experience. "A love of the Western might just be an inherent tendency, a predisposition like left-handedness or color-blindness," she once remarked. "I guess my writing Westerns can ultimately be attributed to my slow and staggering acceptance of myself, to accepting as worthwhile the things I loved most and had been educated out of. I love the West, perhaps not all of its reality, for much of it was cruel and hard, but certainly its dream and hope and the damned courage of people trying to live within its demands."

For almost a decade after the appearance of *Dead Woman's Trail*, Haseloff at the behest of Irwyn Applebaum at Bantam tried writing a major historical novel based on the life of Cynthia Ann Parker. In the meantime, her books vanished from the racks and Bantam Books was acquired by a German cartel whose management had little inclination to exploit back list or encourage publication of new Western fiction outside of pulp Western series such as "Rivers West." Starting over at the beginning, something she had done successfully with the first incarnation of *Ride South!*, Haseloff reworked her story into the kind of traditional book-length novel with which she is most comfortable. In this form her sixth Western story, *The Chains of Sarai Stone* (Five Star, 1996), was scheduled for publication and she intends in future novels to carry forward her charting of life on the frontier during the last years on the plains of the wild Comanches.

I do not know if it is something about Arkansas and its close connection in the previous century with the Nations—Judge Parker's court is featured prominently in *Bad Man*—or the undying emotional impact of the War between the States—*Marauder* is set in this period—but Arkansas writers such as Douglas C. Jones and Cynthia Haseloff have created new, vivid, and captivating narratives using these periods and themes as well as the time when the Comanches roamed free. In a way they have taken all of us back to reflect poignantly on the unresolved and tragic issues which were at stake in those times and have charted the devastating impact these upheavals from the past have had on the American consciousness *and* our collective unconscious ever since. This same vitality can be witnessed as well in other regions, in the Western stories of Gary D. Svee, Frank Roderus, Stephen Overholser, Tim Champlin, as well as in the works of older masters such as Lauran Paine and Dan Cushman.

It has been a long journey, and a fruitful one, from the earliest intimations and whispers to the point we have reached with this final story. It is taking nothing from Cynthia Haseloff's power and magic as a storyteller to say that without Zane Grey, and Max Brand, and Willa Cather, and Walter Van Tilburg Clark, and Dorothy M. Johnson, and Les Savage, Jr., and T.V. Olsen, and so many more, we could not have attained this plateau where it is become self-evident to all readers that the

Western story grew out of the very land which first gave it birth and could not exist without that land, both the physical land where a change in the weather can mean the difference between life and death and that spiritual terrain so unique, the land *just before* the land beyond the sun.

REDEMPTION AT DRY CREEK
1994

"I HAD A SON ONCE," THE RAGGED PREACHER SAID. "But his mother drowned him like a blind pup. Maybe it was because it was my child; or maybe it was because food was already scarce and bad winter was yet comin' on. I do not know why she killed him. I stood there on the river bank and watched her. And I do not know why I did not stop her. Maybe I figured it were hers more than mine; or maybe I figured I done her enough hurt without makin' her drag my child through the rest of her life; or maybe I was just hard as nails and did not give a damn for her or the boy or anything else.

"But I cannot get shut of them . . . that woman holding that kicking screaming, living baby under the cold water 'til it was quiet and limp. When she threw him out of the water by his heels like a big fish, I kneeled down and looked at him lying there on the white river rocks, blue as if he'd been painted. A beast has more feeling than I had for that baby.

"I have often looked at the faces of the men I have killed, and I have known I killed them before they could kill me, and that was enough. But I do not know why I let her drown the boy."

"I wasn't going to drown my son," the woman said.

326

"Reckon not," the Preacher said, sitting beside her. "Ain't no water in a dry creek. You'll have to figure another way."

"I ain't thinkin' on killin' my boy," the woman said. "That ain't my thought."

"Death be here, woman," the Preacher said. "You have some thought a-drawin' it here."

The woman dropped her head and said nothing. The ragged man beside her was right. Her thoughts had been that morning on death, but not to drown the boy. She had seen that morning that there was nothing but the day's worth of food left. After they ate it, there was nothing—nothing but to die.

She had come to the shade tree looking out on the dry creek and sat with the boy, Thom, in her arms. *"Why back in the old country,"* she had said to Thom, *"I done some foolish things, but it were a forgiving land."* She looked at the wet spot near the bank, the last small run of the water still beneath the earth. Her mind went back then to the old country, and she remembered.

"I woke up determined it were Marmie's birthday. I woke up determined to have her a birthday. I had heard of a birthday lately, just a dab of a article in a yella newspaper about a queen over in England or somewheres a-havin' a birthday, and ever'body a-honoring her and givin' her presents for her birthday. They just picked a day to have her a birthday which weren't her real birthday. Marmie did not know when she was born, though she had all us children wrote down in the Book. And so she never had no party. So I got the idea from that paper you could pick, pick any day you wished, and have a public birthday like that queen.

"There we were alone for the men, and many days

327

from the settlement. And I was determined to give Marmie a birthday. There was Marmie with the ten of us younguns and Selah's nine and five more children with Mary. Marmie made bread every morning in a hollered out log big enough for you to lay down in and stretch out. I's young and feelin' big to do. I figured I'd put the little 'uns to gathering, and I would make Marmie a blackberry cobbler for her birthday. The berries was thick, big as your thumb. Oh, my, Thom, they was pretty and good, too.

"I made up my cobbler and set it on the table, set it in front of Marmie with a bunch of flowers we picked. That was the first time she ever sat first I could remember. And she said she was proud . . . mighty proud . . . to have a girl could make up a cobbler so nice and wait on her Ma. The little 'uns couldn't think nothin' 'cept eating so she cut it and took the first bite like I said to be special for her birthday. She chewed that cobbler, and the piece got bigger in her mouth. No happy light came in her eyes. She looked at me so sad. 'Annie, it's salt,' she said.

"I had grabbed up a bag of salt and used it fer sugar. All the pickin' lost. All the wood gatherin' lost. All the rollin' out and mixin' up lost. All the butter and cream and flour lost, too. And the gift plum ruined for one misthought, and Marmie disappointed in me on top. I started to cry, and all the little ones began to cry.

"And, suddenly, Marmie started in a laughin', laughin' like music, and she hugged me up, and held me, and laughed. 'Why child,' she said, 'you give me the best gift . . . to be needed. *Old cobbler ain't nothin'.' And she began to throw that cobbler around at the children. They threw it back and at each other. We all had blackberry stains and seeds all over us so we had to*

328

go to the spring and wash.

"Afterwards we all got busy and got more berries, and Marmie made a bigger cobbler, and we ate 'til we hurt. It were a fat country, Thom, the old country, full of green trees and water and berries enough for two big cobblers. Amen."

She had rocked the boy in her arms past noon. He did not fret but lay against her with his black hair stuck to his small round head. She had sometimes fanned the hem of his coarse cotton shirt over his bare legs. The wind had borne against them, stirring the dry leaves the dying tree dropped. Sometimes the sand had cut them when the wind rose hard. The woman had covered the child with her body and had turned her back away from the dry creek and looked at the house.

The house was a ramshackled kind of thing, abandoned before they came. The wind drove against the adobe bricks, dissolving them back into their native earth, carrying them over the land. The boy's father had thrown a *gringo* lean-to of logs against the mud walls. He had dug a root cellar beneath it and had planted a peach orchard in the sandy land. There had been water then.

But the man had seen the dry coming the second year. One morning when the woman got up, he was gone and the horses and the steers. He had taken the gun, too. That had been months back. Annie thought he'd return. By the time she understood he would not, she had a little garden of potatoes and beans and corn besides the peach trees. There was still food in the cellar. She had trapped rabbits that came to the garden, and once she had cut the throat of a thirst-starved deer who had come to the spring. She had dressed it, and there was meat for her and the boy. She had figured to stay 'til she figured out what to do.

The sun took the corn. The peaches never made but knobs. And the potato vines began to die. She had carried water to the vines in the morning and in the evening, and the ground drank the water so that there was barely a shadow where the water had touched it.

The sun had burned hotter and higher 'til the beans rattled in their shells. Annie made a shade over the potato vines where she could. She carried water morning and evening. This was not a country for potatoes, but she knew potatoes, and she strove for them to live because a person could live on potatoes.

The creek began to dry, and the spring became a trickle, and, then, a few drops. There was some to drink, but none for the garden. They ate the dying fish and the beans and the stored food, not all at once, but little by little, the woman eating less and less to feed the child.

Finally, Annie decided to walk with the boy to the town. They started out, climbed the hill behind the house like the man had done. And there they sat down. Annie did not know the way from there. It was a long way, a hundred miles maybe, and they did not know anyone in the town or have any money for food.

She and the boy went back to the house. They gathered berries and any nuts that they had missed along the creek. Coming home with a little firewood and a rabbit, they saw the Indians digging away at the spring, filling their dry gourds by drops, wetting their horses' muzzles. The woman and the boy slept in the brush that night.

When the Indians rode away, they went home and found that the Indians had taken everything that was left, even the coffee and sugar that Annie had hoarded for the company that might one day come. Annie laughed as tears ran down her dry brown cheeks. *"Sure enough,"* she had said, *"her company had been served."*

Annie looked at the ragged man beside her. Beyond him a raven settled onto the creek bank and drank from the spring. There were other ravens walking about in the dry creek. Annie's eyes ran over the evil black birds and the man. He was tall and thin. Coarse, unkempt hair stuck out over his head. A sparse beard covered his sunken cheeks. The coat he wore was black and frayed at collar and cuffs. His elbows poked out at holes in his sleeves. The white shirt beneath his vest was spotted and stained with the red clay of this land. She remembered he'd spoken of killing his child, of killing men, of her thoughts drawing Death to the place.

"Are you Death?" Annie asked.

"Not Death, woman," the Preacher said. "Death is gorged on this land, but I am hungry. Fix me something to eat while I sit here in the shade a spell and think."

"Did them birds come with you?" she asked.

"They did," he said. "They are my friends, and we cannot eat them. They have preserved my life in this lonely land by bringing me carrion morning and evening. I was well until the spring I lived by played out, and the Lord directed me to this place."

"The Lord didn't direct you here if he cared about you," the woman said.

"Hush, woman," the man said. "Get my supper . . . just a small corn cake."

"There ain't no corn, mister. Not a wormy kernel. We ate them. The only thing left is a couple of dried up potatoes. The boy and I are going to eat them. Then . . . ," Annie looked around at the empty land, no longer even yellow beneath the drought, but sucked dry of all color, "then, I figured, we'd just wait to die."

"I'll take one of the potatoes," the Preacher said.

"I do not think you will," Annie said. "I do not know you, mister. I do not know where you come from or how you got here. And from what I've seen and heard, I do not like you. You have no call on me?"

"I'm the Preacher," the man said.

Annie laughed. "There it is, then, just like Pa said. Where there's a mouthful of food, there'll be a preacher. You're bound to be a Methodist."

"Shut up," the Preacher said. "Make the supper, woman. You'll have your pay."

"Oh, no," Annie said. "I've had my pay of all the preachers they ever was. Preachers pay with worthless script. Preacher prayed for my Ma, and she died. Prayed for my little brothers and sisters, and they was took off, too. Prayed my Pa would come home. He never did. Finally, when I was left to make my way the best I could, a preacher run me out of town. I been run out of lots of places since, but you ain't runnin' me out of this one. This is where me and my boy and you will die, Preacher."

The Preacher studied the woman's face. His eyes softened. "Fix the supper, woman," he said quietly, looking into her pale eyes. Annie's jaw set and her eyes flared hot hate at the Preacher. "Fix all there is. We'll eat it together."

Annie carried the listless boy back to the house and laid him on the quilt-tossed bed where she could see him if he moved. "Damn," she said reaching into the bin where the potatoes were stored. "Just damn. What are you doin', Annie, feedin' a preacher your last morsel? Pa's rollin' in his grave if he's dead."

Annie found a potato and reached back for the other. Her fingers closed over it. Withdrawing her hand she brushed against another. "Um," she said, "well, there's one a piece. Ain't that nice. Pa's spinnin' for sure me even thinkin' that."

Annie built her little fire thoughtfully, carefully placing each small branch, building the coals on the bed of ashes. "But Ma ain't. Reckon she'd be pleased there was somethin' for the Preacher. There, Preacher, this potato and the good it brings you is for her sake. Even though she was deceived, she believed. It's for her sake not your own I'm givin' it to you. So eat hearty of the miserable thing. It is all you will get from me."

The Preacher came in when the meal was prepared. His face was washed. His hair lay in place. He blessed Annie's food, thanked the Lord for her generosity, knowing Annie did not want to be generous.

"Reckon your God knows that's a lie if he's God," Annie said. "I ain't generous to you, Preacher. I just had a memory of someone. I gave you what you got for *her* sake."

"Yes," the Preacher said. "And why did she give?"

"'Cause she was an ignorant woman who believed in things that can't be."

"Maybe such things can be, *must* be." There was a pause. "I'll take the loft for my sleeping quarters," the Preacher said then. And he climbed the rawhide-tied ladder to the small room.

Annie watched him with her mouth set. "Sure," she said, "you just take whatever you want. Make yourself to home."

"I won't wake you when I get up," the Preacher said. "I'll be out early . . . visiting with the Lord."

"You just make sure you don't visit my bed on the way out, or I'll kill you dead," said Annie.

The Preacher leaned over and looked down into the

lower room. "What is your name, woman?" he asked.

"Annie," she said. "Annie Caudle. My boy is Thom."

The Preacher disappeared. Still sitting at the table, Annie heard him moving things about in the little room. "Well, Thom," she said to the child on the bed, "we got us a boarder."

The next morning, when Annie crawled out of her tumbled bed still clad in her dirty dress, she saw the Preacher sitting beneath the dying tree beside the dry creek. He had taken a chair with him and sat comfortably, one long leg crossed over the other, reading his Bible, looking occasionally toward Heaven. The ravens were perched in the tree above him.

Annie and Thom walked down to get the water that had collected overnight in a pitcher left at the spring. The Preacher never looked at them. His lips moved, but Annie could not hear any words. The boy looked at him while Annie lifted the pitcher and set an empty one in its place.

"Shoot," Annie said, catching the boy's stare, "pray 'til you turn purple." She gave the boy a little water. "Rinse it around your mouth good before you swallow." She watched the boy. He dutifully rinsed before he drank each mouthful she gave him. At last, he looked up into Annie's face. Her eyes softened. "You're a good boy, Thom." She gently touched his head. They walked back to the house with the pitcher.

In the evening the Preacher came in with an armful of small branches. "I gathered these on my walk," he said. "They'll do for the supper fire."

"There ain't nothing to cook," Annie said.

"Look again, Annie," the Preacher said. The woman's lower lip thrust out. "Do it, please, Annie, for Thom's sake."

"You are the cruelest person I ever met, teasing me with the boy's life."

Still looking at the Preacher, Annie reached into the dark dry recesses of the bin. "There . . . !" she started to say in proof of the emptiness of the bin. But she stopped. "Well, I'll swear." She bent lower, peering into the darkness. When she straightened, she held four good-sized potatoes in her dirty hands.

Annie made their supper on the hearth while the man rocked Thom. After they ate, the Preacher again climbed to the loft. Annie climbed back into the unmade bed and wondered how she had missed the four potatoes until she fell asleep.

The next morning the Preacher was at the dying tree beside the dry creek when Annie and Thom went to get the water. The ravens were gone.

"Where are them old black birds?" Annie asked.

"They are not needed now," the Preacher said. "The Lord has released them."

"The Lord," Annie said. "Most likely they know the water's about gone here. If I's a bird, I'd be gone too. They'll probably come back to pick our bones, though."

"Annie, Annie, what has made you so sour?" asked the Preacher with a smile.

"Preachers," Annie said, and went back to the house.

Each morning the Preacher was at the dying tree beside the dry creek when Annie and Thom went to get the water. Whenever she looked out, he sat with the Book in his lap, tipped back in the chair against the tree. He read and prayed. Each evening he brought a little wood for a fire. And each evening Annie found a few potatoes she'd missed. As the woman and the child began to recover their strength, the strangeness of the day's routine began to gnaw at Annie's mind.

"I know there ain't that many potatoes I missed," Annie said to the boy. She sat in the midst of the tumbled bed which she had long before ceased to make, falling into it in exhaustion and, later, in the stupor of hunger. "I've a mind to tear out them boards and just see what's down there." Annie stood up. "I'll do that. I'll prove to my own mind that there ain't no 'taters. Then I'll talk to that Preacher."

Annie started toward the potato bin. She stopped in the middle of the dirt floor. She turned slowly toward the open door. Beyond it, the Preacher sat under the dying tree beside the dry creek.

"You'll prove it, Annie, old girl," she thought. *"Then where'll the food come from? He's a gettin' them potatoes somewhere and puttin' 'em in the bin while we sleep. If I make a fuss, he'll have to stop. Then where'll Annie and Thom be?"* Annie was standing in the middle of the floor.

"Come on, Thom. Let's walk out to the old garden and have us a look. Maybe them 'taters did make it. Maybe all that water I carried done some good. If I find he's been diggin' my own potatoes and feedin' 'em to us a few at a time, I'll run his preacher's behind off this place."

Annie and Thom found no signs of digging in the burned-up garden.

That evening the Preacher came again with the firewood. Annie found the potatoes that could not be there, and they all ate their fill.

"Preacher," Annie said, "where do you reckon all them potatoes are comin' from? I mean I might have missed a few, but not all these that's been feedin' us these past days."

The Preacher stood up and walked toward the ladder.

"The Lord, Annie," he said, looking back at her.

"The Lord?" Annie said quietly. "And why is He so generous to us, Preacher?"

"Because you have given me a place, Annie," he said.

"I don't believe the Lord puts them potatoes in that bin," Annie said.

"Why not, Annie?" asked the Preacher. "If you plant potatoes and tend potatoes and the year is right, don't you have potatoes in the garden?"

"Why sure I do," Annie said. "I worked it with my own hand."

"Your own hand had not done too well before I came, had it, Annie? But you still have confidence in what you do and what you see, what you wretch out of the earth for yourself. Suffice it for now, God's of a mind to be generous. His way is always yea and amen. His way is always deliverance."

The Preacher went up the ladder and disappeared.

Annie rested her head on the table. *"This's too complicated for me,"* she said to herself. *"Ain't nobody, including the Lord, ever been generous to Annie Caudle."* Annie lay quietly, still thinking. *"Well . . . Marmie was generous. Better than ever I deserved."*

The next morning when Annie and Thom returned with water to the house, Annie stood in the doorway a long time and watched the Preacher. Later she brought out the bed clothes and shook out the sand and red dust. She turned the mattresses and remade the beds. When the Preacher came with his firewood, the cabin was set in good order. Annie had on a clean apron. She prepared the potatoes, and they all ate 'til they were full.

"You reckon the Lord is so good to you 'cause you let your baby be killed and 'cause you killed all those men, Preacher?" Annie asked. "Or does He just overlook that? Is that why you pace the floor at night? Seein' all them dead faces?"

The Preacher tipped back in his chair, resting his forearm on the table, looking at Annie. "It is the nature of God to be generous, Annie." His eyes were direct and very soft in the firelight.

"Most folks would say you deserve to burn in Hell," Annie said.

"That is fair to say about most folks," the Preacher said. "We are all eager for justice. That is why I killed those men. I figured they *deserved* to die. The better way is to embrace them, consume their hate with love . . . reconciliation . . . redemption."

"Shoot," Annie said. "Sugar candy grows on bushes. You didn't let that baby be killed for justice. You was just plain mean to the core no matter what you tell yourself or how pretty you try to make it out."

The Preacher rubbed his eyes with his thumb and ring finger. "You are right, Annie. I have been thinking on the boy. I had a deep cold place in me. I was mean to the core. I had a curiosity about how mean I could be? I think with the boy I found the limit of the blackness . . . there was nothing worse . . . though there were a lot of dead men and ruined women after that."

"And so God fergive you, and you're good all through and through?" Annie said. "God may, but *I* still think you are a sorry thing."

The Preacher smiled. "Good night, Annie."

He went to the loft.

Annie threw herself on the quilt top. "That's what I think. He's a sorry thing. Just got religion. Religion's his disguise. He'll show his spots. A leopard don't change his spots."

Annie went to sleep and dreamed of leopards and

338

spots and the torn and bloody innocent prey they consumed . . . .

Before daylight, she sat up straight up, fully awake. "I reckon we best get out of here 'fore he does show them spots. It just ain't safe here. We're stronger now. Maybe if we walk down the dry creek a ways, we'll get some place, find some help."

Annie got up. "Thom," she said, shaking the boy awake. "There's a piece of moon left. We're going to walk down the dry creek to find us a town where we can live and be safe. Get up, son. There's some potatoes left from supper and water in the jug. Come on, now."

Annie closed the door softly as she and Thom left the shack. She did not hear the Preacher's shout. "Hallelujah! The drought is broken. The rains have started up country. We'll see the manifestation today."

Awake then with his revelation, the Preacher came eagerly down the ladder on his way to the dying tree beside the dry creek. The Preacher passed the beds. The forms of the woman and the child were curled deep in the covers. He smiled. The air was already colder, he thought. He opened the door and stood smelling the light fragrance of distant moisture. The first sparse drops hit the earth kicking up dust, bouncing off the hardness of this land. "Get up, Annie! Get up, young Thom!" he said. "Come, see gentle forgiveness."

He turned into the room. Neither form stirred. He went to Annie's bed and shook her. The piled covers dissolved beneath his hand. "Dear God," the Preacher said.

He ran from the house toward the tree and the creek. Annie's footstep had nearly filled beside the spring. The pitcher lay on its side. Further downstream, he found another track near a small pool in the middle of the dry creek.

The Preacher began to run.

"Annie!" he shouted. "Annie, the rain's up country. Annie, *flood*!"

Even as he ran the noise of the wall of water came to him. The water wall pushed passed him as he threw himself onto the bank. He ran along the edge trying to catch the water, losing the race. "Annie," he shouted, but the sound of the water absorbed his words.

Still the Preacher ran. He ran and, at last, he saw a small bit of color—Annie's shawl tangled in a tree. The dry creek tumbled with water and debris from above the homestead. Creek banks of dry sand had collapsed trees weakened by the drought into the boiling waters. The Preacher searched the tumult for the woman and child. "Annie," he shouted. "Annie!"

He reached down to get the shawl and found the woman. The Preacher caught Annie by her shoulders and pulled her from the flood onto the bank. He dragged her away from the edge.

"Thom," she said. "Thom."

The Preacher looked up and began to search the shore for the boy. He ran along the bank looking at the debris, cutting his face and arms on the limbs of the trees that still clung to the high banks. He stopped suddenly. The child was jammed face down in the crotch of a tree. Holding the brittle limbs, the Preacher fell into the flood, racing the raging current for the small body bobbing loose from the tree. He grabbed the boy's ankle. Then, pushing his shoulder against the tree, he lifted Thom from the fork and pulled him to his chest.

"Thom!" the woman shouted. "Preacher, do you have him?"

The Preacher handed her the boy, then used his legs

to shove himself off the tree and up onto the clay bank. He rested long enough for air to enter his seared lungs.

Annie held the boy, rocking him gently. "Poor, Thom," she said. "So cold."

The Preacher caught her shoulders. "He's blue. Give him to me, Annie." He pushed her gently aside and began to rub the child's arms and legs.

"His breath is gone, Preacher. He ain't breathing," she said. "You took him from me like I knew you would from the beginning!" Annie picked up a rock and struck the Preacher with her weak force on the side of the head. A small trickle of blood appeared.

The Preacher caught her hand and gripped it. "Hold with me, Annie. Hold with me. I ain't your enemy." He jerked her to him and began to pray. "Lord, have You brought further calamity upon this woman with whom I sojourn by slaying her son?"

Then, the Preacher sat over the boy, holding the woman. He seemed to be listening. "No, of course not. By God, he ain't. Get up, Annie. We've a fight to make."

The Preacher stood up. Putting the boy's body over his shoulder, he lifted the woman to her feet.

"He ain't breathing. His breath is gone," she said.

"Don't say nothing now, Annie," the Preacher said quietly. "Now ain't the time."

Inside the shack the Preacher lay the child on the bed. Annie fell beside him and caught him in her arms. "He's blue. He ain't breathing."

The Preacher closed the door. "Get away, Annie. Give me your son."

The Preacher waited.

Annie looked up into his eyes. "He's gone," she said.

The Preacher touched her lips to silence with his

fingers and took the boy from her. He held the limp body with one arm as he climbed to the loft.

"Preacher," Annie said to his back, "Preacher, make him live. Oh, dear God, please listen to this man I been so hard on. If he's your man, I'm sorry for all I said and thought again' him."

The Preacher lay the small lifeless child on the neatly made bed. He stood looking at the boy's face, then sat down beside him. He pulled the cover over the cold body. Finally, he stretched himself on top of the child and held him.

"God," he said. "I ask You this: let this child's spirit come back to him. I ain't willing to let him go."

He held the boy, rubbing his arms. Suddenly anger flashed in the Preacher's black eyes. "Death, you come out of the shadows and show your ugly self and hear me! I recognize your work. You've come again to rob, to kill, and to destroy! But you'll get no help from me this time. I won't let this child go, and you can't take him. I'm telling you that in Jesus's name."

The rain was gentle when the Preacher came down. Annie lay asleep where she had crawled in exhaustion onto the bed. He quietly made a fire and set water on to boil while she slept. He hung the boy's small shirt over a chair back and moved it toward the fire.

"Thom," he said to the boy, standing in his spare shirt with the sleeves rolled up to disclose the child's small hands, "your mother is worn out from all the hard times and the struggle. Why don't you take her a dry blanket and lie down beside her 'til she wakes up?"

The boy pushed his mother's wet hair aside from her forehead and kissed her. "Marmie," he said. "Wake up, Marmie. The Preacher's brought us home safe."

Annie opened her eyes. She caught the boy and

pulled him to her. Tears ran down her cheeks as she kissed his eyes and nose and ears and cheeks and mouth.

"I figured you was diggin' up my own potatoes on the sly," Annie said to the Preacher, "and puttin' them in the bin for me to find. I knew you was foolin' me. I knew it, but I wasn't just sure how."

The Preacher smiled. "Annie, Annie. Could it be that God is good, whether a woman plants a patch of potatoes and a man digs them or it comes some other way?"

"I never thought it likely," Annie said. "Pa always said you had to wrestle everything away from the hard-assed old bustard, and then He'd short you. Looked like Pa was right to me after Marmie and the others died."

Annie looked at the boy as she held him unable to let him go. "I been wrong when I thought I was dead sure right before. Why one time I ruined a whole blueberry cobbler taking salt for sugar. It looked just right 'til we bit into it, too. I ain't saying I know what you done here, Preacher. I'm saying, thank you."

"It all begins with that, Annie," the Preacher said. "All belief begins with that . . . the knowledge that you have a debt to One greater than yourself."

SELECTED FURTHER READING

THE TWO PRINCIPAL REFERENCE SOURCES FOR AUTHORS of Western and Frontier fiction are the second edition of *Twentieth Century Western Writers* (St. James Press, 1991) edited by Geoff Sadler and the *Encyclopedia of Frontier and Western Fiction* (McGraw-Hill, 1983) edited by Jon Tuska and Vicki Piekarski. The former is limited only to authors who wrote in the 20th Century and has no illustrations and generally short and not always accurate entries whereas the latter includes authors from the previous century as well as from the 20th Century. The second edition of the *Encyclopedia of Frontier and Western Fiction* appeared in 1996. Most of the authors included in this second edition are examined in depth in terms of their works and their bibliographies and filmographies (where they exist) are complete, some also having short fiction bibliographies as well. Where little is known of the biography of an author whose work is nonetheless significant, mini-entries in a special section have been included discussing their work. There are also numerous articles including one of considerable length on "Pulp and Slick Western Fiction" and another on "Artists and Illustrators." Illustrations include book jacket covers, pulp magazine covers, stills from motion picture versions, and author portraits.

In the recommendations which follow, titles of novels are to be found under the principal name of an author followed by works under pseudonyms where these apply. Citations are to first editions. Many of these titles have been reprinted or will be reprinted and it is suggested that the interested reader consult the most recent edition of **Books In Print**. This is a list of personal recommendations. If an author has been omitted, it is simply because for whatever reason I could not cite a novel about which I did not have some reservations, or because space simply did not permit me to cite every author who has written a Western story. No ranking here. These are all good Western stories. It is wrong to ask or expect more, although a particular book might well come to mean more to us as a reader.

EDWARD ABBEY; *The Brave Cowboy* (Dodd, Mead, 1956), *The Monkey Wrench Gang* (Lippincott, 1975).ANDY ADAMS, *The Log of a Cowboy* (Houghton Mifflin, 1903).

CLIFTON ADAMS; *Tragg's Choice* (Doubleday, 1969), *The Last Days of Wolf Garnett* (Doubleday, 1970); as Clay Randall, *Six-Gun Boss* (Random House, 1952).

ANN AHLSWEDE; *Day of the Hunter* (Ballantine, 1960), *Hunting Wolf* (Ballantine, 1960), *The Savage Land* (Ballantine, 1962).

MARVIN H. ALBERT; *The Law and Jake Wade* (Fawcett Gold Medal, 1957), *Apache Rising* (Fawcett Gold Medal, 1957).

GEORGE C. APPELL; *Trouble at Tully's Run* (Macmillan, 1958).

ELLIOTT ARNOLD; *Blood Brother* (Duell, Sloan, 1947).

VERNE ATHANAS; *Rogue Valley* (Simon and Schuster, 1953).

MARY AUSTIN; *Western Trails: A Collection of Short Stories* (University of Nevada Press, 1987) edited by Melody Graulich.

TODHUNTER BALLARD; *Incident at Sun Mountain*

345

(Houghton Mifflin, 1952), *Gold in California* (Doubleday, 1965).

S. OMAR BARKER; *Little World Apart* (Doubleday, 1966).

JANE BARRY; *A Time in the Sun* (Doubleday, 1962).

REX BEACH; *The Spoilers* (Harper, 1906), *The Silver Horde* (Harper, 1909).

FREDERIC BEAN; *Tom Spoon* (Walker, 1990).

P.A. BECHKO; *Gunman's Justice* (Doubleday, 1974).

JAMES WARNER BELLAH; *Reveille* (Fawcett Gold Medal, 1962).

DON BERRY; *Trask* (Viking, 1960).

JACK M. BICKHAM; *The War on Charity Ross* (Doubleday, 1967), *A Boat Named Death* (Doubleday, 1975).

ARCHIE BINNS; *The Land Is Bright* (Scribner's, 1939).

CURTIS BISHOP; *By Way of Wyoming* (Macmillan, 1946).

TOM W. BLACKBURN; *Raton Pass* (Doubleday, 1950), *Good Day to Die* (McKay, 1967).

FRANK BONHAM; *Bold Passage* (Simon and Schuster, 1950), *Snaketrack* (Simon and Schuster, 1952), *The Eye of the Hunter* (Evans, 1989).

ALLAN R. BOSWORTH; *Wherever the Grass Grows* (Doubleday, 1941).

TERRILL R. BOWERS; *Rio Grande Death Ride* (Avalon, 1980).

W. R. BRAGG; *Sagebrush Lawman* (Phoenix Press, 1951).

MATT BRAUN; *Black Fox* (Fawcett Gold Medal, 1972).

GWEN BRISTOW; *Jubilee Trail* (Thomas Y. Crowell, 1950).

SAM BROWN; *The Long Season* (Walker, 1987).

WILL C. BROWN (pseudonym of C.S. Boyles, Jr.); *The*

Border Jumpers (Dutton, 1955), ***The Nameless Breed*** (Macmillan, 1960).

EDGAR RICE BURROUGHS; ***The War Chief*** (McClurg, 1927).

FRANK CALKINS; ***The Long Rider's Winter*** (Doubleday, 1983).

BENJAMIN CAPPS; ***Sam Chance*** (Duell, Sloan, 1965); *A* ***Woman of the People*** (Duell, Sloan, 1966).

ROBERT ORMOND CASE; ***White Victory*** (Doubleday, Doran, 1943).

TIM CHAMPLIN; ***Summer of the Sioux*** (Ballantine, 1982), ***Colt Lightning*** (Ballantine, 1989).

GIFF CHESHIRE; ***Starlight Basin*** (Random House, 1954);

as Chad Merriman, ***Night Killer*** (Ballantine, 1960).

WALT COBURN; ***Mavericks*** (Century, 1929).

DON COLDSMITH; ***Trail of the Spanish Bit*** (Doubleday, 1980).

ELI COLTER; ***The Outcast of Lazy S*** (Alfred H. King, 1933).

WILL LEVINGTON COMFORT; ***Apache*** (Dutton, 1931).

MERLE CONSTINER; ***The Fourth Gunman*** (Ace, 1958).

WILL COOK; ***The Wind River Kid*** (Fawcett Gold Medal, 1958);

as Frank Peace, ***The Brass Brigade*** (Perma Books, 1956);

as James Keene, ***Seven For Vengeance*** (Random House, 1958);

as Wade Everett, ***Fort Starke*** (Ballantine, 1959).

JOHN BYRNE COOKE; ***The Snowblind Moon*** (Simon and Schuster, 1984).

DANE COOLIDGE; ***Horse-Ketchum of Death Valley*** (Dutton, 1930), ***The Fighting Danites*** (Dutton, 1934).

BARRY CORD (pseudonym of Peter B. Germano); ***Trail Boss from Texas*** (Phoenix Press, 1948).

EDWIN CORLE; ***Fig Tree John*** (Liveright, 1935).

JACK CUMMINGS; ***Dead Man's Medal*** (Walker, 1984).

EUGENE CUNNINGHAM; ***Riding Gun*** (Houghton Mifflin, 1956).

JOHN CUNNINGHAM; ***Warhorse*** (Macmillan, 1956).

PEGGY SIMSON CURRY; ***So Far From Spring*** (Viking, 1956).

DAN CUSHMAN; ***Stay Away, Joe*** (Viking, 1953), ***The Silver Mountain*** (Appleton Century Crofts, 1957), ***Voyageurs of the Midnight Sun*** (Capra Press, 1995).

DON DAVIS (pseudonym of Davis Dresser); ***The Hangmen of Sleepy Valley*** (Morrow, 1940).

H.L. DAVIS; ***Honey in the Horn*** (Harper, 1935), ***Winds of Morning*** (Morrow, 1952).

IVAN DOIG; ***The McCaskill Family Trilogy: English Creek*** (Atheneum, 1984), ***Dancing at the Rascal Fair*** (Atheneum, 1987), ***Ride With Me, Mariah Montana*** (Atheneum, 1990).

HARRY SINCLAIR DRAGO; ***Smoke of the .45*** (Macaulay, 1923);

as Will Ermine, ***Plundered Range*** (Morrow, 1936); as Bliss Lomax, ***Pardners of the Badlands*** (Doubleday, Doran, 1942).

HAL DUNNING; ***Outlaw Sheriff*** (Chelsea House, 1928).

ROBERT EASTON; ***The Happy Man*** (Viking, 1943).

GRETEL EHRLICH; ***Heart Mountain*** (Viking, 1988).

ALLAN VAUGHAN ELSTON; ***Treasure Coach From Deadwood*** (Lippincott, 1962).

LOUISE ERDRICH; ***Love Medicine*** (Holt, 1984).

LESLIE ERNENWEIN; ***Rebel Yell*** (Dutton, 1947).

LOREN D. ESTLEMAN; ***Aces and Eights*** (Doubleday, 1981).

MAX EVANS; *The Hi Lo Country* (Macmillan, 1961), *Rounders Three* (Doubleday, 1990) [containing *The Rounders* (Macmillan, 1960)].

HAL G. EVARTS, SR.; *Tumbleweeds* (Little, Brown, 1923).

CLIFF FARRELL; *West With the Missouri* (Random House, 1955).

HARVEY FERGUSSON; *The Conquest of Don Pedro* (Morrow, 1954).

VARDIS FISHER; *City of Illusion* (Harper, 1941).

L.L. FOREMAN; *The Renegade* (Dutton, 1942).

BENNETT FOSTER; *Winter Quarters* (Doubleday, Doran, 1942).

KENNETH FOWLER; *Jackal's Gold* (Doubleday, 1980).

NORMAN A. FOX; *Rope the Wind* (Dodd, Mead, 1958), *The Hard Pursued* (Dodd, Mead, 1960).

STEVE FRAZEE; *Cry Coyote* (Macmillan, 1955), *Bragg's Fancy Woman* (Ballantine, 1966).

BRIAN GARFIELD; *Valley of the Shadow* (Doubleday, 1970).

JANICE HOLT GILES; *The Plum Thicket* (Houghton Mifflin, 1954), *Johnny Osage* (Houghton Mifflin, 1960).

ARTHUR HENRY GOODEN; *Guns on the High Mesa* (Houghton Mifflin, 1943).

ED GORMAN; *Guild* (Evans, 1987).

JACKSON GREGORY; *The Silver Star* (Dodd, Mead, 1931), *Sudden Bill Dorn* (Dodd, Mead, 1937).

FRED GROVE; *No Bugles, No Glory* (Ballantine, 1959).

FRANK GRUBER; *Fort Starvation* (Rinehart, 1953).

BILL GULICK; *White Men, Red Men, and Mountain Men* (Houghton Mifflin, 1955), *They Came to a Valley* (Doubleday, 1966).

A.B. GUTHRIE, JR.; *The Big Sky* (Sloane, 1947), *The*

Way West (Sloane, 1949).

E.E. HALLERAN; *Outlaw Trail* (Macrae Smith, 1949).

DONALD HAMILTON; *Smoke Valley* (Dell, 1954).

C. WILLIAM HARRISON; *Barbed Wire Kingdom* (Jason, 1955).

CHARLES N. HECKELMANN; *Trumpets in the Dawn* (Doubleday, 1958).

JAMES B. HENDRYX; *The Stampeders* (Doubleday, 1951).

O. HENRY (pseudonym of William Sydney Porter); *Hearts of the West* (McClure, 1907).

WILLIAM HEUMAN; *Gunhand From Texas* (Avon, 1954).

TONY HILLERMAN; *Skinwalkers* (Harper, 1987).

FRANCIS W. HILTON; *Skyline Riders* (Kinsey, 1939).

DOUGLAS HIRT; *Devil's Wind* (Doubleday, 1989).

LEE HOFFMAN; *The Valdez Horses* (Doubleday, 1967).

RAY HOGAN; *Conger's Woman* (Doubleday, 1973), *Fortuna West, Lawman* (Doubleday, 1983), *The Whipsaw Trail* (Doubleday, 1990).

L.P. HOLMES; *Summer Range* (Doubleday, 1951); as Matt Stuart, *Dusty Wagons* (Lippincott, 1949).

PAUL HORGAN; *A Distant Trumpet* (Farrar, Straus, 1960).

ROBERT J. HORTON (writing as James Roberts); *Whispering Cañon* (Chelsea House, 1925).

EMERSON HOUGH; *The Covered Wagon* (Appleton, 1923).

JOHN JAKES; *The Best Western Stories of John Jakes* (Ohio University Press, 1991) edited by Bill Pronzini and Martin H. Greenberg.

WILL JAMES; *Smoky the Cowhorse* (Scribner, 1926).

DOUGLAS C. JONES; Any (*and Every*) Novel This Author Has Written!

MACKINLAY KANTOR; *Warwhoop, Two Short Novels of the Frontier* (Random House, 1952).

PHILIP KETCHUM; *Texan on the Prod* (Popular Library, 1952).

WILL C. KNOTT; *Killer's Canyon* (Doubleday, 1977).

TOM LEA; *The Wonderful Country* (Little, Brown, 1952).

WAYNE C. LEE; *Petticoat Wagon Train* (Ace, 1978).

ALAN LEMAY; *Old Father of Waters* (Doubleday, Doran, 1928), *Winter Range* (Farrar and Rinehart, 1932), *The Searchers* (Harper, 1954), *The Unforgiven* (Harper, 1957), *By Dim and Flaring Lamps* (Harper, 1962).

ELMORE LEONARD; *Escape From Five Shadows* (Houghton Mifflin, 1956), *Last Stand at Sabre River* (Dell, 1959).

DEE LINFORD; *Man Without a Star* (Morrow, 1952).

CAROLINE LOCKHART; *Me Smith* (Lippincott, 1911).

JACK LONDON, *The Son of the Wolf; Tales of the Far North* (Houghton Mifflin, 1900), *The Call of the Wild* (Macmillan, 1903), *White Fang* (Macmillan, 1906).

NOEL M. LOOMIS; *Rim of the Caprock* (Macmillan, 1952), *The Twilighters* (Macmillan, 1955), *Short Cut to Red River* (Macmillan, 1958).

MILTON LOTT; *The Last Hunt* (Houghton Mifflin, 1954).

GILES A. LUTZ; *Stagecoach to Hell* (Doubleday, 1975).

WILLIAM COLT MACDONALD; *Powder Smoke* (Berkley, 1963).

ROBERT MACLEOD; *The Appaloosa* (Fawcett Gold Medal, 1966), *Apache Tears* (Pocket Books, 1974).

FREDERICK MANFRED; *Conquering Horse* (McDowell Obolensky, 1959).

E.B. MANN; *The Valley of Wanted Men* (Morrow, 1932).

CHUCK MARTIN; *Gunsmoke Bonanza* (Arcadia House, 1953).

JOHN JOSEPH MATHEWS; *Sundown* (Longmans, 1934).

GARY MCCARTHY; *Sodbuster* (Doubleday, 1988), *Blood Brothers* (Doubleday, 1989), *Gringo Amigo* (Doubleday, 1991).

DUDLEY DEAN MCGAUGHEY (writing as Owen Evens); *Chainlink* (Ballantine, 1957);
as Lincoln Drew, *Rifle Ranch* (Perma Books, 1958).

LARRY MCMURTRY; *Lonesome Dove* (Simon and Schuster, 1985).

D'ARCY MCNICKLE; *Wind From an Enemy Sky* (Harper, 1978).

N. SCOTT MOMADAY; *House Made of Dawn* (Harper, 1968).

WRIGHT MORRIS; *Ceremony in Lone Tree* (Atheneum, 1960).

HONORÉ WILLSIE MORROW; *The Heart of the Desert* (Stokes, 1913), *The Exile of the Lariat* (Stokes, 1923).

CLARENCE E. MULFORD; *Corson of the J.C.* (Doubleday, Page, 1927), *Trail Dust* (Doubleday, Doran, 1934).

D(WIGHT) B(ENNETT) NEWTON; *Crooked River Canyon* (Doubleday, 1966), *Disaster Creek* (Doubleday, 1981);
as Ford Logan, *Fire in the Desert* (Ballantine, 1954).

NELSON C. NYE; *Not Grass Alone* (Macmillan, 1961), *Mule Man* (Doubleday, 1988);
as Clem Colt, *Quick Trigger Country* (Dodd, Mead, 1955).

FRANK O'ROURKE; *Thunder on the Buckhorn* (Random House, 1949), *The Last Chance* (Dell, 1956), A *Mule for the Marquesa* (Morrow, 1964).

STEPHEN OVERHOLSER; *A Hanging in Stillwater* (Doubleday, 1974), *Field of Death* (Doubleday, 1977).

WAYNE D. OVERHOLSER; *Draw of Drag* (Macmillan, 1950), *The Violent Land* (Macmillan, 1954), *Cast a Long Shadow* (Macmillan, 1955);
as Joseph Wayne, *Land of Promises* (Doubleday, 1962);
as Lee Leighton, *Law Man* (Ballantine, 1953).

LAURAN PAINE; *Trail of the Sioux* (Arcadia House, 1956), *Adobe Empire* (Chivers North America, 1993);
as Richard Clarke, *The Homesteaders* (Walker, 1986).

F.M. PARKER; *Skinner* (Doubleday, 1981).

LEWIS B. PATTEN; *Death of a Gunfighter* (Doubleday, 1968), *A Death in Indian Wells* (Doubleday, 1970), *The Angry Town of Pawnee Bluffs* (Doubleday, 1974), *Death Rides a Black Horse* (Doubleday, 1978).

GARY PAULSEN; *Murphy* (Walker, 1987).

CHARLES PORTIS; *True Grit* (Simon and Schuster, 1968).

JOHN PRESCOTT; *Ordeal* (Random House, 1958).

GEO. W. PROCTOR; *Walks Without a Soul* (Doubleday, 1990).

BILL PRONZINI; *Starvation Camp* (Doubleday, 1984).

WILLIAM MACLEOD RAINE; *The Sheriff's Son* (Houghton Mifflin, 1918), *Ironheart* (Houghton Mifflin, 1923), *The Desert's Price* (Doubleday, Page, 1924), *The Trail of Danger* (Houghton Mifflin, 1934).

JOHN REESE; *Jesus on Horseback* (Doubleday, 1970).

EUGENE MANLOVE RHODES; "*Pasó por Aquí*" in *Once*

in the Saddle (Houghton Mifflin, 1927), ***The Trusty Knaves*** (Houghton Mifflin, 1933).

ROE RICHMOND; ***Mojave Guns*** (Arcadia House, 1952).

CONRAD RICHTER; ***Early Americana and Other Stories*** (Knopf, 1936), ***The Sea of Grass*** (Knopf, 1937), ***The Lady*** (Knopf, 1957).

Frank C. Robertson; ***Fighting Jack Warbonnet*** (Dutton, 1939).

LUCIA ST. CLAIR ROBSON; ***Ride the Wind; The Story of Cynthia Ann Parker and the Last Days of the Comanche*** (Ballantine, 1982).

FRANK RODERUS; ***The 33 Brand*** (Doubleday, 1977), ***Finding Nevada*** (Doubleday, 1984), ***The Outsider*** (Signet, 1988), ***Mustang War*** (Doubleday, 1991).

MARAH ELLIS RYAN; ***Told in the Hills*** (Rand McNally, 1891).

MARI SANDOZ; ***Miss Morissa, Doctor of the Gold Trail*** (McGraw-Hill, 1955).

JACK SCHAEFER; ***The Kean Land and Other Stories*** (Houghton Mifflin, 1959), ***Monte Walsh*** (Houghton Mifflin, 1963).

JAMES WILLARD SCHULTZ; ***Red Crow's Brother*** (Houghton Mifflin, 1927).

LESLIE SCOTT; ***Blood on the Rio Grande*** (Arcadia House, 1959).

JOHN SHELLEY; ***Gunpoint!*** (Graphic Books, 1956).

GORDON D. SHIRREFFS; ***The Untamed Breed*** (Fawcett Gold Medal, 1981).

LUKE SHORT (pseudonym of Frederick Dilley Glidden); ***Dead Freight for Piute*** (Doubleday, Doran, 1940), ***And the Wind Blows Free*** (Macmillan, 1946), ***Vengeance Valley*** (Houghton Mifflin, 1950).

LESLIE MARMON SILKO; ***Ceremony*** (Viking, 1977).

BEN SMITH; ***Trouble at Breakdown*** (Macmillan, 1957).

CHARLES H. SNOW; *Six-Guns of Sandoval* (Macrae Smith, 1935).

VIRGINIA SORENSON; *A Little Lower Than the Angels* (Knopf, 1942), *Many Heavens* (Harcourt Brace, 1954).

ROBERT J. STEELMAN; *Surgeon to the Sioux* (Doubleday, 1979).

CHUCK STANLEY; *Wagon Boss* (Phoenix Press, 1950).

WALLACE STEGNER; *The Big Rock Candy Mountain* (Duell, Sloan, 1943).

GARY D. SVEE; *Spirit Wolf* (Walker, 1987), *Sanctuary* (Walker, 1990).

JOHN STEINBECK; *The Red Pony* (Covici, Friede, 1937).

GLENDON SWARTHOUT; *The Shootist* (Doubleday, 1975).

THOMAS THOMPSON; *Brand of a Man* (Doubleday, 1958), *Moment of Glory* (Doubleday, 1961).

WALKER A. TOMPKINS; *Flaming Canyon* (Macrae Smith, 1948).

LOUIS TRIMBLE; *Crossfire* (Avalon Books, 1953).

WILLIAM O. TURNER; *Place of the Trap* (Doubleday, 1970).

W.C. TUTTLE; *Wandering Dogies* (Houghton Mifflin, 1938).

WILLIAM E. VANCE; *Death Stalks the Cheyenne Trail* (Doubleday, 1980).

ANNE LEE WALDO; *Sacajawea* (Avon, 1979).

MILDRED WALKER; *Winter Wheat* (Harcourt Brace, 1944).

BRAD WARD (pseudonym of Samuel A. Peeples); *Frontier Street* (Macmillan, 1958).

L.J. WASHBURN; *Epitaph* (Evans, 1988).

FRANK WATERS; *The Man Who Killed the Deer* (Farrar and Rinehart, 1942).

JAMES WELCH; *Winter in the Blood* (Harper, 1974).

JESSAMYN WEST; *The Massacre at Fall Creek* (Harcourt Brace, 1975), *The Collected Stories of Jessamyn West* (Harcourt Brace, 1986).

RICHARD S. WHEELER; *Winter Grass* (Evans, 1983), *Fool's Coach* (Evans, 1989).

STEWART EDWARD WHITE; *Arizona Nights* (McClure, 1907).

HARRY WHITTINGTON; *Vengeance Is the Spur* (Abelard Schuman, 1960).

JEANNE WILLIAMS; *No Roof But Heaven* (St. Martin's Press, 1990), *The Longest Road* (St. Martin's Press, 1993).

JOHN WILLIAMS; *Butcher's Crossing* (Macmillan, 1960).

CHERRY WILSON; *Empty Saddles* (Chelsea House, 1929).

G. CLIFTON WISLER; *My Brother, The Wind* (Doubleday, 1979).

CLEM YORE; *Trigger Slim* (Macaulay, 1934).

CARTER TRAVIS YOUNG (pseudonym of Louis Charbonneau), *Winter of the Coup* (Doubleday, 1972).

GORDON YOUNG; *Days of '49* (Doran, 1925).

OTHER BOOKS BY FRED C. SHAPIRO

RACE RIOTS NEW YORK 1964 (WITH JAMES W. SULLIVAN)
WHITMORE

RADWASTE

RADWASTE

FRED C. SHAPIRO

RANDOM HOUSE
NEW YORK

Portions of this work previously appeared in different form in *The
New Yorker.*

Library of Congress Cataloging in Publication Data

Shapiro, Fred C.
Radwaste: a reporter's investigation of a growing nuclear menace.

1. Radioactive waste disposal—United States.
I. Title.
TD898.S48   363.7'28   81–40238
ISBN 0–394–51159–X   AACR2
Manufactured in the United States of America

24689753

FIRST EDITION

For Paul Shapiro, Mary Shapiro and other people's children.
This is a fine mess we've gotten you into.

FOREWORD

Since 1977, when I set out on *The New Yorker* assignment that led to this book, I have talked to hundreds of people about radwaste, and before anything else, I want to express my gratitude to those who took time, and in some cases went to considerable effort, to give me the information in this book. I also would like to acknowledge the reporting assistance of James W. Sullivan. However, the perspective I have brought to this subject is entirely my own, and I want to acknowledge that it was formed in a high school chemistry class.

This was 1947, the first man-made atomic reaction had been initiated five years earlier, but Bartram Cadbury, my teacher at Friends' Select School in Philadelphia, wasn't lecturing about nuclear physics, but rather good scientific practices, when he posed a question that went something like this: "Suppose I gave you all the money and all the facilities it would take and assigned you to produce an acid so powerful it would dissolve any substance—what would be your first step in going about it?" There were a number of responses from the class about setting up series of distillation experiments, but the instructor shook his head to them all. "Suppose you ever got such an acid," he said, "what could you keep it in? The first thing you have to determine in any experiment is, when you get whatever it is you're going after, what are you going to keep it in?"

That's my prejudice on thirty-nine years (so far) of nuclear wastes, and I gladly acknowledge it.

F. C. S.
New York 1981.

CONTENTS

RADWASTE

1
QUANTITIES

An appropriate place to begin a book on nuclear waste is at a level clearing about three quarters up the slope of a steep hill in Palos Forest, a park preserve approximately 20 miles southwest of Chicago's Loop. Buried here, under 2 feet of soil and then a foot-thick concrete cap, and guarded only by a stone marker headed "Caution Do Not Dig," are the world's first reactor-made wastes. In a technical sense, they are not the first radioactive wastes—those are in Bavaria, and they were created in 1789 from the first separation of uranium oxide from pitchblende ore—but the materials entombed in Palos Forest have their own claim on history. They are the first wastes of the scientists who generated the first man-made nuclear reaction at the University of Chicago in December 1942. About a quarter of a mile to the south of this clearing, at the crest of the hill which has no name, is another clearing, and beneath it rests the only known remains of the graphite reactor that Enrico Fermi and his team put together on the squash courts of the University of Chicago. It was disassembled and reconstructed in 1943 near this hill at what was then the site of the world's first nuclear engineering laboratory, Argonne, and then buried at the top of the hill in 1956 when Argonne moved to another site 2 miles away.

At that time, the Palos Forest site, about 20 acres, reverted to the control of the Cook County Forest Preserve District. Tenanted now primarily by hawthorne and scrub oak, the hill that is the preserve's most prominent feature is frequented only by white fallow deer, backpackers, motorcyclists and occasional camping vehicles. The deer and smaller animals drink surface water that recently has been found to contain uranium and plutonium well above normal levels; the human visitors drink from wells that are collecting measurable quantities of tritium, the radioactive isotope of hydrogen. Tritium isn't toxic or chemically any different from hydrogen, and all water contains infinitesimal quantities of it. In the wells used by visitors to Palos Forest, however, this isotope has been measured at more than two thirds the level permitted in drinking water by the federal Environmental Protection Agency. I'll try not to become technical in this book—but for the record, the EPA maximum is 20 nano—or billionths—of a curie per liter. Water from one of these Palos Forest wells has been measured as high as 14. These levels fluctuate and fortunately are higher in the fall and winter when the wells are little used than they are in the spring and summer when recreational use of the preserve is at its peak. Because atoms of tritium, unlike those of other radioactive substances, do not combine with atoms in tissues, blood or bone, they are generally secreted from the body within two days. Primarily for that reason, the maximum permissible concentration of tritium in drinking water has been set at twenty-five times the maximum permissible concentrations of other radionuclides. Even so, Howard Morland, an anti-nuclear activist, calculates in *The Secret That Exploded* that 6 milligrams, or .00021 ounces of pure tritium, ingested at one sitting, would remain within the body long enough to emit a radiation dose that would be fatal to a person of average weight.

Department of Energy scientists at Argonne concede that lingering tritium levels are a concern—and this is a word chosen after consultation with federal officials anxious not to appear either unheeding of, or upset by, a phenomenon of radioactive contamination that they admit they do not fully comprehend.

The last known wastes were deposited in 1949 in what was then an open trench on the Palos Forest hillside. Tritium has a half-life of only 12.3 years—and yet the concentrations monitored in the wells in the winter of 1979–80 reached 12.5 nanocuries. Annual averages are dropping down at an average of 15 percent a year, the Department of Energy says—in the winter of 1980–81 the high reading reached only 6.5 nanocuries—but what they are doing at even this level 31 years after the last waste deposits, when radiological intensities should have decayed to less than 20 percent of their original levels, is described as "difficult to understand" in a survey prepared by the Division of Environmental Control Technology of the Department of Energy. The same source also reports concentrations of uranium and plutonium well above expected levels on the surface of a meadow that is about 50 to 200 feet down the hill from the clearing. The uranium levels were registered at 10 picocuries per gram, which isn't much (a pico is a millionth of a millionth), but is still about thirty times normal. The plutonium average of .2 picocuries per gram is four times the level that the Department of Energy study considers "a common concentration for fallout plutonium."

Officials at Argonne, which is now one of twelve national research laboratories, admit that despite considerable investigative effort, they don't really know the complete nature or the volumes of the wastes that are buried within the Palos Forest hill, or Plot A as it is designated on their records. "We'd have a better fix on contamination levels if we knew exactly what was in there," said Roger Mayes, one of a party of five Department of Energy executives and technicians who escorted me there. "The problem is that in the early days of the Manhattan Project, everything was carried on in secrecy, and as a result, records for types of waste and quantities that have been buried here are non-existent."

Officially, it is the position of the Department of Energy, as stated in an undated "executive summary" of radiological survey results, that "there is no measurable radiation dose resulting from the radioactive materials buried there which could be experienced by members of the public visiting the site or anyone living in the vicinity." As a practical matter, however, the contamination findings have been sufficient to earn Palos Forest a place on a list of twenty-six former nuclear sites that have been given priority for remedial federal action. In the meantime, the site continues to be popular. "Come up here on a weekend in spring," said Jake Sedlett, one of the Argonne physicists who collects samples of the soil and water there, "and you'll find motorcyclists, hikers, campers and a lot of loving couples strung out all over this hill."

Had I encountered any of these visitors (excluding the loving couples, of course), I would have asked if they knew of the findings of surface contamination and isotopes in the wells. As it was, on a chilly weekday morning in early spring, my federal escorts and I had the park to ourselves. On the way down the hill, we stopped at one of the three wells in which the tritium had been measured at its highest concentrations, and I asked Edward Jascewski, the Energy Department's responsible health and safety official why, as a precautionary measure, this and the other two wells were not simply filled and covered. "From a radiological point of view, we don't think there is a hazard in them yet," he said, "and from a governmental point of view, we aren't sure we should spend the money unless it becomes necessary." In the meantime, however, the remedial actions now under active consideration by the Department of Energy appear to be considerably more expensive. These range from a maximum effort of carving off the entire top of the hill —reactor, waste trench and all—and depositing it within a federal reservation somewhere, to a minimum one of laying asphalt covers over the clearings above the waste trench and the reactor shell in order to reduce the drainage that is carrying the tritium seepage. For the time being, in any case, the wells remain open and unmarked by warnings, available to anyone with the muscle to pump the tritiated water up from the underground streams. Before I left Palos Forest, I did just that and tasted the liquid. It had, I reported to my federal escorts, a pleasant, rather mild mineral flavor. For the record, though, I think I should add that of the five government officials who had assured me of the safety of the water, only one, Dr. Sedlett, chose to share in the drink.

My visit to Palos Forest, part of a pilgrimage of sorts to the site of the first reactor-generated wastes, came just about 3 years after the issue and problems posed by nuclear-waste disposal impressed themselves upon me at what I had at first expected to be a rather routine federal hearing in New York. That hearing dealt with the transportation of spent reactor fuel through New York City, a subject I'll get back to in Chapter IX, and subsequently I set out to learn more about what both nuclear industry executives and environmentalists now battle over in the name of radwaste. Many of those I have sought out for information on this subject, and in particular government and corporate officials, have asked me about the extent of *my* qualifications to report on this nuclear issue. This is not an unfair question, and I think it should be answered here: I have no qualifications to deal with scientific information beyond a liberal arts college education and twenty-five years' experience as a newspaper and magazine reporter.

Accordingly, I make no claim that this book deals other than in passing with any of the scientific or technical aspects of the subject. This is, instead, a layman's report on how much radwaste there is, what forms it takes, what has already been done about it, and what is proposed to be done about it. If there have been, as Paul Turner of the Atomic Industrial Forum estimates, 5,000 technical studies on the problems of nuclear wastes (Michael Brown, in his book on toxic wastes, *Laying Waste,* puts the number at 5,600), I can't claim to have read more than a fraction of them. Instead I have talked to as many of those in both government and industry who have responsibilities in nuclear-waste disposal as I could reach, and to environmentalists who have concerned themselves with its hazards, and have traveled across the country to see for myself radwaste as it exists in the land (and the oceans around it).

To begin with, what *are* nuclear wastes? The Nuclear Regulatory Commission defines them officially as "those radioactive materials which are of sufficient potential radiological hazard that they require special care and which are of no present economic value to the nuclear industry." What troubles me most about that definition is that public perception and scientific recognition of "sufficient potential radiological hazard" has already changed and will continue to change as wastes pile up and nuclear consequences (or lack of them) become increasingly apparent. A lesser problem, perhaps, is the uncertainty of what is and what is not of "present economic value to the nuclear industry." In 1977, when government policy changed to bar the reprocessing of spent-fuel rods from commercial reactors, these once-valued by-products of power generation became de facto wastes—even though they still are not financially accounted for as such. By the same token, the government is supporting a substantial research effort, principally at Sandia Laboratories in New Mexico, to develop acceptable uses for nuclear by-product materials, and an example of "waste" already promoted out of that category is uranium depleted in the fissile isotope 235 which has been extracted to enrich the fuel of reactors. This heaviest, and therefore most penetrating, of natural elements, now stacked up in the form of uranium fluoride at enrichment plants, has recently become valuable to the armed forces as source material for armor-piercing bullets and projectiles.

My own definition of the subject matter of this book is, therefore, both less technical and less qualified: Radwaste is any material emitting above-background levels of radiation and which has no present use. How much nuclear waste is there, and what forms does it take? The following inventory figures were compiled in, or derived from, an excellent running scoreboard kept at Oak Ridge National Laboratory by five scientists, W. L. Carter, B. C. Finney, C. W. Alexander, J. M. McNair and J. O. Blomeke, under contract to the Department of Energy. The ORNL figures, and, in fact, nearly all government measurements of radwaste quantities are metric. (A cubic meter is equal to slightly more than 35.3 cubic feet.) I intend to take the liberty here, and elsewhere in this book, of converting most of these official metric figures back to more familiar American measurements. Since the Nuclear Regulatory Commission, in the language of one of its own documents, "is unable to quantify the relative risks of various waste categories," I'll deal with them here, and in subsequent chapters, in the following order:

URANIUM MILL TAILINGS: These are obviously the first radwastes produced, and they comprise nearly a hundred times the volume of all other waste forms. Because the milling process is unable to remove more than 90 percent of the uranium in the ore, and because other radioisotopes remain mixed in with the contaminated residues, these tailings, piled up sand-dune-like around the mills, retain 85 percent of the radioactivity of the excavated ore. From these dunes emanates radon, a radioactive gas which is one of the decay products of thorium, radium and the residual uranium. In 1980, the Oak Ridge survey reported a total of 2.955 billion cubic feet of tailings at 19 active uranium mills and at 25 inactive sites, most, but not all of them, in the Western states. This volume is increasing at the approximate rate of 141 million cubic feet each year.

HIGH-LEVEL WASTES: Uranium is irradiated in government reactors to create plutonium for nuclear weapons and in medical and research reactors for a variety of purposes. When fuel assemblies are removed from these reactors, the plutonium and the unfissioned uranium are separated by chemical processes, and the wastes created by this "reprocessing" work are called "high-level." Contrary to general belief, the term "high-level," as contrasted with "low-level" in waste categories has nothing to do with radioactive intensities—except outside the United States among nations which have adopted the 1978 radwaste classifications promulgated by the International Atomic Energy Agency of the United Nations. The American classification based solely on source has resulted in the anomaly of some "low-level" wastes that are more immediately dangerous than their "high-level" counterparts. Legally, however, the United States restricts its use of "high-level" to the Code of Federal Regulations (Part 50, Appendix F) definition of "those aqueous wastes resulting from the operation of the first cycle solvent extraction system, or equivalent, in a facility for reprocessing irradiated reactor fuel."

In 1980, there were 10.2 million cubic feet of these highly radioactive materials in the United States, and despite an extensive program to reduce volumes by additional evaporation, we were adding to high-level waste inventories at the rate of 85,-000 cubic feet annually. Accumulation of these additional volumes will also be substantially increased by the Reagan Administration's decision to emphasize the production of existing atomic weapons and to deploy new ones.

Although they were originally entirely liquid, some of the military wastes that are now buried within massive underground tanks at the Hanford Atomic Energy Reservation in Southeastern Washington State have been chemically neutralized to form salt cake, and others, at Hanford and at the Savannah River Plant in South Carolina, have precipitated into sludges; at the Idaho National Engineering Laboratory near Idaho Falls, the effluents from the reprocessing of nuclear submarine fuel are calcined—turned into powder—and held in steel bins. A very small proportion of reprocessing wastes, about 78,000 cubic feet, or about 582,000 gallons of liquids and sludges, is contained in 2 underground steel tanks at West Valley, New York, which was the site of the only American attempt to reprocess spent fuel commercially.

COMMERCIAL SPENT FUEL: Uranium undergoes a much longer "burn-up time" within power-producing reactors than it does within military or research reactors, so commercial spent fuel is the most radioactive form of radwaste, even though it had not attained the status of "high-level" by the end of 1980. (Legal steps are under way to reclassify it, however.) Since these assemblies have not been reprocessed since 1972, they have been piling up underwater in pools, nearly all of them at the sites of 73 American reactors. By the end of 1980, there were 28,315 of these spent-fuel assemblies comprising 8,206 tons of uranium, with another 5,775 more expected to be discharged in 1981, and 175 more due to be imported into this country from nations with "Atoms for Peace" treaties with the United States.

Fuel-assembly compositions vary according to reactor types. Nearly all American reactors producing commercial power today are of the boiling-water or pressurized-water forms. Typical pressurized-water assemblies hold up to 264 uranium-filled zirconium fuel rods that are 13.5 feet in length and .37 inches in diameter; most boiling-water assemblies hold 64 fuel rods that are 14.3 inches long and .49 inches in diameter. Assuming that it was possible to dispose of these wastes in their present form (which it definitely is not because of the heat they radiate and because of criticality considerations), the 1980 stock of 28,-315 assemblies would comprise a volume of 122,000 cubic feet.

TRANSURANIC WASTES: Transuranic is a term applied to the man-made elements higher than uranium on the periodic table—neptunium, plutonium, americium, and so on. There was no such waste classification as transuranic, however, until 1970, when the Atomic Energy Commission decreed that all materials containing transuranic elements to the extent of 10 nano (or billionths) curies per gram be segregated from the low-level (or non-reprocessing) wastes and stored where they can be readily retrieved. This retrievability, however, has less to do with any possible dangers these elements might pose to the environment in their present shallow burial vaults than it does to their possible future value. By fiscal year 1980, 24 million cubic feet of transuranic wastes had been buried at eight governmental and five commercial sites, with another 1.9 million cubic feet placed in retrievable storage after 1970. (These figures do not include an estimated 494 million cubic feet of soil that may have been contaminated either by transuranics leaking from ruptured or insufficient waste containers or by the residues of thirty-five "broken arrows," the Defense Department's code name for accidents which have involved nuclear bombs or warheads.) The volume of transuranics increases by approximately 25,400 cubic feet annually, and in its upcoming remedial action programs, the federal government expects to find and store 17,650 cubic feet more each year through the year 2000.

LOW-LEVEL WASTES: The term "low-level" is less a classification than it is a grab bag. Briefly stated, any radioactive discard that is not a product of reprocessing, is not contaminated by 10 or more nanocuries of transuranic elements, and is not uranium mill tailings, is low-level waste. Materials consigned to low-level burial range from such innocuous substances as the solidified residues of isotopic liquids intended for injection into hospital patients to such lethal radiation emitters as cobalt sources used in radiotherapy or coolant filters and control rods that have been removed from the cores of nuclear reactors. Between these two extremes are medical and research wastes, contaminated tools and equipment from power reactors, a good deal of plastic rubbish, gloves and shoe covers which are only radioactive-suspect, as well as the solidified residues from the conversion, enrichment and fabrication plants which produce nuclear fuels. By 1980, according to ORNL's tabulation, 23.6 million cubic feet of low-level waste was buried at six commercial sites (only three of which are still in operation) and 62.2 million cubic feet at seventeen Department of Energy sites. This material is expected to accumulate at the annual rate of at least 3.3 million cubic feet on the civilian side, and 2.4 million cubic feet from governmental operations.

PROSPECTIVE DECONTAMINATION AND DECOMMISSIONING WASTES: Like everything else, radioactive materials and facilities wear down or become obsolete and must be discarded. The seventy-three currently operating commercial reactors and ninety-three military and research reactors are expected to be in service no longer than 40 years before they become too radioactive to operate safely, and then they, too, will become low-level wastes, along with the vessels of 141 reactors already decommissioned, and the nuclear components of 126 reactor-driven ships, most of them submarines. Add to this the unknown quantities of discarded radioactive materials that the Nuclear Regulatory Commission permits to be "stored" in shallow burial trenches at power-plant sites; an estimated 19.4 million cubic feet of former Manhattan District and Atomic Energy Commission facilities that recent federal surveys have found to be contaminated to some degree; an estimated 10.6 million cubic feet of contaminated or suspect material from surplus Department of Energy nuclear sites—everything from fuel-reprocessing facilities down to the earth scraped from waste-treatment settling ponds—and finally an unknown, but certainly massive, quantity of materials from both currently operating and already decommissioned commercial nuclear facilities licensed by the NRC and the states.

While these vast quantities of radioactive materials have been accumulating since the invention of the atomic reactor in

1942, the United States government, in the words of a 1977 report by Comptroller General Elmer B. Staats, "has never articulated a firm policy on how it intends to manage, over the long term, either federal or commercial nuclear waste. Because of this there has also never been a clearly defined, technically feasible long-term waste management plan." And President Carter, in a 1980 message to Congress: "For more than 30 years, radioactive wastes have been generated by programs for the national defense, by the commercial nuclear power program and by a variety of medical, industrial and research activities. Yet past governmental efforts to manage radioactive waste have not been technically adequate."

Not only hasn't there been a policy, there hasn't even been a long-term governmental agency responsible for the formulation of such a policy. The Manhattan Engineering District, which built the bombs that ended World War II, yielded in 1946 to the Atomic Energy Commission, which, in effect, was cut in half in 1975 to form the Nuclear Regulatory Commission and the Energy Research and Development Administration, and in 1977, ERDA was reorganized as the Department of Energy. (And still another reorganization may be in the works if President Reagan keeps a campaign pledge to abolish DOE and redistribute its functions.)

As might be expected, scientists and government administrators blame each other for this nuclear-waste stalemate. Both politically and technically, radwaste was, as Carroll Wilson, the first general manager of the Atomic Energy Commission once put it, "not glamorous; there were no careers; it was messy, nobody got brownie points for caring about nuclear waste." As a matter of fact, what the United States Geological Survey was later to acknowledge as "the first serious examination of waste containment," did not take place until 1955, when the National Academy of Sciences brought sixty-five researchers to Princeton for an interdisciplinary seminar on the subject. Even subsequently, according to Harvard Professor Harvey Brooks at a 1976 seminar on waste management, "the whole problem had little prestige or glamour among the scientists and engineers who were being attracted to the new and growing field of nuclear energy. The few competent people who chose to work in the field got little recognition for their efforts." This also held true on an institutional level. In 1980, I asked Donald Oakley, director for waste programs research and development at Los Alamos National Scientific Laboratory, where atomic weapons are designed, why so little radwaste research had been performed there. "This lab looks on itself as a pretty tony place," he said. "It likes to take on those projects which have the highest intellectual requirements, and in waste management, you don't have that, so we simply haven't competed for much of the R and D [research and development] funding."

On the other hand, there never really has been that much research funding for scientists to compete for. Rustum Roy, one of the scientists who *has* received professional recognition for work on nuclear wastes—he now heads the Materials Research Laboratory of Pennsylvania State University—blames "the people who ran the Atomic Energy Commission's Division of Reactor Technology," for whom radwaste was a subsidiary responsibility. "They said screw the waste, let it sit there. So everybody let it sit there. Ninety-nine point five percent of the nuclear budget went into making reactors, and what was left over went into this squeal of the pig, this reactor garbage, and so nothing developed in the more than twenty years that we neglected the cleanup cycle." The budget numbers bear out Roy. In its early years, the Atomic Energy Commission allocated only about $40 million annually to handle the waste that was being produced and only about $5 million a year (and not all of that was always spent) on research on what to do with it. What did it need research for anyway, since, as the commission noted in 1959, "waste problems have proved completely manageable in the operation of the commission and of its predecessor wartime agency, the Manhattan District, Corps of Engineers, U. S. Army." Professor Daniel Metlay, of Indiana University's Department of Political Science, was assigned by the Nuclear Regulatory Commission, AEC's partial successor, to analyze prior official attitudes toward radwaste, and wrote in a report published by the NRC in 1978 that "for most of the commissioners, waste was simply unpleasant and unglamorous. For example, Dixy Lee Ray [the AEC's last chairman], according to two persons interviewed, would simply 'turn up her nose' when the subject was mentioned in meetings."

Even in the 1980s there are still those who at least figura-

tively turn up their noses at the consideration of the tough and
politically unpopular decisions that radwaste disposal is necessarily going to involve. "There's No Hurry on Nuclear Waste,"
the New York *Times* headlined a leading editorial on December 27, 1979, and then followed this up in August of 1980 with
an editorial declaration that "a couple of decades' waste won't
make the disposal problem significantly more difficult." In the
same month, across the continent, the Portland *Oregonian*
headlined its editorial on the subject "Nuclear Waste Trip Can't
be Rushed."

On the other hand, the Atomic Industrial Forum, a non-profit
organization of nuclear executives in government and business,
is pressing for immediate government action on radwastes, and
as part of its public relations effort, it has compiled the following
chronology of initiatives taken—and withdrawn—since 1957 on
the disposal of high-level wastes:

1957: National Academy of Sciences–National Research
   Council recommends high-level waste be buried in bedded salt deposits.

1957–1961: . . . studies on the feasibility of this proposal.

1961: Results of this study are reviewed by NAS-NRC,
   which recommends further study.

1963–67: . . . studies [conducted] under the name of Salt
   Vault (eventually to be located near Lyons, Kansas).

1963: Calcining demonstrated.

1965: AEC begins to convert liquid wastes . . . to salt cake.

1966: Subsequent NAS-NRC committee continues to advocate deep salt burial.

1968: Committee on Radioactive Waste Management established by NAS-NRC at request of AEC . . . reviews
   . . . programs for solidification and disposal.

1969–70: Conceptual design [developed] for a prototype
   facility to bury reprocessed HLW in salt . . .

1970: Panel on disposal in salt mines meets to hear presentation on burial of radioactive waste in bedded salt . . .

1970: AEC declares that all commercially generated HLW must be solidified within 5 years after reprocessing and delivered to a federal repository within 10 years.

1970: AEC tells state of Idaho that . . . waste stored there will be removed by 1980. This plan is predicated on availability of storage facility near Lyons, Kans.

1971: Congress directs AEC not to proceed with Lyons project until its safety can be certified.

1972: AEC abandons Lyons project.

1972: AEC announces retrievable surface-storage facility to hold military and commercial high-level waste for up to 100 years . . .

1975: ERDA gives up plans for early construction of retrievable surface-storage facility.

1976: ERDA sends letters to thirty-six state governors informing them of plans to conduct field investigations . . . part of plan to have a deep geological repository in salt available by 1985 . . .

1977: DOE announces plan for government to accept title and custody of commercial . . . spent fuel and to store it in away-from-reactor facilities pending availability of deep geologic repository.

1978: DOE issues draft report of Task Force for Review of Nuclear Waste Management [composed of representatives of fourteen federal agencies]. Included is statement that 1988, not 1985, is earliest that deep geologic repository can be available.

1978: DOE conducts a series of local hearings on its proposed Waste Isolation Pilot Project to be built near Carlsbad, New Mexico.

Left off this AIF chronology since it was not specifically a waste-disposal initiative, although it certainly affected waste-disposal programs and plans, was President Carter's 1977 decision, in the interest of nuclear weapons non-proliferation, not to allow commercial spent fuel to be reprocessed at all. Also subsequent to the preparation of the chronology came yet another flip-flop on the Waste Isolation Pilot Project. In February 1980, President Carter acted to scrap it, and less than a year later, after he left office, the Department of Energy reinstated it in a somewhat different form. It will now be a repository for government-produced transuranics and, for limited demonstration purposes only, a small quantity of unreprocessed military spent fuel. The DOE now projects the time frame of 1997 to 2006 as the earliest possible date for the establishment of a geologic repository for commercial spent fuel.

At present (1981), the formulation of nuclear-waste policy is the responsibility of eight governors, five state and local government officials, a spokesman for several Indian tribal councils and the heads of four federal executive agencies who comprise the State Planning Council on Radioactive Waste Management, a body appointed by President Carter in February 1980 to write what its chairman, South Carolina Governor Richard Riley, calls "a plan for a plan."

Indiana University's Professor Metlay, in a paper submitted at a 1979 symposium on radwaste management, points out that "as one initiative regularly failed and was replaced by another, public confidence was further undermined, the government's credibility was reduced, and additional obstacles to problem-solving in the future were erected." William L. Rankin, a researcher for the Human Affairs Research Centers of Battelle Memorial Institute in Seattle, in a survey of public-opinion polls dealing with the subject, reported that "in 1960, about 13 percent of the public questioned the safety of waste-disposal methods, and no respondent opposed nuclear power because of waste-disposal problems. By 1974, 52 percent of the American public believed that the disposal of nuclear wastes was a serious problem associated with nuclear power." However, it is Rankin's feeling—or at least it was in 1978 when he reported it to the American Nuclear Society—that "a majority of the public has confidence in the ability of technologists to solve the problems."

Others, however, have already begun to wonder how long

that majority will hold. In July 1976, Harvey Brooks, applied physics professor at the John F. Kennedy School of Government at Harvard, and a leading academic proponent of the nuclear industry, predicted in an address that "should nuclear energy ultimately prove to be socially unacceptable, it will be primarily because of the public's perception of the waste-disposal problem." And from the other camp, Lorna Salzman, mid-Atlantic representative of Friends of the Earth, led off a December 1978 article in *New Ecologist:* "If any issue has the power to shut down the nuclear industry, it is the disposal of radioactive wastes. To the general public it poses a more insidious and intractable threat than any other aspect of the nuclear fuel cycle. Hostility to dumping plans continues to mount, and is hitting the industry where it hurts."

Encouraging, if not actually fomenting that hostility, of course, are the various campaigns, in the courts and in the streets, of national environmental organizations like the Friends of the Earth, the Sierra Club, the Union of Concerned Scientists and the Natural Resources Defense Council, the last of which (talk about "hitting the industry where it hurts") was successful in 1978 at the federal appeals court level in requiring the Nuclear Regulatory Commission to conduct what it calls "a rule-making proceeding" to assess its own degree of confidence that radwaste *can* be safely disposed of eventually. "Once a series of reactors is operating," the court held, "it is too late to consider whether the wastes they generate should have been produced . . ." For more than 20 years now, the NRC and its predecessor AEC have simply been citing a 1957 finding of a National Academy of Sciences advisory committee on nuclear-waste disposal that "radioactive waste can be disposed of safely in a variety of ways and in a large number of sites in the United States," and nobody is in much doubt now that the NRC will eventually uphold the safety of nuclear-waste disposal, but the fact that the agency could be forced formally to consider the question 35 years after the first production of radwaste stunned nuclear advocates.

There are, of course, still those in government and industry who hold with Dr. Edward Teller, who is usually described as "the father of the H-bomb," that "waste disposal is a political problem, not a technical problem," and with Dixy Lee Ray, who went on from the AEC to become governor of Washington and to tell a reporter in 1980 that radwaste transportation and management are "simplicity itself. Of all the kinds of hazardous, toxic, dangerous things that are carried, radioactive wastes are probably the most easily handled and the least dangerous." However, in 1980, after a campaign that focused in part on the quantities of radwaste at the Hanford reservation, Miss Ray lost her bid for reelection, and Washington voters approved a referendum that would have the effect of limiting the quantities of low-level and transuranic wastes that could be brought into that state.

Like Miss Ray, many of those I have talked to in government and the nuclear industry have made, sometimes vociferously, the point about the waste hazards of other fuels. "Are you going to write about coal ash and acid rain?" Leo Macklin, a frequent New York spokesman for the Atomic Industrial Forum, responded when I asked him about aspects of the transportation of radwaste. To summarize this argument:

More direct radiation is received by people living downwind from coal-fired power plants than by those downwind from nuclear generators—a result of the release of microscopic particles of uranium which the coal contains at concentrations estimated by the nuclear industry at 1.8 parts per million. And non-radioactively, according to the Atomic Industrial Forum, a 1,000-megawatt coal generator discharges up the stack about 3,000 tons of particulates, 190 metric tons of hydrocarbons, 6 metric tons of aldehydes, 3.3 metric tons of zinc, a metric ton of lead and a metric ton of arsenic. A 1980 Canadian government report blames the sulphur dioxide effluent of coal and oil-fired plants for the acid rain which it says will destroy the fish population of 48,000 lakes in that country by the year 2000— as it has already emptied 170 lakes in the Adirondack Mountains of New York. At peak capacity, an average coal plant also puts out as much as 600 pounds of carbon dioxide every second, and this is said to be a principal factor in the "greenhouse effect," which scientists fear may raise world-wide temperatures. After a 5-year, $4.3-million federally supported research effort by faculty members at ten universities, the Ohio River

Basin Energy Study reported in 1981 that air emissions from coal-fired power plants apparently contribute to the deaths of up to 8,000 Ohio Valley residents annually.

And a Tennessee Valley Authority report maintains that coal fly ash, which is buried, contains radium at concentrations that may exceed Environmental Protection Administration limits.

Even the "soft" energy sources have environmental problems. It is probably safe to say that the thirty hydropower dams spread across the Columbia River are more responsible for the decline of that watercourse's fabled salmon than the effluent of the reactors—there were nine at one point—on the Hanford Atomic Energy Reservation. White-water enthusiasts are now fighting the damming of rivers and streams as valuable fishing and canoeing resources. The innovators of solar power, too, have to deal with the fact that photovoltaic cells, which are the driving force in these systems, contain arsenic, selenium and cadmium, all of which are perpetually toxic. Geothermal energy, like coal, turns out to have a considerable off-gas problem, and geothermal steam harnessed by a demonstration plant in Utah was recently found to contain dangerous levels of natural arsenic. Even the wind turns out to have drawbacks. In the Netherlands, environmentalists are fighting wind power on the ground that clusters of windmills will endanger birds, create noise pollution, spoil views and interfere with television reception, and in Vermont, a proposal to generate power from a windmill atop Lincoln Mountain is opposed by local residents who say it will detract from the region's natural beauty.

When it comes to relative danger potentials, Dr. Jerry Cohen, of Lawrence Livermore National Laboratory, has compiled a list of substances "which, on the basis of unit mass ingested were more lethal" than the plutonium which could conceivably be released in a nuclear-waste repository accident. Another scientist, Dr. John Gofman, emeritus professor of medical physics at the University of California in Berkeley, maintains that a pound of plutonium, perfectly distributed and ingested, could cause 338 million lung cancers, but Dr. Cohen's list of substances that have an even greater catastrophic potential includes botulism toxin, belladonna, hemlock, oleander extract and parathion and a number of similar insecticides. Lead is also a poison, he points out, "and if persistence is a major consideration, then lead with an infinite half-life is certainly a worse problem than plutonium. Yet we hear no advocates of rocketing waste lead to the sun or talk of committing it to the bowels of the earth under perpetual surveillance . . . Why?"

A ready answer to Dr. Cohen's question is that plutonium and other radioactive materials don't have to be inhaled or ingested to be harmful. Mere exposure to them at sufficient intensities or for sufficient lengths of time destroys cell tissue with effects that can be fatal, or, if the cells are in the reproductive organs, genetic. Botulism toxin and belladonna may be killers, but at least they don't have the capability of mutating future generations. In the State of New York's submission to the Nuclear Regulatory Commission's rule-making proceeding to assess its confidence in high-level waste disposal, Attorney General Robert Abrams calls it "no exaggeration to say that exposure of a significant number of people to the plutonium from a waste repository could threaten the genetic integrity of the human race."

Even the National Academy of Sciences–National Research Council panel on radioactive-waste disposal, which held in 1957 that radwaste certainly could be disposed of safely, took the occasion to warn that "unlike the disposal of any other type of waste, the hazard related to radioactive wastes is so great that no element of doubt should be allowed to exist regarding safety." In 1966, a successor NAS-NRC panel, in a report to the Atomic Energy Commission, held that "there should be no phenomenon involved in any of the waste disposal schemes that is not completely understood."

When it comes to analyzing the dangers of radioactive contamination, several nuclear physicists I have talked to have made the point that in most cases levels are only detectable because of the development of monitors of such sensitivity that they measure the emanations of pico (or millionths of one millionth) curies. True enough, but the curie is itself a measurement of thousandths of millionths, or 37 billion, atomic disintegrations every second, the standard having been fixed at the emission rate of one gram of pure radium (and named, of course, after Madame Marie Curie, who isolated the element).

I'm aware that background cosmic and fallout radiation are inevitably part of everyone's life, but when it comes to the question of how much radiation above this is sufficient to cause damage, I'm willing to stand on the professional assessment of Nobel laureate Hermann J. Muller: "There is no amount of radiation so small that it cannot provide harmful effects," as well as the introductory postulate of the 1972 report of the National Academy of Sciences' Advisory Committee on the Biological Effects of Ionizing Radiation: "No exposure to ionizing radiation should be permitted without the expectation of commensurate benefit."

Another form of this numbers game that nuclear scientists and environmentalists sometimes play is the characterization of "long" and "short" radioactive half-lives. Thorium 232's 10 billion years, more or less, is certainly long, and polonium 214's, in the ten thousandths of a second, obviously short; but what about, for example, strontium 90, with a half-life of 28 years? Most health physicists measure by ten half-lives, when a radioactive substance will have decayed to less than a thousandth of its former quantity, to calculate its "safe life." In environmentalists' arguments, however, this objective is reached only after 20 half-lives, when the material will have decayed to less than one millionth of its former quantity. My own perspective on this, for what it's worth, is that anything that will still be around in sufficient quantities to present a hazard of radiation without "the expectation of commensurate benefit" to my (as yet unborn) grandchildren has a half-life long enough to require a commitment from its producers to its permanent isolation from the biosphere.

In 1971, Alvin J. Weinberg, then the director of Oak Ridge National Laboratory, coined the often-quoted phrase "Faustian Bargain" for this commitment. "We nuclear people have made a Faustian bargain with society," he said in the Rutherford Centennial Lecture delivered at the annual meeting of the American Association for the Advancement of Science. "On the one hand, we offer . . . energy that is cheaper than energy from fossil fuel. Moreover, this source of energy, when properly handled, is almost nonpolluting . . . But the price that we demand of society for this magical energy source is both a vigilance and a longevity of our social institutions that we are quite unaccustomed to . . . Is mankind prepared to exert the eternal vigilance needed to ensure proper and safe operation of its nuclear energy system? This admittedly is a significant commitment that we ask of society . . ."

"Eternal vigilance" is certainly a "significant commitment"— a hell of a commitment in fact—equal to the price we are asked to pay for liberty. Even the federal Environmental Protection Agency limits its "reliance on institutional controls" in America to "about 100 years." Does that mean that I am reporting on radwaste from the viewpoint of an opponent of nuclear power and a nuclear defense? I don't think so. What I do think is that a calculation is overdue, not only of the economic and political costs, but of the social consequences cited by Dr. Weinberg, in disposing of nuclear wastes by the best available technology. And whether or not the United States produces another nuclear watt of energy or another nuclear weapon beginning with the moment you read this, there remain 39 years of wastes already produced that still must be dealt with by the best available technology.

Arguably, present defense strategy—and past and future atomic-weapons proliferation—make retreat from a nuclear defense improbable, if not impossible. Nor do I think it feasible— or advisable—to turn the clock back on atomic medicine. When it comes to electricity, however, I think it is past time to count all the costs of what is called "the back end of the nuclear cycle." Only when these are added to the better-known expenses of nuclear-power generation will it be possible to calculate the entire cost that will ultimately have to be paid for electricity that we have already consumed. And as Norman Cousins points out, "later generations will have to pay the price for the way we meet our energy needs today." Just as we, today, are now only beginning to comprehend the environmental, social and economic costs of the atomic wastes that were first dumped in 1942 into a trench on a hill in Palos Forest.

2
MILL TAILINGS

Unlike other forms of radwaste, which are hidden away below the ground, nearly all uranium mill tailings are heaped up on the surface of the earth. At Lewiston, 10 miles north of Niagara Falls, in New York, a 165-foot concrete silo that contains 1,757 tons of processed tailings is, in fact, a local landmark. Granted, 1,757 tons is a very small drop in a very big bucket of 140 million tons, which is the approximate weight of the 1981 national inventory of 2.955 billion cubic feet of this form of waste; however, like the radwaste at Palos Forest, the tailings at Lewiston are historic—and also like the radwaste at Palos Forest, they are putting forth measurable levels of radioactive contamination into the surrounding environment.

Mined originally for radium in what was then the Belgian Congo and is now Zaïre, these tailings were brought to America before the outbreak of World War II by Edward Sengier, the then manager of the Belgian corporation, Union Minière, who had both the foresight to recognize the strategic importance of the material and the means to keep it out of the hands of the Axis powers. On his own initiative, Sengier loaded the ore onto a freighter and brought it to New York where, without any further idea of what to do with it, he stored it in a warehouse in Staten Island. It was still there in 1942 when a Manhattan Engineering District officer looked up Sengier in New York to ask his advice on acquiring a sizable quantity of Congo ore for a secret wartime purpose. As it turned out, Sengier's material, from which only the radium had been extracted, was also extremely rich in the uranium that subsequently fueled Enrico Fermi's first University of Chicago reactor and its replacement at Argonne Laboratory—unquestionably some of the radioactivity now leaching from Palos Park originated from this shipment—and eventually this became the fuel of the uranium bomb at Nagasaki. (The Hiroshima bomb was composed of plutonium also fissioned from this uranium.)

Even as it fulfilled its wartime purposes, however, Sengier's ore, code-named K-65, left a radioactive trail across the Eastern United States before it ended up in the concrete silo at Lewiston. So rich is it, even after its wartime refinement, that unextracted concentrations of uranium still within it exceed those of uranium now being mined commercially, and scientists monitoring it believe that decay of some of this uranium has already produced a kilogram of radium, making the silo, in effect, the repository of the world's largest known quantity of that radioactive element.

Built originally as a dynamite-production facility in World War II, and camouflaged as a farm (hence the concrete silo), the Lake Ontario Ordnance Works originally comprised 1,500 acres. The known quantity of 20,489 tons of radwaste dumped there during and after the war were, however, confined to a central 190 acres, with the remainder of the site sold off in a number of transactions. Immediate neighbors of the facility now include one of the nation's largest toxic-waste disposal facilities, a regional school and, across a country road, a trailer campground.

The present contract caretaker of the fenced-in facility is one of the nation's leading nuclear firms, National Lead of Ohio, and the chief of the three-man crew employed to monitor the instruments that take periodic air and water samples around the site for radiological tests is Joseph Kirchue, a short, pleasant man in his sixties, who went to work there in the mid 1950s. Kirchue professes himself completely unworried by the fact that his predecessor on the job, James S. Schmidt, and another

worker both died of cancers diagnosed while they were working at LOOW. "I live only ten miles down the road," he says,
"and I come here sometimes seven days a week because I like
the place."

Driving me around the site, Kirchue points out that the silo,
although the most prominent feature of the facility, is not, in
fact, the repository of most of the ores now of radiological concern. More than four times as much, or 8,227 tons, of Congo ore
mined subsequently to K-65 lies at the bottom of two 19-foot-
deep vats within a building now half buried in the earth. Also
inside a concrete structure are 1,878 tons of radioactive sludge
from the processing of pitchblende ore, and, nearby, where
they were simply dumped on the earth in 1946, lie 8,235 tons
of radioactive tailings also from pitchblende. "To eliminate a
potential dust hazard," a contractor noted several years ago,
this pitchblende tailings pile was covered with topsoil and
seeded in 1964. Even so, radioactive radon gas continues to
seep through this cover, and scientists are now attempting to
determine whether a further asphalt or concrete topping will
significantly reduce these emanations.

It is the silo, however, that is the principal attraction for most
of those who seek out the site in the northwestern corner of
New York. Vented at the top and lined with concrete at its base,
it is set well apart from other buildings at the facility. "There
was an inspection in 1964," Kirchue said as we circled its base,
"and they found the tower was shaling—concrete does shale—
so a contractor came in and put an additional five-inch liner
around the tower up to a hundred ten feet, which is as high as
the material goes. The stuff inside—we took the last sample in
1977 through a porthole—is orangy, yellow, greenish clay. It's
damp, but we aren't getting any leaching through the concrete
base, and that's it."

But is it? Even reinforced, the concrete silo is beginning to
show the effects of age, and air samples collected above its
rooftop vent show radiation readings of 5 to 10 microrems per
hour, which is about eighteen times background. In any case,
something is going to have to be decided soon on what to do
about the radwaste inside it. Under the contract Sengier negotiated with the United States for his Congo ore, only the ura-

nium was sold to the United States; the tailings, rich in other metals as well as the unremoved uranium, remain the property of Afromet Corporation, the successor company to Union Minière. The federal government agreed in 1958 to store the material at LOOW for another 25 years, but with that lease about to run out in 1983, Afromet's current president, Ralph Sorum, says he doesn't know what's going to be done with it. Afromet is reported in the press to be negotiating with the Department of Energy either to take over the material or to renegotiate its LOOW lease indefinitely, and while Sorum refused to confirm this, he did concede to me that selling it outside government channels "would be a hassle. Look at all the Nuclear Regulatory Commission regulations that will have to be met just for packing and moving it to a refinery, and then I can't just sell the stuff to John Doe."

Conversely, though, "the stuff" in the silo and lying around it can't be left at LOOW indefinitely. Extensive levels of contamination are now being measured at many of the 27 air monitors and 19 wells that Kirchue and his men sample on the site. An environmental survey in the fall of 1979 found radon concentrations that are double New York State's permissible limit at the fence at the southeast corner of the facility, and readings taken at nearby residences extend up to three times background. Radioactive contamination has also been found in soil as deep as 20 feet below the site and in a ditch which bisects it. In 1972, this ditch was scraped and the land from it reburied to clean it of some of this contamination. A study completed last year found it extensively contaminated, again primarily by radium measured at levels as high as 1,660 picocuries—the state's limit is 5. The source of this radioactivity is believed to be pipes leaking from buildings where tailings and pitchblende are stored; its eventual destination, through several streams, is Lake Ontario.

In February 1981, a New York State Assembly Task Force on Toxic Substances charged that the LOOW site had been "singularly ill-suited" for the storage of radioactive waste in the first place, and that the land now being used by the toxic waste-disposal facility had never been adequately decontaminated either of radwastes or of dangerous TNT residues.

Environmental surveys are performed in and around the remaining ordnance works property by researchers from Battelle Memorial Institute of Columbus, Ohio, who are now experimenting with asphalt coverings to determine their effectiveness in containing the seeping radon. In July 1980, I asked Joseph Dettorre, projects manager and chief senior researcher on these studies, what would eventually happen to the radwaste there. "The next thing that gets done in terms of overall site disposition is to do a full decontamination and decommissioning study of alternatives," he said. "We have to determine what can feasibly be done with all that material." Dettorre has his own personal hope for the site—he'd like to see it turned into an environmental laboratory for the study of the disposal of mining radwastes—but he doubts the prospects for that, and he thinks that eventually the site will somehow be decommissioned: "The whole job, if you could do it for less than $30 million, you'd be ahead of the game."

In the meantime, Joseph Kirchue and his two assistants continue their indefinite patrol at Lewiston. Despite Kirchue's liking for the place, he is willing to concede that working at LOOW entails some discomfort. Several years ago, the facility's waste-water treatment system was donated to the town government, which appears to have accepted it under the belief that the federal government would pay for the necessary decontamination work. When that expectation failed to materialize, the town simply shut the system down, leaving the LOOW caretakers to rely on a chemical toilet.

"I don't know what they're going to do about the rest of the stuff, but I have a great idea about what to do with the silo," Kirchue told me. "Put four Pratt and Whitney engines around its base and rocket it off the face of the earth [in fact, there are a number of federally subsidized researchers now considering the feasibility of doing something very much like that with the longest-lived high-level wastes]. With our luck, though, the damn thing would just go straight up and then come straight down again."

Although uranium mill tailings are the least radioactive form of radwaste, because of their sheer volume the federal Environmental Protection Agency believes that they may present "the greatest environmental impact of all waste forms over the years." One of the most prominent academic proponents of the nuclear industry, University of Pittsburgh physics professor Bernard Cohen puts forth the contrasting view, though, that consuming the uranium in reactors is, in effect, "cleansing the earth" of radioactive contamination that heretofore existed primarily below the surface. One answer to that argument is that only 15 percent of the radioactivity in the ore ever makes it into a reactor (and only a small fraction of that is actually consumed). The unseparated uranium and the other actinides that comprise the other 85 percent, instead of decaying away harmlessly within deep geological barriers, is being left to radiate uncontrolled for the most part on the surface of the earth.

The extraction of only enough uranium to fuel a single 1,000-megawatt light-water reactor for a year requires the generation of 106 tons of tailings. The American operation of 73 commercial power, 145 military production and propulsion, and 93 research reactors, plus the provision of uranium for foreign sales, requires the mining of more than 20,000 tons of uranium every day. This ore, from 29 open-pit and 193 underground mines, is shipped to 19 operating mills, where it is pulverized and ground fine enough to pass through a mesh of 40 wires per centimeter, processed in a torrent of water to remove the uranium, which averages about two tenths of one percent by volume, and then poured into settling ponds. From there the fine tailings are conveyed to piles reaching as high as 100 feet. There are 43 sites with tailings piles in the West and one within the city limits of Canonsburg, Pa., where some of the K-65 ore was milled. A Sierra Club publication maintains that levels of radium 3,000 times federal guidelines have been recorded beneath what was once the settling pond there, accessible to drainage into streams that run to the Ohio River, a source of drinking water in Western Pennsylvania. The Department of Energy concedes that contamination extends from 2 to 6 feet below the surface of the entire 19-acre site but maintains that "river water quality has not been affected." The tailings at Canonsburg actually predate the development of the nuclear reactor by more than 30 years. Built in 1911, the mill extracted

radium from carnotite ore—the gram of radium presented by
President Wilson to Madame Curie in 1916 was refined at Canonsburg, and in 1942, some of the rich K-65 material was processed there. After the shutdown of the mill, the land was sold
in 1966 to a development corporation which now attempts to
operate it as an industrial park. However, the recently publicized presence of 15,000 tons of tailings and approximately
185,000 tons of contaminated soil, in the words of the Department of Energy's survey of the site, "inhibits future growth of
the area."

Visually, tailings piles differ greatly—if you've seen one, you
very definitely have not seen them all. The grains themselves
range from yellow-orange to dirty-gray according to processing
methods, and once piled, this material tends to take on characteristics from its environment. For example, the 2.3 million-ton
pile on 111 acres in the metropolitan area of Salt Lake City, in
the political jurisdiction of South Salt Lake City, appears much
like any other overgrown municipal land-fill. Nearly 2 million
tons of crusted uranium and vanadium tailings from a mill
demolished in 1970 lie in the shape of a 20-foot-high horseshoe
in the midst of a nine-square-block warehousing and light-
industrial area, and they are separated from the surrounding
streets by nothing more substantial than two strands of unbarbed wire and a small, easily jumped ditch which carries
tailings leached from the pile by rain water to the Jordan River,
which connects Utah Lake and the Great Salt Lake. There are
radioactive-danger and no-trespassing signs around the perimeter of the site, but you have to look for them, and they appear
to have been ignored both by midnight rubbish dumpers and
by several area contractors—to date, aerial surveys have identified forty-two sites in the metropolitan area that appear to
have been built on contaminated fill taken from these pilings.
I stopped at one of the factories that border the site to ask
several workers if they knew what the nearby mounds contained. Two of the three people I asked did not—the third
correctly identified some of the material as uranium ore but said
he was not concerned about the possibility of radioactive contamination from it.

On the other hand, a 17-million-ton (so far) pile still being

built outside of Grants, New Mexico, by United Nuclear–
Homestake Partners is one of the most impressive man-made
sights of the Southwestern desert. Approximately a hundred
feet high, rounded at the corners, it resembles a half-mile-
square football stadium surmounted by a roadway complete
with streetlights which permit trucks to continue the piling
work at night. Seen in the sunset, though, the pile reflects the
yellow-orange glow of the sands that comprise it. The mill that
feeds this piling is accessible from the highway that runs out of
Grants, but on the other three sides, the piling itself is fenced
only by strands of unbarbed wire. A "Caution, Radioactive Material" sign is visible if you look for it; more prominent, however, are "Private Property—No Trespassing" signs. Perhaps a
hundred yards from the base of the piling, across a gravel road
from the site, are a number of house trailers on more-or-less
permanent foundations. (In its draft environmental-impact
statement on uranium mill tailings, the Nuclear Regulatory
Commission calculated possible effects on a hypothetical
"nearby" resident presumed to live 2 kilometers downwind
from a mill—many of these trailer homes were less than half
that distance away, and to the south, toward Grants, a housing
development in progress appears to be closer than 4 kilometers,
a downwind radius from the typical mill within which the statement maintains that federal non-occupational radiation standards cannot be met.)

The problem posed by uranium tailings piles goes far beyond
the question of aesthetics in both the desert and municipal
environments, however. Downstream from piles in the uranium belt of western New Mexico, the Environmental Protection Agency reported in 1975 that shallow aquifers that are
water sources have been "grossly contaminated with selenium
attributable to excessive seeping" from mill tailings. Selenium
is not radioactive, but in toxicity it is comparable to arsenic.
Radioactive contaminants at levels above maximum permissible concentrations have also been measured in water supplies
in this region. A 1973 publication of the International Atomic
Energy Agency of the United Nations warns that "if strong
winds and dry conditions are common [as they are in New
Mexico and Utah], it may be necessary to stabilize the piles in

some way to prevent the transport of dust clouds to populated areas. If the piles are exposed to weathering and to water leaching, attention must be given to the water runoffs . . . ." From all appearances, no such attention has been given to the pile near Grants, and only a limited and partial cover of dirt was ever applied to the Salt Lake City pile, which has been called by Utah Governor Scott Matheson "the largest microwave oven in the West." (By right, however, that title belongs to the working Kerr McGee Nuclear Corporation pile at Ambrosia Lake, N.M., which is estimated to contain more than 23 million tons of pilings, more than ten times the Salt Lake City accumulation).

In addition to runoff contamination, tailings piles pose the more immediate hazard of emissions of the radioactive gas radon. A relatively short way-station on the uranium-238–to–lead-206 decay chain, radon 222 is formed in the decay of radium 226, and its half-life is only 3.8 days. In this short gaseous period, however, these atoms have the capability of spreading alpha, the most virulent form of radiation, wherever the winds take them. Should the radon atoms happen to decay within someone's lungs, or should their solid daughters, unstable isotopes of polonium, bismuth and lead, be inhaled, even in their microscopic proportions, there is the possibility that these particles will lodge within tissue and, continuing to radiate, they could cause fibrosis and lung cancers.

Of course, not all paths of radon exposure emanate from tailings piles. Uranium miners are also subject to overexposure to it. Basing recent findings on statistics compiled by the National Institute of Occupational Safety and Health, the Health Research Institute, which is allied with Ralph Nader, noted an excess of 173 lung cancer deaths (over probabilities) in a study group of 4,146 men who worked in the pits before 1946. An even more likely place than a tailings pile or a uranium mine to suffer radon exposure may be your own unventilated basement, particularly if your home was built with, or is proximate to, minerals laden with traces of isotopes. The National Radiological Protection Board estimates that radon is responsible for fifteen cases of lung cancer for every million inhabitants of homes with typical ventilation, and the 1979 draft of the Nuclear Regulatory Commission's environmental-impact statement on uranium milling estimates a potential for 1,594 annual American deaths from exposure to radon emanating from building interiors, 1,162 from the gas emanating from the earth, and only 6 from tailings piles.

But the problem with tailings, no matter how imposing they may appear in mesa-like piles in the desert, is that they can't be expected always to stay where they're put. As early as 1969, it was estimated that 3 million tons of these fine grains had been blown or washed into the Colorado River watershed. In a study of three inactive mills reported in the 1972 Symposium of the Health Physics Society, one was found to be subject to "dust devils, the miniature cyclones of desert areas," and as a result, isotope concentrations measured 75 feet downwind from this pile "approached or equaled non-occupational MPC [maximum permitted concentration] values." Another tailings pile subject to the effects of high winds is at Durango, Colo., where the United States Vanadium Corporation refined uranium from 1943 to 1963. The Durango pile, built on the banks of the Animas River, eventually grew to a height of 230 feet, and in 1966 the federal Water Pollution Control Administration found it necessary to warn Coloradoans and New Mexicans downstream who drank from the river that they were being exposed to three times the maximum permissible exposure from radium 226 and strontium 90. More alarming even than these river measurements were the levels of isotopes found in water organisms. Radium alone was measured in river plants and creatures at ten thousand times its concentration in the river.

In 1980, the Environmental Protection Agency, after a two-year study, reported the finding of 22,795 of what it called "anomalies" of higher-than-background radiation levels in towns around abandoned mills. It has also been estimated by a government contractor that $126 million in remedial actions taken at twenty-two inactive mill tailings piles would avert 46 cancer cases in the next 25 years and 339 in the next century. The need for such remedial action—and soon—on mill tailings piles is stressed even by nuclear proponents like Professor Cohen of the University of Pittsburgh. "There's no evidence that any member of the public has been injured by radon from the tailings," he told me recently, "and the thing that knocks radon out [of his projections of future nuclear health statistics] is that I am assuming the tailings are being taken care of; if they are not covered, I will have to back off."

In fact, something is being done both about inactive mill-tailings piles and those that will be built. In its 1980 final generic impact-statement on uranium milling, the Nuclear Regulatory Commission added to its future mill-licensing considerations "remoteness from populated areas, hydrogeologic and other environmental conditions that will be conducive to keeping the contamination in the tailings away from usable ground-water sources, and the potential for erosion, disruption and dispersion of the tailings by natural forces." It didn't entirely rule out piling the material above the earth's surface, but it did specify as a "prime option," wherever practicable, "placement below grade, either in mines or specially excavated pits" (but not in deep mines or deep pits that have already been excavated to get this ore, since advantages of these disposal options would be outweighed by the environmental and financial costs of getting them into these mines, and because the tailings could then be reached by ground-water flooding). Also to be required is a minimum of 10 feet of a "full self-sustaining vegetative cover" or rock cover "to reduce wind and water erosion to negligible levels."

Twenty-five inactive or abandoned tailings piles also are scheduled to be cleaned up—at government expense. In 1978, after years of wrangling over who would pay what costs—the federal government sought a 75 percent–25 percent split with the states; the states thought the United States should pay the entire bill—Congress adopted and President Carter signed the Uranium Mill Tailings Radiation Control Act, which put the mills under the licensing authority of the NRC in the first place, and provided a 90 percent–10 percent split with the states on twenty of the piles, with the federal government paying the entire amount on five others on tribal lands. Altogether these twenty-five sites are estimated to contain 28 million tons of tailings, with perhaps about 12 million pounds of residual uranium—of which 2.6 million pounds is considered potentially reclaimable. The tailings also contain quantities of vanadium, gold, silver and molybdenum, but at current (1981) market prices, "reclamation will be very marginal at any of our sites," says Richard Campbell, a stocky, white-haired retired Air Force colonel who is in charge of the federal program. Working out of a basement office at the Department of Energy's Albuquerque Operations Office located within Kirtland Air Force Base, Campbell has watched the projected cost of his project escalate from $126 million, which the Department of Energy projected in 1978, to "$480 million in 1980 dollars, or $780 million if you escalate for inflation over the seven years we are mandated to work in."

On the average, these sites have been inactive for about 15 years, and Campbell told me late in 1980 that preliminary surveys showed that it might be feasible to stabilize sixteen of them in place, but that the other nine—in Salt Lake, Canonsburg, Shiprock, N.M., Durango, Grand Junction, Gunnison and two at Rifle, Colo., and Riverton, Wyo.—would probably have to be moved. The question, of course, is moved where?

"That's what we're working on right now," Campbell said, "trying to find candidate disposal sites for these nine piles. An expensive part of this is going to be transport—we're estimating about ten cents a ton-mile to move the tailings, so it's important to minimize distances—we're looking for a maximum radius of thirty miles.

"Now, at Durango, for example, there is an attractive site about 12 miles away, and it looks like we can run eighty to ninety truckloads a day and move the 1.55 million tons of tailings in about three years." At the ten-cent-per-ton-mile estimate, the cost of this transport would be nearly two million dollars—but of possibly even greater consequence could be the political costs. A thirty-mile shift, in most, if not all, cases, would require the crossing of one (or possibly more) political jurisdictions. How is a township, or in some cases a county, to be persuaded to accept a hazard that its neighbor is trying to get rid of? (Of course, this question is not exclusive to mill tailings, or even to nuclear waste.) There are also jurisdictional questions to be resolved within the federal government itself. An overanxious would-be contractor's attempt to develop a tailings-disposal site in southeastern Utah or western Colorado in December of 1980 brought Campbell a rebuke from the district

manager of the Bureau of Land Management, who protested
that the effort "has thus far succeeded in alienating a substantial
number of local citizens, as well as failing to establish a working
relationship with my office."

"It *is* a very delicate political operation," Campbell concedes.
"We start at the office of the state's governor, and from there
we get an interface working with the towns and counties—we
are trying to be very careful not to make people feel that it is
us, the feds, who are going to make the decision and then
confront them with it. At Durango, for instance, we have a
coordinating group with representatives of the Chamber of
Commerce, county government, the local bar, medical association, a college and a local public-interest group. Our commitment is to come before them every time they want information
and to present them with the alternatives under consideration
before every decision is made." And what if all the proposed
alternatives are rejected by the local board? "Then we leave it
to the state to work out. The law says the states pay only 10
percent, but they have to take over the burden of dealing with
local governments."

Whether the tailings piles are moved or not, there still will be
a considerable environmental impact simply in digging holes
big enough to bury them in, in accordance with the 1980 NRC
licensing recommendation, covering these pits with an asphalt-
like emulsion to form a gas-proof membrane—and then piling
10 feet of earth on top of that. Campbell is somewhat sensitive
to kidding about a newspaper headline (over a story about the
decision to require the asphalt emulsion) announcing that the
Department of Energy was planning to "pave the desert" with
18 acres of tailings. One of his biggest problems, however, will
be the finding of approximately 494 million cubic feet of earth
that will be required to put all twenty-five sites under the requisite cover—the 2.6 million tons of tailings at Ambrosia Lake,
N.M., will need 87 million cubic feet of earth: "I'm afraid we'll
create a bigger problem just digging up that amount of cover
to put it on top," Campbell says. "We're looking now toward
ways that will be the most economic and feasible."

Will this mammoth effort—and expense—be effective? At
least at first, the asphalt membrane and cover should trap and

hold the radon long enough so that when it decays again into a solid, it will still be contained. The law establishing the program requires an emission standard of 2 picocuries per square meter of surface per second, which is about double the normal background rate in the Western states. The unanswered question, of course, is how long this containment will hold. To keep it intact, Campbell concedes, the buried tailings sites will have to be protected from grazing animals, and he therefore is skeptical about the "vegetative cover" approved by the NRC in its uranium milling environmental-impact statement. Some desert plants, he points out, put roots down more than ten feet and could pierce the asphalt membrane. "Right now, we're considering covering the sites with riprap [irregular stones], but even after that, the Department of Energy has a responsibility for long-term management and surveillance. Obviously each of these piles is going to be a maintenance chore for as long as there is someone around to look after the fencing."

Also skeptical—for want of a better word—both about the vegetative cover and the durable qualities of asphalt are three members of a research team that for the past 5 years has been working at Los Alamos Scientific Laboratory to devise a better method of isolating tailings. "At one site where a commercial operator asphalted over a piling ten or fifteen years ago, we checked back and found problems," said David Dresen, staff manager of the team. "Gophers had penetrated the cover and brought tailings back to the surface." "Another of the inactive sites, at Tuba City, had a man-made cover," his associate, Caroline Meis, put in, "and the first reports [in 1968] were that it was grand and glorious, but within two years it started to degrade. Now you can hardly find a trace of it."

However, even if Campbell is eventually successful in isolating the tailings under asphalt at or around the twenty-five inactive sites, piles at the nineteen active mills are growing at a faster rate than either the government or private industry now proposes to keep up with. The Nuclear Regulatory Commission says these licensees "must develop definitive programs meeting the technical and financial criteria" in its new regulations, but the legal question of whether or not the estimated 157 million tons of tailings at the active mills are "grandfathered" out of reach of the NRC's recent regulations is expected to take years to work its way through the courts. And beyond that there is the pragmatic question of whether even the wealthy mining industry has the financial capability to meet these safeguards. If it is going to cost $780 million, as Campbell believes, to dispose of 25 million tons of tailings at the inactive sites, where will the money come from to dispose of more than five times that amount? Even the General Accounting Office, which is not noted for liberality in questions dealing with federal appropriation, notes that more than half these tailings were generated in producing uranium for defense and national research programs, and in 1979 it recommended assistance to mill owners faced with expense of "retroactive stabilization."

On top of this, add the cost of stabilizing more than three times the present quantity of tailings that will have to be produced at perhaps sixty additional mills if the United States is to meet present goals. According to the NRC's 1979 draft generic environmental-impact statement on uranium milling, an additional total of about 539 million tons of tailings "is estimated to be generated by conventional uranium mills over the time period 1978 to 2000." More recent estimates of demand cut this quantity 20 percent to 30 percent, and there is also the increasing success of an unconventional method of mining, the "in-situ leach" process, a method of extracting uranium oxide without mills, without tailings, and even without having to send men or machinery underground to dig out the ore. In "solution mining," as it is also called, sodium bicarbonate and hydrogen peroxide are combined to form a "leachate" (there will be more about leachates and their effects on buried waste in subsequent chapters), and this is injected within a high-pressure stream of water into an underground aquifer. The chemicals oxidize the uranium, permitting it to be dissolved in the water, which is then pumped up to the surface, run through an ion-exchange column to deposit the uranium, and then reinjected back into the aquifer again.

A great advantage of this method is that instead of 250 to 1,000 pounds of tailings for each pound of uranium produced, the waste is reduced to a pound of chemicals to be buried as low-level waste for each pound of uranium. A disadvantage is that the process requires the expensive drilling of a number of wells, both to inject and withdraw the water and to monitor the field around the aquifer to insure that there are no "excursions" of the injected fluid. Mobil Oil, to cite one company, has had commercial success with this method in Texas aquifers in the 400-foot range; Mobil engineers at Crownpoint, N. M., where the aquifers are 2,000 feet deep, report only results that have "encouraged" them to plan another such pilot.

Not all engineers are comfortable with solution mining, however, and several years ago another company, Wyoming Mineral Corporation, had to shut down a solution mine after an "excursion" of fluid worked its way through an overlying formation that had been thought sufficient to contain it. "The problem," said one mining specialist I talked to about this method, "is that the action all takes place hundreds or thousands of feet down, and we have to monitor it indirectly, so we don't always know what's going on down there."

Nor is all uranium susceptible to solution mining. The geology has to be right: an aquifer of porous sandstone enclosed by sufficiently thick formations of denser rocks. The production of tailings continues, therefore, at the 1980 rate of about 20,000 tons (from which about 40 tons of uranium oxide have been extracted) every day. At Los Alamos, where they are working on developing a better "envelope" than the asphalt membrane, the tailings research team is also experimenting on methods of treating the ore during or just after the milling process—dewatering or stabilizing the tailings in cement are two possibilities—to reduce their later hazard when piled. In this, however, as the research team's alternate leader, James Steger, concedes, "practical economics are involved, and the practical reality is that long-range economics are not considered as much as the shorter-term interests of the mining industry."

Another practical factor is that radiological and non-radiological concerns over mill tailings inevitably overlap. Mining firms worry that restrictions now imposed on uranium tailings will be applied next to other spoils piles. Copper ore, for example, contains uranium not removed during milling, and copper tailings piles may therefore produce as much radon as uranium tailings piles. The other side of that coin is that the non-radiological pollutants of uranium mill tailings may be transported by ground water or through the "vegetation cover" recommended by the NRC, posing more hazards to wildlife and man than radon and the other isotopes.

"We're looking at things like molybdenum, arsenic, selenium and vanadium that we don't think have received as much attention as they deserve," says David Dresen, of the Los Alamos team. "Molybdenum and selenium we've already found to be very mobile, and both are taken up by native plants that would grow on tailings piles. We've found concentrations in some of these plants in the laboratory that would be above levels that could be toxic to growing animals. Last summer, at the NRC's request, we did a few studies near an active pile (of about 1.15 million tons of tailings) near Canon City, Colorado, and what we came up with, in particular, was molybdenum which had been transported a considerable distance from the tailings. Also in the ground waters used for irrigating small agricultural fields, we found evidence of molybdenum accumulation and high levels of it in vegetation in an area where University of Colorado researchers tell us they have had cases of molybdenosis."

Again apparently as a matter of "practical economics," this pile, fed by a mill of the Cotter Corporation, continues to grow unstabilized. "This is an area where the mining interests are pretty prominent," says a member of the Los Alamos team. In one notable example, however, long- and short-range economics coincided to benefit a mining firm, Ranchers Exploration, which held the rights to a small (704,000 tons) pile which had been dumped by prior owners only 10 feet above the bank of the San Miguel River at Naturita in southwestern Colorado. In the winter of 1977–78, this company, at its own expense, dug up these tailings and trucked them to clay-lined pits it had dug 10 miles away. The purpose of this move was commercial: The material was subjected to an acid leach to recover residual uranium and vanadium, but subsequently covered by 2 feet of earth, the tailings were out of harm's way the following year when the San Miguel flooded and inundated the original site of the pile.

The reprocessing of these tailings was reported only marginally profitable, but at least Ranchers Exploration was able to report to its stockholders the avoidance of the substantial legal liability that now faces the United Nuclear Corporation in the contamination of the Rio Puerco, a stream that runs through Gallup, N.M., into Arizona. United Nuclear's 3,800-ton-per-day mill at Church Rock, N.M., was completed in 1977 with a compacted clay dam appraised by Department of Energy officials as "state of the art," to contain the tailings that are produced in a slurry and diverted into a settling pond. On the morning of July 16, 1979, for no apparent reason, the dam broke, sending a 3-foot crest of 100 million gallons of radioactive water (later estimated to contain 1,100 tons of tailings) into the nearly dry bed of the stream and contaminating it for at least 80 miles. Radiation in the Rio Puerco was measured at the outset at 100,000 picocuries per liter—the federal maximum permitted concentration for this form of contamination is 15 picocuries— and even though Gallup doesn't draw drinking water from this stream, several nearby Navajo villages do.

An alarm went out to the residents of Gallup to keep away from the Puerco, but word got to the Indian villages too late to keep from contamination ten children found playing on its banks. Since then, United Nuclear has been trucking 10,000 gallons a day of potable water to replace the Navajos' supply, but the Indians have found it difficult to keep their livestock from drinking from the river. "Our cows don't read press releases," a Navajo leader has pointed out.

Four months after this spill, after rebuilding the dam (and presumably improving on its "state of the art" technique), and scraping away and removing about 3,800 tons of river-bottom sand to be disposed of as low-level waste, United Nuclear was permitted to reopen its mill. However, an official of the New Mexico Environmental Improvement Division has estimated that a minimum of 50 miles of river bottom really should be removed, pointing out to the Chicago *Tribune* that even in the scraped sections, crusted radioactive salts appear on the surface of the water after each rain, and "when the river dries up, you have dust blowing. People in the area might be living there 20 years or 30 years and be exposed to the dust."

In the end, the Federal Environmental Protection Agency citation United Nuclear received for discharging uranium mill process water without a permit may prove to be the least of the company's legal liability in the spill. A hundred twenty-five Navajo families have filed damage suits asking $100,000 apiece, and in 1980, a company attorney predicted the filing of three hundred more actions in tribal courts.

The Church Rock accident is only the largest of six recorded tailings dam failures; two floods and six pipeline ruptures also contaminated American watercourses radioactively between 1959 and 1977. And in 1962, there was a spill of one of the piles (for no obvious physical reason except that it may have been built too steeply) that sent 200 tons of tailings into the Cheyenne River at Edgemont, S.D. Most of this material later was found to have been washed into a drinking-water reservoir downstream.

And so far we've been lucky. The effects of water spills of tailings piles, serious as they are, have been minor when compared to the possible consequences should a tornado ever smash into an unstabilized pile—and according to the draft report of the Department of Energy's Task Force on Nuclear Waste Management, "at none of the sites can the tailings be considered adequately stabilized for long-term storage." In drafting its generic environmental-impact statement on uranium milling, the Office of Nuclear Material Safety and Safeguards of the Nuclear Regulatory Commission assumed that its model mill would be built in a Southwestern region where "thunderstorms occasionally spawning tornadoes are frequent in spring and summer," and although it calculated the dosages that might be expected should this model mill be hit by a typical tornado of 360-mile-per-hour winds—the maximum dose of radiation would affect residents living 2.5 miles from the site—it did not include a calculation of what might happen should the tornado miss the mill and instead "lift" the tailings pile.

Barring such a catastrophe, however, the principal "diversions" of tailings into populated regions will probably continue to be man-made. For years, before the radioactive potential of uranium, thorium and phosphate mill tailings was realized, these fine sand-like materials had been sold—or often simply just given away—to contractors who used them for sanitary fill, for the formulation of cinderblock, or for the construction of concrete foundations. Two of the more generous donors of these tailings were the Amax Uranium Company and the Climax Uranium Company in the city of Grand Junction in western Colorado, and between them they gave away more than 300 tons of uranium mill tailings between 1952 and 1966 before federal and state Public Health Service inspectors traced substantially elevated levels of radioactivity in hundreds of Grand Junction buildings to radon emanations from their foundations.

In 1972, Congress authorized a 75 percent–25 percent split with the state to pay approximately $15,000 per home and $75,000 per commercial building, including temporary relocation costs, to get the tailings out from beneath Grand Junction structures; despite this subsidy, the work has not gone smoothly, partly because some owners of the affected buildings are not convinced of the need for the work and see no need to inconvenience themselves even if the rehabilitation is free, and partly, according to the General Accounting Office in 1978, because "the program is having considerable difficulty in getting enough contractors to do the cleanup work, because they appear to be more interested in doing other work."

It is the estimate of Robert Ramsey, who heads remedial-action programs within the Department of Energy's nuclear-waste management organization, that eventually about eight hundred structures will qualify anyway for this rehabilitation. I asked what was being done with the tailings that were being removed and was told that the State of Colorado had established a repository adjacent to the original pile of 1.9 million tons of tailings left behind when the mill that produced them shut down in 1970. Therefore they are still in Grand Junction, behind a dike at the confluence of the Colorado and Gunnison rivers, and, according to the Department of Energy, "in times of high water, the river surface is above the base of the tailings pile and may cause minor leaching." The agency's 1979 report on the status of the inactive uranium piles also concedes that radiation levels in the vicinity, a largely industrial section of the city next to a heavily populated area, "are slightly elevated as a result of radon emanation from the tailings."

Have these elevated levels of radon and radiation from the piles and from the foundations of hundreds of buildings had observable effects on the people of Grand Junction? A Colorado Department of Health study of residents of some of the tailings-supported houses describes its results as "inconclusive," although levels of leukemia in Mesa County, where Grand Junction is located, have been reported at twice the state's average. "There is no scientific evidence yet to indicate an association with uranium mill tailings," Dr. Anthony Robbins, the state's health director, told a Los Angeles *Times* reporter recently, "but the reason for concern is clear."

The people of Grand Junction may have been the first Coloradoans to have been informed that they were living and working on top of radwaste, but they weren't the last. Like the material at Canonsburg, the radioactive tailings subsequently uncovered in Colorado date back to the early 1900s and the mining of radium used in the treatment of cancer. Radiation levels three times higher than the standard for non-radiological workers were recently measured at a Denver site where radium was once refined—but which has been for at least 30 years devoted to the manufacture of bricks. An ensuing search of state records led the Environmental Protection Agency to even older contaminated sites in Denver, Boulder, Central City and Montrose. Officials are still searching the region between Gateway, Colo., and Moab, Utah, where it is believed that Madame Curie herself may have buried radwaste in 1903 when she spent several months concentrating radium ore.

Less frequently found than uranium or radium mill tailings are the spoils of thorium, a radioactive metal which is coming into prominence, particularly in Canada, as a reactor fuel. An advantage of thorium is that plutonium is not formed in the reaction of the thorium fuel cycle. Like uranium, however, thorium decays into the gaseous radon 222, which was, in fact, called thoron when it was first isolated.

However, until the relatively recent development of this nuclear employment, thorium was only in limited use—in alloys fashioned into bulb filaments and in electronic tubes, and as the incandescent component of gas mantles. A principal American refiner of it, a plant on a 43-acre site in West Chicago, Ill., stopped active milling operations in 1973. Six years later, an Environmental Protection Agency inspection found 45,000 tons of thorium tailings left behind were radiating up to 50 millirems per hour on the surface of this pile, which meant that anyone exposed to it for just ten hours would receive the *annual* dosage limit for members of the public not employed in the nuclear industry.

Unfortunately, this facility, the Lindsay Light and Chemical Co., also appears to have been generous with its tailings before 1967 when it was acquired by the Kerr McGee Nuclear Corporation. The Chicago *Tribune* reported recently that eighty-one sites in West Chicago register radioactivity levels that exceed the Nuclear Regulatory Commission standard for unrestricted access of 2 millirems per hour. Town authorities have now fenced off four of these, including a part of the local park where radiation levels matched the 50 millirem-per-hour readings of the plant tailings pile, and another, almost as high, at the town dump. Biophysical tests have shown that a number of former Lindsay employees and the plant's present caretaker have detectable levels of radon on their breath. Kerr McGee has begun work on dismantling the factory, at an estimated cost of $5.3 million, and plans to bury the debris and tailings under a clay cover; it is, however, denying liability for the remedial actions necessary to clean out the tailings that were given away before it acquired the plant.

Less of a radiological problem than uranium or thorium mill tailings, but used much more widely in foundations and concrete blocks, is phosphate slag, which contains traces of uranium and therefore emanates some radon. Between 1953 and 1978, when the Environmental Protection Agency warned against the practice, more than 2 million tons of this slag, a by-product of the production of phosphoric acid at the Tennessee Valley Authority center at Muscle Shoals, Alabama, was sold to concrete block manufacturers who sold their product to builders operating in Mississippi, Alabama, Tennessee and Georgia. A preliminary study conducted last year on behalf of a task force which consisted of members of the TVA, EPA and the health boards of the four states indicated that "an imminent health hazard does not exist," but called for additional studies, which TVA says it has now contracted for.

Even if it is eventually determined that a health problem

does exist from this slag, effective remedial action is certain to be a long time forthcoming. Nearly forty years after Edward Sengier's K-65 ore came to America, its tailings, although targeted by several planned cleanup programs, were still adding to radon and radiation levels at Lewiston, N.Y., Canonsburg, Pa., and in the vicinity of a long-since-forgotten rock-crushing facility at Middlesex, N.J., where the material was ground and analyzed. The Department of Energy, after finding that two previous decontaminations of the former Perry Sampling Plant —later a Marine Corps Reserve training center—have been insufficient, is now embarked on a third. In 1981, at a cost of approximately $5 million, contractors began the work of scraping the entire 18-acre site as well as portions of twenty-eight adjoining properties, cleaning up a bordering ditch contaminated for half a mile, and completely excavating the lawn of the rectory of a nearby church where grass has been flourishing for more than 20 years on top of donated radioactive uranium tailings.

3
HIGH-LEVEL WASTES

There are only two places in the United States where high-level nuclear waste actually can be seen. One is at the Hanford Atomic Energy reservation in Washington State, at a facility where cesium and strontium capsules of it are fashioned. The other is down in the basement of the Savannah River Plant Laboratory, where scientists work on gallon-size samples of it with robot arms called master-slave devices operated from behind 5 feet of leaded glass. Visually, the stuff in Savannah River's "caves" looks much like crude oil or the kind of thick grease used in heavy-duty lubrications. "What we're doing here," Bruce Ferguson, the laboratory's research supervisor, told me, "is taking five- to six-liter samples of actual sludge melt and putting it through the same kind of processing in miniature that we're doing on the [Savannah River] reservation with simulated waste. The scale is perhaps one two-hundredth or one three-hundredth of the actual operation. The idea is to see if these real wastes behave in the same way the simulated wastes we are experimenting with in full-scale operations behave, and so far we have found a very close correspondence between what we're doing here and the synthetic waste."

If this seems to be a convoluted process—testing small quantities of authentic materials to see if results conform with data obtained from experiments on substantial quantities of synthetic materials that are being examined to see if their behavior will conform with that of immense quantities of authentic materials—that's what radwaste requires. In gallon-sized beakers like the one I saw it in at Savannah River, high-level sludge gives off temperatures of up to 392 degrees Fahrenheit and radioactivity of up to 10,000 curies. Working with it is necessarily—and increasingly—expensive. In 1980, senior master-slave operators were making more than $25,000 a year, and scientists, of course, commanded much more. About double the 1980 figure—$58.8 million—was budgeted for long-term waste-management technology in 1981, and almost all this money was to be spent on figuring out what to do with the 10.2 million cubic feet of high-level waste awaiting disposal at the end of 1980 at four American locations. In descending order of quantity, these are the Hanford Atomic Energy Reservation, in the southeast corner of Washington State, which has nearly twice as much as the other sites put together; the Savannah River Plant, near Barnwell, S.C., and about 25 miles from Augusta, Ga.; the Idaho National Engineering Laboratory, about 40 miles west of Idaho Falls; and the Western New York Nuclear Service Center, at West Valley, about 30 miles south of Buffalo, where the only commercial (as contrasted with governmental) spent fuel was ever reprocessed in the United States.

In addition to being the volume leader for storing high-level waste (as it also is for low-level and transuranic wastes), Hanford is the oldest of these reservations. Originally a 570-square-mile tract of farms widely scattered on the desert plain and three small towns (including the town of Hanford) on the banks of the Columbia River, this site was cleared of 1,200 residents within 30 days in early 1943 for the construction of nine reactors that produced the plutonium for the bomb dropped on Nagasaki (the Hiroshima bomb element was uranium enriched at Oak Ridge, Tenn.). To hold the wastes from the reprocessing of these first nuclear fuels, the Manhattan Engineering District, which was the World War II atomic energy authority, contracted for the building of what became a succession of 149 tanks of increasing size—eventually they reached capacities of a million gallons—that were dug into the earth in two areas 5 to 7 miles south of the Columbia.

The bottom and side plates of these tanks are composed of three eighths of an inch of carbon steel; Congress' Joint Committee on Atomic Energy was subsequently informed by Hanford engineers that although the design life of these tanks had been conservatively set at 50 years (a time span that will begin to expire in 1993, incidentally), hot-cell tests had indicated that carbon steel, when exposed to wastes fresh enough to boil spontaneously, would corrode at the rate of only one ten-thousandth of an inch a month. This should have given these plates 300 years of integrity, and possibly longer, since the thermal output of reprocessing liquids drops below the boiling point after 5 or 6 years. Despite these assurances, the first leaks came in 1958, after only 15 years of tank life, and so far leaks totaling more than 450,000 gallons have been confirmed in 26 of these vessels, with the integrity of 32 others now considered "questionable."

Because these massive cisterns-within-concrete vaults are buried at least 7 feet under the surface, and because it may take several weeks before seeping nuclides can be detected in adjacent monitoring wells, confirming suspected leaks requires a judgment based on instrumentation that is not always precise —and when it has been accurate, it has not always been heeded. This was the case in 1973 with the reservation's largest and most embarrassing leak of 115,000 gallons, which occurred just after additional volumes of waste liquids had been pumped into 106-T, a 533,000-gallon tank constructed in 1944. The liquid level after the pumping operation was measured at 178.9 inches on May 2, and in the absence of a vacationing supervisory technician, according to the Atomic Energy Commission report, this information "was recorded in the static tank farm inventory log and left on the office desk. The day-shift supervisor has stated that he did not review the information because of the press of other duties."

Subsequent excerpts from the commission report:

"On May 7, the weekly liquid level reading for Tank 106-T was recorded at 174.0 inches. Information was logged in the static tank farm inventory log in the day shift supervisor's office. He did not review it.

"On May 14, the weekly liquid level reading for 106-T was recorded at 167.9 inches. The information was logged in the static tank farm inventory log. It was not reviewed by the day-shift supervisor."

And so it went. On May 21, the level was measured at 160.4 inches; on May 30 at 152.7 inches and on June 4 at 149.2 inches. It was not until the supervising technician returned from vacation that it was realized that the tank had lost approximately 14 percent of its contents, a radioactive inventory of 327,000 curies. On June 6, the remaining liquid was pumped to a spare. A number of remedial measures were taken subsequently to tighten up tank-farm procedures, including the computerization of instrument monitoring readings, and the twenty-five tank leaks thereafter were, at least, caught before they reached such extensive proportions. However, these changes hardly appear to have addressed what the Atomic Energy Commission in its eventual report considered to be the underlying cause of the 106-T spill: "There was no effective redundancy in the system to assure that a leak undetected by those primarily responsible for detection would be detected by somebody else, or to alert management's attention to any breakdown in the system." Also, in the opinion of Professor Daniel S. Metlay, of the Department of Political Science of Indiana University, in a book of essays on waste-management principles that the Nuclear Regulatory Commission published in 1978, "by increasing the technological complexity of the detecting system without increasing the assurance of compliance in the non-technological elements needed for implementation, e.g., without assuring that workers follow the new procedures better than they did the old, the overall reliability of the system is likely to decrease. Such an outcome is almost an inevitable result of thinking that focuses primarily on technological solutions."

As a more practical matter, a decision was made to allow the wastes in the tanks to boil themselves dry into salt-cake and sludge forms after several years in the tanks, rather than to keep piping water in indefinitely to cool them. While this eases the maintenance problem for the time being, it will, in the end, make the wastes extremely difficult to retrieve from the underground tanks, if and when a permanent repository is ever opened for their disposal. In the end, they may have to be mined out like coal.

Add to the quantities of high-level liquids believed to have spilled from the tanks another 50,000 gallons that the environmentalist Natural Resources Defense Council estimated by 1974 to have come from leaks in pipes and transfer spills, and you come up with a total of half a million gallons. Nothing has been done, and possibly nothing feasible can be done, to remove this material from the soil, and the General Accounting Office reported to Congress in 1974 that 5 to 10 square miles of the reservation, in the waste areas, "is so grossly contaminated" that it probably never can be cleaned up.

Yet if radioactive liquids must be spilled or poured onto the ground anywhere, the desert of the Columbia Plateau might appear to be the best possible place. Volcanically deposited silts and gravel underlie the reservation's sands to a depth of 150 to 300 feet above the water table, and a 1978 report by a National Academy of Sciences–National Research Council panel studying Hanford wastes postulated that a leak of almost twice the volume that federal officials concede to have spilled from the high-level tanks would take a minimum of 3 years to seep down to the water table and 20 to 30 years after that to make its way to the river, and by that time, it concluded, "the radioactivity of most of these nuclides would be less than their respective maximum permissible concentrations . . . In this panel's view, a leak of even this magnitude would result in no significant radiation hazard to the surrounding population."

A less sanguine view of seeping nuclides is taken by the Natural Resources Defense Council, an environmental organization which has been engaged since 1975 in federal court litigation seeking to require the Department of Energy to submit the high-level waste facilities at Hanford, the Savannah River Plant and the Idaho National Engineering Laboratory to licensing examination by the Nuclear Regulatory Commission. In addition to turf-preservation, an obvious reason for DOE's reluctance to submit to this was provided in 1979 testimony on the Hanford tanks by then NRC Chairman Joseph Hendrie before

a Senate subcommittee: "I'll tell you flatly right now, those
tanks are unlicenseable." The NRC, he said, would "try to shut
down that whole operation."

The NRDC's petition cites concern in 1973 by Hanford's own
environmental monitors that plutonium leaked into the soil
might "be converted to more soluble, more toxic complexes by
soil microbial mechanisms of detoxification or energy assimila-
tion as has been demonstrated for other metals." Filed with this
petition is the testimony of Marvin Hendrickson, who was until
1971 the supervisor of nuclear safety technology for the power-
generating reactor still operating at Hanford. His point was that
1966 tests had predicted that liquid radioactive iodine would
require a hundred days to travel the distance, less than a thousand yards, from the reactor's waste trench to the Columbia, a
time span that would permit its radioactivity to decay by a
thousandfold. However, in actual practice, he said, "the travel
time from crib to river was as little as two to four days, thus
providing little delay time for iodine to decay. The careful and,
I believe, conscientious laboratory work simply did not predict
the situation which occurred in the field."

In 1979, I toured Hanford in company with two members of
a subcommittee of the House of Representatives Science and
Technology Committee, Congressmen Mike McCormack, of
Washington, and Jack Lloyd, of California, several aides to congressmen and congressional committees and a group of reporters. McCormack, a Democrat defeated in the 1980 Reagan
sweep, was one of the strongest proponents of nuclear energy
in the Capitol, and at Hanford, the status of "Atomic Mike" as
a visitor to be escorted around the reservation was, to under-
state it, incongruous. A research chemist by profession, he
worked at Hanford for twenty years before his first election to
the House in 1970 as a representative of the district which
encompasses the reservation, and for most of the tour, while a
government bus carried us over the desert plain, it was McCormack who pointed the landmarks out to all of us, including the
Department of Energy officials who were his ostensible guides.
Not the least of these was the spot not far from the main Hanford road where about a decade ago contamination monitors
came across a highly radioactive coyote carcass on the desert

plain. "The coyote," McCormack theorized, "had gotten rabbits that apparently had been drinking from a pool of the leaked waste. Since then, they send guys out into the desert with vacuum cleaners to pick up coyote droppings for radiation tests." In 1978, the discovery of such radioactive items as an intensely contaminated swallow's nest—apparently the birds picked up mud from a pool formed by seeping radwaste—and contaminated mouse droppings found behind a Hanford building's candy-vending machine, led to the posting as contaminated of 21 separate areas comprising 80 acres.

The decision to allow high-level wastes to boil dry into salt cake and sludges, in order to make it easier on the weakening underground tanks, required the construction at Hanford of a laboratory that is unique among nuclear reservations, and the Waste Encapsulation and Storage Facility, an otherwise unremarkable concrete building lined with hot cells, was a principal stop on the tour with Congressman McCormack. The long-lived heat-emitting isotopes of cesium and strontium now must be stripped chemically from the wastes, and they are precipitated here in the form of cesium chloride and strontium fluoride, and then pressed into double-walled cylinders 50 centimeters long and 6.4 centimeters in diameter and placed in one of 10 concrete-lined water basins.

The strontium, cased within a metallic alloy, radiates at 450 rems per hour at a distance of one meter (5 rems per year is the maximum permissible dose for adults working in the nuclear industry) and gives off surface temperatures of 430 degrees Celsius. The cesium, inside stainless steel, gives off more radiation but less heat—1,500 rems per hour at a distance of one meter and 200 degrees Celsius.

By 1979, 75 percent of the strontium and 85 percent of the cesium had been stripped from the wastes in the Hanford tanks, and a small proportion of this had been packed into capsules. A score or so of these were stacked up in a holding pool at the far end of the facility when I toured it, and even under 11 feet of water, they emitted a fluorescent green glow (called the Cherenkov effect, it is caused by radiation emissions that pass through water at a speed faster than light) that was clearly reflected from a mirror through the 5-foot-thick leaded glass

window of the hot cell. Projections call for the eventual production of 3,500 of these capsules at this facility, which is about 8
miles south of the Columbia River. The National Academy of
Sciences–National Research Council panel that reported on the
Hanford wastes in 1978 warned of possibly disastrous consequences should a flood in the river somehow reach these capsules. It calculated that "a quantity of water equal to the total
flow of a thousand years" of the Columbia would be required
to dilute the strontium to a dose risk that might be considered
acceptable to the public; the cesium, the panel estimated, could
be sufficiently diluted by only 10 years of the entire flow of the
river.

An alternative to storing these capsules in the WESF pools
might be burying them, but the NAS-NRC panel advised
against it, since it seemed likely that the emitted heat "would
melt any ordinary rock material." The scientists unsuccessfully
urged a temporary halt to the stripping of cesium and strontium
from the wastes. The capsules, they conceded, are now "safely
out of the way in their cooled water basin, but the basin will
require continual monitoring and maintenance. The surveillance that the different forms of waste would require would
have to be maintained for at least 600 years to permit the major
radioactive isotopes to decay to harmless levels, and such a
period is long compared with the stability of political and social
institutions." In fact, this period is just about three times as long
as there has been a United States of America.

The cesium and strontium are not being stripped from the
high-level wastes accumulating in underground tanks at the
Savannah River Plant in South Carolina. Instead, the more than
68 million gallons (before evaporation) of liquids, salt cake and
sludge are kept under continual refrigeration within carbon-
steel tanks that are buried under 9 feet of soil. There have been
far fewer leaks at Savannah River than at Hanford, which is
fortunate, since wastes spilled at the South Carolina reservation
have far less distance to travel and fewer natural barriers to
overcome to be transported off-site. The water table at Savannah River is only an average of 40 feet below the earth's surface,
compared to Hanford's average of 150 to 300 feet. Additionally,
this reservation is crossed by several streams and marshes that

feed into the bordering Savannah, which the Department of Energy's environmental-impact statement says "is used for fishing, both commercial and sport, and pleasure boating downstream of the plant, and also as a drinking water supply at Port Wentworth, Ga., for an effective consumer population of about 20,000, and at Hardeeville, S. C. (Beaufort-Jasper Water Treatment Plant), for a consumer population of approximately 50,000."

The Savannah River Plant began operating on a 300-square-mile site in 1955, principally as the replacement for Hanford in turning out plutonium from reactors and extracting heavy water for weapons use. The waste produced in the reprocessing of this fuel comes in alkaline form at the present rate of about 1.5 million gallons a year. Keeping these wastes manageable, or "flocculent," as the Department of Energy describes them in its environmental-impact statements, requires 2 to 4 miles of cooling coils in each tank and 3,000 mega (million) watt hours of power annually. The Webster's Second Edition definition of flocculent is "of the appearance of wool; woolly; flocky," but flocky (flaky) or not, the Savannah River wastes are as dangerous as any other high-level liquids, and last April the Department of Energy calculated within them a total of 750 million curies of radioactivity.

Unlike the first tanks at Hanford, all the vessels at Savannah River have been built with double steel walls; in the reservation's history of high-level waste management, only one spill from a tank is known to have escaped this extra barrier. In 1960, about 700 gallons overflowed the space between the double walls of Tank No. 16 and seeped into the bottom of its concrete vault. According to the waste-operations environmental-impact statement, almost all this liquid was contained in the vault, "and the quantity of waste leakage into the soil was limited to a few tens of gallons of waste containing about seven curies of radio-activity per gallon [primarily cesium 137]." However, it conceded, "because the tank bottom is below the surface of the water table, the radioactivity that reached the soil also immediately reached the ground water." It maintains, however, that extensive monitoring has shown radiation migration of only a few feet in the ensuing years.

There are two other notable aspects to this spill: First, it turned out not to have been caused by one single fracture but by as many as 134, which were subsequently observed by cameras mounted on periscopes, and second, as at Hanford T 106, monitoring indications of the extent of this leakage were persistently disregarded. The seeping wastes were first spotted in November 1959, beginning to fill the annular cavity, but no corrective action was taken until the following September, after a spurt of subsequent leaks filled this space and the wastes overflowed the 5-foot height of the exterior tank wall for about 6 hours before a transfer pipe could be activated. After the wastes were pumped down to a level below the worst of the 134 cracks, the tank continued to be used, although at reduced capacity, for another 12 years, until 1972.

So far there have been leaks in the interior walls of 8 other Savannah River tanks; to the present, fortunately, these have been self-sealing—the salt that seeps through the crack dries and acts as a plug. However, this plugging characteristic causes, as well as prevents, waste accidents. In May 1967, 200 gallons of liquid containing an estimated 1,500 to 2,000 curies of cesium reached the ground after a vertical inlet riser into a tank became plugged with this crystallized salt. Most of this cesium was subsequently trapped by a storm sewer, although about 32 curies of it was measured in the next 7 months in a creek that runs to a Savannah River swamp, and it is estimated that an additional curie from it still reaches this swamp each year. In 1974, health physicists from the Du Pont Corporation surveyed affected portions of this swamp on the border of the reservation and found gamma radiation levels of 30 to 590 millirems per year above background (approximately 100 millirems per year). However, since hunters and fishermen would be exposed to only a fraction of this in the few hours they might spend there, it held that "no restrictions on use of the swamp are considered warranted, nor are remedial actions needed." Not entirely persuaded of the logic of this is Marvin Resnikoff, a physicist who is director of the Sierra Club's radioactive waste campaign, who points out that these hunters and fishermen usually eat the deer and fish that do spend all their time in the swamp, and thus they are exposed to considerably more radiation than normal.

Attention of the scientific community was drawn to the

Savannah River reservation in 1955 at the first forum ever held to determine what might be done with high-level wastes. One of the proposals suggested to the sixty-five scientists of various disciplines who met at Princeton, and subsequently investigated by a panel of the National Academy of Sciences–National Research Council, was to put them, either in liquid form or solidified, into caverns to be drilled out of crystalline bedrock beneath the reservation. In 1966, after looking at the data from preliminary borings and finding that the plant had been constructed over four identifiable aquifers, including the Tuscaloosa, a principal fresh-water supply of the Southern United States, a majority of the committee recommended that the site be dropped from consideration, but the Atomic Energy Commission voted instead to continue studying the site's suitability for a long-term geological repository. This investigation actually continued six more years, until 1972, when a committee of the South Carolina state legislature asked the governor of the state to point out to the federal government that "there are more suitable locations for such storage." (Apparently the Department of Energy later came to the same conclusion: Its Task Force for Review of Nuclear Waste Management noted in February 1978 that the first nuclear reservation to be studied in the environmental-impact-statement process would be Savannah River, "based on its generally less favorable environmental characteristics, and therefore the relatively greater need for alternate disposal of high-level wastes at that site.")

"A letter from the governor of Georgia, a guy named Jimmy Carter, also helped stop it," says Edward Goldberg, who is now the director of the Department of Energy's Waste Management Project Office at Savannah River. "There was a lot of concern about having to drill through the Tuscaloosa Aquifer to get to the bedrock—if there was an earthquake [and Savannah River is in a high-probability earthquake zone] would we poison the whole Southeast?"

The Savannah River plant may have lost the repository, but it did become the lead office for investigation of the waste-solidification processes, and scientists there are currently pursuing studies of the feasibility of forming high-level radwaste into monoliths of borosilicate glass, the reference option selected by

the Department of Energy from twenty-three primary alternatives and thirty-one other proposals. "After evaporation and
processing of the sixty-eight million gallons we've generated
here, we figure we have already cut the volume down to
twenty-three million gallons, and solidified, we'd come out with
a million gallons of glass and sixteen million gallons of leftover
salt which would meet the criteria for disposal at a low-level
burial ground," Goldberg said. "The plant would take five to
seven years to build and five hundred people to man. We'll be
ready to go to Congress in fiscal year 1983 for authorization, and
we think we can bring in the total facility for $1.5 billion."
(Other published estimates, however, put this figure as high as
$3 billion, with $55 million already having been spent on planning and preliminary work.) "We already have the technology
and the experts here, and we believe we ought to proceed with
it."

In the meantime, while officials there—and everywhere else
—await the implementation of a final high-level waste-disposal
plan, the liquids at Savannah River are being moved from the
original 24 tanks into 27 new tanks, a program that is expected
to take about 7 years. "The new-type tanks will hold 1.3 million
gallons," Goldberg explained as we drove up an earthen ramp
to what will be the "farm" of 14 of these tanks sited beside an
operating low-level and transuranic burial area. "We're building these new tanks in a doughnut shape," he continued. "The
central column helps hold up the roof. We found that a lot of
the cracks in the old-type tank were the result of stress corrosion, so now we're heat-treating these new tanks in place—they
reach 1,100 to 1,200 degrees before we allow them to cool down
slowly." Even so, he conceded, the design life of these new
vessels would be no longer than the fifty years that the original
single-walled tanks at Hanford had been expected to last.

I asked why the high-level waste tanks at these two reservations had been made of carbon steel rather than the more expensive stainless. For the alkaline wastes at Savannah River,
Goldberg said, "our research people tell us stainless might not
be a better choice." Goldberg referred me to the appendix of
the environmental-impact statement on long-term management of Savannah River's wastes, which maintained that stain-

less had been considered—and rejected—by several technical panels on the grounds that it is no better at holding alkaline liquids. "Besides," Goldberg added, "we don't see any reason economically for stainless, since we don't intend to leave this stuff in the new tanks more than forty years."

At Savannah River, in addition to seeing an actual sample of high-level waste, I was allowed to walk up to—and on top of—one of the tanks destined to hold these liquids. Eventually each of these vessels will be hidden away inside a vault of concrete 3 feet thick and then buried under soil—in a year or so, the farm will resemble a gradually sloped plateau. At the time of my visit, however, massive cylinders of concrete had only just been constructed around the bases of several tanks. "Each vault is continuously poured so there are no cold seams in it," Goldberg said. "We will have the capacity to put pumps inside after we seal it, but we don't want to until we have to because this way the concrete stays leak-tight." The uncompleted doughnut-shaped top of a tank I walked upon was a thicket of pipes and openings—a glance down several of these revealed a web of monitoring devices and cooling coils which extended 33 feet to the tank bottom. "We'll be running dehumidified air through the annular space between the outer and inner tank walls," Goldberg explained, "because if we don't, the tanks will sweat in this humidified climate, and, in addition, we can monitor it to detect any leak in radioactivity."

The estimated price of each of these new tanks is a little less than $10 million, or about $250 million for all 27 tanks in both new farms, and on top of this, add another $150 million to pipe the wastes to their second "temporary" location. Not all can feasibly be moved, however, since 5 percent of the sludge, the most radioactive fraction of the wastes, has hardened to the point where the Department of Energy believes "attempts to flush it out would be hazardous." For as long as this sludge is retained in the old tanks, they, too, will require cooling and maintenance.

By contrast with Hanford and Savannah River, there have been no accidental releases of liquid high-level wastes at the Idaho Chemical Processing Plant at the Idaho National Engineering

Laboratory, where the fuel of the Navy's submarine and the federal government's research reactors is reprocessed. Radioactivity from this activity is funneled high into the Idaho sky and injected down into one of the region's principal aquifers quite deliberately.

Covering 893 square miles, which begin about 30 miles west of Idaho Falls, INEL was established in 1949 as the National Reactor Testing Station (before that it was a Navy gunnery range). Even larger than Hanford, it holds, in addition to the reprocessing plant, a radioactive waste-management complex for low-level and transuranic materials, as well as seventeen currently operating reactors. The nuclear submarine was developed at INEL in 1952, and the reservation was the site in 1961 of the only deaths directly attributed to reactor operation—three workers died in an accident associated with a premature core criticality at a prototype breeder reactor.

Unlike the liquids stored at Hanford and Savannah River, the high-level wastes building up at INEL since 1963 are in the solid form of calcine, a powder that resembles yellow salt. It is no less radioactive this way, but reduced to one eighth its former volume, it is much easier to manage. This acidic powder is swept pneumatically into stainless steel bins 12 feet in diameter set in clusters of as many as seven inside concrete silos that rise from 50 feet underground to 17 feet above the surface. Although originally constructed in 1963 only for demonstration purposes, this calcining facility had solidified 4 million gallons of liquid wastes into 62,800 cubic feet of calcine powder by the time I visited it late in 1980, and a new $90 million plant, and two new sets of storage bins—the fifth and sixth respectively—were under construction to handle a backlog of 2.5 million gallons of acids now held in eleven cooled underground stainless steel tanks behind the Idaho Chemical Processing Plant.

"This arrangement is the best high-level waste management you're going to see," J. P. Hamric, director of Nuclear Fuel and Waste Management Operations at the Department of Energy's office in Idaho Falls, told me before I went out to look at the calcining facility. "We can assure people that the material after it's processed will be safe for five hundred years, because stainless steel in our dry air simply will not corrode away." Although fresh calcined waste reaches centerline temperatures of 480 degrees Celsius, Hamric pointed out that natural air convection reduces the heat radiated by the stainless steel walls of the bins to about 50 degrees above ambient temperatures. In a 1967 experiment, the flow of air was shut off to one bin, and the maximum centerline temperature reached 515 degrees Celsius, which is still under the 750 degrees Celsius at which cesium, the most volatile constituent of the waste, will begin to boil. However, because of its leachability in water, calcine is not considered suitable as a final form for disposal (even though as a temporary holding form it is certainly less leachable than the damp salt cakes and liquids in tanks at the other high-level sites).

In 1979, a subsidiary of Exxon Nuclear Corporation succeeded the Allied Chemical Corporation as the operating contractor of the Idaho Chemical Processing Plant, and Jerry Ritter, a vice-president in the Exxon corporation's technical department, says the calcines originate in five different forms of reactor fuels that have been dissolved in various nitric acid solutions. With the uranium and plutonium removed, the wastes are introduced as a spray over a bed of solidified aluminum oxide granules that have been heated to between 400 and 500 degrees Celsius. The water content of the wastes is quickly evaporated, and a coating of dried radioactive solids envelops the granules, which are then swept pneumatically through stainless steel pipes encased in concrete sleeves to the storage bins.

In the end, however, this liquid-waste treatment process has its own wastes—not all the constituents of high-level liquids are amenable to calcining, and there is also a significant off-gas problem—and these radioactive materials, to the consternation of growing numbers of Idahoans, are being discharged into the air above and the water table below the reservation.

By far the larger source of radioactive emissions is the plant's 250-foot stack. Since reprocessing began there in 1953, more than 7.3 million curies of radioactive isotopes have escaped the ICPP's system of gas filters, absorbers and scrubbers to reach the atmosphere. According to Ritter, however, "radiation levels are multiple factors below allowable release limits. No radiation from our stack has ever been measurable off the INEL site, and only occasionally have we ever detected very low levels off our plant site."

Nearly 98 percent of these radioactive emissions have consisted of the relatively short half-lived (10.8 years) isotope krypton 85. Krypton is a noble gas—which means that if inhaled or somehow ingested, it won't combine with anything in the body and will be exhaled or secreted right out of the system. However, in building the ICPP, the Atomic Energy Commission found a commercial reason to build in a krypton-recovery process which uses a technique of distillation at extremely low temperatures. Great quantities of krypton still go up the stack each year—253,900 curies in 1974, for example—but since 1953, the plant's operators have been able to collect and sell more than 200,000 curies of it, most recently at a price of $12 a curie, to Oak Ridge National Laboratory where scientists are studying uses for the light-emitting gas, one of them in non-electric bulbs that stay lit for years.

As it happened, my visit to Idaho came several months after Nuclear Regulatory Commission officials sanctioned the venting to the atmosphere of 57,000 curies of krypton 85 from the crippled Three Mile Island reactor, rejecting as infeasible suggestions that the gas be collected and possibly recovered. Officials at ICPP shrugged off my question about why what had been found not only feasible but profitable in Idaho should be considered infeasible in Pennsylvania. "We aren't recovering our krypton to meet emission standards," Ritter said, "but because we consider the gas a product. The demand almost exceeds our ability to produce it."

Compared to the stack discharges, far smaller quantities of radioactive isotopes are contained in the waste water that the plant discharges each year, but what concerns Idahoans, to the point where it has become a political controversy, is that these isotopes are being injected directly into the aquifer that provides drinking and irrigation water for the southern half of the state. INEL's reactor testing area discharges of toxic and radiological contaminants are five times those of the ICPP, but these materials go into seepage ponds 450 feet above the water table. By contrast, 390 million gallons of ICPP waste water containing

223 curies of radioactive elements, were poured in 1979 down the facility's 8-foot well to a depth of between 445 and 558 feet —the well's casing is perforated to extend seepage evenly throughout the aquifer. More than 99 percent of the radioactive discharge consists of tritium, but longer-lived isotopes occasionally are also flushed down the well. In December 1958, according to the facility's environmental-impact statement, "approximately 29 curies of activity (7 curies of strontium 90) was accidentally released to the atmosphere from a liquid waste tank at ICPP owing to a leaking flange." In September 1969, 19 more curies of long-lived fission products "accidentally" went down the well.

Under normal circumstances, according to Hamric of the Department of Energy, the calcination plant's discharge to the well consists of "isotopes left over after the liquid waste stream goes through the cleanup process, along with a lot of cooling water and some chemical waste, mainly salt. The stuff goes right back into the water table, which is where the liquid came from in the first place—we pull out the water upgradient and inject it downgradient, and the only material we put into the water that goes any distance at all is tritium, and it won't reach the southern boundary of the site until the year 2000, and by then it will be a factor of ten below the maximum permissible in drinking water."

Coincidentally, the same day Hamric told me this, the Idaho Falls *Post Register* carried an account of a press conference at which Idaho Governor John Evans had called continued operation of this injection well "totally unacceptable." After more than a quarter century of use, this well had abruptly become an. Idaho political issue in 1979 when the Lewiston, Idaho, *Morning Tribune* came across a United States Geological Survey report that salt and tritium from the facility had migrated approximately 12 to 15 square miles, and that the area within a square mile downstream of the injection site contained nonradioactive but toxic chromium in excess of drinking-water standards.

One of the authors of that report is Jack Barraclough, who came to INEL first in 1948 and now heads a USGS hydrology project team. When I talked to him at his office on the labora-

tory, I mentioned that I had been told at the Department of
Energy office at Idaho Falls that thirty wells had been dug on
the reservation just to monitor contamination from the processing plant well. "Yes, but they didn't tell you how long and how
hard we had to fight to get that many wells, did they?" Barraclough responded. The Snake River Plain Aquifer, he told me,
"is difficult because of fracturing. We have thin lavaflows of
basalt here, each one like a pancake separated by sediment
from the ones above and below it, and we figure there are half
a billion acre feet of water in storage and flushing through at
between five to ten feet per day, which means it's going to take
between three and four hundred years for the water now at the
well to reach the reservation boundary."

The nuclides and most of the chemicals being injected at the
well move at slower rates of speed, he added, "and all we've
seen down at the boundary so far is non-radioactive chloride.
Most of the other stuff from the processing plant's well hasn't
moved 2,700 feet in 27 years. We have yet to measure positive
for cesium 137 in any of our monitoring wells, but we have seen
strontium 90. The bulk of the plutonium is held up rather
quickly; we may be able to see it perhaps as far as a mile away
by now. Most of the other elements that circulate at all are short
lived, and they'll decay before they get 45 miles to the site
border."

One of these isotopes, however, is iodine 129, which has a
16-million-year half-life, and many of the others, decayed or
not, can be toxic. Once inside the aquifer, their destination is
the Snake River Canyon, about 90 miles to the southwest between Twin Falls and Boise. From that point on, the Snake is
the primary water source for several hundred miles of Idaho
and Washington before it joins up with the Columbia just below
the Hanford reservation. And even before it reaches the canyon, the aquifer is the source of an annual 1.4 million acre feet
of water pumped up from it for irrigation and water consump-
tion. Idaho Governor Evans is now demanding that whatever
is put into the processing plant well be cleaned up to meet
federal and state water-discharge standards. The remaining nuclides and chemicals, he suggested, could be discharged into
one of the reservation's existing seepage basins. This would

increase surface pollution, but it would at least insulate the aquifer with 450 feet of fractured basalt above the water table. In June of 1981, DOE promised to discontinue use of the injection well in 1987, proposing to replace it either by a deeper disposal well below the aquifer or an evaporative system to discharge nuclides high in the air.

Although Governor Evans called this "a major positive step," Idahoans have also been described as "disturbed" by the construction of the $90-million permanent calciner facility which will replace the "demonstration" plant in 1982, and by the installation of the new bins designed to hold the high-level powder for a minimum of 500 more years. State officials believed they had a commitment from the old Atomic Energy Commission to remove the stored high-level and transuranic waste from the reservation by 1980, and the recent Mt. St. Helens eruptions in Washington have reminded area residents that the INEL region is also subject to the kind of volcanic action that laid down the fractured basalt beneath it in the first place. "I feel confident of the eventual removal of the stored wastes from the reservation," Governor Evans told me when I sought him out while he was attending a meeting of the State Planning Council on Radioactive Waste Management several months after my trip to Idaho, "and in the meantime we're doing what we can to make sure that what goes down that well will meet environmental standards."

The smallest American quantity of high-level waste—at West Valley, New York—is the dismal legacy of the only commercial nuclear fuels reprocessing plant to operate in this country. However, because power-producing fuel is irradiated at least five times longer in reactors than uranium assemblies used to produce weapons-grade material, the radwaste from this reprocessing is proportionately more radioactive than the high-level effluents at Hanford, Savannah River and INEL.

There are at the Western New York Nuclear Service Center 560,000 gallons of high-level acid waste chemically neutralized but bearing an estimated 39 million curies of radioactive elements within a carbon steel tank in a buried concrete vault, and another 12,041 gallons of waste still in acid form, with a radioactive content of about 2.2 million curies, in a stainless steel tank also buried in concrete. Proportionately, the neutralized wastes are more than three times—and still-acid wastes more than ten times—as radioactive as the alkaline wastes at Savannah River. Both these tanks are being monitored and electrically cooled beneath eight feet of earth enclosed in a fenced-off tract adjacent to the massive, and since 1972, inactive reprocessing facility once operated by the Nuclear Fuel Services Corporation.

I stood at the fence of this tract one warm fall afternoon with Dr. Alden Pierce, an ecologist who holds the title of operations manager of the West Valley Plant, and stared at the shack that contains the monitoring instruments of the tanks while Dr. Pierce explained the function of a nearby grove of pipes and vents, some of them occasionally obscured by gusts of steam: "We're required to keep certain systems operating, keep the vents of the tanks filtered, and these steam tracers lead to the filters and outside instruments. And three times a day, once on every shift, somebody goes into that shack and checks the monitoring instruments."

The NFS official had a ready response when I brought up the T-106 Hanford leak: "I assure you we read our monitoring reports very carefully; any drops would be noticed immediately." Perhaps, but while we were watching the above-ground area of the tanks, I noticed a remote camera at the top of a pole inside the fence and asked if anybody was monitoring it. Dr. Pierce had no answer, and in my subsequent tour of the facility I never did see a monitoring screen.

The West Valley tanks were designed to last forty years; they have already held 190-degree liquid waste and sludge in the larger tank and 100–120-degree acid waste in the smaller one for more than a third of that span. Questions have also been raised about the ability of these tanks to withstand seismic pressures—a fault 23 miles to the east of West Valley was responsible for quakes there in 1929 and 1966. Basing its conclusion on a study of the tanks by technicians from Lawrence Livermore Laboratories in California, the Nuclear Regulatory Commission decided in 1978 that these vessels could withstand the stresses of the most severe earthquakes that could be expected to rock Western New York. (Public confidence in the Livermore expertise in this area may have been somewhat shaken, however, when a California quake in January 1980 cracked one of that laboratory's own radioactive waste tanks, a 30,000-gallon vessel that contained only tritium.)

Should either of the high-level tanks at West Valley be weakened either by corrosion or by tremors, their secondary containment systems have already proved suspect, and there may be no way to keep their radioactive contents entirely out of the environment. The tank containing the neutralized wastes rests on a steel saucer designed to hold the first dripping liquids at least temporarily. Unfortunately, the saucer itself is known to leak. "We performed a functional test of our alarm system," Dr. Pierce told me, "and when we added water to the saucer system, some of it came through to the bottom of the vault. We repeated that test a number of times very carefully and then added several redundant alarms and instruments."

Since it is impossible to get close enough to the tank to repair the damaged saucer, any leaking liquid will now run unobstructed down to the base of this tank's concrete vault—and there are questions about the integrity of the vaults. Several years ago, the Sierra Club's Radioactive Waste Campaign, which focuses on West Valley, turned up reports showing that during their 1965 construction, the two 2,850-ton concrete structures had actually been floated three to four feet off their foundations by water that leaked into their open pits. Subsequently, according to Sierra's publication, the *Waste Paper,* inspectors counted "40 radial cracks, with one circular crack 17 feet in diameter. These cracks were patched with cement."

Should a leak be detected in the bases of either of the high-level vaults, spare tanks are standing by, along with a 6.3-liter turbine pump with the capability of transferring the wastes before the leak becomes serious. The problem is that this pump has never been hooked up to either of the waste-holding tanks, and engineers have estimated that it would take a minimum of three weeks to get it hooked up—and they don't want to make this connection until it is required, for fear that the work itself might start a leak. "Under the original plans, three weeks would have been reasonable in line with the built-in containments," Dr. Pierce said. However, as these containments began to appear less and less reliable, Nuclear Fuel Services made what

Pierce describes as "procedural changes" that should cut down on the three-week leaking time. How much less time? "I don't want to speculate on how long it would now take," he said, "because we haven't worked out all the aspects."

Leaving the high-level wastes in the tanks too much longer would be dangerous; getting them out may be more so. This is particularly true in the case of the larger tank with the neutralized acid, since some of its contents have turned to sludge. Collected at the bottom of the tank, the sludge, which contains most of the strontium and the longest-lived isotopes, is estimated to comprise 124,000 gallons. The Department of Energy, in its 1978 study of the facility, subdivided this estimate into "about 15,000 gallons of solid material, mixed with about 109,000 gallons of liquid." Estimates of the volume of sludge are somewhat difficult to pin down, however, since they are necessarily based on measurements taken by NFS engineers who lower a soft-drink bottle into a tank vent at the end of a calibrated string and mark the point at which it goes slack. I mentioned to Dr. Pierce that this "Mark Twain" method of measurement seemed anachronistic in the atomic age, and he pointed out that, although cumbersome, it is certainly as "scientifically precise" as the remote instrumentation on the underground high-level tanks at Hanford and Savannah River.

Physically, this sludge has hardened in the crevices of a lattice of 51 support columns in the base of the tank, and it will be difficult, if not impossible, to flush it out by conventional methods. Conceivably a proportion of it will not yield to high-pressure sluices of up to 3,500 pounds per square inch, which was successful only in removing between 79 percent to 95 percent of the sludge from the first Savannah River tanks to be decommissioned. Since no facility this radioactive has ever been dismantled without first being immersed in water, it is probable that in the end this tank, still containing some sludge, may have to be cut up by operators working remotely from behind lead shields—if it is not, in fact, necessary to construct an actual hot cell around the tank area.

Of course, all this is going to cost money—lots of it—and since 1972, when the reprocessing stopped, there has been the open and divisive question of who will pay it. Legally, New York State built and is the owner of the Western New York Nuclear Service Center, and Nuclear Fuel Services, a 78 percent–22 percent subsidiary of the Getty and Skelly Oil companies (which succeeded the W. R. Grace and American Machine and Foundry corporations respectively) is only a lessee of the 345-acre site and $34-million plant. In September 1976, NFS, which also processes fuel for nuclear submarines at a facility at Ervin, Tenn., formally declared its intention simply to walk away from West Valley (after a loss estimated by New York State officials at $2 million a year for each of its six operating years) at the expiration of its lease, December 31, 1980.

A perpetual-care fund was established in the NFS lease, but payments to it reached only $5 million before the expiration date, and even the 1962 study commissioned by the New York State Office of Atomic Development that provided the basis for this fund warned that the total by now "would need to be $9 million if one assumed inflation on both annual costs and replacement value at 2 percent." The annual inflation rate since 1962, of course, has reached double-digit figures.

For its part, NFS maintains that its physical responsibility and legal liability for the high-level and low-level wastes at the site ends with the lease in 1980. The response of environmental organizations is that the lease requires that the facilities and land be left in "good condition," and in the words of one witness at a recent federal hearing on the future of West Valley, "land with nuclear wastes, cracked vaults and deteriorating tanks in it is not in good condition."

Whether or not additional money can legally be squeezed out of NFS, New York, although an Agreement State (which means that it has compacted to be responsible for its own commercial nuclear development), has turned to the federal government for help, pointing out that although the facility was originally established to reprocess fuel from commercial reactors, 60 percent of the assemblies that eventually passed through West Valley came from federal reactors. The state's request was not unanticipated: Back in 1978, when the General Accounting Office was considering the problem of who would pay for cleaning up the uranium mill tailings in the Western states, one of the negative considerations it offered against federal aid was that such a program "can be viewed as a precedent for the Federal Government becoming involved in the decommissioning of other nuclear facilities. Perhaps the greatest immediate danger of this idea taking hold pertains to the nuclear fuel reprocessing plant at West Valley, N.Y."

The GAO (as usual) correctly called the play. Just as it authorized a 90 percent–10 percent split on the tailings, Congress, after several unsuccessful attempts to get New York to agree to additional low-level waste burial at West Valley or to allow the plant's receiving basin to be expanded to become a temporary holding facility for spent fuel from reactors that had run out of room in their own basins, agreed in September 1980 to put up $250 million of the $285 million then estimated to be the cost of decontaminating the reprocessing plant and disposing elsewhere of the wastes it produced. Solidifying the high-level liquids, dismantling the tanks and moving both somewhere else is expected to be a ten-year job, and since the eventual disposal site has yet to be specified, final costs may exceed even the $285-million estimate—but even if they don't, the minimum price of disposing of this only commercial reprocessing waste in the United States will be about $202 for every pound of the 640 metric tons of uranium that passed through West Valley. In the middle of 1981, the price of uranium fresh from the mills was $28 per pound.

4
COMMERCIAL
SPENT FUEL

Outside of Morris, Illinois, which is about fifteen miles west of Joliet, stands an imposing steel and concrete memorial to the dream of nuclear fuel reprocessing. The General Electric Corporation put $64 million and six years of effort into building what it hoped to call the Midwest Fuel Recovery Plant, before concluding in 1974 that the design just wouldn't work. A persistent engineering flaw did not become apparent until the operation reached the non-radioactive "dry-run" stage, and its remedy was estimated to cost between $90 million and $130 million, an investment which General Electric management declined to make. Now except for occasional tours—"our main business," quips J. R. Fine, who is the facility's manager of relations and administration—the greater part of the building stands empty and desolate. A lone operator mans the plant control room, but his only duty is to keep an eye on the enclosed spent-fuel pool in one of the plant's outbuildings. Originally, this 675,000-gallon filtered and cooled pool had been intended to be only the receiving basin of the reprocessing operation, but more or less by default, it has become an AFR, or away-from-reactor facility for storing spent fuel. General Electric is paid as much as $5,700 per year to watch over each of the intensely radioactive assemblies that utilities in Connecticut, California, Wisconsin and Illinois send to stand indefinitely at Morris.

When I visited the facility in April of 1980, 1,207 assemblies filled 48 percent of the pool's storage positions in 14½-foot-tall baskets, the tops of which were visible under 14 feet of water. Above the waterline, the most notable objects were a crane and, incongruously affixed to the wall, a life preserver. The gallery from which I viewed the pool also held a radiation monitor registering less than one millirem per hour. Just above the waterline, Fine told me, the reading is 6 millirems per hour, and monitors lowered to the depth of the assemblies have registered more than a million millirems.

"When we begin designing this place in 1965," Fine said, "the government told us it would soon be providing permanent disposal facilities for high-level wastes, but fortunately our engineers didn't believe it, so they designed this pool to be able to hold five years of high activity from our reprocessing operation, as well as the incoming wastes [spent fuel] to be reprocessed."

After giving up on the reprocessing, General Electric figured it might as well earn back some of its losses by offering utilities a place to store excess spent fuel, and went so far as to receive NRC permission to increase the facility's storage capacity from 750 to 1,850 tons of assemblies. The licensing application for the expansion was withdrawn, however, after President Carter, in his 1977 decision to bar reprocessing, specified that the federal government would take the spent fuel from the utilities upon the payment of a one-time fee for disposal.

Unable subsequently to project a continuing market for its spent-fuel-holding capacity, General Electric decided simply to restrict storage at Morris to utilities that originally contracted for its fuel, and with which it shares the cost of operating the fifty-eight-employee (not including patrol guards) facility. "With regard to the cost of storage at Morris, we forecast a range of $10,000 to $12,000 per metric ton per year, in 1977 dollars," Bertram Wolfe, general manager of fuel recovery and irradiation products of GE's Nuclear Products Division, told the House of Representatives Oversight Committee in August of 1977. "We currently estimate that the capital costs for a new storage facility would range between about $40,000 to $80,000 per metric tons of storage space depending on the size of the facility." However, he added, with national spent-fuel policy as uncertain and variable as it was (and still is), "it's virtually impossible to move ahead on a commercial basis . . . For example, it's not plain how long the fuel will be stored in one of these facilities. They are very capital intensive (and) if you build it on the basis of a twenty-year lifetime, and the government makes a rule that after five or after ten years it has to be shipped to a government storage facility, then you're left with a facility that is underutilized."

Whether the Morris pool will also turn out to be underutilized will eventually depend on the outcome of litigation that followed a December 1980 act of the Illinois legislature, which overrode a gubernatorial veto to ban spent-fuel shipments from states that have bans on importing radwaste from Illinois. The only reactor with plans to make shipments to Morris in 1981 is in California, a state which has such a radwaste embargo, and its owner, Southern California Edison, and General Electric have sued the State of Illinois in federal court, and are, in turn, being sued by Illinois to halt the shipments.

If and when these shipments are resumed, they will arrive at Morris in 25-ton (truck) or 65-ton (rail) casks which are picked up by the pool's overhead crane and unloaded in a receiving pit beneath at least 10 feet of water. In 1972, one of these shipping casks swung free and banged into the side of the basin, rupturing its liner and spilling 2,000 gallons of radioactive water from the pit—this has been the only accident recorded so far at Morris.

Three or four pressurized-water assemblies or nine boiling-water assemblies are stacked into each of the open-ended pipe-like baskets that are locked vertically into position on the 900-square-foot floor of the Morris basin. Thus enveloped, the zirconium-clad fuel rods are not visible through the pool water; however, Fine told me, the pressurized-water reactor rods "have a dull black look—boiling-water fuel looks like it has rust spots on it." Nor was there, in midday, a visible Cherenkov effect—named for the Russian physicist, P. A. Cherenkov, who first identified and explained the glow that is caused by radiation passing through water in excess of the speed of light passing through water. However, the Morris official told me that a few months before my visit, "we totally blacked out the building for a test, and after five minutes or so, we were able to spot a very faint glow—more white than blue. One time, too, we got an assembly that was only a hundred twenty-three days out of the reactor, and for a while that gave off a noticeable Cherenkov."

In addition to radiation and heat, the water of the pool also inevitably takes on some of the fuel's nuclear content. "In the early days, we operated with about thirty curies in the pool water," Fine told me, "but we've improved the filtering system, and now we're running with about one curie." Plant manager Eugene Voiland maintained that the pool water is now so free of radioactivity that it could meet drinking water standards. It would make a pretty warm drink, however, since only an elaborate electric cooling system keeps the Morris water at between 75 and 90 degrees. Fine told me of a 1979 test when the cooling system was disconnected "for a month, and the temperature got up to 117 Fahrenheit, and at that point the evaporation effect equaled the decay heat and stabilized it." At this temperature, though, the water evaporated at a rate of about 1,500 gallons a day, and there is also a persistent leak of about 12 gallons a day beneath the receiving basin gate—which means, according to Fine, "that even if something happens to disconnect all the water, we'd have about two hundred days before the water level drops to uncover the top of the fuel baskets." The heat and evaporation rates will rise with the increasing quantity of fuel in the basin, however, and if the pool is ever completely filled, this margin of safety will drop to only 9 days.

What could possibly happen to cause such a shutoff? Nuclear opponents point out that Morris is just across the road from three reactors at Commonwealth Edison's Dresden Nuclear Power Station. "What would happen if operators had to abandon the Morris operation storehouse for a prolonged period in the event of a major accident at Dresden?" the Illinois *Times* of Springfield asked rhetorically in a 1980 article. Also questioned by environmentalists is the wisdom of building up the nation's largest inventory of commercial spent fuel, which is the most dangerous form of radwaste, within fifty miles of Chicago and within half a mile of the Illinois River—and in a region that is high in both tornado and earthquake probabilities.

General Electric officials maintain that their pool of reinforced concrete lined with stainless steel is built to last "in perpetuity." Perhaps it is, but the fuel rods it holds are not. Eventually, the zirconium cladding will begin to yield to the demineralized water flowing past and around it at a constant 250 gallons per minute. A recent study cited to a House of Representatives subcommittee put this safe life at a minimum of 50 years—for fuel that was in good condition when removed from a reactor. The trouble is that not all the fuel in the Morris pool is in good condition. Some—GE officials are reluctant to say how much—of the 144 tons of assemblies it is storing from the Dresden facilities had to be removed from the boiling-water reactors just across the road long before their expected expiration dates because leaking radioactive gases had been found to be filtering through the zirconium cladding.

In any case, a tour of the Morris plant is not calculated to reinforce a visitor's willingness to rely even on the firmest of engineering guarantees. After we left the swimming pool, Fine led me past a three-dimensional scale model of the reprocessing facility that General Electric had expected to provide its access to the nation's burgeoning nuclear-fuels market. I asked what had gone wrong with it.

"It was this little doohickey right here," Fine pointed to a miniature calciner at one end of the model. "The uranium, after it was dissolved in acid, would go through this to be converted from a nitrate to an oxide. The entire process was remotely operated, and at this point we had fifteen heaters to bring the material up to the necessary temperature—in the pre-operational tests, these heaters kept burning out, and there was no way we could replace them remotely. We would have had to redesign the entire system, and in addition to the hundred-thirty-million-dollar additional expense, we figured it would have taken us four more years to get the requisite licensing approvals."

There were at the end of 1980, seventy-three operating commercial reactors in the United States, with another eighty-seven either under construction or firmly planned. By 1985, these are expected to have discharged 68,435 boiling- and pressurized-water assemblies. By that time, too, America will also have begun to *import* spent fuel rods from commercial reactors abroad. Since the mid-fifties, the United States has been accepting spent fuel from overseas reactors established for research purposes under President Eisenhower's Atoms for Peace Program. In 1979, approximately 5 tons of this spent fuel was delivered from twenty-eight facilities in twelve different countries —most of it entered through the port of Portsmouth, Va., to be trucked to Savannah River for reprocessing. Now the United States has promised to assume responsibility for what President Carter has said will be "limited" quantities of spent fuel that will be exported to this country from commercial reactors in nations that support American non-proliferation goals. In its projections, the Department of Energy is calculating that 10 percent of the commercial fuel rods discharged from reactors in qualifying nations will begin to arrive here in 1983, and by 1985, 1,520 of these assemblies will be added to the American inventory for a total of 69,955 assemblies in indefinite storage in the United States.

Since 1977, it has been American policy that the nuclear fuel in these assemblies would not be reprocessed, and even should this policy change in the Reagan administration, commercial reprocessing could not be expected to resume for several more years, although a facility tested in pre-production runs at a capacity of 3.9 million tons a day already exists at Barnwell, S. C., next door to the Savannah River Plant. This plant was designed under the corporate sponsorship of the Allied Chemical Corporation, Gulf Oil and Royal Dutch Shell, which got together in 1971 to form Allied General Nuclear Services, and to build its reprocessing facility on 1,740 acres deeded by Congress from the SRP site. Agnes, as this plant came to be called from its corporate acronym, didn't seek to utilize any new reprocessing technology, but it also didn't produce an ounce of fuel. After an investment estimated by one of its officials at $562 million (although the General Accounting Office reckons it only at about $250 million), Agnes was stopped before startup by a waste-management restriction added to the Code of Federal

Regulations, a requirement that the waste liquids and the plutonium from the reclaimed spent fuel would have to be solidified within five years of production, and, moreover, solidified at the reprocessing site before they could be shipped to a repository whenever one was opened. Meeting these additional qualifications, the company estimated, would require the spending of at least another half-billion dollars, and possibly as much as $650 million. By 1981, this range had grown in federal estimates to between $1 billion and $1.5 billion. This expenditure would be in addition to more than $100 million which Congress appropriated in "research grants" to keep Agnes alive between President Carter's ban on reprocessing in 1977 and the inauguration of President Reagan.

In the intervening years, however, even South Carolina officials who in the beginning worked hard to bring the facility there (to the point of building a highway to it and naming it Osborn Road after AGNS vice-president Kenneth Osborn) began having second thoughts about the operation. "I'm opposed to reprocessing if we're going to be left with more liquid high-level waste, which is the most dangerous stuff," South Carolina Governor Richard Riley told me in 1980. "We're trying to get the research going to get the stuff at the Savannah River Plant solidified, and praying there isn't an earthquake between now and when they do it, so I sure don't want to accumulate more of it 'temporarily' with no place to put it and no way to solidify it. That shouldn't have been done in the beginning of the weapons system, and I sure don't want to see it done in the civilian mode until we are able to regulate it." Not that it's much consolation to Agnes investors, but, as it turned out, if reprocessing had started there in mid-1978 as planned, the operation would have been choked by high-level wastes by 1981. A. Eugene Schubert, president of the corporation, admitted to the Joint Congressional Committee on Atomic Energy in 1976 that Agnes' waste tanks were designed on the assumption that the federal government would take prompt responsibility for the high-level liquids, and that the facility had a capacity of holding no more than 2½ years of its full production.

Also on the Nuclear Regulatory Commission back burner, after the expenditure of millions in design funds, is an application by the Exxon Nuclear Corporation to build a reprocessing center on the Oak Ridge, Tenn., nuclear reservation. This plant, intended to reprocess 1,500 metric tons annually, would have turned out a solidified calcine waste and provided interim storage for 7,000 tons of spent-fuel elements.

Arguments have been made against reprocessing on both financial and environmental grounds. The 1977 Ford Foundation study, *Nuclear Power Issues and Choices,* concluded that "the international and social costs far outweigh economic benefits, which are very small even under optimistic assumptions." In 1977, Robert Fri, acting administrator of the federal Energy Resources and Development Administration, conceded to the House Oversight Committee that the "net economics" of reprocessing "balance out to about zero. The economic value of the material in the spent fuel is just about equal to its cost. It may even be less." Environmentally, although recycling the waste uranium and plutonium sounds like a good idea, the effects may also outweigh the benefits. There are 450 synthetically produced nuclides in spent fuel at the moment it is ready for removal from a reactor, and according to Mason Willrich, a professor in both international law and nuclear physics, in the authoritative book *Radioactive Waste Management and Regulation,* reprocessing results "in additional dissemination of the radionuclides originally contained in the spent fuel and the consequent generation of many waste streams with different physical forms and chemical compositions." The volume of the transuranic, and therefore longest-lived, elements would also increase to up to three times its proportion in the spent fuel.

Certainly the one commercial reprocessing facility ever to operate in the United States, the Nuclear Fuel Services plant at West Valley, proved both financially and environmentally expensive. In one published report, its operators are said to have lost $40 million, and in each of the 6 years that fuel actually was reprocessed there, from 1966 to 1972, NFS employees received exposures that were two or three times higher than at comparable reprocessing plants abroad. In the most spectacular of fourteen incidents of exposures reported to the Nuclear Regulatory Commission, a filter, apparently being operated at pressures beyond manufacturing specifications, tore into shreds which spewed out the plant's 200-foot stack to spread contamination outside the building. In 1972, the Atomic Energy Commission cited operators of the facility for "failure to make reasonable efforts to maintain the lowest levels of contamination and radiation," and Dr. Karl Z. Morgan, a professor at Georgia Institute of Technology and one of the nation's leading health physicists, wrote in 1976 that "with regard to environmental contamination and potential exposure," the NFS plant "has made about all the mistakes one could imagine in relation to poor health-physics practices, of excessive releases of radioactive contamination, and storage and burial of radioactive contaminated materials. Future plants must not repeat this poor record of operations."

So far, no American plant has been given the opportunity to —although reprocessing continues or is planned in fifteen (so far) other countries. Research into it here is also continuing— a Brookhaven National Laboratory analyst has identified thirty-two different techniques that have been proposed in the literature of nuclear science—and James Shipley, leader of a Los Alamos task force studying nuclear non-proliferation safeguards, has made a plea for completion of Agnes and its takeover by the federal government in order to test the feasibility of what other nations are doing.

In February 1981, President Reagan's energy secretary, James B. Edwards, a former governor of South Carolina, announced his support for a federal purchase or lease of Agnes, although he told members of a Senate subcommittee that actual reprocessing of commercial spent fuel there "will have to wait a while."

In addition to reprocessing nuclear fuel, it is also possible to breed it. If quantities of a "fertile" radionuclide are wrapped, like a blanket, around the shell of a reactor fueled by a "fissile" radionuclide, the fertile atoms capture excess neutrons from the reaction and are converted into fissile atoms, producing, under optimum conditions, 1.24 times the number of fissioning atoms that fed the reaction in the first place. By the end of 1980, breeder reactors were operating in France, the United Kingdom, the Soviet Union, and although it seems to have been virtually forgotten since 1974, at the Shippingport Atomic Power Station in Pennsylvania.

Breeder technology was first demonstrated in 1951 at the

Idaho National Engineering Laboratory (then the National Reactor Testing Station), and the first breeder to produce electricity suffered a core meltdown in 1955 at INEL. Then in 1967 the first commercial-power breeder, the Enrico Fermi No. I unit at Monroe, Michigan, suffered a disabling meltdown which resulted in no injuries but which was memorialized by writer John G. Fuller in a book entitled *We Almost Lost Detroit* (a conclusion that the facility's corporate sponsors vociferously dispute).

The still-operating 60-megawatt breeder at Shippingport is, in effect, a recycling of the first American power reactor jointly constructed by the federal government and the Duquesne Light Co. in 1957. After fifteen years of normal power generation, it was remodeled to breed fissile uranium 233 from fertile thorium 232. This thorium form of breeder, strongly promoted by Navy nuclear administrator Hyman Rickover, was endorsed by his former staff aide, President Carter, specifically because it did not breed plutonium (although uranium 233 can also, with greater difficulty, fuel nuclear weapons). By 1981, according to the General Accounting Office, $518 million had been spent on this demonstration program, with another $450 million still to be spent before 1989 or 1990, when the Department of Energy says it will then shut down the reactor to determine its breeding effectiveness.

The other form of breeder does create plutonium: Specifically, it turns non-fissile uranium 238 into plutonium 239. In addition to this disadvantage, plutonium breeders must be cooled by molten sodium, which is extremely volatile, but which, when heated to more than 500 degrees, facilitates the passage of neutrons from the fuel core to the breeder blanket. Thus, the liquid metal fast breeder reactor (LMFBR), which, in addition to generating power, makes a nuclear fuel out of previously almost useless "depleted" uranium.

There are fifteen known isotopes of uranium, and only seven tenths of one percent of the element in its natural form consists of the fissile isotope 235. In order to sustain an effective chain reaction, the uranium put into reactor fuel assemblies has to be enriched to at least 3 percent of the 235 isotope—weapons-grade material requires at least a 90-percent enrichment. This physical process is accomplished by gas and centrifuge diffusion (and soon will be done by laser excitement), but the end result, building up since the dawn of the nuclear age, is a stockpile of approximately 280,000 tons of uranium that has been *depleted* in the 235 isotope. This material consists almost entirely of uranium 238, the raw material of the LMFBR blanket.

When President Carter decided in 1977 not to proceed with this form of breeder, his decision left unconstructed on the banks of the Clinch River, near Oak Ridge, Tenn., a 375-megawatt LMFBR on which $1 billion had already been spent. Although formally sponsored by a consortium of 753 utilities, nearly all the money that had already been paid out for this project was governmental. Altogether, the General Accounting Office has estimated $5 billion had been spent in developing "the federal government's most heavily funded nuclear concept." Included in these appropriations was $700 million spent to build a sodium-cooled, but not breeding and not power-producing "fast-flux test" facility reactor at Hanford in Washington to test LMFBR components. Even without components to test, this project was completed anyway, and like Agnes at Barnwell, the Clinch River breeder was also kept alive by "research" funding grants from Congress—$172 million in fiscal year 1981 alone.

The change in administrations in 1981 appeared to have brought both the nuclear industry and the LMFBR new leases on life. President Reagan, while cutting all other energy programs, awarded nuclear power an additional $81 million and restored the Clinch River breeder's authorization (presumably to the embarrassment of his economy-minded budget director, David Stockman, who as a congressman had described the project as "the nuclear breeder lobby looking for a large, uneconomic subsidy"). Construction of the breeder—the latest estimate is $3.2 billion—was deleted from the proposed 1982 budget by the House Science and Technology Committee, but later restored by the full House. However, even if Clinch River is not canceled again by yet another administration, the reactor is not expected to provide power before 1989, and it will take at least until the year 2007 before it breeds enough plutonium both to compensate for the fuel it will have already used and to provide enough to fuel another reactor. Inevitably, though, the resumption of plutonium breeding will require the renewed production of civilian high-level wastes, since the plutonium bred in the LMFBR must be reprocessed to separate it from the uranium 238 blanket in order to put it in fuel form.

In any case, obtaining new sources of fuel wasn't the principal problem reactor operators faced going into the eighties—getting rid of fuel that had already been consumed was. The Oak Ridge surveyors reported that in 1980 spent-fuel assemblies were piling up in reactor spent-fuel pools at the average rate of 253 assemblies or 48 tons of uranium per reactor per year.

Even more than high-level reprocessing liquid, spent fuel is the most immediately dangerous form of radwaste. Although the uranium put into a reactor is so barely radioactive that it can be shipped in ordinary commerce, it has been estimated that 26,800 curies of radiation are formed each day for each megawatt of thermal power produced in the reactor. Fresh from the reactor, a spent-fuel assembly gives off a lethal radiation dose at a distance of 10 yards in ten minutes until it is shielded in water or otherwise. Even after a century, according to a National Research Council draft report, "the characteristic parameters" of ingestion hazard, radioactivity and thermal power from spent-fuel assemblies "are relatively more hazardous [than high-level reprocessing waste] by a factor of about twenty." And eventually, there is the reasonable question of how long spent fuel can last underwater in its present form before its increasingly brittle zirconium cladding cracks, releasing radioactive gases and allowing solid isotopes to contaminate the pool. According to the Department of Energy, "there are no obvious degradation mechanisms which operate on the cladding which would be expected to cause failure in the time frame of fifty years or longer." Since the nuclear-power era began in 1957 at Shippingport, Pa., the age of some of the first commercial spent fuel is approaching half that time span now.

Of course, getting spent fuel rods into and out of underwater storage, and moving them around within it, requires a good deal of circumspection and remote handling. Including the Morris mishap with a fuel container, the Department of Energy reported that by April 1980 there had been a dozen "abnormal events" involving leaks in spent-fuel pools, and in one case, when a boiling-water assembly being removed from a reactor was dropped about 30 feet through water, landing on another assembly, a radiation release required a temporary evacuation of the reactor room. Even in accident-free handling, the DOE concedes, "some radioactive crud particles may detach from the fuel surfaces during fuel handling and storage; if fuel failures occurred during reactor residence, fission products absorbed on the crud layers will desorb slowly during pool storage."

The buildup of these assemblies in pools at reactor sites has led to what *Fortune* magazine in 1979 called a "constipation" problem in the American nuclear power industry. According to Robert Fri, who was acting administrator of the Energy Research and Development Administration in 1977 when he testified to a House oversight subcommittee, this malady "has deep historical roots which go back to a time ten or so years ago when the Atomic Energy Commission took the view that once . . . reactors had been developed, much of the rest of the fuel cycle—virtually everything except the permanent disposal means—would come about by natural industry action. For a variety of reasons, subsequent experience showed that view to be incorrect. Reprocessing, for example, which was assumed to come into being as quite a natural evolution of the fuel cycle, ran into all kinds of technical and policy problems."

Since its "natural industry action" has, indeed, been blocked, primarily for reasons of nuclear non-proliferation, it is the view of the Edison Electric Institute, which speaks for American power utilities, that "it appears to be the government's responsibility to accommodate safe storage for the spent fuel and its final disposition. As an initial step, the government should provide storage at an early date and also provide assurance to the utilities that sufficient storage capability will be made available to permit uninterrupted operation of their nuclear power plants." Additionally, the institute said in its 1977 statement, the government "should compensate the utilities for the net salvage value of the spent fuel" as if there were reprocessing. A rough estimate of this "salvage" value of the fissile isotopes remaining in spent-fuel elements discharged each year by a

1,000-megawatt boiling-water reactor is $10 million, and since one of these reactors puts out a hundred seventy-five assemblies each year, and each assembly weighs 605 pounds, that works out to slightly more than $57,000 per assembly, or about $94 a pound. If there were reprocessing, a General Electric spokesman says wistfully, his company would place the value of each spent assembly at $250,000, which works out to about $413 per pound. This is about fifteen times the 1981 price of $28 for fresh uranium.

In 1979, Representative Morris Udall, then chairman of the House subcommittee on energy and the environment, urged as a licensing requirement for nuclear power plants the provision of 50 years' capacity for spent fuel storage; the massive swimming pools that this would require would be about twenty times the size of those built at the sites of the first commercial reactors when operators assumed for design purposes that they would be required to hold spent fuel for only six months, or until its isotope content had declined from about 180 megacuries per metric ton at discharge to 4 megacuries per metric ton. Boiling-water reactors discharge one third of their cores each year, and some of the early pools were built to hold no more than one and one-third full cores, with additional room to accommodate a "full core reserve," or all the rods within the reactor in case they had to be dumped in an emergency.

The first thing to go was this "full core reserve"; as early as 1978, Congress was informed that the oldest of three reactors at the Oconee plant of Duke Power in South Carolina had been granted permission by the Nuclear Regulatory Commission to operate without this emergency safeguard. Lee V. Gossick, the NRC's executive director for operations, sought to reassure members of the House Oversight and Operations subcommittee that "there are no safety reasons that require the immediate unloading of a full core." The full-core reserve concept, he testified, "has been traditionally maintained by the utilities to withstand even the most severe events with the fuel still in the reactor vessel. Consequently, no reactor is designed to depend on removal of its core as a safety measure. The redundant emergency core-cooling system and the high integrity of the reactor vessel provide assurance that cooling and storage in the reactor vessel of the fuel is safe under all conditions."

There were also several intermediate expedients available to some utilities: Carolina Light and Power Co. shipped some of the excess spent fuel from its H. B. Robinson Nuclear Plant at Hartsville, S.C., by special train to an emptier pool at the Southport, N.C., site of its two Brunswick reactors; the three utilities operating the San Onofre reactors at San Clemente, Cal., called upon General Electric to store 150 tons at Morris. However, 25 of the 73 operating plants would still have lost their full-core discharge capability by the mid 1980s had not their operators prevailed upon the NRC to consider the expansion of spent-fuel capacities, not by altering the physical dimensions of the pools themselves, but by permitting the stacking of the assemblies closer together. This is called reracking, and the reason it involves license-amendment proceedings is that there is a considerable question of safety involved.

For obvious reasons of nuclear criticality, the stacking of 5.5-inch-wide boiling-water assemblies and 8.4-inch-wide pressurized-water assemblies has always been limited by regulation to 95 percent of the concentration that might permit the initiation of a chain reaction within a pool. Originally, assemblies were emplaced at a much greater spacing—as far apart as 12 inches from the center of one boiling-water assembly to the center of the next, and a 21-inch center-to-center separation for pressurized water assemblies. It is possible to bring the centers as close together as 8 inches for boiling-water assemblies and 12 to 15 inches for pressurized-water assemblies without going over the 95 percent factor, and still further, to 7-inch spacings for boiling-water fuel and 10 inches for pressurized-water fuel if the stainless steel or aluminum racks are filled with boron compounds, which, in engineering terms, "poison" the chain reaction by capturing neutrons.

This is bringing them pretty close together, however—and as the Department of Energy points out, this option requires "periodic checking of the continuing presence of poison in the control racks."

Of course, the closer the assemblies are stacked, even in boron-poisoned racks, the hotter the water in the pool becomes, and the greater the load put upon the plant's cooling system. In testimony prepared on behalf of the Illinois attorney general in opposition to a petition for reracking a pool serving two pressurized—water reactors at Zion, Ill., the Sierra Club's Marvin Resnikoff, a nuclear physicist, estimated that in the event of a failure in the cooling system and an inability to replace water, it would take only 141 hours for the water level to drop far enough to expose the tops of the reracked fuel assemblies. Zion won NRC permission to rerack anyway, more than doubling its pool's capacity from 340 assemblies to 868. By March of 1981, the commission had received 59 applications for modifications of the pools at the existing 73 power reactors, and had, to that point, granted 50 and had not denied any. The largest increases so far approved are three and a half times the original capacity at the Connecticut Yankee pressurized water reactor at Haddam Neck and the twin pressurized-water reactors at Prairie Island in Minnesota. On paper, some of these reactor pools will have gained as much as nine years' additional discharge capacity, but even so, reracking is only a stopgap. As many as twenty-eight commercial reactors will run out of capacity anyway by 1990.

This problem of crowding reactor pools has not snuck up exactly unnoticed on nuclear planners, who have always recognized that some form of intermediate storage facility will be required either for spent fuel or for reprocessing wastes until a final repository can be established and licensed—and that will be at least 10 years after a site for it is finally chosen. Back in 1972, when reprocessing of commercial spent fuel was still the favored planning alternative, the Atomic Energy Commission announced an intention to construct a Retrievable Surface Storage Facility, location unspecified, that would hold all the high-level waste that would be generated through the year 2000. The RSSF won the endorsement of a Panel on Engineered Storage of the Committee on Radioactive Waste Management of the National Academy of Sciences–National Research Council, which studied three possible concepts—storing in water basins, in an air-cooled vault, and in sealed storage casks stacked outdoors—and came out in favor of the individual storage casks, partially because this approach "is passive and thus requires a minimum of operating service or surveillance." Conservatively calculating the need for such a facility through the year 2010, the panel estimated that by then 75,000 stainless steel canisters

12 inches in diameter and about 10 feet high would be filled with wastes. Surrounding each of these canisters with a carbon steel casing and standing these on a thick concrete base of 1,100 acres, or a little less than two square miles, would be an expensive undertaking, it conceded, requiring a peak employment of 330 workers and costing more than 1.5 billion 1973 dollars.

The RSSF got as far as a draft environmental-impact statement, which was attacked not only by environmental organizations but by the federal Environmental Protection Agency, which gave it an unsatisfactory rating primarily because it held that the government was going about the waste-disposal process backward. Since the final disposal process and site would inevitably determine the temporary storage process and site, the Energy Research and Development Administration, after it was formed from the old AEC, was urged to stop looking for expedients and to get to work on an ultimate repository. As one of its first actions, therefore, ERDA withdrew its request for funds to construct the RSSF; two years later, however, the project was reincarnated in the 1978 budget request as SURFF, for Spent Unreprocessed Fuel Facility. Other than the physical form of the waste to be stored—fuel assemblies would simply be stacked until it was determined whether or not they would be reprocessed—there weren't many discernible differences between RSSF and SURFF, which was conceived by engineers at the Savannah River Plant as a facility with a capacity for 6,000 metric tons of fuel assemblies, and it was estimated that this could be built on a government reservation for only $290 million by September 1985.

SURFF went by the boards too. As the General Accounting Office reported in 1978, "utilities are finding it difficult to select a course of action, lacking Department of Energy information on cost, schedule, location and terms and conditions. As of now, it is economically advantageous for them to expand their current storage pools and build more than to anticipate such decisions from DOE."

The next time the storage signals were changed—from the surface, passive-cooling concept back to pools—so was the nomenclature. SURFF became AFR (for Away-From-Reactor), and the NRC obtained from the engineering firm of Stone and

Webster a generic design for such a facility with a capacity of 1,300 metric tons, which it said could be built for an estimated $20 to $30 million. Splitting the difference, this works out to $5,342 for each of the 4,680 boiling-water assemblies, or $12,-821 for each of the 1,950 pressurized-water assemblies that such a facility could contain. However, Raymond L. Dickeman, the president of Exxon Nuclear Corporation, testified to estimates more than double these figures at a House subcommittee hearing in 1977. In Dickeman's calculations (later confirmed by Atomic Industrial Forum estimates), the capital costs of building an AFR would range "between $40,000 and $50,000 per metric ton of storage space in 1977 dollars. Escalation is assumed to occur at 8 percent per year." Of course, charges for shipping the fuel to an AFR, operating the facility, and then shipping the fuel to a subsequent disposal facility and operating that, would all be additional.

Along with the accident at Three Mile Island on March 28, 1979, and scaled-down projections of long-range increases in power demands, this increasing realization of the escalation of spent-fuel costs appears to have considerably diminished the enthusiasm of utility executives for nuclear generation: fifteen planned reactors were either canceled or indefinitely deferred in 1979 and 1980. One of these, at Sterling in Cayuga County in Western New York, appears to have been hit from all directions. It had been approved in January of 1978 by the State Board of Electric Generating Siting on a three-to-two vote—the swing ballot having been cast by a member who recorded his vote only on the condition that its spent pressurized-water assemblies would be stored off-site. How this was to be accomplished remained an open question until several months after the Three Mile accident, when the board decided there was insufficient demand for the 1,150-megawatt plant anyway and voted to cancel it—at a reported loss of $72 million in planning and engineering fees incurred by its four utility sponsors.

When it submitted authorizing legislation to Congress in February 1979, the Department of Energy accompanied it with a fact sheet listing five possible choices for locating an AFR. These were the existing facilities at Barnwell, Morris and West Valley, one that might possibly be constructed on Tennessee Valley

Authority property, and one called Greenfield, which is a governmental euphemism for an unchosen site. One Greenfield under consideration in Washington and at DOE offices in Germantown, Maryland, was as far away as possible: In March of 1979, officials of the Japanese government let it be known that they had been consulted about cooperating on a study of the feasibility of using a Pacific island—Wake, Palmyra and Midway were principal candidates—as a joint AFR site. However, that part of the world is particularly sensitive to nuclear innovation, and, citing the bomb-test contamination of Bikini and Enewetak (formerly called Eniwetok) atolls, the South Pacific Forum, which represents a dozen independent nations, including Australia and New Zealand, passed a resolution of condemnation against "any action which represents further exploitation of the Pacific for nuclear purposes in ways which disadvantage the people of the Pacific."

Hawaii Senator Spark Matsunaga effectively killed Greenfield-in-the-Pacific by tacking onto a bill authorizing funds for American territories a provision that would require congressional approval of any nuclear-waste storage facility to be constructed on a Pacific island (and promising his constituents that he would insure that such approval would never be given). President Carter called this an "unnecessary impediment to the orderly conduct of this country's nuclear non-proliferation policies," but signed the bill in March of 1980.

Another island somewhat closer to home also received brief Greenfield consideration. This was Pelican Island, which is about 2,000 feet out in the Gulf of Mexico from downtown Galveston, Texas. In a sense, Pelican, which is the site of Todd Shipyards Corporation's nuclear division, already had been an AFR facility. When the nuclear ship *Savannah* was decommissioned in 1972, she left behind for a short time thirty-two reactor fuel assemblies destined for shipment to the Savannah River Reprocessing Plant. Most of the 300,000 gallons of water contaminated by those assemblies is still on the island where, as early as 1970, Todd had established a sideline in storing low-level radwaste. However, since that operation had already proved itself something less than an environmental and commercial success—and had become, in fact, a statewide political issue—Texas Governor Bill Clements said in 1980 that he would "unequivocally reject" Pelican's use "for the storage of any form of high-level nuclear waste."

If the South Pacific and Texas were reluctant to welcome Greenfield, the Tennessee Valley Authority, at least at first, was eager to build an AFR for the United States. In June 1978, TVA, which by then had three reactors operating at Browns Ferry, near Decatur, Ala., and plans to construct thirteen more, offered to build a storage facility which would have had a capacity for 4,500 metric tons of spent fuel—more than three times the capacity envisaged in the NRC's generic design. In return, TVA chairman David Freeman asked the federal government to pay only for "costs incurred over and above those incurred to meet TVA's own needs." The Department of Energy welcomed the TVA plan, at least to the extent of listing it among its five options, but after several exploratory talks, according to Hugh Parris, TVA's manager of power, the proposal "kind of died."

In the end, not only did TVA decide not to build an AFR for the federal government, it scrapped its plan to build one just for itself, and chose instead the option of reracking its existing pools and building spare pools at the sites of its reactors under construction. The multiple pools would cost more to build and to operate than the single AFR pool, TVA conceded in a special report, but it pointed out that both the AFR construction and restraints likely to be put on operating it "are subject to future changes which TVA cannot control. Under such conditions of uncertainty, the benefits of waiting for better information may outweigh the potential savings of an early decision to build a central facility. It appears that TVA could respond appropriately and safely to a wider range of future developments by starting on the path to onsite storage."

Pending possible designation of a new "Greenfield" (at one point Exxon Nuclear officials had pointed out that the site of their never-begun reprocessing facility at Oak Ridge might be suitable for an AFR, but this suggestion has not so far been pursued), the most likely spent-fuel storage option appeared to be a governmental takeover of one or more of the existing spent-fuel pools at Barnwell, West Valley and Morris. The facility with the most present and potential capacity is Barnwell, where a 400-metric-ton pool, expandable to 1,750 metric tons, now stands entirely empty. However, Agnes officials say that while they'd be glad to sell the whole place to the government for the money they've already spent on it, they have no interest in running it only as an AFR. South Carolina Governor Richard Riley, who is chairman of the State Planning Council on Radioactive Waste Management, also told me he'll do all he can to block the temporary storage of spent fuel there "until DOE can come up with a timetable for the permanent waste repository to make sure Agnes is only temporary. I don't think South Carolina ought to be the answer to the whole national problem. If we let them put all the rods in South Carolina, quote, temporarily, unquote, when we go to Congress to get them out, we'll have two Senators interested in moving the assemblies and ninety-eight saying, 'Well, let's put it off.' I am not going to sit back and let them put all the nation's problems down here and say it is just temporary. I keep saying, 'Tell me when you're going to move it and where you're going to put it, and then we'll have something to talk about.' "

In New York, however, Governor Hugh Carey, if he did not actually support use of the Nuclear Fuel Services spent-fuel pool as an AFR, did veto a 1979 bill intended to ban that use. On the other hand, Carey also refused to ratify a 1979 agreement—eventually superseded by the congressional legislation which established the 90 percent–10 percent split for the cost of solidifying the high-level waste in the tanks—that would have called on the federal government to pay all the cost of solidification of the high-level liquids, up to $500 million, in return for the use of 85 metric tons of capacity now remaining in the 248.5-ton pool. (Like GE at Morris, NFS now stores, at a fee, excess assemblies from utilities that had contracted to use its reprocessing service.)

In June 1980, the General Accounting Office strongly recommended that use of the spent-fuel pool and remaining capacity at the West Valley low-level burial site be obtained as a quid pro quo for financial aid in cleaning up the site: "Making Federal assistance for West Valley contingent on New York's making the facilities available to help solve its own and national waste management problems is a practical solution." Conceivably, continued nuclear use of the West Valley plant might bring some prosperity back to Cattaraugus County, where unemployment is well above the national average, and to the Town of Ashford where, local officials say, half the farms in operation twenty-five years ago are no longer being worked. However, only three out of eighty-two (by my count) witnesses who testified at a Department of Energy hearing in the auditorium of West Valley's Central School in February 1980 favored any continued nuclear use of the facility, and one of these proponents, Charles W. Couture, a director of the West Valley Chamber of Commerce, brought down a chorus of booing when he specifically favored use of the spent-fuel pool as an AFR facility.

The mood of the vast majority of those who attended the hearing—about a hundred fifty spectators at one point filled rows of chairs set down on the high-school basketball court—was with Carol Mongerson, a nearby resident who is chairman of the locally based Coalition on West Valley Wastes, when she warned the federal panelists that area residents would fight designation of the site as an AFR "with every means open to us, not just now, during the decision process, but on and on. Through every step of the way you will meet nothing but resistance."

Making my way out of the auditorium later, as the hearing was concluding, I encountered several members of the League of Women Voters who had attended the session as observers. "I agree with the people who told them we don't need any more wastes until we can deal with those we've already got," reflected Mrs. Marie Sawinski, who said she would be reporting to the League's East Aurora–Elma chapter near Buffalo. Her white-haired, cane-carrying colleague, Mrs. Elizabeth Gibbs, also of East Aurora, said she was impressed by "how many different groups were represented. The participation was excellent, and even when people disagreed with a speaker, they weren't too disruptive." Were you there when the representative of the West Valley Chamber of Commerce was booed? I asked her. "You bet," Mrs. Gibbs snapped. "I booed him myself."

Several days later Mrs. Gibbs dropped me a note summing up the perceptions she would be reporting to her League of

Women Voters chapter. "As we drove home through West Valley," she concluded, "observing its gently rolling wooded hills, providing cover for so much wildlife, looking so peaceful, so rural, so unspoiled, certainly one of the most beautiful areas of New York State and one of God's loveliest creations, we felt very sad that mankind had desecrated it with a nuclear reprocessing plant, with its high potential for destroying and mutilating not only human life but this entire fragile ecology now and for generations to come."

Similar sentiments were offered less eloquently at the hearing by a spokesman for Iroquois tribesmen from the nearby Cattaraugus Indian Reservation, a member of a Buffalo labor coalition, several teachers, and more than fifty local residents, including Henrietta Gurwitz, the operator of a dairy, who told the government panelists that "the people of West Valley have had it up to here. They have lived with these nuclear wastes for seventeen years. A lot of people didn't come here today because they feel that the Department of Energy won't listen to us anyway, that we will have this AFR crammed down our throats."

In effect, however, the matter was taken out of the department's hands by Congress and President Carter when they approved legislation mandating the West Valley cleanup without linking it to the use of the spent-fuel pool—which pretty well left Morris as the front-running AFR candidate. The pool there has a present capacity of 750 metric tons of assemblies, and at the end of 1980 was reported to be holding 318 tons. General Electric has indicated a willingness to sell the entire facility for $30 million, and the General Accounting Office has concluded that it would cost $24 million more to expand the pool's capacity by 1,100 metric tons. "For about $54 million," it noted, "DOE can acquire 1,450 metric tons of interim spent-fuel storage space, which may be enough, according to our data, to handle away-from-reactor storage needs through at least 1988."

Another pragmatic advantage that Morris enjoyed, as plant manager Eugene Voiland pointed out when I was there, is that its pool "is licensed and operating; West Valley's is licensed to store, but it is not now open for more fuel to come in. Barnwell's never has been licensed. In terms of availability, Morris is the best place."

Nevertheless, several months after my visit—and Voiland's AFR pitch—the Illinois legislature passed its ban on importation of spent fuel from states that ban Illinois radwaste. Predictably, this was matched early in 1981 by a South Carolina legislature resolution intended to bar the establishment of Agnes' so-far-unused pool as an AFR to hold spent fuel from utilities with no South Carolina operations. It is possible, and may even be probable, that both these bans could be nullified either in the courts or by a federal takeover of either Morris or Agnes well before 1985, which is the Department of Energy's "deadline" date for establishing an AFR. In that event, however, the government will still have to contend with a degree of public opposition quite remarkable in states heretofore considered friendly to nuclear development. The South Carolina resolution noted that that state "is already storing more than its proportionate share of radioactive wastes and materials," and in Illinois, the state with the largest number of commercial reactors—seven operating by the end of 1980 with another ten planned or in construction, ten thousand residents petitioned the Illinois Commission on Atomic Energy to oppose a Morris takeover.

"The people of my district and throughout the State of Illinois do not want the federal government to assume that white elephant for the purposes of storing—even temporarily—high-level spent nuclear fuel rods," State Senator Jerome J. Joyce testified in August 1980 to the Senate subcommittee on rural development. "The people of my district have just recently been made aware of their newly found role as the 'nuclear waste babysitter of the nation.' Yes, the people living in Morris, Illinois, are becoming frightened." Joyce's opposition is not without significance. In addition to representing the district which comprises Morris, the senator later represented Illinois as an adviser to the State Planning Council on Radioactive Waste Management.

If an AFR should ever have to be designated, Morris is probably still the best bet for it. However, with the inauguration of the Reagan administration came yet another change in policy.

In February 1981, the new Republican Secretary of Energy, James B. Edwards, explained his opposition to temporary storage of spent fuel on much the same grounds that the federal Environmental Protection Agency offered for opposing it in 1972: "If we go to AFRs," the secretary told a Senate subcommittee, "it means we've put off the tough decision" on selecting permanent disposal sites and modes. He also promised an Illinois congressman "100 per cent support for finding alternatives" to Morris.

Not surprisingly, considering this history of blunted initiatives, most utilities have long since begun discounting any federal promises to relieve them in the foreseeable future of the spent-fuel assemblies piling up at their reactors. In 1979, the General Accounting Office contacted the owners of fifty-seven nuclear power plants that indicated they would require AFR storage by 1988 and found that "because of their critical storage situation, many utilities are not counting on the Department of Energy to provide storage space but are developing plans to solve their own storage needs. In fact, several utility representatives told us they did not feel that DOE would ever have a spent-fuel storage program, and they were excluding DOE's program from their planning base."

5

TRANSURANICS

Every three years, Max Schletter's crew takes down a portable, air-supported building, moves it 240 feet forward on a 150-foot-wide asphalt pad at the Idaho National Engineering Laboratory, and then puts it up again. Left behind when the building moves on are drums and bales stacked 16 feet high, capped with nylon-reinforced polyvinyl, and then buried under 3 feet of earth. The drums and bales contain radwastes that are transuranic, which means they consist of man-made elements heavier than uranium, mostly plutonium, but including measurable quantities of neptunium, americium, curium and others. Any radwaste contaminated to the extent of 10 nano (or billionths) curies per gram of these elements must be packaged and stored in such a way that it can be retrieved intact for at least twenty years. Roughly 36 percent of the transuranic waste produced in the United States until 1987 is destined to be stored on the asphalt pad which is part of an 88-acre radioactive waste-management complex administered by Schletter, an engineer. His formal title is manager of waste-management operations in the waste-management program of E. G. and G. (for Edgarton, Germeschausen and Grier) Idaho, a subsidiary of a Wellesley, Mass., nuclear contractor.

"Our first pad was filled in 1975," Schletter told me as we entered the airlock that contains the pressure inside his balloon-like building. "Now we're a little less than halfway along our second pad." The cavernous interior of the air-supported structure looks like an empty hangar, with the bales and drums stacked four and five high at the far end. "We didn't begin storing transuranics retrievably like this until 1970," Schletter said, "but a few years ago we did a test on some of the early drums we buried, 135 of them from when TRU [as transuranic waste is now called] was intermingled with low-level waste. We dug these up and ran them through an ultrasonic test, and while we found some evidence of surface corrosion, there was no evidence the drums had deteriorated below limits."

I asked what had been done with the material from the 135 drums after the test. "We packed it back into drums and boxes and stored them retrievably on the pad," he said. "It was a hassle, but we had everybody wrapped in disposable paper suits, and in the end we kept them all within the limits set down for radiation exposure. In fact, the only real accident we've had here was in 1970 when a fork-lift operator punctured one of the drums—after we cleaned that up, we redesigned the fork lift." He pointed to a lift that was moving drums not by supporting them with the customary forks from underneath, but rather by clutching them two at a time from the outside.

At the end of 1980, about 1.3 million cubic feet of waste, most of it plutonium, representing 74 percent of all government-stored transuranics, rested on Schletter's pads, with another 2.3 million cubic feet buried nearby. About 95 percent of this material came from Rockwell International's Rocky Flats plant 16 miles from Denver, where plutonium assemblies are fabricated for nuclear weapons. Rocky Flats puts out 2.2 million pounds of liquid and solid radwaste each year, and while the transuranic component of this material originally was dumped into trenches at low-level burial grounds, it is now carefully segregated and safeguarded at INEL, with the intention of processing it through a $355-million incinerator to be built someday at the laboratory, and then shipping the ashes to the Waste Isolation Pilot Project, an underground repository expected to be constructed in salt beds near Carlsbad, N.M., and now scheduled to be opened in 1987 for a cost now estimated to exceed $1 billion.

"It has taken us quite a while to settle on what we're going to do with it," Schletter concedes, "but that's the advantage of storing it out here—our evaluation is that it will last for a minimum of forty years in this dry Idaho environment, and the Department of Energy requirement for retrievability is only twenty years, and since some of our waste has only been here half that, we have more time to study our alternatives."

A somewhat less enthusiastic report on the Idaho environment's effect on transuranic waste, and vice versa, was submitted in 1976 by members of a National Academy of Sciences Committee who conceded that although waste packaged, stacked and retrievably stored as it is now comprised less of a problem than earlier transuranics that had simply been dumped into trenches, "waste containers that had been stored in stacked pits for twelve years were in poor condition, mainly due to corrosion. Contamination levels were as high as five nanocuries of plutonium per gram soil in this area . . ." Also found with the barrels stacked seven years were "cardboard cartons containing Rocky Flats Plant filters . . . the cardboard had disintegrated, and soil contamination was at a relatively high level of 0.1 to 1 nanocuries of plutonium per gram of soil . . . Migration of the plutonium was limited. Most of the contamination outside the barrels was found within 15 centimeters (six inches) of the waste containers. At the oldest site excavated, contamination of about 0.1 nanocuries of plutonium per gram of soil was found one meter (three feet) below the barrels . . . It is postulated that it moved by way of fissures in the basalt . . ."

For what it's worth, the people of Idaho had a firm and formal commitment from the old Atomic Energy Commission that these Rocky Flats materials would be on their way out of the state right now. This as-yet-unfulfilled commitment stemmed from a $20-million fire which burned 8,800 pounds of plutonium at the Colorado plant in 1969. A subsequent investigation resulted in a shipment of 1,400 barrels of plutonium-contaminated waste to INEL, then called the National Reactor Testing Station, and the discovery by many Idahoans that their state had been burdened by this form of defense waste since the Rocky Flats plant began operations in 1953. Idaho Senator

Frank Church thereupon obtained from AEC Chairman Glenn T. Seaborg a formal letter of commitment in June of 1970 promising "transfer of such wastes from NRTS, which we hope to start within the decade." In the next ten years, wastes continued to come to INEL—one of the more notable shipments was of 10,800 cubic feet of soil contaminated by plutonium contained in oil buried in drums discovered in 1976 after their corrosion had spread radioactivity throughout a Rocky Flats storage field—but at the end of 1980, the selection of an ultimate repository for all this transuranic material was no closer than it had been a decade before. Given this ten-year increase in volume—and in costs—a 1979 Sierra Club estimate of the cost of excavating the INEL transuranics and moving them to a repository projected in New Mexico ranged from $750 million to $1 billion.

This cost, of course, will continue to escalate as long as Max Schletter's air-supported building continues to crawl across the Idaho plain, leaving behind an annual spoor of approximately 91,000 cubic feet of transuranic waste bales and barrels stacked beneath a 3-foot berm. "I think we'll only be able to get one or two more moves before we have to replace this weather shield," he says. "They wear out after eight or nine moves; we won't run out of pad for another five years, though, and then there's plenty of room out here to build a third one."

Transuranic is the longest-lived form of radwaste, but this material is often less immediately dangerous than other isotopes. Most transuranic elements emit alpha radiation, which is easily shielded, even by paper. An isotope of americium, which has a very low radiation intensity, is commonly used in smoke detectors sold for home use, and plutonium powers some pacemakers. In pure form, though, some of these transuranics are pyrophoric—they tend to ignite spontaneously upon exposure to air—and a 3-percent pyrophoric content limit has been established for Rocky Flats waste shipments, and a one-percent limit has been proposed for packages eventually disposed of at a repository.

In addition to alpha, however, some transuranics also emit beta rays, and the more penetrating gamma radiation. Waste

packages that register 200 millirems per hour on the surface or
10 millirems per hour at a distance of one meter—about 17
percent of the governmental transuranic waste expected to be
generated through the year 2000—will continue to have to be
handled remotely. In addition, according to the Transuranic
Waste Management Program Strategy Document issued by the
Department of Energy in 1980, "about two percent by volume
of the (already) stored TRU waste has high beta and gamma
radiation levels, up to thirty thousand rems per hour, and its
thermal output may be a few hundred watts per container."
These wastes are buried in upended concrete culverts or stainless steel–lined pipes typical of ones I was shown at Oak Ridge
National Laboratory in Tennessee. At the summit of a small hill
cut open to accommodate a garage-like concrete facility housing a waste compactor, a row of concrete caps 3 feet thick
marked the location of a dozen 10- to 15-foot storage wells that
hold four 55-gallon drums stacked on top of each other. "We're
probably thirty or maybe thirty-five feet above the water table
here," a laboratory official told me, "and we have space for
about fifteen hundred drums on this hill, and we're building
another facility of the same capacity."

Fortunately, most transuranic material does not require this
isolation, and if the concentration of it in contact-handled waste
is less than ten billionths of a curie per gram it can be buried
without segregation in low-level facilities—and even the federal Environmental Protection Agency has recommended that
this concentration factor be raised to one hundred. However,
at least partially because transuranics are considered more potentially valuable than other isotopes, the level at which this
waste is set aside to be put into retrievable storage has not so
far been changed. In any case, few assay procedures are sophisticated enough to measure accurately down to ten billionths, or
one one hundred millionth of a curie, so the Department of
Energy assumes, in the language of its environmental-impact
statement on the Management of Commercially Generated
Radioactive Waste, "that all wastes from locations that might
cause contamination levels above 10 nCi/g of waste are considered to be TRU suspect and are combined with known TRU
wastes for treatment."

Since nearly all TRU waste is generated either in government facilities or in ten civilian plants that engage in government-sponsored nuclear fuel and weapons work, the Department of Energy has been given responsibility for managing this form of radwaste along with high-level material. Before 1970, however, when contact-handled TRU was routinely mingled with low-level waste, it was sent off for shallow burial at both commercial and government disposal sites in about equal proportions.

Originally, five of the six disposal sites that were operated commercially in the United States accepted these transuranics. By 1980, all these facilities had barred this form of waste. In fiscal year 1979, however, of the more than 26 million cubic feet of transuranic waste in the national inventory, 12.8 million cubic feet had already been buried commercially. The largest recipient of them was the nation's first privately operated nuclear-waste burial ground at Maxey Flats, Ky., where approximately 4.8 million cubic feet of transuranic material that now appears to have met the 10-nanocuries-per-gram definition was disposed of in a 13-year period. The Department of Energy's present estimate is that 152 pounds of transuranic elements was buried in the Maxey Flats trenches—and some of this material is now seeping out of them.

In 1970, only seven years after this facility had been opened, Kentucky inspectors discovered radioactive contamination off-site, and the federal Environmental Protection Agency measured plutonium levels as far away as a kilometer from the dump. The latter finding was particularly disturbing, since plutonium is thought to have little mobility through soil—the plant's operator, then called the Nuclear Engineering Co., but which in 1981 changed its name to the U.S. Ecology Corporation, a subsidiary of the industrial firm of Teledyne, had predicted that this element would not be measured beyond half an inch in 24,000 years. In a little more than a decade, however, plutonium was also being measured as deep as 35 inches below the Maxey Flats trenches and in wells and streams as far as two miles away.

"Living just under the hill that Maxey Flats . . . is located on, I am very concerned," Rosena Carswell, of Route 2, Hillsboro, Ky., wrote in a letter submitted to the House subcommittee on energy in 1976. "We have a herd of beef cattle that are drinking water from Rock Lick Creek and many families drinking water from vein-fed wells coming out of this hill; also, there is dairy cattle in this area . . . Maxey Flats should be closed down immediately and strong monitor measures taken to determine if waste already in the grounds there is leaking out . . ."

Although Maxey Flats was, in fact, forced to close in that year, the migration of the plutonium and other radionuclides continues to be measured off-site. Mrs. Carswell and her Eastern Kentucky neighbors have indicated that they consider the cause of this unexpected mobility of plutonium to be an academic question—they simply want it contained—however, the phenomenon does have wide-ranging implications for the U.S. Ecology Corporation, which operated four of the original six commercial low-level disposal sites, and for radwaste management in general. Its officials have attributed the migration to unexpectedly heavy rainfall causing "surface water runoff which carried off traces of plutonium and other isotopes resulting from minor spills on-site during burial procedures."

In fact, the facility did have problems with surface runoff and flooding of burial trenches. In 1972, it was cited by the state for the latter, along with burial of unauthorized material and disposal of liquid wastes directly to trenches designed to hold only solids. Additionally, scientists who have studied the problem for the government have attributed some isotope migration to unexpectedly large fractures in the shale underlying the Maxey Flats topsoil, and to the same kind of chelate reaction that makes solution mining of uranium feasible. The original hydrology tests on plutonium and other nuclides had been carried out for the most part on pure samples of these substances, and in the case of plutonium, scientists of the Atomic Energy Commission had satisfied themselves that its chemical and physical characteristics would make migration "unlikely." Unfortunately, however, most of these tests turned out to have little relevance to the actual conditions in the Maxey Flats trenches, since neither there nor anywhere else are these elements discarded in pure form. Just as combination with hydrogen peroxide and bicarbonate of soda loosed uranium compounds under the soil and freed them to travel in water, so it was believed did the chemical solutions from reactor and nuclear decontamination processes operate on buried plutonium-bearing waste compounds.

Such is the dangerous potential of plutonium that not only can its unexpected mobility cause problems, so can its unexpected immobility. In 1972, this caused a scare at Hanford, where approximately 30 million gallons of liquids containing 1.3 million curies, mostly of uranium and plutonium, had been *deliberately* percolated into the soil along with more than 130 billion gallons of reactor cooling wastes and steam condensates which also contained trace amounts of fissile uranium and plutonium. The most radioactive of these waste streams were dissipated through one or more of the reservation's 177 "cribs," that have been described in the Hanford environmental-impact statement as having been constructed by "digging a ditch about 20 feet deep and up to 1,400 feet long, backfilling with rock and covering with an impermeable membrane and soil. A pipe running the length of the crib is designed to distribute the liquid uniformly along the crib length."

One of these ditches, called the Z-9 trench, had received over a 7-year period approximately 84 pounds of plutonium contained within a million gallons of metal scrap recovery liquids. Theoretically, this plutonium was supposed to filter down uniformly into the soil of the trench; in fact, as monitoring showed, the fissile material had been retained within a foot of the floor, raising the possibility of a concentration of a critical mass of it and a subsequent nuclear reaction. Whether this reaction could have been of sufficient force to pose a great hazard remains in dispute. "If a criticality had occurred, there could not be an explosion," L. E. Bruns, of Rockwell International's Hanford Operations, told a 1975 seminar on nuclear-waste management. "It would give a high radiation field, many instruments would warn personnel of the radiation, the critical mass would be neutralized [he didn't say how], and there would be no harm to man." In environmental-impact statements it has compiled, the Department of Energy maintains that "energy releases in a criticality excursion are self-limiting in that when the concentration of nuclear material becomes high enough to cause the momentary chain reaction, the chain reaction causes a very minor type of explosive force, thus blowing the nuclear materials apart and halting the chain reaction." In any case, the Hanford trench was hastily excavated, at an approximate cost of $7 million, and the plutonium-contaminated soil transferred to retrievable storage.

The official euphemism for the type of accident that might thereby have been averted is "inadvertent criticality," and Zhores A. Medvedev, a dissident Soviet biologist working in England, maintains in a controversial book, *Nuclear Disaster in the Urals,* that just such an event within a waste trench, or something very like it, reached massive explosive proportions in early 1958, causing hundreds of casualties and contaminating beyond habitability at least 40 square miles near the town of Kyshtym in central Russia. Medvedev mentioned his theory of a disaster caused by an explosion in transuranic wastes almost in passing in an article about Soviet science that the biologist wrote in the British publication *New Scientist* in 1976, but it caused a furor by postulating exactly the kind of accident that nuclear scientists have maintained can never happen. The then head of the United Kingdom Atomic Energy Authority denounced Medvedev's conclusion, based on deductions from reading Soviet scientific reports on cesium and strontium contamination in the area, as "rubbish."

The Soviet government has never confirmed, officially or unofficially, the occurrence of such an accident; however, Medvedev's theory has been supported by Russian émigrés who have reported that an unknown terrible event certainly caused the evacuation of the area he described and by Soviet cartographers who without explanation have deleted the names of thirty small communities from maps of the region. Subsequently, the nuclear establishment at least appeared willing to concede in the words of Sir John Hill (the same British official who had originally dismissed the Medvedev findings) that "something very unpleasant happened in the Urals about twenty years ago."

Still the argument continued on whether or not the cause of this disaster could have been a nuclear-waste storage accident until early in 1980 when Critical Mass, a Ralph Nader organization, obtained the release of an analysis completed by four scientists in the Environmental Sciences Division of Oak Ridge National Laboratory, where they had access to Central Intelligence Agency data as well as translations of Soviet publications. Their conclusion was that it was a radwaste accident, probably in tanks that contained scrap transuranics from military weapons production: "The scope of the incident, in human terms, was not well defined, but appeared to involve some loss of life (magnitude undetermined), the evacuation of the civilian population from a large area, and the appearance of a restricted, radioactive contamination zone." A possible cause of this accident was suggested in a 1979 letter to the publication *Science* by Freeman Dyson, of the Institute for Advanced Study at Princeton as "an autocatalytic fission reaction that might have occurred underground if plutonium-containing wastes from a chemical separation plant had been carelessly discarded . . . If an underground solution of plutonium once became critical, the reactivity would increase rapidly as the temperature rose. The whole mass might become strongly supercritical at a temperature of about 2,000 degrees Centigrade, causing an explosion that would spread over the surrounding countryside the long-lived fission products which had accumulated in the ground together with the plutonium . . ."

Soviet Russia is, of course, not the only nation reluctant to talk about its "inadvertent criticalities." By 1976, however, it was reported in *Scientific American* that in the United States "there have been twelve accumulations of critical mass, five of them in chemical processing plants or laboratories." Typical, perhaps, of those that have involved radwaste is the 30-second "inadvertent criticality" that took place in 1959 at INEL's Idaho Chemical Processing Plant. According to a 1960 report, this probably was caused when concentrated uranium-nitric acid was accidentally transferred from a hot cell into a waste-collection tank holding transuranically contaminated process equipment. INEL's environmental-impact statement estimates that about 350,000 curies, mostly in the form of radioactive noble gases, but also containing some radioactive iodine, fluorine and bromine, were discharged into the environment "in the form of a gaseous 'cloud' released from the ICPP stack."

Like the management of spent fuel and high-level waste,

transuranic waste storage and disposal requires consideration of environmentally affected criticality factors. The Panel on Waste Solidification of the National Research Council was writing specifically about spent fuel as a solid waste form in a repository when it pointed out in a report held back from publication in 1979 by the National Academy of Sciences that "the presence of plutonium and uranium make the possibility of criticality a concern if the repository were breached, water were to enter, and the fissile materials were arranged in a suitable configuration." This might be something for the Nuclear Regulatory Commission to keep in mind in its regulation of the nuclear burial ground established on the site of the West Valley facility 30 miles southeast of Buffalo, N.Y. According to a Department of Energy study, the NRC-licensed burial ground at West Valley contains "spent fuel hulls; fuel assembly hardware; failed process vessels and large equipment; degraded process solvent absorbed on suitable solid medium; and miscellaneous packaged trash, including laboratory wastes, small equipment, ventilation filters and other process-related debris," along with 42 spent-fuel rods that ruptured in transit from Hanford, where they were to have been reprocessed. These rods, containing a little more than a thousand pounds of special nuclear material, were hastily encased in cement and dropped into a column dug 165 feet below the surface, where there is at least a possibility that water from 2 sub-surface aquifers may have already begun rearranging some of these fissile materials in the "suitable configuration" that the unpublished National Academy of Sciences report warned about.

In West Valley's adjoining—and far less deep—commercial burial ground, which is licensed only by the state, approximately 8 pounds of transuranics are believed to have been mixed in with about 2.3 million cubic feet of buried low-level radwaste. Because transuranic did not exist as a distinct waste category until 1970, calculations of TRU deposits before that date are at best approximations. However, the Oak Ridge survey estimates a total of nearly 2,000 pounds of transuranic elements buried at five of the six commercial sites and at eight government facilities. The Albuquerque, N.M., operations office of the Department of Energy has lead responsibility for formulating transuranic disposal plans, and in a 1980 "strategy document," it calculated the volume of this transuranic waste at government sites at 11.7 million cubic feet. The ORNL survey projects that this inventory will increase in 1980 by a little more than 200,000 cubic feet, nearly all of it accumulated in weapons-related work. Industrial production of TRU waste, although greatly reduced since 1972, when the last commercial spent fuel was reprocessed, still continues from research and from civilian fuel-fabrication work, and its 1980 volume is projected at 52,844 cubic feet. The commercial repository at Hanford, the last civilian site to accept transuranics, began barring this form early in 1980, and according to the Oak Ridge survey, "it is not known at this time where future industrial TRU waste will be stored." Probably, however, it will eventually be combined with chemical process residues, discarded machinery and tools, casting crucibles and molds, glass, gas filters, metal, rubber, plastics, firebrick, paper, rags and clothing contaminated above the 10 nanocuries per gram minimum that now finds its way to the pad at INEL or to similar but smaller storage sites at Hanford, Los Alamos, the Nevada Test Site, Oak Ridge or the Savannah River Plant.

A larger problem, at least in terms of volume, is the quantity of soil that has been contaminated by transuranic elements to the extent that, like the earth that received the waste leaks at Hanford, Savannah River and the plutonium-contaminated oil from Rocky Flats, it itself must now be classified as a transuranic waste. The Transuranic Waste Management Strategy Document estimates that there are about 494 million cubic feet of this dirt—roughly 42 times the volume of all other transuranic solids. Of this, about 338 million cubic feet, contaminated by about 440 pounds of plutonium, comes from waste-disposal spills, and the remainder from "accidental discharges or spills."

This second category, quantity of plutonium unspecified, includes ground that has been scraped from the sites of some 35 "broken arrows," nuclear bomb or missile accidents. The two most spectacular of these have been the 1966 and 1968 crashes of B-52s armed with nuclear bombs at Palomares, Spain, and Thule, Greenland. Dirt and rubble from these accidents has been sealed in metal drums that are buried in 20.5-foot-deep concrete cylinders six feet in diameter at the Pantex plant near Amarillo, Tex., where the weapons were originally formulated. So far, about ten of these cylinders have been filled by an approximate quantity of 5,800 cubic feet of dirt which contains about 7 pounds of plutonium from the weapons accidents that, according to the Department of Energy, has been "mixed with and diluted by the debris so as to render recovery virtually impossible."

The unsalvagable pieces of the "broken arrows" that can be distinguished from the general debris eventually are shipped to "classified-waste" disposal sites. The exact weight and volume of the contents of these are, of course, classified information. However, two of the largest and most secure of these installations are at Hanford and at the Nevada Nuclear Test Site, and at both places, burials and monitoring procedures must be carried out only by those with nuclear, or Q, clearances—which adds a significant expense to this form of radwaste disposal.

There is also a transuranic waste that is noteworthy simply because it is believed to exist—but can't be accounted for anywhere. This is MUF, the government's perfectly descriptive acronym for its strategic nuclear "material unaccounted for." From time to time, the government and commercial plants where weapons-grade uranium and plutonium is fabricated and enriched come up short on their production lines. Because these materials are processed as gases and liquids, as well as in solid form, accounting for them is an extremely sophisticated procedure which requires a good deal of estimating. An explanation frequently proffered for many of these inventory differences is that, in one way or another, the strategic nuclear material has been dispersed in various waste forms. In the words of a 1977 ERDA report on Strategic Special Nuclear Material Inventory Differences, "Small amounts of SNM form fractions of the waste streams which are uneconomical and difficult to recover or measure and, as part of normal operating losses, are properly disposed of."

Of course, MUFs are not measured for purposes of establishing waste inventories, but rather to check on potential thefts of fissile nuclear material. The International Atomic Energy Authority estimates that 17.6 pounds of plutonium is sufficient to make a bomb, and it is believed that only slightly more enriched uranium 235, about 19.8 pounds, would be required for weapons purposes. Although it has never officially confirmed the finding, the Central Intelligence Agency has indicated that 200 pounds of enriched uranium that disappeared in 1965 from a Nuclear Materials and Engineering Corporation plant at Apollo, Pa., were somehow diverted to Israel. However, in some cases where diversions are not suspected, the inventory differences have been even larger. In the three gaseous diffusion plants where uranium is enriched, losses of 264, 339 and 706 pounds (at Union Carbide's Nuclear Division plant at Paducah, Ky.) were reported in one 6-month period in 1976–77. A subsequent tightening up of procedures led to the closing for a 3-month period of the Erwin, Tenn., atomic submarine fuel plant operated by Nuclear Fuel Services (the same Getty-Skelly subsidiary that operated the West Valley reprocessing facility) when a 48-pound shortage—later scaled down to 11.7 pounds —was discovered in 1979. (Environmentally, this Erwin plant seems to be operated on something of a par with NFS's West Valley work: At least part of the cause of this MUF appears to have been a blocked pipe which in August 1979 diverted a cloud of uranium in powder form right up the plant's stack. Later, when the inventory difference was scaled down, the reported proportions of this accident and the subsequent contamination had to be increased. Eventually, the Nuclear Regulatory Commission calculated that the diversion accounted for 6.6 pounds of uranium, or enough to give a dose of as much as 250 millirems, or two and a half times the annual background dose, to nearby residents.)

Government plants have MUFs, too. In 1977, the Energy Research and Development Administration totaled cumulative shortages at all plants under its control through 1976 as 3,366 pounds of plutonium, 1,519 pounds of enriched uranium 235 and 55 pounds of uranium 233. Just one of these facilities, the Savannah River Plant, has been caught short 320 pounds of special nuclear material in its operations between 1955 and 1978. When I visited Savannah River in 1980, I mentioned to Ed Goldberg, the director of the Department of Energy's waste project office, my belief that unless this material had been illegally diverted, it necessarily had to turn up as one or another form of radwaste. Several weeks later I received a response from David Peek, one of his assistants, who wrote in part: "The inventory difference results primarily from the difference between the amount of plutonium calculated to be produced in the reactors, and the amount actually measured when the material is dissolved at the separations facility. In addition, uncertainties in the measurement of many transfers of process solutions and the measurement of inventories contained in numerous vessels in the separations facilities contribute to the reported inventory difference. Transfers to the waste tanks are a measured removal from the separations process and are subject to measurement uncertainty . . ."

Three hundred and twenty pounds still seems to me to be a significantly large "measurement uncertainty," however, particularly when calculated for material as closely guarded and monitored as plutonium. In any case, it appears safe to predict that numbers and quantities of MUFs will continue to increase with increases in the production of weapons-grade material. Shortly before the 1980 elections, the Pentagon, which was then adding only "a few hundred" warheads annually to its nuclear arsenal, received permission from the Carter administration to stockpile in the 1980s an additional 2,000 MX missiles, 5,000 sea-launched Trident missiles, 1,500 air- and ground-launched missiles and 1,000 bombs. President Reagan's Secretary of Energy, James B. Edwards, has indicated he may want further increases, and that, in any case, he will seek to step up weapons research.

In addition to increasing MUFs, this future defense production will inevitably increase the volume of defense radwastes beyond the projections of the Oak Ridge National Laboratory surveyors and lead to an intensification of political and technological pressures to do something about disposing of them permanently. At the Albuquerque operations office of the Department of Energy, I talked to Anibal L. Taboas, who is in charge of transuranic waste research programs that were budgeted at more than $25 million in fiscal year 1980. "My responsibility is making sure we have adequate technology for getting this waste into acceptable forms for transport and disposal," he said. "We're going at the problem from several different directions. First, we're trying to see if we can reduce generation of the form and to improve our instrumentation so we can make better assays of transuranic-suspect material. There's a huge saving if we can establish that something is less than the ten-nanocuries-per-gram limit. We estimate that it costs us two hundred fifty to two hundred seventy-five dollars to store commercial transuranic waste as opposed to $5 or $6 per cubic foot to dispose of low-level wastes.

"Then we're looking hard at incineration, which will get rid of organic materials that build up gases, and even better, give us a volume reduction of up to a hundred to one—we'd save two ways. And we're making a substantial effort toward immobilization of this waste into a single form. Unfortunately, some of the forms we've been experimenting on up till now will not accept a high metallic content of some of the components of transuranic scrap—contaminated aluminum, for example—so we're looking at a host of alternatives which may or may not be similar to what they're looking at for high-level waste, which is much smaller in volume."

Basically under consideration are three forms of volume reduction: Compaction, incineration and bituminization. The last of these involves mixing the wastes with bitumen or asphalt heated to temperatures that will boil off water within organic materials. This process has been employed in France since 1965, with a claimed reduction in volume of fivefold to twentyfold. However, according to the federal environmental-impact statement on the Management of Commercially Generated Radioactive Waste, "it is uncertain whether bituminized waste forms will meet waste form criteria for repositories."

Compactors hooked up to high-efficiency particulate air filters have been employed for some time by both governmental and industrial plants turning out transuranic and low-level wastes. Volume reductions range up to ten to one—at the compactor in use at the Transuranic Waste Treatment Facility at INEL. I asked Max Schletter how long the machine could be operated before it became too radioactively contaminated to be worked on. "The machine will fail mechanically before that happens," he promised.

Incineration offers the greatest volume reduction—however,

here again the gas effluent has to be filtered and cleansed of its radioactive components. In addition, incinerators can be troublesome to operate: Non-combustibles have to be mechanically segregated from the wastes that feed them; filters in the off-gas system tend to block up and need to be frequently replaced, and the radioactivity which concentrates in the ash and unburned solids can present a formidable handling problem. However, incineration of radwastes, including transuranics, is now practiced at seventeen governmental facilities. My visit to Savannah River included a look at a ceramic electrically heated incinerator now being tested for the combustion of plutonium and other alpha-emitting wastes. "We started in 1975 by reviewing what everybody else was doing with this kind of problem," Edward L. Albenesius, a Du Pont engineer in charge of the testing told me, "and we came up with this British design —they've been burning plutonium-contaminated waste on a test basis there since 1973." With a few adaptations of design, Albenesius expects the Savannah River incinerator to produce an off-gas decontamination ratio of one part in ten billion— "that's what we're shooting for"—and a volume reduction factor of eighty: "It'll cost $12 million, and we hope to have it operational in 1984."

Already in operation for more than three years at Los Alamos Scientific Laboratory is the "Blue Goose," a two-tiered natural gas-fueled incinerator which Thomas Keenan, group manager of the institution's waste-treatment development facility, walked me past. "The principal advantage of this unit is that it burns very, very slowly," Keenan said. "By controlling the air that gets to the waste, we slow down the burning, and that cuts down on particulates. The gases are scrubbed in a high-efficiency particulate air filter and cooled by water in an enclosed loop, so it never is contaminated by the emanation. In the three years we've operated, we've never had a release of radiation. We not only exceed federal standards, we exceed all present state standards, and everything that's gone up our stack has been as pure as baby's breath."

The incinerator, in the basement of the waste-treatment facility, is composed of a series of connected box-like chambers operated from a central control panel. "Glove boxes"—compartments equipped with built-in gloves—allow protected manual access to the materials within. The transuranic waste is consecutively burned, first at 1,500 degrees Fahrenheit and then at 2,000 degrees, in furnaces one atop the other. The upper, higher-temperature furnace is in turn topped by a massive venting pipe leading to filters, blowers, and eventually to the plant stack. "The ash is dropped automatically into a pit, and we can easily break up any lumps that form in it," Keenan said. "Mostly, however, it comes out fluffy, and right now it is being immobilized into pellets that we are experimenting on—people at the lab are trying to see if they can find a way to recover the plutonium out of it." The Blue Goose, which achieves a volume reduction factor of eighty to one, was built at a cost of $2 million "entirely from off-the-shelf components," Los Alamos visitors are told. "Add another million to pay for a building, and in reducing waste storage and disposal costs alone, it should pay for itself inside of two years."

In fact, the Blue Goose and Savannah River's much more expensive ceramic electric prototype are two of five incinerator candidates now being evaluated for incorporation into the pending transuranic-waste strategy program. The others are a fluidized-bed incinerator (not unlike INEL's fluidized-bed calcinator) at the Rocky Flats Plant, a cyclonic incinerator (excess air above that required for combustion keeps burning temperatures relatively low) at Mound Laboratory, which produces plutonium triggers at Miamisburg, Ohio, and a slagging pyrolysis (temperatures high enough to melt contaminated soil) incinerator yet to be built at a projected $355-million cost at Max Schletter's Radioactive Waste Management Treatment Facility at INEL. This device is not expected to become operational until 1990, and a reason for its extraordinary cost—nearly 30 times the Savannah River prototype and 177 times the Blue Goose—is that it is being designed to burn more than 2 tons of transuranic waste each hour and to incorporate the resulting ash and non-combustibles into a molten slag that will be drained and poured into bricks or molds suitable for disposal in the repository for transuranics. Four prototypes of slagging pyrolysis incinerators already burn non-radioactive garbage for European municipalities, and the technique has also been demonstrated in facility tests in Florida, but before this planned one begins to consume any of the stored transuranics at INEL, some Department of Energy officials are betting privately that additional modifications of the design will almost double projected costs to $600 to $700 million. The incinerator is also opposed politically by members of a Pocatello anti-nuclear group who feel that its installation at INEL will only attract more transuranic waste there.

No matter how much money is invested in volume reduction ("Designing new incinerators is DOE's version of reinventing the wheel," a critic of the department's program maintains), transuranic ash or slag or solid residues will have to be disposed of somewhere. One of the first acts of the incoming Reagan administration was the reinstatement in the budget of a 22-year-old plan to establish a government Waste Isolation Pilot Project now expected to cost more than a billion dollars—on top of a $100-million planning expense—by the time it is constructed near Carlsbad, N.M.

WIPP started out in 1959 as a project of Oak Ridge National Laboratory; in 1963, it was sited as Project Salt Vault in bedded salt near Lyons, Kans. Although it was not disclosed at the time, several canisters of spent fuel from a government reactor were buried within test borings at an existing mine there, but the Kansas project was abandoned after 1971 when an attempt to solution-mine salt a half-mile away disclosed the pressure of a previously unsuspected fissure near the site—commercial mine operators revealed they had pumped in 175,000 gallons of water that had simply disappeared.

Reincarnated in 1974 as WIPP, and reformulated as a repository for defense transuranic waste being held retrievably in storage, mostly at INEL, the project settled down again 26 miles east of Carlsbad, N.M. There in bedded salt at least 2,000 feet below the surface, government engineers planned to excavate caverns that would accept 1.2 million cubic feet of contact-handled and 10,000 cubic feet of remote-handled transuranic waste each year. WIPP's planners believed that given a continuing production of a quarter of a million cubic feet of this waste a year, they would have caught up with the entire transuranic backlog by the year 2000.

Then in 1977, the mission of the facility was changed again: In addition to the transuranics, it would become a pilot repository for military high-level wastes, and in this capacity it was decided that it would be subject to licensing by the Nuclear Regulatory Commission. This proposal, to require civilian licensing of a facility originally designed to meet the needs of the defense program, which produces almost all the transuranic waste and currently all the high-level waste in need of disposal, eventually provoked the opposition of the congressional armed services committees. The following year, the Interagency Review Group on Nuclear Waste Management, which President Carter had established to advise him on radwaste policies, proposed that the high-level waste not be put into WIPP, but that in addition to the transuranics, the facility be established as a pilot repository for a maximum of 1,000 canisters of spent fuel. "The purpose of the WIPP site was changed in midstream," Dr. Darleane Hoffman, of the staff of the Los Alamos Scientific Laboratory, wrote in a formal presentation to the Senate Subcommittee on Science, Technology and Space in 1978, "leading to assertions that the government did not know what it wanted, or still worse, was not telling all of its intentions. And people asked, if the purpose of the site could be so easily changed, what was to prevent further changes?"

The proposal to mingle civilian and military radwaste in a single repository drew additional fire even from officials of the Department of Energy, which has oversight authority over both sources, and from House Armed Services Committee Chairman Melvin Price, of Illinois, who wrote the Department in September 1979 that his committee was also "unalterably opposed to subjecting a defense program to licensing and regulatory control." On February 12, 1980, just a little more than a month after signing a bill funding construction of the repository for transuranics, President Carter canceled it, pointing out in a message to Congress that WIPP "is currently authorized for the unlicensed disposal of transuranic waste from our national defense program, and for research and development using high-level defense waste. This project is inconsistent with my policy that all repositories for highly radioactive waste be licensed, and that they accept both defense and commercial wastes."

In the end, though, Carter's action allotted $22 million toward further study of the New Mexico site for possible use as a high-level waste repository, and a subsequent refusal by Congress to revoke WIPP's $28-million appropriation to begin actual excavation led to skepticism in both Washington and New Mexico as to whether the project had, in fact, been canceled. In June 1980, a letter to the editor of the Carlsbad *Current Argus* suggested that as a practical matter a Waste Isolation Pilot Project "weather vane" be erected atop the paper's building to indicate on a daily basis whether the project was alive or dead.

During this period of uncertainty, I visited WIPP's office in Albuquerque, more than 300 highway miles northwest of the proposed repository, and found scattered in a dozen large offices—filled with filing cases containing surveys, scientific reports, plans and specifications—a group of project executives with undiminished enthusiasm for the disposal concept. "WIPP may not be the only solution," said Ray Mairson, manager of the project for Westinghouse, the principal contractor. "In sixty years it may not even be seen as the best solution, but right now salt is the medium in which we have the most answers." After five years of test drilling, he maintained, nothing has turned up in 73 holes drilled around the periphery of the proposed repository to indicate that anything might have damaged its integrity: "The salt bed has been there for millions of years, and if water had reached it, it would have long since disappeared, so we think we can be confident of isolation for a long period of time. In other rocks, you have to assume some ground water will get in."

"Even those who feel we don't know enough about what happens when you put high-level wastes into salt agree we know enough to put transuranics into salt, because the kind of geological problems that are blocking high-level disposal don't occur with transuranic wastes," said Dr. Wendell Weart, the manager of waste-management technology for Sandia Laboratory—and the engineer who has been longest associated with studies of WIPP.

"What we're hoping to do with the money we have is to downbore two more shafts," explained John Treadwell, a Department of Energy project associate. "The first of these will be steel lined ten feet in diameter to allow us to get twenty-one hundred feet down to the repository level, and then we'll have to build a second shaft six feet in diameter that will be a safety escape. Eventually we hope to connect these two shafts with an underground drift, or tunnel, and then we'll drill northward and excavate a small design-verification area to test our engineering assumptions. The drift and the design area are contingent upon future funding, but we believe we'll have the money to complete the two shafts in a year and a half."

I asked the engineers how they felt about WIPP's then uncertain position on pending federal budgets. "My personal opinion is that it's a tragedy," said Mairson, the project manager. "I was involved for many years in designing reactor plants; certainly it has been a much less difficult job to design this repository than a new reactor plant. How long are we going to have to sit on the surface and hash over old information?"

"Nuclear power is the real issue," said Weart, "and the easiest way to attack it is through the question of waste disposal. We need to go ahead, not because we are in any danger from spent fuel in the reactor pools, but because of the public's increasing perception that there is no solution to waste disposal and never will be. Really, we're between a rock and a hard place. Our critics say, 'You don't know enough to proceed with WIPP,' but the only way we can find out more is to go ahead and build the project. They don't want to allow us to do that, though, so what their argument gets down to is that we don't know enough, so they aren't going to let us learn."

As Weart conceded, his "critics" have been successful in marshaling New Mexican opposition to WIPP. A statewide poll conducted at about the time of my 1980 visit found 63 percent of a voter sample against the repository, with 26 percent favoring it and 11 percent undecided. However, to the gratification of the engineers and executives who had worked so long to plan it, the project was reinstated on January 23, 1981, the day after President Reagan's avowedly pro-WIPP energy secretary, James B. Edwards, was sworn in. Without notice either to the

State of New Mexico or to the Interior Department's Bureau of Land Management, which controls the use of some of the 18,-960 acres involved, Department of Energy officials flew to Albuquerque to make the announcement.

Two weeks later, the Albuquerque *Journal* was reporting that "red protest signs are springing up on lawns around the state as part of a statewide campaign [against WIPP]," and New Mexico's attorney general, Jeff Bingaman, was announcing that he would seek to determine "if the state has a legal position it can pursue through the courts." He wrote Secretary Edwards that the reinstatement of the project "without first resolving the state's legitimate legal and public health and safety concerns, is a flagrant abuse of federal power and a breach of trust with the government and citizens of New Mexico." He did file a federal court suit, but withdrew it when DOE promised to recognize the state's right to health and safety recommendations on the project; a parallel suit by environmentalists remained pending.

Unless the courts intervene, however, drilling of the repository's two vertical shafts will be under way by the end of 1981. At an approximate depth of 2,150 feet some 100 acres of salt will be mined out (the resulting 340,000-ton spoils pile will reach a maximum height of 60 feet on a 30-acre site east of the shafts) in order to construct more than 100 underground chambers, with separate areas for remote- and contact-handled transuranic wastes and for a limited quantity of defense high-level wastes. To fulfill WIPP's original "pilot" function, 40 canisters of this material are scheduled to be put into the repository temporarily for demonstration purposes while the mine is filled to its approximate capacity of 6.5 million cubic feet.

Beginning in 1987, the transuranic wastes stacked on INEL's asphalt pads are scheduled to be dug out from under their earth cover, incinerated and shipped to New Mexico. By 2003, if the repository is not to be brought under NRC licensing requirements, the high-level canisters will have to be removed before the mine is then sealed, with the intention of removing forever from the biosphere its burden of long-lived dangerous radioisotopes. Where the high-level canisters will then be sent, and where the transuranic wastes produced after that date will be disposed of, remain open questions.

6
LOW LEVEL—
GOVERNMENTAL

In May of 1980, I drove out to look at the hydrofracture well at
Oak Ridge National Laboratory with Adolphus L. "Pete" Lotts,
the facility's director of nuclear-waste programs. ORNL is operated for the Department of Energy by the Nuclear Division
of Union Carbide Corporation, and Lotts, a metallurgist, has
attained a higher degree of scientific recognition than other
waste-management executives I met on my visits to nuclear
installations around the country. In 1976, he received the government's E. O. Lawrence Memorial Award for leadership in
the development of the high-temperature gas-cooled reactor
fuel cycle. The following year, he told me, "I asked for this job.
My perception is that waste management has not always been
assigned to the best technical people, and before 1977, there
was no integration of waste programs here. I was promised a
budget that would allow me to hire a few good assistants and
work out a coherent approach to the problem, and I saw the
assignment as an opportunity to bring what we had learned
from the rest of nuclear technology to bear on waste management."

If Lotts is unique, so is Oak Ridge's hydrofracture process.

Although haphazardly packaged waste solids are still thrown
into low-level trenches in Melton Valley, south of the laboratory's complex of buildings, its liquid wastes have been for more
than 15 years confined by both geological and chemical barriers
—and, in fact, Oak Ridge is the only facility in the country that
does anything more to these effluents than to allow them to
settle in ponds or to pour them into wells.

Most of the 150,000 gallons of liquid wastes that are collected
and processed at the laboratory each month come from radioisotope production, cooling and shielding of research reactors,
decontamination of hot cells and laboratory research, and the
principal nuclear contaminants in it are cesium 137 and strontium 90—but not in sufficient concentrations, I was told, to
cause self-heating problems. "We take this waste and put it into
one of two steam-operated evaporators," Edward King, a waste-
process engineer, told me, "and after it is concentrated by factors of twenty-five to 30 to one (the resulting off-gases go
through filters and scrubbers and eventually up a two-hundred-
fifty-foot stack at the center of the laboratory complex) we
pump the remaining effluent out to Melton Valley in stainless
steel pipes to tanks where it is held for hydrofracture."

Physically, the hydrofracture facility is hardly prepossessing.
On a knoll in the valley stand five 100-foot tanks, several trailers
which serve as offices and locker rooms, high-pressure pumping
machinery and an assortment of pipes leading to a well that
extends down a thousand feet into a formation of shale more
than a hundred feet thick. "The first hundred feet of the pipe
has a ten-inch case," Lotts told me, "and after that, it's six inches
in diameter all the way to the bottom. We hold the waste in the
tanks until we're ready to pump it, and then we mix it with
cement and fly ash that have the chemical properties necessary
to hold the most mobile fractions of the waste, the cesium and
strontium.

"The well casing is slotted at the appropriate depth to allow
us to pump water under pressure out into the shale there to
fracture its layers. Then we pump out the water and pump in
the cement waste slurry, also under pressure, and that enlarges
the cavity and spreads the mixture further into the shale. Then
we follow that with more water to make sure the whole grout
is piped out." A crew from Halliburton, Inc., a firm primarily

engaged in pumping oil wells, requires three days to complete a pumping operation, and an artist's projection of the effects of this work showed thirty to forty irregular wafers of concreted waste inserted like pancakes between layers of shale.

"We've been pumping since 1966, and we've just about used up our first well. Approximately two million gallons went down here, maybe a little more, and we haven't spotted any contamination at all in any of the monitoring wells. As a matter of fact, the only physical effect we have been able to determine is that we do have an uplift of a few thousandths of an inch in the hill. We're about ready to move the operation to a new well on the next knoll a few hundred yards away, where we've already built eight fifty-thousand-gallon holding tanks within a concrete vault."

At the time of my visit, the Halliburton contractors were finishing up on the original well with an experiment to determine the feasibility of including minute pellets of solidified waste within the grout, and several weeks afterward I received a report on the results from Jim Alexander of the Department of Energy, who reported that these efforts "ended with the slot at the well casing or the fracture itself in the formation being plugged with pellets." Consequently, he said, the only solid materials that appeared amenable to hydrofracture were the ashes of incinerated wastes: "This should present no problem, since the ash would have a consistency similar to materials that we presently utilize in the grout."

In fiscal year 1981, the laboratory expected to spend more than $2.5 million on its liquid and gaseous waste operations, $180,000 for technical work to improve its hydrofracture mix, and another $2 million to design and develop a low-level waste pilot facility, and these three items comprised more than half its radwaste management budget of $8.5 million. "Our waste-management program is the only one that's increasing in size and level of effort," Joseph Lenhard, a research and development manager in the Oak Ridge Department of Energy office, told me, "and in the 1982 budget, the trend will be even more marked."

Until the opening of the first commercial nuclear waste repository in 1962 at Beatty, Nevada, all radwaste, whether government or commercially produced, was the responsibility of first the wartime Manhattan Engineering District, and then the old Atomic Energy Commission. In retrospect, many of the liquid effluents of World War II atomic-weapons production appear to have been disposed of expediently without much consideration of environmental consequences. In February of 1981, a New York Assembly Task Force on Toxic Substances uncovered evidence that 37 million gallons of radioactive water from uranium ore processing at Tonawanda (a town on the other side of Niagara Falls from the Lake Ontario Ordnance Works where the ore tailings are still stored) had simply been poured into 5 wells previously used for drinking water. The task force also obtained a document in which the disposal in the 150-foot-deep wells was recommended by executives of the Linde Air Processing Co. plant to the Army "because our law department advises that it is considered impossible to determine the course of subterranean streams and, therefore, the responsibility for contamination could not be fixed." Subsequently, the plant's present owner, Union Carbide, confirmed the well dumping of nearly twice as much radioactive water, 67 million gallons, but said that current sampling of drinking wells in the Tonawanda area shows no abnormal radioactive contamination.

Low-level solid residues of these early days were supposed to be sent either to one of the seventeen land disposal sites which succeeded the trench at Palos Forest, or to be dumped from barges operating off the Atlantic and Pacific coasts. Again many years after the fact, evidence has been uncovered to indicate that not all these ocean disposals were made in accordance even with the comparatively less restrictive disposal regulations of the time. In December of 1980, a now retired Navy pilot told New Jersey environmental officials of three Atlantic dumping missions he and his crew flew from a field near Philadelphia in October of 1947 to drop shielded nuclear wastes in October of 1947. Former Lieutenant Commander George Earle IV said his four-engine bomber was loaded three times with a total of approximately six tons of radwaste canisters, and "we were told to fly as low and slow as possible to avoid having any of those things break open, so we went out to sea and dumped it, and nobody asked any questions." Later, he said, when he went to look up his flight records on these three missions, they were not to be found in the files. After his testimony was publicized, Earle subsequently told a reporter, he received "a call from a Navy pilot who's in the Middle West who said that he'd made six similar missions out of Noah's Island [at San Diego]."

The known ocean disposal between the years 1946 and 1970 amounts to 94,673 curies of activity dropped from barges in depths of up to 12,000 feet in ten sites, including three off British Columbia. (These figures, of course, do not include the curies contained in a submarine reactor that the Navy has admitted dumping into the Atlantic or the two nuclear submarines, the *Thresher* and the *Scorpion,* lost in 1963 and 1968 accidents in the Atlantic.) The preponderance of this material was simply sealed in 55-gallon or 80-gallon drums lined to 75 percent of their capacities with concrete as both shielding and ballast, and dropped at three principal sites, two of them off the Farallon Islands about 50 miles from San Francisco, and the third about 120 miles out in the Atlantic off the southern tip of New Jersey. As a "rare event" (it was so characterized by the Navy's Radiological Defense Laboratory in 1960), an insufficiently ballasted canister would float, and in such cases it would be breached and sunk by gunfire—thus its radioactive content would begin leaking even before it hit bottom. In any case, barging these canisters far out to sea was expensive (and there was always the question of whether they ever really got all the way to the dump site or were simply dropped over the side as soon as the craft got out of sight), and in the 1960s, increasing use began to be made of a dump site only 12 miles off Boston in Massachusetts Bay.

The protests that followed disclosure of this site were in no way mollified by the AEC's citation of a 1962 report of a National Academy of Sciences–National Research Council Committee on Oceanography. Although it approved the concept of ocean dumping, this panel urged the establishment of 9-by-9-nautical-mile disposal areas that would be "remote from seamounts, trenches, canyons, coastal basins and submarine cables; avoid unusually deep covered bottoms and not be disposal areas for other purposes." Massachusetts Bay failed to qualify on several of these counts, and even this recommendation was given by the NAS-NRC committee despite an admission that the waste canisters would inevitably leak and that bottom organisms and underwater plants would ingest some of the leaking wastes, and although dangerous levels would not be reached, "it is apparent that *a greater total exposure of the population to radiation may result* [emphasis in the original] from this stimulation."

As the panel pointed out in its introduction, "human beings do not drink much sea water, but they eat much sea food . . . The problem is not one of simple physical diffusion of soluble chemical elements through the sea, but rather one involving not only this and the circulation and chemistry of sea water, but also the behavior, ecology, biology and biochemistry of the creatures of the sea, the physiology and biochemistry of man, and that principal connecting link—man's great fisheries, both sport and commercial."

In addition to its high costs and the environmental protests provoked by it, ocean dumping also led to international complications. In 1959, the government of Mexico filed a diplomatic protest which effectively blocked announced plans to open a dump site in the Gulf of Mexico, and in 1961, the World Health Organization asked its members to prohibit "all discharge of radioactive wastes into water courses or the sea, to the extent that the safety of such discharge has not been proved." Sea disposals were ended by the Atomic Energy Commission in June of 1970, for stated reasons of economy, and in 1972, Congress put radwaste ocean dumping under the jurisdiction of the Environmental Protection Agency. This is still the only radwaste activity over which the EPA exercises regulatory authority, but it is hardly likely to approve any renewal of sea disposal, given its research into what has happened to the waste that has already been dumped into the ocean.

In 1976, Robert Dyer, an EPA oceanologist, reported that an underwater photo study of the Farallon Island sites revealed that one quarter of the 50,000 drums there had ruptured. In addition, plutonium contaminants of the sediments of the Pacific bottom were up to 25 times higher than the maximum concentrations that could have resulted from fallout. In 1976, William D. Rowe, deputy assistant head of EPA radiological programs, assured a House energy subcommittee that this contamination "is only five billionths of a gram per kilogram of dry sediment . . . well below any marine environmental concentration of health significance." According to Rowe, "the only route of exposure to man likely to occur at these depths (3,000 feet) would be via the ingestion of contaminated edible marine fish. But marine fish are not known to concentrate plutonium to any appreciable extent . . ." With that reassurance, however, came a report on what Rowe called an "observation of specific interest," the discovery of large white vasiform sponges "seen growing on both intact and breached containers." Since these sponges ranged up in size to a previously unheard of 4 feet, Rowe conceded, they "probably represent a new genus." He called it "extremely unlikely," however, "that there is any correlation between the size of these sponges and the contents of the drums."

This was supported to an extent by Dyer, the oceanologist, who told the committee that the one specimen of these previously unknown sponges that he had been able to retrieve showed no sign of radioactive contamination. In the deeper, 6,000-foot Farallon Islands site, he said, "although we didn't see these particular sponges we saw other species of sponges that didn't grow as large but are still present on waste containers containing the same kinds of waste. They also grew on rocks and showed the same growth on both the waste containers and the rocks."

Follow-up studies to the EPA report conducted by W. Jackson Davis, a professor of biology and environmental studies of the University of California at Santa Cruz, cited elevated radiation readings monitored in cod netted near the Farallons and other fish caught off the California coast from 1976 to 1978. Dr. Davis' conclusion was "that the scope and magnitude of radioactive contamination of the Pacific Ocean could be greater than previously realized."

In the long run, however, the findings of the EPA oceanologists who investigated the principal Atlantic site in 1975 appear even more disturbing. After a three-day search by divers and a research submarine at depths of between 9,000 and 12,000 feet, the scientists emerged to report that they could find no trace of any of the 14,300 waste drums that were supposed to have been dumped 120 miles off the southern tip of New Jersey —leading to a suspicion that the marine contractors who did the disposal found a more accessible location closer to shore. On the other hand, they did find 11 barrels of radioactive waste that weren't supposed to have been dumped in this sector (perhaps these are the barrels Commander Earle dropped in 1947), and had measured cesium 137 in sediments around one of these that had breached. This contamination had not spread to marine life on the sea bottom, the EPA said, but subsequently it reported it had found significant levels of radioactive americium in two fish caught well off shore.

Even if the United States moratorium on ocean radwaste dumping becomes permanent, contamination of the seas and marine life within them is certain to increase. Reactors must be sited on rivers or lakes in order to have access to vast amounts of water needed as coolant, and inevitably they return some proportion of their radioactivity to the waters. The 1957 license granted the first American commercial reactor, a 60-megawatt pressurized water plant at Shippingport, Pa., permitted the discharge of as much as 50 curies of tritium and 6,200 millionths of a curie of other isotopes per day into the Ohio River, provided that the annual daily average of discharges did not exceed 10 curies of tritium and 1,590 millions of a curie of the other isotopes.

Since 1971, discharges from commercial reactors have been limited to 20 pico (one millionth of one millionth) curies per liter, and the American Nuclear Society maintains that the "typical" nuclear power plant discharge is in the range of one to 10 picocuries, compared to domestic tap water, which averages 20; ocean water, 350; whisky, 1,200; and milk, 1,400. Not all discharges are "typical," however. While this book specifically is not about nuclear reactor operations, the fact is that reactor accidents have a significant potential and history of burdening watercourses—and eventually lakes and oceans—with radwaste, principally contaminated cooling waters. For example, Metropolitan Edison, the operator of the Three Mile

Island plant, still plans on filtering and treating, but eventually discharging into the Susquehanna River—and therefore into Chesapeake Bay—the approximately 650,000 gallons of cooling waters that filled the containment building of its crippled reactor after the March 1979 accident. Nor does it require an accident of Three Mile proportions to contribute contamination to a river. In 1971, the Northern States Power Co. plant in Monticello, Minn., allowed 50,000 gallons of untreated, or only partially purified, cooling water to reach the Mississippi. No alarm was sounded to warn of this release until after some of the radioactive liquid had been taken into the St. Paul, Minn., water system. Tritium, the principal contaminant of reactor effluents, has a 12.3-year half-life, and will therefore retain nearly all its radioactivity by the time it reaches the seas.

Unfortunately, many other nations are even less particular than the United States about the contaminants they release into the oceans. Britain routinely discharges high-level liquid effluents from its Windscale reprocessing plant through a pipe which extends more than a mile into the Irish Sea. In addition, Britain is one of eight nations which avail themselves of a 2-mile-deep Atlantic site designated by the European Nuclear Energy Agency more than 600 miles southwest of Land's End for low-level (defined by the United Nations' International Atomic Energy Agency as material with activities of less than one curie of alpha radiation or 100 curies of beta-gamma radiation per metric ton) radwaste. In the Pacific, the Soviet Union does not admit to disposal of any of its radwaste at sea—and, in fact, it advocates in the United Nations a ban on this form of dumping. Japan evoked protests from Australia, New Zealand and several island territories by announcing plans to drop between 5,000 and 10,000 radwaste drums at four sites about 500 miles southeast of Tokyo in 1981, and in February of 1981 it agreed to postpone these drops for at least an additional year.

Fortunately, the oceans have received only a small fraction of the low-level radwaste that has been the responsibility of the United States government. The Oak Ridge National Laboratory surveyors inventoried more than 62 million cubic feet of this material that has been buried in shallow trenches at 17 installations. Although maintaining these trenches and containing the radioactive contamination within them is a part of the "housekeeping" budgets of each of these sites, at the Albuquerque Operations Office of the Department of Energy, Robert Lowrey, whose title is director of waste management and transportation, keeps an eye on the continuing production of this waste: "My office is responsible for assuring that each of our contractors has a formal program for the management of waste, and we audit their programs. Someone from this office goes and performs what we call a quality-assurance audit, and the results of it can be quite serious for contractors because it quite possibly can impact on their fee." As Lowrey explains them, however, these audits appear for the most part to be more checks on documentation—to make sure that the proper programs are in place and that the proper forms are being filled out in the proper manner—than they are on-site inspections of waste-disposal work or trench maintenance. "You go to a place," Lowrey explains, "and while they may be reducing volume, for example, in a number of ways, they may not have a formal program for the process. They're doing it, but we require them to document it."

Also under Lowrey's direction, several of the smaller low-level sites are to be consolidated or phased out. In 1980, work began on exhuming some low-level material from a burial site at Pantex, the nuclear-weapons plant near Amarillo, Tex. "They only have four thousand cubic feet, all easily retrievable," Lowrey said, "and they only generate an average of a hundred fifty to two hundred cubic feet a year, primarily of depleted uranium. We asked ourselves if we really needed a permanent burial ground there and decided we didn't. Nevada operations agreed to take them, so we're now shipping those wastes to the Nevada Test Site." (It is not part of Lowrey's program, but the Nevada Nuclear Test Site, although listed as a single low-level disposal facility for accounting purposes, has actually buried low-level wastes, mostly the residues of weapons tests, in thirty-five locations over the 1,350-square-mile range, and Department of Energy managers there, too, are working on a program to consolidate some of these disposals.)

In addition to the Nevada sites, principal low-level repositories are maintained at Hanford, Savannah River, Oak Ridge National Laboratory, Los Alamos Scientific Laboratory, Idaho National Engineering Laboratory and Sandia National Laboratory in New Mexico. Lesser but still-active repositories are maintained at the Feed Materials (for nuclear weapons) Production Center at Fernald, Ohio; three uranium gaseous diffusion plants at Oak Ridge, Paducah, Ky., and Portsmouth, Ohio; the Y-12 weapons fabrication plant at Oak Ridge, and at Lawrence Livermore National Laboratory in Livermore, Cal. Inactive dumps, in addition to Pantex, are at plants which once processed uranium at Weldon Springs, Mo., and Niagara Falls, N.Y., and at the Brookhaven National Laboratory on Long Island, N.Y.

For the most part, these facilities were chosen upon considerations of economics and proximity to weapons-production operations, with environmental factors given very little weight—in fact, the United States Geological Survey, the government's principal earth-sciences agency, was not even consulted in many of these selections. In May 1976, George DeBuchananne, chief of USGS's office of hydrology, testified to the Joint Congressional Committee on Atomic Energy that although his agency had been called on to study prospective sites for nuclear-power plants, laboratories and processing plants, "the survey has worked only peripherally on high- and low-level radioactive waste disposal problems . . . Prior to the 1975 fiscal year, the survey's role in radioactive waste disposal has been primarily one of investigating problems . . ."

"You felt the USGS could have more input into this whole process," Representative Manual Lujan of New Mexico asked, "and that its abilities are not being utilized quite as much as they could, is that correct?"

"I would say that the earth science has not been called upon to its fullest extent in the past," DeBuchananne replied diplomatically.

In 1943, the Oak Ridge region in Eastern Tennessee was selected—primarily on the grounds of its remoteness—as the site for facilities that would enrich the uranium that the Hanford reactors turned out and produce the plutonium that would fuel the atomic bombs. Oak Ridge is no longer remote; it is 15 miles of easy highway driving from Knoxville, and its three low-level burial sites, at the National Laboratory, the gaseous diffusion plant and the Y-12 weapons components factory, concentrate within a 10-mile radius more than 8 million cubic feet of radwaste in a region with an average annual rainfall of approximately 53 inches (more than at any other American radwaste disposal site), a water table only 5 to 15 feet below the surface (some trenches began filling with water as soon as they were dug), and a limestone and shale ground formation that is deeply and frequently fractured.

Actually, it should have hardly required the expertise of the United States Geological Survey to warn the wartime Manhattan Engineering District and its successor, the Atomic Energy Commission, that these factors would combine to make difficulties in the containment of radioactive contamination. "We had the first leaky burial ground, so we have had to become damn well expert on the problem," J. A. Lenhard, assistant manager of energy research and development in DOE's Oak Ridge office told me last summer. Nevertheless, the AEC chose the laboratory's burial ground as one of the two national sites for disposal of the first commercial low-level wastes from 1960 to 1962 (the other was the Idaho National Engineering Laboratory, then the National Reactor Testing Station), and as the Southern Regional Storage Area for government-produced solid low-level waste from 1955 to 1963. Between them, these two designations account for about 1.5 million cubic feet of buried solids in Melton Valley.

Also in this valley, excavated settling pits received more than 4 million gallons of liquid wastes containing 57,000 curies of activity between 1951 and 1956. The first of these pits was in operation only two and a half months before significant levels of radiation were measured downhill from it. The practice of liquid disposal into settling pits continued at the laboratory until 1966, and according to Conrad P. Straub, author of a 1964 study on low-level wastes published by the Atomic Energy Commission, "the bulk of the residual radionuclides is retained close to its point of introduction. This accumulation of radionuclides is a radiation hazard to maintenance and research personnel. A radiation survey made on May 16, 1957, in the immediate vicinity of the three pits then being used showed maximum radiation levels of three and four thousand millirems per hour at the edge of one of the pits."

Three to 4 rems per hour is a lot of radiation (current EPA guidelines limit the permissible dose to nuclear workers to 5 rems per year), and while it was possible to warn Oak Ridge personnel away from the area, the laboratory had less success in keeping migratory fowl and wildlife out of harm's way with chicken wire strung over the ponds. Eventually, contamination filtered out of these basins anyway and into White Oak Lake, a 55-acre artificial pond formed by the damming of White Oak Creek on the southern boundary of the laboratory. The lake acquired a following of ducks, some of which were killed, and upon analysis found to have accumulated substantial levels of radioisotopes in their flesh; other birds, trapped, banded and released, were later reported to have been killed—and presumably consumed—from Canada to Texas. Other ecological studies turned up insects with high levels of radiation and apparently deformed fish.

White Oak Lake has now been drained, but when I visited Oak Ridge in the summer of 1980, I asked Jim Alexander, a Department of Energy spokesman, whether this sampling program was still being continued in and around White Oak Creek and was told it was, as "part of our general environmental surveillance which covers various types of organisms that represent different components of the ecological food chain. Analyses to date indicate only trace amounts of radioactivity." And as to the deformed fish: "Several years ago, one . . . study involved sampling small-size fish from White Oak Lake. In the collection, there were a number of fish that had body anomalies. Some had malformed spines that gave them a humpback appearance and others had malformed eye structures . . ." Alexander went on to point out, however, that "in all fish populations there is a certain amount of malformation," and that many such mutations come from non-radioactive chemicals (which, of course, are also contained in the laboratory's discharge), and that "consequently the malformations probably should not be attributed to radioactivity."

I subsequently looked up this study, published June 25, 1956,

in the *Bulletin of the American Museum of Natural History,*
and its findings and conclusions speak for themselves. Louis A.
Krumholz analyzed semi-annual nettings of wildlife from the
lake for three years before it was drained and all the fish killed
chemically in 1953, and reported that the fish had fed on plank-
ton organisms that "selectively concentrated radiophosphorous
in greater amounts than any other radioactive element." The
rates of growth of these fishes he found to be "noticeably slower
and the lengths of the life spans were markedly shorter, than
those of fishes of the same species from nearby reservoirs."

Krumholz calculated that "the fish in White Oak Lake received the equivalent of more than 57 roentgens of external
irradiation from the surrounding water each year during their
entire lives . . . it can safely be assumed that the internal dose
was several times that of the external dose . . . Certain individual
black crappies and bluegills concentrated radiostrontium in
their skeletal systems in amounts 20,000 to 30,000 times as
great as those in the water in which they lived . . ."

In addition to the fish mutations mentioned by Alexander, it
was also observed by Krumholz that "two species of fish, the
white crappie and the redhorse, although relatively common in
the lake in 1950, had apparently been unable to maintain their
populations and had gradually disappeared from White Oak
Lake during the three-year study period. By April 1953, all the
white crappies were gone, and fewer than forty redhorse remained. Furthermore, . . . there had been no successful repro-
duction of the species since 1949."

Although significant radioactive discharges into White Oak
Creek were reduced when the laboratory began hydrofracturing its liquid wastes in 1966, they were by no means eliminated.
The laboratory also has had problems in the disposal of solid
low-level wastes—not the least of them is determining what was
buried in the Melton Valley trenches before 1959, when records were destroyed in a fire. Edward King, the laboratory's
waste-process engineer, drove me to the facility's current
waste-disposal area—its sixth—where we found an assortment
of containers, including open garbage cans, sealed 55-gallon
drums and cardboard boxes, lying at the bottom of an open
trench about 12 feet deep. "The waste is brought here in any-

thing that will get it into the hole safely," King said. "When the trench is within three feet of being full, we cover it over with earth, and on a continuous basis, we fill and grade to try to reduce the amount of water which might infiltrate and to keep trees from taking root on the site so there are no root cracks down deep."

As often happens in radwaste management, an attempt to reinforce these grounds-keeping protections has backfired. In 1974, James O. Duguid, then a health physicist in ORNL's Environmental Sciences Division, reported to an AEC environmental-protection conference on the undesirable effects of uncontaminated fill deposited as an extra cover on top of trenches at a 23-acre disposal area where 3.2 million cubic feet of waste, nearly half the laboratory's inventory of solids, had been buried through 1959. This additional fill, he said, "increased the surface elevation and also increased the permeability of the surface soil," with the result of increasing the leaching rate of the buried waste, causing "one to two curies of strontium 90 to be transported" every year. "In some locations in the burial ground," Duguid found, "trenches behave like tilted bathtubs. The trench fills with ground water, which then spills over the lower end of the trench and appears in surface seeps." In 1976, a National Academy of Sciences–National Research Council panel also investigated this burial ground and found indications that "water is moving through the solid waste and carrying contaminants away from the disposal site."

On top of that, once again there is a problem posed by the organic chelates, compounds frequently used in decontamination work, which combine with radionuclides and free many which would have otherwise been absorbed in soil or combined with rock to travel in water. In 1978, Duguid, who has since moved to Battelle Memorial Institute's Columbus, Ohio, laboratories, and Jeffrey L. Means and David A. Crerar, members of the Department of Geological and Geophysical Sciences at Princeton, collaborated on a report published in *Science*, which held that such an agent, ethylenediaminetetraacetic acid (EDTA), was at work on the waste in the Oak Ridge trenches.

"The use of EDTA and similar compounds in decontamination operations, and therefore their presence in low- and intermediate-level waste in the United States and the rest of the world is widespread," they wrote. "Throughout the world, low- and intermediate-level radioactive waste is being buried along with chemicals that are likely to cause the migration of hazard- ous isotopes such as plutonium over the long term. Indeed, trace levels of radionuclides are being released by groundwater transport at many radioactive waste disposal sites in this coun- try, and migration of radioactive transition metals, rare earths and transuranics is probably being aided by chelates such as EDTA."

Whether from liquid or solid waste, radioactive contamina- tion from Oak Ridge gets into one of several creeks that empty into the Clinch River, which flows 16 miles southwest to King- ston and its confluence with the Tennessee, which in turn flows to the Ohio and the Mississippi. The water filtration plant of the city of Kingston is upstream from the mouth of the Clinch, but the *Environmental Monitoring Report* for Oak Ridge points out that "under certain conditions of power generation . . . Clinch River water may move upstream in the Tennessee River and be used as the source of water for the Kingston Filtration Plant." According to the 1979 edition of this report, "analysis of water samples collected at the juncture of White Oak Creek and the Clinch River indicated that the yearly average concentration of radionuclides was approximately 16 percent of the applicable concentration guide for uncontrolled areas." Not stated in this edition was the fact that this yearly average concentration has reached as high as 88 percent in 1976.

Over a short-term period, too, average concentrations may be increased markedly by heavy rains. Louis G. Williams, pro- fessor emeritus of biology at the University of Alabama in Tus- caloosa, has reported the finding several days after the passage of Hurricane David in 1979, a "slug" of contaminated Tennes- see River organisms, containing "concentrations of cobalt that were six thousand times higher than background and concen- trations of strontium and cesium eight to ten thousand times higher." In response to that disclosure, Dr. Stanley Auerbach, director of the Environmental Sciences Division at Oak Ridge, told a reporter for the newspaper *Newsday* that he was "not at all surprised that after something as drastic as Hurricane David, there was a buildup of strontium and cesium. When you move that much water over that large an area, you are going to move some of the cesium and strontium into the rivers."

On my visit to Oak Ridge, I talked to Dr. Auerbach about some of these problems. "This is an exceedingly complex terrain," he conceded, "with a high rainfall and a high water table, and a thirty-five-year history of operations, beginning when the philosophy was dilute and disperse [contamination] to the present philosophy of concentrate and confine. Back in the early 1960s, we switched to new modes of disposal, and our choice was to put it into closed pits located on knolls of shale, which has a strong affinity for most of the waste constituents. A lot of the strontium-90 seepage from the burial grounds has been rectified, and the seepage pits have been filled in and covered with a thick layer of asphalt. All you can see now is a tennis-court-like thing all completely covered over. What burns me is guys who don't even come here but write articles saying that nothing has changed since the early days at Oak Ridge. Look at the waste pits now and check our current practices, and you'll see how much they've changed."

The Savannah River Plant has even more buried governmental low-level waste than Oak Ridge—its 1980 inventory of 11.9 million cubic feet of solids makes the South Carolina facility the second largest civilian or governmental low-level dump after Hanford. According to the Savannah River Waste Management Program Plan, the low-level trenches, 20 feet deep and 20 feet wide, were dug in "clayey sands averaging about one third clay" in a 195-acre area located midway between two of the high-level-waste tank farms about 6 miles from the plant boundary, but only about half a mile from a stream called Four Mile Creek. Four Mile is one of six tributaries of the Savannah River that drain through the plant and the adjoining swamp, where background levels six times normal have already been reported (see Chapter III). The 1974 Du Pont survey which measured these levels maintains that five of these six tributaries, including Four Mile, have "experienced increased flows from reactor cooling water and have received low-level liquid radioactive discharges at some time during the operating history of SRP."

Radwaste disposal in these trenches is a complex operation. In addition to the mandatory distinction from transuranic wastes (which are themselves divided into radiation-emission categories for different modes of asphalt-pad storage nearby), low-level materials are divided into two subdivided categories, low-level and intermediate. In the low low-level category, waste radiating less than 300 millirads per hour at the surface of an unshielded container is handled and buried separately from scrap uranium. In the intermediate low-level category, separate burial trenches are maintained for irradiated reactor fuel-housing components, tritium waste contaminated with lithium-aluminum melts, and miscellaneous waste in cardboard boxes. I got a passing look at the surface of this low-level area on my visit to Savannah River in May of 1980. A solitary crane bearing Army markings was at work depositing waste in a trench a few hundred feet from the sort of windsock normally found at small airports. "When we bury waste, we want to be sure that the people doing it stand upwind," explained Donald Nichols, area superintendent for Du Pont, the facility's contractor. "If the wind is high, we won't bury it at all—we wait for another day." Nichols pointed to a pair of hard-hatted, coverall-wearing men drawing water up from a roadside well casing. "We have more than two hundred of those monitoring wells in the burial ground and the perimeter," he said. "The subsurface water here moves only about a tenth of a foot a day, so it isn't really something we need continuous monitoring on, and most of this soil is high on clay, which is extremely good for holding plutonium. We've gone back and taken borings out of some of our early trenches and haven't found any migration, not even to the edge of the trench."

According to the 1980 Savannah River Waste Management Program Plan published a month before my visit, however, "extremely low concentrations of alpha and beta radioactivity have been measured in all wells at the burial site." Also, in August 1978, "increased concentrations of tritium were measured . . . later that year, a tritium outcrop from the burial ground was measured in the effluent stream . . . to Four Mile Creek. This outcrop resulted from 25 years of erosion of the effluent stream, causing the stream bed to fall below the ground-water table." Remedial measures already under way include repair of the eroded ditch and an engineered trench to replace the effluent stream, after which, according to the plan, "tritium in ground water from the burial ground will be decayed to insignificant levels before reaching a natural out-crop in Four Mile Creek."

At Hanford's governmental low-level disposal sites, which contained 16.4 million cubic feet of solids in 1980, the principal method of contamination transport is not water but fire and the wind. Because of its dry climate, Hanford is particularly suscep-tible to range fires—122 of these between the years 1964 and 1973 are tabulated in its environmental-impact statement. Two of these swept over governmental low-level burial grounds, and in the larger of these, in August 1955, radioactive particulates were carried by winds 1,500 feet beyond the burial site. High radiation readings at that distance required a scraping of the earth, with the contaminated soil then added to the low-level waste inventory. Even without a fire, the desert winds have carried contamination around Hanford from some of its settling ponds or retention basins that had been allowed to dry up, either to effect repairs or because of an extended shutdown of the facilities, primarily reactors, that drained cooling waters or other effluents into them. The function of these ponds is to allow the radioactive contaminants to settle out of the water, and the expectation is that these isotopes will, for the most part, decay in the ground before they can reach the water table and begin the second leg of their journey to a waterway. If the ponds are ever allowed to dry up, however, many of these isotopes are left in particle form upon the earth's surface, and on seven occa-sions between 1954 and 1964, high winds swept up masses of these radioactive particles and deposited them in fan-shaped areas downwind. Once, in December 1957, the receiving area had to be posted as a radiation zone. "Seasonal rains fixed con-taminant in soil," the Hanford environmental-impact state-ment maintains. An earlier such incident, in March 1954, spread particulate contamination over 20 percent of an area that is the site of two reactors and borders the Columbia River. "No particles above ten millirads per hour were found outside [the] area," the Hanford EIS says. "Roadways were water flushed and the concentrated activity was removed to the burial ground."

And sometimes the winds have help. The swallows that scooped up mud from a radwaste trench at Hanford in 1956 marked their flight path with a ground trail of contamination to the other side of the Columbia River where they built their contaminated nest. And in early 1960, according to the Hanford EIS, animal burrows were found in liquid waste trenches, and "radioactive feces from coyotes and rabbits were subsequently spread over surrounding sagebrush-covered desert land to east, south and west of trenches. The bulk of radioactivity remaining is fixed in rabbit droppings scattered over approximately four square miles of ground surface."

At two government waste-handling facilities the earth-filtration protections afforded by settling ponds are deliberately bypassed by operations that put radwastes directly into deep wells that either enter or approach the subterranean water table. One of these, at the Idaho Chemical Processing Plant at INEL, was covered in the chapter on high-level wastes. However, the laboratory's environmental-impact statement also lists five accidental discharges of low-level material that exceeded water-quality standards from 1954 through 1969. In the largest of these, in December 1958, approximately 29 curies of activity, including 7 curies of strontium 90, were "accidentally released" from "an unknown origin in the plant system." At the Nevada Test Site, liquid wastes from cattle and swine dosed with nuclides in studies at a laboratory farm are poured down a formally entitled "Post Shot Sample Hole" 1,000 feet deep (but still 200 feet above the water table) into an underground cavity formed by an underground nuclear explosion. In addition, highly radioactive core samples of test borings made after weapons explosions have been put into 6 drilled holes ranging in depths up to 200 feet. Tower debris and the remains of vehicles and structures subjected to nuclear-bomb tests are shoved into a subsidence crater formed by one such test before 1967, and just about filled by now—however, scores of equally suitable craters dot the range.

The draft of the Department of Energy's 1980 program budget estimated that $4.7 million would be spent during fiscal year

1979 on developing better long-term technology for low-level waste disposal, with $10.6 million expected to be spent for this purpose in fiscal year 1980 and $17.5 million in fiscal year 1981. At least one Department of Energy official, Dr. Goetz Oertel, director of nuclear-waste products in the Germantown, Md., headquarters, questions the need for such a sharp increase: "People will come some day and tell us we've been wasting millions in trying to be 100 percent sure of everything. Certainly all this effort is worthwhile on high-level waste, which is very dangerous stuff and has to be handled correctly and safeguarded for centuries and beyond. But low-level stuff is under control, and a lot more so than chemical wastes. There's a radiophobia in this country that I think is irrational because people don't accept the fact that the risks can never be zero."

7
LOW LEVEL—
COMMERCIAL

The most recently opened of the six American commercial
low-level waste repositories is Barnwell, which is outside the
town of Snelling in Barnwell County, S.C. The 200-acre site, just
a short distance east of the Savannah River Plant, is owned by
the state and leased to Chem Nuclear, a corporation headquar-
tered at Bellevue, Washington. In May of 1980, I visited Barnwell with my son Paul, who took pictures for me, and we were
shown around the site by John Ott, a thirty-five-year-old former
nuclear submariner who has the responsibility of verifying that
shipments to the facility meet legal and safety specifications.

At the electronically operated gate, where we were issued
hard hats and clip-on pencil-like dosimeters, eight trucks bearing radioactive warnings waited for clearance: "It's a slow day,"
Ott said. "Sometimes we have trucks backed up all the way to
the highway." Each driver, he continued, "will submit his
paperwork to our health technicians. They'll scrutinize it to
make sure there's nothing in there that violates our burial license [liquids, even those absorbed in solidifying materials, and
transuranics are barred at Barnwell], and they'll conduct radiation surveys to make sure that shippers have complied with

Department of Transportation regulations. If we find the shipment passable, we submit the paperwork to the resident inspector of the State Department of Health and Environmental Control, who does the same surveys, reviews the same paperwork and conducts the same inspection of the vehicle. If he approves it, it is cleared for off-loading."

Although the vehicles and the exteriors of the reusable casks that contain the wastes are monitored in these checks, the actual waste packages themselves remain uninspected, and are not even monitored for radiation until the casks are unloaded by a crane at the trench sites. Sometimes, however, even these gate inspections can be quite productive—South Carolina inspectors issued a total of 61 citations against 41 trucked shipments during one 3-month period in 1979. Most of these are vehicle-safety infractions, though, and even if there is a radiological problem, as Ott points out, "there is no such thing as too radioactive for us to take. If the shipper violated Department of Transportation regulations in hauling it down here, we can't violate them again by refusing to bury it. What happens if there's a problem with the vehicle is that we quarantine it after off-loading, and it has to be fixed before it's put back on the road. The ultimate penalty is that the shipper will be barred from sending radwaste into South Carolina until it changes its procedure and convinces the State to write a rescinding order."

More often, however, and usually by way of a first warning, a fine and a temporary suspension are enforced. In July of 1980, for example, South Carolina's Department of Health and Environmental Control fined the New York State Power Authority $1,000 and ordered it not to ship for a month after a cask of metallic-oxide trash from the Fitzpatrick Nuclear Power Plant in Lycoming was found to give off a surface radiation reading of 300 millirems, 100 over the Department of Transportation limit.

From the gate, Ott took us out to the burial area. "This is really good clay you're walking on," he told us. "It holds the water after a rain, and it goes down all the way to the water table, which is thirty-five feet deep." At the side of a trench a flat-bed truck was being unloaded by a crane and a crew of eight men, one of whom had climbed up a ladder to the top of the shipping container and was unfastening the bolts holding its cover. "The riggers wear green hard hats," Ott explained, "the guys in the uncolored hard hats are laborers, the man in the white hat is a quality-insurance inspector, and the one in the orange hat is a health-physics technician—every load we handle requires the presence of a health-physics man." The health-physics technician was wielding what looked like a fishing rod over the cask being unloaded. "At the end of the pole is a teletector," Ott told us, "which is an instrument that monitors up to 1,000 millirems, which really isn't unusual for these shipments." Cleared by the teletector reading, a laborer climbed back up the ladder and attached a line which enabled the operator of the crane to hoist from the cask's interior a pallet holding six sealed 55-gallon drums, swing it over the trench, and unceremoniously drop in the drums.

"Unlike the federal low-level sites, we never bury cardboard containers," Ott said. "Everything's in drums or liners, but even so, our trenches are really the waste containers, and they're a hundred feet wide, a thousand feet long and up to twenty-one feet deep, which puts the bottom fourteen feet above the first water-bearing sands. We're about finished filling trench thirty-two right now, and in a few weeks when it is filled, we'll pack clay on the top, compact it, then pile two and a half to three feet more of clay on, so there will be at least five feet of clay on top of the waste, and water just will not go through it. Then we'll put topsoil on top of the clay and seed it. We run a monthly inspection program over the top of the filled trenches looking for cracks and settling. Also, there are monitoring pipes every hundred feet all the way through the trenches, so we'll be able to tell if water ever does get into the trenches."

Some distance from the working trench, in the approximate center of the burial ground, was a smaller, fenced-off trench where Ott told us particularly radioactive material, "up to 20,-000 rems per hour," is buried. "The problem here is that the best instrument we have measures only up to 10,000 rems. When we get a really hot load, reactor pump or valve seals or drains or some of the isotope-manufacturing stuff, we bury it here." At this trench, he pointed out that the crane operator is shielded by a row of concrete blocks, and the material is unloaded and maneuvered into place with the help of a remote-controlled camera.

As we returned to the gate, Ott told us that only thirty of Chem Nuclear's force of two hundred workers are involved in the actual burial operations, and that most of Barnwell's workers live, as he does, in the immediate area. "Do you think we'd bring up our kids around here if we didn't think it was safe?" he asked rhetorically. "We've never had a fire here or a radioactive release. At the rate we're going, filling up two trenches a year, we figure we have burial capacity in excess of thirty-nine years of shipments, and after that, I don't know why they can't make a golf course out of the place."

Ott and other Chem Nuclear executives we spoke to at the site made a persuasive case for low-level disposal with safety at Barnwell. A few minutes later, however, a hitch developed when we stopped at the gate to turn in our hard hats and dosimeters. The form filed with the dosimeter issued me showed that its dial read 10 millirems when I received it. The dial upon turning it in read 20 millirems, which meant that I had received 10 millirems of exposure out on the burial grounds. After a short conference between Ott and a security officer, it was announced that my dosimeter had been misread when I received it; the 10-millirem reading was erased from the form, and 20 millirems was entered—certifying that I had received no radiation. Subsequently, as we were driving away from Barnwell, my son described himself as "impressed" by the safeguards and security precautions that had been explained to us. "If they doctor the forms for ten millirems," I asked him, "how can you be sure they aren't doing the same for thousands of millirems radiated by the materials they handle every day?"

Reporting on commercial radwaste disposal, no less than other corporate topics, requires a checking and comparison of often-limited and invariably partisan information that can be obtained from company spokesmen, workers and government regulators. To give a few examples from our visit to Barnwell:

According to the Chem Nuclear official who explained the mechanics of the trench-drainage system, "We have never during the lifetime of this site had waste sitting in water, and that's saying a lot"; according to Brookhaven National Laboratory scientists, that's saying too much. Their 1979 survey found trench water samples that contained cesium 137, cobalt 60 and manganese 54. "Water is usually not present in the trenches at the Barnwell site," the Brookhaven report notes, "except during the winter rainy season."

The Bureau of Radiological Health of the South Carolina Department of Health and Environmental Control has also published a document which brings into question the efficacy of some of those gate inspections that are twice performed by Chem Nuclear and state inspectors. Many waste shipments arrive in Chem Nuclear's own tractor trailers, it points out, and in those of two other companies, Tri-State Motor Transit and Home Transportation Co. Chem Nuclear maintains terminal facilities just outside the Barnwell gate and the other two companies have nearby terminals on the road leading to it. Although the state inspectors have access to all three, the bureau's document points out, on many occasions, the tractor hauling the shipments unhitches the waste-bearing trailer at the terminal and takes off uninspected. The trailer is checked by workers of the trucking firm there, *at the end of its journey,* and any mechanical defects found are remedied before it is hitched to a rigorously maintained "yard tractor" and hauled the last few hundred yards to the Barnwell gate.

Most disturbing in retrospect was a casual mention by a Chem Nuclear official that on the weekend of our visit to the repository, residents of the nearby town of Snelling had been invited to picnic beneath a large tree that stands in a small fenced-off area at a corner of the burial ground "just to let people know that they can come out and get this close to the site and be perfectly safe." I wonder if those who accepted this information were told that a state survey conducted in 1978 determined that the picnic area had the highest average radiation measurements recorded along the site's fence line, a daily average of 3.5 millirems which is 14 times the average daily background rate of .25 millirems.

Charges have also been made that radwaste disposals in excess of legal specifications have taken place "off the books" at Barnwell. A former accounting supervisor at the facility charges that spent-fuel assemblies from Boston Edison's Pilgrim nuclear power plant were illegally buried there in 1977, along with three trucks of liquid wastes, which are also barred. She says they were simply driven into trenches and buried whole. Early in 1980, South Carolina and Nuclear Regulatory Commission investigations cleared Barnwell, but several months later I asked John Martin, director of the NRC's waste-management programs, about the extent of the federal probe. "Our inspection and enforcement people checked it well enough to see that the state did a thorough job in its investigation and the charge was unfounded. In addition, our folks checked to make sure that every stick of Boston Ed's fuel was accounted for."

I wondered whether the investigations had included digging up the Barnwell spot where the fuel assemblies and the liquid waste were said to have been buried. "It's a little like investigating a murder," Martin said, "if somebody tells you Joe Jones is shot and his body is buried, and you find Jones and he isn't shot, police can be sure the charge is unfounded." However, in such cases, I pointed out to him from a background as a police reporter, I would still expect investigators to do some digging at the spot just in case the witness had mistaken the identity of the victim.

Like the Department of Energy inspections of radwaste handling procedures of its contractors, the NRC's inspections of the low-level waste sites in Agreement States are, for the most part, paper exercises. At Barnwell in the 1980 probe, it appears that the NRC staff ratified state investigators' audits of the commercial operator's inspection of the bills of lading submitted by the producers. According to a presentation NRC made to the Joint Committee on Atomic Energy in 1976, its inspectors also make annual unannounced inspections during which they "pay particular attention to the following areas: The overall organization structure . . . training, retraining and instructions to workers, radiological protection procedures . . . available instruments, equipment and facilities for radiation protection, receipt and transfer of radioactive materials, personnel radiation protection, notification and reports to NRC, environmental monitoring." In short, everything is checked but the waste packages (which at Barnwell are only

monitored at the gate to make sure they have been sufficiently shielded to pass legally through interstate commerce,
and again, gingerly, at the trenches by the teletector to reduce radiation exposure to the burial crew) and the condition
of the waste trenches themselves.

Six commercial waste repositories have accepted low-level
waste for burial in the United States, and the smallest of these
and the only one not located in an Agreement State—which
means that first the Atomic Energy Commission and later the
Nuclear Regulatory Commission was responsible for licensing
and monitoring it—is at Sheffield, about 50 miles west of Morris
in northern Illinois. Although Illinois chose not to enter the
Agreement State program, the state did acquire the 20 acres
used for the disposal purpose, and it leased them in 1966 to the
Nuclear Engineering Co., the Teledyne subsidiary which has
since been renamed the U.S. Ecology Corporation. In 1966, it
also operated the commercial repositories at Maxey Flats, Ky.,
Beatty, Nev., and at Hanford. NECO opened Sheffield's five
trenches to disposals in 1967, and by April 1978 it had filled
them with a little more than 3 million cubic feet of material
containing more than 7,000 curies of isotopes. Additional land
was available to expand the repository, but NECO's attempt to
rezone it suitably was successfully opposed by Illinois officials.
"A previously unknown subsurface layer of sand was discovered
beneath the site by the United States Geological Survey," a
Strategy Task Force of consultants reported to the Department
of Energy in a 1980 planning document for low-level wastes.
"The fact that sand transmits radionuclides faster than other
soils may have contributed to the state's unwillingness to expand the site." In fact, the consultants pointed out, tritium
has already migrated in ground water "a few meters" off the
Sheffield property.

When it found itself unable to expand the Sheffield site or to
accept further wastes, NECO attempted to turn its lease on the
property back to the state, which was reluctant to accept it—
and understandably so, since all but $50,000 of a "perpetual
care" fund collected from disposal revenues had already been
spent by the time the trenches were filled in 1978. The DOE's
Strategy Task Force on low-level waste disposal made the point

that most of the studies that provided the bases for these funds at commercial sites "have not addressed the effects of inflation or possible changes in tax structure, nor have they considered the resources that may be necessary for corrective actions."

Legally, then, it appeared in 1980 that the five states—Nevada, Kentucky, New York, Washington and South Carolina—which licensed commercial low-level repositories under the Agreement States program, would ultimately have to shoulder a substantial part of this "perpetual-care" expense. According to a Nuclear Regulatory Commission statement, this program was enacted in 1959 "to recognize the states' interest in atomic energy activities, to clarify the respective responsibilities of the states . . . and to provide a statutory means by which the [now superseded] AEC could relinquish to the states (a) part of its regulatory authority . . ." By 1980, twenty-six states—Alabama, Arizona, Arkansas, California, Colorado, Florida, Georgia, Idaho, Kansas, Kentucky, Louisiana, Maryland, Mississippi, Nebraska, Nevada, New Hampshire, New Mexico, New York, North Carolina, North Dakota, Oregon, Rhode Island, South Carolina, Tennessee, Texas and Washington—had entered into compacts with the federal government and were administering approximately 11,900 licenses. Institutional and industrial nuclear generators and commercial disposal sites are covered in this program, but not nuclear power plants or federal facilities.

The first commercial dump was opened at Beatty in 1962, before Nevada joined the Agreement State program, but Kentucky became the first of the Agreement States in 1963 specifically so it could expedite the establishment of Maxey Flats—supposedly this facility was expected to attract other nuclear industries to the state, an expectation that went largely unrealized. Leasing and subsequent licensing of the 252-acre parcel was pursued despite a warning by Atomic Energy Commission surveyors that they had been unable to draw "firm" conclusions on "the geologic suitability of the proposed burial site to assure there would not be transport of radioactive materials through ground water to surrounding streams." When this "transport" did begin to manifest itself even with transuranic plutonium (see Chapter V), the Kentucky legislature in 1976 enacted a 10-cents-per-pound tax on waste to be disposed of at Maxey

Flats. Added to the 4-percent gross levy the state already
charged as lease rental, this effectively put Maxey Flats out of
business in December 1977, after approximately 4.8 million
cubic feet of low-level waste had been deposited in its trenches.

Maxey Flats was not the first of the commercial low-level
dumps to have to shut down, however. That distinction, again,
belongs to West Valley in upstate New York. There really are
two adjoining burial grounds at West Valley, a 22-acre state-
licensed area of shallow trenches that was operated as a commercial sideline to the reprocessing plant, and a 7.2-acre area
licensed by the AEC, and later the NRC, which accepted only
the wastes produced at the plant and buried them in holes up
to 165 feet deep. More than 2.3 million cubic feet of waste
containing approximately 710,000 curies of isotopes was buried
in the commercial repository from November 1963 to March
1975, when rain water broke through the top of the first of
three trenches that eventually overflowed.

The weakness, as usual in radwaste operations, turned out to
have been derived from a strength: in this case, it was West
Valley's renowned "silty till," a claylike glacial drift that is considered impermeable to water, and was, therefore, preferred as
a containment medium. Indeed, the till was impermeable so, as
the Department of Energy reported later, it exerted a "bathtub
effect," and rain water seeping into the trenches simply built up
until it broke through the ground surface. Eventually, 1.7 million gallons of radioactively contaminated water had to be
pumped from the West Valley trenches; the water went first to
holding lagoons, where as much as possible of the contamination, radioactive and otherwise, was filtered out, and then it was
allowed to flow into off-site streams in which, an NRC spokesman has declared, radioactivity, although not of a "significant
level," has already been measured. In February of 1980, Harold
Ironshield, a representative of the Black Hills Alliance of Indians, testified at a federal hearing on the future of the facility
that "if West Valley is leaking, then Cattaraugus Creek is contaminated. My concern is Cattaraugus Indian Reservation
twenty miles downstream. People from the reservation fish in
the creek for food on the table. Indian children swim in the
creek, because that is the only place they can go." At the west-

ern edge of the reservation, the Cattaraugus drains into Lake
Erie, the water source for a number of cities.

Since these overflows began, the covers of the West Valley
low-level trenches have been reinforced, and when I visited the
site in December of 1979, Dr. Alden Pierce, Nuclear Fuel Services' operations manager, took me to look at the burial ground
—it resembles a long golf fairway regularly mounded length-
wise by the covers of trenches that have been marked at both
their ends by standing stone monuments. "We mow this grass
cap regularly," he said. "If we see any settling, then we regrade
it. We monitor the trenches, and we have had some indications
that water levels are still increasing slowly. However, that isn't
an imminent threat. The point I'd like made is that this plant
has never violated its technical specifications. As a matter of
fact, our goal was to shoot for releases of less than 20 percent
of what we're allowed, and in recent years it has been even less
than that. It's not that the trenches overflow uncontrolled.
When the water in the trenches gets to be a problem, we pump
it out and treat it in our holding lagoons, and we test it before
we release it, and not once in the history of our entire operation
have the alarms on the radiation monitors in Cattaraugus Creek
gone off."

Nor were the 1975 overflows, which did by-pass the treatment lagoons, solely the fault of Nuclear Fuel Services, which
had been blocked by the State of New York for three years from
pumping out the trenches. According to a report of the General
Accounting Office, the state "claimed the pump-out procedures
NFS suggested were inadequate. The State asked NFS to pro-
pose new procedures . . ." No proposal was received, and no
state action was taken either until after the trenches overflowed, when permission for the pumpouts was belatedly given.
Even now that pumpouts have been resumed, sporadic accidental discharges still take place, although, as Dr. Pierce points
out, the radiation releases still remain "within our technical
specifications." In November of 1980, for example, workmen
buttressing one of the trenches penetrated its cover and
released 800 gallons of contaminated water to run down Cattaraugus Creek.

University of Pittsburgh physics professor Bernard Cohen, a

leading academic proponent of the nuclear industry, points out that "the water in the creek was never made unsafe for drinking, and no one received as much total radiation exposure from it as he would receive extra exposure from spending one minute in Colorado, where [background] radiation levels are twice the U. S. average," and in an article in *Public Utilities Fortnightly*, he claimed after making a survey of the site that needed improvements could be made on the trenches for only $1.5 million. New York State's estimate of the cost of putting these trenches into good repair is $5 million, which is, coincidentally, the full amount of the escrow fund put up by Nuclear Fuel Services to cover the decontamination of the entire West Valley property, high-level waste tanks, reprocessing plant and all. In any case, provisions have been made to absorb this escrow fund in the $285-million budget which the federal Department of Energy and the State of New York are preparing to pay for the solidification and removal of the high-level wastes and the decontamination of the reprocessing plant. Since the federal-state agreement made for this work does not appear to cover remedial work at the low-level grounds, the question of who is now obligated to pay for these repairs that are needed at present, and thereafter for the perpetual maintenance of the commercial disposal trenches, is now being litigated. NFS says it never made much of a profit on this operation—in 1975, when it closed the trenches it was charging only 15 cents per cubic foot of buried waste—and that it has fully met its legal obligation by providing the $5-million escrow fund. Only a State Supreme Court order kept it from abandoning the burial grounds at the end of 1980.

By that time, though, the Sierra Club's Radioactive Waste Management Campaign had succeeded through a freedom-of-information proceeding in uncovering geological data which, if borne out in future testing, could indicate that migration of isotopes from several of the West Valley trenches is much more likely than had previously been thought possible. Apparently (and it is charged that this was known to state geologists as early as 1974), not all the trenches were excavated entirely within the impermeable silty till. The Sierrans say that at least 3 (out of 14) cut through a 100-by-200-foot "sand lens," a layer of sediments which would facilitate lateral isotope transport out of the burial ground. With support from a locally based Coalition on West Valley Nuclear Wastes, the nationwide environmental organization is calling for exhumation of all the West Valley low-level waste and its relocation to above-ground bunkers, a project which it estimates would cost $200 million.

The closings, in chronological order, of West Valley, Maxey Flats and Sheffield have left in operation only three of the original six commercial low-level repositories, Barnwell, Hanford and Beatty, in western Nevada. Like Maxey Flats, Sheffield and the Hanford site, Beatty is operated by the U.S. Ecology Corporation, formerly the Nuclear Engineering Co., the Teledyne subsidiary which, to its credit, discovered early in 1976 and reported that significant amounts of quite radioactive material had been illegally diverted from burial by some of its employees.

As hearings before a House of Representatives subcommittee subsequently disclosed, the Beatty facility had become known to its residential neighbors as "the store," since it was the source, at discount prices, of large quantities of tools and materials that were later found to have been substantially radioactive. However, the most flagrant example of diversion by several Beatty workers turned out to be the use of a contaminated concrete mixer that among other extra-curricular projects, laid down a radioactive floor at a local saloon.

The Nuclear Regulatory Commission later sought criminal sanctions against Beatty's operator, the first—and so far only—such action it has ever taken against a corporation, and Nuclear Engineering paid a $10,000 fine. Perhaps even more important than this precedent was what the House hearings brought out about the control of nuclear waste under the Agreement States program. "The problems at Beatty," testified Roger Trounday, director of the Nevada Department of Human Resources, "reinforced our awareness of the state's lack of resources to deal with emergency situations." Only two health inspectors had been assigned to enforce Nevada's nuclear regulations, and it turned out that even they didn't have access to the necessary radiation-monitoring instruments. Yet when the state called on the federal government for help in locating the material that had been diverted from Beatty, it was told, according to Trounday, "that the emergency was a state problem, and it was the state's role to take the lead. This is analogous to a well-trained fire department—all the latest fire-fighting equipment—with the chief asking, 'Just how would you like us to go about putting out this fire?' "

Eventually, the federal Environmental Protection Agency and the Nuclear Regulatory Commission did have to go in and put out the Beatty "fire," conducting a radiological sweep of almost every home in the town and its surrounding ranches. Among the contaminated items picked up and returned for burial at the site were sheets of plywood that had been used in the construction of a playground and a radioactive-materials shipping container that had been converted to a drinking water cistern. In addition to the court fine, the Beatty managers suffered a short suspension of their operating license. This was their first, but others would follow.

According to the Oak Ridge surveyors, the three remaining commercial low-level sites still operating at the end of 1980 had utilized only 120 acres in waste burial and had an additional 283 acres of capacity left to fill. In addition, another 400 acres could be purchased and added to the Beatty site, and 900 more acres, well over a square mile, has been leased by the State of Washington at Hanford and could be made available for future low-level burial.

The Department of Energy calculates that each square foot of land surface should be sufficient to hold a volume of 7.5 cubic feet of low-level wastes, with a ten-to-one factor considered an "achievable objective." Even at the 7.5 ratio, however, and without figuring in increasing use of such volume-reduction practices as incineration and compaction, and without expanding either the Beatty or Hanford sites, the 283 remaining acres calculates out to more than 92 million cubic feet of capacity, enough for 27 years at the 1980 generation rate of 3.4 million cubic feet. Yet that isn't to say that trucking radioactive trash all the way across the country to three sites, from New England to Barnwell or Hanford, for example, is economically, environmentally or politically acceptable. Understandably, voters in

Washington, Nevada and South Carolina are showing increasing resistance to having dumped in their three states the commercial radwaste of all fifty states. In 1980, Washington State's environmentalists succeeded over the opposition of the state's governor, Dixy Lee Ray, the former AEC chairman, in putting on the ballot a referendum intended to bar the use of the Hanford commercial site to out-of-state wastes. The nuclear-waste issue figured largely in the subsequent campaign, and when it was over, Governor Ray was out of office and the ban was law, with an effective date of July 1, 1981. Enforcement of the embargo was stayed, however, on June 26, by Federal Judge Robert J. McNichols in Spokane. The measure, he ruled, "violates both the [federal] supremacy and the commerce clause of the U.S. Constitution. Should this ruling be overturned on appeal, there is an exception to the Washington embargo for medical wastes and for the non-medical wastes of any Northwestern states that agree in a formal regional compact to accept the burden of some of the hazardous, but non-nuclear, wastes produced in Washington.

This Hanford referendum is a manifestation of a radwaste "states-rights movement" that appears in retrospect to have been initiated in April 1979 by South Carolina Governor Richard Riley. Physically slight and soft-spoken, Riley had campaigned for office at least in part on a promise that South Carolina would no longer offer "the path of least resistance" to the dumping of nuclear waste at the Savannah River Plant and at Barnwell, which at that time was receiving 80 percent of the nation's low-level commercial disposal. In May of 1979, several weeks after the accident at Three Mile Island, Riley took the unprecedented—and possibly illegal—step of barring at the South Carolina border two truck tankers full of the first wastes cleared from the Pennsylvania facility. "Suddenly we got word that an awful lot of stuff was coming down here that had to be buried real fast," Riley's nuclear advisor, Dr. John Stucker (later the executive director of the State Planning Council on Radioactive Waste Management which Riley chairs), recalls the incident. "The thing was that nobody seemed clear on just what the trucks contained."

Legally, Riley may have created a bar to federally protected interstate commerce, but as it turned out, it was the federal government, through the Nuclear Regulatory Commission, that backed hurriedly away from this confrontation. Subsequently, Harold Denton, the NRC's chief staff executive at Three Mile confirmed that the shipments had exceeded Barnwell's bans on transuranic and liquid wastes. The first highly radioactive sludges from the accident had to be trucked back to Pennsylvania and then all the way across the country to Hanford where, predictably, they figured prominently in the referendum campaign. At the end of 1980, the Three Mile cleanup was generating two or three trucked shipments of wastes per week to Hanford.

Riley's next step was to extend Barnwell's ban on liquid wastes to include even liquids that had been solidified in an absorbing material, most often vermiculite. This action hit particularly hard at hospitals and laboratories which had been solidifying the bulk of their wastes in this manner, but the problem, as Ott explained to me at Barnwell, was that these medical wastes tend to escape the absorbent in time, and that many contain the same sort of organic solvents that have speeded the migration of isotopes at other repositories. "They break down the ion-exchange property of clay, which means that if it leaches out of the containers, it can get out of the trenches."

Then in July of 1979, Riley got together with Dixy Lee Ray, of Washington, and Robert List, of Nevada, and as Riley later testified to a congressional subcommittee, the three governors agreed "to mutually ban any violator of laws, rules or regulations concerning the packaging and/or transporting of low-level nuclear wastes. They also joined in calling for the NRC and the Department of Transportation to enforce their regulations in this matter." More informally because of the interstate-commerce regulations, the three governors also served notice to the rest of the nation that one way or another they would begin cutting back on the quantities of radwaste they would allow to be shipped to their states.

"What I said in the very beginning," Riley told me in August of 1980, "was that I saw a national problem that South Carolina was on the way to becoming the entire answer to, and that's what projected me into taking a leading role in nuclear-waste disposal. It seemed like the only way to deal with a problem that affected my state a great deal, not only because of the dump, but because of the transport. We have trucks going through the state all hours of the night and in and out of our ports, so it was my judgment that we could jump up and down and raise hell, but the only way I, as governor, could effectively handle the problem in my state was to try and bring out some response nationally. I tried to do that in a reasonable way—at least I think it was reasonable, although the people getting squeezed seemed to have thought otherwise, even though it was a very gentle squeeze initially."

However, Riley allowed the timing of his "very gentle squeeze" to be dramatized, not very gently, by nearly simultaneous suspensions of shipments to the Nevada and Washington low-level dumps. If any one development can be said to have stunned an entire industry, it was the action taken by Governor Dixy Lee Ray, the former chairman of the Atomic Energy Commission and one of nuclear power's strongest proponents—she once called radwaste disposal "the biggest contemporary nonproblem"—in temporarily barring shipments of wastes from reaching the commercial-waste repository at Hanford. The ostensible cause of this October 4, 1979, edict was the arrival on the two previous days of three defective shipments: On one truck, three out of six boxes that contained radioactive scrap iron and gravel had broken open, with some of the contaminated contents lost en route; on a second, one of seventy-five barrels of cobalt 57 was found to be leaking onto the floor of its trailer, and the third, carrying 74,000 pounds of depleted uranium, was 20,000 pounds overweight, and although the load was properly packaged, the truck carrying it from California had fourteen individual equipment defects, including defective brakes, defective steering and a flat tire. The timing of the governor's action, only two days after she had defended the Nuclear Engineering Company operation at a Capitol press conference, provoked skepticism from the Olympia press corps, one member of which pointed out to the governor that vehicle and load inspections supposedly performed during the entire 20-year history of the commercial repository had turned up only one other defective shipment, in October of 1978.

For her part, Governor Ray reported her own incredulity on the previous evening, when she attempted to notify the Nuclear Regulatory Commission of her forthcoming action, "there was no one there to receive the information. The telephone operator in Washington, D.C., had a telephone number for NRC, but there was no one there, there was no emergency number and no twenty-four-hour manning. I can assure you there was at the Atomic Energy Commission when I was there as chairman . . . I believe that the Nuclear Regulatory Commission is so busy playing 'what if' games and delving into theoretical studies and testifying before the Congress that they're now incapable of carrying out their normally assigned duties. And they are not, I repeat, they are not doing the proper job on the everyday work, shall we say, the nuts and bolts of things that they're supposed to be doing on inspection of licensees and assuring the citizens of this country that any transportation or shipment of radioactive materials is being properly handled at the point of origin." (The after-hours phone-manning situation complained of by Governor Ray is apparently little improved. In October of 1980, when a massive leak led to the shutdown of the Indian Point Number 2 reactor, Consolidated Edison officials in New York called the NRC in Washington and reported the emergency situation to an automatic phone-message recording device.)

Three weeks after the suspension of shipments to Hanford, it was Nevada Governor Robert List's turn to be shaken by the discovery of yet another radwaste impropriety at Beatty—and to shake up the nuclear industry by shutting that facility down indefinitely. What provoked List's action was even more serious than a deficient waste shipment, although it had been preceded three months before by the arrival at Beatty of a delivery of reactor cleaning solutions found to have leaked liquid contaminants all the way from Michigan, and two months before that, by the spontaneous combustion of another truckload of medical wastes in a parking area outside the disposal site—ten workers were slightly contaminated in putting out the fire. These two incidents resulted in temporary suspension of the repository's license; then, on October 25, 1979, members of a United States Geological Survey crew, searching for routes of possible contamination, dug 40 to 60 feet beyond a Beatty waste trench and punctured one of 5 waste drums inexplicably buried outside the disposal area. The USGS workers were sprayed with liquid wastes, and this was one incident that the facility's operator could not blame on outside truckers. The State's Public Health Director, Ralph DiSibio, called it "irrefutable evidence to our satisfaction of gross mismanagement," and Nuclear Engineering Company's operating was suspended until, it was announced, proceedings could be undertaken to revoke it permanently. "We mean to make it stick," said DiSibio.

With the two other dumps closed, Governor Riley of South Carolina initiated his "very gentle squeeze" by obtaining state action which amended Chem-Nuclear's license at Barnwell to require the facility to reduce receipts of low-level radwaste each quarter until October 1981, when the site would be burying 1.2 million cubic feet, exactly half its prior quota. While he was at it, the governor also renegotiated the escrow fund to be paid for perpetual care of the wastes from 16 cents per cubic foot up to a dollar by April 1981 and $2 in 1984.

There is a legal question of whether the state could enforce the cuts, but it became moot when Chem-Nuclear chose not to challenge them. During my visit to Barnwell, I asked E. T. Brooks, communications officer for the Washington State-based corporation, why it had not gone to court. "We are here pretty much due to the good graces of the state," he said, "and we recognize that from the South Carolina standpoint, the commercial waste-disposal situation is ridiculous, so we are in support of what the governor is doing. We may not agree with everything he does, but we hope it will lead to the opening of some other sites." In any case, it appears that Chem-Nuclear won't lose much of its Barnwell income: It was permitted to increase its disposal charge from $3.60 to $6 per cubic foot, and later to $7.71, and although this last fee is nearly ten times the 80 cents per cubic foot charged shippers in 1974, Barnwell's reduced quotas remain filled.

The simultaneous shutdowns of Beatty and Hanford and the cutbacks at Barnwell caused an understandable outcry. In 1980, the Nuclear Regulatory Commission admitted to congressional probers that because many licensees are now regulated under Agreement States programs, it was unable to say exactly how many generators of low-level waste there are. It is known, though, that more than 3,300 medical centers, hospitals and clinics in the United States are certified for the practice of nuclear medicine, and the radwaste they and research laboratories generate accounts for approximately 25 percent of all material requiring low-level burial. Power-plant wastes range from merely radiation-suspect items like workers' shoe coverings up to intensely contaminated filters—according to the Department of Energy, a large 1,000-megawatt power plant can be expected to generate about 35,000 cubic feet of low-level wastes per year. About half these wastes must be shipped and disposed of in shielded containers, and in total, power-plant wastes comprise 43 percent of commercial low-level materials buried at disposal sites. Fifteen government operations, including naval submarines as a single generator, contract for 14 percent of this capacity, and industrial radwaste fills the final 18 percent.

This industrial radwaste classification includes such highly intense wastes as are produced in the manufacture of cobalt 60 sources of up to 10,000 curies which are used in industrial, as well as medical x-ray machines. These sources are shipped and employed inside permanently sealed containers, and after the intensity of their radiation emissions decreases to 30 percent of the original activity, they are returned to their manufacturers for recycling or disposal. Among other commonly used radionuclides in industry are radium 226, still used in electron tubes, gauges and luminous products, and iridium 192, used in radiation-control equipment and in several industrial x-ray devices. Uranium depleted in the enriched 235 isotope which has been concentrated to fuel reactors and weapons is also finding increasing uses. Late in 1980, I visited the Los Angeles plant of a company called Netco which turns out uranium armor-piercing bullets under a Navy contract.

Shavings of uranium turned out by the lathes that machine these bullets are pyrophoric, meaning that they tend to ignite spontaneously, "which means we have to be particularly careful with our wastes," Russell Sherman, Netco's vice-president, said, pointing to a row of small black containers not unlike 5-gallon paint cans. "We layer those cans at the bottom with two inches of sand, then we put in two inches of uranium chip turnings, two more inches of sand, two more inches of turnings, and so forth—each can takes four inches of uranium sandwiched with sand before it's sealed." The Netco plant also turns out liquid wastes—its lathes have to be operated under a continuous stream of cooling water—and this effluent, Sherman told me, "has to be solidified with vermiculite absorbant which the waste-disposal company brings us. In the end, we get less liquid, only twenty-five gallons, than we do absorbant into each fifty-five-gallon drum. When we fill these, we seal them—each drum has a tie-down bolt—then on goes the radioactive label, and the can waits for the shipping company to come and take it to Beatty."

And if Beatty and the other low-level repositories no longer accept the shipments? By way of response, Sherman pointed out a largely unused section of his factory's floor space. Nothing but a desire for good housekeeping would prevent the stacking of waste cans there indefinitely—or, at least, until Netco's production contract runs out—and if the contract is renewed and the space is eventually filled? "Then we find more space," said Sherman.

One option not available to Netco and to many industries licensed under Agreement States programs is on-site burial of the wastes; however, the Nuclear Regulatory Commission does permit its licensees, and specifically power plants, to bury low-level wastes 4 feet below the surface of their sites (compared to a 5-foot minimum depth required at the commercial burial sites) indefinitely if they wish. In 1980, the General Accounting Office attempted to learn how many licensees were burying this waste, but, it reported, the Nuclear Regulatory Commission was unable to supply either a figure or a list of facilities that availed themselves of the burial option: "According to three different NRC officials, such a list does not exist because a license is not required for that action. Licensees simply do it and then NRC inspects them afterward." Nevertheless, the GAO found a potential "for storage of low-level wastes at nuclear powerplant sites for the operating lives of the plants, and perhaps for permanent disposal at some sites." It recommended congressional consideration of this potential, even though it conceded that many power plants, built on the banks of rivers or the shores of lakes or oceans might not be "technically acceptable for traditional shallow-land or deeper burial of low-level wastes," and that "on-site storage only defers the inevitable need to dispose of the waste, and would add one more task to eventually decommissioning a nuclear powerplant site."

However, indefinite storage or on-site burial are seldom feasible options for the chronically space-short hospitals and medical-research institutions that produce 25 percent of the nation's commercial low-level waste. Radiologically, a good proportion of the material shipped by these facilities even decays into stability before it ever reaches the burial ground. The Oak Ridge Laboratory survey also estimates that by volume nearly half the medical and biological waste consists of the residues of radiological preparations ingested or injected into patients, and scintillation counters, which are combinations of a small quantity of phosphors mixed with a very slightly radioactive liquid, usually tritium. Tissues or blood samples taken from patients who have ingested or been injected with isotopes are put into vials of this fluid, and the phosphors in the counter convert the emitted radioactivity into flashes of light which, counted in a photomultiplying device, indicate the proportion of radioactivity absorbed by the tissue or blood sample under test.

Paradoxically, the much greater amount of radioactivity which the patient eventually excretes as a result of these tests is not legally considered to be, or controlled as, a nuclear waste. "If I give a patient a hundred-millicurie drink on Monday or Tuesday," a medical technician told me, "I know that by Wednesday, ninety millicuries of that radioactivity are on their way down the toilet." This toilet disposal is in addition to the one curie per year of radioactive liquids which NRC licensees are permitted to release into sanitary drains, but which some licensees—hospitals in particular—refuse to do as a matter of conscience. While this short-lived contamination flows into rivers through sewer systems, however, between 84 million and 159 million only slightly radioactive scintillation counting vials containing between 200,000 and 400,000 gallons of liquids containing only about 11 curies in all, had to be dispatched to low-level commercial sites in 1980. The carcasses of animals used in nuclear medicine and research also made a large contribution to these sites as well, approximately 80,000 cubic feet of burial space compared to approximately 400,000 cubic feet of space taken up by the scintillation counters. In 1981, the Nuclear Regulatory Commission, in effect, decontrolled both scintillation counters and most carcasses of animals killed in nuclear studies, permitting both to be sent to sanitary landfills. It also authorized its licensees annually to dispose of in sewers or bury as much as 5 curies of tritium, one curie of carbon 14, and one curie of other isotopes.

Not all the medical wastes that still find their way to the low-level commercial repositories are radioactively as innocuous as scintillation-counting liquids and animal carcasses, however. At Barnwell, Ott told me that "some of the hottest stuff we get" comes from the production of radioisotopes and the fabrication of medical radiation sources, primarily cobalt 60. In use, these shielded sources usually contain about 3,000 curies each. Of lesser intensity, but still dangerous, are the wastes shipped by firms in the production of iodine, iridium and radium pharmaceuticals, as well as technicium, strontium, iron, mercury, selenium and other isotopes used in diagnostic tests.

In 1980, after the reopening of the Hanford and Beatty sites, and at least the temporary easing of the low-level waste-disposal crisis, I asked Philip M. Lorio, health-physics officer for Columbia University and Columbia Presbyterian Hospital in New York, and the 1980 president of the metropolitan (New York) section of the American Nuclear Society, about medical radwastes.

"I'll tell you right from the beginning," he said, "we have to find better ways of disposing of our medical wastes. What we do now is take radioactive liquids mixed with toxic and flammable liquids like toluene or xylene, and pour them into five mil [five thousandths of an inch] polyethylene bags along with enough vermiculite to absorb the liquids to meet Department of Transportation regulations, put the lot into a 55-gallon drum, put a cover on it and ship it. In the scale of balances, this is a terrible technique. Those drums are very thin, they can be punctured easily, and the vermiculite doesn't really hold the toluene or xylene, which, in addition to being chemically toxic, is flammable. If the drum is punctured, those chemicals could start a fire, and several times they have.

"Still, for many years this has been the cheap and easy way to dispose of medical wastes—put them in a can and say to somebody, 'Get it out of here.' Now it's no longer cheap. For just one fifty-five-gallon drum, it costs us two hundred twenty-five dollars, including the vermiculite, and we get rid of only about twenty gallons in each drum—the rest is the absorbant. Solid waste is cheaper, only a hundred fifty-five dollars per drum, but since we ship from twenty-five to thirty solid and liquid drums each week, you can see it's beginning to run into money."

Early in 1981, Edward Mason, radiation-protection officer at the University of Chicago, estimated the charge for shipping that institution's approximate annual total of 160 55-gallon drums of radwaste to Hanford at "fifty thousand dollars and rising fast. The cost has doubled over the past two years." Nor is shipping the only expense. Mason announced that the university would have to clear a warehouse and arrange for additional security exclusively for the storage of radwastes being held temporarily at two hundred fifty individual campus laboratories.

One way to cut down on this shipping and storage cost would be to incinerate the greater proportion of hospital and research radwaste that is combustible. Lorio has proposed this at Columbia, but incineration would require amendments to the institution's nuclear licenses, and Dr. Leonard Solon, director of the New York City Bureau of Radiation Control, says he would oppose these because of the possibility of widespread contamination in the event of a failure in an incinerator's gas filters. "If one does break," he maintains, "you won't know it until too late —after the stuff gets out."

Still, there are jurisdictions in which medical and research radwaste is incinerated—although the number of institutions that do it is uncertain. In a published report, the Nuclear Regulatory Commission said that sixty-one of its non-agreement state licensees used incineration as a volume-reduction technique. When pressed, however, the NRC was able to provide the General Accounting Office with a list of only twenty operating radwaste incinerators—and even this lower figure surprised Department of Energy officials who had recently awarded the University of Maryland a contract for a demonstration study to determine whether the process is commercially feasible. "When DOE officials heard that many institutions are already incinerating their waste on a practical basis," the GAO pointed out, "they conceded that someone could seriously question their demonstration contract."

In addition to incineration, there is compaction: The Department of Energy estimates that 24 percent of the hospital and university sources of wastes employ this volume-reduction technique, although the percentage of those that have hooked their compactors up to the kind of high-efficiency particulate air filters in use at DOE facilities is unknown.

By and large, however, most American hospitals and research institutions were caught unprepared without any way of getting rid of their radwaste or cutting the volume of its production after Beatty and Hanford were shut down in October of 1979. A spokesman for the Society for Nuclear Medicine told members of the House Committee on Science and Technology that the crisis had the potential for halting radiation treatment and diagnosis procedures in many hospitals within 7 to 10 days, and Nobel Prize laureate Rosalyn Yalow testified that the Veterans Administration hospital where she practices in New York "is filled with yellow barrels with 'radioactive-material' warning labels which cannot be disposed of." The institutional responses to this backup varied. Yale University announced it would store barrels of radwaste in an unused building previously devoted to nuclear research; Massachusetts General Hospital asked its physicians to defer radioactive diagnostic tests for as long as possible, and Harvard, among other institutions, put its faith in Todd.

Todd Shipyards is a national—and diversified—corporation. Its facility on triangular Pelican Island in the mouth of Galveston Bay is now primarily occupied with the production of instrument control panels. Beginning in 1970, however, and growing out of its melancholy experience servicing the nuclear ship *Savannah,* decommissioned in 1971 after a decade of unprofitable operation, the shipyard had been developing a sideline in storing and concentrating liquid radwaste destined for low-level disposal. Three other Texas facilities have in the past stored limited amounts mostly of local hospital radwaste—and presumably still do—but Todd had the benefit of an NRC license, necessary for its storage in a pool until 1973 of the *Savannah*'s spent-fuel rods, and a largely underutilized section of its 200-acre shipyard on the island and a work force of approximately fifty employees.

Todd made no secret of its radwaste storage work; neither did it publicize it. In retrospect, not much of a stir appears to have been caused in southeast Texas by a September 1979 article headlined "Todd's Halfway House for Nuclear Garbage," that appeared in *In Between,* a Galveston County monthly publication, although it disclosed that tanker trucks pulled onto the island "a dozen or so times a year" with the contaminated cooling effluents from reactors in California, New Hampshire and Arkansas reactors as well as those from Navy submarines, and that this liquid was held for up to a year for the decay of short-lived isotopes, then filtered and discharged into Galveston's ship channel.

Just a month later, however, with the announcement of plans by Harvard to ship to Galveston, according to the Dallas *Times Herald,* "reaction from town fathers verged on shock." Galveston's mayor, E. "Gus" Manuel, said he hadn't even been aware that Todd was storing nuclear wastes until he read that some of this material had been diverted from Barnwell to "right across from our population center." The Galveston City Council passed a resolution asking Todd to stop accepting new waste accounts—and that, apparently, drew the attention of the chairman of the Texas State Senate's Natural Resources Committee, A. R. "Babe" Schwartz, who represents the Galveston district. At a meeting of his panel, Schwartz pointed out that Pelican Island, 19 feet above sea level, had been vulnerable in the past to Gulf of Mexico hurricanes, and he speculated on the effect of high winds on barrels of radwaste stacked in the open only 2,000 feet from downtown Galveston. "From June to September, nothing you put on Pelican Island can be guaranteed to stay there through a 200 mile-per-hour wind," he said. (Senator Schwartz also delivered a notable response when a colleague argued in a legislative debate that the wastes at issue were only low-level: "There ain't no such thing as low-level death.")

Texas Governor William P. Clements, Jr., also appeared annoyed to learn from the Schwartz Committee hearing that 80 percent of Todd's shipments came from out of state, and, specifically, that two of the major accounts were California power plants. "Governor Brown can take care of his own waste," he told a reporter. Not exactly coincidentally, Texas' health commissioner, Robert Bernstein, looked up Todd's permits and found that they stipulated that wastes not be held for more than a year and that no more than 2,000 drums should be accumulated. At that point, Todd had an inventory of 11,000 drums, some of them more than 3 years in residence. In something of a compromise, Bernstein raised the storage maximum to 5,000 drums but ordered Todd to divest itself of at least the excess 6,000.

Beatty had reopened by then—January of 1980—but even so, Todd, as others before it, was to find that there is more to getting rid of radwaste than simply loading barrels onto a truck. In February 1980, the shipyard's deliveries to Beatty were suspended for a month after a waste drum arrived there radiating 4 millirems, or twice the permissible dose, on contact. Then two months later, when one of its drums, supposedly carrying only material that had been solidified, arrived at Beatty leaking water, Todd's shipments were indefinitely suspended by the Nevada facility, and subsequently wastes first sent to Texas had to be trucked north almost transcontinentally to Hanford.

Todd also had its troubles at home. In January 1980, a bottle popped from the lid of an uncapped waste drum and scattered a radioactive powder which was tracked around by several employees—eventually contamination was detected on the clothing of thirteen men, and although no health effects were determined, that accident seems to have been the factor that led Todd to decide to get out of the nuclear-waste business. Two days later, its lawyers announced that the company would accept no more radwaste "except to fulfill the contracts that it has with hospitals and institutions that will expire within a year." Unfortunately, not even that action was the end of Todd's difficulties—in the following May, a fire apparently started by the flammable chemical toluene destroyed a compactor and the building housing it.

Still, when a reporter visited C. W. Hathway, manager of Todd's nuclear division at Pelican Island in the summer of 1980, the executive blamed "politics and politicians" for driving his division out of the radwaste traffic: "The company took a look at the situation and found that we were doing maybe one percent of Todd's business and getting ninety-nine percent of the publicity. We were forced out because these people made conditions such that we didn't want to continue.

"The question I have now," he continued, "is what is to prevent some unscrupulous operator from going into the nuclear-waste-disposal business, collecting about a million and a half dollars in cash and skipping with a million of it, leaving a big pile of nuclear waste behind him? Todd has assets; we had to be responsible because we could be held accountable, and that's not necessarily true of most of the other people now handling nuclear waste, some of them in what we call 'bicycle shops,' working out of a garage or warehouse. If such people get into trouble, the state has no leverage, and they can walk away from it."

In April of 1980, one of Todd's smaller competitors, a company called Nuclear Sources and Services, Inc., did apply for a Texas license to evaporate contaminated liquids at a building in Centerville, about 150 miles inland from Galveston, and to store up to 5,000 drums of radwaste in an abandoned school building not far away in Leon County. Leon County also has the distinction of housing a natural salt dome that the Department of Energy is considering as a candidate site for a high-level waste repository, and a protest against both the high- and low-level proposals drew more than 20 percent of the county's population of 9,000 to a protest meeting in October of 1980. A petition circulated there eventually received 7,000 signatures.

NSSI appears to have had its own radwaste-handling problems in the recent past. According to a Texas newspaper, this company's shipments were once barred from Hanford, and since 1978, it had received eight citations at its Houston plant from the Texas Department of Health. Nevertheless, the firm's proposal to expand into Leon County remained under active consideration by that department until March of 1981, when a Texas House of Representatives subcommittee approved a bill that would establish stricter standards for radwaste containment—and provide for a $100,000-per-day fine for violations. At that point, NSSI's president, Robert Gallagher, said these measures would make continued operation in Texas economically unfeasible and set an April deadline for his firm to stop accepting even medical wastes.

Subsequently, after hearing testimony from representatives of Texas hospitals who said they had run completely out of room to store radwaste drums—one Houston institution had been stacking them up on its roof—the Texas Legislature approved, and Governor William Clements signed, a measure that will permit the state itself to establish and supervise a low-level repository, but only for wastes generated within Texas. Conceivably, like the Washington referendum, this restriction could be overturned in federal court under a United States Supreme Court ruling several years ago that lifted a New Jersey ban on out-of-state shipments of non-radioactive wastes to one of that state's disposal facilities. In any case, the Texas Legislature still faces a considerable political hurdle in selecting an actual site for the repository. Ron Bird, a lame-duck State Representative who took responsibility for drafting the 1980 enabling measure, concedes that Texans "think low-level nuclear waste sites are just about as popular as new prisons."

Uncertain though its prospects may be, the Texas proposal appears to have been the most positive 1980 response to a federal plea made to each of the states during the October 1979 low-level disposal crisis that they take action "to develop additional disposal capacity to correct the present imbalance." Nuclear Regulatory Commission Chairman Joseph Hendrie conceded in a telegram to each of the governors that "there may be a misconception that the NRC has a moratorium on development of any additional low-level waste disposal capacity. This is not the case."

The obvious source for that "misconception" about an NRC

moratorium is the NRC itself—and a 1978 recommendation by a Department of Energy Task Force for Review of Nuclear Waste Management that the federal government remove low-level waste-disposal licensing and regulation from the Agreement State program, and that the Department of Energy "acquire ownership and control" of operating and inoperative commercial low-level repositories and submit them, along with any to be built in the future, to licensing by the NRC. This proposal never got anywhere either—and, in fact, it is specifically opposed by the State Planning Council on Radioactive Waste Management, which succeeded the Interagency Review Group on Nuclear Waste Management, which succeeded the DOE Task Force.

Before it was countermanded, however, the Task Force recommendation had the effect of thwarting plans that would have established a seventh commercial low-level facility near Cimarron in northeastern New Mexico. The sponsor of this application was Chem Nuclear Systems, which operates the Barnwell facility, and according to the firm's president, Bruce Johnson, $620,000 had been spent in planning this repository before the application met unexpected obstacles that Johnson attributed to a letter from NRC staff members to state officials suggesting that the application be held up, for three years if necessary, until the federal-state licensing issue was resolved.

Whatever the result in 1978, it also appears that the low-level waste crisis of 1979 was also resolved, at least temporarily, by just such a warning that a continuing backup of this material would, unavoidably, require federal intervention. The NRC let it be known that it had called on the DOE to prepare a contingency plan for opening some of its low-level sites for commercial waste. Not entirely by coincidence, the three DOE sites selected were Hanford, the Nevada Test Site and the Savannah River Plant, which just happen to adjoin, or in the case of Hanford, contain, the three commercial sites at issue. This had something of the effect of an ultimatum—the governors would either allow use of their commercial sites or face resumption of the shipments to facilities within their states over which they would have no control at all. Riley, who had never completely shut off disposal at Barnwell, kept South Carolina's scale of restrictions on shipments in effect, but Ray and List allowed Hanford and Beatty to reopen in November 1979—the latter after firing off an angry telegram to the President protesting any use of the DOE sites as "a subversion of states rights for regulation and control of our own destiny with regard to the safety and welfare of our citizens."

The ball is now back in the states' court, and specifically it is being put in play by the State Management Council on Radioactive Waste Management which Riley chairs and on which the governors of Nevada and Washington sit—Dixy Lee Ray has been succeeded in Washington by John Spellman, a Republican with somewhat less of a history of promoting nuclear causes. In the fall of 1980, the State Planning Council for Radioactive Waste Management secured from Congress one of its principal recommendations, authorization for the states to form low-level-waste regional compacts. The National Governors Association proposed the operation of six regional sites which after the 1985 effective date of the legislation would be obligated to accept only the commercial low-level radwaste originating in their particular regions, and at that time, presumably, Washington State will be freed by the courts to ban from Hanford Reservation's low-level commercial burial grounds wastes from states that have not entered into a compact with it.

Although it has obtained this authorization for the regional compacts, the State Planning Council has been less successful in persuading Congress to enact some of its other recommendations, and principally the establishment of "a special discretionary fund which would confer benefits to host states, tribal governments and local communities" to compensate for the undesirability of being a host or a neighbor of a low-level radwaste facility. Also overlooked toward the end of the fourth decade of the nuclear age was the council's wistful request that somebody in authority, presumably the Nuclear Regulatory Commission, finally get around to specifying for the record exactly what is defined by the term "low-level nuclear waste."

8

DECONTAMINATION AND DECOMMISSIONING

The radioactive shell of the Enrico Fermi Fast Breeder Reactor is locked in solitary confinement within a 72-foot-tall, windowless containment building inside a 6-foot fence on the shore of Lake Erie at Lagoona Beach, near Monroe, Mich., which is about halfway between Detroit and Toledo, Ohio. Outside the fence in May of 1980 were all the signs of construction for the completion by 1982 of a 1,093-megawatt boiling-water reactor that will be Enrico Fermi Unit Number 2, but only Detroit Edison health physicists unlock the gates of the fence enclosing Fermi Unit Number 1 these days to check for signs of spreading contamination and to monitor pressure gauges on the inert gases which still must be maintained on the reactor vessel, and several times a year a Nuclear Regulatory Commission agent inspects the condition of the whole desolate place.

When it was brought to criticality in 1963 after 7 years of construction work, the 61-megawatt sodium-cooled Fermi 1 seemed destined to symbolize a new era of commercial nuclear breeder reactors. Today, however, it is symbolic primarily of a lack of consideration given the decontamination and decommissioning of radioactive facilities that for one reason or another have reached the end of their working lives.

Fermi 1's career was foreshortened in 1966, after only three years of tests, by the fuel-meltdown accident that John G. Fuller has written about in a book entitled *We Almost Lost Detroit.* Detroit Edison, which enlisted the support of twenty-three nuclear engineering, manufacturing and utility companies to finance the project under the corporate structure of the Power Reactor Development Company, adamantly denies that there was ever any danger to the public from Fermi 1—and has, in fact, distributed a rebuttal entitled *We Did* Not *Almost Lose Detroit.* Whether or not Detroit was almost lost, the breeder as a reactor prototype suffered a severe setback. It took four years to clear the core and discover the cause of the meltdown—a segment of a zirconium conical flow guide at the bottom of the reactor vessel had broken free and had blocked sodium coolant from reaching two of the fuel sub-assemblies—and by the time the reactor finally was started up again and run up to full power capacity in 1970, it was only two years away from its licensed fuel-burnup limit. When the Atomic Energy Commission, then beginning to plan its own breeder reactor at Clinch River, declined to increase its funding of the Fermi, and a fund-raising drive among the corporation's contributors also fell short, the reactor was shut down in December of 1971, and its decommissioning ordered a year later.

Approximately $130 million was spent over a 16-year period to plan, construct, operate and decommission Fermi 1, and in the end this effort produced only 32 million gross kilowatt hours of power for the Detroit Edison system and an estimated 6,524 grams of plutonium 239 that were never stripped from the uranium blanket which in the end the AEC charged $1.6 million to bury at the Idaho Chemical Reprocessing Plant grounds at INEL. The ninety-nine subassemblies of the Fermi's core fuel were shipped off to the Savannah River Plant ostensibly for reprocessing, but one of the reasons this has not yet taken place, I was told by a Department of Energy official, is that "there is no present demand for fuel at the Fermi enrichment (of 25.5 percent fissile uranium)." In any case, PRDC paid another $1.8 million to get this spent fuel off its hands, plus the cost of fabricating special casks for the material and shipping it.

The company was able to give away slightly more than 30,000

gallons of its non-radioactive sodium from the secondary loop —it took the heat from the primary loop and passed it on to the water which generated the steam that drove the plant's turbine —but it had a hard time disposing of the 77,000 gallons of radioactive sodium from the reactor vessel and the primary cooling system. The U. S. Ecology Corporation, the operator of active repositories at Beatty and Hanford, at first agreed to bury the Fermi 1 coolant at Beatty, but then encountered resistance from Nevada regulators. Washington State officials wouldn't allow the radioactive sodium to be disposed of at Hanford either, but eventually PRDC was able to get the AEC to take most of it off its hands for use in the Clinch River Breeder—with Fermi 1's operators, of course, committed to paying shipping and insurance charges, and storing the material on the site until 1984. "After that," a Detroit Edison executive told me (and "after that" could be a considerable period of time, since Clinch River was not until 1981 budgeted for construction), "the government will either tell us where it wants this stuff sent or it will have to pay *us* to store it."

Fermi 1's steam turbine was salvaged by Detroit Edison to provide peaking power from a fossil-fueled boiler also erected at the site, and the unit's main steam generator was sent to Japan at the expense of Japanese utilities that sought to test it; the reactor's fuel-assembly nozzles and equally radioactive chips from the disassembly of the fuel were buried at Maxey Flats, as was the bulk of the contaminated network of steel pipes, and the liquid wastes generated during steam cleaning and decontamination operations. Salvageable material and tools with radiation counts well below maximum permissible concentrations were sold as scrap, and the residual heat-transfer and piping systems were filled with nitrogen and carbon dioxide gas still maintained under pressure. The decommissioning has so far cost $6.9 million, with a lot more expense still to come when (or perhaps if) Fermi 1 is eventually dismantled and its shell and buildings finally disposed of.

Eldon L. Alexanderson was the assistant superintendent of the reactor while it was operating and has been the general manager of the decommissioning work, and he and Gary Frost, a senior reactor operator, showed me around what remains of the project, beginning at an office building still in use by the operators of the fossil-fuel boiler and turbine which are on stand-by to provide peaking power for the Detroit Edison system, and by the architects and engineers at work on the construction of Fermi 2. This building also contains what remains of Fermi 1's control room—many of the instruments have been removed; others still bear warning tags affixed to them during the reactor's shutdown—and on the floor immediately below the control room there is an electrical relay room which had been the focal point of the breeder's instrumentation. "After we got the go-ahead for decommissioning in 1972," Alexanderson said, "we called in a junkman, and as I recall, the guy gave us a couple of hundred dollars for the whole relay system."

Leaving the office building, we passed through a locked gate in the fence into Fermi's Fuel and Repair Building, where my first impression was of both disrepair and disaffection. Daylight was visible through holes in the roof and puddles had formed on the concrete floor, and a 6-foot-high replica of Mickey Mouse had been sketched on the exterior of the steel-lined concrete wall which contained the spent-fuel pool. While Fermi 1 operated, however, Alexanderson maintained, "I think this was an unusually clean plant. We didn't get contamination all over the place because we were operating with sodium, and because of its volatility, you have to be very careful with sodium to begin with."

From the top of the fuel-handling pool, where a bridge-controlled crane used to maneuver—"all that machinery has been sent off to ordinary low-level burial," Alexanderson said—we looked down 40 feet to its concrete base where, according to Frost, "we still get forty millirems per hour on contact." This is after the pool has been decontaminated as far as possible by steam-cleaning its interior surfaces and then painting them with a plastic insulating material. The radiation readings taper off to half a millirem per hour at the top of the pool where we were standing.

Following steel tracks that had once guided a fuel-handling vehicle down a wide corridor, we entered the containment building; Frost groped for a light switch, and the shell of Fermi 1 appeared. Towering out of the gloom 30 feet above the floor level, it was surrounded at its base by three levels of 55-gallon drums that had been stacked up on skids. These drums—630 of them, I was told—contain slightly more than half of the primary cooling sodium now in storage for Clinch River. "It's good clean stuff," Alexanderson said. "We estimate half a curie or less in the entire 70,000 gallons here and in tanks next-door." Radiation readings from the drums themselves have dropped, Frost said, from 20 millirems per hour when they were filled and stacked there seven years ago to a present 9 millirems.

The remainder of the sodium is in three 12,000-gallon tanks in the nearby sodium storage building—which we were able to enter only after Frost had hammered open a rusty padlock with a rock. This building, too, had holes in its roof and water an inch deep in puddles on the floor. "There's no need spending money on the plant as long as we're not operating anything in it," Alexanderson explained. "The only radiation is contained inside the tanks—two in here are full of sodium and one is half full— and in the pipes buried underground. I say that unless there's some need for this space, we might as well just leave the place —it's harmless the way it is—for about fifty more years when the radioactivity, which was about four thousand curies when we shut down, should be only a single curie. I don't think you'd even have to use remote cutting tools to cut the plant apart then, and the cost in dollars and exposure would be a hell of a lot cheaper."

I mentioned the possibility of a terrorist or a natural disaster in the meantime. "What could either one do?" Alexanderson asked. "Blow up a lot of harmless sodium? Most of the radioactivity now is inside the stainless steel of the pipes and the fuel pool walls. To get it out, you'd have to dissolve the steel in nitric acid."

And the eventual cost to dismantle the remaining plant and restore the site? "I don't think anybody has ever really made a good estimate of that," Alexanderson said as Frost locked the perimeter gate behind us, "and considering the uncertainty of inflation, I don't think it's even worth spending money now to make an estimate. In 1972, it didn't make any sense to do anything other than what we did—obviously, the surveillance costs we're paying are fairly substantial, but at least they're lower here than they would be elsewhere because we're building the other plant."

For the indefinite future, therefore, while water leaks in through the roofs of its service buildings, Fermi 1 stands under its passive gas cover, a nuclear expense deferred to be paid by another generation, and a symbol largely ignored by the architects and engineers pressing forward with the construction of Fermi 2 several hundred yards away.

Sooner or later everything wears out, and nuclear plants are no exception. However, primarily because of the radiation induced within their originally non-radioactive components, reactors and other major nuclear facilities may become dangerous to operate—or even approach—long before they show signs of physical deterioration. Because of these increasing levels of induced radioactivity, the Nuclear Regulatory Commission limits the operating licenses of commercial reactors to 40 years—and there is a question of whether the 1,000-megawatt-and-above reactors that have been brought on-line in the last several years will be able to operate that long. The 200-megawatt Dresden I unit, which Commonwealth Edison started up in 1960 at a cost of $18 million, had to be shut down by 1979 for decontamination—85,000 gallons of chelates will have to be flushed through its pipes and shipped to Hanford for burial—before it can be permitted to begin the second half of its licensed life span. The work is estimated to cost $36 million, twice the reactor's construction cost, and early in 1981, the utility had not decided whether or not to make the investment.

The era of commercial nuclear power is now well over 20 years old—the first civilian reactor, a 60-megawatt joint project of the Atomic Energy Commission and the Duquesne Light Co., began operations in 1957 at Shippingport, Pa. Many of the nuclear officials I have talked to tend to dismiss "D and D," as they call it in conversation, as a minor nuclear problem, easily resolvable when the time comes to get around to it. Well, the time is coming, and as the General Accounting Office pointed out in 1977, not even the Nuclear Regulatory Commission has "paid much attention to one of the biggest problems that may confront the public in the future—that is, who will pay the cost of decommissioning power reactors. It has not made any plans or established any requirements for advanced accumulation of funds for decommissioning reactors or any facilities it licenses with the exception of uranium mills."

In addition to the 73 commercial reactors operating at the end of 1980 and 8 that have already been decommissioned, there are in civilian hands more than a thousand atomic-particle accelerators, used in nuclear research and the manufacture of isotopes; 21 fuel-fabrication plants and 19 active and 25 inactive uranium mills. Portions of these facilities take on dangerous intensities of induced radioactivity with time and will have to be disposed of at low-level radwaste sites. Eventually, these D-and-D costs will probably turn out to be greater than the costs of building the facilities in the first place.

In 1978, for example, Battelle Memorial Institute closed down the plutonium-fuel-fabrication facility it had operated for 20 years at West Jefferson, Ohio, and according to Joseph Dettorre, the institute's manager of projects, the 7,000-square-foot, one-story building cost $750,000 to $1 million to build, and will cost "somewhere between $3.5 million to $4 million to decommission. We're still in the process now [in July of 1980] of digging out and analyzing material. All the glove boxes have been removed, cut up, put into containers and shipped off to low-level burial at Hanford. Several rooms have been decontaminated down to levels for unrestricted use; mostly it's just a matter of washing down the walls, which are concrete blocks sealed with epoxy, but we have found penetrations [of contamination], and in those cases, we've had to take out pieces of block and do some sandblasting."

I asked whether it might not have been cheaper simply to demolish the entire building. "Not really," Dettorre said. "That would have required us either to have incurred tremendous shipping and disposal costs in sending all that material to Hanford, or we would have had the expense of surveying every piece of the rubble to determine that it was not contaminated and could go to a sanitary landfill."

In fact, every facility or object in nuclear use today, as well as a vast quantity of material and structures that are no longer in use, but stand like Fermi 1 awaiting demolition, are candidate low-level wastes. However, it is reactors, built to withstand the most tremendous pressures and the most intensive radiation known to man, that present the toughest disposal problems. Several small government units that have been dismantled have had to be flooded and cut apart remotely by tools operated from behind concrete shielding—and, of course, at the end of these procedures, the contaminated tools and shielding must then also be disposed of as radwaste. In terms of volume and cost, the numbers are staggering.

Most D-and-D estimates are based on the reference base of a 22-megawatt boiling-water reactor at Elk River, Minn. This unit, which went critical in 1962 and was shut down for economic reasons in 1968, was owned by the old Atomic Energy Commission, and its dismantling to grade level was accomplished over a 2-year period ending in August 1974 at a cost to the federal government of $6.2 million. The most expensive item in accounting for this charge was $1,249,000 paid for the shipment of 86,379 cubic feet of radwaste, and the burial of it at the Sheffield, Maxey Flats and Hanford repositories—at a time when commercial low-level disposal fees were only a small percentage of what they are now.

Of course, the Elk River reactor was a pipsqueak compared to reactors coming on-line today. The Atomic Industrial Forum says that the average volume of radioactive waste estimated to be produced during the course of dismantling a 1,150-MW nuclear-power reactor is 594,000 cubic feet. This may be an underestimate—the 1978 Department of Energy Task Force for Review of Nuclear Waste Management estimated up to 800,000 cubic feet of low-level material for reactors above 1,000 MW— but accepting the AIF figure for the sake of argument, just burying that amount of waste at Barnwell's 1981 charge of $7.71 per cubic foot would amount to nearly $4.6 million—with packaging in shielded containers and transportation extra. Moreover, the AIF estimate works out to a ratio of 516 cubic feet of D-and-D radwaste per megawatt of reactor capacity; apply that to the 53,957 megawatts of capacity rated for the 73 commercial reactors operating in 1980, plus 7 decommissioned units waiting to be dismantled, and the result comes to slightly more than 27.8 million cubic feet of candidate low-level waste, or about 30 percent of the 92 million cubic feet that remained of the nation's commercial low-level burial capacity in 1980.

But that's just the *commercial* reactors. At the same time, there were 87 operating and 64 decommissioned test, research and university reactors; 16 operating and 38 decommissioned military production, process and research reactors, and 126 operating and 6 decommissioned submarine propulsion reactors destined for eventual burial at federal sites. The unused burial capacity of federal reservations is, of course, much greater than that of the three commercial sites, but even so, in 1979, Energy Department Deputy Undersecretary Worth Bateman warned the House Committee on Science and Technology that "alternative disposal methods may be used to handle potential increases in waste quantities, particularly from decommissioning."

Faced with these massive disposal volumes and costs, it has been the understandable tendency of both utility and governmental managers to put off dismantling reactors indefinitely, to "mothball" them (Fermi 1 is an example), or perhaps go a little further and entomb them in concrete until less expensive disposal methods—or less restrictive regulations—come to be accepted. The Nuclear Regulatory Commission defines mothballing as "a state of protective storage." Fuel assemblies, coolant and mobile wastes are removed from the reactor and its spent-fuel pool and shipped to low-level disposal. The reactor containment building is then simply locked up under 24-hour security and monitored at least once a week physically and radiologically to check for possible contamination leaks. Including Fermi 1, four of the eight decommissioned civilian power-producing reactors have been mothballed; the first to undergo this procedure was a 17-megawatt unit that four Southeastern utilities erected in 1963 near Parr, S. C. After four years of unremarkable operation, this unit was shut down as unprofitable and mothballed in 1967, and its site has been described by the Columbia *Record* and the State as "South Carolina's first nuclear ghost town—a mothballed, rusting but still radioactive power plant surrounded by climbing vines and overgrown weeds."

Entombment is somewhat more extensive than mothballing.

The steam pressure vessel and the internal working parts of the reactor are sealed within the containment building with additional steel and concrete barriers—the whole structure is more or less surrounded by an impenetrable concrete shell. This, of course, is more expensive at first than simple mothballing, but the security requirements are less—the facility is enabled to depend on automatic intrusion alarms rather than 24-hour surveillance. However, periodic maintenance and annual radiation checks are still necessary. Two reactors, at Piqua, Ohio, and Puerto Higuera, Puerto Rico, were entombed in 1966 and 1968 for $1 million and $1.6 million respectively.

These Ohio and Puerto Rico units were only 50 megawatts, even smaller than the 61 MW Fermi 1, which cost $6.9 million just to mothball. (This can't be counted as typical, however, since most of the expense derived from the disposal of Fermi 1's atypical uranium-breeder blanket and sodium coolant.) For the kind of large boiling-water reactors in the 1,000-MW range that are now being brought on-line, the Atomic Industrial Forum estimated in 1975 the immediate costs of mothballing at $2.8 to $3.1 million, entombment at $7.1 to $9.5 million, and dismantling at $33.6 to $39 million. Although the Nuclear Regulatory Commission has adopted these estimates in calculations which it updates for inflation, McKinley C. Olson, author of *Unacceptable Risk: The Nuclear Power Controversy,* maintains he was shown a 1974 Atomic Energy Commission study which estimated a $100-million cost to dismantle an 1,100-megawatt plant. Apparently the AIF/NRC estimates are even suspect within the federal establishment. Paul Giardina, chief of the radiation branch of the New York region of the Environmental Protection Agency, testified at a 1979 hearing before the New York State attorney general that "it has been EPA's experience . . . that little attention has been paid to D and D both from an economic and feasibility standpoint. This void may lead to certain underestimations with regard to the cost of a nuclear facility . . ."

At first glance, it would seem to make good financial—and radiological—sense to let a decommissioned reactor rest under guard for a century or longer until its most intensely radioactive constituent, cobalt 60, decays away to insignificance—logically,

a greater proportion of the dismantling can be accomplished
without extensive use of remote tools and greater quantities of
the waste can be disposed of in less expensive sanitary landfills.
(However, the Sierra Club's Marvin Resnikoff, a physicist,
makes the point that the shell of a large boiling-water reactor
in typical use will at decommissioning contain 171 curies of
nickel 59, with a half-life of 80,000 years, as well as lesser quantities of long-lived iron 55 and carbon 14.) Utilities can also absorb
a portion of their continuing surveillance costs by building new
facilities, either nuclear or non-nuclear, proximate to decommissioned reactors and using some of their non-nuclear facilities
and equipment—as Detroit Edison has availed itself of Fermi
1's steam turbine and office building.

Ultimately, though, even if the effects of inflation are disregarded, the fixed dollar costs of monitoring and surveillance and
property taxes on a completely non-productive reactor and its
grounds over a hundred-year period render mothballing the
most expensive of the three alternatives and just about balance
the financial positions of entombment and prompt dismantling.
A comparison of the long-range costs of the three alternatives
is contained in a nuclear consulting company's estimate in 1979
on expenses involved in dismantling, or entombing or mothballing two 1,264-megawatt units Detroit Edison planned to build
in St. Clair County, north of Detroit. For mothballing, surveillance for a century (at $606,300 per year), and then disman-
tling, the total was $123.4 million; for entombment, a lesser
degree of surveillance for the century (at $242,000 per year),
and then dismantling, the total was $109.8 million. Prompt
dismantling and disposal was estimated to cost $110.5 million.
Presumably Detroit Edison took these estimates into consideration the following year when it decided not to build the reactors.

Not as easily entered onto accounting ledgers is the aesthetic
effect on future generations of these mothballed and entombed
reactors. "Our children and our grandchildren face the prospect of hundreds of 'tombs'—totally useless monuments built by
their ancestors—dotting the countryside from sea to shining
sea," Illinois State Senator Jerome J. Joyce testified in 1980 to
the Senate Subcommittee on Rural Development. "In Illinois

alone, in the area where I farm and where I hope my family will farm for hundreds of years to come, there will be no fewer than fourteen nuclear reactor crypts. These crypts will stand out like eerie headstones in a cemetery. And that cemetery just happens to be some of the best farmland in the world."

Aesthetics aside, the Atomic Industrial Forum puts the cost of mothballing now and dismantling after a hundred years at four thousandths of a cent per kilowatt hour of electricity. That's quite a minuscule figure, but since very few utilities have made *any* advance D-and-D provisions, and since the Edison Electric Institute estimates that by the end of 1980 a total of 2,513,280,000,000 kilowatt hours of power had been generated by fission since the early 1950s, the present D-and-D bill, for power already consumed, comes out to something like $10 billion.

Of course, the numbers become astronomic with inflation. In 1980, Consumers Power of Michigan estimated the cost of decommissioning and dismantling its 72-MW boiling-water reactor at Big Rock Point at $92 million, but stressed that this was in 1979 dollars. To keep up with inflation and have the funds ready to do the job after the end of the plant's licensed life in 2003, a spokesman told a reporter, would require the collection of $526 million by that time.

Another case in point is Indian Point 1, a 265-MW boiling-water reactor on the Hudson River above New York City. Consolidated Edison of New York shut it down in 1974, after 12 years of operation, and waited until December of 1980 to file a "decommissioning plan" with the Nuclear Regulatory Commission. This "plan," however, only spelled out Con Ed's decision to wait until 2006—when its second Indian Point reactor, an 873-MW unit, will have reached its licensed limit—to decide what to do with both of them then. The utility's president, Arthur Hauspurg, cited State Public Service Commission estimates that dismantling and removing both reactors would have cost $51.65 million in 1977 and will cost about $246 million after 2006. Shortly before the plan was filed, however, the utility's chief of mechanical and nuclear engineering, Arthur Flynn, told a committee of the Westchester County Board of Legislators that dismantling might not take place, in the end, until 2036, and by then, he said, "who knows what it will cost —$500 million, $1 billion? It's like figuring the cost of a 747 going to the moon based on today's 747 configuration. We've seen construction costs multiply by a factor of ten in just ten years."

Whatever reactor D and D will eventually cost future generations, few utility operators are asking today's rate-payers to contribute to it. According to a report of the Washington State Public Interest Research Group, "of the 67 commercial reactors operating at the end of 1977, only six had made provisions to pay for decommissioning." The General Accounting Office took its own survey of thirty-two utilities operating forty-eight reactors in 1977, and reported that only seventeen of these utilities had even established depreciation accounts (which they admitted frequent borrowings from) to begin providing for future decommissioning from current receipts.

Environmentalists and nuclear opponents want more than easily raided depreciation accounts for D and D, however. They have asked state public service commissions to require reactor operators to furnish bonds or set up escrow accounts. Against that, there are two accounting reasons for not making such provisions. The one industry spokesmen prefer to point to is that absent such a fund, they are obligated to deduct each year of depreciation from the rate base on which consumer bills are calculated. "Any fund approach," Rochester Gas and Electric pointed out in a 1979 submission to the New York State attorney general, "whether requiring cash up front, or one paid into over the life of the plant, will significantly increase the cost of electricity to consumers." An equally strong disincentive, not often mentioned by the utilities, to the establishment of such a fund is that it would be taxed as income over the years the money was taken in. If there is no such fund, the utility will also benefit from a mammoth deductible business expense when it actually pays for the work.

Not having such a fixed fund requires a gamble that when the time comes, the operators of reactors will have in hand the mammoth sums that will be required to decommission and dismantle them. (Borrowing the money, although theoretically possible, would probably be difficult, since banks customarily look with much more favor on lending money or underwriting bonds for building something—which then becomes an asset to be claimed against—than they do to providing the capital for what will wind up, if everything goes right, as a vacant lot.) The 1977 position of the Nuclear Regulatory Commission, as expressed by Lee V. Gossick, its executive director for operations, was that these charges, which he called "a small factor in the overall cost of operating a nuclear power plant," should be funded "out of current revenue," and he called it "reasonable to assume that the decommissioning and subsequent maintenance costs would be charged to operating expenses either in the year they are incurred or amortized over a period of years according to the policy of the rate-making regulatory authorities."

But what happens if there is no "current revenue," as is the case with the West Valley Reprocessing Plant, or if the facility never brought in the income that will cover these charges and seems unlikely to do so in the future, as is the case with Three Mile Island Number 2? The accident that crippled that plant on March 28, 1979, came only three months after the reactor was put into commercial service. General Public Utilities, a holding company that owns Metropolitan Edison, the central Pennsylvania utility that owns the reactor, held $300 million in insurance coverage on the plant, but by early in 1981, more than two thirds of this had been spent on decontamination work and in the payment of $26 million in claims filed by nearby residents and businesses affected by the accident. GPU estimates that at least $1.3 billion more will have to be spent to clean up the plant and put it back in operation by 1986 at the earliest. In the meantime, it is suing Babcock and Wilcox, which built the reactor, for $500 million, and the federal government for $4 billion, because, GPU charges, the Nuclear Regulatory Commission failed to alert it to safety defects highlighted in the 1977 failure of a valve at the Davis-Besse Nuclear Power Station at Oak Harbor, Ohio. It was a defect in an identical valve, the company says, that initiated the sequence of events which led to the Three Mile accident.

Of course, these suits are a long way from resolution, and in the end neither one may result in compensatory payments to

GPU which, since the accident, has only been able to persuade the Pennsylvania Public Utilities Commission to grant it limited rate increases covering the costs of purchasing replacement power and keeping Metropolitan Edison from becoming the first American public utility to declare bankruptcy since the Depression. According to Congress' General Accounting Office, it is "questionable" whether Metropolitan Edison "will be able to obtain the necessary funds to pay its share of Unit 2 costs and maintain its present electric power system." As the GAO notes laconically in its April 1980 report, most prospective lenders "appear unwilling to invest in a utility system whose current and future financial viability is in doubt."

And ultimately even if GPU, the parent company, is able to bring Three Mile Unit 2 back into profitable operation—and even if it never suffers another such accident—it still must find a way to pay for the eventual decommissioning of that reactor as well as Three Mile Unit 1 and two other reactors which another subsidiary operates at Toms River and Oyster Creek, N.J.

The federal government also has a significant D-and-D burden —one it didn't pay much attention to until prodded by a 1977 GAO report entitled in part, "A Multibillion Dollar Problem." To this point, there are more than five hundred decommissioned and about-to-be-decommissioned radioactive federal facilities, ranging in size from reprocessing plants and reactors down to leaching ponds (eighty-one of them at Hanford) and isotope-handling glove-box sets. The Oak Ridge survey estimates that a program to clean up former Manhattan Engineering District and Atomic Energy Commission sites, and another concentrating on Department of Energy surplus facilities, will generate slightly more than 30 million cubic feet of low-level waste, plus about 365,000 feet of transuranic material. Since this is slightly less than half the volume of approximately 62 million cubic feet of low-level material buried at all Department of Energy sites at the end of 1979, the department concedes in a program-summary draft for fiscal year 1981 that "this new large volume will require additional burial ground capacity."

Moreover, federal D-and-D estimates seem to be as understated as commercial ones. To cite just one example, the Army concurred with a commercial survey in 1978 that 7,000 cubic feet of radwaste would have to be removed to decontaminate Frankford Arsenal in Philadelphia. Eventually 50,000 cubic feet of contaminated rubble was shipped from there to Barnwell, and Rockwell International, which did the work, negotiated an increase of $1.8 million in a $6.8-million contract.

The Department of Energy's manager of Remedial Action Programs is Robert W. Ramsey, who spent 11 years at the Savannah River Plant working on production and research programs before becoming involved in radwaste management in 1970. In March of 1980, I tracked him to one of the smaller offices in the massive complex of buildings that the Department of Energy took over from the old AEC at Germantown, Md. "What we're going to do," he said, "is consolidate the wastes from the five hundred projects at seventy locations—fifty of them will be at Hanford. The idea will be to pull everything to where the waste tanks are, put it in one place so it won't encumber too much area, and then manage intensely those locations where we are committed to dispose of this waste. Our goal is to do this by the year 2000, when we would hope to be current, and we've estimated costs for achieving it would be between $500 and $700 million, although if we have to move the waste great distances, those numbers could escalate, and since that was our 1977 figure, escalate for inflation, too."

Even with those escalations, the $500- to $700-million figure seems unrealistic. Before the Department of Energy was formed in 1977, its predecessor, the Energy Resources and Development Administration, calculated an expenditure of $2.5 to $3 billion to decommission facilities that were then excess—and the General Accounting Office said its auditors "do not believe this is a credible estimate," both because ERDA failed to furnish sufficient data to support it, and because a contractor for the prior Atomic Energy Commission had estimated back in 1972 that just decommissioning the Hanford plant—high- and low-level waste-disposal facilities excluded—would cost $4 billion. An additional D-and-D cost is the money that will be required in the not-too-distant future to retire three uranium-enrichment plants now about 30 years old. Surveys reported at Oak Ridge National Laboratory have indicated that decommissioning these plants at Paducah, Ky., Oak Ridge, Tenn., and Portsmouth, Ohio, as well as one now planned to replace the one at Portsmouth, could cost $570 million, an estimate that the General Accounting Office says has not been factored into the price that commercial power plants pay for their uranium fuel.

A proposal that the Nuclear Regulatory Commission began considering at the end of 1980 would save at least a portion of this cost by allowing the unrestricted sale of scrap metals or alloys contaminated by "de minimus" quantities of enriched uranium or technetium 99, an isotope formed in the fissioning of uranium. The Department of Energy estimates that the smelting at Oak Ridge of alloys with less than 5 parts per million of the technetium and 17.5 parts per million of the uranium would produce approximately 10,000 tons of nickel, 1,750 tons of copper and 35,000 tons of steel, which in 1977 it expected to be able to sell for approximately $41.6 million. A draft environmental-impact statement prepared by the Office of Standards Development of the NRC considered the potential use of these metals in the fabrication of such products as desks, belt buckles, bone pins, iron tonics, frying pans and structures and calculated that a "worst-case scenario" of transport, manufacture, distribution and use of the contaminated scrap in these items would yield a cumulative radiation dose of only 80 person rems. However, it warned, "if the smelted metal alloys were used in objects having large surface areas, such as truck cabs, desks, buildings, etc., the radiation doses to individuals could be higher . . . and the population doses would be increased."

In addition to attempting to win permission to recycle very slightly radioactive scrap, the Department of Energy has been holding down some of its decontamination and decommissioning expense by finding new nuclear uses for contaminated facilities that it once scheduled for dismantling. An example cited by Ramsey as his "favorite success story" is E-MAD (engine maintenance assembly and disassembly) at the Nevada Nuclear Test Site. This huge hangar-shaped facility contains what is believed to be the biggest operating hot cell in the world (or so it was described to me on a visit I later made to the test site). Built in 1965 for $55 million to assemble, test and disassemble nuclear rocket engines, the 25-foot by 45-foot cell stands 25 feet high and is worked on three levels. After the demise of the nuclear rocket program, the facility was scheduled for decontamination and dismantling until 1978 when it was reactivated as a test center for commercial spent fuel. "If we didn't have that facility, we'd have to build one like it," Ramsey said. "Many of these installations from the past represent a good deal of unused genius and technical excellence—things like the nuclear rocket development program that got shot down along the way. They're perfectly good and usable for today's programs, but instead, more often than not, we end up dismantling and wasting these sites or leaving them derelict in the desert. I wonder how long we can afford to keep wasting our genius that way."

Ultimately, though, the number of federal nuclear facilities prematurely abandoned for programatic reasons is probably smaller than the number declared excess because they have taken on too much of a radiological burden to make their continued use feasible. For example, in April of 1979, the world's first nuclear submarine, the *Nautilus,* its reactor removed, joined the mothball fleet at Mare Island Naval Shipyard at Vallejo, Cal. By the end of 1980, 5 more atomic submarines had been decommissioned, and America's active nuclear fleet at that time included 102 more nuclear-propulsion submarines, 3 aircraft carriers (one, the USS *Enterprise,* carried 8 reactors); 8 frigates and a deep submergence vessel. Eventually, decontamination and decommissioning provisions must be made for these as well as the 34 nuclear subs, 2 carriers and a frigate under construction in 1980. A September 1980 article in the publication *Science* reported that the Navy was seeking to convince the Environmental Protection Agency to lift its ban on ocean dumping—at least to the extent of allowing the scuttling of decommissioned nuclear vessels over deep-bottom areas.

Also destined to be added into the candidate-waste totals is the radwaste produced by cleanups of federal facilities found to have been inadequately decontaminated in the first place before they were sold to private owners or turned over to public use—the Palos Forest hill is an example. In 1974, after a search of records, the Atomic Energy Commission said it had been unable to find sufficient documentation of decontamination for 73 of 126 such sites or facilities once used by it or by the Manhattan Engineering District. Eventually 26 of these were determined, some of them more than a decade after decommissioning, to register radiation levels that the DOE says "appear to exceed rules for unrestricted release." One of the first of these scheduled by Ramsey for remedial action was a New Jersey tract where the contamination has been traced in part to 1942 and the brief passage there of the K-65 Belgian Congo ore that went into the building of Fermi's Chicago reactor—the material which now reposes in and around the silo at Lewiston.

The site of the former Perry Sampling Plant stands about 5 miles north of New Brunswick, on Mountain Road in Middlesex Township, New Jersey, between a row of houses and a culvert for the Lehigh Valley Railroad. Fenced off from the street and its immediate neighbors, the 18-acre tract contains two buildings; the smaller, one story of whitewashed cinderblock, faces the road. Behind it is a cavernous two-story structure where the old K 65 ore was ground and chemically tested back in 1942. Uranium ore continued to be processed there until 1955, and after that to be stored there until 1966 or 1967, when the site was purportedly decontaminated for the second time—a first attempt was made in 1950 while the plant was still working on the ore. Cleared for unrestricted occupancy in this second effort, it was claimed for use by a reserve motor transport battalion of United States Marines—the processing building made an excellent barracks, gymnasium and training center, and the smaller building was the outfit's headquarters—until 1977, when the Department of Energy's check of formerly utilized sites turned up abnormally high radiation readings in and around the larger building's sump. Apparently rubble and dust from the exceptionally radioactive K-65 lode had simply been swept up and deposited there.

The sump itself would present only a minor cleanup problem, but the contamination has spread over the years. The DOE survey found radium at levels of more than 2,400 picocuries per gram—the Environmental Protection Agency's recommended limit is 5—in and near a drainage ditch south of the site, and 208 picocuries per gram as far away as a quarter of a mile downstream. The Marines had hoped to save the buildings, but even after ventilation was increased, radon levels in the larger structure continued too high for unrestricted use. And, as is often the case when tailings are involved, radioactive fill was found beneath nearby sites. Aerial surveys led technicians to a residence a few blocks away and to the rectory of a Catholic church about a mile distant. Both appeared to have been constructed on foundations of radioactive tailings taken from the plant.

In the summer of 1980, just before the third decontamination of the Perry site, I drove to Middlesex to talk to John Cavendish and Robert Kispert, executives of National Lead of Ohio, one of DOE's principal nuclear contractors. In addition to operating its own uranium feed-materials production plant at Fernald, Ohio, the company holds the maintenance contracts for the Lake Ontario Ordnance Works (the site of the silo filled with tailings), and for two sites at Weldon Springs, Mo., where uranium-refining wastes were once processed. Cavendish, a former chemical process foreman now in his early sixties, became director of NLOO's decontamination and decommissioning division when it was established in 1979; Kispert, in his mid-forties, is head of the division's engineering department, which has drawn up a forty-one-page book of specifications for the work, which, Cavendish explained, will begin with "the laying of an impervious asphalt storage pad 300 to 400 feet that will be large enough to handle all the contaminated soil in this job. It will be constructed with perimeter trenches that will discharge into a controlled basin with air and water radiation monitoring.

"Then we'll clean up the two properties, the church and the residence, where the fill was used. It's possible, and our surveys give us some reason to hope, that the fill was not put beneath the buildings themselves but used to build up the surrounding land. That would make our decontamination job easier, but we won't know, though, until we begin the digging and take samples.

"After that, we'll scrape [a surface layer from] twenty-eight properties, three or four industrial, the rest residential, which border the plant, and decontaminate the drainage ditch, which we may have to clear for half a mile. We'll take all the material we scrape up and put it on the asphalt pad, seal it in a rubber covering—we call it an envelope—and cover that with a couple of feet of topsoil. In the final stage of the work, we'll dig up the envelope and move it and its contents to the yet-to-be specified final disposal repository, take down the buildings and decommission the entire site."

Cavendish's "ballpark estimate" on the total cleanup was $5 million, "including the cost of replacing the birch and silver maple trees around the perimeter of the plant—not that you can really replace an adult tree." I asked what the reception had been in the neighborhood to this new decontamination, and according to Kispert, it was "pretty good so far. We presented our plan at a public meeting called by the mayor of Middlesex, and about eight or ten people from the community showed up to listen. The vibes, as far as we can tell, are that people are glad to see that the work is finally going to be done."

The neighbors I talked to along Mountain Road, on some of the properties that will have to be scraped, seemed less glad than resigned to the decontamination. Ken Kohl, who restores furniture at a workshop a few doors down the street, said he bought his property two years earlier without knowing the site's history. "They've sent us all the surveys—the file's as big as a phone directory, and the results are so much Greek to me. But as far as I'm concerned, that plant doesn't bother me—hell, it's been there for years."

Next-door, I found Mrs. Mary Volgy, whose garden has been found to register radiation levels that are up to ten times the Environmental Protection Agency's recommended limit. "After they told me that, I didn't eat anything out of the garden last year," she said, "but the woman next-door to me, and she's even closer to the processing building, she has a garden and she ate from it. What can I say? They do what they want, these people, and they don't count me much, I don't think. I never went to any of the meetings they held; nobody from around here did—what could we say?"

The Department of Energy's fiscal year 1981 program summary draft lists the work at Middlesex and the other twenty-five sites to be decontaminated as part of an overall remedial-action program which also includes the cleanup of 25 inactive or abandoned mill tailings piles, and says it expects to spend $50 to $70 million annually on these efforts—and on a program to remove tailings from beneath buildings in Grand Junction, Colo. Since Richard Campbell, director of the inactive mill tailings work, told me he expects to spend $480 million over the next 7 years, there would not appear to be much left for Ramsey's remedial-action work for at least that period, but in any case, the DOE appears to have made a better start than the Nuclear Regulatory Commission and the Agreement States at cleaning up some of the still-contaminated nuclear sites that they are responsible for.

In principle, civilian nuclear licensees are supposed to present proof of decontamination to unrestricted use before they are allowed to turn over a site or go out of business. However, ever since 1971, when a manufacturer of sealed radiation sources simply abandoned a plant near Clinton, Tenn., leaving behind a $110,000 decontamination job, which the state and federal governments agreed to share, increasing numbers of discoveries of inadequate—or nonexistent—D-and-D work have been made. Just a few examples from the past three years:

March 1978: Workmen remodeling a pipe factory at Washington, W. V., send up violent eruptions of sparks every time they put shovels into the ground. An NRC team finds "unacceptable radiation" in the soil from thorium and flammable zirconium which appear to have mixed together after "discreet burials." The site's former occupant, a division of the Amax Corporation, denies responsibility and points to a previous occupant, the Carborundum Corp. The question of responsibility is still pending; the firm that planned to occupy the site has relocated elsewhere.

October 1979: Arizona Governor Bruce Babbitt calls out the National Guard to help state Atomic Energy Commission technicians pack up drums of tritium and ship them to storage at an Army depot after a Tucson plant which made luminous signs and digital instruments was ordered closed for repeated off-site contamination. The plant's immediate neighbor, the Tucson public school central kitchen, also had to be closed after one of its cakes was found to be laced with tritium at concentrations more than twice the maximum permissible in drinking water. The cost of decontamination fell entirely on the state and city —the firm, American Atomics, declared bankruptcy. Several months later, the Tucson City Council banned the local manufacture of most products using radioactive material.

January 1980: Michigan authorities checking for non-nuclear contamination at a chemical plant outside Lansing turn up 300,-000 buried barrels of low-level wastes. Apparently these derived from the processing of ore years before by a company that had sold the plant to its present, unaware, operator.

February 1980: In Between, a Galveston publication, reports Texas Department of Health data on eight different sites that have been contaminated by operations of a peripatetic—and now defunct—company that produced shielded radiation sources used in petroleum exploration. One of these sites is now partially occupied by an office building for Brazoria County, a few miles south of Houston.

March 1980: The State of Georgia moves to take over the decontamination of the Luminous Processes Co. plant in Athens. The company, which produced watch dials and instruments illuminated by radium and tritium, has gone out of business, and a contractor hired for the work has walked off the property, leaving, above ground and unguarded, a highly contaminated septic system and barrels of waste taken from it.

March 1980: The *Village Voice* in New York reports that the National Park Service is having second thoughts about converting the former site of United Nuclear Corporation's plutonium research center near Pawling, N.Y., into a way station on the Appalachian Trail. The plant shut down after a 1972 accident which blew powdered plutonium—the most dangerous form of the most dangerous element—out two windows of the place. After a $3-million decontamination, the property was purchased for $900,000 in 1979 by the Park Service—which appears to have been unaware of residual contamination which its contractors have now measured in the soil and in aptly named Nuclear Lake, where the plant used to be allowed to pour 1,000 gallons of its radioactive effluents annually under a federal discharge permit. The Nuclear Regulatory Commission official who released United Nuclear from its license, William T. Crow, maintains that the entire tract was decontaminated to "the most restrictive criteria we had in the United States." Nevertheless, the Park Service now finds it necessary to keep caretakers at the site to tell hunters and hikers of its history and to warn them that they visit it at their own risk.

Late in 1980, I talked to Crow and his boss, R. G. Page, acting chief of the NRC's uranium-fuel licensing branch at the agency's office in Silver Spring, Md., and they told me of measures that have been taken in the past several years to strengthen decontamination requirements for nuclear operations that seek to give up their licenses. "Even before we issue a license," Crow pointed out, "we specify in it that the plant eventually will have to be decontaminated to a point where we can release it for general use."

"Then, before we let the license expire," Page put in, "we also require its holder to perform a survey and determine that all levels of contamination are reduced to below specified levels —that survey can cost anywhere from $20,000 to $100,000 for a large installation—and even after that, we ask our own inspection and enforcement people to confirm that these limits have been met. For some of the really large installations, we may even call in outside contractors to help in the verification."

Page also told me that like the Department of Energy, the NRC is going back in its files to see whether it can determine if its AEC predecessor may have prematurely released licensed sites without verifying their decontamination. This check, however, only includes licenses in the non-Agreement States, and those that may have been released before a state signed the agreement. Beginning with eight thousand dockets, the number of these suspect sites was reduced to two hundred, "operations with either large quantities or long half-lives." Eventually the number of files found not to contain documentary proof of decontamination was reduced to fifty. "On those," Page said, "if we can't finally establish that a conformity study was made, we'll go out and do it ourselves."

For the most part, however, Page's responsibilities deal with emergency planning and licensing of uranium facilities. "Decontamination work," he told me, "is a smaller part of that effort." I asked how many people the NRC has working full time on insuring present D and D and checking on past lapses. "Well," said Page, not at all nonplussed, "actually not one full person. Essentially, I handle it myself, and I'd estimate that it takes up about one one-hundredth of my time."

9
TRANSPORTATION

In twenty-seven years as a reporter, I have covered plenty of disorderly—sometimes even chaotic—public proceedings. However, the Department of Transportation's June 13, 1980, hearing in New York City dealing with the transport of nuclear materials, and specifically of spent reactor fuel, was the only one I thought really might end in a riot. I feared for the safety of the three DOT officials and their clerks—and the fact that this event took place in the auditorium at New York Police Headquarters Building should be an indication of the emotional frenzy that the issue of radwaste transport arouses.

The purpose of this all-day hearing (it began shortly after nine-thirty and, with recesses for lunch and dinner, ran until a few minutes before eleven in the evening) was to receive public comment on a DOT ruling that proposed to overturn restrictions that New York City and more than a hundred other jurisdictions have maintained on radioactive materials transport. In New York, these restrictions have been challenged by Brookhaven National Laboratory, which operates two reactors out on Long Island, and by the Long Island Lighting Company utility, which has a reactor under construction—there is no land route off Long Island which does not pass through New York City. The city's position is that spent fuel can be barged around it, but Brookhaven says this is even less practical than the security precautions enforced upon its shippers before the city enacted its total ban in 1976. For the preceding fifteen years, Brookhaven spent fuel moved through the city only after midnight under heavy guard—and by one of the most circuitous and environmentally impacting routes that could have been devised. To get from Nassau County on Long Island to the New York City approach to the George Washington Bridge across the Hudson River to New Jersey, these shipments, in effect, traveled the circumference of a horseshoe, detouring nine miles for what amounted to a tour of some of the most crowded streets of the Borough of Queens and midtown Manhattan.

The cause of this detour is that a direct route, from one prong of the horseshoe to the other, would have traversed either of two Long Island Sound bridges that are operated under the independent jurisdiction of the Triborough Bridge and Tunnel Authority, which had routinely banned nuclear shipments in 1961 after its insurance carrier raised premiums for the coverage. I have checked the Triborough files on this, and I find it interesting that neither the city, nor the nuclear industry, nor the shipping companies, and not even Brookhaven, which had to assume the extra expense of this detour and the subsequent security precautions it required, ever challenged the Authority's ban by so much as a letter of protest until after the city embargoed the shipments altogether by an amendment to its Health Code. The author of this amendment is Dr. Leonard Solon, the director of the City Health Department's Bureau of Radiological Control, and it is his contention that the city's population density makes both the Triborough Authority bridges and the mid-Manhattan routes unacceptable: "Spent fuel shouldn't move through the city period," he once told me.

Of course, if New York City is allowed to block spent fuel, what is to prevent towns and cities, even entire states, from adopting the same restriction? This question was specifically argued at a Ford Foundation forum in 1978 when Dr. Solon was asked by Columbia University professor of chemistry and nuclear engineering Charles F. Bonilla how he proposed "to deal with the mayor of New London, Conn. [which had just adopted a similar ban], who says, if it's not safe enough for New York, why should it be safe enough for New London?"

"In public health," Solon responded, "the size of the population at risk is one of the most important considerations focused upon."

"Would you say that if the expected consequences [of a disastrous release from a spent-fuel cask] were an order of magnitude lower, the risk would be tolerable?"

"No, sir," the city official replied. "You're not going to get me into that trap. One death is unacceptable; ten thousand deaths is a catastrophe."

Eventually, the New York embargo did spawn others—New London, for instance, imposed its ban after Connecticut newspapers disclosed that the Brookhaven spent-fuel casks barred from New York City were crossing Long Island Sound on the New London ferry. By 1980, according to a Department of Transportation survey, more than a hundred cities, towns and counties adopted restrictions on nuclear transport, many of them based on the New York ordinance, and several copying its language word for word. In December of that year, Illinois became the first state to attempt—by legislative act over a gubernatorial veto—to bar spent-fuel shipments. This legislation, now under challenge in federal court, is specifically intended to stop further shipments of irradiated assemblies to Morris. The clincher, however, was probably Missoula, Mont., which adopted a New York–type ban in February of 1980; Missoula is in the path of Interstate 90 and spent-fuel casks are too heavy to be carried on possible alternate routes around it, and this restriction, if unchallenged, would have required a 350-mile detour by government spent-fuel shipments on commercial carriers to Hanford and on Three Mile Island decontamination wastes bound for disposal at the commercial low-level site. Injunctions were obtained against its enforcement, and the DOT moved ahead with its rule-making proceeding with the intent of overturning all these bans. Public hearings and meetings are a requisite for this kind of action, and these were held in Akron, Ohio; Eugene, Ore.; Union City, Cal.; Philadelphia, Atlanta, Chicago, Denver, Seattle, Boston and ultimately and finally, New York.

The New York hearing at the Police Headquarters Building

in lower Manhattan began decorously enough. Robert Paullin, associate director of the Office of Operations and Enforcement of DOT's Materials Transportation Bureau, introduced himself and his colleagues—Douglas Crockett, a departmental counsel, and Russell Toth, an executive in the Bureau of Motor Carrier Safety—and set forth DOT's reason for making the proposed ruling: "It is estimated by the Census Bureau that there are approximately 53,000 jurisdictions in the United States ... Each of these jurisdictions could conceivably have its own peculiar and differing restrictions on the carriage of radioactive material ... Most people would agree that this multiplicity of differing local transportation requirements presents an entirely unworkable situation."

Two principal arguments against the transport acknowledged by the federal agency are the horrendous consequences that conceivably might result in the event of an accident or, worse, the deliberate sabotage of a spent-fuel cask in the heart of New York or of any city with many thousands or millions of residents, as well as the fact that no matter how thick the shielding, even truck casks weighing 22 tons and railroad casks weighing 100 tons and more are unable to contain all the radioactivity of the irradiated fuel assemblies they carry. The radiation that escapes, while it is not considered sufficient to cause measurable damage to any one person's health, would nevertheless be transmitted to pedestrians, to the occupants of passing cars, and —as New York City Mayor Edward Koch, the hearing's first witness, pointed out—to the residents of apartment buildings "which literally straddle" the approaches to the George Washington Bridge. Barging the casks off Long Island, the mayor maintained, would be "the safest method of conveyance along the congested East Coast."

The mayor departed to applause—not always the audience response to his appearances at New York public forums—and the 116 witnesses who followed him for seven-minute turns at the podium were received by an audience which peaked at about 250 midway in the day with a degree of enthusiasm that varied according to the militancy of their positions against the transport—the loudest applause being given to those who expressed vociferous opposition to nuclear energy in all its manifestations. One speaker appeared on behalf of the Purolator Courier Corporation, which, among its other enterprises, delivers radioactive isotopes to hospitals, and though he took no position on spent-fuel transport, he supported the DOT's proposed rule as a way of heading off any future local restrictions on medical shipments—an argument that brought forth boos, hisses and catcalls. This response was mild, however, compared to the one evoked by the opening remarks of Dr. Matthew Cordaro, vice-president for engineering of the Long Island Lighting Co., the utility that had announced that beginning sometime after 1983, it intended to ship spent fuel from its reactor under construction at Shoreham, N.Y., through the city. A pandemonium arose that made it impossible to hear either him or the federal panelists as they called for order. It was not until Dr. Paullin threatened to end the hearing at that point that the utility representative was permitted to read through his presentation. Thereafter, he was interrupted only once—by a burst of sardonic applause after he warned that bans like New York's, "if carried to an extreme could ultimately force the shutdown of numerous operating nuclear plants." The applause subsided when he continued, ". . . and a concomitant loss of electricity for millions of Americans."

Long Island Lighting's objections to water transport of the spent fuel included the additional cost—the utility has estimated this at $500,000 per year—and the contention that "it has yet to be demonstrated that water-borne transportation is inherently safer than overland shipment." This second point was disputed even by Crockett, DOT's counsel, who stated that federal surveys give water transport a safety preference. Dr. Cordaro's final argument was beyond rebuttal, however. The vessels carrying spent fuel must eventually dock somewhere, he pointed out, and "if Northern coast cities such as New York are allowed to ban these materials for alleged safety reasons, would other port and inland areas across the country continue to accept such shipments?" Then, with an understandably sarcastic, "Thank you for this opportunity to present our views," he left the auditorium stage—to a chorus of boos.

The backgrounds and interests of those who recorded their opposition to spent-fuel transport were extraordinarily diverse.

In New York City, I have not often heard representatives of the East Side Republican Club and the Village Independent Democrats offering testimony on the same side of an issue. Nor do I recall previously such a degree of accord between statements offered on behalf of community organizations representing on one hand the residents of Sutton Place luxury apartments, and on the other, Harlem housing projects. Even city-suburban barriers and state lines were transcended. Public officials from Rockland and Westchester counties and representatives of community organizations in those counties registered their support for the city's spent-fuel ban, and so did witnesses from New Jersey and Connecticut. Eventually, the ubiquitous origins of these arguments became an argument in itself. "Doesn't it strike you as significant that people everywhere are expressing the same sentiments and making the same demands?" Mitzi Bowman, a spokeswoman for a Connecticut organization called Stop, asked the panel.

After the dinner session, however, these reasoned presentations gave way to a kind of revolutionary rhetoric on the order of "Our next meeting will not be across a microphone but across a barricade," and worse, torrents of abuse directed not so much at the projected shippers of spent fuel as at the panelists themselves. In its last hours, the hearing caused me to recall accounts of political trials in China at which defendants were forced to listen without response to calumnies heaped upon them by parades of witnesses. In addition to being likened to Adolf Eichmann, they were called lackeys, bastards and worse. One young man stood at the lectern and simply repeated, "Go to hell, go to hell, go to hell," until the chant was taken up throughout the auditorium.

Still worse were threats directed at the panelists individually by people identifying themselves as teachers, lawyers (two said they were law clerks to New York judges) and doctors. The nadir of this was reached by a biophysicist with a doctorate who said he was working at Rockefeller University; his threats included one to "watch your three heads crushed like overripe watermelons." At a later point, a witness left the lectern to shake his fist in the faces of the three panelists. When this happened, and on several other occasions, a police sergeant (and I had to keep reminding myself that this was taking place at Police Headquarters) made an appearance at the front of the auditorium and remained there until order was in some measure restored.

Although the hearing was scheduled to end at nine, increasing numbers of protestors were still entering the auditorium at that hour—summoned apparently by some of the more vociferous nuclear opponents who had announced an intention to keep the hearing going, specifically by not allowing the DOT panelists to leave. As these reinforcements turned up and registered to speak, the session was extended—first until ten and then until eleven. The auditorium continued to fill, and at about ten-thirty one of these newcomers demanded that the hearing be extended indefinitely, claiming—correctly, I later determined—that 134 speakers remained to be heard.

However, some of those then taking their turn at the lectern were repeaters speaking under names that were different from the ones they originally supplied. The 117th, and final, witness was one of these, a young woman, who worked herself up to an emotional peroration. "The Department of Transportation," she cried, "is a sneaky, slimy creature rising from a nest of other slimy creatures!" As she left the lectern, half a dozen police officers ran down the aisles and cordoned off the stage while the panelists, their clerk, and the stenotypist quickly gathered their papers and were taken under guard out a back door. I never did hear a formal adjournment of the proceeding, and it is my belief that this sudden conclusion, ten minutes before the expected confrontation, was a pretty good piece of police work—arranged to forestall a rush onto the stage that I, and most other members of the audience, expected at eleven. Caught by surprise, the clamorous demonstrators in the audience milled around uncertainly for several minutes, but eventually allowed themselves to be shepherded out onto the street.

I called Crockett a few days later at DOT headquarters in Washington, and he told me that he and his colleagues had been hidden in a police parking lot until it appeared they could be safely allowed to leave in cabs. "There's no question that it's going to take weeks for some of us to stop shaking," he said, "and look, for some of us, this kind of thing just gets our backs up on the original issue."

Nuclear proponents in government and industry I've talked to have been at a loss to explain why nuclear transport, even above reactor siting and waste disposal, has become a focus for what some of them like to call "radiophobia." In February of 1980, the New York *Times* maintained in an editorial that "the presumption of safety in transit seems valid . . . Spent fuel, the most dangerous nuclear cargo, is probably no riskier to ship than liquified natural gas or the other explosive chemicals that are routinely trucked around the country." True enough, but at least liquid natural gas and these other cargoes don't irradiate the people they pass. As the NRC concedes, "since the electromagnetic radiation emitted from a package cannot be reduced to zero by any finite quantity of shielding, the transport of radioactive materials will always result in some population exposure."

Most transport exposure is received by those involved in the shipments (who should, at least, be aware of the nature of the materials they are handling). Less than half is absorbed by people who may or may not have been made aware of the radioactivity of the shipment as it passes them (or they pass it) in transit. Minuscule as these exposures are, they add up. According to Georgia Institute of Technology Professor Karl Z. Morgan, the dean of health physicists, in some cases "the estimated population doses from the shipment of irradiated fuel and radioactive waste are greater than those from the operation of the reactor from which they are shipped."

In its final *Environmental-Impact Statement on the Transportation of Radioactive Material by Air and Other Modes,* the NRC estimated a total 1975 population dose from radioactive shipments at 9,750 person rems, and calculated that this would increase to 25,400 person rems annually by 1985. "The predicted result of public exposure to this radiation," it says, "is approximately 1.19 latent cancer fatalities and 1.7 genetic effects in 1975 and 3.08 latent cancer fatalities and 4.4 genetic effects in 1985."

In 1978, after I began reporting on the New York ban, I

discussed these figures with a Brookhaven scientist, Dr. Walter Kato, the laboratory's associate chairman for reactor safety, and he made three points: "The 1.2 latent cancer fatalities per year should be compared with the 336,000 annual deaths due to all types of cancers . . . 30 percent of the 9,702 person-rem population dose is due to passenger exposure in aircraft carrying principally radioisotopes for medical use . . . about 26 percent of the normal population dose is a result of truck crew exposure." His conclusion was that "the hazards associated with transportation of radioactive materials under proper governmental regulations are minimal."

Minimal or not, the fact remains that people along the route of radioactive shipments must accept some degree of risk from nuclear fuel which may or may not (as is the case in New York City from the Brookhaven shipments) have given them any direct benefit. The most eloquent protest I have so far recorded against the imposition of this risk was offered at a radioactive-materials transport hearing I attended in New York back in November of 1977. Suki Ports, a Manhattan resident, was responding to a contention by a spokesman for nuclear shippers that the risk of being killed in an accident involving radioactive transport is only one in 200,000,000,000. "Your probability statistics don't interest me," said Mrs. Ports, who is raising two children in an apartment near the George Washington Bridge approach followed by the shipments before they were banned by the city. "I recently lost both my husband and my mother to cancer, and now I am a resident of an area where you are proposing to introduce what you say is an infinitesimal possibility of cancer or leukemia. Add as many zeroes to that figure as you like, and I still don't think one mother in my neighborhood is willing to take a chance that it could be her child that is hit by that infinitesimal possibility."

Subsequently, I have asked many of the industrial and government nuclear executives I have met how they'd reply to Mrs. Ports, and a representative and, in my opinion, the most comprehensive answer was provided by Leo Macklin, who heads a corporation involved in fabricating spent-fuel casks and transporting waste and is also chairman of a transportation subcommittee of the Atomic Industrial Forum. "Simply by going about every day in the normal life of the city, she has already chosen to accept that risk," he said. "She has chosen to work and live in this society with energy systems that involve risks, radiological and otherwise. If she's ready to live in a pup tent in a desert without any electricity, she might have a case, but as long as she stays here in present-day society, she is, in effect, offering to take this risk. All I can say is that in thirty years of nuclear transport, there has not been one death directly attributed to radiation from it, and that's not just in the United States but the whole world. I don't know if you consider that statistically significant, but I do know it's the best that can be done."

Of course, there have been casualties from nuclear shipments involved in traffic accidents that have had no radiological consequences. In 1973, for example, the driver of a tractor-trailer hauling a spent-fuel cask was killed after the vehicle ran off the road near the Savannah River Plant. The cask suffered only scratches and no radiation was released. On the other hand, despite Macklin's contention, there has been at least one death that can be attributed (although not legally) to a spill from a nuclear shipment in 1963. A warehouseman at a Jersey City truck terminal handled a seeping package later found to contain gold chloride contaminated by plutonium, and according to court papers, some of this plutonium, entering through a small cut on the man's hand, later caused a rare sarcoma. After the warehouseman's death in 1973, his widow accepted an out-of-court settlement of $300,000 to drop an appeal of a lower-court decision that no casual relationship between the cancer and the spill had been established.

The Critical Mass Energy Project, part of Ralph Nader's Public Citizen organization, keeps tabs on nuclear transport, and its report on 1979 lists a hundred and twenty-two accidents, with seventeen of them involving some contamination. Additionally, the organization says, "the near-total lack of adequate or coherent inspection or record-keeping activities by local, state or federal agencies of atomic shipments constitutes a major shortcoming in the radioactive transportation system. Because of major deficiencies in the tracking of such shipments, the reported accident rate understates the actual magnitude of transportation mishaps." The General Accounting Office also cites sixty-four incidents between 1969 and 1972 that were not reported as accidents but required some degree of decontamination work.

Although the numbers of radwaste cargoes are not separately broken out in accident surveys, the Nuclear Regulatory Commission's environmental-impact statement on transportation estimated that 7 percent of the shipments in 1975 were waste consignments, and it expected this to increase to 11 percent by 1985. In computing exposures, because of distance factors and curie content, radwaste accounted for 15 percent of the radiological risk in 1975 and is expected to account for 24 percent by 1985. Also because waste lacks intrinsic value, it is more likely to be carelessly handled than other nuclear cargoes, and therefore it probably accounts for a greater share of accidents. Sixty-eight of the 122 nuclear transport accidents listed by Critical Mass in 1979 affected cargoes either within South Carolina on access highways leading to Barnwell or occurred outside of the state but headed for Barnwell or other South Carolina nuclear installations. One of the more spectacular of these was the spilling onto Interstate Highway 24 near Monteagle, Tenn., of 46 drums of cobalt and cesium wastes from a Barnwell-bound truck that overturned.

For the purposes of transportation, federal law holds that materials of intensities less than .002 micro (millionths) curies per gram of material, "and in which the radioactivity is essentially uniformly distributed, are not considered to be radioactive materials." Above that, radioactive materials must be transported in accordance with the regulations of one or more of the following agencies: The Department of Energy, the Postal Service, the Coast Guard, the Federal Aviation Administration, the Interstate Commerce Commission, the Department of Transportation, the Nuclear Regulatory Commission and the Agreement States. Most nuclear shipments for defense purposes are made by the Department of Energy, and civilian shipments are regulated principally by the DOT and the NRC. A memorandum of understanding between these two agencies, last updated in 1979, gives the DOT responsibility for regulating packages and carriers of smaller quantities of low-specific activity non-fissile material, while NRC specifies shipping requirements for packages that may contain as little as one one thousandth of a curie of high-intensity materials, transuranics in particular, or as many as 1,000 curies of tritium. In 1979, in answers formulated to questions posed by a Senate subcommittee, the NRC maintained that this joint responsibility had led to "good working relationships . . . between the two agencies, and lines of communication are well established at all levels . . ."

Nuclear opponents maintain, however, that the result has been that neither agency concerns itself sufficiently with nuclear transport. A principal cause of the shutdown of the Beatty and Hanford commercial low-level repositories in 1979 was the arrival at both of dangerous, improperly packaged shipments, and in allowing Hanford to reopen, Washington Governor Ray enclosed with her executive order a letter from NRC's then chairman, Joseph Hendrie, conceding that the low-level disposal crisis had been "further exacerbated by instances of careless packaging and transport. Regulations and requirements were not being followed. It is clear that the federal agencies have fallen short in the vigorous enforcement of their own regulations. On this latter point, NRC and the Department of Transportation are taking further steps to tighten up our regulatory efforts in our inspection and enforcement activities."

In fact, both agencies have cracked down—to an extent—on nuclear shipment violations. In calendar year 1980, inspectors for DOT's Bureau of Motor Carrier Safety carried out 258 radiological safety checks (out of 3,362 vehicle inspections overall), and the agency also increased its scale of penalties: Fines that used to average less than $1,000 for violations of nuclear packaging or shipping standards were increased to a maximum of $10,000. DOT has also proposed to Congress a $25,000 maximum fine and the possibility of a jail term of up to ten years for violations that cause injury or death.

Most of the radiological safety checks that were carried out in 1980 took place at positions that DOT and NRC inspectors established at the three commercial low-level sites—which means that defects in the shipments and inadequately shielded waste packages were not discovered until *after* they had been transported hundreds or thousands of miles on the highways.

Nevertheless, according to Leo Higginbotham, chief of the radiological safety branch of the Nuclear Regulatory Commission's Inspection and Enforcement Division, "the emphasis we were giving to shipments to these three sites began to manifest itself, and things got better." He estimates that ten of his inspectors are still pulling 3- to 5-day tours "a week out of each month out at the sites." On one of these joint NRC-DOT visits to Hanford from October 1 through October 4, 1979, 8 of 14 vehicles inspected had to be placed out of service after the discovery of either mechanical or radiological violations.

In nuclear transport, a "package" can be anything from a vial containing a minute quantity of tritium up to a 97-ton cask containing spent fuel. The NRC expects the annual number of packages transported to more than double between 1975 and 1985, when it projects a total of 5,570,000. If, as it also predicts, radwaste then accounts for 11 percent of the total number of shipments, this will work out to 627,000 packages containing 1,110,000 curies.

Generally, because it is cheaper, most radwaste is shipped by truck or van, although, according to the NRC, each driver "could receive as much as thirty millirems per shipment." Additionally, the Department of Energy states in a publication of its Division of Environmental Control Technology, "a few members of the general public could receive as much as one millirem per shipment, or about one five hundredth of his annual permissible exposure."

Altogether, the NRC concedes in its environmental-impact statement on transportation, "shipments by truck produce the largest population exposure, resulting from relatively long exposure times at low radiation levels of truck crew and large numbers of people surrounding transport links." The "large numbers of people surrounding transport links" may not be aware they are receiving any radiation at all from nuclear cargoes passing them on the highways, and even the drivers and truck crew members usually have to guess at the amount of exposure they receive, since there is no regulatory requirement that they wear radiation-detecting film badges. In 1978, the South Carolina Department of Health and Environmental Control checked a Purolator terminal in Columbia, and its inspectors reported that "corporate management had suggested that we accept the company film badge records . . . It was determined through conversations with . . . employees that they had never been issued company film badges." (One practical result of this inspection was a suggestion to Purolator officials that nuclear packages henceforth be placed as far to the rear of vans—and away from drivers—as possible. Apparently the firm had not until then been alerted to this obvious radiological precaution.)

Tri-State Motor Transit, which carries more nuclear cargoes than any other trucking company, badges drivers on some—but not all—radioactive shipments. "It isn't required, but it is company policy," Earl Rutenkroger, nuclear specialist at the company's headquarters in Joplin, Mo., told me. "If we're moving new fuel, for instance, we wouldn't need badges; but if we're carrying wastes that give off radiation to any extent, we would use them. And so far, at least, we have not had any bad exposures. No badge has yet been returned with significantly high readings."

I asked whether drivers who carried these shipments received extra pay. "Drivers who handle routine radioactive shipments don't," he said, "but those who are assigned to spent fuel and strategic quantities of nuclear materials do get incentive payments—it's not hazardous duty pay, though, but compensation because the requirements in carrying those materials add so many things over and above what we normally expect of a driver and a crew. Also, these guys get paid by the mile they drive, and a lot of the things they have to do with these materials slow a load down, so they can't make as many miles as they normally would, so we try to make sure they at least break even on these shipments, and, if possible, end up a little ahead."

Also subject to interpretation is the applicability of the one-millirem-per-shipment estimated dose that the Department of Energy says "a few members of the general public could receive." Presumably, this dose would be transmitted to "those few members of the general public" unlucky enough to be subjected to unwitting exposure to the shipment at truck stops or gas stations. In 1979, a witness from a suburban New York environmental organization, Rockland Citizens for Safe Energy, presented to the state's attorney general pictures of a truck later determined to be carrying 80,000 curies of mixed fission products in the parking lot of a roadside diner at a crowded intersection. The truck, parked amid a number of other vehicles, was not only unattended—for at least half an hour its motor had been left running.

As for all other cargoes, shipping charges for radwaste are rapidly being jacked up by the oil crisis. In 1975, the cost of a one-way trip of a thousand miles or more for shipments not exceeding 73,000 pounds (including the weight of the truck) was 89 cents per mile. The 1981 long-haul tariff was $1.50 a mile, plus a 16½ percent fuel surcharge, which means that sending a truckload of hospital wastes, for example, from New York for burial at Hanford, costs approximately $4,645.

These shipping costs do not, however, include the costs of the packaging. The first packaging requirements, formulated by the Interstate Commerce Commission in 1948, permitted as much as 2.7 curies of nuclides to be shipped in containers previously approved for the transport of hazardous materials. The enactment of stricter controls was less of an effort to cut down on radiation exposure to the handlers of these packages than it was to reduce the exposure to film often found to have been fogged after it was carried on the same truck with radioactive shipments.

Petitioned by the international film companies, the United Nations International Atomic Energy Authority proposed standards—the principles of which were later adopted in the United States—that placed the primary emphasis in packaging on emitted radiation. Current limits now permit maximum intensities of one rem per hour measured 3 feet from the external surface of a package inside a closed vehicle used exclusively for this transport, and 20 millirems at the surface of the vehicle. In vehicles in common commerce, the limit is 200 millirems per hour at any point on the package surface and no more than 10 millirems per hour at any point 6 feet from the surface of the vehicle.

Most radwaste is shipped in Type-A packages—55-gallon drums and wooden crates are examples—which are required only to maintain their structural and shielding integrity during normal accident-free transport. In an accident, it is assumed that these Type-A packages would be breached but that their contents would not be widely dispersed and would not radiate more than one rem per hour at a distance of 10 feet.

Nuclear materials that would produce a significant threat to public health in the event of an accident, spent-fuel hulls, for example, or, as a general rule of thumb, anything over 20 curies, must travel in Type-B packages, lead-shielded casks or reusable overpacks which are essentially double-steel-walled boxes with fire-resistant foam fillers. These must be designed to contain their contents and maintain shielding integrity in the event of a hypothetical accident which throws the package off the truck or train and into a fire of 1,475 degrees Fahrenheit. (This is the temperature of the largest-scale gasoline fire likely to occur on a highway—as from an overturned tank truck.)

A and B packages are also labeled according to emitted intensities: Those radiating less than half a millirem per hour on the package surface take white one-striped trefoil (the propeller-shaped radiation symbol) labels. Between that and 50 millirems per hour, a package must bear a yellow two-striped trefoil, and above 50 millirems to the maximum permissible 200 millirems, a yellow three-striped trefoil. Only trucks and trains carrying yellow three-striped labels are required to bear "radioactive" placards.

Two kinds of nuclear shipments require safeguards over and above Type-B packaging restrictions. Transports of special nuclear materials, 5,000 grams or more of enriched uranium or 2,000 grams of fissile uranium or plutonium, are accorded special escort protections, including seven or more armed guards, to prevent diversion by terrorists or national enemies. For irradiated spent fuel, on the other hand, the extra protection essentially is assumed to be the package.

Unlike almost all other radwaste, spent fuel travels primarily by train. Because of the ban on reprocessing of commercial uranium, only a handful of power-plant assemblies were shipped from utility reactor pools in 1980—some California spent fuel was sent to Morris and some transfers were made between reactors with full pools to reactors with emptier ones. Most of the three hundred spent-fuel shipments made during the year were of foreign or government assemblies destined for reprocessing at Hanford, Savannah River or INEL. Approximately 90 percent of these shipments were made over reluctant railroads.

Since 1974, the American Association of Railroads has been trying to free its members of the obligation of carrying spent fuel and high-activity materials in common trains with other cargoes, and an association of twenty-two Eastern lines has now taken to the Supreme Court an ingenuous appeal that the "lamentably poor" safety record of railroads makes this mode unfit for carrying these nuclear cargoes in routine commerce. The railroads have suggested that they be permitted to restrict these materials to exclusive-use trains that will move no faster than 35 miles per hour—with shippers, of course, paying an extra tariff. So far, however, the federal courts have upheld an Interstate Commerce Commission finding that common-carrier protections are sufficient and that "no other mode of transportation is more suited to the economical carriage of these materials than train carriage."

Whether it is carried on trains or truck trailers, spent fuel must be shielded in casks made out of lead and steel (and in some cases depleted uranium) in order for these shipments to meet the surface emission limit of 200 millirems per hour. Then, because of the heat radiated by these assemblies, the massive vessels containing them must be filled with water or antifreeze, and some are additionally cooled by mechanical blowers to maintain their surface temperatures below 180 degrees Fahrenheit. In England, the *Sixth Report* of the Royal Commission on Environmental Pollution describes such a cask carrying spent fuel as "in effect a small-scale nuclear installation, with fuel, moderator and coolant." Also as in a reactor, the fuel assemblies must be precisely placed—and held in place in the event of an accident—to prevent an inadvertent criticality.

Formidable as spent-fuel casks are, they must be loaded—and unloaded—under 15 feet of water, and sometimes, like other nuclear packages, they are improperly handled and transported. In November 1978, Battelle Pacific Northwest Laboratories checked 3,939 shipments of spent fuel in casks and found 16 "incidents" of improper packaging. In one case, impact limiters were not properly installed; on five occasions, casks arrived at destinations with higher external radiation readings than permitted in transport; the closure bolts were not properly closed on 6 casks; on one, closure bolts were missing altogether; vent valves on 2 casks were not closed, and on one cask, in the only case where a substantial release of radiation was known to have taken place, a closure seal was found to be leaking.

Early in 1981, a total of 15 casks—9 truck and 6 rail—was available for shipping spent fuel from boiling-water and pressurized-water reactors in the United States. Most of the truck casks are designed to carry no more than 2 boiling-water assemblies—one, weighing 36 tons, can carry up to 7 such assemblies. The rail casks, made by two different manufacturers, can carry up to 10 pressurized-water and 24 boiling-water assemblies apiece.

With an annual volume of only about 300 spent-fuel shipments a year, these present 15 casks are less than fully employed, and a number of older models already retired now add to D-and-D waste inventories. However, if its plans for a repository for spent fuel are realized, the Department of Energy sees a need for approximately 44 rail casks and 14 truck casks by 1997, and 203 rail and 33 truck casks by 2005.

Overseas in countries where spent fuel is being reprocessed either for government or commercial use, 53 rail and 8 truck casks were known to be in operation in 1980. A principal supplier of these casks is Transnuclear, a company jointly owned by French and German utility corporations (American interests also hold a 10-percent share). Leo Macklin, who chairs the Atomic Industrial Forum's transportation subcommittee, is the chief operating officer of Transnuclear at its American office in White Plains, New York, and he says his company's plant at Lyons, France, is now building 5 casks capable of holding 12 pressurized-water or 32 boiling-water assemblies to United States NRC standards "because we have faith that American spent fuel will have to move sometime."

Macklin declined to disclose the complete price his company now receives for fuel casks, but he says "a rough figure is $5 million for a rail cask, although some of our competitors, Nuclear Assurance in Atlanta and National Lead Industries, for example, claim to be able to do it for less. A truck cask should cost you $1.5 million." In addition to selling casks, Transnuclear and the other companies also rent them for sporadic consignments.

Transnuclear's cask designer is Kurt Goldmann, a nuclear engineer with about 25 years of industry experience "in everything from military reactors to sodium-cooled systems." And I asked him to outline the process for building a cask and getting it licensed. "Before you do anything," he said, "you have to read up on the regulations of the International Atomic Energy Authority—for the most part, the United States NRC has been adopting IAEA specifications about three years after they have been put into effect.

"Essentially, what the NRC tells us is that if we follow its guides, it will accept our design, but if we go outside them in any way, we know they're going to look very carefully at it. So this NRC regulatory guide gives us an outline and quite a lot of detail to begin with, and it describes the procedures that will be used to evaluate the safety analysis report we have to furnish."

The rail cask that Goldmann has designed, and the Lyons plant now produces, is a container of 12 inches of steel wrapped around 8 inches of lead—"I defy you to penetrate it with anything," the engineer says—weighing more than 100 tons unloaded. "It cost about half a million dollars to design, and that's not counting the $83,000 that the NRC charges just to review our safety analysis, which takes a minimum of a year, and after that, they come up with questions which we have to answer, so it takes maybe two or three years for licensing on top of a year in preparation."

Quality-assurance control of spent-fuel casks is carried out by Sandia National Laboratories in Albuquerque, which is responsible for confirming that these containers will be able to withstand a 30-foot drop onto an unyielding surface, a 40-inch drop onto a cylindrical spike 6 inches in diameter, a 1,475-degree Fahrenheit fire lasting 30 minutes, and immersion under 3 feet of water for 8 hours. Computer-modeling procedures and scale-model tests indicate that the casks now in service will pass these tests, and Sandia has subjected actual casks to tougher ones. It has compiled reels of movies showing casks mounted on trailers surviving intact after being hurled by rocket-driven sleds into a reinforced concrete wall, first at 60 miles per hour and then at 82 miles per hour, another cask coming through an 80-mile-per-hour grade-crossing crash with a locomotive, and one burning for longer than 30 minutes in a fire hotter than 1,475 degrees. This last film was shown by a Sandia engineer after a federal hearing at West Valley in February of 1980, and after its conclusion, one of the area residents asked these obvious questions (which I admit had not occurred to me):

"Did you have a heat source inside the cask when it burned?"

"Well, no," the engineer said.

"Spent fuel is hot enough to boil water; if you had that kind of heat on the inside, wouldn't it make a difference on how much heat the cask can withstand on the outside?"

"Well, yes," the engineer conceded.

Other questions have been raised about the Sandia tests, many of them in the literature of the Sierra Club's radioactive-waste campaign. Its points include the fact that cooling fins had been built onto the obsolete casks that underwent these tests, that these fins at least partially cushioned the impact of the crashes. The new generation of casks now in service has no fins—they turned out to raise a decontamination problem. Also, it is highly conceivable that a cask could fall much farther than 30 feet onto concrete (from an approach to the George Washington Bridge, for example), and finally that many hazardous cargoes now on the highway, diesel fuel, for one, burn at temperatures well in excess of 1,475 degrees.

"Besides, what they don't tell you," Marvin Resnikoff, director of the Sierra project, says, "is that a few minutes after they turned off the camera, they discovered leaks in the cask that underwent the fire test." In at least partial support of these and other questions raised by environmentalists about the adequacy of the testing procedures appears to be a Nuclear Regulatory Commission decision in 1979 to pull two Nuclear Assurance Co. casks off the road after the discovery of metal warping in their inner linings—this after the pair had logged 295,870 spent-fuel miles.

In the summer of 1980, I raised these points with Robert Jefferson, manager of the Nuclear Materials Transportation Technology Department in the Transportation Technology Center that the Department of Energy established in 1979 at Sandia. Jefferson is one of the nuclear industry's most active spokesmen—he estimates he gives a hundred speeches a year "to anyone who will listen" emphasizing the safety of nuclear transport. He conceded at the outset that a crack "six inches long and four thousandths of an inch wide," did develop in the pressurized cask undergoing the fire test after the cameras were turned off. "It was a failure of the outer skin, and some of the lead shielding did seep out in the form of lead oxide, but there was no failure in the containment—the fuel would still be safely enclosed."

Is the 30-foot drop test sufficient? "The key word in that test is that it's on an 'unyielding' surface. Concrete by itself isn't enough to be called unyielding. To make an unyielding surface you have to cover concrete with a minimum of two inches of steel armor, and when we did this and we dropped the casks onto that surface, they bulged, but they didn't break. Hell, we did better than that, we dropped a cask two thousand feet onto compacted soil from a plane going a hundred thirty-five miles per hour, and although there was some distortion, it remained intact."

Is the fire test valid without an interior heat source? "A heat source inside would really have made very little difference. We calculated that it would have taken a ninety-minute fire to melt all the lead; the interior heat source might have cut this to eighty-five minutes. Actually, though, we found better protection than we expected, since we hadn't figured that the charring, on the outside of the cask, would slow the transfer of heat into the inner shell, so now we think we may have been conservative on our ninety-minute figure."

What about the casks that had to be pulled out of service because of interior warping? "What happened there was that in order to increase the shielding, the manufacturers had welded copper onto steel. The problems caused by dissimilar-metal welding are widely known, but originally nobody viewed that as a problem because these weren't structural members of the casks. When the manufacturer did discover the problem—and I think it's significant that it was the manufacturer that discovered the problem and reported it—the condition wasn't too difficult to correct on five out of seven Nuclear Assurance casks, and they are now back on the roads."

And the contention that all the casks now in service are essentially untested—that the testing has been done only on computer and scale models? "True enough as far as the argument goes, but you have to realize that these are the tests that are accepted on massive engineered structures. You design a bridge, for example, to take a rolling load, and the only way to test that bridge is to let the public put the rolling load on it. Look at high-rise buildings. Do architects test them after they're erected to see if they can pull them down? Our tests are done to verify that the basic engineering done in the designing of the casks is adequate, and we think they've shown that it was —and then some."

In the final analysis, however, even if the casks can withstand pressures of normal use and reasonable accidents, there remains a question of possible sabotage or terrorism—the commercial nuclear chain is obviously most vulnerable when shipments of irradiated fuel are on the roads or the rails. The Department of Energy ships fissile defense materials on the highway in "mobile vaults," insulated and armored trucks equipped with immobilization and defense features and usually disguised as moving vans, and these are escorted by equally innocuous-appearing panel trucks or small vans containing armed escorts.

Shipments of irradiated fuel, on the other hand, have been traveling in plain view for the most part, on placarded trailers pulled by tractors manned by at most a driver and an escort. Security is expensive, and the position of the nuclear industry, in the words of an American Nuclear Society booklet, is that spent fuel "is inherently safe from theft because of the high level of radioactivity." As for terrorism, the Department of Energy points out in one of its booklets that the casks "will withstand high-power rifle or machinegun fire, even with armor-piercing bullets, without penetration. . . . The casks would also withstand explosive attacks, such as one might expect with a satchel charge (several sticks of dynamite) or small bombs or plastic explosive charges that might be surreptitiously placed on the vehicle or dropped from an overpass. Even small thermite bombs would have no serious effects."

Physics Professor Bernard Cohen is a principal academic proponent of the nuclear industry, and when we discussed this point in his office on the University of Pittsburgh campus, he conceded the "possibility you could kill a fair number of people if you really worked at blowing up a spent-fuel shipment under the right conditions. Of course, if you blow up anything in the middle of Times Square at rush hour, you'll kill a lot of people. Once I decided to sit down and see how many ways somebody could kill ten thousand people, and I came up with a dozen methods, none of which used anything nuclear. Put poison gas into the ventilators of a large building, bomb a football stadium, those sorts of things. They'd all be easier than blowing up a spent-fuel shipment in the heart of a city. If terrorists want to kill a lot of people, that is not one of the better ways."

Possibly, but in its 1980 draft environmental assessment on Transportation of Radionuclides in Urban Environs, the Nuclear Regulatory Commission projects a possibility of 2,492 deaths (combining immediate and latent cancer fatalities by release of contamination and those caused by exposure to radiation from material not dispersed from the cask) and $3 billion in damages as a worst-case estimate from blowing up a spent-fuel cask at lunch hour in downtown New York. Also to be considered is the psychological damage that a terrorist might achieve by hijacking a shipment on the road and simply spiriting it out of sight. In May of 1979, the General Accounting Office concluded that federal agencies weren't being sufficiently protective of nuclear materials in transit.

Private security is expensive, of course. The 1977 report of the Nuclear Energy Policy Study Group of the Ford Foundation estimates that all suggested security improvements, including continuous communication channels for shipments on the road, would add one or 2 percent to the cost of nuclear-generated electricity. It might be less expensive to allow the military to take over the job of guarding spent-fuel shipments, but this is opposed by, among others, retired Air Force Lieutenant General E. C. (Moose) Hardin, a deputy assistant manager of the

Albuquerque Operations Office of the Department of Energy, which coordinates waste transport policy.

"I want spent fuel to stay a part of 'common-carrier commerce,'" Hardin said. "I want to contribute to the acceptance of the nuclear option, and I don't want to let transportation become the millstone around its neck. I would hate to see the country become full of federal nuclear inspectors, and I also would not like to see county police chiefs or state fire marshals meeting every radioactive shipment."

Under recent procedures, however, these county police chiefs and state fire marshals and other public-safety officials who would be called on to respond to an accident or act of terrorism involving a nuclear shipment have had no advance notification of them—and many even were unaware that irradiated spent fuel was being moved through their jurisdictions. In 1980, the New York Public Interest Research Group polled civil defense and emergency-response coordinators of towns and counties along the route of spent fuel coming through New York State from Canada for reprocessing at Savannah River, and of 31 officials contacted, 24 were unaware of this transport. A few interesting informal responses were also catalogued: "Hoo boy," said one county director of emergency preparedness when asked what his role would be in containing damage from a radioactive transportation accident. The mayor of one town along the route, when asked about local training for such an eventuality, responded, "I'm jogging every day in preparation, so I can get the hell out of here when an accident happens."

In October of 1980, after prodding by congressional resolutions asserting a public right to know the routes of spent-fuel shipments (and after the Potomac Alliance of Washington had verified and published several), the Nuclear Regulatory Commission agreed to make them public. It has also proposed another, still-pending, rule that will require licensees doing the shipping to notify governors of the expected times of arrival and departure of shipments from state boundaries, with these itineraries to be treated as confidential and only passed on to local law-enforcement and public-safety officials "as if it were national security information."

The release of the routes came several months after the NRC tightened up specifications for protections of spent fuel in transit, particularly when it is traveling on highways in urban areas —defined as communities with a population of 100,000 or more —or within three miles of such communities. In these areas, shipments are to be escorted either by local law-enforcement officers or by two trained and armed guards in separate vehicles equipped with radiotelephones to summon help if necessary. As a last resort, the trailers actually doing the hauling are to be equipped with devices that will immobilize the vehicle. These are to be operated from the tractor cab "when it is apparent that an attempt is being made to gain unauthorized control over the shipment, and there is no likelihood of avoiding capture through flight or early interdiction by local law enforcement agency response forces."

On the last day of the Carter administration, however, the Department of Transportation affirmed its intention to keep spent fuel moving through New York City and other jurisdictions that have sought to ban it. The rule published in the *Federal Register* on January 19, 1981, gives the states broader powers in selection of routes (and encourages them, in turn, to give local communities a say in making these determinations), but pointedly specifies that "a state cannot make transportation between two points impossible by highway."

The DOT said it "agrees that 'high consequence' accidents in densely populated urban areas should be of great concern, but not to the extent that public policy on hazardous material routing should be formulated solely on the basis of avoiding such 'worst case' accidents." And what about bans posed by independent highway facilities like New York's Triborough Bridge and Tunnel Authority? The DOT rule also lifts bans on the passage of radioactive material through "urban vehicular tunnels used for mass transportation," but granted states the right to determine "that a safer route exists which does not require the use of tunnels and other facilities" (so if New York officials still deem it to be "safer," they will again be able to keep spent fuel from Long Island off the Triborough Authority bridges by detouring it through the middle of Manhattan).

Before the DOT ruling takes effect on February 2, 1982, a

number of jurisdictions, including New York City, are expected to appeal it in the federal courts; if they are unsuccessful there, challenges of the resumed shipments in the street will have to be anticipated. As an appendix of the NRC's own draft environmental assessment of *Transportation of Radionuclides* puts it:

"If transportation policy fails to account for public concern for the potential consequences of future incidents, social impacts will likely increase, and radioactive materials transportation will encounter increased resistance . . . The political and legal attention given such transportation may escalate with the general controversy surrounding nuclear power. This attention may ultimately prove to be of more significance in decisions regarding the transportation of radioactive materials than strictly technical concerns."

10
RUSSIAN DOLLS

A Russian doll is one that opens up to reveal a doll within it, and that opens up to reveal yet another doll, and so on down to a nut-sized doll that rests deep within the interior of all the others. Rustum Roy, professor of the solid state and director of the Materials Research Laboratory at Pennsylvania State University, keeps such a Russian doll on his desk at the school's Materials Research Laboratory to explain his ideas on the disposal of high-level radwaste. Roy advocates putting it behind a sequence of engineered and geologic barriers that offer independent guarantees of isolation.

Roy's is not a unique approach—other scientists make the same point in other ways. What promoted this scientist into maverick status in the American nuclear community has been his persuasive—and publicized—attack on the make-up of what has been accepted throughout the world as the innermost doll of the eventual radwaste containment package. Since 1953, when a vitrification, or glass-making, process was formulated at Brookhaven National Laboratory, it has been virtually taken for granted that high-level waste in calcine form, or spent fuel dissolved in acid and heated until the liquid becomes a calcine, would be melted in furnaces along with frit, and the resulting mixture would be cast into monolithic glass blocks for repository disposal.

According to Roy, however, "glass chews up" under temperatures and pressures that could reasonably be expected in a repository. In 1978, he was chairman of a committee of eight scientists designated by the National Research Council to study waste solidification, and their report, pulled from the presses only hours before its scheduled publication by the National Academy of Sciences, called the glass form only "currently adequate for use in a first demonstration system."

"For the implementation of a large-scale solidification program," the Roy panel maintained in comparing waste-form alternatives, "glass may also be adequate, but on the basis of our analysis, *it cannot be recommended as the best choice* [emphasis in the original], especially for the older DOE wastes. In fact, a modest R & D [research and development] effort may well provide alternative first or second generation solid forms whose long-term stability and ease of processing are superior to glass."

In June of 1978, this report was unanimously approved by the Roy panel's parent National Academy of Sciences Committee on Radioactive Waste Management, and prepublication copies were subsequently sent out. Among those who responded adversely were the Department of Energy, which by that time had awarded approximately $60 million in vitrification research contracts and had selected glass as the waste form for the immobilization of high-level wastes in a $2.8-billion plant it planned to construct at Savannah River, and Battelle Pacific Northwest Laboratories, which had done most of the research studies on vitrification.

DOE's and Battelle's protests caused the National Academy of Sciences to stop publication of the report the following September, on the morning that it was due to be printed, and after an independent review, the academy decided to scrap it permanently—several thousand copies were later printed and distributed by the Nuclear Regulatory Commission, which had paid $93,237 in grants for the research. "I heard that in the end it got a wider circulation than any other NRC document," Professor Roy said later. "That's what usually happens to books banned in Boston."

It is at least ironic that this objection to vitrification came from Penn State's Materials Research Laboratory, which is known as a center for development of uses of glass. For the particular task of isolating radwaste, however, Roy objects to glass both from a process and a product standpoint. Vitrification, he points out, requires the highest temperatures of all the candidate waste-management processes—the $12-million incinerator I saw under test at Savannah River is designed to reach 1,150 degrees Centigrade. "In industry," Roy wrote in *The Bridge,* a publication of the National Academy of Engineering, "operations in the 1300 Centigrade plus range notoriously require continuous maintenance. No such high-temperature process has ever been operated in a remote 'canyon'-type operation." A canyon-type operation is one in which materials are processed sequentially in inaccessible hot cells controlled from shielded corridors, and, in fact, it was the failure of remote high-heating elements in just such an operation that led to General Electric's decision not to start up its Morris Reprocessing Plant, with at least a $64-million loss. "From a product viewpoint," Roy also maintains, "glass is ineluctably metastable [which the Random House dictionary defines metallurgically as chemically unstable in the absence of certain conditions that would induce stability, but not liable to spontaneous transformation]. Most silicate glasses are highly reactive."

However, the point that Dr. Roy says he would like to stress is that evaluation of all the candidate waste forms "should not be made independently of the other components of the Russian doll." These, from the outside going in, he specifies as "geographical isolation, deep-mine location, geological emplacement in a carefully selected hydrologic and seismic regime, tailored overpack—we're leaders here at Penn State in overpacks [materials that would be packed around the waste in the repository], suitable containers, and at the core of it all, the waste form itself. It, too, can be a Russian doll and consist of a composite with primary containment phases, coatings, matrices and so on."

This Russian doll within a Russian doll, Roy says, could be a "pellet of nearly theoretically dense ceramics . . . embedded in a lead matrix and sheathed in an outer layer of one to two centimeters of pure lead." This "Fort Knox" waste form, he maintains, "is now so chemically resistant that the releases which can be obtained under any conditions in the surface 1,000 meters of the earth probably cannot exhibit significant amounts of radioactivity."

Ultimately, however, it is the feeling of Roy (and a number of nuclear scientists I have talked to) that not even high-level and spent-fuel radwaste requires such extensive isolation. "With current technology, we can make it as safe as breakfast food, but when the public gets the bill, wow," Roy told a reporter in 1978. And in 1980, at his laboratory office at Penn State, he reflected that "in the radwaste game, it has become part of a misconception that people will accept inefficiency. Big bucks are going to come by making unnecessary glass plants, and the Department of Energy says that after all their research, they don't want to find out anything that will contradict what they've spent so much money to learn. I say, if nuclear energy is stopped because of all this unnecessary radwaste expense, well, it couldn't happen to a nicer bunch of guys. I still think the nuclear option is the way to go, but these people pushing it at DOE don't help the cause, that's for sure."

The scientific—and to some extent the political—signals on the disposal of radwaste are called in Columbus, Ohio, on the southern border of Ohio State University's campus, at the Battelle Memorial Institute, which has been described by its hometown newspaper, the Columbus *Dispatch,* as "probably the only United States institution with the capability and with the reputation for politico-economic neutrality to undertake this task with the credibility the American public might accept."

Battelle, established in 1929 in the will of Gordon Battelle, a steel magnate, budgeted $367 million in research on more than 2,400 projects in 1979, including the Office of Nuclear Waste Isolation, which came to it in July 1978, after two years of operation at Oak Ridge, where it was managed by the Union Carbide Corporation. The general manager of ONWI is Neal E. Carter, a nuclear engineer and the former research manager of the Nuclear Technology Department at Battelle's Pacific Northwest Laboratories, which is the principal scientific contractor at the Hanford Reservation, where most of the research work on the glass waste form has taken place. In his last three years at Hanford, Carter also sat on the Richland, Wash., City Council, an experience which he now finds helped prepare him to face the political and social issues that have become an increasing part of his work. "The waste-isolation program started small back in 1976," he told me when I spent several days at Battelle in the summer of 1980, "but our portion of it in 1980 has grown to $87 million, and it will be approximately $100 million next year. It's a five-year renewable contract, so it technically expires in 1983, but it's cancelable by the government at any time, just to keep me responsive.

"The real challenge is that the program has to achieve three levels of consensus, political, societal and technical—and these involve a lot of people. The political aspect addresses such things as dealings with Congress, which gives us the money and the laws. Societal means that somehow we have to communicate sufficient confidence to the public so that it believes the problem to be solvable, and that the way we are going about it is reasonable. If there isn't a consensus to that, politicians aren't going to support radwaste disposal solutions that the voters don't want.

"Technically, one major accomplishment of our program is a new emphasis on a longer-lived waste package, and we're beginning to move on the establishment of a better regulatory environment for the two federal agencies principally involved, the Department of Energy and the Nuclear Regulatory Commission. Our problem with them is that their regulations have been very quantitative and numerical. We think they should set general performance objectives that the entire system will have to meet, but not go so far as to set numerical qualifications for each of the elements in the total system. We think that restrains us—the regulations almost wind up designing the system. We feel that you need only the specifications that are restrictive enough to tell you when you have achieved the desired performance goals."

To some extent, however, these numerical criteria that Carter and some of ONWI's other engineers object to are required because the high-level and spent-fuel disposal system is, in effect, being designed backward. From a scientific—and economic—point of view, it would make better sense to begin by specifying a repository mode, and then designing the waste-packaging protections that will best complement it. Obviously, for example, the elements of the canister that will contain the waste form will differ according to whether it is going to be shot into space, which is one proposed solution, or left to melt into Antarctic ice sheets, which is another. Unfortunately, political considerations require that the packaging protections be demonstrable before a repository site is selected, and as a result, a substantial proportion of ONWI's budget is being spent collecting information on solutions that its analysts realize have little or no chance of ever being pursued—much less implemented.

As attractive as some of the more esoteric of these proposals seem to the scientists working on them, they are destined to languish in file drawers because of a recommendation to concentrate on mined repositories that was made by the National Academy of Sciences as far back as 1957. As the Department of Energy points out to the Nuclear Regulatory Commission in its proceeding evaluating its confidence on whether wastes can safely be disposed of, "the expansion of the current waste disposal program has built on work conducted for over 20 years." It also maintains that "the design and construction expertise required to build a mined geologic repository is currently available in the United States. Operating expertise will be available by the time the repository is ready for waste emplacement." Other federal agencies agree, although perhaps with a little less certainty, that a geologic repository is the place to begin disposing of high-level radwaste and spent fuel—even the United States Geological Survey, which went on record as recently as 1978 in a published circular which declared that "some key geologic questions are unanswered, and answers are needed before the risk associated with geologic containment can be confidently evaluated."

However, other disposal options have not received the same degree of emphasis that went into scientific investigations of mined repository proposals, and they therefore present even more unanswered questions. The principal alternatives—and some of the arguments against them—are:

PARTITIONING AND TRANSMUTATION: This involves a chemical separation of the different elements of the wastes—as strontium and cesium are now being stripped from high-level reprocessing liquids at Hanford—and bombarding each of the long-lived transuranics with neutrons until it fissions or fuses into a stable element, or at least a shorter-lived radioisotope. Among the drawbacks of this method are the extraordinary amounts of power required—possibly as much as was generated in the reaction that created the waste in the first place—the radioactive exposure to workers that would be entailed, and ultimately the fact that even fusion reactors, not expected until 2010 at the earliest, will only transmute about 10 percent of their target transuranics each year, inevitably leaving waste fractions that would have to be disposed of in another fashion anyway.

DISPOSAL INTO SPACE: In an error-free and energy-abundant world, this would probably be the way to go. The most dangerous transuranics would be separated from the other wastes, put into a capsule and rocketed off the face of the planet, perhaps into the sun or to a point midway between the earth and Venus, where they could be expected to orbit harmlessly for a million years. The obvious drawbacks are the risk of an aborted shot (as the British Royal Commission's *Sixth Report* on environmental pollution puts it, "the consequences of even one failure that resulted in the release of the wastes into the atmosphere would be so serious as to make the method quite unacceptable at present"), and again, because power requirements would make it uneconomic to rocket all the wastes, the need for another disposal system for the remainder.

DISPOSAL AT THE SOUTH POLE: The wastes, suitably packaged, would be placed on Antarctic ice and simply allowed to melt their way down to the land mass below where, the Department of Energy assumes, "several thousand feet of solid ice would isolate the waste from the surface." Drawbacks include the difficulties of handling the dangerous materials properly in transport in the hostile environment, and the fact that scientists believe there is a layer of unfrozen water just above the bedrock, and they do not yet know its destination or flow rate. Additionally, the United States is a party to a 1959 treaty on Antarctica which specifies that "the disposal there of radio-active waste material shall be prohibited."

BUILDING A REPOSITORY ON AN UNINHABITED IS-LAND: Suitably deep rock formations and isolation conditions exist on a number of islands both close to and far distant from our shores. However, as the Department of Energy points out, "the effects of severe ocean storms and tsunamis (tidal waves produced by undersea earthquakes or eruptions) must be considered." So must international relations; indications that the United States and Japan were considering joint funding of a $3-million study of the feasibility of building a spent-fuel storage facility on one of the islands southwest of Hawaii, brought a 1979 protest from the South Pacific Forum of twelve nations.

DISPOSAL UNDER THE SEABED: It would also be possible to deposit wastes deep below the sediments of the ocean floor, emplacing them beneath thousands of feet of ocean water within thick red clay that is believed to have been undisturbed for 10 million years or more. The wastes would be packed into bullet-shaped canisters which would fall through the water and dig themselves into the bottom for about 100 feet—the clay sediments would then be expected to fill up the holes behind them. Drawbacks include a lack of knowledge of the possible effects of the heat of the wastes on the stability of the sediments. There is also the possibility that, like the drums of low-level wastes dropped off the Farallon Islands, the heat of the high-level materials will attract bottom-dwelling creatures which could initiate the transport of contamination through the food chain. Again there are also international considerations—the 1971 International Seabed Treaty restricts this mode of disposal.

ROCK MELTING: Proposed in 1972 by Lawrence Livermore Laboratories under the since-discontinued name of DUMP (for deep underground melt process), this concept envisions the excavation of 200,000-cubic-foot cavities within silicate rock formations 7,000 feet below the earth's surface. High-level liquid wastes would be poured down into this cavity, and after it was sealed, these liquids would be expected to melt their way into the rock, enlarging the cavity over a 90-year-period to an expected volume of more than 130 million cubic feet. After that time, however, the diminishing heat would allow the rock to resolidify, eventually trapping the waste. Drawbacks to this concept include the possibility of inadvertent criticality if the wastes are not properly dispersed throughout the cavity and the possibility that the heat and the subsequent cooling effect could weaken the rock formation, allowing ground water to reach the wastes when, as the Department of Energy points out, they are "most mobile during the period of greatest fission hazard."

DEEP WELL INJECTION: Essentially this is an extension deeper into the earth of the hydrofracturing technique employed at Oak Ridge since 1966. Shales, which are essentially muds turned into rock, would be drilled into to depths of 1,600 feet, and then fractured by the injection of high-pressure jets of water. The water would then be pumped out, and high-level wastes, liquified and mixed with ash and cement to form a slurry, would be pumped in. The result would be a vertical succession of cemented waste wafers stacked pancake-like around the circumference of the well. The Soviet Union makes extensive use of this method for low-level liquid radwaste. For high-level materials, however, there is, again, a need to protect against inadvertent criticalities after the waste solidifies. Also, even for other-than-radioactive wastes, injection well disposal has come under suspicion since 1966 when seismic evidence appeared to involve operations at the Rocky Mountain Arsenal's 12,000-foot injection well, the nation's deepest, in a series of tremors in Colorado.

VERY DEEP HOLE: Theoretically, it would be possible to drill approximately 6 miles through rock formations in tectonically stable areas in order to pierce the mantle of the earth. Wastes poured to that depth would be isolated from the biosphere as effectively as if they were shot into space. Unfortunately, man has not yet been able to drill that deeply. Mineral-exploration probes have reached 4 miles, but vast pressures at that depth have made it impossible to keep these holes open. Going farther, the Department of Energy says, "would require a tremendous advance in the state of technology."

With the exception of the sub-seabed proposal, which is managed at Sandia Laboratories in New Mexico, progress (or the lack of it) in the development of these and several less-feasible alternatives to mined repositories is tracked at ONWI by Ralph Best, an engineer with particular experience in radioactive-waste transport. "The decision is pretty well made that mined repositories will be acceptable," he concedes, but it is Best's responsibility "to evaluate the other alternatives as they develop more or less on their own. Just to give an example, the National Academy of Sciences is pursuing a deep-drilling project, and we are looking at the information that is coming out of it to see if there is anything we can learn that will benefit our programs."

The data he collects, Best says, "gives us knowledge about the differences between the concepts and the risks and affects future decisions about where to allocate our resources, and ultimately how to dispose of radwaste. Besides, there always has to be something in our back pockets in case we need it. Who's to say we won't get a breakthrough that points the way to space disposal, for example? Right now, though, I don't think we have to spend the money for full-scale research and development of alternatives when everything I've seen so far shows me that the mined repository will be acceptable from a health and safety point of view."

Even Eric Rice, a Battelle astronautical engineer who is program manager for the study of space disposal options, agrees that a "mined repository is the best way to go at this point in time." Along with two National Aeronautics and Space Administration coauthors, Claude C. Priest and Robert F. Nixon, Rice published in the journal *Astronautics and Aeronautics* a comprehensive proposal to employ the space shuttle to rocket 11,000-pound packages of radwaste transuranics into earth orbit. Detached from the shuttle in space, the waste package would then be propelled on a 160-day voyage into a solar orbit.

I asked Rice how he would answer the safety question of an aborted mission with the subsequent possibility that a waste package might break up in the stratosphere to scatter radioactive particles and dust around the earth. "By designing a package that can withstand the fire and heat of reentry and the shock of impact," he said. "The concept would require us to design a package so strong that if it landed here in Columbus, we could go out and retrieve it without any adverse effect. We think we have the capability of doing this, but we can't prove it because we don't have the money to do a design test."

Rice makes the point that the interplanetary rockets all carried SNAP (space nuclear auxiliary power) generators, "and right now seven thermal generators with nuclear fuel are orbiting the earth on satellites, and these were all designed to reenter the atmosphere safely and strike the earth without adverse consequences." Ultimately, though, Rice yields to the other principal argument against space disposal—that it cannot conceivably handle the radwaste volumes, and that an alternate disposal method would still be needed. "But I still think that if we were to open our newspapers this morning and find that for one reason or another, mined repositories had been ruled out, we would be looking to space for our eventual solution."

The sub-seabed program is the one alternative to mined repositories that is not under Battelle supervision. Research on it is coordinated at a trailer office at Sandia in Albuquerque, and I talked there to Richard Lynch, manager of the laboratory's waste-management and environmental-programs department. "Our subseabed research began in 1973," he said, "and even if the United States builds and successfully operates a mined repository, we still won't curtail our program.

"We're looking at putting the waste in the middle of a stable tectonic plate out in the middle of the ocean, for example, west of Hawaii, where even the geology is boring. At one time, we thought we might drill into the rock below the sediments on the ocean floor, but we gave that up, and now we expect the sediments themselves to demonstrate the main containment function. We've gone down in them a few tens of meters, well below the depth of bottom burrowers, but it's still an open question whether bacteria might migrate down to reach the wastes. We are also concerned about possible radiation impacts on the fauna that are there, although so far, we haven't seen anything that would turn us off. In any case, this is not just a paper study —it will have a tremendous impact on the state of understanding of ocean sections, and I also think we are developing a knowledge capability that the United States needs. Even if we decide not to pursue a sub-seabed disposal program, there are other nations with less of a geological endowment than we have that will go ahead, and what we're learning here will make us a better critic of their approaches."

If a mined repository has, in fact, been decided upon, several questions about that mode of disposal still remain open. These include the nature of the waste form to be buried in it, the make-up of its protective packaging, and even the rock that the repository will be mined from. Despite the efforts of Dr. Roy and several other prominent physicists, the leading contender among waste forms is still borosilicate glass. The principal arguments for this medium, as listed by the Department of Energy in its environmental-impact statement on long-term management of defense high-level radioactive waste, are that the "technology is well developed and uses simple, easily available materials"; that glass will accept all the non-radioactive elements in the waste and most of the radionuclides—the exceptions are the noble gases and cesium, iodine and ruthenium, which "may have to be partially recycled from an off-gas system during glass formation"; that it will accept relatively high waste loadings; is amenable to casting in large monoliths compatible with relatively inexpensive steel canisters; and that these monoliths are "structurally strong, have good impact resistance and a high heat capacity [and] good resistance to water leaching . . . at expected repository conditions."

The kicker to this, of course, is the "expected repository conditions." Deep underground, these could be expected to include both elevated temperatures (from the decay heat of the waste) and increased pressures. Researchers at Battelle Pacific Northwest Laboratories, the principal promoters of radwaste vitrification, have now confirmed some of Professor Roy's claims that borosilicate glass crumbles under these adverse environmental factors. A Stanford University test on vitrified radwaste in brine (one of the rock media candidates is salt) exposed to 300-degree-Centigrade temperatures and high pressures showed disintegration in only one day.

One possible response to this is to formulate a better glass, which is what Theodore Litovitz and two colleagues at the Vitreous State Laboratory at Catholic University in Washington have done. "Ancients found they couldn't make pure silica glass because they couldn't get the temperatures high enough," Litovitz explained to me one afternoon late in 1979. "But the Egyptians found long ago they could make a crummy glass at lower temperatures just by adding alkali. It's this alkali content that now causes glass to be leachable."

The solution, developed out of Vitreous State's work with optical fibers, was to fabricate a highly porous glass without sizable proportions of alkali. When crushed into a dry, porous powder, this silicate material absorbs liquid wastes into its pores, and when the powder is again heated to 800 degrees Centigrade, well below the temperatures required by borosilicate glass and just above the temperature at which cesium, radwaste's most volatile element, begins to boil, according to Litovitz, "this porous glass collapses and becomes transparent, a perfect piece of glass, and now the cesium and the other radioactive substances are trapped in its crystals."

Critics of the "thirsty glass" procedure, including Dr. Roy, call it too complicated and point out that some ceramics, if equally treated, would accommodate much higher proportions of waste. Still, Litovitz and his colleagues, Pedro Macedo and Joseph Simmons, patented their process in 1980 and received a $723,000 DOE research grant for its development.

Anxious to get on with a working demonstration of radwaste disposal, the American Nuclear Society has urged relegation of thirsty glass and thirsty ceramics to "second-generation design," and getting on with the work in borosilicate glass. In the Germantown, Md., offices of the Department of Energy, G. H. Daly, who heads the Division of Waste Products Technology, says that "glass is still the reference point. You have to select one in order to write the environmental-impact statements, and logically, you choose one you know a reasonable amount about, and you evaluate it for costs and impacts and then evaluate the others against it. Of the ten or twelve alternatives suggested, we want to narrow the choice down with a fair amount of intensive laboratory-scale work to three or four to undergo the most expensive large-scale engineering process development and testing that look at both the costs and reliability of each of these and stack them up against each other. Probably around fiscal year 1984 we'll be in a position to select the best alternative."

In 1981, DOE expected to spend approximately $21 million —more than twice the 1980 figure—in research grants for qualifying waste-form characterization tests. In addition to the borosilicate and high-silica glass forms, the principal candidates are:

CALCINES AND SUPERCALCINES: Calcines are powdered wastes of the type gathering in the bins of the Idaho Chemical Processing Plant. Liquid wastes are atomized and dried at high temperatures, and these can either be stored as powders or pressed into pellets. Supercalcines are calcines combined with silicates to produce synthetic mineral forms which can be sintered into ceramic waste forms. Under normal temperatures, this is so far one of the most fire resistant and leach resistant of the alternatives, but at high temperatures, its leachability increases above other forms.

CONCRETES AND CEMENTS: These forms have the advantage of being well developed historically. Researchers at Oak Ridge National Laboratory and Penn State's Materials Research Laboratory are now testing concretes formed under elevated temperatures and pressures with a view toward increasing their isolation capability. So far, however, these forms appear to offer only moderate fire, temperature and pressure resistance.

GLASS CERAMICS OR TAILORED CERAMICS: Glass ceramics are devitrified glasses; clay ceramics are generally aluminum-silicate based. Mixed with radwaste, they appear durable chemically, but apparently radiation in some way may impair their crystal structures—it is thought that these may not be able to accommodate the decay of some isotopes to different elements without shattering.

SYNROC: These are synthetic titanate materials which Australian National University Geochemistry Professor A. E. Ringwood developed to hold radwaste, basing them on analogues of minerals that have persisted naturally without substantial leaching or erosion for thousands of years. Liquified radwaste would be blended with melted synroc at the ratio of one part to nine, and the resulting mixture would be pressed inside its eventual container at temperatures of up to 1,300 degrees Centigrade. Synroc is the only alternative so far to demonstrate low leachability at temperatures in the range of 350 degrees Centigrade; it is also best in fire resistance. However, it has a low waste-loading factor and is considered inflexible as a process.

MONAZITE ANALOGUES: Researchers at Oak Ridge National Laboratory have created artificial forms of monazite, a mineral found in sands in some areas. Monazite may naturally contain and isolate atoms of uranium and thorium within its lattice-like crystals. So far, studies have shown these analogues to have low leachability under elevated temperatures and pressures. As yet, however, large-scale production of these artificial crystals has not been accomplished.

METAL MATRICES: Yet another Russian doll. Calcines or glass beads or marbles or ceramic pellets can be embedded in molten metal. The advantages are better heat transfer and reduced brittleness and leachability. Oak Ridge National Laboratory is also working on a composition it calls "cermet" (for ceramic particles uniformly dispersed within a metallic phase). Although this appears to offer excellent stability and fire resistance, it inevitably adds another layer of complexity and inflexibility to the waste-disposal process.

Eventually the Department of Energy's environmental-impact statement on long-term management of high-level radioactive wastes approaches Professor Roy's "Fort Knox" Russian doll by envisioning the possibility that calcines or super-calcines could be coated with "impervious materials such as carbon, alumina or silicon carbide" before they are placed within a metal matrix. This layering of process upon process would be enormously expensive, of course, but as Roy pointed out when I talked to him at Penn State, "to do all these things together, or if they like, one after another, will still be cheaper if they'll only start doing them now than if they keep putting it off to select the theoretical best one in some distant future."

Whatever the chemical and physical composition of the waste form, eventually it goes into some kind of can—or canister, as the government prefers to call it. Under any name, this container has to be chemically compatible with the forty-seven different elements in spent fuel (exclusive of cladding), and with the elements that will comprise the sleeve and overpacks that will surround it in the engineered-barrier system. "We're taking the approach that the packaging ought to last at least a thousand years without any release," John Martin, director of the Nuclear Regulatory Commission's waste-management branch, told me. "Basically, that means the canister will have to carry the freight for that length of time." After the millennium, according to the NRC's published criteria, releases should be limited to one part in 100,000 of the packaging contents per year.

At ONWI, Samuel Basham, with 25 years of experience in developing reactor operating systems, is now manager of engineering development, and he points out that these stringent containment requirements are only the most recent stage of an evolution of packaging criteria that began with "more or less of a grocery bag. Originally, geologists said packaging couldn't be given any credit at all for containing the waste within a repository." I asked if, in fact, it would be possible in 1980 to design a package that would be demonstrably impenetrable until 2980. "We think it's do-able with the knowledge we have today," Basham said, "and with the kind of investment that people now seem willing to make."

There is one engineering question that appears to have been fully resolved, and that is the shape of the canister—and therefore of the waste form within it. It will be a cylinder. According to Basham, a doughnut-shaped alternative would have provided more surface cooling area but was rejected because of engineering problems: Present plans call for the package to be fabricated in a factory directly over the repository, and the cylinder would be easier to lower remotely through a tube to the emplacement area. The circumference of the cylinder will necessarily be limited, however, both by the diameter of the shaft through which it will be lowered and by the thermal power of the waste itself—if the cylinder is too fat, cesium at the center of the package could be subjected to temperatures that approach its volatilization point. Cylinders that have been designed for the Savannah River vitrification demonstration plant measure 24 inches in diameter and are 8 feet long.

Actually, as Basham points out, "packaging includes everything between the waste form and the host rock," so, his responsibilities also include the design of a corrosion-resistant sleeve to hold the canister, an ion-absorbing overpack (ceramics, graphite, carbon, glasses and several cements are under study), and eventually a backfill material which the Department of Energy specifies will have to be "relatively impermeable to water by reason of its physical and chemical properties." These protections will, of course, all have to be compatible with each other—and yet not so compatible that they will fuse chemically and make it impossible to dig out the waste package any time in the next century if that becomes necessary. Inherent in the system, according to Basham, is a "retrievability option" in case anything not yet foreseen does go wrong with the repository, or if future generations find acceptable ways to make use of the spent fuel.

If the shape of the canister has been settled, its composition has not. Savannah River Plant engineers completing the borosilicate glass demonstration project have indicated that carbon steel might offer greater protection than stainless steel —and be cheaper as well. Environmentalists and some nuclear engineers point out, however, that the experience of the leaking underground tanks at Hanford hardly inspires confidence that carbon steel can meet the 1,000-year no-release requirement. Apparently disregarding the cost factor, Gosta Wranglen, a professor at Sweden's Royal Institute of Technology, would not only use stainless steel, but for additional protection he suggested gold-plating the canisters and then electroplating a thick layer of copper onto the gold. Of course, this gold and copper would be, as the United States Geological Survey has pointed out, "an attraction for human intrusion." Eventually Sweden decided on a titanium container wrapped in lead and quartz sand and overpacked with bentonite ion-absorbing clay.

Another frequently suggested container material is lead, but Basham points out that "after a thousand years, the lead will be more toxic in itself than the remaining other waste products. It's a serious concern to bury a chunk of high-purity lead." On the other hand, he has even graver doubts about some of the recently developed metallic alloys: "It's easy to fabricate them; what's harder to do is demonstrate that they will last for thousands of years. Some of this stuff, we have gathered experimental data on for ten years. Big deal. The other nine hundred and ninety-nine will have to be an extrapolation. On the other hand, we have some high-nickel irons in meteorites that we can show have withstood exposures of twelve thousand years, and some early cements that go back something like three thousand years. Rather than take one of these new alloys that are easy to fabricate and try to demonstrate that it will hold up, I think it will be more practical to take a material we know has good exposure characteristics and work on how to build a can out of it."

Of course, the primary—and ultimate—protection is the rock medium itself. The Department of Energy says it hopes to qualify by 1985 "four or five sites in three or four different types of rock with potential." Until recently, this "potential" was expected to be offered only in bedded salt, found in half a dozen states, and specifically at the WIPP site in eastern New Mexico; domed salt, inland from the Gulf coasts of Mississippi, Louisiana and Texas; granite that is found along the East and West coasts and in the Lake Superior region, and basalts concentrated in the Pacific Northwest. Added to these in the National Waste Terminal Storage Program announced by President Carter in February 1980 were welded tuffs, which are essentially volcanic ashes that have been welded by their own heat into dense rock formations, and argillaceous rocks, which were formed from clay. Inclusion of these latter two candidates has widened the Department of Energy's exploration program to include all the contiguous states, with the possible exception of Delaware.

BEDDED SALT: This was the first of the possible disposal media to be explored, beginning in 1963 at Lyons, Kansas. Principal advantages are its demonstrable isolation from water

—its very presence indicates an absence of flooding for centuries—and its plasticity. Fractures in salt are rapidly filled in naturally and healed. Additionally, it is resistant to damage by heat and radiation and has a high thermal conductivity.

In nuclear-waste considerations, however, advantages have an abrupt way of becoming disadvantages. Salt's plasticity, for example: In October of 1979, Nuclear Regulatory Commission analysts told the Department of Energy they would need more evidence that the "creep behavior of salt under thermonuclear loading" wouldn't foreclose the retrievability option. Salt also turned out not to be as dry as originally thought. In fact, it is now considered possible that droplets of water in the salt beds could be attracted by the heat of the waste to merge in a brine that would quickly corrode most prospective waste packages. "Special materials with the potential to provide a suitable canister in brines exist," the United States Geological survey said in its submission to the NRC's confidence rule-making procedure, "but their cost, availability and reliable fabrication must be carefully considered."

Another disadvantage of salt is that its presence usually indicates nearby pockets of natural resources that may have been mined in the past (as at the Lyons site), or conceivably could be mined into unwittingly in the future. Even salt's insularity from ground water has now been challenged by relatively recent discoveries of breccia pipes (water conduits naturally formed from rock), believed to have been created when insoluble anhydrite formations that separated salt beds from underground aquifers were somehow penetrated. However, Wendell Weart, Sandia Laboratories' technical advisor for WIPP, assured me in September of 1980 that its site 25 miles east of Carlsbad, N.M., is "well away from the aquifer and reef where breccia pipes have been found"—which is fortunate, since three days after President Carter left office, the Department of Energy announced it was canceling his cancellation of the project and going ahead with plans to build "a research and development facility to demonstrate the safe disposal of radioactive waste resulting from the defense activities and programs in the United States." In addition to the transuranics from Idaho, this repository will accept, for its "demonstration" purpose, 40 canisters of high-level defense waste instead of the spent commercial fuel which originally aroused the opposition of the congressional Armed Services Committees.

SALT DOMES: These rose from beds deep in the earth, apparently squeezed by pressures through overlying rock fractures. They may be as extensive as 4,000 acres in area and up to 17,000 feet in depth. Most are now considered stable, which means they are believed to have stopped rising, and the Department of Energy already stores oil reserves in pockets mined out from several. From an original list of 263 domes studied as possible radwaste repositories, researchers have narrowed the number of prospects to 3—2 in Perry County in Southeast Mississippi, and one near Minden, about 30 miles east of Shreveport, La. The candidacy of salt domes appears to have withstood a bizarre accident in November of 1980 when a dome in active use as a salt mine under Lake Peigneur at Jefferson Island, La., was pierced from above by an oil-drilling rig. The ensuring whirlpool sucked barges and the rig down into the flooded mine, as the Washington *Post* described it, "like so many bits of soap going down the bathtub drain." Fortunately no one was injured.

GRANITE: These formations contain plutons, large bodies of unfaulted rock apparently formed as a single unit deep below the surface. Granite is strong and dry, with good heat tolerance and low permeability for water. The French have been storing high-level reprocessing wastes in granite caverns at La Hague in Brittany without reports so far of detrimental effects. Granites, however, are brittle and will deform under high pressure and high temperatures, and, according to the Department of Energy's draft environmental-impact statement on management of commercially generated waste, "thermal expansion of particular minerals (granite contains quartz, feldspar, hornblende and mica) may be sufficient to cause ruptures of rock and surface heave." Also, an Oak Ridge National Laboratory researcher, J. O. Blomeke, writing in a 1976 symposium on "Nuclear Power Safety," warned that natural joints and existing fractures in granites outside of plutons will allow "appreciable natural permeability," and that "even if rocks of this type could be found adequately isolated from circulating ground water, it would be difficult to guarantee their integrity over the very long hazardous lifetime of the wastes."

BASALT: This dense igneous rock shares characteristics of strength with granite, although its ability to conduct heat is lower. Near the surface of the earth, basalt is usually stratified with sandstone aquifers; however, deep formations appear extensive enough to accommodate a repository. One of these formations, as it happens, underlies the Hanford Reservation, which already holds nearly 65 percent of American high-level wastes, and consequently basalt has been under test as an isolation medium almost as long as salt. According to Raul Deju, director of the Hanford Waste Isolation Program, nothing has been found so far that would disqualify it, and, in fact, researchers at Pennsylvania State University's Materials Research Laboratory have found that under radiation, it combines with water to form a mineral that may turn out to be a better isolator than the original rock.

However, in 1980, in the thirteenth year of exploration tests in the Northwest's Columbia Plateau, faults discovered in the basalt beds below Hanford indicated greater vulnerability to earthquakes than previously suspected. Additionally, according to the Washington Public Interest Research Group, "the Columbia Plateau is undergoing a gradual downwarping (one foot every three hundred years), and joints in the basalt will develop with progressive subsidence. Drilling and constructing a repository would enhance the permeability of the basalt, and the effect of heat from the waste on groundwater flow would increase pressure within the rock, possibly causing it to fracture."

TUFFS: There are two forms of this volcanic rock, porous and welded. Porous tuff, which is naturally compacted volcanic ash, soaks up water—low-level wastes have been buried in it with good results at Los Alamos. Welded tuffs have additional strength and sufficient density. However, just the fact of the existence of either one is confirmation of volcanic activity in a region. Zeolite (a hydrous silicate mineral) tuffs have good sorptive properties—they would combine chemically with escaping radionuclides to hold them within a repository. The Geological Survey warns though that "phase changes starting at about 150 degrees, to 200 degrees Centigrade cause the release of free water and may preclude use of zeolitic tuffs for the disposal of hot wastes."

SHALES OR ARGILLACEOUS ROCKS: These have low permeability and the virtue, to a lesser degree than salt, of flowing under pressure, so that fractures will be self-healing. However, shales are layered into relatively weak formations; they generally contain a good deal of moisture, and again the Geological Survey warns of a possible "phase transition" that could occur when heat of the wastes began to boil off the moisture trapped within the shales: "Interaction among preexisting minerals, volatile components and waste will be promoted by high temperatures. Experience from the Geological Survey's geothermal studies indicates that hot moving fluids may alter existing minerals and form new ones, thus causing significant changes in permeability . . . accompanied by volume changes and attendant stress on the confining medium."

Before shales and tuffs were brought into its exploration program, the Department of Energy estimated the costs for building 2,000-acre repositories holding 160,000 canisters containing 68,000 metric tons of spent uranium fuel in the four original candidate media. These were calculated at $2.170 billion for bedded salt, $2.490 billion for domed salt, $3.150 billion for basalt and $3.150 billion for granite. If DOE should now, as it proposes to do, build a minimum of four sites—and they should be in these particular media—the total cost estimate would be $10.940 billion, which works out to slightly more than $18.28 per pound of spent fuel, in 1980 dollars, with the costs of transportation and temporary storage to be added on top of that. So far, however, according to the General Accounting Office in 1978, the Department of Energy "has failed, as of yet, to demonstrate" that "engineered structures can blend with geologic features in a way that radioactive isolation can be relatively assured for the next few thousand years."

Ultimately, of course, the "no-action alternative of leaving radwaste undisposed of indefinitely while the search for relative assurance of isolation drags on also leads to risks of accidents and inevitable exposures. One of the most controversial nuclear documents—beyond even the unpublished report of Rustum Roy's panel—is the 1976 report of Dr. Thomas Mancuso of the University of Pittsburgh and two British researchers, Dr. Alice Stewart and George Kneale, who came to the conclusion that low-level exposures received by workers at the Hanford Atomic Energy Reservation were responsible for a 5-percent additional risk of cancer.

The Mancuso data did not differentiate between waste-management and other operations at the reservation, but by volume 64 percent of the high-level wastes, 66 percent of the buried transuranics and 24 percent of the commercial low-level wastes are beneath Hanford soil, and even the scientists who have disputed Dr. Mancuso's findings agree that waste burdens at Hanford have contributed significantly to the risks whatever they are.

After matching the mortality and exposure records of 3,500 men and women who worked at Hanford after 1944, Mancuso and his co-researchers reported that low-level exposures had been responsible for inducing 41 excess deaths among 832 workers known to have died of cancer.

When I visited Hanford in 1979, I discussed these findings with Carl Unruh, manager of Battelle Pacific Northwest Laboratory's organizational and safety programs and with Dr. Sidney Marks, who succeeded Dr. Mancuso in analyzing the mortality data after the University of Pittsburgh researcher's contract was terminated by federal energy officials who made no secret of their dissatisfaction with his analysis. "We have looked at the Mancuso report," Unruh said, "and we think its statistical approach is incorrect." Specifically, he explained, the figures did not take into account what he called "the healthy-worker effect." Hanford contractors, he pointed out, require new employees to pass physical examinations and therefore, "most of those who come to work here tend to be healthier than the general population—that means they don't die of other causes as often as other people, and so they live longer to die of cancer."

Dr. Marks, like Dr. Mancuso, is both a physician and a statistician, and although he conceded that low-level radiation at Hanford may have been responsible for "three or four" excess deaths, "we feel his use of the numbers represents an exaggeration. For instance, he included six breast cancer deaths among women. We found there was one woman who had absorbed a really high proportion of radiation. Remove her from the study, and our breast cancer deaths come out less than average. Now, I'm not saying this would show that our radiation has a beneficial effect; what I am saying is that there really isn't enough data to pin down absolute statements."

Several months after my trip to Hanford, I sought out Dr. Mancuso at the University of Pittsburgh, and was fortunate enough to time my visit to coincide with one from his co-researchers, Dr. Stewart and Mr. Kneale. "The key thing," Dr. Mancuso said of their study, "is the latency of cancers—we used the concept of establishing the earliest cohorts that met the long latency periods." I asked Dr. Stewart (who became known as "the mother of radiation epidemiology" after her studies in the early 1950s linked fetal x-rays to the incidence of cancer among infants) how she answered Dr. Marks's criticism that the inclusion of the woman who had absorbed a "high proportion" of radiation skewed the study's breast cancer data. "You can't exclude anybody because they look bad or good," the English physician said. "That's against the rules of this whole game. And besides, although [her exposures were] exceptional for a woman, she was hardly exceptional from the whole."

And what about the "healthy-worker" effect? "That's a strength, not a weakness," Dr. Mancuso put in. "We didn't compare Hanford workers against the general population but against each other. It's an internal control of the study that all those in it were hired under the same procedures and given the same diagnostic tests and medical surveillance."

"What set the cat among the pigeons," concluded Dr. Stewart, "was George Kneale's finding that the mean radiation dose received was distinctly higher for people who died of cancers than for those who died of other causes. This clear-cut difference remained after all sorts of other discrepancies were ruled out."

In the long term, however, the furor that arose over the cancellation of Dr. Mancuso's research contract—and its assignment to Dr. Marks, who had been his federal contract officer before taking over the research at Battelle—exceeded even the dispute over the mortality findings. It is Mancuso's contention that the work's original concept called for a long period of delay before making evaluations in order to allow the gathering of data over latency periods of 20 to 30 years. In 1974, however, Dr. Samuel Milham, a researcher for Washington State's Department of Social and Health Services, did an independent study of the death certificates of 842 Hanford employees and reported finding significantly more than average numbers of cancers. Subsequently, Dr. Mancuso says, his federal contract officers called on him to publish findings that would refute these conclusions, but he refused, "saying that what I thought we had was false negatives. At that point the average length of time between exposure and death was fifteen years, and certain lung cancers take twenty-five to thirty years to develop."

When the federal government did announce that the Mancuso contract would be canceled in 1977—to that point $6 million would have been spent on it without apparent result—the University of Pittsburgh researcher called on the help of Dr. Stewart and Mr. Neale, and their preliminary findings, published in the authoritative *Journal of Health Physics,* set off a debate that still divides epidemiologists over whether radiation at doses long considered innocuous could have been responsible for the excess of 5 percent cancer deaths among Hanford ex-employees. Four years later, in 1981, the General Accounting Office was still complaining, in the title of one of its reports, that "Better Oversight [is] Needed for Safety and Health Activities at DOE's Nuclear Facilities."

Overshadowing this argument, though, is another that has arisen over the question of whether the Department of Energy canceled Mancuso's contract because his early results were not what had been expected. In 1979, Congress' General Accounting Office looked into allegations that the government was attempting to establish an official "line" which researchers had to support or face the loss of their contracts, and although its report came down on the side of the Department of Energy, it also raised serious questions about the subsequent assignment of aspects of the Mancuso study to Dr. Marks, his previous contract officer, and Battelle. Concern was expressed about "the image that results in an agency developing and improving nuclear power while at the same time using the same contractors to study the safety of nuclear power. The ramifications of this problem extend much beyond Dr. Mancuso's study to all of the similar research projects being carried out under these circumstances." In her account of the Mancuso debate, Constance Holden, a writer for *Science*, the publication of the American Academy for the Advancement of Science, makes the point that "the radiation research community has lived almost entirely off the energy and defense establishments. The situation is conducive to a monolithic approach to research and makes for at least the appearance of a conflict of interest. It also means that for anyone seeking objective scientific advice it is practically impossible to find someone knowledgeable who was not trained with AEC money."

11
CONSULTATION AND CONCURRENCE

This book began on the slope of a hill outside of Chicago where the first radwaste is buried; this last chapter begins in the Climax Mine, a radwaste burial demonstration facility that is 1,400 feet below the surface of a hill of granite in the northern sector of the Nevada Nuclear Test Site. David Miller, a public relations officer for the Las Vegas Operations Office of the Department of Energy, and I have driven about 90 miles northwest of Las Vegas and descended in a mine elevator to a surrealistic sort of subway tunnel—except that it is cleaner and better lit than any transit tunnel I've ever seen. Between tracks that stretch about 200 feet before us are 17 circular 5,000-pound concrete covers spaced about 10 feet apart, and beneath 11 of these covers, in steel-lined circular holes 18 inches in diameter and 15 feet deep in the granite, are spent-fuel assemblies. With the exception of the spent fuel put into the Lyons, Kansas, salt mine in 1968—and then hastily removed—these are the first American assemblies to be buried. And they, too, are destined to be exhumed by 1985.

I walked through the Climax tunnel in September of 1980, after the assemblies had been in place for a little less than 6 months, and at that time was able to detect no signs of thermal effects. Nor, as Miller stressed, had monitoring turned up any indication of radiation contamination. "The six wells that don't contain the assemblies hold electric heaters to simulate the thermal effect, and after the spent fuel was emplaced, we brought in health physicists with radiation monitors and challenged them to determine which of the holes contained the spent fuel and which held heaters. They couldn't tell the difference, and when they compared notes later, they told us there were higher readings around the holes that didn't hold the spent fuel because of the natural uranium and thorium in the rock."

At first glance, it appears that, like subway tunnels elsewhere, this tunnel has also been defaced by graffiti: Daubs of red spray paint are visible everywhere beneath the mesh of a heavy wire screen that covers the walls and reaches 20 feet up to form a canopy below the arched rock ceiling. "Before we put any of the fuel in here," Miller explained, "we painted each of the cracks visible in the rock. If at the end of the experiment, there are new cracks, we'll know they were caused by the heat. But we don't really expect them."

Then why the protection afforded by the screen? "You have to remember that when granite does give way, it gives way in big chunks," Miller said. Another point is that the mine is only a mile or so from the Yucca Flat nuclear-weapons testing area. "We make our own earthquakes here," the DOE spokesman explained. (Later, one of the engineers working in the mine mentioned—before he realized he was talking to a reporter—that a bomb test before the spent-fuel assemblies were emplaced had caused structural damage to some of the vertical shaft's engineered supports "even if it didn't blow any granite around.")

Nuclear security comprises another obstacle to the conduct of radwaste experiments at the test site. The Department of Energy would like to publicize the progress of its disposal programs, but bringing in reporters, or, in fact, anyone without atomic-energy Q clearances, requires complicated advance arrangements and escorts. On the other hand, the site offered a rather substantial engineering advantage. The vertical shafts that lead down to the experimental tunnel were drilled out for nuclear-weapons tests. "So we got a multimillion-dollar excavation without it costing the waste-disposal program a dime," Miller pointed out.

The subsequent cost to mine out the 200-foot-long subway tunnel and two narrower tunnels without tracks which parallel it on both sides and contain electric heaters was $8 million. According to Miller, each of the electric heaters in the three tunnels puts out "approximately the same amount of heat as an iron," and hundreds of radiation and heat sensors are hooked up to cables which snake up through the tunnel shafts to surface trailers filled with dials and gauges and experimental controls. Within the central subway tunnel itself, though, the most imposing visible object is a massive transporter crane which received the fuel assemblies as they were lowered down the secondary vertical shaft and deposited them in the experimental wells that are centered between its tracks. "We brought that down in pieces," Miller said with some pride, "and assembled it here. It can be operated remotely from the surface, but it was sufficiently shielded that the operator was able to be down here when it was moving the waste." Although the actual transport of each element from the surface to its eventual dry well required only 4 to 5 hours, the assemblies were brought in separately at two-day intervals because of elaborate rehearsals and measurements required for each emplacement. Later, I asked one of the project's engineers about DOE projections that 40 such canisters of spent fuel could be installed in one day. "They're living in a different world," he said.

From the mine, Miller drove me about 30 miles to the site of the E-MAD (engine maintenance assembly and disassembly) facility operated by Westinghouse. This is the site of the world's largest operating hot cell, a heavily shielded enclosure behind concrete walls, where radioactive materials are inspected by closed-circuit television cameras and manipulated by master-slave devices operated from behind 5-foot-thick leaded glass windows. Seventeen spent-fuel assemblies within steel canisters were received at this facility in 1979. Eleven have been placed in the Climax mine; five now rest in 25-foot-deep dry wells that are spaced 20 feet apart outside the hangar-like

E-MAD building, and one has been put into one of a pair of nearby above-ground steel-reinforced concrete silos.

The dry wells are being monitored to record canister temperatures, soil temperatures near the wells and radioactivity levels, and the silos, 21 feet high, 9 feet in diameter, standing atop a 6-foot-thick concrete pad, are being tested as prototype away-from-reactor storage units (even though the AFR concept is, for the time being anyway, no longer under consideration). One is an empty control, monitored for purposes of comparison with the other silo, which has held a spent-fuel canister since December of 1979. According to David Durrill, deputy manager of E-MAD, the inside temperature of this silo reached 250 degrees Centigrade the following August, and "now it's slowly beginning to come down." The spent fuel used in the Nevada Test Site experiments, Miller put in, "all came from the Turkey Point reactor pool in Florida. On the average, it was two and a half years out of the reactor, but some of the elements were as recent as a year out." I asked Durrill if its heat had had any effects either around the dry wells or the cask. "Not so far as I've been able to see," he said. "Thermocouples on top of the cask with the fuel in it show that the temperature at the top is only whatever the sun makes it, and as long as I've been watching anyway, as many birds fly in to sit on it as sit on the control cask."

The following day at the Department of Energy's building in Las Vegas, I again brought up the question of environmental effects at both the mine and E-MAD with Robert Nelson, whose nuclear experience includes four years on the staff of Admiral Hyman Rickover and subsequent management positions with the Atomic Energy Commission and the Federal Energy Administration, and who is now director of the DOE's Waste Management Project Office (WMPO, or Wimpy as it is unofficially referred to). "I think it's important to point out that we have put spent fuel into the ground an the world hasn't come to an end," Nelson said. "We have predictions that show the rock in the mine will distort, and the instrumentation has started showing those kinds of movements. You may have seen on the floor of the tunnel some very fine hairline cracks [I hadn't], but they are the only visible effects we've seen, and so far they conform very closely to what was predicted."

In passing, Nelson mentioned that he'd been having a problem getting enough commercial spent fuel to carry out the tests. "We could use another ten assemblies, and we'd really like to get some boiling-water elements—the ones we have from Turkey Point are all pressurized water." I said I wouldn't have thought there would be any difficulty in persuading utilities to turn over as many assemblies as the government was willing to take out of their crowded pools. "In addition to the insurance and liability problems like who indemnifies whom and for what," Nelson said, "the generators still cling to the hope of reprocessing, and they want to hang on to the uranium in case it ever does become of economic value again."

If more spent fuel does become available for testing, however, Nelson and members of his WMPO staff are looking at the feasibility of turning the southwest quadrant of the 800,000-acre test site into a more or less permanent radwaste disposal demonstration area. The Climax mine where the granite is under test isn't in this quadrant, but a formation of tuff now being drilled into for electric-heater tests is. In addition to its deep water table—a minimum of 660 feet below the surface—this area has the advantage of already being monitored radiologically to collect data on nuclear-weapons tests. The disadvantage is that this tract lies just to the west of Frenchman's Flat, where many of these tests take place, and just to the east of a part of Nellis Air Force Base Bombing Range. "Do you think it would be a good idea to put a repository right in the middle between them?" Nelson asks.

In fact, there are those both in and out of government who do favor using part of the Nuclear Test Site for radwaste disposal, and among them is Isaac J. Winograd, a prominent research hydrologist with the United States Geological Survey. He has suggested to the Department of Energy, and published in *Science,* a proposal to use a 322-foot-deep crater formed by a 100-kiloton nuclear explosion about 7,000 yards from the Climax mine for the disposal of transuranic or high-level wastes, maintaining that the potential for diffusion or transport of nuclides would be much less there, 5,900 feet above the water table, than at projected mined sites that are below the water table and from 2,000 to 3,000 feet below the earth's surface. However, the determination of the Pentagon, supported at first by the DOE in its submission to the Nuclear Regulatory Commission's proceeding to consider its confidence in spent-fuel disposal, was that "waste isolation activities must not interfere with the prime mission—nuclear weapons testing."

By the same token, however, if a repository for commercial spent fuel is considered unacceptable for any reason at the Nevada Test Site, which is the most contaminated land in the United States, by the government's own declaration beyond conceivable hope of ever being returned to unrestricted use, how will the Department of Energy ever convince the people of any other locality that they and their descendants will not be harmed by the siting of such a repository close to their homes?

Yet a repository, or at the least an away-from-reactor storage facility, has to be established if power plants are not to run completely out of capacity in their reracked and expanded spent-fuel pools. Between 1986 and 1990, according to Department of Energy figures, the pools at twenty-eight reactors will be filled to their new capacities, and the operators of these plants will either have to ship their spent fuel somewhere or shut down. The managers of several utilities have already cited the spent-fuel disposal crisis as a principal factor in their decisions not to build nuclear generators. According to the General Accounting Office, these utility executives "have stated they cannot afford to put themselves in a position in which their operation of power plants depends on schedules and projects for nuclear-waste disposal over which they have no control." As early as 1976, the California Legislature had enacted—and Governor Jerry Brown had signed—a measure that would prohibit further nuclear-power-plant construction "until the State Energy Commission certifies that the federal government has approved, and there exists, a demonstrated technology or means for the disposal of high-level nuclear wastes." California utilities have challenged this (so far successfully) in the federal courts, but in 1980, after Oregon voters had approved a similar proposition, the chairman of Pacific Power and Light Co., Don Frisbee, said nuclear power there had been "pushed over the cliff."

When it comes to defense radwaste, however, Pentagon, Department of Energy and congressional officials allow no state or local interference with their prerogative to establish and operate repositories on any land under federal control. In 1980, a Washington *Post* editorial described the House and Senate Armed Services Committees as "appalled by the thought that state governments, citizens, environmentalists and others might have any say over what happens within their jurisdiction." To make it clear that the effluents from weapons production were not ordinary radwaste, these two committees ruled that the government's radioactive waste would now be called "defense by-products" and handled apart from commercial material.

By any name, of course, military and commercial radwastes are much the same thing (although commercial fuel does spend more time within reactors and therefore its wastes are considerably more radioactive), and Congress had originally decreed in 1974 that both should be accommodated within the Waste Isolation Pilot Project, which would be the first demonstration repository. It then became the policy of the Executive Branch, as decided by President Ford in 1976, that the construction and operation of WIPP would be licensed by the Nuclear Regulatory Commission, and further that this NRC construction and licensing authority would be extended to subsequent repositories that would follow WIPP, and which would also accept both military and civilian forms of high-level waste. In 1979, however, Illinois Representative Melvin Price, chairman of the House Armed Services Committee, declared his "unalterable opposition" to allowing the civilian NRC even this slight measure of control over the defense-funded WIPP, and in February 1980 President Carter announced the cancellation of the demonstration repository.

In President Reagan's administration, WIPP has now been resuscitated. Once again it is being funded as a "demonstration" that high-level radwaste can be safely contained, although unreprocessed spent military fuel will replace for this purpose the much more radioactive civilian spent fuel. As a result, WIPP will not now come under NRC jurisdiction. However, present plans at least call for any subsequent repositories that the DOE constructs for commercial fuel assemblies still to be licensed by the commission. This unprecedented regulation of an operation of one federal agency by another is not only going to be time-consuming, it will be expensive. The NRC itself concedes that "the regulatory costs . . . would be expected to range in the millions of dollars, depending on the option selected, involving such factors as increase in staff resources and contractual costs for technical support for both agencies. Beyond that, the ultimate costs of such regulation, taking into account such things as cost of possible remedial action, cost of potential delay in DOE programs, and impacts on NRC's presently assigned waste management regulatory program, could run to billions of dollars."

Some of that money is already being spent. The NRC has contracted with two of the national laboratories to advise it on criteria to be used to evaluate the forthcoming DOE license applications and the subsequent preparation of environmental-impact statements. At Brookhaven National Laboratory on Long Island, a $2.6-million program to develop tests that will demonstrate the acceptability and future performance of engineered containment safeguards has been assigned to Donald G. Schweitzer, a photochemist with recent experience in radiation damage studies and radwaste projection studies.

As Schweitzer sees it, his program will show the DOE how it will have to "demonstrate the accuracy of the claims it makes on the safety of the proposed repository system. I will strongly suggest to the NRC that before it considers anything, that DOE shows that it will be reproduceable. The waste forms and any engineered forms of the package that look promising will first have to be tested over and over by DOE, and after that, we will do our own NRC evaluations."

An obvious—and important—question about this procedure is how closely the two federal agencies should work with each other. Early in 1981, Edward Hanrahan, NRC's staff policy evaluation director, proposed at an open meeting a strictly arm's-length separation: "My concern is having agreements made in Washington without the public being involved and them thinking it's a federal railroading job," he said—only to be squelched by Commission member Joseph Hendrie, President Carter's designated chairman, who called the proposal "garbage" and who maintained that "that's not the way this agency has conducted business since Day One."

Hendrie won the argument. According to Schweitzer, "the NRC point of view is that its responsibility is to carefully monitor the DOE program as it generates the repository's design so that mistakes aren't made—we have ongoing meetings on a weekly basis. I think the result will be a much better way of licensing high-level waste disposal procedures than, for example, we've had with the other wastes." However, even with the closest cooperation, the commission is on record as estimating that it will take a minimum of four years to review a repository construction application—and the DOE in its planning has allotted five.

Considering the inherent problems, even five years from designation to the start of construction of a radwaste repository is probably a highly conservative estimate. In addition to having to run the gauntlet of public hearings ("If we chased the examiners off the stage at a transport hearing," an environmentalist said to me recently, "can you imagine what will happen at a repository hearing?"), both federal agencies can expect to face extensive challenges in state and federal courts. Predictably, these challenges will be joined by the attorneys general of the affected states. By 1981, thirteen states had enacted legislation intended to bar their eventual designation as a repository host, and even though these bills appear vulnerable any time the federal government chooses to challenge them in court, at least fifteen more states were reported to be considering laws adopting some of the language of the first section of the bill passed in the New York Assembly in 1979:

"The legislature hereby finds and declares that the establishment of a permanent federal nuclear waste repository in New York State presents a potential threat to the health, safety and general welfare of the people of such state. The legislature further finds that there has been no proven technology which has been developed which has been demonstrated to be safe and reliable for the handling and disposal of high-level radioactive nuclear wastes. In addition, neither the federal government nor the nuclear industry has prepared reliable cost estimates for the ultimate disposal and perpetual care of radioactive nuclear wastes and spent fuels."

This legislation was eventually vetoed by New York Governor Hugh Carey, at least partially on Constitutional grounds. The precedent is Northern States Power Co. vs. Minnesota, a 1971 case in which state officials were blocked from attempting to enforce reactor emission standards that were more restrictive than Atomic Energy Commission limits when the United States Supreme Court held that the 1954 Atomic Energy Act gave the AEC (later the NRC) "authority and responsibility" over the regulation of nuclear "production and utilization facilities." Manuel Real, the judge who overturned the California ban on reactor construction, held this to mean only that "the regulation of nuclear energy [is] reserved to the federal government." The question of whether "production and utilization facilities" will also be held to mean spent-fuel repositories appears to be facing a prolonged legal battle which undoubtedly will be appealed back to the Supreme Court.

Regardless of the interpretation of the Supreme Court's holding in the Minnesota case, there is one state, Louisiana, that argues that it possesses a blanket immunity against radwaste disposal within its borders. In 1978, in return for an agreement allowing the Department of Energy to stockpile oil in several Louisiana salt domes, then Secretary of Energy James Schlesinger promised that state a veto against the future siting of a high-level repository. The General Accounting Office subsequently took a dim view of Schlesinger's legal authority to make that promise, but although it was formally withdrawn, Louisiana officials have continued to garner official assurances that their state, alone among the fifty, will not have to accept a repository without the consent of its Legislature. In the 1980 elections, promises to that effect were exacted from both President Carter and Ronald Reagan. "If the citizens of this country are to have confidence in its government," the latter wrote, "such agreements must be honored. They will be in my administration."

New Mexicans should be interested to hear that. They, too, had once been promised a "veto," and by the same Secretary of Energy, James Schlesinger, who made the promise to Louisiana. In 1978, Schlesinger told New Mexico officials that WIPP would not be sited there without their consent. However, in the 1979 federal law that established the demonstration repository, the state was granted only the right to "consult and cooperate" on the project. In 1981, the New Mexico governor, Bruce King, was accorded only the courtesy of a phone call on the morning of the afternoon that the Department of Energy announced that WIPP would, after all, be constructed near Carlsbad. The state's role, New Mexico Attorney General Jeff Bingaman was later quoted as saying, had diminished "from veto power to concurrence to consultation to cooperation to absolutely nothing."

Of course, if Louisiana's veto promise is ultimately kept, and that state is off the hook, that leaves Mississippi squarely on it. Exemption of the candidate Louisiana salt dome near Shreveport effectively limits the choice in that medium to two southeastern Mississippi prospects. Predictably, Mississippi and thirty-four other states under active consideration as repository hosts argue that if Louisiana has a veto, they should have one, too. Whether they do or not is the focus of a policy that the Department of Energy and its Battelle contractor call "consultation and concurrence," or C. and C., for short.

Since 1979, DOE has, in fact, significantly expanded its consultations with the states on radwaste problems; it is having more difficulty, however, in defining "concurrence" to the satisfaction of both the states and the federal government. (The definition in the second edition of Webster's New International Dictionary is "a meeting of minds; agreement in opinion; union in design; consent—implying joint approbation.") The Nuclear Regulatory Commission held a workshop in Atlanta in 1979 with representatives from thirty states, and its report of the meeting maintains that "concurrence was generally understood to be a process by which the states could raise questions to federal authorities and have them resolved satisfactorily, first concerning the broad technology and later concerning site-specific issues. States further suggested that nonconcurrence by a potential 'host' state would have the effect of holding the project in abeyance until the problems are resolved."

An obvious question is how a state is going to acquire the

knowledge and data it will need to argue effectively against conclusions that will be reached by DOE and NRC scientists who will have the primary expertise in the field and who will control the computer models which will point the way to the eventual repository selections. The NRC's answer has been a recommendation for a $500,000 federal grant to each affected state each year during the review process, since "as a matter of equity . . . the federal government should defray the costs reasonably incurred by the state in protecting the interests of its citizens," and inevitably, it concedes, "disposal of wastes in geologic repositories involves irreversible commitments, made in the face of unavoidable uncertainties, that may present some degree of risk to people for hundreds or thousands of years. It is in this context that the active participation of the state is most needed."

And if after all the consultations, the grants and the scientific arguments, what happens when the voters of a state either through a referendum or through their elected officials say "The hell with it, we don't concur; stick it someplace else"? To blunt the effect of that probability, the Department of Energy has embarked on an effort to involve as many states as possible in the early stages of its consultation and concurrence program. (There has been speculation that, in fact, this is what led the department to expand its geological explorations to include tuffs and shales, which originally appeared to have been passed over as candidate media—"the public relations tail may be wagging the scientific dog," a government researcher has observed.)

At Battelle, the consultation and concurrence programs are being coordinated by Donald Keller, manager of ONWI's communications department. "For a lot of politicians," he believes, "the real issue is how they can avoid appearing to make the decision—I know some of the governors would prefer not to. But as this is working, as we accumulate the technology and approach the point that a decision has to be made, we hope the choices will be clear to everybody involved. If we have agreement in the technical community that certain sites qualify and that others don't, we'll be in a better position than we are now."

Do you give the states a veto? "No, you don't. You give them something in-between." Such as? Keller wasn't quite sure. He was convinced, however, that "when you have a national commitment to solve the waste problem, when you have a Congress and President elevating it to a point where there is national recognition that it must be solved, and it will be solved, then the states will be ready to share in the responsibility of solving it."

Another question under study is whether the states and/or affected localities should be given additional financial incentives beyond the NRC's proposed $500,000-a-year grant for research for accepting a radwaste repository. Keller doesn't think these inducements will be necessary, but on a practical basis, ONWI's general manager, Neal Carter, a former member of the Richland, Wash., City Council, says that "given present federal policies, there is no place I would rather live in the future than next-door to a federal nuclear waste repository—especially in a small town with good political leadership. I'd get everything I'd want from the feds, and a lot more than I deserve." And as to a veto, Carter says, "the states should be able to influence the process in a significant and meaningful way, but that isn't tantamount to a veto." Significantly, WIPP, the demonstration repository for military wastes, was reinstated in January 1981, without anything more than a promise to the governor of New Mexico that he would have a right to federal "consultation and cooperation."

In July 1980, I flew to Wisconsin with Carter and Keller to preview the consultation-and-concurrence process at a hurriedly arranged public hearing at the State Capitol at Madison. Heading the federal delegation was Colin Heath, a veteran of the NASA and ERDA establishments, who is director of DOE's Office of Waste Isolation. One afternoon several weeks before, Heath had been working up a letter to governors setting out procedures that would be followed for "keeping state officials informed of the progress of the [exploratory] work" when he received an angry phone call from Wisconsin Governor Lee Dreyfus, who had just read in his hometown newspaper, the *Capitol Times,* that four counties in his state, along with parts of the Upper Peninsula of Michigan and Northeastern Minnesota were being explored for possible repositories in granite.

Waiting to confront Heath at the public meeting that Dreyfus somewhat icily summoned him to were representatives of Minnesota and Michigan, a couple of Wisconsin congressmen, a number of state legislators (one of whom was pointed out to me as having gained recognition by announcing his opposition to "a nuclear suppository in my district"), the capitol press corps, and at least four hundred vociferous no-nuke demonstrators.

The unexpected size of this last contingent led to something of a problem in arrangements. Originally scheduled in the governor's antechamber, a formal room with a capacity for about a hundred spectators, the hearing had to be moved to the chamber of the State Assembly, where the crowd of spectators filled the visitors' galleries and overflowed onto the Assembly floor to occupy the desks of the state's legislators. From a table hastily erected before the speaker's rostrum, Governor Dreyfus led off the meeting by spelling out pointedly what "consultation and concurrence" meant to him: "A partnership that will have to be based on openness, trust and certain processes and procedures, in which the state will not only participate, but, if you will, Mr. Heath, monitor."

The response of the Department of Energy official was both lengthy and cautious. "The point I want to emphasize is that we are not talking about doing anything tomorrow," Heath said. "We are talking about taking the necessary time to examine these questions in detail." Eventually, he continued, the Department of Energy hoped to qualify "at least three" sites in differing geological media in separate parts of the country. In any case, he said, the earliest conceivable date for actually putting spent fuel in a repository would be 1996.

The question that Heath was called upon most often to answer—it was posed in a number of forms throughout the afternoon—was, if Louisiana could have a veto, why not Wisconsin? "Really," the Department of Energy official responded at one point, "everybody who has studied this problem has said that if there is an ironclad veto, the process won't work. You're just inviting fifty states to veto, and you're back to square one." In that case, came the next question, "has any thought been given in your department to a moratorium on future nuclear plants, because obviously between now and when we dispose of it, we are going to have more and more waste?" "Some thought was

given to it," Heath conceded, "but our feeling is that we don't
have the authority to declare such a moratorium. That authority
belongs to Congress or to the Nuclear Regulatory Commission.
I think it's appropriate that they have the power to do that and
not the DOE."

And in the meantime, until 1996, when the first repository
presumably would be ready to accept them, what would be
done with the spent-fuel assemblies crowding the pools at reactors? "Is Wisconsin under consideration for an Away-from-
Reactor site?" asked a member of the state's Public Service
Commission toward the end of the hearing. "The answer is that
Wisconsin is not," said Heath, "but this whole region is. We are
interested in considering it, and we are asking the states to help
us in this responsibility."

Earlier in the afternoon, such a disclosure, that the Lake
Superior region was under consideration not only for a disposal
repository but for a surface-storage facility (this, of course, was
before the 1980 election and the subsequent Reagan administration decision to forego this option), would have brought roars
from the overwhelmingly anti-nuclear crowd. However, by this
time—it was well after four and the hearing had droned on for
more than three hours—the visitors' galleries had just about
emptied. Governor Dreyfus, too, had slipped out of the chamber, taking with him most of the reporters. After a concluding
murmur, the "consultation" wound down to what the DOE
officials later agreed was a satisfactory conclusion. "It may turn
out," one of them said later on the plane back to Washington,
"that the only way to get a consultation-and-concurrence program going is to leak it to the press."

This question of a state veto, coupled with the question of
whether the Nuclear Regulatory Commission will be permitted
even limited authority over defense "by-products" stymied
congressional attempts in 1980 to impose a high-level waste
solution. A House of Representatives approach principally promoted by Arizona Democrat Morris Udall, would have required
the Department of Energy to choose four repository sites by
1985 and the President to choose among them by March 30,
1987, with an anticipated objection by the host state to be
sustained only by a vote of both Houses of Congress (an amend-

ment to allow this veto to be sustained by only one House was defeated). This proposal was blocked in the Senate, most notably by Armed Services Committee Chairman Henry Jackson, because of the licensing authority it gave the NRC.

The Senate's bill was put forward by Louisianan J. Bennett Johnston, who, since his state's unofficial exemption, has become Congress' foremost advocate of action on radwaste disposal (asked by a reporter where he thought the first repository should go then, Johnston replied "somewhere other than the salt domes of Northern Louisiana"). The Senate would have required the Department of Energy to take title to the spent fuel and to spend $300 million to build AFR's until some indefinite time when a repository (and just to make sure, the way the bill was worded would appear to have excluded a salt-dome candidate) was opened. This foundered in the House, however, because it established only a very weak and ambiguous state right to "consultation and concurrence." These two policy questions were also being wrestled with in the meetings of the State Planning Council on Radioactive Waste Management, which President Carter established in 1980 with the intention, he said, of formulating "this country's first comprehensive waste-management program."

The state council, which met at 3-month intervals in different locations around the country, is, in effect, a successor to the Interagency Review Group of federal departments, which succeeded the original Department of Energy Task Force for Review of Nuclear Waste Management. This latest body, which President Carter appointed in February of 1980, consisted of the governors of Connecticut, Idaho, Maryland, South Carolina, Virginia and Washington, the secretaries of the Departments of Energy, Interior and Transportation and the administrators of the Environmental Protection Agency, four state and county legislators from Kansas, Minnesota, New York and Wisconsin, the mayor of New Orleans and a tribal representative, who is Peter MacDonald, chairman of the Navajo nation of New Mexico. Also participating with the standing of "observers," are legislators from Illinois and Mississippi, appointed at the request of their states, and John J. Ahearne, member and former chairman of the NRC.

Rather prudently, President Carter named as chairman of this panel Richard Riley, the governor of South Carolina who had been principally responsible for bringing the shortage of low-level disposal capacity to national attention. In turn, Riley appointed as the council's executive director John Stucker, a professor of government on leave from the University of South Carolina, and he established an office in downtown Washington, where he coordinated a staff of seven analysts borrowed from the Departments of Energy and Transportation, the Nuclear Regulatory Commission and the United States Geological Survey.

Not surprisingly, considering Governor Riley's 1979 role in restricting shipments to Barnwell, the first problem the council addressed was low-level waste disposal, and its first preliminary recommendation, for authorization for the states to enter into regional low-level waste management compacts, was passed by Congress in 1980. By April of 1981, the Legislature of Idaho had authorized that state's governor to sign such a pact with other Northwest states that agree to conform with packaging and transportation requirements that will be set by the State of Washington for continued disposal of low-level wastes at Hanford. Later, when it took up transportation, the council voted to recommend that the Department of Transportation be designated the ultimate authority in routing radioactive shipments, but urged that states and tribal governments be given "primary responsibility for designating substitute and additional highway routes." In situations like New York City's, it recommended that "consideration of alternative modes of transport, such as rail and barge . . . should emphasize, but not be limited to, public health and safety considerations."

In considering the issues of high-level waste disposal, the council for the most part supported the position of the House of Representatives. It called for "the primary emphasis of the national program" to be placed on permanent isolation of spent fuel "from the biosphere"—which runs counter to Senator Johnston's proposal for AFR's—and it supported NRC licensing (and the enforcement of provisions of the National Environmental Protection Act requiring the drafting of environmental-impact statements) for repositories for commercial spent fuel.

More or less in response, the Department of Energy has, since the inauguration of the new administration, proposed to Congress that it be given budgetary authority to sink shafts and begin characterization studies at three sites—including, after all, a welded-tuff formation at the Nevada Test Site. The other two candidates would be a basalt formation at the Hanford Reservation and a salt formation at a location to be determined by 1983. Based on the results of the studies, the DOE would select one of these by 1985 to begin construction of a T&E (test and evaluation) facility in which up to 300 packages of solidified high-level waste would be placed by 1980 in a mode designed for retrieval if necessary.

Faced with this change in federal signals, the State Planning Council put itself on record to the effect that a T&E facility "is technically justified," but urged a requirement that "after a specified period of time the [commercial] wastes emplaced in a T&E facility be withdrawn unless DOE has made, or there has been approved, an application to the NRC to license the facility as a permanent repository." It added that "the principles of consultation and concurrence . . . should be fully applied." The council also, for the first time, promulgated what might be considered at least a radwaste definition of consultation—"involves sharing of information on planned activities and the right of states/tribes to review, comment and make recommendations on such activities"—and concurrence—"an incremental process involving the growth of public confidence and the development of a technical consensus that the waste-management program can be accomplished with acceptable risks to public health and safety and with acceptable socioeconomic costs."

Applying these definitions to the process of siting either a full-scale commercial high-level waste or spent-fuel repository or a T&E facility, the council, after considerable discussion, offered the following procedure: Affected states and tribes would be authorized "to petition the President for a formal review of their objections to the selection of a site for detailed site characterization," and if the President, after this review, denied their appeal, the affected jurisdictions would be enabled to petition Congress later "for a formal review of their objections to a decision by DOE to seek long-term protection of a site judged to be qualified for a repository. These objections should be considered by Congress using expedited procedures and should be overridden only by affirmative action by *both* Houses of Congress."

The principal dissenter in the preliminary votes that led to the formulation of this recommendation was Sheldon Meyers, the Department of Energy's deputy assistant secretary for waste management. "If what this council wants is to provide a veto, why don't you come out and say that?" he asked at the final meeting of the panel in June of 1981.

"We spent two months working on a definition of what we meant by consultation and concurrence, and it is not an absolute veto," Governor Riley responded.

"Not absolute, but it may do the same thing," the DOE official observed.

Whether these policy initiatives will be heeded in the Reagan administration remains to be seen. There is at least a probability that they may be specifically reversed, since the pre-inauguration Republican Party transition team had recommended the replacement of Governor Riley as chairman, the dismissal of Dr. Stucker and the entire staff and the "reorientation of the mission of the State Planning Council" in order to change what it saw as this body's "adversarial relationship with DOE." By the time the Republican administration took office, however, the council was only seven months short of its reporting deadline of August 12, 1981, and it was allowed at least to make its final recommendations to President Reagan without any such "reorientation of the mission."

In 1980, before the election, I talked to Governor Riley about the council's work in achieving a consensus on such difficult issues as the consultation-and-concurrence procedure. "It's a little like pulling eyeteeth," he said, "but that's the point: If eyeteeth need pulling, you have them pulled. We get a fair number of disagreements, but you expect that in a policy board. People have to develop a feeling of being treated fairly although they are involved in a very complex system that most of them don't yet understand. They have to be comfortable with us and also realize that no answer is going to be perfect."

To sweeten the pill for the residents of regions ultimately selected as repository sites, the council has urged the federal government to "accept the responsibility for socioeconomic impacts resulting from such repository development . . . Federal government impact payments should be [made] to states or tribes to distribute, in accordance with impact experienced, to affected jurisdictions." For low-level repositories also, the council urged Congress to "create a special discretionary fund which would confer benefits to host states, tribal governments and local communities."

There is, however, one American community that already is next-door to a low-level repository and which has so far given every indication that it would gladly welcome a high-level repository—without any more federal inducements than it already has. This is the southeastern Washington town of Richland, which likes to bill itself as "the town the atom built." It was, in fact, part of the Hanford Atomic Energy Reservation until 1958, and now it and its neighbors in the Tri Cities region, Pasco and Kennewick, encompass the residences of most of the 12,000 full- and part-time workers already employed on the reservation—during the Carter administration, annual budgets at Hanford reached $600 million a year, and the Washington *Post* has estimated that two thirds of the 110,000 residents of the three towns "are economically dependent on the nuclear industry."

There is a concern among environmental groups, and in particular the Natural Resources Defense Council and the Washington Public Interest Research Group, that Hanford, one of the three sites that has now been recommended by DOE for characterization for the proposed T & E facility, will ultimately be chosen as a repository site not because of any possible superiority in its underlying basalt, but because, as a reporter for the Seattle *Post-Intelligencer* wrote in 1980, it "offers a near-magic combination of ingredients—pro-nuclear public opinion, support by community leaders and the backing of an uncritical press." The *Tri-City Herald* itself headlined announcement of the repository possibility in 1979: "WASTE COULD BE $20 BILLION HANFORD BUSINESS."

In addition to the payroll incentive, there is the pragmatic

position taken by the General Accounting Office, which maintains that since cleaning up Hanford, if it is indeed possible,
"would be prohibitively expensive," first consideration should
be given to determining whether it or any of the other "existing highly contaminated reservations are acceptable" as high-
level repositories. (On the other hand, back in 1966, the
National Academy of Sciences advised the Atomic Energy
Commission that "none of the sites at which radioactive
wastes are being stored or disposed of is geologically suited for
safe disposal.")

Most of the Department of Energy executives I've talked to
have conceded that a jurisdiction's willingness to accept a repository will ultimately influence the siting decision. Before his
resignation in 1980, Undersecretary of Energy John Deutch,
who had headed the federal Interagency Review Group on
Waste Management, told me that in his view the problems
involved in locating a nuclear-waste repository weren't very
different from those of siting other controversial facilities—airports, for example. "I don't think there is any magic medium for
disposal," he said. "What is extremely important, though, is the
total characteristic of a site. You must assess specific geological
environments and hope you'll be able to choose among a large
menu of sites, all of which are deemed to be technically adequate, and then select the one that is presumed to be possible
or easiest to do."

Given its considerable public support—the Richland chapter
of the environmentalist Sierra Club is even reported to have
taken a pro-nuclear position—and the fact that 64 percent of
the military high-level wastes are already in the underground
tanks there, Hanford certainly seems "easiest to do." However,
Sheldon Meyers, the highest-ranking Department of Energy
official now dealing exclusively with radwaste—his title, deputy
assistant secretary for nuclear waste management, puts him on
an organizational plane with Admiral Hyman Rickover, the
deputy assistant secretary for naval reactors, and Robert L.
Ferguson, the deputy assistant secretary for nuclear reactor
programs—doesn't see Hanford as a shoo-in. "If basalt turns out
to be technically suitable, fine, we might well site a repository
there," Meyers said, "but none of the policy-makers I've talked

to in Washington or anywhere else is saying we'll go through a charade and then pick the reservation."

I asked about the increasing costs of radwaste disposal. "I don't think we are going to price nuclear out of the market," he said. "We think the whole waste cycle will add only 3 percent to the entire cost of nuclear power, and the way the prices of oil are rising, we think nuclear will end up looking like the golden sunset people used to think it was."

There are, however, forecasts from equally responsible sources that could turn Meyers' "golden sunset" into a stormy night. Just by itself, the DOE's own repository disposal and away-from-reactor storage projection exceeds his 3 percent estimate: According to the Atomic Industrial Forum, American reactors generated 251.1 billion kilowatt hours sold at an average (DOE estimated) price of 4.5 cents per hour, for an approximate nuclear income of $11.3 billion. The same reactors were expected to discharge 1,530 metric tons of spent fuel in 1980. This latest DOE estimate for repository disposal and away-from-reactor storage costs is $371 per kilogram. At $371 per kilogram, 1,530,000 kilograms of spent fuel comes to $568 million, or just about 5 percent of $11.3 billion.

This, of course, is only for the storage and disposal of the spent fuel. Commercial power's radwaste accounts payable file should also include bills for the disposal of its low-level wastes, annual provision for decontamination-and-decommissioning expenses, and ultimately, the stabilization of the uranium mill tailings generated in the production of the fuel.

These commercial tailings are not now being stabilized—and the mining companies have no plans to stabilize them. Eventually they have to be, however, and a cost estimate can be extrapolated from the government's present program to clean up 28 million tons of tailings produced in its service at a cost that Richard Campbell, the Department of Energy's program manager, estimated at a minimum of $480 million. That's $17.14 per ton. The Union of Concerned Scientists' specialist in radioactive waste management, Ronnie Lipschutz, estimates in his report (*Radioactive Waste,* Ballinger, 1980), that 105,600 tons of tailings are produced each year in the production of fuel for a single 1,000-megawatt reactor. This works out to 105.6 tons per megawatt of capacity; American nuclear capacity in 1980 was

53,600 megawatts, so it seems fair to estimate that 5.7 million tons of tailings were produced in commercial power service. At $17.14 per ton, that rounds out to $98 million per year for tailings work.

Similarly, it is possible to extrapolate future decontamination-and-decommissioning costs, in this case from 1980 projections that dismantling a 1,000-MW reactor now or mothballing it now and dismantling it later will cost approximately $100 million either way. This works out to a $100,000 per megawatt factor which, multiplied by the 1980 generating capacity, rounds to a total of $5.4 billion that American ratepayers eventually will owe. Assuming (generously) the full life span legally allotted to reactors, 40 years, and spreading the D-and-D charge over that period, then the average annual expense (very little of which is now being provided for) should be $135 million.

By contrast with these much larger expenses, the costs of disposing of reactor low-level wastes are for the most part being handled on a pay-as-you-go basis. According to a survey commissioned for the Department of Energy, the reactors sent 1,-265,680 cubic feet of low-level material to commercial repositories in 1978, and 75 percent of this went to Barnwell, where disposal fees reached $7.71 per cubic foot in 1980. Beatty and Hanford charged somewhat less, but since waste transport expenses (which vary according to shipping distances) should also be counted—and haven't been—$7.71 would be a conservative estimate. Assuming no increases from the 1978 volume, the low-level disposal cost for commercial reactors was approximately $9.7 million. A tabulation of these annual commercial power radwaste costs rounded off to millions is:

Spent-fuel storage and disposal	$568
Mill-tailings stabilization	98
D and D	135
Low-level disposal	10
	$811 million

These predictable costs work out to 7.2 percent of the $11.3 billion that nuclear power billed in 1980—and the only one now being assessed ratepayers is the $10-million low-level disposal charge. According to the Washington *Post* in December of 1980, the Department of Energy suppressed a study made for its own Energy Information Administration Office of Economic Analysis that concluded that commercial nuclear power had received $6.5 billion in federal subsidies for these past and future unpaid radwaste management costs—the figure was 16 percent of the $39.9 billion in total subsidies which commercial power was calculated to have received since its inception. When this study was finally released in 1981, after the departure of its author, Joseph Bowering, from government service, the $39.9-billion figure had been reduced to $12.8 billion, a figure even lower than an Atomic Industrial Forum estimate of $15 billion to $17 billion. Among the accounting revisions that accomplished this change in the DOE estimate was a complete subtraction from the total of Bowering's estimate of $6.5 billion in commercial radwaste-management and disposal subsidies— apparently on the grounds that since most of the waste still remains undisposed of, the money already spent on it cannot yet be considered to be a subsidy.

Eventually to be added onto these known radwaste management expenses incurred by commercial power are a number of costs that can only be guessed at in 1981. These would include waste-decontamination costs for future reactor accidents (somebody, for example, is going to have to pay the $1.6-billion cleanup bill at Three Mile Island); the costs of the increased safeguards and escorts that the NRC has ruled must accompany shipments of spent fuel; a portion of the cost of incentives that will probably have to be paid to site a repository; a significant share of the increased radiological protections that will in the future be required for waste operations or shipments (the Office of Management and Budget suggests for accounting purposes that the prevention of a single man-rem of exposure be budgeted at $1,000); increased costs incurred in regulating waste operations and shipments as an integral part of other nuclear operations; and increasing federal research expenses for commercial wastes—the DOE's 1981 research and development appropriation for commercial waste management was $246 million.

Now for some really big numbers. Just to build and operate

four full-scale repositories for commercial spent fuel it proposed in 1980 to establish in different geological media, the Department of Energy has calculated a cost of $10.9 billion. (This would be in addition to the unspecified cost of creating, operating and eventually decommissioning the "T & E" facility.) However, as nuclear-power proponents point out, the spent fuel of commercial reactors comprises only 10 percent of the volume of high-level radwaste. Add projections of the costs of disposal for the other 90 percent, the military and governmental high-level wastes, and the costs skyrocket in proportion. In the 1978 report which the National Academy of Sciences chose not to publish, but which the Nuclear Regulatory Commission did distribute, Professor Rustum Roy's panel accepted estimates that the costs to solidify and bury defense high-level wastes would approximate $30 billion. Roy told me subsequently he had seen credible estimates that reached $50 billion. "The disparity is so large," he said, "that obviously no one knows for sure what the real number is."

But whatever that "real number" is (or was in 1980) it is certain to be much larger by the time actual construction work begins on the first full-scale commercial high-level-waste or spent fuel repository, in 1992 at the earliest. Nuclear power's foremost academic proponent, University of Pittsburgh Professor Bernard Cohen, who would like to see this work begin much sooner, has estimated that delays in going ahead and actually disposing of this waste are already costing American ratepayers $2 million a week, or more than $100 million a year simply because of inflation. "What's really going to cost us is more delay," he said. "Spread construction of facilities out to twelve years instead of completing them in five, and you double the costs." Ultimately, Professor Cohen's estimates on inflation may turn out to be conservative. Early in 1980, a DOE spokesman estimated that delays on just one repository, WIPP, first projected at a cost of $355 million, but increased to $650 million by then—and now estimated at more than a billion dollars—was costing taxpayers $5 million per month from inflation alone.

Yet despite this inevitable inflation, several environmentalists I have spoken to have indicated that they will continue to oppose and try to delay every radwaste-disposal program, no matter how sound its merits. "I will not accept waste in my state or any other state until they stop making it," Lorna Salzman, mid-Atlantic representative of Friends of the Earth, has said. "If they want to find a waste solution, let them start at the source." The administration of President Reagan, however, has started out not by pressing for waste solutions (although WIPP has been restored to the budget), but by stepping up efforts that will produce it. The only form of energy support not cut in the new President's 1982 budget was nuclear power, which got an $81-million increase. On the military side, the new Secretary of Energy, James B. Edwards, has promised the congressional Armed Services Committees to undertake "drastic" improvements in the production rate of 3 new nuclear warheads which were being added daily to increase the 1980 arsenal of 2,300 strategic and 22,000 tactical nuclear warheads, and in August 1981, President Reagan approved the additional production of neutron, or enhanced-radiation, artillery shells and missiles.

Given this increased impetus, the radwaste surveyors at Oak Ridge National Laboratory will have to increase the quantity projections they made in 1980 for the year 2000. According to their published report, they expected by that time the number of commercial spent-fuel assemblies either disposed of or awaiting disposal to be approximately 321,300, amounting to nearly 100,000 tons of the most radioactive form of waste—with another 11 million cubic feet of almost-as-radioactive high-level liquid waste in tanks. (The National Resources Defense Council calculates that the combined curie content of this material will exceed 10 billion.) Low-level waste inventories, by the year 2000, are predicted to exceed 376 million cubic feet, with another 11 million cubic feet to come from decontamination of surplus facilities and an additional 30,000 cubic feet from stored and buried transuranic waste. Finally, there should still be, in the year 2000, 11.3 billion cubic feet of uranium mill tailings.

I have tried in this excursion through "the back end of the nuclear fuel cycle" to cover the political, financial and, to a degree, the technical options, for dealing with these quantities of radwaste—and to report on some of the consequences of not having done so before now. In my research, I received cooperation from both proponents and opponents of nuclear power and a nuclear defense, and I hope I have reported fairly the positions of both—which doesn't mean that I don't have my own view on these issues. To borrow a metaphor I've heard from those on both sides of this debate, it appears that the nuclear camel got his nose into mankind's tent in 1942, when Enrico Fermi and Manhattan Project scientists initiated the chain reaction—and created the first radwastes. In the nearly 40 years since then, some Americans have been engaged in welcoming the camel and making him as comfortable as possible while others have been trying to drive him out. Me, I think it's time to housebreak the beast before he takes over the tent.

APPENDIX

EXECUTIVE SUMMARY OF THE REPORT TO THE PRESIDENT
BY THE STATE PLANNING COUNCIL ON RADIOACTIVE WASTE MANAGEMENT
AUGUST 1, 1981

During the decade of the 1970's it became increasingly apparent that government was unable to resolve the institutional barriers which prevented sound waste management practices from being implemented. The State Planning Council on Radioactive Waste Management was established by the President in order to address this problem.

As a nation, we have learned that sound technical solutions to the problems of waste disposal cannot be carried out without public acceptance. The key to gaining the public's confidence is a process of decision making which is open and accessible to elected officials from all levels of government. The Council believes that such a process can be put in place through a renewal of the traditional principles of our federal system of government.

A PARTNERSHIP FOR WASTE MANAGEMENT

State, local, and tribal officials must become working partners with the Federal government in making the crucial decisions about how radioactive wastes will be handled, transported, and ultimately disposed. This partnership presupposes a willingness on the part of public officials to undertake cooperative efforts to resolve waste management problems which affect their overlapping jurisdictions. It rejects the alternatives of either an arbitrary imposition of decisions by the Federal government or arbitrary actions by state, local, or tribal governments to block waste management activities.

A workable and effective partnership must include, first the full sharing of information and plans regarding waste disposal activities among all levels of government and, second, the opportunity for state, local, and tribal governments to participate effectively in waste management decisions which affect their jurisdictions. Finally, although the partnership will vary, depending on the type of waste involved and the nature of each governmental entity's authority, the principle of partnership should apply to all aspects of radioactive waste management regardless of the source of the wastes.

We have arrived at the point where it is important to decide not only what is to be done, but also how we will do it. A process of decision making must be established that will allow the American people to have confidence in the results of that process. There will be remaining uncertainties no matter what the decisions are. Only confidence in the process which leads to those decisions will enable us, as a society, to carry out safe and practical solutions to the disposal of our radioactive wastes.

HIGH-LEVEL WASTES

As a country, we have developed national policies which enable us to gain the benefits of nuclear technology, but the activities which produce these benefits also produce inherently dangerous wastes. State, local, and tribal officials are now contending with a vast array of proposals and promises related to either having large amounts of high-level and transuranic wastes stored in their midst or the prospect of having large amounts of this waste buried in their midst. Industry, likewise, has been hampered in its ability to plan for the management of its own waste materials. The end result is that none of us is certain about our fate in this matter because of changing Federal approaches to the problem.

The Federal government should continue to provide assistance to the states during the transition phase of implementing this new policy, and the Federal regulatory agencies should complete the regulatory framework to support this policy. Finally, the Congress should authorize the transfer of properly decommissioned low-level waste burial sites to the Federal government for extended care.

SPENT FUEL

The President and the Congress should firmly maintain the current national policy of industry responsibility for the interim storage of spent nuclear fuel. A consistent commitment to this policy, coupled with Federal assistance in the development and demonstration of new storage technologies, will provide utilities with the incentive required to prepare for the additional storage capacity required for their spent fuel.

In addition, Federal and state authorities must take action, consistent with their obligation to protect public health and safety, to mitigate potential institutional obstacles to spent fuel storage proposals. The NRC should put forth regulations specifying a timely licensing process for existing and new storage techniques. States in cooperation with local and tribal officials should take appropriate actions to facilitate implementation of safe and reasonable proposals for the storage of spent fuel within their boundaries. Our national policy should not permit one part of the country to avoid the burden of spent fuel management in the hope that the Federal government will transfer that burden elsewhere.

TRANSPORTATION

A regulatory framework that applies to all radioactive waste shipments must balance both national uniformity and the states' traditional authority to regulate transportation within and through their boundaries for the protection of public health and safety. This requires that the Federal government work with state, local, and tribal officials in the development and enforcement of transportation regulations. It also implies that arbitrary actions by state, local, and tribal governments to block reasonable highway routing of radioactive waste could increase risks to public health and safety.

A uniform national routing system should be finalized with uniform standards for advance notification of certain shipments of radioactive materials and wastes for use by appropriate state, local, and tribal officials. States should be encouraged to take the lead, in partnership with local and tribal governments, for developing and implementing emergency response plans and procedures for transportation accidents involving radioactive materials and wastes.

CONCLUSION

In formulating its recommendations, the Council has been instrumental in building an active dialogue among state, local, and tribal officials, among Federal agencies and non-Federal officials, and with industry and public interest groups. As a result of this dialogue, a consensus has been achieved on the basic principles for national policies for radioactive waste management. The responsibility now rests with elected officials from all levels of government, working together, to establish and carry out these policies. A continuing formal dialogue among Federal, state, local, and tribal officials would strengthen this intergovernmental partnership and facilitate the task of implementing these policies.

Confidence that we in government can resolve this difficult issue will not be gained by further promises that programs are in place and that high-level wastes will some day be safely disposed of. We need Congress to enact legislation that establishes the national policy and the intergovernmental framework for the permanent disposal of high-level and transuranic wastes.

The legislation should prescribe a technically conservative national repository program with target time schedules to ensure that key objectives are met. The emphasis of the legislation should be on permanent disposal rather than temporary or long term storage of these wastes. The national program for more than a quarter of a century has been, in effect, temporary storage. It has represented our national policy by default, and this policy must be changed.

The legislation should also specify a consultation and concurrence process for state and tribal participation in the national repository program. This process should include a conflict resolution mechanism to be used in case consensus is not achieved between the Federal government and a state or tribe on a proposed repository site. State and tribal governments must be held accountable for the participation of local officials in this process.

Adopting the principle of consultation and concurrence does not mean granting a veto. The Council does not support the right of any state or tribe to veto a decision to site a permanent repository. What we have proposed is a framework for intergovernmental relations that is a reaffirmation of the Federal principles of governance. A national repository program can be implemented if it guarantees the legitimate right of state and tribal governments to be involved in decisions of vast importance affecting the future of their citizens.

Finally, the program authorized by Congress should apply to all high-level and transuranic wastes regardless of their source. We will not gain public acceptance for a national repository program if the American people perceive that different programmatic and institutional procedures have been put in place for the disposal of wastes which, from the perspective of public health and safety, are essentially the same.

The President must ensure effective coordination among the various executive branch agencies responsible for carrying out the national repository program. State and tribal governments must begin to establish procedures which will enable them, and officials from their local jurisdictions, to participate in the national program. These actions can be taken prior to final Congressional action.

LOW-LEVEL WASTE

The Congress, through the Low Level Radioactive Waste Policy Act of 1980, has established a national policy which makes states responsible for ensuring the safe disposal of low-level radioactive wastes. The act encourages states to carry out this responsibility on a cooperative regional basis through the formation of interstate compacts.

In the seven months since this policy was established, considerable progress has been made throughout the country toward stabilizing low-level waste management; progress which would not have occurred in the absence of a clear statement of national policy. Several states have enacted legislation that will facilitate the creation of new disposal sites. An interstate compact has been created in the Northwest, and nine states in the Southeast are negotiating a compact for submission to their state legislatures in 1982. States in the Northeast, Midwest, and South Central regions are working toward similar arrangements.

INDEX

ABOUT THE AUTHOR

FRED C. SHAPIRO has been reporting since 1954, when he got out of the Army and joined the staff of the Portsmouth, Va., *Star.* His subsequent newspaper employers were the Philadelphia *Daily News,* the Baltimore *News-American,* the New York *Journal-American* and the New York *Herald Tribune.* Since 1965, he has been a staff writer at *The New Yorker.* A series of three articles in that magazine dealing with confessions subsequently found to have been extorted from an innocent defendant won the 1969 Robert F. Kennedy Foundation Journalism Award for outstanding magazine coverage of problems of poverty and discrimination. These articles were expanded and published under the title of *Whitmore* by Bobbs-Merrill. In 1974, a New York *Times Magazine* article on a public school for emotionally troubled children won the magazine prize of the National Council for the Advancement of Education Writing. In addition to *The New Yorker* and the *Times Magazine,* his articles have appeared in *American Heritage, Washington Monthly, Esquire, Ms., the Columbia Journalism Review, Holiday, New Times, Philadelphia Magazine* and the Boston *Phoenix.* He is also coauthor, with James W. Sullivan, of *Race Riots New York 1964,* published by Thomas Y. Crowell in 1964. He lives in New York City with his wife, Iris, and their two teen-aged children.